# GLORIA! GLORIA!

## A TALE OF FORMENTERA

By

## Glyn Gowans

Grosvenor House
Publishing Limited

This book is published by
Grosvenor House Publishing Ltd
Link House
140 The Broadway, Tolworth, Surrey, KT6 7HT.
www.grosvenorhousepublishing.co.uk

A CIP record for this book
is available from the British Library

ISBN 978-1-83615-124-1

# PREFACE

I conceived and commenced writing this book during a blissful three-month stay on Formentera in 1995. I already knew the island well, having holidayed there several times from the early 1980s. Even in 1995, mobile phones were still something of a novelty; 'smart phones', laptops, tablets and 'social media' had yet to undermine Formentera's heavenly isolation from much of the hurly-burly of 'civilisation', despite its proximity to Ibiza. To communicate with the outside world, I relied solely on a public telephone in a pueblo to which I would cycle once or twice a week. I suffered no inconvenience. Life went on.

GMG, Witham, Essex, 2024

# MAP OF FORMENTERA

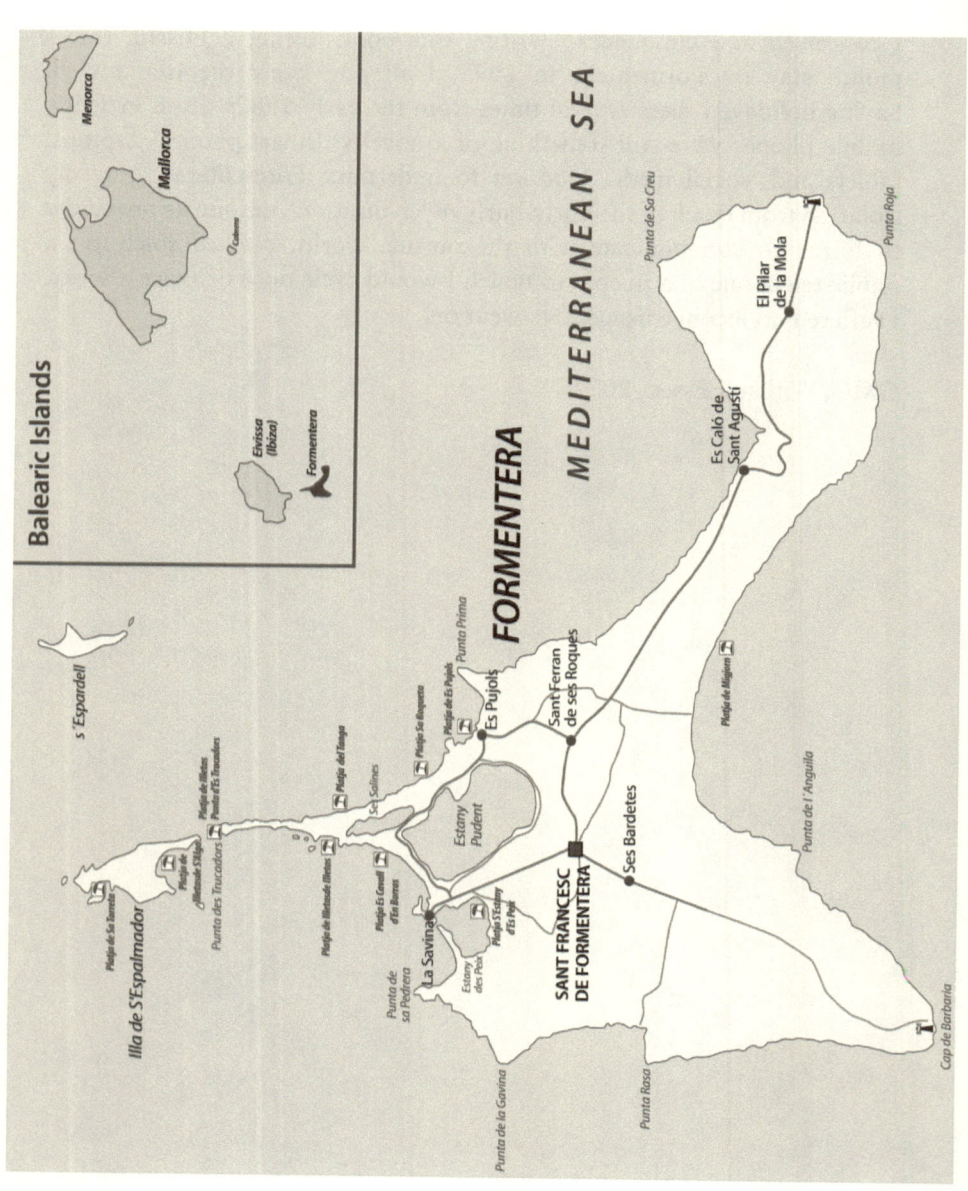

# CHAPTER 1

'Our associates in Montevideo have now checked the death certificate, and it confirms Quisling's story. Einstein *did* die of salmonella poisoning.'

As the import of the latest piece of intelligence from Uruguay sank in, the lawyers sitting around the conference table awaited the reaction of Mr Sonny Start, the president of their firm's most important client, SI (pronounced 'ess-eye'), formerly Start Industries. His demeanour, however, indicated a complete lack of emotion, but then, as a self-effacing Texan with a gentle voice, he was something of a rarity. He was certainly an atypical leader of the international business community – a leader, to boot, who had only just celebrated his fortieth birthday but looked more like a thirty-year-old sportswear model.

The gentle, soporific purring of the air conditioning had come to dominate the meeting room. Start appeared mesmerized by the Dallas skyline shimmering in the July heat on the other side of its tinted windows. Several of the younger lawyers, keen to impress, were on the point of making seemingly pertinent remarks when, without averting his gaze, Start said softly: 'So, Trent, all the pieces of the jigsaw *seem* to fit together, but I have the feeling that the picture we get isn't the one on the box.'

It was typical of the homespun allegories with which Start's colleagues were familiar; two of the acolytes wrote it down.

'How do you mean exactly, Sonny?' asked Charles Weigel, SI's senior in-house counsel and Start's right-hand man.

Start placed his hands together as if about to pray, and studied his perfectly manicured nails. 'That's the weird thing, Charlie. I just don't seem to be able to put my finger on it. I guess it's just a gut feeling that something's not quite right about all this. Don't you feel the same?'

Weigel did not, but in view of the nature of the president's query, he suspected that his own judgement might be defective. Nodding his head, he managed a seemingly affirmative 'Hmm'.

Start suddenly switched his attention to Trent Purkey, the gaunt middle-aged head of the Intellectual Property Department of Swinehart, Crudge, Idol & Purkey, one of Dallas's largest law firms. It was in their palatial offices that the meeting was taking place, despite the invariable rule that whenever Start required advice in person, Swineharts would go over to SI's offices in neighbouring Fort Worth. But the matter on which

Purkey had first been asked to advise just a week earlier had, according to Weigel, raised such critical issues of security that the president himself had decreed that all meetings would take place at Swineharts. Consequently, Purkey had decided that code names should be used to minimize the risk of any unauthorized personnel becoming aware of the nature of their discussions. So far, however, he'd only succeeded in causing confusion.

'What's your view, Trent?' asked Start, his dark brown eyes focusing on the lawyer's bow tie – white spots on a navy-blue background. Start detested bow ties. 'Are you still of the view that we should proceed with ... um ... "Operation ...? Actually, Trent, just for this meeting, can we dispense with the codes?'

'Well ... OK – if you're sure?' *Christ! Don't sound so patronising!* 'Of *course* we should go on the offensive, Sonny – can't see we've got anything to lose.' As usual, Purkey's legendary self-confidence boosted the morale of his junior colleagues. He was not one of those 'on the one hand-on the other hand' breed of lawyers who drove clients to distraction. 'When I say, "we've got nothing to lose", Sonny,' Purkey continued, leaning back in his chair with his arms folded, 'the way I see it is simply this. First, there are the indisputable facts. Einstein – Vosene Pesto, I mean – worked as a research chemist for that soap outfit back East–'

'New Jersey,' snapped one of Purkey's junior colleagues eagerly, 'and code-named "Seaweed" – Groovy Soaps.'

Purkey waved a hand dismissively. 'Wherever – whatever. ... OK, Pesto's employment contract stipulated that anything she invented belonged to Groovy. During 1991, we – SI that is – buy Groovy, together with all its inventions and rights against employees, and Pesto transfers to our Texas research facility. One day in January 92, she doesn't turn up for work – disappears – without trace. We inform the FBI, but they get nowhere. All we know is that she was last seen driving away from her condo that day with some guy in his mid-thirties.

'Now, roll forward five years, OK? A few weeks ago, Quisling – sorry! – *Nickel* – that weirdo Luke Nickel – contacts you, Sonny, claiming to be Pesto's widowed husband. He tells a fantastic story about her inventing some amazing new kinda soap while still working for Groovy – an invention she kept all to herself until Nickel persuaded her to disclose it to that British outfit ... um ... WSD, the owners of Goblin Soap, and–'

Purkey snorted, shaking his head. 'Jesus! I'd love to know what in God's name ever made those Brits choose that dumb brand name.'

'It's Victorian,' chirped another keen assistant.

'Victorian?'

'Sure, like in Queen Victoria. She was amused by their jingle "Goblin Gobbles Grime". They still use it – WSD, that is, formerly Weetwoods' Soaps and Detergents ... and ... and...' She fizzled out: Purkey's glare looked career-threatening.

Start sighed: he wanted to ask Purkey why he'd chosen the code name 'Quisling' for Nickel, but no way was he going to look stupid in front of all these Ivy League guys. Anyway, Purkey had already raced on.

'... and, of course, none of us was at the first meeting which you, Sonny – and Charlie – had with Nickel. Still, even though I say so myself, I think I'm a pretty good judge of character. I've interviewed hundreds of potential witnesses over the years, and when someone's not telling the truth, well, I *always* sense it. Subject to a couple of minor cosmetic elaborations or trivial distortions, I believe he's legit. And let's face it, most of what he's told us checks out. He *was* Goblin's U.S. distributor. He *did* stay at the Holiday Inn near the airport on that night in January 92. And those two Goblin directors *were* booked into adjoining rooms. The following day, Pesto and Nickel *did* fly to Montevideo via Mexico City using false passports – I don't know how you got that info, Sonny, and I don't *want* to know – and those Uruguay investigators have confirmed that people answering to their descriptions began living together as man and wife under assumed names in Montevideo some months later. Frankly, there's no doubt that Goblin bought them new identities.

'Now, Nickel has shown us copies of several agreements between the Brits and Pesto giving Goblin ownership of Eureka – let's just call the invention that for simplicity, Sonny, OK? – and requiring her to assist them in getting it into commercial production. They look hastily drafted to me, but in one sense I think that makes them even more credible. If the Goblin guys were anxious to get her on board and grab Eureka, they wouldn't have spent weeks getting fancy contracts drawn up.'

'Maybe,' Start murmured. His eyes were following one of Swineharts' junior attorneys – a tanned Adonis – who was moving around the table, offering top-ups of chilled mineral water and orange juice. 'They could be fakes,' he added without looking at Purkey.

'I can sniff out fakes, Sonny. I'd bet anything you like they're the real McCoy.'

'I never bet,' Start responded coldly.

'No, of course not. ... Anyway, there are the Eureka notebooks Nickel showed us. The handwriting matches the Pesto specimens in her old SI file – absolutely no doubt of that. And although the formulations seem crazy–'

'I couldn't stop laughing when Nickel first showed them to us,' Weigel interjected. 'He got real upset.'

3

'Quite,' snapped Purkey: he'd no time for the in-house lawyer, whom he regarded as an overpaid supernumerary. 'But the point is that your lab people have made Eureka successfully, and the stuff seems to work.'

'"Seems to",' Sonny repeated. He was gently stroking the five o'clock shadow on his chin and staring again at the huge windows. 'Our guys also say that we could never make that "stuff" commercially just with those notebooks. There'd have to be *years* of research costing hundreds of millions, and ... well, Vosene's ... dead – or so we're told.'

'Ah, but that's precisely the point, Sonny,' Purkey chirped. 'The Goblin guys have done all that. Their published accounts for the last few years show that since Pesto's disappearance their R&D budgets have soared. We know they've built two new plants in Kenya and Sri Lanka, and through their media contacts our guys in England have been told that every business editor has been invited to WSD's HQ for the launch of something *real* important on August fourth.'

Start sighed loudly and raised his eyebrows with just a hint of melodrama.

'Oh, come on, Sonny,' Purkey declaimed, 'you can't really believe it's all a coincidence – a *mass* of coincidences – surely?'

Start finally met Purkey's gaze. 'What I find slightly difficult to swallow, Trent,' – his voice was so quiet that Purkey and several others around the table leaned forward – 'is that a hard-headed businessman who was prepared to sell his soul to the devil five years ago, should now come clean because he's so full of remorse. I mean, that sob story about blaming, um ... Goblin and himself for Vosene's death – the mix-up in the Montevideo hospital that would never have happened had they stayed in the States. ... And I still don't understand why there should have been such a long delay between her death and the issue of the death certificate – or, for that matter, her cremation. I think he's hiding something from us.'

But Purkey had no such concerns: Swineharts' lawyers in Uruguay had convinced him that hospital officials who were fearful about negligence claims from relatives of deceased patients could indeed delay the issue of death certificates and the release of corpses through bribing the relevant officials, just as Nickel had alleged. And, as for his motives for 'coming clean' at this stage, Purkey believed it all came down to money – it always did.

'Look,' he argued, 'before Pesto's death, Nickel had gotten used to an extravagant lifestyle. And although he has assurances from WSD that he'll be paid royalties on sales of Eureka on the same terms as those set out in their old agreement with Pesto, no one has any idea what those sales – and hence the amount of his royalties – might be. And he fears that because of the illegalities surrounding Pesto's defection from us to WSD, the Brits

4

might renege on the deal, and he wouldn't be able to sue. He wants the security of a big lump sum payment now. He probably wants to buy a yacht or–'

'So, Trent,' Start interjected, 'why doesn't he just go to Goblin and ... well ... blackmail them? "Give me a bag of dough, or I go to SI Corporation and–"'

'Because, Sonny,' Purkey snapped, stunning his colleagues, 'he's probably calculated that on his own he can't really hurt them. But he knows that *we* can – with his help. In fact, if we're successful, they're so overstretched they could be staring bankruptcy in the face. It wouldn't be the first time that patent litigation has destroyed a great business.'

Purkey's reference to devastating corporate warfare seemed to electrify the atmosphere. He wanted this case badly: it could be one of the biggest, most exciting, high-profile and lucrative cases of his career. He'd already convinced himself that SI was in a no-lose situation. He straightened his bow tie and pursued his cause relentlessly.

'Look, there's every indication Goblin's about to launch Eureka. We've got a guy who's prepared to give us sworn depositions confirming everything he's told us. I say the jigsaw fits *and* matches the picture on the box, Sonny. The Brits will probably say they acted in good faith – rely on technical legal arguments to protect themselves – the invention clauses in Pesto's contract with Groovy were oppressive and void – or try and do some deal. Either way we'll get at the truth. We could end up owning a gold mine for peanuts. At worst, you lose a hundred thousand bucks on lawyers' fees.

'Hell, Sonny, our London lawyer guys say that if Nickel's telling the truth, we've got enough to get a temporary restraining order to prevent Goblin from launching Eureka. Put yourself in their shoes – pissing their pants about the bad publicity, being labelled technology thieves, buying new identities in Uruguay, secret labs, et cetera, et cetera! The media would have a field day. And don't forget,' he added chuckling, 'with their "royal warrant" gimmick, the Queen of England is Goblin's most famous customer!'

There was some polite tittering, but it quickly fizzled out as soon as the culprits realised that Start had not joined them.

Purkey instantly adopted an expression of deadly seriousness. 'I say we go for the jugular, Sonny.'

*

The drive back to Fort Worth didn't take as long as Start had expected, but then they'd missed the worst of the evening rush hour. Weigel sat in the rear of the limousine with him. They'd driven over together at midday in order to touch base on their tactics when dealing with the Swinehearts people; Weigel himself had only just returned from Uruguay. Start's bodyguards, Chuck and Bob, were right behind them – in a Jeep with black-tinted windows. Former marines and veterans of the 1991 Gulf War, Start rarely travelled anywhere without them; he particularly enjoyed their company at Dallas Cowboys and Texas Rangers games.

It was as they drove past the freeway exit to the airport that Start said: 'Do you still think we were right not to tell him?'

Weigel stared at the chauffeur. 'Can Dwayne–?'

'He can't hear anything through the screen. You know that.'

'Yeah, but ...' Weigel took a few more moments before answering Start's question: he was not quick-witted. But behind his undistinguished facade lay a core of plain old-fashioned common sense. 'I don't think *anyone* needs to know – definitely not Purkey. He can be very prissy.'

Start nodded slowly: 'prissy' summed up Trent perfectly.

'No,' Weigel continued, almost whispering, 'seeing how she's dead and the SI team she worked with has been disbanded – *they'll* never tell what went on at that place – and the records have been destroyed ... well, I think it's all best forgotten.'

'Yeah, but perhaps she told Nickel – about "that place".'

'She probably did – almost definitely.'

'So, maybe she – or he – told *them*.'

'"Them"?'

'The English.'

'Ah ... possibly.'

'So, if we attack them now, they may use that as a weapon in their counter-attack, Charlie.'

Weigel ruminated on this hypothesis as he watched the traffic streaming eastwards on the other side of the freeway. Finally, he said: 'I don't think you need have any concerns on that score, Sonny. First, it would be a two-edged sword. What she did for us ... well, I bet those Brits have been doing the same stuff in secret for years. Secondly, they'd have no real evidence against us – just hearsay.'

Start opened the drinks cabinet below the glass screen; as usual, it only contained non-alcoholic beverages. He poured two glasses of mineral water and handed one to Weigel.

'Do you remember her, Charlie?'

'Einstein? – *Pesto*? Vaguely. Pretty kid but geeky. Typical scientist.'

'Her death, the certificate an' all ... I don't know, I still feel–'

'Are you trying to tell me that you're having doubts now about instructing Trent to go ahead? We can still stop–'

'No! I won't have him think ... When I say I want something done–'

'OK. I get it.'

Start drained his glass and put it back in the cabinet. 'Are we tailing Nickel?'

'Sure – and his hotel room here is bugged – *and* the house and phone in Montevideo – the whole caboodle. Nothing suspicious so far. By all accounts, he's a manic-depressive alcoholic.'

Start grunted contemptuously.

A few blocks from SI's headquarters, the Start Tower – one of downtown Fort Worth's few landmarks – Weigel asked: 'Are you in the office tomorrow, Sonny? I'd like to run through the main points of the new Microsoft group software licences. Shouldn't take more than twenty minutes. What time would suit you? We could get it over first thing – say eight-thirty? Is that OK? ... Sonny?'

The limousine was slowly descending the ramp into the Start Tower's underground car park. Weigel turned his head and looked at Sonny's face. His eyes were tightly closed, and in the clinical glow of the fluorescent lighting it suddenly struck Weigel that Sonny's youthful looks were slipping away – hints of crows' feet and a couple of rogue silvery hairs in the black brush of his military-style crew cut. Sonny was growing old; he was human after all.

Dwayne pulled up before the private non-stop elevator to the Senior Executives' offices on the thirtieth floor.

'Misty,' whispered Start. Then he opened his eyes and blinked. He cleared his throat. 'Eight-thirty would be fine.'

'*Misty?*' queried Weigel with obvious surprise.

Start shot him a glance. 'Excuse me?'

'You said "Misty".'

'Did I?'

'Sure. Is everything OK? Is she still studying at–?'

'I was just thinking ... well, about that report we got from those London investigators and all that material on the CEO of ... er–'

'You mean Goblin's Lord Weetwood?' interjected Weigel in hushed tones: he was eyeing Dwayne, who'd exited to summon the elevator for his master. 'He sounds like one heck of a screwball. Did you read all that stuff about model railroads? In fact, the whole family sound kinda crazy – like characters out of a P. G. Wodehouse novel, or – even better – Evelyn Waugh. Beryl, the gold-digger wife who spends most of her time on the French Riviera chasing studs. The "Honourable" Caroline, the candy-addicted egghead daughter drooling over dusty manuscripts. Her twin brother, the "Honourable" James, the psychotic who's been locked up in

Weetwood's castle ever since his best buddy was blown away at that weird school in Scotland two years ago. Probably a fruit if you ask me – Jesus!'

Start bristled as the elevator doors opened and a beam of warm, non-fluorescent light flooded out: he demanded traditional illumination technology throughout his working environment; it was more flattering. 'Hmm,' he replied icily. 'I thought it was all sort of … sad.'

Having no idea what sort of 'characters' Charlie was alluding to, Start filed a mental picture of a large colonial-style wooden house belonging to some New England society folks called 'Peachy': one more reference to check on overnight. He didn't catch the other author's name – at least he assumed they were both authors.

'So,' Weigel asked delicately, 'what does Weetwood have to do with … um … your daughter?'

Start straightened his tie. 'I don't know – nothing of course. It's a fine machine,' he added briskly, looking in the direction of Weigel's sherbet-yellow Jaguar E-type.

'Hmm? … Oh yeah! It sure is.' Weigel smiled broadly. 'She was delivered while I was in Uruguay. Come and sit behind the wheel for a minute. You can take her for a spin if you like.'

'Can't. You know I'd end up driving her all night. I need to check on a few things upstairs.'

'"Too much work and no play–"'

'Don't worry about me, Charlie. But if *you* don't get home soon, your … your–' *Damn it, what's his wife's name?*

'I'm going! I'm going! Just wait a second though and hear the Jag's engine.'

Weigel trotted over to the E-type. Within seconds, the car park was reverberating to the engine's throaty roar. A few jerky manoeuvres and much squealing of tyres brought it over to the elevator.

Start was shaking his head. 'I hope you don't drive home like that!'

'You bet!' yelled Weigel. 'We're not getting any younger! See you tomorrow, Sonny.' And with a mock military salute to his nonplussed boss, the Senior Counsel roared away in a cloud of exhaust fumes and burning rubber, the roadster weaving dangerously between the concrete columns.

Start remained stationary in the open elevator as the booming echoes subsided. He felt tired and vexed. *Too much work and no play. … We're not getting any younger. Was Charlie trying to tell me something in a roundabout way? … Probably not. He isn't the amateur therapist type. What a thought! And yet, do I really know Charlie? The way he drove the E-type! He's always had boring sedans. Then he turns fifty and wants a sports car. And once behind the wheel, he acts like a college freshman!*

Start thought of his own college days and managed a smile, but the flicker of nostalgia dissipated almost immediately, for in rapid succession he saw video images of a baby and a fuzzy Xeroxed photograph of a pompous-looking businessman in a three-piece suit. ... Something in a newspaper ... something about–

He trembled. *Weetwood! And Misty! Why do I keep–?*

'Ready, boss?' asked Chuck as he and Bob entered the elevator and took up their positions on either side of Start; the ex-marines seemed to dwarf him.

'Ready.'

Grimacing, Bob said: 'I didn't like the colour of Weigel's Jaguar.'

*

Endive Rinso, Dallas's pre-eminent 'interior creator', had been honoured by Sonny Start to 'create' not only the Start Tower's Senior Executives' Suite but also its Penthouse. Luckily, the bizarre results had pleased her client, particularly his own office with its potbelly stove, panelled walls of distressed timber, and what looked like cattle pens housing a 'Conference Module' and 'Secretarial Unit'. But then Sonny had spent his early years in abject poverty on a farm near Waxahachie some forty miles to the south-east of Fort Worth, biographical details he proudly admitted to all and sundry. The only child of God-fearing Baptists who never travelled far from Waxahachie, Sonny had not shone academically. But prowess on the sports field at high school had won him a scholarship to the Texas Christian University in Fort Worth, where he soon became the best of buddies with one Garth Appleby Junior, a fellow TCU footballer. Garth had a red Italian roadster and his own apartment; Sonny soon moved in. Garth dealt only in one-night stands before he met Carmen. Eighteen, beautiful and Mexican, she worked illegally in a supermarket. Sonny resented her presence. The first time he found Garth bedding Carmen and one of her friends, he decided to move out. Garth begged him to stay; Sonny stayed.

The night of Misty's conception remained something of a blur. It had been Garth's birthday and he and Sonny had thrown a party; everyone got stoned. It was still dark when Sonny awoke in an empty living room, lying on a carpet of cigarette ends, half-eaten food and abandoned beer cans. He had to pass Garth's room to reach his own. The sight of Carmen performing fellatio proved irresistible. After Sonny committed the mortal sin, Carmen seduced him.

When Carmen discovered her pregnancy, she'd no doubts about the father's identity: Garth, she averred, had 'a problem'. The tests proved her right; Sonny believed it was God's punishment for his own wickedness.

9

And so he married her, hoping it would atone for his sins. His parents never forgave him: Carmen was Mexican, Catholic and poor. But she was delighted with her U.S. citizenship, which was all she'd ever wanted. There would be no divorce: they needed each other.

To support wife and child, Sonny abandoned TCU and joined an uncle's aluminum cladding business in neighbouring Arlington. Within a few years, he'd acquired control. But it wasn't enough to be good at selling, negotiating and deal making: one needed contacts, people in the right places, connections. Sonny tried his best: every spare moment he'd be on the golf course or working out in the gym of one or other of the country clubs to which he belonged. But in the locker room or bar, Sonny bombed: conversation was not his forte; dirty stories revolted him.

Luckily, Carmen was sexy, gregarious and keen to further her husband's career – and, thereby, her own status. By contrast, she loathed housewifely duties and coping with a frighteningly precocious little girl, Misty. And so, once seized of Sonny's marketing deficiencies, Carmen stepped enthusiastically into the breach. With a Latin-American exuberance that impressed and thrilled all but the most puritanical of Texans, she was soon throwing parties for the Great and Good of their city and its hinterland, and procuring the vital reciprocal hospitality. Very quickly, the Starts began to make all the right contacts. Sonny's business boomed, and Carmen discovered the heady cocktail of charitable causes and the Arts. And when 'Start Aluminum Cladding' was transmogrified into 'Start Industries' and then 'SI Corporation' with a Wall Street flotation, she found herself inundated with trusteeships of ever more prestigious institutions.

Meanwhile, Misty receded still further into the background; schooling in the East seemed the most appropriate course for both parents. What Sonny knew of her life over the last decade had mainly been gleaned from regular and meticulous auditing of his personal bank statements, supplemented by memoranda from Carmen's secretary. Consequently, he was aware that Misty had attended Brynamman, a very expensive boarding school near Newport, Rhode Island. Two years at Harvard had followed, but she'd dropped out – some garbage about charity work – and was now living in New York; her account at Chase in Boston had recently been transferred to a Manhattan branch to which her current monthly allowance – a most generous $4,000 – continued to be paid. Sonny had no need or desire to know anything more. His only concerns had been to ensure that she was fed, clothed, housed and educated in a manner befitting her status up to her coming of age. In his mind such responsibilities had been properly discharged. Anyway, as he reminded himself on the rare occasions his daughter's existence occurred to him at all, it had been Misty's choice to spend almost all her vacations with those snooty Brynamman friends of hers. That was the East for you.

Ironically, the media saw Sonny as both a loving husband and father; their interviews with an unswervingly loyal Carmen confirmed these impressions; Misty never gave interviews. Despite their loveless, sexless relationship, neither Sonny nor Carmen was aware of any specific marital infidelity. They merely assumed that, in accordance with their first post-marriage compact, each had been wholly discreet – as, indeed, was the case. In any event, while Carmen resided at *SonCar* – a mansion in Fort Worth's most exclusive suburb – Sonny spent his weekday nights in the Start Tower penthouse; his workaholic image proved convenient.

*

Sonny had made a few phone calls, dealt with his faxes and emails, and cooked a tasty supper of his own creation in the penthouse's kitchen: unlike Carmen, he didn't enjoy being waited upon; in fact, he found cooking therapeutic. Having eaten, and with a cup of herbal tea for company, he'd tracked down the meaning of 'quisling' on the Internet, but Charlie's 'Peachy Woodhouse' – or whatever it was – had totally eluded him. Frustrated, he'd abandoned the exercise and retreated to the master bedroom to take a shower – his third of the day.

Drying himself, Sonny carefully studied his muscular body in the bathroom's floor-to-ceiling mirrored walls. '"Not getting any younger",' he scoffed. 'Hah!' He put on a robe and returned to the living room, wondering what he could usefully do before turning in. After a few minutes of flicking through the pages of the consultants' report on his proposed acquisition of a bookstore chain in the Pacific North West, he sighed and thought of Bob and Chuck in their quarters down the hall. No doubt they'd be watching a movie in the den – sitting there in shorts and sleeveless T-shirts enjoying each other's company.

'I wish I had a *real* friend,' he whispered. 'I wish–'

But there was no point wishing: it was impossible; it always would be.

With his head bowed, he wandered into the bedroom, slipped naked under the sheets, and, not for the first time in recent months, cried himself to sleep.

# CHAPTER 2

At Bobbins, a Victorian neo-Gothic 'castle' ten miles east of Manchester in the Pennines' foothills, twenty-year-old the Honourable Caroline Camilla Weetwood was sitting at the monumental desk in her beloved library. On this sultry evening in early July, despite habitual contentment with her own company, Caroline took some comfort from the knowledge that she wasn't alone in the vast rambling pile. Doubtless, her father was ensconced in his attic retreat, playing with 'Crewe Junction'; James, her twin brother, would be moping in his second-floor hermitage; and the garrulous housekeeper, Mrs Duffle, was surely glued to the television in the staff flat, watching some romantic nonsense while her dull husband, Ron, the Weetwoods' chauffeur and factotum, enjoyed a few hours of freedom down at the pub in nearby Muckley-in-Dribbledale.

As the heiress to the mighty Goblin soap empire, Caroline could have been excused the occasional anxiety attack about her safety. And yet, due to disinterest in the world beyond academe, she'd never considered her security at all. But since returning home from university two weeks ago for the summer vacation, her equanimity had steadily begun to evaporate. Indeed, such was her bewilderment over this novel feeling of nebulous insecurity that she was no longer able to concentrate on her beloved work for more than half an hour or so, even here in the library's sanctum; previously, it had always operated like some magical time machine transporting her back to the place and era of whatever historical text she was studying.

Caroline's passion for history had begun at the age of eleven when she was sent to St Ethelburger's Ladies' College in Cheltenham – 'Burgers' as pupils and staff called the venerable boarding school. Already rather plump and unathletic, she was an immediate target for name-calling and bullying. Becoming increasingly introverted, she turned to books and chocolate for company. Although no genius, she had a good memory for facts, an attribute that helped to endear her to the Head of History, Miss Angela Tudworth. At the end of her first year, Caroline won the Dame Hilda Bex-Bissell Memorial History Prize. She'd never won anything before.

At Burgers, Caroline had no true friends. Frankly, she didn't care, preferring her own company. In any event, she soon appreciated that her chances of becoming a great historian were negligible without total dedication to her studies. Year after year, therefore, she kept winning the Bex-Bissell prize, an achievement which even made some impression on her parents – albeit neither of them ever possessed a detailed knowledge of her scholastic progress: Lord Weetwood had a world-class business to run; his wife, Beryl, enjoyed a hectic social life.

Professor Marjorie Pangbourne of Durham University's Department of the Age of the Enlightenment had written some of Caroline's favourite history books – her seminal works on Louis XIV in particular. When she was fifteen, Caroline wrote to Professor Pangbourne to tell her so. They were soon corresponding about Versailles, Mazarin, Colbert and so forth; in due course, Pangbourne began signing her letters 'Love, Pongo'; in her final year at Burger's, Caroline's application to read History at Durham proved successful. Now, after two years of sedentary undergraduate studies, she'd ballooned, a state of affairs exacerbated by a lack of interest in her own appearance: tracksuit bottoms, baggy T-shirts, trainers and anoraks comprised her standard garb. And although she possessed a pretty face, it was ruined by savagely-cut golden hair, which conjured up paintings by Breughel; myopic blue eyes squinting behind thick black-framed spectacles exacerbated matters. In consequence, few students had attempted to befriend Caroline; those that had done so were either fellow geeks or mercenaries motivated by her soap-heiress status. In truth, misanthropy rendered all their efforts unproductive.

Bobbins' library reverberated with what sounded like a small explosion as Caroline violently closed the book she'd been trying to study.

'I'm *not* becoming paranoid,' she muttered. '*I – am – not.*' Shaking her head, she anxiously surveyed the chaotic piles of books, papers and assorted maps that littered the desk. 'It's already Thursday evening, a most unwelcome guest is being inflicted on me for the weekend, and I'm hopelessly unprepared for my secret mission.' She groaned and buried her head in her hands.

*

The bizarre business had all started when, only a few days into the vac, Pongo had telephoned Caroline out of the blue from Durham and dropped a bombshell: Professor Hugo Shackleton of Cambridge had suffered a stroke and was unable to give his much-heralded series of lectures on 'George III and the Revolutionary War' scheduled for the Harvard Summer School. The organizers had asked Pongo to step into the breach, which necessitated cancelling her six-week 'vacation' on a Mediterranean island studying priceless manuscripts owned by a German millionaire. She couldn't possibly let Harvard down – or her old tutor, Shackleton. Emphasising the 'absolute confidentiality' of what she was about to disclose, Pongo added that, having examined just a few photocopied pages of the manuscripts, she was convinced they were Louis XIV's secret diaries – indeed, that they would finally reveal the identity of the legendary Man in the Iron Mask.

Despite Caroline's long-held belief that 'MIM', as Pongo called him, had never existed, she was flattered by the Prof's extraordinary request for her, a mere undergraduate, to step into the driving seat of 'Project MIM'. Nonetheless, Caroline reminded Pongo that she'd planned to spend the vacation completing her degree dissertation on Neville Chamberlain's 'appeasement' of Adolf Hitler: she'd prove that Chamberlain had actually laid the foundations of the Allies' ultimate victory in World War II – a subject Pongo herself had advocated, notwithstanding its tenuous links to 'the Age of the Enlightenment'. A roar came down the phoneline: 'Good God, girl, don't be a bloody chump! Six weeks in a luxury villa on the heavenly, tranquil island of Formentera would be an ideal venue for completing both Project MIM *and* the sodding dissertation! Get packing!'

Within hours, Caroline's panic multiplied when she received a fax with the Prof's promised list of Project MIM research materials. To her dismay, there were just six references: the *Encyclopaedia Britannica*, four standard textbooks on seventeenth-century France – all of which Caroline had studied at Burgers and now regarded as infantile – and Alexandre Dumas's novel *Dix Ans Plus Tard ou Le Vicomte de Bragelonne*, the third and final part of which had been translated into English as *The Man in the Iron Mask*. Pongo, it seemed, had done little to prepare herself for Project MIM. It was all very puzzling.

In a sense, the unproductive research which Caroline undertook during the next few days provided a degree of comfort: hardly any contemporary source materials containing references to The Man in the Iron Mask were known to exist. Nevertheless, historians of great eminence agreed on one thing – that he *had* existed, albeit that his mask was actually made of black velvet. But this research also worried Caroline, for it began to dawn on her that although she'd prided herself on being an expert on Louis XIV, she'd never before given much thought to this mysterious prisoner. It was as though she'd dismissed the whole thing as a bit of romantic nonsense, nothing more than a fictitious creation of Dumas's – a product of what she'd always regarded as a rather silly novel because of its cavalier distortion of history. Had she become an academic snob? Or had she become lazy – merely content to digest and regurgitate the works of others? Perhaps she wasn't destined to follow in the footsteps of the great Pangbourne after all.

*

Caroline gasped as she saw a man fall from a mighty cliff. *No – not fall – pushed!*

14

As if awakening from a dream, she stared perplexedly at the library's great Gothic window. The sun having set, the vaulted chamber was now illuminated solely by the twilight filtering through the leaded glass. She switched on the desk lamp, took a deep breath, and told herself to get a grip. For a few minutes she scanned her ever-expanding list of things to take on the trip. Then she tried to read a few more pages of the only guidebook on Formentera that she'd managed to procure so far. The text, however, soon became a blur. After a while, she found herself staring at a photograph of a lighthouse.

'"The Lighthouse of El Pilar",' she read aloud, '"was the inspiration for Jules Verne's *Lighthouse at the End of the World*".' It was perched dramatically at the edge of cliffs that plunged hundreds of feet into a very blue Mediterranean. 'There was no one there,' she murmured hesitantly. 'I never saw ... It was just a trick of the light. He–

'*Stop* it! Get back to work. You've only got three days – *three* days!'

Caroline searched the desk for her pen, only to discover that she'd been gripping it all the time. 'You sillyosity,' she hissed. Spotting a half-eaten Mars bar protruding from an upturned open volume, she added: 'I bet you can't get *them* on Formentera.' But as she was about to add 'Mars bars' to her shopping list for Mrs Duffle, the pen fell from her fingers. Printed at least a dozen times in large block capitals on the top sheet were the words '**WHO WAS HE?**' Caroline stared in horror: she'd no recollection of writing them.

She kept telling herself that the oft-repeated question could only relate to the tantalising mystery of the identity of the masked prisoner – no one else. Her mind raced: *I've become obsessed with him.* And that would surely account for the sense of uneasiness – indeed, *all* the bizarre thoughts – which had recently been troubling her. She'd been torturing herself: Pongo had handed her the opportunity of a lifetime, and she, the student who owed so very much to the great woman, had been ungrateful and unworthy. Selfishly, she'd wanted to stay at home rather than help the Prof out of a jam. But because she'd been bitten by the MIM bug, the mystery which had intrigued so many fine historians now had her well and truly hooked too. And if the solution lurked in the Formentera manuscripts, she would find it.

'Me,' Caroline whispered as if not to break the spell, '... me.' She felt a tingle of excitement. 'I could be famous!'

It was certainly an evening for swings of emotion.

'Resentment, ingratitude, guilt,' she muttered, reaching for the remains of the Mars bar as the effects of dinner began to wear off, '– that's what all this tosh has been about – getting myself organized for the trip, completing the MIM research, fitting in my dissertation.' She even managed a little chuckle as she swallowed the masticated chocolate. But her smile evaporated as she suddenly recalled the strange tone in Mrs Duffle's voice when serving the first course at dinner that evening.

*

Caroline was dining alone with just the Formentera guidebook for company: her father, aloft with his trains, was dining off a tray; James, who was addicted to television and computer games, always ate in his room.

'You haven't forgotten, Miss Caroline,' sneered Mrs Duffle, 'that your American *friend* arrives tomorrow morning, have you?' It was the way Mrs Duffle had emphasised 'friend' which Caroline found particularly irritating. Mrs Duffle's discourtesy, however, was not something she'd time to dwell upon: she was more concerned with the import of the reminder and a desire to avoid any indication that she had indeed forgotten that the arrival of her former 'penfriend' was imminent: Project MIM had pushed all thoughts of the horrid visit out of her head. Glazing over with undisguised disinterest as Mrs Duffle droned on about the guest's collection from the airport and her board and lodging, Caroline ruminated yet again on her absent mother's outrageous presumption.

The unwelcome tidings had hit Caroline like a tsunami on the day of her homecoming for the vacation, when Ron Duffle collected her at Stalybridge station off the Durham train. Before he'd even completed loading her luggage into the Jaguar, Duffle had begun babbling about the 'incredible' news – that 'Miss Caroline' had a friend coming to stay! He was soon to discover something even more incredible: she'd no idea what he was talking about. Caroline never engaged in lengthy discussions with the Duffles, but on that grim day she'd no option: they were the only people who could shed any light on the mystery. There would have been no point in questioning her father on his return from Soap House – WSD's world headquarters in neighbouring Goblinville – as he invariably took no interest in domestic affairs. Although James was at home, he'd given every impression of being deranged for the last couple of years. As for her mother, Caroline was unsurprised to learn that Beryl had already made her way to the *Villa Gobelin*, the Weetwoods' estate on the French Riviera at St-Jean-Cap-Ferrat, where, according to Mrs Duffle, she planned to remain until late September. And so it was that over several cups of tea in the kitchen, Caroline discovered the housekeeper's version of the affair.

About a month earlier, Mrs Duffle had been serving breakfast to an unusually cheerful and talkative Lady Weetwood, who, in due course, confessed to having answered the telephone the previous evening, only to find herself talking to 'an American girl'. To her ladyship's astonishment,

16

she claimed to be someone with whom Caroline had regularly corresponded for some years while at Burgers. Initially, she'd doubted the girl's veracity, but detailed interrogation convinced her of the caller's *bona fides*: she mentioned a prestigious girls' school in New England, studies at Harvard, and a legal career in New York.

In brief, the American was planning a summer trip to Europe. Her first stop was England, and because Caroline had once written so voluminously and enthusiastically about the glorious architecture and scenery of Manchester and its environs, she'd allotted a whole weekend to the region, and very much hoped she could spend it with Caroline at 'Bobbins Castle'. Mrs Duffle distinctly remembered Lady Weetwood saying that it was high time Caroline had 'a friend' – especially someone who was 'a paid-up member of the international jet set'. A flurry of transatlantic communications during the following days resulted in an instruction from her ladyship that a 'Miss Misty Start' would be joining Caroline for the first weekend of July. Not unreasonably, Mrs Duffle assumed that her ladyship had liaised with Miss Caroline and that she'd acceded to her old penfriend's request for accommodation.

Mrs Duffle was now stunned to learn that Caroline was wholly ignorant of the matter and had had no contact with 'Miss Start' for some two years. Mrs Duffle suggested that in view of her ladyship's hectic preparations for her lengthy stay at the *Villa Gobelin*, she must have simply forgotten to contact Caroline. But Mrs Duffle was not Beryl's best advocate. Caroline believed that her mother had acted maliciously: it was the sort of practical joke which would have appealed to her warped sense of humour.

And so, Caroline had found herself presented with a *fait accompli*. Furthermore, she and Mrs Duffle concurred that Lord Weetwood would be wholly ignorant of the imminent invasion of his precious sanctuary. But then, even if her mother had taken the trouble to inform him of any aspect of the American's visit, Caroline knew it would have gone in one ear and out the other. For a day or two, Caroline had considered all kinds of excuses to wriggle out of the irksome arrangements made on her behalf, but she simply didn't possess the sort of cunning or malice which motivated her mother's every thought and deed. Project MIM's materialization, however, provided her with the perfect excuse to remain at home while 'Misty' spent her mercifully brief stay touring Manchester's 'sights'. Ron Duffle and the Jaguar would be placed at her disposal – Lord Weetwood rarely left the house at weekends – and Caroline even weighed up the pros and cons of slipping Duffle £10 to keep the pest away from Bobbins for as many hours as possible. Significantly, she chose not to tell Mrs Duffle anything about the nature of her 'penfriend' relationship.

In truth, she'd never told anyone, but then it had been something she'd tried hard to forget.

Throughout Caroline's days at Burgers, Angela Tudworth ran SELCOPEL, the St Ethelburger's Ladies' College Penfriend League. A proud 'Old Burger' herself, she'd been an enthusiastic participator in the League since her teens; she was still corresponding with seven 'girls', albeit the replies to her letters from all but one had become somewhat irregular. It was this most loyal of correspondents, Miss Betty van Heusen, who wrote to Angela in autumn 1992 with a request which quite stunned her. Betty taught 'American English' at exclusive Brynamman, Rhode Island. Thanks to their long and intimate relationship, Angela and Betty had done much to cement links between their schools; over the years, many students had become SELCOPEL penfriends. But when Angela read the request in Betty's letter that autumn, she feared a serious setback to all their good works. A Brynamman 'superb all-rounder' had heard of 'a sad, lonely Burgers lass' who desperately needed 'a pal'. All attempts in Cheltenham to befriend her had failed. Betty's girl was convinced she was 'up to the task.' Could Angela effect an introduction and persuade the English youngster to put pen to paper?

The 'superb all-rounder' was Misty Start; the 'sad, lonely lass' was Caroline Weetwood.

Enclosed with Betty's letter was Misty's curriculum vitae. Angela read it with mounting horror: Misty was more than an all-rounder – she was perfection personified. In addition to her accomplishments as an amateur thespian, dazzling violinist and polyglot linguist, Misty also possessed an armful of trophies for sporting achievements and devoted a considerable portion of her free time to various charitable and environmental causes. It was all very impressive for a fifteen-year-old Texan.

And that was why Angela found herself in such a dilemma: Caroline was the American's antithesis; any kind of friendship between them was surely impossible; someone had committed a wicked deception. But to ascertain the truth she'd have to conduct an embarrassing investigation – one that could provoke an almighty transatlantic rumpus involving at least *two* billionaire fathers. Thus, Angela decided to let fate take its course. In any event, she doubted that Caroline could be persuaded to join SELCOPEL: the girl's anti-social attitudes had frequently been the topic of gossip in the staff common room. Yet, softened up by tea and chocolate cake in Miss Tudworth's study, and feeling pity for her pleading history mentor, Caroline suddenly found herself volunteering to serve the League.

Alas, subsequent analysis of Misty's curriculum vitae led Caroline to the conclusion that she was the victim of a conspiracy involving those beastly

18

fellow pupils who'd long striven to make her life a misery. Nonetheless, during her three remaining years at Burgers she honoured her SELCOPEL commitments and wrote her mandatory fortnightly letter to Misty. Initially, she'd expected to receive only one or two replies: those responsible for the 'joke' which had been played on both Miss Tudworth and herself would soon get bored as the fun wore off. But, to her dismay, the replies kept coming – long, earnest and excruciatingly detailed reports of Misty's glorious achievements at Brynamman, supported by photographic evidence – including countless snaps of a startlingly beautiful and athletic teenager being awarded silver cups. It was, Caroline concluded, all too good to be true.

Caroline's last letter to Misty was mailed a week before she made her final and long-awaited farewells to St Ethelburger's. Yet, she received a further three letters from Misty during the following months, which caused her to wonder whether the American *wunderkind* had been genuine all along. Having written three years' worth of wilful gibberish to Misty, however, Caroline refrained from ascertaining the truth.

*

Ensconced in Bobbins' library on the eve of Misty's arrival, Caroline dwelt on the comforting thought that if all went according to plan, she might only have to suffer the American at dinner – apart from meeting her at the airport in the morning and on the drive back to Muckley. Accordingly, fortified by her chocolate snack, Caroline stretched her flabby limbs, scribbled '**MARS BARS!!!**' on a scrap of paper, and recommenced her MIM research with fresh determination. She resolved to summarize the salient facts which she'd ascertained of the lives of the two men whom most reputable historians had shortlisted as the primary candidates for the Man in the Iron Mask – an Italian diplomat and a French valet, albeit she'd yet to identify any credible reason why either of them should have been subjected to life imprisonment *in a mask*. This was what she hoped to discover in the Formentera manuscripts, or – and she prayed this would be the case – that MIM had been someone far more important, such as an elder brother of Louis XIV – whether a twin or not – as both Voltaire and Dumas had suggested. That would certainly shock many historians – and make a name for herself!

And so, poring over her text books and scribbling furiously, Caroline finally managed to forget about her visitor from across the Pond – and, more importantly, the bizarre sensation which had first manifested itself shortly after Pongo Pangbourne's momentous telephone call: that someone – or something – was constantly watching her, a sensation which had materialised yet again that very morning when she'd taken one of her infrequent strolls through the grounds.

Caroline was not prone to flights of fancy, but, nonetheless, she'd been followed. That, in truth, was what she'd suddenly felt down by the lake, although she hadn't seen or heard anything that could have reasonably led her to this worrying conclusion. Yet, returning to the house as fast as her excess weight and feeble physique would permit, something made her turn and look back when she finally reached the top of the long flight of steps that connected the parterre's upper and lower terraces.

A man was standing beside one of the great elms on the far side of the lake – staring straight at her. She blinked and he disappeared.

For the first time in her life, Caroline had felt real, uncontrollable fear. 'I'm going mad,' she'd murmured, '– just like the rest of the family.'

# CHAPTER 3

As the crow flies, the picturesque village of Muckley-in-Dribbledale – plain 'Muckley' to locals – lies about a mile from Bobbins. On its village green stands the quaint Cob o' Coal Inn, and in one of its half-dozen chintzy guestrooms, Rory Devlin – a former Goblin laboratory technician – was unsuspectingly lighting the fuse of his current mentor, Ursula Klinker.

'We should have stuck to my original plan,' whined Devlin, 'and just blackmailed them. I mean, so many things can go wrong with kidnapping. And she could always identify us – even if she never sees our faces. That's assuming, of course, that you can abduct your ... your *victim* in the first place. But Caroline's a weirdo! She *never* goes out – well, hardly ever.

'You said it was going to be easy, Ursula, identify her routine and then – bam! But after almost a fortnight lurking in those bloody bushes, well, I think we're wasting our time. And I'm going cross-eyed staring through those sodding binoculars. I mean, it's not as though she works in some office from nine to five so we know when she sets off for the bus stop, or that she picks up the kids from school at a particular time, is it? That blob just sits in that bloody library for hours on end, reading and stuffing her face with chocolate. And then when she *does* go out for one of her rare strolls – never at the same times – she keeps pretty close to the house. I'm telling you, Ursula, it's bloody hopeless. If you want to know the truth, I'm sick of–'

'*Scheisse*! Shut your damned, moaning mouth, or I'll–'

The road atlas that Klinker had been studying spun across the room and hit a glass vase containing a motley assortment of wild flowers on top of a chest of drawers. Ricocheting, it smashed on the polished floorboards below the sash window.

'You just don't know when to stop, do you? On and on and on ...' Klinker closed her eyes, and, breathing deeply, mentally counted to ten. When she opened them, Devlin was still sitting bolt upright at the other side of the double bed, staring at the vase's remains. His mouth was wide open and there was a look of fear in his eyes. She picked up a packet of cigarettes from the bedside table and began to light one.

'Go and clear it up,' she hissed.

Bristling with indignation, Devlin turned to look at her, just as she exhaled a cloud of smoke in his direction. He pulled a face and attempted to blow it back.

'What the hell did you do *that* for?'

Not knowing – or caring – whether he was referring to the vase or the smoke, Klinker ignored him.

'We'll have to pay for it, you know,' Devlin bleated.

'Don't be stupid.'

'We will. They check – they always do in hotels. And–'

'If you don't stop bloody moaning' – she was punctuating each syllable with a stab of her cigarette within inches of Devlin's face – 'I'll–'

'You'll *what*?'

Klinker took another long drag, but this time blew the smoke towards the low ceiling of exposed wooden beams. 'Never mind. Now be a good boy and go and clear up the mess.'

'Why do *I* have–?'

'Just *do* it! And while you're up, empty the ashtray.'

Devlin glared at her for a few moments; she glared back. Momentarily, he forgot about the smashed vase. He wished she'd wear something in bed, at least until the lights were switched off: she had the flattest woman's chest he'd ever seen. She'd claimed to be fifty, but he'd seen her passport: she was fifty-five. In fact, with that prune-like skin, thanks to all the sunbathing over the decades, the sad cow looked more like sixty.

He suddenly realized that she was smiling at him. Averting his gaze, he got out of bed, pulled on a pair of boxer shorts, and began performing his chores. Klinker watched him in silence, admiring his tanned, wiry body with its covering of curly light brown hair. He was in his late twenties, the age she preferred.

*

Rory had first met Ursula almost exactly a year ago at the remote La Jenny naturist camp on Aquitaine's Côte d'Argent, some thirty miles west of Bordeaux. Although a practitioner for some years, he'd not previously sampled the pleasures of La Jenny. Ursula, by contrast, was a regular, and the instant she set eyes on him she accurately identified his type.

Misfortune had been Rory's constant companion since the age of eleven and his arrival at John Lennon College, a comprehensive school in a tough Nottingham suburb. Due to his delicate physique and health, it proved a hostile environment for the nurturing of his intellectual pursuits. Unable to finance a private education, his doting parents finally decided to undertake the schooling of their only child within the protective walls of the family home. Initially, Rory welcomed their commitment, but the law suit commenced by the disapproving local education authority generated a barrage of embarrassing publicity. Moreover, the rocketing costs of the litigation pushed the Devlins into the hands of loan sharks; the strain on

22

the health of Rory's father, which had never been strong, undoubtedly contributed to his fatal heart attack. And then, within days of the funeral, Mrs Devlin suffered a nervous breakdown, whereupon her son's ignominious return to John Lennon College became inevitable.

In due course, however, Rory did manage to secure admission to the equally undistinguished Stonehenge University – formerly Mid-Wiltshire Polytechnic – to read Physics and Chemistry. Armed with a degree of sorts after three uneventful years, he headed north to Goblinville and the glum block of laboratories adjoining WSD's headquarters, Soap House. Thanks to his boyish good looks, Rory swiftly acquired two ardent admirers – fellow technician, Melanie Meld, and the recently appointed Head of Research, Dr Mark Dumpwell, who had eagerly recruited him. Melanie, who was the same age as Rory, exuded jollity and gregariousness – qualities which, perhaps, compensated for her lack of stature: she was just five feet tall. Mark did not wear his homosexuality on his sleeve; his colleagues believed he was just a regular good-looking guy in his early forties who enjoyed the carefree life of a bachelor. After all, he was an ardent supporter of Manchester United, and, as an enthusiastic officer in the Royal Air Force Volunteer Reserve, he never missed an opportunity to mention his pilot's licence. On Friday and Saturday nights, however, and sporting the latest designer clothes favoured by the most fashionable members of the 18-30 set, Mark cruised the bars and clubs of Manchester's 'Gay Village' around Canal Street.

It was Melanie who made the first move: she invited Rory to her stone cottage in Saddleworth for 'a snack' one evening. He found himself enjoying a candle-lit supper for two with a Gloria Estefan CD playing on 'REPEAT'; she managed to remove his trousers before pudding. Thereafter, she was like a limpet. Mark, who had developed an all-consuming infatuation, seethed. He'd inherited Meld from his predecessor and had instinctively disliked her from the outset. Now, Rory's manipulation into a cosy embryonic marital relationship before his very eyes generated such a degree of loathing that he lapsed momentarily into irrationality.

In her office mail one morning, Melanie received an anonymous typed note from 'a friend', informing her that it was in her very best interests to know that Rory Devlin suffered from genital herpes. The 'friend', of course, was Mark and the contents of his note – typed on pink stationary bordered with a variety of hardy annuals and complemented by a matching envelope exuding Channel N$^c$ 5 – were wholly untrue. Nevertheless, Melanie assumed the worst – as Markl had hoped – and the ensuing row with Rory in a corridor attracted the attention of most of the laboratory staff; the defamed party's earnest denials only served to exacerbate the volume and vehemence of their repetition. Finally, Rory snapped: with the aid of a fire extinguisher, he devastated thousands of pounds' worth of sophisticated equipment. It was not the outcome Mark had anticipated, albeit Melanie did promptly resign.

Rory's prosecution for criminal damage caused Mark considerable distress: too thorough an investigation could have revealed his complicity. But these fears proved groundless: the case was ineptly defended. While serving his six months' sentence in an open prison, Rory's mother committed suicide. Mark came to offer sympathy, but lust and sentimentality proved a fatal combination. His exceptionally venomous remarks about Melanie finally alerted Rory to the possibility that Mark, for some reason, had played a role in his downfall.

Mrs Devlin's demise resulted in Rory's inheritance of a modest semi-detached house, which, to his surprise, was valued at £130,000. Within a few months of his release, he'd sold it, rented a bedsit in Oldham, grown a moustache and shoulder-length hair, bought a small second-hand car, and begun stalking Mark. Swiftly discovering his penchant for Canal Street's nightlife, the penny finally dropped. Rory's numerous homicidal schemes proved a waste of time: even before he could make a decision on the most appropriate mode of execution, Mark was appointed Technical Director of WSD's Latin American Division in Montevideo, Uruguay. Sitting disguised in the hostelries frequented by his former colleagues, Rory's eavesdropping on their conversations about Mark's departure had initially overwhelmed him with depression. But then it occurred to him that Uruguay might offer far better opportunities for subjecting his former boss to a gruesome death.

It didn't take Rory long to locate Mark's Montevideo apartment or his places of work – both official and unofficial. At the latter, a small nondescript industrial unit on the city's outskirts, he witnessed deliveries of numerous dogs. After three months of near-continuous surveillance, and having amassed sufficient evidence not only to destroy Mark but also to make a lot of money for himself, Rory returned to Europe for a well-earned rest. Within days, having seen an advertisement for La Jenny in one of his naturist magazines, he was naked and pushing a trolley through its well-stocked supermarket. As chance would have it, he and Ursula Klinker had simultaneously reached for the last jar of Bonne Maman fig jam; it crashed to the floor after first bouncing off his left foot. Ursula immediately barked orders to a terrified assistant to clear up the mess, and frogmarched Rory to her chalet for his bruise to be treated. Promptly after applying herbal ointments, she gripped his penis.

It was after this first coupling and while his foot continued to throb, that Ursula interrogated Rory about his life. The schnapps probably made him say more than he would have wanted. His account of what he'd gleaned in Montevideo of Mark Dumpwell's secret project aroused a terrifying outburst of expletives in both German and English.

'Filth! These *Schwein* who do the research on animals should all be put into camps and—' With shaking hands, Ursula lit another cigarette. After a few drags, she said calmly: 'We must punish them – including your Dr Dumpwell – just like the others.'

'"Others"?'

During the following days, as they wandered nude through the pine forests and along the empty beaches, Ursula disclosed few details of her secret 'organization' for animal liberation. She was more forthcoming about her background: her late father was a baron; there'd been Swiss boarding schools, marriage at eighteen to an Argentinean rancher, revolution – divorce. For the last 'twenty years or so' she'd lived frugally on various small annuities, globetrotting as a very independent traveller. It had all sounded rather exotic and Bohemian to Rory. In fact, although it was true that Ursula had travelled to most countries of the world *with a coastline*, she'd done so as a marine insurance investigator based in Hamburg. Starting in a minor clerical position, she'd risen through the ranks, thanks to possessing all three necessary attributes for a successful claims investigator: thoroughness, stubbornness and cynicism. At fifty, and still unmarried and childless, she'd retired early on a modest pension.

Notwithstanding Ursula's age and flat chest, the combination of sun, sand, blitzkrieg sex and animal horror stories during that fortnight at La Jenny had been enough to hook Rory: he agreed that they should pool resources in the noble struggle for animal rights. Their first campaign would be directed against the evil WSD and its henchman, Dumpwell. Rory's modest plans of blackmail were transformed, Ursula scoffing at the sum he'd had in mind. And as her stratagem began to take form during the months which followed – they were soon cohabiting in her little house in the forests to the south of Munich – Dumpwell seemed to drop out of the picture, while kidnapping and the Weetwood family came very much into focus.

*

From the bathroom, there was the sound of running taps. Ursula sucked viciously on her cigarette and focused on the ash hanging dangerously at its tip. 'Hurry up, for Christ's sake, Rory! What are you doing in there?'

'I'm *coming*!' he snapped, trotting out and proffering a wet ashtray.

'You only had to *empty* it. It didn't need the disinfecting.'

Rory raised his eyebrows and rolled his eyes. 'Do you want it or not?'

'You could have dried it.'

'I was about to dry it when you–'

'*Scheisse*! Now the ash has fallen on the bed.'

'I suppose that's *my* fault. Perhaps if you obeyed the hotel's rules – perhaps if you just used common sense and didn't smoke in bed–'

'Don't start that again! Don't ever tell me–!'

There was a tremendous banging on the wall behind the headboard as a man roared: '*Another sound from you two and you'll be out in the fucking street! There're people trying to fucking sleep in here!*'

Twisting round to face the source of the remonstrance, Ursula snarled evil-sounding phrases in German. 'Scum!' she added. 'I said they were common.'

Rory sat down on the bed. 'It's not *them*,' he whispered. 'They left for Edinburgh two days ago. Actually, I thought they were rather nice.'

'"Nice",' Ursula mimicked.

'Yes. Nice. They reminded me of my parents, if you *must* know.'

Ursula detected the note of pathos, and resolved to change the subject. 'Come on, Rory, get back into bed. Let's have a sensible discussion about Miss Weetwood. I really don't believe things are as black as you paint them.'

Rory sighed heavily. 'I'm tired, Ursula.'

'I'm tired too, *Liebling*, but we really need to sort things out.'

Rory changed his position, and ended up sitting cross-legged facing her on his side of the bed. '*You're* tired? Ha!'

'Yes, Rory. I know you've had a hard time here, but–'

'You can say that again!'

'– but I have not been sitting on my backsides all day for the last week reading, sunbathing and sipping the cocktails, you know.'

'No?'

'No. As well you know it.'

'I suppose life at the cottage must be pretty exhausting.'

Ursula tutted and stubbed out her cigarette in the wet ashtray. 'So, what do you think I've been doing there?'

Rory raised his shoulders. 'Dusting? Making it nice and homely for "Miss Weetwood"? I know – installing a torture chamber. That's more in your line, I suppose.' His smirk quickly disappeared. 'Just joking, love.'

She reached out and stroked his right foot. 'Kidnapping is not a matter for the joking.'

'I know. I–'

'For a start, I've had to do a lot of reconnaissance around the cottage.'

Rory frowned. 'I hope you've been ... discreet.' He bit his lip. 'You *were* wearing your wig, I hope?'

She snorted and reached for her cigarettes. 'Darling, I'm a professional, remember. This is not the first time–'

'Do you have to smoke another? You've only just put one out, for God's sake.'

'It helps me think and we've got a lot to sort out before I go back to the cottage tomorrow. Now, stop interrupting. ... I've cleared out the attic. Did I tell you? I would have preferred a cellar but the attic will be OK. And I've got us stocked up with food. And I drove over to Leeds – what a dump! – and bought the handcuffs and ankle shackles.' Rory's mouth fell open. 'I told you any good sex shop would have them. They were having a sale – two for the price of one. So I got two pairs of each. And yes, I *was* wearing the wig and I spoke in my best American accent. The assistant even asked me which part of the States I came from!' Rory managed a smile. 'And I got the masks from some joke shop in Bradford.'

'What sort?'

'Two gorillas.'

'Not very original but I suppose they'll do.' A worried expression immediately returned to Rory's face. 'I still don't know how we're ever going to get our hands on her. The blackmail thing–'

'*Ach*! Just wait a minute. I've got some ideas.'

'And – and – what about the owners of the cottage – or their agents? They might come and check on the place. ... The laundry – don't they change towels and–?'

'We're doing our *own* laundry. Jesus! I've told you all this before.'

'I don't remember.'

'You don't listen.'

'I do.'

'You–' She breathed deeply. 'The owners live in London, and we've told the agents you're an author who needs somewhere remote for a month and–'

'Yes, yes! Of course I remember *that*. I'm not an idiot, but–'

'And I've found the perfect place for the drop.'

Rory glared. 'Where? How? I thought we were going to choose it together.'

'It's not a new car, *Liebling*. Anyway, it was purely by chance. I'm sure you'll agree it's perfect. I took a wrong turn driving over this evening and ended up on a minor road on the moors between Halifax and Huddersfield. It's so wonderfully bleak up there, and the road runs straight for at least a kilometre. That's what I was checking in the atlas before ... There's a ruined stone hut and lots of these drystone walls and not a living creature – apart from sheep – as far as the eyes are seeing.'

Rory looked unconvinced. 'Well, I say there's safety in numbers. I still think a big railway station, or a department store – somewhere in Manchester. *Your* place sounds too exposed, too–'

'You've seen *too* many movies. Stations! Department stores! Either some thief walks off with the briefcase containing the money or half the crowd are plain-clothing policemen.'

Rory's eyes bulged. 'Oh! So you *do* think they might go to the police?'

'Yes – no! I mean–'

'That's the merit of the pure blackmail scheme, don't you see? Weetwood would rather die than have his reputation destroyed. You know, all that public school, stiff upper lip, "I say, old boy, not quite cricket" crap. He'd never *dare* involve the police. And it's so much simpler.'

Ursula leaned back against her pile of pillows. 'I love the way you say "Weetwood",' she said softly. 'You really do hate him, don't you? ... *Detest* and *despise*.' She enunciated the words carefully. 'And so you should, most definitely.'

'Don't *you?*'

'Of course, for his lies and cruelty. ... Every time I think of what has been happening in Montevideo – is happening now – as we speak ... well, it makes me so angry, so sick. I wish I could lock *him* up and give *him* a taste of his own medicine. Is that how you say it?'

Rory nodded. He was trying hard to appear empathetic but feared that she'd see through his performance. What truly irritated him was her order of priorities, for whenever she embarked upon one of her diatribes against Weetwood, she always appeared more concerned with his crimes against third parties than those which had been committed against himself. Whether or not this was a false impression, the fact was that she invariably invoked the former as the principal justification for their proposed acts of retribution against the Weetwoods and the source of their wealth.

As if reading his mind, Ursula's face became a picture of theatrical compassion. 'But all that,' she said in a voice oozing desolation, 'is nothing to what he and his henchmen – especially that pig Dumpwell – did to you. The scars will probably never heal and–'

'Please, Ursula. Don't. I'll have nightmares and–'

'I'm sorry, Rory, but sometimes we have to remind ourselves why we're here – why they have to be punished. Jesus Christ! They humiliated you, destroyed your career, they' – she leaned forward and gripped his arm – '*killed* your mother, Rory.'

*There, she's said it, her coup de grâce. She's redeemed herself.* 'You don't need to remind me.'

'I do, especially when you start moaning about a few hours of observation, a couple of days of spying. Hell – you spent *weeks* in Montevideo following Dumpwell! You were even planning to *kill* him. *You*! Of course, you didn't have the slightest idea how to go about it, and knowing what I know now, I think you would have probably – how do you say it in English? – "chickened out"?'

Rory glared at her. 'Maybe we *should* still kill him. He's the one really responsible for–'

'*Ach*! He's only a minion. He just obeys orders. We have to go to the *top*. Surely you can see that, can't you?' Rory was about to say something and then hesitated. 'Yes?' Ursula prompted. 'Come on, what is it?' But she knew what was coming: she could read him like an open book.

'Well ...'

'*Ja?*'

'Well, don't get mad, but why ... why don't we just blackmail them? I mean, we've got *photographs* and–'

'Rory, Rory, *Rory*. I've told you so many times that we should not rely on all the Montevideo stuff as our *only* weapon. What if they called our bluff and told us to do our worst? They'd deny everything. Weetwood's company is a multi-billion-dollar multinational. They could press a button and clear up their act in Uruguay before we could pick up the phone to the ... I don't know – the *Daily Mail* or the BBC. There wouldn't be a trace of Dumpwell or his team ... or their victims. But if we use that stuff as *part* of our arsenal, then Weetwood will realize we really mean business, that we're not just a bunch of amateurs. He'll be tearing his hair out wondering how we found out – and what else we might know. And he'll definitely not risk – I mean, he'll believe that if he doesn't play the ball, we really will carry out our threats to do some very nasty things to his fat little girl.'

Not for the first time, Rory looked as if he might have finally been convinced of the merits of her arguments. 'I'd still like to do something to Dumpwell one day,' he murmured.

'Oh, I think I – *we'll* be paying him a visit in the not-too-distant future.'

Feeling thirsty, Rory went to fetch two glasses of water from the bathroom. As he set one down on the bedside table next to Ursula, he said: 'All right. I can see the force of your argument, but that still leaves us with the problem of getting our hands on Caroline.' He moved around to his side of the bed, removed his boxer shorts, and got under the sheets.

Sensing that Ursula's lack of response was an indication of an admission of fallibility, he warmed to his theme. 'I mean, if Weetwood himself was our target, at least we'd have a definite routine to work around. He leaves for Goblinville every morning at precisely the same time – almost to the second. It's the same when he comes back in the evening, like a railway timetable.'

'Well, he would, wouldn't he?' sniggered Ursula, squeezing one of Rory's nipples.

'Ouch! That hurt!'

'Don't be such a baby.'

'Well, it did.' Rory pretended to be discomforted for a few moments and then pinched Ursula on the shoulder. 'Why?' he asked.

Ursula glanced at her shoulder and then at Rory. 'Why what?'

'Why would he be like a railway timetable?'

'Because ... *Mein Gott*! Don't you remember *anything*?'

'I can't remember every little detail.'

'You copied his entry in *Who's Who* and–!'

'Shush! Keep your hair on!' And then, realizing what he'd said, Rory stared at her shaved head and thought of her wig. He spotted it on the dressing table and started to giggle. To his amazement, Ursula saw the joke, and, thanks to her addiction to nicotine, managed a rasping chortle. It was the first time either of them had laughed in a very long time. But the amusement, such as it was, rapidly evaporated.

'Anyway,' Ursula finally said, 'that *Who's Who* thing says Weetwood is crazy about railroads. He owns one of the world's largest toy train collections.'

'Model *railways*,' Rory corrected smugly.

'Precisely! Ah, so you *do* remember, *Liebling*?'

Rory nodded. 'Of course,' he lied, 'I was just joking.' He stared for a few moments at the chintz curtains swaying gently on either side of the open windows. They seemed to inspire him.

'Look, now that we know Caroline is a bit of a problem, why don't we reactivate the idea of abducting Weetwood himself? Seems obvious the more you think of it. He's the one responsible for everything. He's got the money and all his movements are predictable. ... I mean, down one of the narrow lanes near the house, it would be easy to block the road as he's driving to work – being driven, I mean – and I'm sure that chauffeur bloke wouldn't be a problem. He doesn't look as though he could fight his way out of a paper bag, and ...'

Ursula allowed Rory to drone on for some minutes, her blood pressure slowly mounting as a potentially explosive mixture of frustration and exasperation bubbled up inside her. She forced herself to stop listening and imagined conducting the Berlin Philharmonic in a performance of Bruckner's Ninth Symphony. As she brought the First Movement to its cataclysmic conclusion, she experienced one of her favourite visions of a world cleansed of its entire population by nuclear war – with just herself surviving. She'd not made any provision for Rory Devlin in her bunker.

'You haven't been listening to a word I've been saying, have you?' he whined.

'Frankly, no. Who are you going to negotiate with – Weetwood's board of directors or just one of them? Which ones do you trust? What do you know about *any* of them? Or maybe you had Lady Weetwood in mind? Perhaps you see the vacuous Beryl making her way across the windswept moorland in high heels and a cocktail dress to make the drop?'

'I ... There's the son.'

'Nobody's seen *him* for *two* years, Rory. And I hope you're not going to try and convince me that Fatty Weetwood could do something sensible if her father were kidnapped. ... You're not, are you?'

Rory snorted and threw his head back onto the pillows.

'The fact is, *Liebling*, fathers invariably have soft spots for their daughters. And Weetwood is also the only character in this scenario who'll definitely be able to get a large amount of cash organized at very short notice. And he's the one most affected by the Montevideo angle. Do you honestly imagine that he'll have told his wife and kids about all that? Do you?'

'I suppose not. ... If only ...'

'If only *what*?'

'Well, I was just thinking that if Lady Weetwood hadn't gone to France, *she* might have been the ideal candidate.'

'*Scheisse*! Aren't you forgetting your gossiping barmaid downstairs, that Mrs' – Ursula flicked a hand dismissively – 'Mrs ...?'

'Umpleby.'

'That's the one. *Mein Gott*, just *three* nights ago you phoned and told me what she'd said! Remember? They hate each other – Lord and Lady Weetwood. The impression I received, Rory, was that he'd *pay* us to abduct her – or vice versa.'

Rory fidgeted with embarrassment. 'Maybe Mrs Umpleby was exaggerating.'

Ursula lit yet another cigarette and puffed at it frenetically. She glanced at the alarm clock: it was already well after midnight and she wanted to make an early start in the morning.

'Oh, I nearly forgot,' Rory said breaking the silence. 'Talking of Mrs Umpleby, I was walking back from the Weetwoods' last night and took a short cut along the river and then through those woods and–'

31

'There's a cottage with horrid gnomes in the garden.'

'You've got it. Well, the cottage belongs to none other than Mrs Umpleby.'

Ursula stared at him blankly. 'Is that it? How fascinating! I–'

'Just a minute! I haven't finished. God! You're so impatient. ... That Duffle bloke – the Weetwoods' chauffeur – his car was parked in the lane at the side of the cottage and the two of them, him and Umpleby, were in it snogging like a couple of teenagers.' He beamed at Ursula triumphantly. 'What about that for a bit of gossip? Mind you, I should have put two and two together before. After all, he comes down here every night for a drink. I don't blame him. You should see his wife! Even through binoculars she's gruesome. And then when she was serving me breakfast the other morning – Umpleby, not the chauffeur's wife – I was doing my "interested tourist" routine, like "Who owns that big estate up the road? Is it open to the public?" and so on. Well, she just couldn't resist showing off and putting on this pathetic posh voice and telling me she knows Lord and Lady Weetwood's chauffeur – "butler" she called him – and what a wonderful gentleman he was and everything. And what a sad life he'd had what with his parents being killed in a freak accident and being brought up by Dr Barnardo's – that's a home for orphans.'

Rory shot a coy glance at Ursula, who was also propped against the pillows with her arms folded. Her eyes, however, were firmly shut. He wondered whether she'd nodded off or was just bored. He resolved to press on.

'They were standing at a bus stop and this car went out of control. It mounted the pavement and ran them down. He was a lecturer at Manchester University – the driver, that is. He'd been out boozing. And you'll never guess what Mrs Umpleby said to me.' Ursula remained motionless. 'She leaned over me as I tucked into my bacon and eggs and whispered "That's why Mr Duffle hates Germans, love. The driver was German, you see. I'm only telling you because I know your friend's one, and if Ron – that's Mr Duffle – hears her talking in the bar one evening, he might go a bit funny. I suppose if my folks had been killed by a drunk *German*, I wouldn't be too fond of them neither."'

Rory wondered whether he was twisting the knife too much. He looked at Ursula out of the corner of his eye. Nothing. She reminded him of an Egyptian mummy; it was not the first time he'd thought so. He began to reach for the light switch, just as the mummy's eyes shot open. Jumping and gasping, he watched with mounting fear as Ursula's head turned to face him. Her eyes were burning into him and she was grinning crazily.

'I – I–' he stammered, fearing another one of her verbal or physical assaults.

'A drunk *German*?' she hissed. 'He hates *Germans*, does he?' Rory's body tensed as she leaned towards him. 'You've *done* it, *Liebling*! You've *done* it! You've found the Achilles heel – unwittingly of course – of the Weetwoods!' Then she lunged, seized his head with both hands, and pressed her hot, smoky lips to his.

# CHAPTER 4

George Reginald Weetwood, 3rd Baron Weetwood of Muckley-in-Dribbledale, Chairman and Chief Executive of WSD plc, was sitting on the lavatory. He often retreated to his favourite cubicle in the Directors' Washroom at Soap House: it was the only place in the whole building where he could escape from his colleagues and the incessant bombardment of electronic communications. It was particularly safe from his extremely efficient secretary, Patricia Spigot. The other day, Miss Spigot had even suggested taking a mobile telephone on his trip to 'the loo', just in case, as she'd put it, 'that important call from Jakarta comes through while you're inconvenienced. I could call the mobile and let it ring three times as a sort of signal and ...'

Her employer's expression of utter contempt was enough to remind her that she was treading on very thin ice.

Weetwood surveyed the walls of his deliciously phone-free refuge, a cubicle decorated with wallpaper that reproduced an attractive William Morris design. He'd chosen the designs for all the cubicles in the Directors' Washroom, but he liked this one the best. He sat wishing he was somewhere else – preferably on the footplate of a mighty Pacific steam locomotive hauling a crack express from London to Glasgow in ...1937? ... Yes, a very good year! The *Coronation Scot* came to mind and he hummed the first few bars of the eponymous tune. Then, imagining mighty pistons pumping rhythmically away, he began to chuff quietly.

Oh, but this was getting him nowhere! The board meeting at ten-thirty loomed, and, as usual, he felt uneasy about the likelihood of Dame Diana Tenby-Jones – the sole non-executive director – proving troublesome: Dame Diana spoke her mind.

For years WSD had done very well without 'non-execs', and Weetwood had been free to pack the board with men – until two years ago no woman had ever held a senior position at Soap House – who were clearly his intellectual and social inferiors. Yes, he'd inherited the barony granted to his self-made millionaire grandfather, but he could never forget his schooldays at Harrow, where, because of his mild Lancashire accent and industrial background, he'd been mercilessly ridiculed. Nevertheless, he'd managed to survive the ordeal and scrape into Cambridge by the skin of his teeth; perhaps his father's endowment of several 'Weetwood Scholarships' at undistinguished Lloyd College had had some bearing in the matter.

George had buried himself in the study of Natural Sciences; train-spotting was his sole recreation. He finally ended up with a Lower Second, and, after coming down in 1961, joined the family firm. For the next ten years, he devoted himself to Goblin, remaining a bachelor and almost wholly celibate. Then, aged 31, he met Beryl Partridge.

Beryl had been born and raised on her parents' vast sisal estate in Kenya; the 1950s Mau Mau rebellion almost bankrupted them. In 1969, when drink and malaria finished them off, nineteen-year-old Beryl became a typist in the Nairobi office of Goblin's Kenyan subsidiary. Two years later, George Weetwood paid a visit – ostensibly to acquaint himself with Goblin's East African operations. Beryl grasped the opportunity with total dedication. Thanks to exhaustive research, her *coup de grâce* was an invitation for Weetwood and herself to dine at Nairobi's exclusive Muthaiga Club with Lord and Lady Delarue. 'Jumbo' Delarue, who'd been at Eton with Beryl's father, had recently retired as chairman of East African Railways, a fact which had persuaded the initially reluctant Weetwood to accept the invitation: in truth, his visit's prime objective was to savour the delights of the powerful steam locomotives still thundering along the 'Lunatic Line' between Mombasa and Kampala.

After dinner and their farewells to the Delarues, Beryl offered to drive Weetwood back to his hotel. For a while, they indulged in mundane conversation. Then, during a lull, Beryl inquired in a very off-hand sort of way: 'Does the 4:23 still run from Norwich to Liverpool Street? I always used to catch that when I was returning to Roedean after my holidays with relatives in Norfolk.'

Weetwood, who was almost nodding off, came alive. 'Ah ... well, if I remember correctly, Miss Partridge, in the summer timetable the 16:23 now departs at 16:30 – Saturdays excepted of course. During weekdays it has a full restaurant car service. There's a buffet at weekends.'

'How interesting!' There was a pause as Beryl groped for a suitable introduction to her next nugget. 'The engines we have here,' she finally ventured, 'are massive, you know. I just love watching them at work in the freight yards. Would you like to pop over now and have a gander? The best time to see the yards is at night when the long freight trains are being assembled. The place is awash with engines chuffing around.' Beryl bit her lip: 'chuffing' sounded a bit *Thomas the Tank Engine*-ish. Perhaps he'd think her a fool.

Weetwood, however, was thrilled. 'I should be delighted. I do hope I'm not keeping you up too late, Miss Partridge?'

Beryl laughed. 'Not at all – my pleasure!' She turned off the highway and drove to a slightly elevated spot adjacent to some dimly lit freight yards. Several articulated locomotives were at work, and the smell of their exhaust steam, which Weetwood found so intoxicating, wafted around them on the cool night air, mixed with the wood smoke from fires burning in the shanties on the other side of the tracks.

'This is *wonderful*,' he murmured ecstatically.

Beryl briefly empathized – and then unzipped his flies.

When it was all over, Weetwood said in a faraway voice: 'I can truthfully say, Miss Partridge, that this even surpasses the most thrilling experience of my life. I was seven – just after the end of the War – and returning to my prep school, accompanied by Nanny Blotch. We were changing at Crewe when the *Duchess of Hamilton* roared through – with all her casing gleaming. Pre-war, she often used to haul the *Coronation Scot* – streamlined of course. The driver waved and it gave me *such* a thrill. Well, I got so excited I ... I had an accident in the nether regions, so to speak, and Nanny took me into the ladies' room and thrashed me with her umbrella.'

Barely listening, Beryl was confused, but then twigged that the 'Duchess' must have been some kind of engine.

'The driver waved at *me*!' repeated Weetwood ecstatically.

Beryl thought him pathetic. 'How *wonderful*!' she enthused sweetly.

A month later, Weetwood married Beryl in Nairobi's Anglican cathedral. Thereafter, sexual contact was minimal – and fruitless – for six dull years. Then, in 1977, he was elected chairman of SADMA, the United Kingdom Soap and Detergent Manufacturers' Association. Consequently, Beryl felt obliged to accompany him to Torquay for that year's SADMA Annual Conference. Both town and conference were infinitely worse than she'd feared. Furthermore, the Imperial Hotel had committed the cardinal sin of allocating the Weetwoods a suite with a double bed – not two singles as booked by Miss Spigot. The management professed ignorance and impotence.

After three interminable days, the conference concluded with the traditional dinner dance and a speech by the Minister of State for Regional Development, the Earl of Birmingham. Beryl's heart sank as she took her seat on the top table next to a Mrs Sheila Clutterbuck of Clutterbuck's Novelty Soaps. A Yorkshire widow in her late forties endeavouring to look twenty-five, Sheila had won SADMA's Exporter of the Year Award: she'd identified an insatiable market in the Far East for her extensive range of taboo phenomena reproduced in traditional English scented soap.

'Me lavender willies go down a bomb with Jap women,' Mrs Clutterbuck proclaimed proudly after the formal introductions, 'while Taiwanese executives can't get enough of me honeysuckle doggy-do's. Come on, lass, drink up!'

After thirty minutes, Beryl was mercifully paralytic. The barriers came down as Sheila described her sexual exploits on the Costa del Sol: since her husband's fatal heart attack five years earlier, she'd treated herself to an annual pilgrimage to Marbella and a succession of one-nighters. At some point in the discourse, Beryl began to experience a strange attraction towards her own husband, 'that boring old fart, George' as she'd branded him. Indeed, through the alcoholic haze his profile appeared almost noble. Perhaps it was time to put an end to the gossip about their marriage and procure an heir to the barony.

George, by contrast, was preoccupied with Lord Birmingham's apparent alcoholism: his imbibing of the Top Table's Château Haut Brion was awesome. Birmingham had insisted on 'Weetwood' keeping up with him, but secretly preferring German whites, George had imbibed without enthusiasm. Nevertheless, his consumption had exceeded an entire bottle by the time the dancing began; even when sober, dancing was not his forte.

Locating his suite proved challenging when George finally managed to detach himself from the dishevelled mass of intoxicated soap executives and their spouses. At some point, he discovered Beryl draped seductively across a bed, dressed in a revealing black silk negligee – a garment loaned by Sheila Clutterbuck. Beryl pounced; George was too stunned to resist. He lay back and thought of Nairobi and the *Coronation Scot*; Beryl pictured 'Pepe', a pool attendant at Marbella's Don Carlos Hotel, whom Sheila had described pornographically.

Some nine months later, the twins were born.

After Torquay, all sexual relations between George and Beryl ceased: he preferred locomotives; she craved the likes of 'Pepe'. Invariably after dinner, George would retire to his 'bedroom' and immerse himself in the operation of his colossal train set – a reproduction of Crewe Junction covering no less than 900 square feet. Bespoke software even enabled him to operate the entire railway timetable for Crewe over a typical 24-hour period. Not infrequently, he would set the controls for all-night operation and drift to sleep to the sounds of his own railway world, complete with recordings of train whistles and station announcements. Within the walls of his 'bedroom', George was the absolute ruler of a minutely regulated miniature world. No one was ever allowed in. Perfection!

*

George looked at his watch and tutted: it was 10:25; he'd better get himself to the Boardroom! He listened carefully to make sure the coast was clear. Nothing. Nonetheless, he flushed the unused lavatory: he didn't want any of his colleagues to get the idea that he used the washroom as a refuge. After washing his hands, he straightened his SADMA silk tie before the mirror and permitted himself a brief and rare moment of vanity: for a man of fifty-seven he could still pass for fifty, even if he said so himself. His frame was as lean as ever – unlike most of his co-directors with their paunches – and, at just over six feet, he towered over all of them. But George's pride and joy was his full head of fine, golden hair – not as thick as it once was, but still impressive. Yes, in his traditional three-piece suit – immaculately pressed as always – starched white shirt, and gleaming black brogues, he was a picture of sartorial elegance that had 'CHAIRMAN' stamped all over it.

And so, reassured that he was ready to go on stage, George stepped out into the wide, oak-panelled corridor. Opposite, stood the Boardroom's massive medieval-style double doors. He stared at them and sighed heavily.

WSD plc's Soap House, the headquarters of Britain's largest family-owned company, was one of the two neo-Gothic monstrosities built almost a century earlier by George's grandfather, Albert, the 1st Baron; Bobbins was the other – named for his beloved wife, Roberta, whom he always called 'Bobbins'. It was Albert who'd founded Goblin Soap, built Goblinville – the 'model village' of mock-Tudor 'cottages' for his 5,000 Lancashire workers – and made Goblin a household name across the globe. When he died in 1935, the reins of power formally passed to his equally dynamic son, Eustace, the 2nd Baron. After the War, Eustace ensured that the company was in the forefront of the liquid detergent revolution and the development of special powders for the new automatic washing machines. He also saw to it that Goblin was the first soap to be advertised on British television when commercial broadcasting commenced in 1954.

Many analysts believed that the company's Golden Years ended in 1972 with Eustace's death and George's accession to the chairmanship. Indeed, the corridors of power at Soap House had become serenely calm: in so far as any deliberate corporate policy could be discerned on his part, it could be best described as 'consolidation', for George was neither entrepreneurial nor predisposed to any form of proactive behaviour. On the very rare occasions when he thought about the matter at all, he saw himself as the competent commodore of a grand ocean liner that embodied some wondrous form of perpetual momentum. However, although the days of excitement at Goblin might have died with Eustace Weetwood, at least there was a steady hand on the tiller – or so it appeared.

Soap House's boardroom – the bridge of George's liner analogy – was monumental; one architectural historian had described it as 'a shrine to commerce'. Resembling a medieval banqueting hall, the predominant features were dark wood panelling, a hammer-beam roof, two vast stone fireplaces – one at each end of the room – stained-glass windows depicting the history of soap, and full-length portraits of the three Barons Weetwood and their spouses. It was all a far cry from an office block in the City or Canary Wharf.

Cocooned on this Friday morning from the harsh, ugly realities of the outside world, and sitting in his throne-like chair at the head of the long board table, George had relaxed since the start of the meeting some fifty minutes earlier. David Chopping, the Finance Director, and Export Director Miles Brancepeth-Tring – 'BT' to his colleagues – were locked in argument about the performance-to-budget figures in the last quarter for the Pacific Islands Zone – 'PIZ'. It was all getting rather personal.

'Gentlemen, gentlemen,' George finally intervened, 'we still have some *very* important items on our agenda to discuss. These matters of budgetary detail can be dissected at our next relevant sub-committee meeting. We certainly should *not* be subjecting our non-executive director to issues which don't involve broader policy dimensions.' He smiled condescendingly at Dame Diana Tenby-Jones. Dame Diana, however, did not reciprocate: she looked even more aggressive than usual.

'As we seem to have finished Item 8,' she barked, 'I'd like to raise a fundamental issue now rather than under Any Other Business. I have to get back to London for a jolly important meeting of the Royal Palaces Merchandising Board.'

George sighed.

'Anyway,' she continued swiftly, 'I believe everyone will get my drift when I say "washroom".'

As usual, Dame Diana was completely wrong: there were puzzled faces around the board table. George, however, knew what was coming, thanks to an insulting letter he'd received from the old bat some days earlier.

'I am a *woman*,' she boomed – George raised his eyebrows, '– you are *men*.'

George switched himself off and returned to the doodle he'd started twenty minutes earlier when Chopping had launched his monthly attack on the Marketing Director, Ged Mellow. On this occasion the misdemeanour was an 'extravagant' film location for the latest Goblin TV commercial: Finance had sanctioned Mallorca; Marketing had opted for St Lucia – something to do with the right, or wrong, sort of palm trees. George had lost interest after a few minutes. Instead, he'd indulged in one of his board meeting traditions – map making. He'd drawn the outline of a large island state and then added some major rivers and a sprinkling of cities and towns. Slowly but surely, he'd connected them by various railway lines, having carefully considered such matters as whether to divert the mainline from A to B via X, or simply to connect X by a branch to the mainline. His final task was to decide on the details of a modernization plan, with the building of some high-speed lines between key centres of population. But which ones? This was the task now exercising his mind as Tenby-Jones droned on.

'... I'm sorry, but I find it intolerable. Why should you *men*' – she spat out the word like a bad olive – 'simply have to trot across the corridor to your deluxe facility – yes, I've popped in there for a recky, and, incidentally, whoever chose the wallpaper should be shot – while I have to trek down three floors to some clinical affair full of half-witted secretaries smoking and gossiping. It's disgraceful! I can tell you that when I was on the board of Marks and Spencer ...'

Seemingly far away, George christened his island state 'New Georgia' in block capitals and boldly decided that the new high-speed line between Reginald Haven and Weetwoodborough would bypass the prosperous but sleepy old spa town of Chipping Goblin. He gave Tenby-Jones another five minutes of haranguing to get the washroom crisis out of her system, and then, as she began to paint a picture of lavatorial splendour at the Root Vegetable Marketing Board's offices, where she'd been Deputy Chairman for some five 'heavenly' years, he silenced her with a theatrical burst of throat-clearing.

'Time is pressing, Diana. What I suggest is that we set up a sub-committee chaired by the Company Secretary ... or yourself, Diana – I'll leave that to the two of you to discuss. Your remit would be to consider the feasibility of installing female washroom facilities here on the Fifth Floor. Is that all right with you?' But before she could open her mouth, he snapped: 'Next item!'

With insincere apologies, Tenby-Jones dashed off. George watched her go without regret: she was like a butterfly flitting from one non-executive directorship or Good Cause to another, one of the new breed of committee professionals. He should never have allowed Beryl to talk himself into appointing her. She'd said Dame Diana had 'influence in high places.' What nonsense! But if he tried to get rid of her now, it would look like weakness – that he was intimidated. No, he was stuck with the lunatic. Thank goodness she had so little time to devote to the company's affairs.

George was still admiring the completed map of New Georgia, when the Company Secretary, Daventry Merryweather, tapped his arm and whispered conspiratorially: 'Shall we proceed with the next item, Chairman – Project Troll?'

George put the map under his notepad and shuffled his board papers unnecessarily. His colleagues had utilized the interruption to the flow of the meeting caused by Tenby-Jones's departure to replenish their coffee-cups and pop across the corridor to the lambasted Directors' Washroom.

'Can we continue, gentlemen?' George enquired headmasterly. 'Now, I want to bring you up-to-date with Project Troll, which, of course, in line with our standard practice has not been specifically referred to in the agenda. And I should not need to remind you that even though the launch of Weetex is only weeks away – more on that shortly – this matter is still *highly* confidential.' Obediently, his fellow directors all adopted expressions of intense gravity.

*

Project Troll originated five years earlier when WSD's then Technical Director, Ernest Barmcake, received a telephone call from Luke Nickel, the President of Nickel Inc., Goblin's exclusive distributor for North America. The American market had never been significant for WSD in volume terms, but, with its Royal Warrant emblazoned on the packaging, Goblin was successfully marketed as a luxury product at a mighty premium. Barmcake, aged 63 – just two years away from retirement – was a down-to-earth Lancastrian who'd commenced his career with the company straight from school as an engineering apprentice. Twenty years his junior, Luke Nickel found him 'a character'; in any event, 'Ernie' appeared to be the only WSD director who ever spoke his mind, or, for that matter – and despite his accent – English that Nickel could understand.

After some gossip about Proctor & Gamble and Colgate-Palmolive, Nickel became serious.

'Ernie, you know Start Industries down in Fort Worth, Texas?'

'Rings a bell, lad.'

'They've a finger in a helluva lot of things from cement to diapers. They recently took over Groovy Soaps of Hokeekokee, New Jersey – pure vegetable stuff – environmentally friendly – wrapped in brown recycled paper – all that kind of shit.'

'So?'

'OK, well some months ago at the Soap In the Twenty-First Century Convention in St. Louis – you should have come – you would have loved it – I met this girl, Vosene – Vosene Pesto. I mean, she's just *fan-tastic*. ... We're so much in love – perfect soul mates. It's a dream come true. ... I've been very lonely since Muffin passed away, you know.'

'Aye, lad, I can imagine.'

'Anyway, turns out she used to be a research chemist with Groovy, but after the takeover she got transferred to this Start laboratory miles out in the sticks north of Fort Worth – Soda Flats – where she's been working on some top-secret thing. I mean, after six Jack Daniels in my motel room last Tuesday night, she told me stuff that seemed real crazy, but–'

'Luke, what are you *bloody* babbling about, lad?'

'Sorry, Ernie. ... OK – in a nutshell – she's discovered some kinda revolutionary process for making soap – soap made so cheaply that – well, she predicts manufacturing costs of only one *tenth* of the industry's best! But she hasn't told the Start guys yet. She hates them. Christ, the things she revealed about what those bastards are doing to dumb creatures! She wants out, but she's kinda trapped, and–'

'Luke, slow down! You're not making any sense.'

'Sorry ... sorry, but I empathize with Vosene so intensely and–'

'Vosene?'

'The love of my life – my angel. Christ, I hope you can help us.'

Some fifty minutes later, after Barmcake had tracked down the Chairman to the Directors' Washroom, George Weetwood sat expressionless in his office as the Technical Director reported his conversation with Nickel.

'I think this Pesto dame could have perfected the Winkelmann Process,' fizzed Barmcake.

'Nonsense, Ernest! You know as well as I do that the Germans tried everything during the War to make soap from seaweed, but–'

'Just hang on a tick, George, and listen.' Barmcake was the only person at Soap House – if not in the entire Goblin Group – who was known to address Lord Weetwood thus. 'This Groovy Soaps outfit was founded by Zip and Alexia Doofer – the Doofer Diet? – the Doofer Clinics? ... No? Never mind. Anyway, in the mid-Eighties they started making soap from pure vegetable substances – moulded into the shapes of endangered species and stuff.'

'Good Lord!'

'Well, it seems the Doofers used to rub themselves every morning with fresh seaweed – they thought it kept them looking young and beautiful – and Pesto was recruited to join a small team of Groovy scientists that were analysing the seaweed with a view to manufacturing and marketing soap containing the "youth-preserving extracts".'

'Americans!'

'Quite. Well, one evening, Pesto was working late and alone in the Groovy lab and decided to take a break and make some tea. As the local water had a nasty chlorine taste, the lass would bring bottles of mineral water to work. She made the tea, but when she took her first sip, it tasted right salty. So, she concluded that, for a joke, one of her daft colleagues had substituted salt water from the seaweed tank for her mineral water. Well, she decided to call it a day and get herself home.

'The following morning, Pesto awoke with flu. It was a nasty strain and a week passed before she was well enough to return to work. As the only tea drinker in the lab, no one had touched the teapot on her workbench, and when she went to make her first brew she discovered this whitish viscous liquid stuff inside. As soon as she started to rinse the pot, the mysterious substance bubbled and frothed like super-concentrated washing-up liquid! She thought it was another practical joke, but all her colleagues professed ignorance. Well, she was ninety-nine per cent certain that the whole thing was a prank, but there was that one per cent nagging doubt.'

George sighed. 'Go on.'

'So, she furtively repeated her experiment, and when she hesitantly peered into her teapot a week later and saw the same whitish liquid, well, she almost pissed herself.'

'Oh *really*, Ernest!'

'Fearing ridicule, she decided to keep the matter to herself until she was sure of her facts. Night after night after everyone had gone home, she analysed the white gunk – Pestex she called it–'

'"Pestex!"'

'– and tried to work out what sort of chemical reactions had taken place. It seemed that a protein in the plankton and alginic acid – that's an insoluble carbohydrate found in brown seaweeds–'

'I'm well aware of that. I *do* have a degree in Natural Sciences from Cambridge, you know.'

'Yeah ... right. Well, be that as it may, when boiled, the protein and the acid were reacting with some molecule in the tea leaves *and* the salt itself, producing a new compound, which, when allowed to cool and stand, would be deposited after a few days. With further evaporation, a solid white cake would be left with very similar properties to ordinary household soap.

'Any road, George, about a year ago the Doofers sold Groovy to Start Industries. The Group's research facilities were merged, and Pesto was offered a job on condition that she moved to Fort Worth.'

'So, she's told the Start people all about her "secret research"?'

'Apparently not. Start owed her no favours and she might have moved all the way down to Texas only to find her face didn't fit. No, she wanted to see how the land lay. Any road, everything began well. Start paid almost twice her Groovy salary, a BMW came with the job, and she got an interest-free company loan to buy her flat. She was based for a while at some lab in Fort Worth studying the effects of artificial colourings on skin tissue. They used volunteer students from the Texas Christian University.'

'A Temple of Learning, no doubt!'

'It all seemed very respectable and she was on the point of telling her boss all about Pestex when one morning he dropped a bombshell. He said she was living up to all his expectations and that she was to be "promoted" to Start's *secret* facility about twenty miles north of Fort Worth to join a "hand-picked" team testing the Groovy products. ... Some place called Soda Flats – I think that's what Luke said. Any road, after the takeover, Start's people had examined Groovy's test results and concluded that their testing on humans was next to useless. They didn't want to make any warranty claims against the Doofers for fear of bad publicity and a slump in sales of the Groovy range.'

'And how were they conducting these "tests"?'

'On rats, chimps and beagles.'

'Ah ... I see.'

'Pesto claims she protested, but was told that if she didn't co-operate she'd be out of a job without a reference and the apartment and the BMW would be repossessed.'

'Pressure indeed!'

'Well, Luke says she can't take it no longer. She's planning to talk to some patent attorneys in Dallas to see if she can file a patent and then start talking to Procter & Gamble or–'

'Procter & Gamble!'

'That's what Luke said.'

'Well, she can't – I mean, we must see her first. She's probably a complete charlatan or a lunatic, but–'

'But we'd better make sure, or, if the production costs are as low as she claims, it could be curtains for Goblin, eh, George?'

Although George found Barmcake verging on the Neanderthal, he was undoubtedly a brilliant engineer with an encyclopaedic knowledge of soap technology. Which was why George's cynicism was a performance: he was secretly terrified, for out of the mists of his nebulous corporate voyage, an iceberg had appeared dead ahead. And so, twenty-four hours later, they were secreted in a motel near Dallas airport. Nickel was already installed, and, despite their jet lag, the Englishmen met with him in his room almost immediately.

'The investigators you asked me to instruct, Lord Weetwood,' said Nickel, 'have confirmed that Vosene *is* twenty-nine and single, she *is* an Arizona State University chemistry graduate, and she does *indeed* work for Start Industries. This morning, they followed her from her apartment in Fort Worth to a heavily guarded single-story building of recent construction some twenty miles away at Soda Flats. Here – it's all in their preliminary report.'

George barely glanced at the document pushed across the coffee table, handing it to Barmcake. 'Yes, I'm sorry you had to engage in that somewhat distasteful business, Mr Nickel, but–'

'No problem. There could be a lot of money at stake – and *do* call me "Luke".'

'Quite.' Staring at a framed poster of the Alamo on the far wall, George added: 'Mr Nickel, however unlikely it may be that Miss Pesto has invented anything of commercial application, it is imperative that WSD should acquire all rights in the "invention" and prevent any dissemination of her research – at least until we're sure that the whole thing is, as I suspect, a load of nonsense.'

'I'm sure she's on the level, sir.'

'You're not a scientist, Mr Nickel. You possess a "degree" in "accounting" from an institution in Minnesota, I understand.'

'I–'

'It would appear that the relationship between yourself and Miss Pesto involves an element of mutual attraction. Now, she may or may not have made a significant invention – I have to confess that some of her behaviour indicates a degree of eccentricity or even madness, but then that is often the case in my experience with inventors. And then she is a woman, an *American* woman, moreover, and–'

'Now just a minute–!'

'Don't interrupt, Mr Nickel. Time is pressing. These are my requirements. First, you will immediately inform Miss Pesto that you've spoken to my company – you'll paint a glorious picture of us, of course – and have discovered that by an extraordinary coincidence one of our directors is in Dallas.' George pointed to Barncake. 'He can just squeeze her into his busy schedule. Naturally, my presence here shall remain a secret.

'Miss Pesto will sign a contract. Our Company Secretary – a solicitor – an "attorney" – has drafted something appropriate – a simple option agreement. In return for selling all her rights in and to Pestex – or whatever she calls it – and keeping all its details secret, she'll receive a lump sum of $200,000 payable in three instalments – $50,000 upon delivery of her formula, $100,000 upon the satisfactory completion of laboratory production of Pestex, and the balance upon WSD's first manufacture of the product in commercial quantities. And she'll also be entitled to a royalty of one per cent of our worldwide Pestex turnover for the first five years of marketing the stuff – if we ever make it. Oh, and tell her, Ernest, she'll have the best laboratory money can buy.

'You, Mr Nickel, will also tell Miss Pesto that you want to marry her – or something. It is indeed fortuitous that your wife died last year, and that you have no children.'

'I – but–'

45

'You must persuade the girl that she should go away with you to South America – at once. Barmcake will make the arrangements to get you to Montevideo in Uruguay. ... We have certain *facilities* there – very hush-hush.'

'Why the hell should we go to–?'

'"*Why*" Mr Nickel? Because your business is on the point of bankruptcy – you've never really recovered since Roger & Gallet terminated their distributorship, have you? Oh, we've had very detailed reports from our Export Director, Mr Brancepeth-Tring. You've been drinking rather a lot, I seem to remember – and gambling – since Mrs Nickel's tragic skiing accident. And I have to tell you that the final nail in the coffin is about to materialize – in the form of the termination of your Goblin distributorship. Mr Barmcake has the formal letter.'

It was Barmcake's turn to push a document across the coffee table. 'Sorry, Luke.'

'You're a ruthless bastard after all, Weetwood,' Nickel finally managed to croak, '– not at all like your image.'

At last, George stared Nickel in the eye. '"Image"?' he queried. 'I'm afraid I don't understand. And frankly, Mr Nickel, I don't think that giving you the chance to make a fresh start with the woman you profess to love, is particularly "ruthless", but then perhaps you Americans also define *that* word differently too. ... Oh, by the way, did I say that in Montevideo we'll get Miss Pesto a new identity – both of you if necessary?'

Vosene Pesto, an attractive if somewhat lanky brunette, was sold Lord Weetwood's plan with surprising ease when she drove over from Fort Worth that evening. Indeed, she was very happy to sign the simple agreement which Barmcake presented to her; Nickel assured her it was a good deal.

'And now, love,' Barmcake said jovially, winding up, 'if you could just also sign this bog-standard Consultancy Agreement. ... For five years you'll provide WSD with such assistance as we may require to get Pestex into production, tested, et cetera – plus options to any other inventions you might make – for a very generous $50,000 a year.'

Vosene signed, smiling angelically at Luke.

'Grand! Sorry about photocopies, love, but them's the best our people could do at short notice. When I get back to England I'll ask our lawyers to send you some pretty ones with them poncey ribbons and seals on.'

In fact, Barmcake never did, but then paperwork was not his forte.

Miss Pesto's disappearance caused her employers some concern; Nickel's disappearance alarmed his insolvent company's creditors. The police were informed, but there was no evidence of foul play, and the trail – such as it was – went dead in Mexico City.

A few corrupt officials in the Uruguayan Department of Internal Affairs transmogrified Pesto and Nickel into 'Señorita Julietta Reborde' and 'Señor Juan Pestana', tragic foundlings who'd been raised by nuns in remote parts of the country. The elopers went along with this subterfuge, even though they thought it an unnecessary part of the extraordinary Weetwood Plan. And, as 'Julietta' and 'Juan', they swiftly married in Montevideo. Comfortably off, Luke was soon enjoying the type of lifestyle he'd long desired: a beautiful home in an agreeable climate, mornings spent swimming, afternoons of golf, and evenings of passion with a woman whom he adored. Only children were absent, but with a young wife he felt sure they would materialize in due course – and certainly once Vosene had performed her part of the bargain with WSD.

Vosene also appeared to be blissfully happy: she had Luke, her own laboratory, and the excitement of witnessing the development of Pestex – or Weetex as the WSD people had renamed it – from laboratory samples to full-scale commercial production.

*

Five years later, amid the pseudo-medieval splendour of WSD's boardroom, George was winding up his summary of the present state of Project Troll. Merryweather had noticed out of the corner of his eye that the Chairman had absent-mindedly started to sketch yet another map on his memo pad: he'd written 'Pestoland' in the top left-hand corner and underlined it twice.

'So, gentlemen, in conclusion, our two production facilities for Weetex in Kenya and Sri Lanka are up and running. Preliminary results show that manufacturing costs are as predicted – in fact, the Kenya plant is operating even more efficiently than we'd hoped. And I'm pleased to confirm that the boffins in the lab here are completely confident that Weetex is one hundred per cent safe. After months of constant scrubbing, or whatever they do, our guinea pigs have suffered no adverse effects. And Marketing–'

'I thought we weren't involved in animal testing,' Brancepeth-Tring admonished, looking puzzled.

'*What?*' snapped George, returning the Export Director's gaze with intense irritation.

'Um, guinea pigs. You said we were testing this stuff on guinea pigs.' Several directors giggled.

'Miles, the "guinea pigs" are *people*,' Merryweather explained with oily smugness.

'People?'

'Well, students at Lancaster University to be precise,' Merryweather added.

'Ah – oh – I *see*. Silly me!'

George cleared his throat. 'If I may be allowed to finish ...? Marketing have – after liaising with me, naturally ... well, Marketing and I have settled on the brand name for Weetex. It will be announced in a month's time on ... on–'

'The fourth of August, Chairman – it's a Monday.'

'Thank you, Daventry ... on the fourth of August at the product launch – here at Soap House. There's been a lot of research for a name which will be internationally acceptable and which we can register as a trade mark in as many countries as possible.'

There were expectant faces as the Chairman's colleagues awaited the disclosure of the much-researched brand name. They were going to have to wait a bit longer: George was adding a few more miles of coastline to Pestoland.

'Now, Marketing did consider Weetex itself, but we agreed it sounded just a bit too agricultural. Then there was Troll. It had served us well as the project name, and, of course, would fit in with the Goblin theme and our brand image. However, Troll was rejected when we ascertained that it's already a highly successful brand of Schnittblumen & Käseglocke, the German ... um ... "sanitary towels" people. So, Marketing programmed their computer-marvel-thing to come up with a gem of a trade mark.'

Brancepeth-Tring emitted the faintest of groans; it was audible yet impossible to trace. As Export Director he was painfully aware of the inadequacies of Marketing's 'computer-marvel-thing': it was programmed by xenophobic monoglots and, therefore, invariably generated names which would be unspeakable, ludicrous or even obscene in many of the world's major languages.

'Gentlemen,' George continued, 'I'm pleased to inform you that our amazing product, which will herald the dawn of a new era of expansion and prosperity for our company eclipsing even the Golden Age of the 1920s and 30s ... um ... Well, the product is to be marketed across the globe as' – he paused dramatically – 'as ... FoamFay.'

There was just a hint of a smile on George's face as he glanced across the room to the portrait of his late father. However, the expressions on most other faces in the now painfully silent boardroom indicated incredulity. While George had not expected cheers or clapping to follow his announcement, he had anticipated some form of dignified acclamation. Consequently, the lack of any positive response unnerved him. He looked at Merryweather, who, as his right-hand man, had been made privy to the choice of name prior to the meeting. Naturally, he'd congratulated the Chairman and assured him that the board would be most pleased. He was now clearly expected to do something supportive. For a start, he grinned broadly.

'Succinct ... mellifluous ... melodious ... *catchy*,' Merryweather chirped, desperately trying to remember all the guff in Marketing's risible report. 'Yes, FoamFay. ... I think it's dashed clever, Chairman.'

Someone chuckled. Everyone looked at Brancepeth-Tring – everyone, that is, except George, who drew a small island off Pestoland's highly indented south-west coast, and, without looking up, proposed that the meeting be adjourned.

# CHAPTER 5

With Ron Duffle at the wheel, the dark-green Jaguar glided along a busy
stretch of motorway which snaked through Manchester's eastern suburbs.
Caroline Weetwood and Misty Start sat in the rear, with Misty endeavouring
to make conversation. It had been a Herculean task ever since they'd met at
the airport an hour earlier. Caroline was as geeky as her weird SELCOPEL
correspondence had strongly indicated. And judging by her clothing and
appearance, two years at university had not brought the kid out of her
shell; being so overweight wouldn't have helped.

'Aren't you hot in that anorak thing?' enquired Misty kindly.

'Um ... no.'

They passed a succession of abandoned textile mills; in the fine drizzle,
the landscape appeared decidedly depressing to Misty. 'I sure am looking
forward,' she said brightly, 'to seeing all those wonderful old buildings in
Manchester you used to write about, Caroline. It really is so, *so* kind of you
to let me come and stay. Jesus! – I've been *so* looking forward to meeting
you and finally putting a face to the name. I just can't tell you what it
means to me.'

The car exited the motorway, and, as it pulled up at some traffic lights,
Caroline continued to stare at the back of Duffle's head, groping for
something to say. Scanning a row of dreary shops, her eyes rested on a
branch of Boots: an advert in the window, featuring a paragon of female
beauty with dazzling white teeth, offered three tubes of Colgate toothpaste
for the price of two.

'I must say, you look even prettier in the flesh than in your
photographs,' Caroline ventured at last, '– I mean the ones you sent with
your letters. I thought they might be of someone else.' She bit her lip.

'Excuse me?'

'Well, I ... er ... I thought – I thought it was all a joke – at first.
I thought you might be ... Of *course* they were *you* – the photographs, that
is. I know that *now*. I mean, I always knew that – I – I–'

'Sorry?'

Caroline unwrapped a boiled sweet, and, after popping it into her
mouth, proffered the bag to Misty.

'No thanks. I never eat that shit. You know, I'm surprised you do, with
your complexion. How much further is it to Bobbins Castle?'

Wondering what she meant by 'your complexion', Caroline rolled the sweet around her mouth for a few seconds before replying. 'It's just *Bobbins*, actually. ... About another thirty minutes.'

'Oh ... right. Well, if you don't mind, I'm going to get a bit of shut-eye. I didn't sleep too well on the plane last night.' Misty closed her eyes; almost immediately, she seemed to become unconscious.

With pursed lips, Caroline glared at her companion for some time, quite fascinated by the intensity of her negative feelings. Yes, it was true that Misty's visit was disrupting her beloved studies and her final preparations for the imminent research trip, but it was more than that. Envy? ... Jealousy? After weighing up these possibilities, she reluctantly concluded that she felt cheated: she'd geared herself up to expect some sort of gregarious clone of herself talking thirteen to the dozen with a grating drawl. How wrong she'd been! There wasn't even a hint of a rotten Texan accent. And although Misty was only wearing jeans and a denim jacket over a dark blue T-shirt, even Caroline had spotted the Armani labels and insignia. Worst of all, her guest was decidedly 'laid back' ... or did she mean 'streetwise'? She remembered her brother using the terms some years back – about a pop star ... Madonna? ... No matter. Actually, she wasn't really sure now what they meant. Nor did she know much about Madonna, come to that.

Caroline unwrapped another sweet, rolled it disconsolately in her fingers, and returned to her study of Misty. *She looks so trim and fit ... and her dark brown shoulder-length hair is like silk. She's ... beautiful – too beautiful if that's possible. Or am I just being spiteful?* But then the snide comment about her own complexion resurfaced. She examined the sweet in her now sticky fingers, opened the ashtray, dropped it in and wiped her hands on her anorak.

*Cripes! If the photographs were genuine, then Misty's letters must have been genuine too. And I wrote all those maliciously tedious and disingenuous replies! Manchester's 'historic buildings' indeed!*

She felt like a criminal who was about to stand trial and had absolutely no defence.

*Oh, Lor'! I hope Goody Two-Shoes doesn't expect to be shown round the works. She certainly doesn't look the type to be interested in industrial infrastructure, despite all those dotty questions she used to ask.*

The drizzle had stopped and the clouds were slowly beginning to lift by the time the Jaguar reached Muckley-in-Dribbledale and pulled up at the crossroads on the village green. The industrial gloom of East Lancashire had been left far behind, and the sight of Muckley's solid eighteenth-century cottages, built from an almost golden sandstone, lifted Caroline's spirits.

51

Despite the absence of traffic, however, the car remained oddly immobile. Scanning the green, Caroline noticed a buxom middle-aged woman in overalls standing outside the front door of the Cob o' Coal Inn – probably the cleaner, she assumed. The woman seemed to be signalling to Duffle. Looking into the driving mirror, Caroline could see him mouthing some words very slowly in reply. They appeared to be 'I LOVE YOU SPANKY' ... 'SPINKY'? ... 'SPUNKY'?

Caroline looked down at her tracksuit-clad legs with embarrassment and coughed rather loudly, whereupon Misty awoke with a yelp, and Duffle pretended to look for his sunglasses.

'Ah – yes – well, I thought so. Yes indeed, Miss Caroline. Looks like your American friend's brought some better weather with 'er. Sun's beginning to poke through.'

Misty yawned. 'What a pretty place! Is this Bobbins?'

Caroline sighed. 'No, no, *no*. This is Muckley-in-Dribbledale. We're almost there – just a few more minutes. I'm glad you've aroused yourself though.'

'Excuse me?'

'I should awfully like to clarify the weekend schedule with you. ... Um, I would suggest that upon our arrival we pop up to your room and take a shower.'

Misty laughed. '"*We*"?'

'*You*, that is, of course. I had a bath yesterday. ... Or, if you prefer, *do* have a bath – whatever. Then a spot of lunch at about ... hmm ... one twenty-five-ish. I can – I mean Mr Duffle can then show you a bit of the house and the gardens – can't you, Duffle? I've got *so* much to do, what with my Spanish–'

'Oh, my pleasure!' Ron enthused, leering at the vision of loveliness in his mirror. All his reservations about 'Yanks' had evaporated as soon as he'd set eyes on Miss Start at the airport.

'Ought to be quite nice if the sun *really* comes out,' Caroline continued. 'That should take us to about three-forty when we – *you* – can have tea. I hope you like cakes. Mrs Duffle has baked quite a few, actually, in your honour. Always jolly yummy.'

'"Yummy"?'

'And then ... well, you'll probably want to read – or something. Then there's dinner with Daddy at seven-thirty *sharp*. He's awfully funny about that. Should be quite good though cos Mrs Duffle's making one of her jam roly-poly puddings and they're awfully yummy too. And then–'

'Look, Caroline – do you mind if I call you "Carrie"?'

'Well, actually–'

'Fine! I'm really very tired after the flight, and I'm not a great eater. So, if it's OK with you, I'll skip lunch and have a rest. That way I can be fresh and wide awake to meet your folks this evening. Is that OK with you, Carrie?'

'Um, yes ... whatever.' *Why protest? If she sleeps the whole afternoon, I can do some more packing. What a spot of luck!*

The car was now winding along leafy lanes flanked by high stone walls, more like the England Misty had been hoping to see.

'So, Carrie, you *too* are off to Europe in a few days.'

'Actually, Misty, the United Kingdom *is* part of "Europe", you know. We are *all* Europeans.'

Duffle half-turned his head. 'I'm *not*! I'm British and proud of it. The worst thing we ever did – join that Common Market.'

Misty chuckled. 'OK, Ron, message received loud and clear! So, it's Spain, Carrie. You told me at the airport, didn't you? Jet lag, I guess.'

Misty's informality with Duffle made Caroline bristle. 'Correct,' she responded curtly. 'Well, actually it's a small island about five miles off the coast of Ibiza, one of the Balearic Islands ... in the Mediterranean.'

'Yeah, I've heard of Ibiza. It's where all those crazy clubs are, right?'

'I really wouldn't know about *that*, Misty, I'm sure. I understand that Ibiza does have a certain *reputation*, but–'

'So why exactly are you going to this little island, Firm–?'

'*Form*entera.'

'Yeah, Formentera. I mean, I don't exactly see you as the sunbathing type, Carrie.'

Caroline emitted a rather silly laugh. 'Oh, I shan't be *sun*bathing. Oh dear me no! The purpose of my visit–'

But the fascinating revelation would have to wait, for the Jaguar was finally emerging from the long avenue of beech trees which led to Bobbins' west facade and its grand entrance.

'Je-sus *Christ*!' enunciated Misty. 'It *is* a fucking castle! Don't tell me – the housekeeper's name's Mrs Danvers, the Hound of the Baskervilles roams the grounds, and Baron Frankenstein lodges in the West Wing!' Her laugh was infectious, and Duffle joined in.

'"Mrs Danvers",' he sniggered. 'Spot on, love!'

Caroline's bemused expression concealed her incomprehension. 'Welcome to Bobbins, Misty,' she said icily, shocked by the appalling expletive.

'It's fantastic – *really*! I love Gothic – so Wagnerian!'

While Caroline clambered awkwardly out of the car, Duffle opened Misty's door and then busied himself with the luggage. Slowly shaking her head, the guest surveyed the sombre pseudo-medieval mass before her with its profusion of towers, spires, buttresses and terrifying gargoyles; the front doors alone would have done justice to any self-respecting cathedral. Bobbins, she rapidly concluded, was vast, dark and very, very ugly; it probably had a lot to account for.

As the two young ladies mounted the damp stone steps, one of the massive wooden doors slowly opened with a spine-chilling creak. Misty gasped: standing in the doorway was the spitting image of the actress who had indeed played 'Mrs Danvers' in the 1930s movie *Rebecca*, except that in this case, Bobbins' Mrs Danvers had bleached blond hair and was wearing some kind of housecoat and white sling-back sandals. *Weird!*

'Mrs Danvers' smiled, revealing a row of very uneven and nicotine-stained teeth. 'Hello, love!' she said cheerfully. 'You must be Miss Start. I'm Vivian Duffle, the housekeeper. Welcome to Bobbins! I hope you had a most enjoyable flight across the Atlantic.' She turned to her husband and the smile disappeared. 'Come on, Ron – don't dither! Get them bags up to Miss Start's room pronto – West Wing, third floor.'

'*Third*!'

'Miss Caroline's orders.'

Misty looked from Vivian Duffle to Caroline and managed an ambiguous grin, but as the guest crossed the threshold into the Victorian gloom, she had a strange premonition that her weekend was not going to proceed in accordance with her meticulous plans.

*

It was mid-afternoon, and in the Yellow Room on Bobbins' ground floor, the Honourable James Cornelius Weetwood was slumped in an armchair before a large state-of-the-art television set – an expensive appliance recently demanded by his mother, even though she was an infrequent Bobbins resident. Barefooted and clad only in an old pair of football shorts and a T-shirt, James looked totally vacant – as if spaced out of his mind after enjoying a massive spliff. It was an impression he'd managed to convey during most of his waking hours ever since receiving the results of his A-level examinations almost two years earlier to the day: Grade Es in Physics, Chemistry and Biology. His parents had also reacted negatively: so much for six apparently dazzling years at a very prestigious – and expensive – boarding school.

His father's comments had been typically minimal: 'I'm very disappointed, er ... James. Of course you'll re-sit. I'm sorry about your friend, er ... Paul. That's the cause of it all. You'll get over it.'

Beryl had been more forthright: 'You're a disgrace to the family,' she scolded. 'I'm leaving for Cap-Ferrat tomorrow. At least at the villa I won't have to explain away this – this ... *embarrassment* to our friends. I always said your relationship with that boy was unhealthy. By the time I return in early October, I expect this mess to have been resolved and your place at Cambridge reconfirmed.'

Later, James wondered about his mother's implicit admission that the guests at the family's French villa would not be 'friends'. In any event, he resolved not to re-sit or go to *any* university: the death of his best friend, *Peter* – his father's inability to remember the name confirmed that the prat was living on another planet – had utterly devastated him.

James and Peter had hit it off from the outset at Glenflannel Academy, an institution in northern Scotland renowned for its unconventional teaching methods. The two boys became inseparable and had spent almost all their holidays together; just before starting their final year, they'd backpacked around Europe. Although never having indulged in anything remotely sexual with each other, Beryl began to fear they were gay; George professed to have no idea what she babbling about. She might have been more at ease had James felt able to tell her about the girls Peter and himself had bedded while island-hopping in Greece, but such a conversation had always seemed inconceivable to him.

James's world fell apart two days before he was due to sit his first A-level exam, when Peter accompanied him into Glenflannel village to mail a letter to Lord Weetwood's sister, James's beloved Aunt Belinda. As they approached the post office, a masked man rushed out brandishing a sawn-off shotgun, and began to run to a waiting car. James froze to the spot; Peter darted forward and tried to stop him with a rugby tackle. In the ensuing melee, the gun went off; the injuries to Peter's head were horrific. The car sped away with the gunman; no one was ever charged with the crime.

Later that day, over a cup of tea and a plate of Bourbon biscuits, Glenflannel's headmaster earnestly advised James to sit his exams, claiming 'that's what Peter would have wanted.' James agreed although it meant missing the funeral in Jamaica; Peter's father was a minister in the island's government.

For the last two years, James had exiled himself at Bobbins. His daily routine was almost invariable: from about midday, when he finally got out of bed, until two or three in the morning, he would sit in his room playing computer games or watching TV. Now, thanks to his mother's latest bout of conspicuous consumption, he'd transferred his allegiance to the set in the Yellow Room, where he would gaze blankly at the giant screen with the quadraphonic sound turned up high. It was an activity of which Caroline still remained ignorant, thanks to Bobbins' vastness and her disinterest in television.

In so far as his parents had given any thought to their son's lifestyle, it appeared preferable to them that it was better for James to be out of sight and harm's way in the family home than displaying his bizarre behaviour publicly, whether by living in a commune – or whatever they were now called – attacking motorway construction workers, or mugging old ladies to pay for some vile drug addiction.

And so it was that within an hour of Misty's arrival, James was being anaesthetized by the long-running quiz show *Stinky Poo!*. There were two teams, each comprising three 'celebrities' – mainly stars of TV soaps. Team A would be provided with a sealed glass jar containing some smell or other, and at the sound of a horn emitting a fart-like noise, their captain would unscrew the top, sniff the jar and then make the appropriate expressions of horror at the evil-smelling contents. The other two team-mates would follow suit. The point was that the smell was supposed to be the most hated smell of one of the members of Team B. But which one? And what was the smell? This was to be unearthed within five minutes by lavatorial interrogation. After each member of Team A had made his or her guess, the member of Team B whose most hated smell lurked within the jar would own up by shouting 'Stinky Poo!'. Then the roles would be reversed. Yes, it was dire, but over ten million people watched every week.

The show was hosted by one-time Manchester United and England captain, Ken Cockle, and as James gazed blankly at the screen, Ken was shouting at Miranda Dubonnet, the rapidly ageing starlet of Channel 4's soap *The Fearless And The Wondrous...*

*

It was the day of the recording and the team members were not exactly hitting it off.

'Come on, Miranda,' Cockle roared, '– only twenty seconds to go! You said that there pong were like carbolic soap, and Magnus has discovered that when "posh" Gwen over there were a kid she lived next to Wright's Coal Tar Soap works. So, lass, who the bloody 'ell do you think it is, yer great puddin'?'

'Darling,' pleaded Miranda, 'stop shouting at me with that horrid northern voice of yours and let me think!'

'Oh for God's sake, Miranda, luvvy, it's obvious. Look at that vicious smirk on Gwen's face.' This was Magnus Lace, bitching as usual. In the Sixties, he'd been the handsome young star of several British films. Now he was bald and fat with the occasional slot on children's TV.

'My dear Miranda, don't fall into the trap,' pleaded Gwen Blackberry disingenuously. 'Are you *sure* it's carbolic? It could be the smell of some cough sweet – a Fisherman's Friend perhaps.'

'Ee,' roared Cockle, 'I bet you've sucked a few Fisherman's Friends in your time, Gwen, chuck!'

Gwen's smile evaporated. 'My God,' she sneered, 'you're such a *vulgar* little man, Kenneth. Why don't you–?' Her words were lost as the camera switched to an ever more hysterical audience who were being frantically induced to try and split their sides by a red-faced studio employee holding up a huge sign bearing the instruction '**LAUGH!**'.

Gwen Blackberry was almost at the end of her tether. Thank God the recording was nearly finished! For over twenty years she'd entertained the discerning BBC Radio listener with her portrayal of the dedicated and permanently middle-aged housewife 'Jessica Muffin', who, in all these years, had never done or said a bad deed or word. *The Muffins* was an institution: it *was* the BBC; it was England – the very best of England – and she, Gwen Blackberry, as Jessica Muffin, the mother-figure par excellence and the keystone of the programme, was the very personification of England itself. This was the world of kindly policemen, village cricket, sheep-dog trials, freshly baked sponge cakes, cathedral choirs, double-decker buses, ivy-clad pubs, pork pies, Bonfire Night, Wellington boots, red telephone boxes. ... And what had she been reduced to? – prostituting her talents on afternoon television with ghastly, common people like Cockle and has-beens like fat old Magnus and brain-dead Miranda. She was definitely changing her agent.

'Come on, love – wake up!' yelled Cockle. 'Still dreamin' about perfectin' the Muffins' recipe for Lancashire Hot Pot? Dizzy Miranda's guessed it's *you*, chuck. So, shout it out! Come on!' He looked quite vicious – almost manic.

For a moment, Gwen thought about walking out. *To hell with them all – and their trashy programme. The very idea of me, Gwen Blackberry, uttering the words 'Stinky Poo' in any circumstances – it's positively grotesque.* She looked around: everyone seemed to be staring at her menacingly. She could imagine what they were all thinking: *The bitch! She's going to ruin the recording. We'll have to have a rerun of the last game.*

Someone from the studio was in front of her, just behind the camera, frantically mouthing 'Stinky Poo!' over and over. She thought of the money she and her husband had borrowed for the new villa in heavenly Formentera, and of the BBC's unexpected delay in the renewal of her *Muffins* contract. She smiled at the audience. 'Stinky ... poo,' she mumbled. 'STINKY POO!' she shouted. '**STINKY POO!**' she screamed. 'Oh Miranda, you're so *clever*, darling!'

*

James watched, but he did not see; he listened, but he did not hear. Almost imperceptibly, a vision of a lighthouse began to form in front of the screen. He blinked and it vanished.

He stirred in his seat: something very strange was happening – something about the room. Perspiring profusely, he suddenly knew that someone was behind him. He wanted to turn around but felt paralysed; he knew whom he wanted it to be. He'd never really believed Peter was dead. It was some horrible, sick joke – it had to be: you don't go down to the post office in a remote Scottish village with your best mate, only to see him get half his face blown off.

With his eyes full of tears, James finally found the courage to turn and face the door.

'Peter? It *is* you, isn't it?'

For an instant he couldn't focus.

'Hi! Sorry – I'm lost. I was looking for Carrie ... Jesus! What the *hell* are you watching?'

James's eyes cleared. The most beautiful woman he'd ever seen stood in the doorway, smiling at him. She smiled just like Peter.

# CHAPTER 6

Caroline was perched on the edge of the single bed in her chaotic study-cum-bedroom. At her feet lay a large open suitcase – inexpertly packed – and a burgeoning British Airways flight bag that had seen better days. Having almost completed her packing, a task prolonged by exhaustive analysis of her lists, it occurred to her that she should check up on bothersome Misty. She glanced at her chunky Swatch: almost quarter to seven already! With considerable reluctance, she heaved herself up, sighed and trudged towards the door.

Trekking along Bobbins' long, echoing corridors contributed significantly to Caroline's limited exercise. When she halted at the top of the main staircase to catch her breath, she was surprised by the sight of James ambling between his room and the adjacent bathroom. Even though he had his back to her, she averted her gaze: save for a towel hanging around his neck, he was naked; his wet hair evinced that he'd had a bath or shower. He was whistling, and the tune sounded like the jolly one that opens Beethoven's Pastoral symphony. Caroline was puzzled: as far as she was aware, James only enjoyed ear-splitting rackets manufactured by 'groups', as she called them. Shaking her head, she recommenced her laboured ascent to Misty's third-floor room.

'Hello, Misty!' she wheezed, letting herself in after a cursory tap on the door.

'Oh hi, Carrie!' Lying on her bed reading a book, Misty seemed embarrassed. She swiftly closed the book and placed it on the bedside table, with the front cover face down.

'Everything hunky-dory?' asked Caroline. 'Had a nice sleep? Feeling peckish?' En route she'd compiled a list of questions to keep the conversation going, but her nervousness had generated a mass bombardment which now left her devoid of ammunition.

'The answers are yes, yes and yes. You look kinda flushed. Sit down.'

Caroline collapsed into an armchair at the side of the bed. 'Thanks awfully. I'll be fine in a sec'.' Casting a furtive glance, she felt a pang of remorse: it really wasn't a very nice room – rather small with a north-facing window and a view of the old stable block. Mrs Duffle had recommended a large guest suite on the first floor with a splendid panorama of the lake, but, out of spite, Caroline had insisted on this drab box.

'Is the room all right?' It was the last question Caroline had wanted to ask, but having exhausted her stock she couldn't think of anything else.

'It's fine,' and, as if to reassure Caroline, who looked dubious, Misty added cheerfully, '– *really*.'

'Jolly good. ... What's that you're reading?'

'Er ... *Eugénie Grandet* ... by Balzac.'

Caroline's eyes bulged. '*Really*? In *French*?' The tone of incredulity was such that she might just as well have said: 'Gosh! I thought Americans were far too dim to learn foreign languages.'

Misty smiled and nodded.

'Golly! I can *read* French quite well – especially seventeenth-century French – but I'm not too good at the spoken stuff.'

'Ah. ... So, as you're off to Spain on Monday – Formentera I think you said on the drive from the airport – how's your Spanish?'

Caroline studied her scruffy trainers. 'I can get by – *buenos días, mañana* and all that. In any event, I doubt I'll have much contact with the locals.'

'Oh?'

'Mm. You see, I'm going there – of *all* places – to conduct some *rather important* research.'

'Research?'

Caroline suddenly remembered Pongo's 'top secret' edict. 'Yes, on ... on Mazarin.' It was the first name that came into her head.

'*Who*?'

'Cardinal Mazarin – you know? – Chief Minister of France? – Louis XIV ...?'

'Oh, *that* Mazarin. ... Why?'

'Well, I – *we* that is – think he may have played a far more significant role in French – and, indeed, European – history than any of us may have ever imagined.'

'In what way?' Misty glanced at her Cartier watch. 'Incidentally, how long is it to dinner? I'm as hungry as a wolf.'

Caroline peered at her Swatch. 'Ooh, about thirty minutes. Seven-thirty *prompt*. Remember? I told you in the car. Anyway, Mazarin–'

'Sorry, Carrie, but don't you need to change or something? I've bathed so I only need to slip into the one concession to formality I've brought with me.' Caroline followed Misty's fleeting glance at a black silk trouser suit hanging on the wardrobe door; it looked very expensive.

'Me? Oh no! Daddy doesn't take a blind bit of notice of my tracksuit bottoms and T-shirts – not like Mummy. Anyway, Pongo and I–'

'Pongo?'

'Gosh! Sorry! Professor Pangbourne at Durham – my university. Anyway, the Prof and I are investigating the theory that' – *improvise, you budding historian!* – '... that ... that neither Louis XIV nor his younger brother, Philippe Duke of Orléans, was the offspring of Louis XIII and his wife, Anne of Austria, but rather of Anne and Mazarin. ... Oh dear, I suppose these names don't mean much to you – if anything.'

'A little,' said Misty, still smiling. 'But Formentera seems an odd place for that kind of research.'

'I'll say! However, there's this frighteningly rich German, Kurt Schmückstück. Apparently, his father made a fortune after the War by buying up enormous stocks of Third Reich flags – the things with swastikas on – and recycling them into utility baby clothes.'

Misty raised her eyebrows and wondered whether she was being taken for a ride.

'He realized,' Caroline continued, 'that people would always put babies at the top of their priorities and make any sacrifices for them. Seems he fiddled his taxes though, and the Schmückstücks had to leave Germany in a bit of a hurry in about 1950. On the other hand, he'd already got loads of money out through the guise of some export-import business controlled by some German friends in Buenos Aires. Anyway, one of these German chums died and Kurt's father bought his flat. Turns out that there were all sorts of secret compartments stuffed full of treasures looted by the Nazis from France. Kurt's father only found this out when he started to redecorate.'

'Really?'

'Mm. The father managed to sell most of the best bits around South America – Argentina mainly. He died a few years ago and Kurt decided to return to Europe and settle in Spain ... Barcelona, I think. He left his mother in Buenos Aires. Well–' Caroline's face suddenly darkened. 'Bother! I'm missing *The Muffins*!'

'Muffins? Before dinner?'

'Oh never mind: there's the repeat on Sunday morning. Anyway, where was I? ... Um ... oh yes! Well, this Kurt bod used to go to Ibiza regularly for holidays and one day took the boat over to Formentera. He instantly fell in love with the place and had a whopping villa built in some gorgeous location. Then last year, one of Pongo's colleagues – a young lecturer – decent cove – very athletic–'

'A guy?'

'No, a lady, of course! ... Ernestine Kirk ... Teeny. Anyway, Teeny went on holiday last May to Ibiza and met Schmückstück in some pub one evening. He invited her over to Formentera and she loved it so much she decided to give up her Durham job and ... well–'

'She decided to shack up with this rich German.'

Caroline sighed. 'Pongo says she's like a companion ... well, sort of. She was awfully upset when Teeny handed in her notice. She'd been one of Pongo's best students and ... Anyway, Teeny moved into Kurt's villa and started rummaging through his library. She was amazed by all the rare and valuable books, and Kurt explained that many of them were part of the Nazi booty discovered in Buenos Aires. One day she came across three beautifully bound notebooks. Something about the handwriting intrigued her. Luckily for us, she had the sense to photocopy a page from one of the volumes and fax it to Pongo – they'd remained good friends, you see. Well, Pongo instantly realised that ... that Mazarin was the author of the journals, and somehow she managed to persuade Kurt to give her exclusive rights of access to them for twelve months. She was supposed to spend the summer there examining them, but something came up – some *jolly* important thing at Harvard. ... I say, aren't *you*–?'

'Shouldn't these valuable manuscripts be returned to their rightful owner, the French state maybe?'

Caroline returned to staring at her trainers. 'Um ... well ... that did occur to me, but Pongo says that their "treasure trove" under Argentinean law, and that under French statutes of limitations ... Well, it's all very technical, Misty. Anyway, Pongo would never get mixed up in anything that wasn't absolutely one hundred per cent pukka.'

Misty was nodding slowly. 'No doubt. ... You seem mighty fond of this Pongo. You're happy then at Durham?'

'Oh yes! It's a smashing university.'

'And you've made lots of friends?'

'I wouldn't say "lots".'

'But you have got *some* good friends? It's just that when you were at Burgers–'

'What did you do this afternoon after your nap? Did Duffle show you around? So sorry I couldn't be your guide, but you can't imagine the amount of stuff I've got to do before Monday, and–'

'No sweat! Actually, I met your brother. We had a good chat, and then *he* showed me around. What a house! And the grounds – wow!'

Caroline looked like she'd just been electrocuted. 'You talked to *James*? ... James talked to *you*? He–?'

'Yeah, he told me about Peter and ... and everything.'

'*Every*thing? I don't believe it! I–! Oh gosh! There's the dinner gong! We'd better hurry!'

As she rose from the armchair, Caroline's bulky frame hit the bedside table, and Misty's book fell to the floor. 'Sorry!' she yelped, but before she could bend down to retrieve it, Misty, whose near-constant smile had evaporated, bounded off the bed and beat her to it.

Turning towards the door, Caroline snapped: 'Come on! Daddy hates unpunctuality.' With another cacophony of gong-beating reverberating around the house, she hobbled out of the room, forgetting that Misty had still to change.

When Caroline finally reached the dining room, her father was pacing up and down before the open French windows. It was a warm, humid evening, and the heavy scent of freshly mown grass drifted in, thanks to a gentle breeze.

'At last! *Really*, Caroline, you sound like a badly maintained Peruvian steam engine of pre-war vintage which has just managed to reach the summit of a particularly elevated stretch of line in the foothills of the Andes. Have a glass of water.' Lord Weetwood started to pour her one just as Misty entered the room with a broad smile; she looked very elegant.

Caroline blushed. 'Um, Father ... er ... may I introduce my *former* penfriend, Misty Start? She's American. Remember, I told you she was coming for the weekend at breakfast yesterday? She's hiking round Europe – or something – for the summer.'

George passed the glass to Caroline and glanced at Misty with obvious disinterest. 'No, I have no recollection of any such communication from you. Be that as it may, Caroline, I'm pleased that we're able to entertain a friend of yours ... finally.' He walked slowly towards Misty and, without looking directly at her, extended his right hand. 'How do you do, Miss ... er ...?'

Assuming she was in the presence of a true aristocratic eccentric of the old school who believed in absolute formality, Misty extended her smile. 'I am delighted to meet you, Lord Weetwood, and to be received in your lovely old home. *Do* call me Misty.'

George looked at the guest enquiringly, for he believed that Caroline had introduced her as 'Miss Something-or-Other'; it would certainly never have occurred to him that the given name of any person could be something as bizarre as 'Misty'. In any event, as he had no interest in the girl, he'd no need to query Caroline's mumbled introduction. If the American was suggesting that he should call her by some ghastly nickname, such as 'Miss D' or 'Miss Dee' – whatever – she was wasting her breath: he'd maintained a lifelong antipathy to nicknames. Indeed, as far as he was aware, he'd never called anyone 'Bob', 'Ron' or 'Ted'.

'Would you like a sherry, Miss ... er ... Domecq's La Ina? We prefer it to Tio Pepe.'

Anticipating a choice, Misty awaited the menu of other refreshments; in truth, she had a craving for an ice-cold beer. She looked at Weetwood expectantly; he looked at her enquiringly.

'Is this a "yes" or did you not understand the question?'

Even though the sarcasm was not lost on her, Misty managed to maintain her smile. 'Oh, excuse me, Lord Weetwood! Sherry would be fine – thanks.'

Caroline did not drink sherry or any other alcoholic beverage. Her usual Coca-Cola was already awaiting her on the drinks table, the garish red can looking somewhat incongruous on its silver coaster. It was a product that George despised; but for Beryl's predilection for Cuba Libras, he would have had it banned. As Caroline snatched the can – the glass of water proffered by her father remained untouched – she observed with some surprise that there were four place settings on the dining table: whatever sustenance her brother had consumed since the start of his self-imposed internal exile had been taken in his room.

'I didn't know my daughter had a penfriend,' George said coolly as he looked over Misty's head and appeared to study a portrait of his father on the far wall; while technically superior to the one in Soap House's boardroom, it was still not a very good likeness. However, the artist had fared better with the panoramic view of the smoking soap works in the background.

'We corresponded when I was at Burgers,' Caroline confessed, glancing sheepishly at Misty. 'Sorry, St *Ethel*burger's. Misty was at Brynamman.'

'Really?' queried George raising his eyebrows. 'You were at school in Wales, Miss–?'

'*Mis-ty*, sir. 'No, Brynamman College – Rhode Island.'

'Ah ... Rhode *Island*. ... And from which part of the United States do you hail ... er–?'

'Texas ... Fort Worth.' Misty sipped her sherry and waited for the next round. Indeed, as she glanced from father to daughter, the whole situation began to appear comical. To make matters worse, Caroline was struggling almost manically to open her Coca-Cola; the task seemed to be degenerating into a life-and-death struggle.

'Ah yes ... Texas.'

'Misty's father makes soap too,' Caroline said offhandedly, glaring at the uncooperative can.

Misty sighed.

George's raised right hand wobbled and a few drops of sherry trickled over the side of his glass. 'Oh?' He seemed on the point of adding something, but instead turned and walked towards the French windows.

'Well, nothing like your outfit, Lord Weetwood,' said Misty. 'I think soap's just a kind of sideline – Start Industries is a conglomerate – not that I know much about the business.'

'*Start Industries*?' croaked George, still with his back turned, '... of Fort Worth? ... You're ... you mean you're Miss *Start* – daughter of – of–?'

'Sonny Start.'

George finally swung round. 'But *how*–? I mean ... *penfriends*?'

'Misty's school and St Ethelburger's operated a penfriend scheme, Daddy. About five years ago, a couple of teachers introduced us, Miss Tud–'

'"A couple of *teachers*"? But that's impossible! ... Why on *earth* didn't you ever tell me, Caroline?'

Staring once more at her trainers, Caroline said meekly: 'I didn't think you'd be interested.'

Silence fell upon the room; Misty felt obliged to break it. 'You have a beautiful garden, sir. James was kind enough to show me around this afternoon. The roses are heavenly and I love that little cottage down by the lake. It looks just like a country railroad station.'

'It *is* a *railway* station, Miss ... Miss *Start*. It once efficaciously served the good people of Clagging, a village some twenty miles distant, until the short-sightedness and accountant mentality of the British Railways Board brought about its closure thirty-four years ago. I had the building taken down and reconstructed here.' He paused. '"James"? ... *James* showed you around?'

'Yes. Excellent guide.'

'James who?'

'Your son, James.'

'My son?'

'Sure! The tall guy – looks like a beefy Tom Cruise but with blond hair and blue eyes, and speaks like Hugh Grant.'

As Caroline's can finally opened with explosive force, spraying her and the table with its brown sticky contents, James breezed nonchalantly into the dining room in Levi's and a dazzling white T-shirt.

'Hi, everyone! Hello again, Misty! *Lovely* outfit! I'm bloody starving. What's for supper, Dad? Hope old Mrs D's pulled her finger out.'

George stared at his ecstatically happy son. He ought to have been pleased that the tedious period of mourning appeared to be over, but no smile or other indication of happiness appeared on his face as frightening possibilities dramatically flashed before him. What on earth was going on? How could it possibly be that Start's daughter was *here* – in *his* house? – a 'penfriend' of reclusive Caroline? – just weeks before the launch of

FoamFay? Was she some kind of spy? And what had she done to James? Had the boy gone completely mad, or was he now on some frightful drug? In any event, he was not accustomed to being addressed as 'Dad', a term he found particularly displeasing. He'd communicate his views on that score in private at the earliest opportunity.

'Well,' George muttered, 'as formal introductions are clearly unnecessary, let's all be seated.' Taking his place at the head of the table, he pressed a button on its underside; in Mrs Duffle's kitchen, an electric bell rang.

For decades, Friday dinners at Clittingham had been something of a sacred ritual, a three-course homage to traditional English food: oceans of soup; great steaming piles of roast or grilled meats; mountains of familiar over-cooked vegetables; swamps of thick brown gravy; mighty dollops of sponge pudding and custard. Beryl, however, was revolted by the spectacle of grown men salivating over glorified school dinners – what she branded 'club food'. In consequence, she'd endeavoured to introduce a veneer of sophistication into Clittingham's kitchen. In George's opinion, this amounted to no more than plates adorned with microscopic portions of obscure meats surrounded by colourful pools of unpronounceable sauces, all garnished with tasteless, odourless and nutritionless sprigs of greenery. But now, with his wife's absence in France, George had expressly instructed Mrs Duffle to produce an English meal *par excellence* – his very words.

Thus, on this July evening, Misty and her three fellow diners were to savour potted shrimps as a starter, followed by roast beef and Yorkshire pudding with boiled new potatoes, carrots, beans and cauliflower. Jam roly-poly with lashings of custard, a delicacy hitherto unknown to Misty, would conclude the feast. To her surprise, Misty found herself consuming substantial portions of each course with relish.

George and Caroline sat through the meal in almost total silence, giving every impression of being only dimly aware of the animated conversations between James and Misty. Over pudding they moved on to Jane Campion's film *The Piano*: Vivian Duffle had chosen it on her most recent weekly visit to the video rental store in Stalybridge, one of the three sources of sex and romance now available to her; television and novels were the others, Ron having manifested no interest in that sort of thing for some years. She'd watched *The Piano* alone last Saturday evening – Ron had escaped to the Cob o' Coal as usual – and on pressing the remote control's rewind button while stroking Kitchener, her beloved feline companion, she'd remarked: 'Well, my little darling, what the bloody 'ell was *that* depressing rubbish all about?' Kitchener made no indication that it was any the wiser, whereupon Vivian decided that *The Piano* must be 'an intellectual film' and that it might, therefore, be of interest to Master James. She'd been correct.

Misty did not share James's enthusiasm for *The Piano*, and enjoyed the opportunity of so informing him across the dinner table. Had Caroline or her father bothered to listen, neither would have had a clue what the others were talking about. George, however, having spent most of the meal convincing himself that the 'penfriendship' was simply one of those bizarre coincidences that occasionally crops up in life, had moved on to deliberating whether to liven up his nocturnal model railway adventures by overriding the computer and staging a truly awesome head-on collision between the up *Royal Scot Express* and a Crewe to Manchester local; there was the danger of a spot of damage to the locomotives, but the 'accident' would justify the mobilization of his breakdown train and, in particular, the steam crane which had been gathering dust in the sidings for some months.

Caroline, by contrast, was mentally rechecking the numerous lists she'd compiled of things to take to Formentera and tasks to complete prior to her departure. She was able to tick off most of them, but had she packed the electric mosquito gadget? And did she have enough of those horrid-smelling tablets to put in it? Should the gadget be packed in her hand luggage? Was it the sort of 'electrical equipment' that one must not pack in one's suitcase? And could she still remember the Spanish translation of the phrase she'd been endeavouring to learn for the benefit of the taxi driver at Ibiza airport? 'Good day. Please take me to the Formentera ferry, sir.'

*Oh, God! – is it Buenos días or Buenas aías? Of course, it could be Buenos díos or even Buenas díos. It really is ridiculous for these foreign languages to have all this masculine and feminine nonsense.*

Meanwhile, Misty launched her main offensive.

'But, James, for Christ's sake, how could an old piano survive a voyage halfway across the world, remain on a beach with the Pacific Ocean pounding around it for days, and then sound like a meticulously maintained Steinway at Carnegie Hall?'

'That's poetic licence!'

'It's *path*etic! And that dumb tune played over and over until one wanted to scream. And it was completely 1980s-ish easy listening. Do you realize that in that entire movie, set in *Victorian* times, Ada – Holly Hunter – never played anything that sounded faintly pre-World War II except five seconds' worth of Chopin?'

'Oh for God's sake, Misty, how pedantic!'

'And the accents! I'm no expert, James, but Holly Hunter had an *Irish* accent. Wasn't she supposed to be Scottish?'

'Well–'

'And Harvey Keitel had a really weird accent. Sometimes he was Scottish, and then he was Irish.'

'But, Misty, do the accents *really* matter? After all, the essence of the story is–'

'I'll tell you what the essence of the story is. An ugly, sad, miserable woman with a piano fetish, but who can only play one lousy tune, travels ten thousand miles across the ocean with an old piano to be ugly, sad and miserable with a husband who tries to be kind and good to her, but who can't understand the piano fetish. She cheats on him and has sex with this dirty, perverted peasant who's shrewdly acquired the piano. The sordid deal is that if she lets him screw her enough, she'll get the piano back. Then the bitch decides she doesn't want the darned piano after all!'

James was laughing. 'With all due respect, Misty, I think that's just a wee bit cynical and, frankly, superficial.'

But Misty was now on her hobby horse, and, aided and abetted by the excellent Château Gloria opened in her honour – the host had stuck to a decent Mosel throughout the meal – fired off one final salvo.

'And worst of all, James, I found the movie disgustingly racist. The Maoris were all portrayed as dirty, stupid, ignorant, perverted, uncouth, money-grubbing, sex-mad degenerates.'

'Not *that* again! I just can't see–'

'Because, James, that's exactly how they came over. Think of the way they played on the beach like imbeciles, how they rubbed themselves against trees for a cheap thrill.'

'Crap!'

'And that interminable tune tinkling away throughout the movie. I felt that if I heard it one more time I'd scream!'

James was about to remind Misty that she was repeating herself, when her clenched fist dropped just a little too forcefully onto the dining table and set the coffee cups rattling on their saucers. George emerged from his reverie of mangled train wreckage and shattered corpses of dreary commuters on the Crewe to Manchester local train.

'Ah, Miss ... *Start*, I see violence from the crime-ridden inner cities of the United States has arrived at our dinner table, albeit in the form of an aggressive debate. However, I'm sure that *without* having to resort to coercive gestures, my son has put forward persuasively the case for the superiority of the European piano over the instruments, such as they are, manufactured in your own country. And now, if you have no objection, I propose to retire to deal with some pressing paper work. I'm sure you'll be well looked after by my son and daughter. Good night.'

Without looking at any of his dinner companions, George pushed his chair back and walked slowly towards the door.

'Good night, Pop,' said James brightly, winking at Misty.

'Good night, Lord Weetwood,' chirped Misty. 'And many thanks for such a lovely dinner.'

Without turning round, George muttered: 'Don't thank me, young lady, thank Mrs Duffle and her *army* of staff. And I'll see *you* ... er, James, in the morning.'

After a few jokes about piano manufacturing, James and Misty rose to take a stroll through the garden. They invited Caroline to join them, but only dimly aware of their presence – the mosquito problem was continuing to bother her – she simply grunted something, which they gratefully took for a 'no'. The happy voices of the attractive couple drifted away.

Caroline lingered, her gaze fixed on the portrait of her grandfather. Did she truly have enough tablets for the mosquito gadget? She had sixty, which should cover an eight-week stay, assuming, of course, that only one tablet per day was required – or rather per night: the beastly things only came out at night, didn't they? But what if her stay was extended? She might, for example, need another week – or even two – to complete the research. What if she fell ill with flu or gastro-enteritis on the day before her planned departure? The *Berlitz Guide to Ibiza and Formentera* said the tablets were readily available in local shops, but could one trust the quality? Were they made to the same exacting standards as those sold in Boots? One thing, however, was absolutely certain: if there was a single mosquito within twenty miles, it would undoubtedly find her. She'd painfully discovered that on the school trip to Venice three years ago. Her legs had blown up like balloons, and she'd had to be sent home by air ambulance after only two days.

*Oh well, if I do have any supply problems in Formentera, I'll just have to telephone Mrs Duffle and get more tablets sent by courier.*

Caroline looked around and was surprised to find she was alone. She considered going in search of her guest and then thought better of it: her crazy brother was obviously doing a good job as host and guide. But then her brows furrowed. 'Blast!' she muttered. 'I forgot to tell Misty about the tour Duffle's taking her on tomorrow. I'll have to go and find her after all. Bother, bother, *bother*!' As she stood up, however, it occurred to her that Misty would probably be happier doing something with James – and vice-versa.

For a few moments, Caroline reflected on James's extraordinary transformation, and it slowly dawned on her that it might have something to do with Misty being the first pretty girl he'd seen in the flesh for two years. 'Well,' she sighed, 'at least some good appears to have come out of her wretched visit.'

And so, with a clear conscience, Caroline returned to the library, intent on finalizing the list of reference materials to accompany her to Formentera. It was while she was debating Item 25 on the list, Alexandre Dumas's *Dix Ans Plus Tard ou Le Vicomte de Bragelonne* – convincing herself that she really didn't need to take a work of fiction – that her thoughts drifted back to Misty and their chat together in her room. Perhaps she'd been indiscreet talking about Project MIM at all, but Misty had been so disarming. Still, it wasn't exactly a gross breach of security thanks to the Mazarin subterfuge. And it wasn't as though Misty was in the history business, so to speak.

A strange feeling suddenly caused Caroline look again at her much-annotated list. She stared hard at Item 25. Her pen hovered above it. She was about to cross it off, when, to her surprise, she said: '*Eugénie Grandet* ... by Balzac.' She tapped her pen a few times. 'Balzac,' she repeated. She'd only glimpsed the cover briefly – a second or two – when the book fell on the floor. Then Misty had snatched it – yes, *snatched* it, with that funny look in her eyes ... not embarrassment, more like ... guilt. Yes, now that she thought about it, it was a *guilty* look. She closed her eyes and tried to reconstruct the scene: her sense of foolishness for bumping into the table; the book lying on the floor; Misty jumping up and–

The title wasn't *Eugénie Grandet*! – there were too many words. They *were* in French, though ... or was she just imagining that now? But the author's name was in large, bold lettering – white on a dark blue background – and it wasn't Honoré de Balzac: it was Alexandre Dumas!

# CHAPTER 7

Whilst Bobbins' Victorian Gothic was not exactly playful, its gardens were delightful, albeit neither George nor Beryl Weetwood could take any credit: the charming terraces connected by massive flights of steps had been laid out by George's paternal grandmother, Roberta – 'Bobbins' – during the decade preceding the First World War. Liberally sprinkled with fountains, neo-classical temples and gazeboes, each terrace afforded glorious views of Goblin Water, a lake formed by damming a small stream that flowed through the grounds.

George's complete lack of interest in things horticultural had much to do with his childhood and tyrannical Nanny Blotch: whatever the weather, she'd required him to make a dozen circuits of the Upper Terrace each morning between eleven and noon. Exacerbated by the estate's elevated position, Master George had regularly been tortured by howling gales and torrential rain, not to mention winter's snow and ice. During the brief summer months, with the sun horribly burning his fair skin, the gardens became a dangerous world of bees and wasps. Consequently, following his father's death in 1972, although George felt obliged to maintain Granny's terraces and herbaceous borders, he remained indifferent to them – as did Beryl, who had no more interest in gardening as she had in any other earthy pastime.

James, by contrast, knew the gardens like the back of his hand; indeed, for the last ten years or so he'd been their only regular visitor, apart from the gardeners. Until his early teens, he'd bounded out of bed almost every morning during school holidays, anxious to depart on yet another expedition into the unknown: in his mind, depending on his mood and which adventure books or films he'd most recently read or watched, the estate could be the Amazon jungle, the mountains of Tibet, or the barren wastes of Baluchistan. On one scorching summer's afternoon, after reading about Jason and the Argonauts, Great-Granny's temples had become infested with multi-headed demons. While his mother graciously supplied tea and cakes in the Orangery to the flowery-hatted ladies of the Dribbledale Conservative Association, he'd scourged Medusa from the Temple of Diana down by the lake. Returning to the house, a stunned silence fell upon Lady Weetwood and her genteel party as a golden, suntanned boy clutching a plastic sword marched past, clad only in sandals and a loin cloth made from a wash leather. Beryl asserted that the 'urchin' was a gardener's 'idiot child'.

James and Misty had strolled as far as the stone balustrade of the second terrace, from which, as the sun began to set, they could enjoy a glorious panorama of the lower terraces and the lake beyond, all bathed in a golden light. The scent of roses was intoxicating, and the tranquillity of the scene was such that neither of them wanted to disturb it. James offered Misty a Camel cigarette. She took one, and he lit it with a disposable lighter bearing a picture of a fat lady in a leopard-skin bikini caressing a man-size banana. Underneath appeared one word: MYKONOS.

Misty laughed. 'As the song goes, that's as "corny as Kansas in August".'

'Yep, you're right. But I like it. Silly, I know. Peter and I each bought one on our last holiday together. We had a great time – getting pissed every night, clubbing until dawn, sleeping all day and ...'

'And plenty of sex?'

'Yeah – I mean ... Don't raise your eyebrows like that! I told you this afternoon, I'm really a very shy guy. I know girls are attracted to me, but on my own I'm hopeless. I just don't know what to talk about. I freeze, and unless I've had about six pints, I'm useless. I can't explain. Peter was *so* different. I mean ... he charmed girls. He made them laugh and feel good.'

'Come on, James! You didn't do too badly over dinner. Perhaps some women liked you more than Peter. Perhaps you–'

'We've talked enough about Peter.' James sighed and shifted uncomfortably. 'Look, I really don't know how to thank you for dragging me out of that crazy state of depression. I suppose you made me talk about ... everything – and you listened. Maybe I just needed someone to talk to. It's not easy around here – as you can imagine!' He wondered whether he should mention that her smile reminded him so much of Peter, but thought better of it.

Misty was still gazing at the lake. 'No big deal. That's me, the good listener. Anyway, after two years of moping about in Dracula's Castle, I bet you were ready to face the world again.'

'Perhaps,' James said softly. 'Actually, I'm quite fond of Bobbins. ... Come on, it's your turn to tell me all about yourself. To be honest – and I know this sounds a bit unkind – but I'm still not really sure why you're here.'

'Thanks!'

'No – I mean ... Well, you told me that your school and Burgers had that penfriend association thing, but you've got to admit that you and Caroline aren't exactly obvious candidates for friendship!'

72

Misty flashed her hypnotic smile. 'Oh, it's a long story, but ... well, my best friend at Brynamman heard from her penfriend at Burgers that your sister was very lonely and ... well ... I-'

'You felt sorry for her.'

'No!'

'Of course you did. *I* did – still do as a matter of fact.'

'Well ... OK, you're right. I took the whole penfriend thing *very* seriously, but then *every*thing was so intense and competitive at Brynamman. ... Anyhow, as soon as Carrie left school she stopped writing. I continued for a few months and then gave up. But I'd think about her from time to time and wonder how she was. You know, those letters of hers were *real* strange. Sometimes I thought – now don't get mad! – I thought she needed therapy.'

'Ha!'

'And when I started planning this trip, it occurred to me that I could kill two birds with one stone. I mean, I wanted to see the North of England – Carrie had written such great things about all the beautiful historic towns – Manchester, Accrington, Oldham, Bolton – places like that, and-'

James was laughing. 'Jesus! Talk about taking the piss! I'd no idea she had it in her!'

'Sorry?'

'Oh nothing. Go on.'

'Well, I also wanted to meet Carrie and make sure she was ... OK ... happy at Durham.'

'Right. And now you've discovered we're *all* bananas!'

'Give me a break!'

'Well, we *are*! Anyway, how come you dropped out of law school? That's what you said this afternoon, didn't you?'

Misty was nodding. 'The pressure at Brynamman to go on to Harvard was awesome. Looking back on it now, I can see that I was virtually brainwashed into opting for a legal career.'

'It wasn't your parents' idea then?'

'My *parents*! You know, James, since I was twelve and booted off to Brynamman, I can count the number of days I've spent with my folks on ... well, I was going to say one hand, but to be fair, on two hands. They never visited me, never phoned me – they never even wrote to me. And when I *did* go home to Texas during vacations, my father was either away on business, or entertaining prospective business partners, or playing golf – or messing around with some mistress or other, I suspect. So, in the end, I preferred to spend my vacations with my girlfriends.'

'What about your mother?'

'Oh God, my mother! She's a woman with a mission. Well, *two* missions, I guess. The first is to get her husband into the White House – or at least the Governor's Mansion – even though my father has about as much interest in politics as he has in watching grass grow.'

'And her second mission?'

'To make Fort Worth the cultural capital of North America. There isn't a committee or society relating to the Arts or Music that she's not a member of. She spends her life championing the causes of new concert halls, art galleries, theatres, ballet schools, refuges for exiled poets – the list's endless. So, if she isn't actually at a committee meeting, concert, exhibition or fund-raising dinner, she's on her way to one, or returning from one, or planning one. It's revolting! You know, if I wanted to talk to either of my parents I'd have to make an appointment weeks in advance. But the fact is I don't want to talk to them, and they sure as hell don't want to talk to me.'

'Your parents and mine seem to have come out of the same mould. They should get together.' James stubbed out his cigarette on the balustrade, flicked it into the rosebushes below, and turned to face Misty.

'Not quite the same mould,' she replied, '– certainly not in the case of your father, James – I haven't met your mom yet. At least he's *around*. You could even have breakfast and dinner with him every day – if you made the effort.'

'Oh, come on! He's *here* yes, but you can't *talk* to him. He's bloody bonkers.'

'Well, a bit eccentric perhaps.'

'No, Misty, he's barking. I mean, he sleeps with his train set!'

'I think that's sort of cute.'

'Hah!'

The setting sun cast a reddish tint over the landscape. A large piston-engine plane droned high overhead. James found the sound nostalgic, and in the lull of the conversation he thought of those Second World War films where the hero, a dashing young Spitfire pilot – David Niven perhaps – would say his farewells to an English rose of a wife – Vivien Leigh came to mind – in a setting such as this. Suddenly, James felt sad: Misty would be leaving on Monday morning. She was looking in the direction of the lake, and he found her profile hypnotic. How could anyone be so beautiful, he wondered.

'Where are you going?' James asked.

Misty was lost in thought, and a few seconds passed before she turned her head and looked into James's eyes. 'Sorry? Going? When?'

'On Monday. You still haven't really told me what your plans are.'

'Oh, right. Um ... well, I'm flying to Paris, and my plan is to spend the summer backpacking around Europe – *Southern* Europe and the Mediterranean, that is. I don't fancy trekking around historic monuments in pouring rain and getting hypothermia swimming in the Baltic.'

'You know, they can have hot summers in Scandinavia, but I take your point. What do your family think of you bumming round on your own, or is that a silly question?'

'First, they don't know. I mean, I wrote to my mom telling her I was coming to Europe and that I'd be back in New York at the end of September. Would you believe, her "secretary" replied thanking me for my letter, "which was receiving her attention"!'

'Don't you think it's a bit risky – a beautiful young woman travelling around on her own?'

Misty squeezed his arm and grinned impishly. 'Why, I *do* declare, Mr James Weetwood, you're making me blush.'

But it was James who was blushing, not so much because of what he'd said, but because of the erection he could feel manifesting itself. Fearing Misty would detect the cause of his embarrassment, he turned and moved closer to the balustrade.

Misty sensed something was wrong. Perhaps James – obviously a sensitive boy – had thought she was making fun of him.

'You OK?' she enquired softly.

'Er ... sure. It's just ... well, I was thinking ...' James, however, could not say what he was thinking, which was that it would be a good idea if he were to accompany her on her trip, or at least part of it. But she'd surely think him presumptuous, or that he was getting fresh. And what if she rejected his proposal? The fear of that made him search for something else to talk about. After all, Misty would be around for another two days, which would give him the opportunity to weigh up the situation.

'I was thinking about Harvard,' James lied. 'I sometimes wonder whether I made a big mistake by not going to university, but after Peter's death ...'

'Yeah, I know. To be honest, Harvard wasn't such a big deal. I mean, everyone was so' – she sighed – 'so single-minded, so determined to get into the right law firm at almost any price. Anything that didn't contribute to achieving that goal was of no interest. It depressed me to think that these people, some of the most gifted in the country, the sort of people who were most likely to be the decision-makers, Congressmen and so forth in twenty to thirty years' time, had no *passion* in them – I mean the passion to change things. It's as if they lived in a different country and not the USA falling apart at the seams with endemic violent crime, drug addiction, and millions of citizens eking out a miserable, terrified existence in decaying inner cities or destitute rural communities, places as bad as – if not worse than – anything you'd find in a Third-World country. Instead, they were – and are – living in a kinda giant Disneyesque theme park.

'To cut a long story short, James, since dropping out of Harvard a few months back, I've been working as a waitress. Most of the allowance my folks pay me – even though I've told them several times I don't want it – is distributed to various charities. One of them is a neighbourhood law centre in the Bronx, and they've taken me on. I start the second week of October. I know it's going to be tough, so I thought I'd treat myself to this trip – paid for out of my waitress tips, by the way – to recharge my batteries, if you will, before battle commences.'

James brushed some ash off his trousers and was relieved to find that the erection had subsided. 'All I can say, Misty, is that whatever the reason, I'm really glad you ended up coming to stay here. ... Look, what about a nightcap before we turn in? A glass of port, brandy, a liqueur?'

'A glass of port! How very English! It sounds wonderfully civilized. Should we ask Carrie?'

'Um, I don't think so. She doesn't drink.'

They both laughed, and as they turned to walk back to the house, Misty playfully tussled James's hair.

*

Down at the Cob o' Coal in Muckley, Ron Duffle was not imbibing exquisite vintage port. His second pint of Ramsbottom's Old Peculiar bitter stood almost empty on the bar in front of him, together with a half-eaten bag of Spofforth's Potato Snacklets; he'd asked for Lancashire Hot Pot flavour but had had to settle for Quiche Lorraine, which, to his surprise, he'd found quite appetizing. He feasted his eyes on Peggy Umpleby, one of the Cob's part-time bar maids – to whom Caroline had spotted him signalling earlier that day. Every feature of her ample body fascinated and excited him, her voluptuous bosom in particular. Being a Friday night, the bar was busy and she was rushed off her feet.

The affair between Ron and Peggy, a forty-eight-year-old widow, had been gathering momentum for the last twelve months. At first, she'd regarded him as just another customer, until a chance remark by Ron over the bar one evening concerning the perils of the 'EEC' and its plans for the 'euro' had united them in a common bond of xenophobia in general and Europhobia in particular. At closing time, Ron offered Peggy a lift, albeit her house was only a five-minute walk away along the lane to Bobbins; he'd no fear of ever being stopped and breathalysed, the local bobbies being mates. It soon became the norm for Ron to drive Peggy home, a fact he'd not attempted to conceal from Vivian. In truth, no one doubted the sincerity and chivalry of Ron's motives: Peggy's cottage was on his route and it was a touch risky for a lady to walk that way alone at night.

Peggy was keen for their relationship to progress; a divorce had even been discussed. Ron had weighed up the pros and cons very carefully. In his eyes it was indisputable that Vivian had lost all interest in things sexual years ago – other than vicariously through her 'romantic' novels and films. On the other hand, he was living in comfortable quarters on a very attractive estate; he and Vivian were well remunerated; there was a generous pension scheme; and, if all went according to plan, a neo-Tudor cottage in Goblinville would be awaiting them upon their retirement in another ten years. Ron was quite sure that were there to be a divorce, the Weetwoods wouldn't retain both of them. So, as Lady Weetwood ruled the roost and Vivan was her 'protégée', he'd be the one to get the chop. There was no doubt about it: the present situation offered him the best of both worlds.

Sitting on his bar stool, Ron experienced an intense feeling of satisfaction as he watched Peggy pull another pint of Ramsbottom's. With two already inside him, all the troubles of the world had evaporated like mist on a summer's morning to reveal a landscape of blissful perfection. And having scaled the perilous cliff faces of the day, he'd now reached the halcyon plateau of the evening, with his goal of further delicious penetrations of Peggy's orifices almost in sight. As he popped a few more Snacklets into his mouth, a young moustachioed and bespectacled man with lank black shoulder-length hair squeezed into the space beside him. It was Rory Devlin.

'Mr Duffle, isn't it?' the stranger asked with a nervous smile. 'I'm told Ramsbottom's your poison. Mrs Umpleby, a pint for our friend when you've a moment, please.'

Open-mouthed with surprise, Duffle revealed the repulsive sight of the Snacklets' semi-masticated remains.

'Oh sorry, Mr Duffle! I've not introduced myself. Hang on, here's Mrs Umpleby with your beer.'

Grinning somewhat conspiratorially, Peggy pushed a pint in front of Ron, picked up his empty glass, and then leaned over the bar; an ashtray was engulfed by her bosom and lost to view.

'Hello, chuck!' she shouted over the noise of the drinkers. 'I see you've met Mr Ganoid.' Rory tried to indicate to Mrs Umpleby that, in fact, he had yet to effect a formal introduction, but she was focusing all her attention on her paramour. 'He's been staying here, Ron, since ... ooh, Monday before last, isn't it, dear?' Rory smiled and nodded. 'With his lady friend – well, she pops in now and then, doesn't she?' Peggy winked at Ron. 'She's foreign, isn't she, dear?' Before Rory could answer, however, she added, '*German*, isn't she, dear?'

'Austrian,' bleated Rory.

'Exactly, dear. Talk about the old buildings they've visited! I never knew there was so many in these parts. It's been a real education for me, I can tell you. Anyway, Mr Ganoid's got a little business proposition to put to you, Ron, haven't you, dear?' Mrs Umpleby glanced at Rory with the sort of look that suggested that the proposition was something to do with robbing a bank. He smiled back at her anxiously. 'Just the pint of Ramsbottom's was it, dear, for old Ron here?

'Hey! Not so much of the "old",' Ron retorted smirking.

'Er – yes,' stammered Rory. 'I mean – no. Two vodkas and tonics as well, Mrs Umpleby, if you'd be so kind.'

Ron watched his beloved's rolling posterior as she bounced over to the other end of the bar. 'So, what's this "*business* proposition", Mr ...?'

'Call me Kenneth ... er – Ken, please, Mr Duffle. ... Well, my partner–'

'The German?'

'*Austrian*. She's out in the garden. ... Look, it's a lovely evening and much quieter there. Perhaps you'd care to join us?'

Mrs Umpleby brought the drinks, and Ron and 'Ken' made their way to the garden. Several customers were sat around ubiquitous white plastic tables with red Martini umbrellas, albeit at this hour they shaded those beneath them solely from moonlight. Electrified gas lights, which had once graced mean streets in Oldham, provided additional weak illumination.

At the most distant table, a solitary seated figure was smoking a cigarette. As Duffle and Rory approached, Ursula Klinker rose, resting her cigarette on the edge of an ashtray. Ron was riveted by the apparition before him: standing like a soldier to attention loomed a tall woman – about six foot he would guess – very thin, wearing blue denim jeans and a matching jacket over a white T-shirt. As for her age, in this light she could have been anything between forty-five and sixty, although the skin on the back of the right hand now extended towards him revealed copious liver spots. But Ron was most disconcerted by the pair of large sunglasses she sported, and a towering mop of orange bouffant hair. He was about to shake her hand, when the thought suddenly occurred to him that perhaps she was blind.

'Lottie, here is Mr Ron Duffle – at last!' There was a note of juvenile triumph in Rory's voice. 'Mr Duffle, may I present my partner, Carlotta Rinderpest.'

Ron's hand went limp as Ursula's bony claw grabbed it. Her small wrinkled mouth opened. 'I am *so* pleased that you have joined us. Sit!'

In a near toneless voice, Ursula promptly launched into a monologue about the 'glories' of the North of England, which she and 'Kenneth' were exploring for the first time. Ron had to admit to himself that, despite her clipped manner, she spoke English very well. She reminded him of the formidable female guide, nicknamed 'the Witch', who had once terrorised Vivian and himself on a coach tour of the Black Forest. This reincarnation was now claiming that the North 'enchanted' her, particularly the windswept moors and the 'bleak' Pennine villages.

'And yesterday,' Ursula continued, 'we drove over to York and spent hours in the beautiful Minster. What a masterpiece of medieval architecture! – don't you agree, Mr Duffle? Neither Kenneth nor I wanted to leave. The experience was so spiritually elevating we felt quite rejuvenated. I attribute some of our emotions to the melodious offerings of the choir, who were performing ... what do you call it in English, Kenneth?'

'Choral evensong, Lottie.'

'Precisely! Have you ever witnessed choral evensong at the cathedral of York, Mr Duffle?' Ron shook his head. '*Schade*!'

A silence fell upon the trio.

Ron was getting fed up. 'Peggy – Mrs Umpleby – said you had some kind of "business proposition" to put to me?'

Ursula exchanged glances with Rory as she lit another cigarette. The lighter was on too high a setting, and a large flame burst into life, cruelly illuminating every feature of her face. The Witch was a prune, Ron thought: she had the look of someone who'd subjected herself to several decades of continuous sun-worshipping in order to achieve and maintain a tan of extraordinary depth. A terribly high price, however, had been paid.

With the cigarette lit and the lighter extinguished, Duffle returned to the matter in hand. 'Well?' he enquired with a hint of irritation.

'Mr Duffle,' said Rory, 'my partner and I should lay our cards on the table.' He stared into his vodka and removed his gold-rimmed spectacles. He swung them around a few times and then, with an air of intense earnestness, put them on again. 'My partner and I,' he continued, 'believe that you are the sort of chap who can keep a secret – the sort of chap who can be trusted.' Duffle's silence seemed to be regarded as an indication of his acceptance of this flattering proposition. 'In fact, if you don't mind me saying so, Mr Duffle – *Ron* – if I may?'

'Of course, lad! That's me name.'

'Thank you. Well, Ron, if you don't mind me saying so, my partner and I are convinced that you are the salt of the earth sort of bloke, the back bone of England, so to speak, who believes in fairness and justice, decency and truth, probity and honesty, fair play and–'

'You see, Mr Duffle,' interrupted Ursula, 'Kenneth and I have been watching you very, very closely for the last five days – now do not get alarmed, Mr Duffle, you have nothing to fear. All will be revealed shortly.'

'"ang on a minute! You've been *spying* on me?'

'I would prefer "observing",' Ursula replied. 'And I can assure you that your ... *friendship* with Mrs Umpleby is of *no* concern to us, no concern at all.' She smiled menacingly as Duffle's mouth fell open. 'Let's move on,' she snapped. 'Look, Kenneth and I represent a German magazine, a very reputable monthly publication renowned for its investigative journalism.'

'It's a sort of cross between *Private Eye* and *Newsweek*,' added Rory.

In shock, Ron stared at his interlocutors, his mouth still open. He was familiar with *Private Eye*: Vivian was always whingeing about the copies that Master James left lying around at Bobbins. She'd even said that the so-called jokes about the Queen were 'treasonable'. As for *Newsweek*, Ron thought it was a programme on BBC 2.

'So, what's this magazine of yours called then?'

'*Schnickschnack*,' responded Ursula.

'Funny sort of name.'

'So is *Private Eye*,' said Rory.

'It's satirical,' explained Ursula, but Ron was none the wiser. 'Our magazine,' she continued, 'is very interested in your employer and Goblin soap.'

'You mean Lord Weetwood? Old Misery Guts? What's so bloody interesting about 'im? He's probably the most boring, strait-laced bugger I've ever met.' Ron gulped another mouthful of Ramsbottom's. 'I suppose Peggy told you I work for his Lordship.'

'Correct,' snapped Ursula, inhaling the smoke from her cigarette as though her life depended on it. 'I must emphasize, Mr Duffle, that what we're telling you is strictly confidential.' She looked around as if for confirmation that no one in the garden would be able to overhear their conversation. 'You see, Mr Duffle, *Schnickschnack* has evidence of some serious matters relating to your Lord Weetwood and his company. I have to warn you that you may be shocked by what you learn this evening. In fact, you may prefer me to stop now and not place you in any danger.'

'*Danger*?' croaked Ron.

'Yes, *danger*, Mr Duffle, but from our investigations – and I can assure you we are always *very* thorough – we believe you are the sort of Englishman who laughs in the face of danger when the interests of justice and fair play are at stake. After all, as you say in your country, an Englishman's home is his castle.'

Ron was mystified as to the 'investigations' that Rinderpest and Ganoid could possibly have undertaken to ascertain his moral fibre, but at least he liked the sound of their conclusions. 'Go on, Miss Rinderpest. I'm all ears.'

'Well, if you're sure? … Our intelligence, Mr Duffle, is that Lord Weetwood has been having secret negotiations with a very large German conglomerate–'

'Schnittblumen & Käseglocke,' Rory interjected.

'Thank you, Kenneth. They are best known in Germany for their Troll range of sanitary towels. Perhaps you've heard of them, Mr Duffle?'

'Er, no, love. Can't say I 'ave, actually.'

'No matter. S&K want to purchase the Goblin soap business, Mr Duffle, and it seems Lord Weetwood is keen to sell.'

Ron's mouth fell open. 'No, no, *no*! I can't believe *that*! Oh *no* – definitely not. I mean, Goblin means everything to Lord Weetwood. And it's not as though 'e's 'ard up or anything like that. No, I think you've got yer facts wrong, my friends. You're definitely barking up the wrong tree.'

Ursula looked at Rory for assistance. 'I know you may find it difficult to believe, Ron, but Carlotta's right. We've a very reliable source within S&K's Stuttgart headquarters. You'll probably be able to confirm our understanding that Lord Weetwood has a passion for steam locomotives.'

'Oh aye, 'e's bloody barmy 'bout them. He's got a train set at Bobbins as big as a football pitch. Well,' he added swiftly as he noticed the expressions of scepticism that met his gaze, 'as big as a tennis court, any road. Aye, the man's potty 'bout trains all right.'

'Precisely. And I suppose, Ron, you know all about the privatisation of British Rail?'

Ron nodded. 'Oh yes. What a bloody mess! Daftest thing that tit John Major ever did. Mind you, what with Labour coming back in May under that nice Mr Blair, I can't imagine anyone wanting to buy another one of them bloody "franchise" things.' Ron snorted into his glass and looked from 'Rinderpest' to 'Ganoid'. The penny seemed to drop. 'You don't mean–?'

'Yes, Ron,' said a smirking Rory, 'Lord Weetwood would like to buy one – several, actually. In fact, our man at S&K tells us that Weetwood wants to sell WSD in order to raise the cash to buy the franchises to run services on the West Coast Mainline from London to Birmingham, Manchester, Liverpool and Glasgow. You see, the rumour is that Blair and his "New Labour" don't really believe in renationalisation and will carry on with the franchising.'

Ron was shaking his head back and forth. 'Oh, my God! The man's mad. I bet her Ladyship will 'ave something to say about this.'

'There's more, Ron,' said Rory. 'Not only would the soap business come under *German* control' – Ron groaned – 'but as part of the deal, as we understand it, S&K would acquire Goblinville and convert it into Britain's first all-*German* holiday and leisure centre.'

Ron's volcanic blast of obscenities caused heads to turn.

'Yes, Mr Duffle,' said Ursula coldly, 'we thought it would come as a shock to you. You must understand that England is a very attractive tourist destination for Germans, particularly those wanting a short break to indulge their craze for shopping and other materialistic pastimes. You see, because London is so expensive these days – the prices of the hotels are absurd! – Germans interested only in the shopping delights England has to offer, will find the prices and *camaraderie* of a place like Goblinville – "Karnivalstadt" as we believe S&K want to rename it – *very* attractive. There would be all-German speaking staff, frequent courtesy coaches to the centre of Manchester for the shopping, and the existing public buildings would be converted into Munich-style beer halls and restaurants serving *sauerkraut* and other German delicacies.'

'But surely nothing can happen to Goblinville?' pleaded Ron. 'It's protected – what d'you call it? – *listed* … as ancient monuments or something, by the Government. The whole thing's a *conservative* area. And what about all the existing tenants? And the people from Goblin who expect to retire there? Bloody 'ell, what about *me* and Mrs Duffle? We've been promised a home there on *our* retirement. Excuse my French, missus,' Ron snarled, staring into what was left of his pint, 'but this bastard, Lord fuckin' Weetwood, can't get away with this!'

Ursula and Rory stared at each other with the briefest flicker of triumph. 'Of course,' said Rory, 'we don't know the precise details of the proposals, but as many Goblinville residents are elderly, a lot of houses will become vacant within a few years by natural wastage. In appropriate cases, S&K would pay people to move out. As for prospective residents, our understanding is that no one has a *right* to live in Goblinville – it's all at the discretion of the Estate Trustees. And as for planning permission, I think you'll find that as there would be few alterations to Goblinville's *external* appearance, there shouldn't be any problems. Anyway, the council would probably do everything in its power to encourage such a massive investment in local tourism.'

In so far as the workings of Duffle's mind ever involved logic, a collapse into total irrationality was now advancing rapidly. Nigh ignorant of history, he had the notion that, with its neo-Tudor houses and fake Baroque palaces of culture and learning, Goblinville was a venerable institution that had graced the Lancashire landscape for centuries. The vision of German tourists goose-stepping in *Lederhosen* along its avenues filled him with abject horror. And what about his own retirement? Never mind that, what about his job if Weetwood sold Goblin? Christ! Wouldn't Bobbins be sold too? After all, there'd be nothing to keep his nibs in the vicinity, and, in all probability, Beryl the Bitch would take up permanent residence at that French villa.

'Ron, are you OK?' Rory sounded quite concerned.

'What? Er ... I'm ... well, I'm just stunned. This has all come as a bit of a shock, lad.'

There was a pregnant pause. Ursula lit another cigarette. 'As I said at the outset, Mr Duffle, what we have told you is *highly* confidential. You will understand that it would be a great "scoop" for our magazine if we could get documentary evidence of the matters we have disclosed to you. And the sooner the story is published, the sooner any opposition to the takeover can be organized. This is where *you* come into the picture. ... We would think that Lord Weetwood must bring papers home and make business phone calls from Bobbins, and we were hoping–'

'You were hoping that I'd steal papers and listen in on phone calls – be your spy!'

'Exactly, Mr Duffle.'

Ron's flushed face was now contorted by an expression of terrifying ferocity. He drained his glass and slammed it down on the table. 'You've come to the right man! What do you want me to do?'

\*

At nine the following evening, the motley triumvirate reconvened around the same table. Sustained by a continuous supply of Ramsbottom's ale, the newly recruited 'spy' recounted in excruciating detail Saturday's comings and goings at Bobbins. As instructed, Duffle had scoured both Lord Weetwood's study and the library for any papers that might refer to the dreaded German acquisition of the Goblin Empire. As far as he could see, however, there was nothing of relevance. The only phone calls he'd been able to monitor on an extension had sounded tedious: from Cap-Ferrat, Lady Weetwood requested the transfer of extra funds to her account at the Nice branch of Crédit Commercial de France to enable her to purchase some jewellery that had caught her eye at Cartier in Monte Carlo. Having reluctantly agreed, Lord Weetwood then phoned a Manchester model shop and ordered three new locomotives for immediate delivery.

'And did he go out at all today, or receive any visitors?' asked Rory, while opening another packet of Snacklets for Duffle.

Ron stuffed three large chips in his mouth before replying. 'Not as far as I know. Just stayed in and played with his trains ... I think.'

'And the rest of the family?' Ursula inquired, as if making polite conversation.

'Well, nothing much to report on that front,' Ron sighed. 'Master James seems to have gone all soppy over his sister's sexy American visitor. The two of them have spent the day mooching around the house and gardens like a couple of lovebirds. The lad's not been out of the house for over two years, you know, and ... and ...' Almost hypnotized by the Witch's orange hair, Ron was beginning to wonder whether it could be a wig. 'Where was I? ... Oh yes. Well, I don't know why he bloody bothers with this Misty What's-her-face cos she's off on her travels round Europe on Monday morning. You know the sort – "Gee it's Friday so this must be Paris".' Duffle's dismal attempt at an American accent produced no obvious reaction from his spymasters.

'This American girl definitely leaves Bobbins on Monday?' asked Ursula, lighting a cigarette.

'Oh yes. I'm scheduled to take her to the airport – bag and baggage.'

Ursula glanced at Rory. 'And then, apart from her brother and father, Miss Caroline will be alone at Bobbins for a week or so, yes?'

'Oh no. Miss Fat Arse, thank God, is off to Spain on Monday, so I've got *two* trips to the bloody airport. The Yank's on a flight to–'

'Caroline's going to *Spain* – on *Monday*?' croaked Rory as Ursula's cigarette plopped into her drink.

'Well, yes. She's off to some island ... to do "research" – that's what *she* calls it, any road – or something. For six weeks, I think. Good riddance, *I* say.'

'Which island?' snapped Ursula as she frantically searched a Marlboro carton for another cigarette. She turned it upside down and shook it violently.

'It's empty, I think, Lottie,' Rory volunteered, nervously playing with his moustache.

'I know it's empty, *Dumnkopf*!' She grabbed a large handbag secreted at the side of her chair, located a fresh pack, and ripped off the cellophane. 'Well, which *island*?' she repeated, her voice now slightly raised.

'Er ... one of them Bally-what's-its.'

'Balearics?'

'Exactly, Ken.'

'Which one?' demanded Ursula.

'What "research"?' whined Rory.

Ron looked from one interrogator to the other. The second question was easier to answer. 'I *told* you – some historical stuff. She's doing History at college, you know.'

'Yes, Mr Duffle, we *do* know. What I require is her destination in Spain – which island?'

Ron was beginning to get irritated by The Witch's attitude. 'Well, I'm not sure. ... Anyway, why are you so keen to know?'

Rory and Ursula glanced at each other, seeking inspiration.

'I understand your puzzlement, Ron.' Rory began slowly. 'The point is that ... well, Miss Weetwood's trip to this Balearic island may not be what it seems.' He paused and took one of Ron's Snacklets. 'You see, she could be acting as a sort of ... go-between.'

'A go-between?'

'Yes,' said Ursula, 'an intermediary between her father and S&K – to avoid *any* leak of this proposed acquisition of Goblin. We know that ... that S&K's president has a villa on one of the Balearics.'

'*Her*? – that tub of lard? You must be joking! She's got about as much business sense as a dog turd.'

'But that could be the whole point, Ron,' said Rory. 'Don't you see? No one would imagine someone like Caroline Weetwood being involved in a multi-billion-dollar takeover? ... So which island is she going to?'

Duffle thought hard. 'OK, I know you have to go there by ferry, and that she's flying to Ibiza. And – 'ang on! You might be right about this go-between thing, cos it's just occurred to me that she's staying at some *German's* villa. My wife told me! Supposed to be loaded ... with a library full of priceless books. That's what Fat Arse is going to study, so *she* says. It's called something like ... "Fermented"?'

'He must mean Formentera,' barked Ursula, '– you know – very popular with naturists.'

'Aye, that's it,' Duffle beamed, 'Formentera.' He was already convinced that 'Fat Arse' was inextricably involved in the dastardly German plot to invade and occupy Goblinville. That was just the sort of dirty, underhand, sneaky thing a slob like her would happily get involved in. Historical research on a Spanish island in midsummer! Who did she think she was kidding with that little Miss Boffin routine?

'So, guys, what next?' Duffle liked the sound of his question: he was finally beginning to feel like a real detective, or, even better, a secret agent. As he awaited his instructions, he knocked back his beer and devoured the remaining Snacklets.

Agent Duffle's orders were specific: to ascertain the precise whereabouts of the villa in which Caroline was to undertake her 'research' in Formentera, the name of her host, and her travel arrangements. He assured his colleagues that obtaining this information from his wife without alerting her attention would be 'a piece of cake'. His prediction proved correct, and on Sunday evening he reported back triumphantly. Arrangements were made for a further Cob o' Coal rendezvous the following evening at nine, when Duffle could be debriefed on Caroline's departure, the results of his continued observation of Lord Weetwood, and his monitoring of Bobbins' telephonic communications.

How addictive was patriotism!

# CHAPTER 8

During supper at Bobbins on Sunday evening, James offered to take Misty to the airport in the morning – she was booked on the 10:30 flight to Paris – but objections were received from his father, who pointed out that he'd not driven a car for over two years, and that his battered Golf needed a major mechanical overhaul.

'In that case,' James countered, 'I'll accompany Misty in the Jag with Ron.'

'Great!' said Misty.

As Caroline needed to leave very early in the morning for her 7:15 flight to Barcelona, she said her farewells when they all finally left the table.

Her father shook her hand. 'Bon voyage,' he said without emotion. 'Will you be away long?'

'Professor Pangbourne thinks it'll take me the rest of the vac – six weeks.'

'Good. ... What will?'

'The research.'

'Ah.' Plainly disinterested, George beat a welcome retreat to Crewe Junction.

'Well,' said James, kissing Caroline on the cheek, 'don't do anything I wouldn't do. And I'm eternally in your debt.' She looked at him quizzically. 'For having such a fantastic penfriend, of course! I just wish you hadn't kept her a secret for so long. And who knows? – I might come and check out this Formentera place – see Ibiza too!'

Caroline bristled. '*Ex*-penfriend, actually. And I'd need my hosts' permission for visitors.'

As James's smile froze, Misty stepped forward and gripped Caroline in a bear hug. 'I'm so glad we've met at last, Carrie,' she said with feeling. 'And I hope you have a great summer and unlock that secret. If you do, maybe you'll write and let me know.'

'I'm bound by obligations of confidentiality.'

Misty hunched her shoulders. 'Well, good luck anyway.' To her own surprise, she added, 'And God bless!'

*

Misty had anticipated an emotional farewell at the airport; after their final passionate kiss at the entrance to Immigration, there were tears rolling down James's cheeks.

'Phone me as soon as you get to Paris,' he pleaded.

'I will.'

'Promise?'

'I promise.'

'If only you'd brought a bloody mobile with you!'

'I wanted to escape!'

Over and over on the drive back to Bobbins, James cursed himself for not having had the courage to ask Misty to let him go with her, but all weekend there'd been that terrible fear of rejection.

'I'm pathetic,' he constantly muttered under his breath.

The journey was also purgatory for Ron Duffle: he couldn't cope with a lad who sobbed like a bloody girl.

*

Sitting alone at the gate, waiting to board her flight, Misty relived the weekend. She was confused. The hours spent with James had been wonderful. He was witty and amusing – and very attractive. Perhaps subconsciously at first, but then purposefully, she'd led him slowly but surely to her bed on Saturday night. He'd been so gentle and loving. But then, with the approach of Sunday evening, the doubts had set in. It was all pointless, of course: she was on vacation; by the end of summer, she'd be back in New York ready to start her new job; James had been through a prolonged trauma – he was now probably over it – and as the heir to an industrial empire, he'd soon be in a three-piece suit clamouring for a seat on the board.

OK, it was a lousy cliché, but they *were* just ships passing in the night. It was best to make a clean break now; in the long run it would prove to be the kindest course of action.

*

George Weetwood was also unhappy on that overcast and humid Monday morning. He sat in his vast office at Soap House and surveyed the piles of faxes, letters, internal memoranda and photocopies of these new-fangled 'emails' meticulously laid out on the desk before him. As usual, Miss Spigot had been performing her secretarial duties since half past seven, albeit as George invariably arrived at ten, he was unaware of this. Perhaps if he'd taken more interest in his working environment, he might have noticed the carefully arranged fresh flowers on the side table every morning, and the highly polished silver letter opener perfectly centred above, and parallel to, his leather-bound desk blotter. Such was Miss Spigot's devotion.

On this morning, however, as on all others, George did not notice the flowers – white and yellow roses today – or that his letter opener was either polished or in any particular position: he was too busy trying to forget the gloomy piles of paper by reliving the hours of railway management he'd enjoyed over the weekend. The *Royal Scot*'s derailment had proved most gratifying! And it had been an inspiration to delay the Anglo-Scottish sleeping car express by fifteen minutes on Saturday evening – such a massive rescheduling of scores of services for the next six hours! That computer had really been put through its paces! He considered organizing something similar when he got home. After all, now that Caroline had left for Spain – was it Spain? – and that Start girl – *bizarre! bizarre!* – had gone, and with Beryl entertaining her cronies at Cap-Ferrat until late September, well, he wouldn't have any obligations to dine downstairs for *weeks*!

A mild thrill shot through his body, but then a cloud appeared on the horizon. Hadn't James been hyperactive all weekend with that frightful Miss Start? He sighed, tutted and shook his head. ... Hang on a minute! Now that she'd departed for Spain – no, that was Caroline ... Paris? ... no matter, the wretch had certainly gone – James, no doubt, would revert to normal and disappear into Bobbins' bowels, wouldn't he? ... So that was all right!

Feeling better, George surveyed Miss Spigot's neat piles with less animosity. A fax in the **PRIORITY** pile caught his attention. It bore a large yellow Post-It, marked '**URGENT**' in red ink – underlined three times. His heart sank. This was all he needed on a Monday morning! Red ink and all that underlining must mean something pretty serious. Perhaps it was another feminist assault from that wretched Tenby-Jones woman about the washrooms. With a loud sigh, he was about to pick up the highlighted communication when the phone rang. He jumped and stared angrily at it for a few seconds before snatching the receiver and snarling 'Yes!'

Miss Spigot was on the other end. *'Good morning, Lord Weetwood. I was just on my way in to see you when a call came through. I'm sorry to bother you, but it's a Mr Smuttle of International Condiments. I don't think we know him or his company, do we? He won't tell me what it's about, but said you'd know and would want to talk to him.'*

George's mind was a blank: the name 'Smuttle' meant absolutely nothing to him. How on earth did these crackpots get through such an elaborate telephone filtering system? 'No, Miss Spigot, I don't know the man. Tell him to state his business or to write to us.'

Detecting the note of irritation in his voice, Miss Spigot assumed that Lord Weetwood had read the alarming fax she'd placed on top of his **PRIORITY** pile; naturally, she had to read all correspondence addressed to him in order to prioritise it. The fax she'd marked '**URGENT**' had certainly come as a shock to her; it had exacerbated her upset tummy. Indeed, shortly before quarter past eight, she'd had to rush down to the Ladies Room on the second floor to be sick. Even now, as she listened to the Chairman's diffident voice, she remained nauseous.

'*I'll try and find out what Mr Smuttle wants, Lord Weetwood. Oh, and in view of the fax from those Dallas lawyers, I've warned all the directors and the company secretary that you'll probably summon an emergency board meeting during the course of the day. By the way, I'm sorry I wasn't at my desk when you arrived. I did want to discuss all this with you ASAP, but I had to go and ... powder my nose. I think the pâté I had for my supper last night was a bit suspect. I'll pop in as soon as I've sorted out Mr Smuttle.*' The phone clicked as Miss Spigot transferred to the outside line.

George slammed down the receiver. What was the damned woman talking about? A board meeting? They'd only just had one on Friday! And what did the pâté have to do with it? With yet another heavy sigh, he returned to the menacing fax and pulled back the Post-It to reveal the name and address of the sender: Swinehart, Crudge, Idol & Purkey, Attorneys-at-Law, 1601 John Wayne Boulevard, Dallas, Texas. There followed column after column of partners' names, and, for no particular reason, he began to read them, shaking his head in disbelief at the sheer callousness of American parents in inflicting such horrors on their offspring. He'd not got very far when the phone rang again.

'Weetwood!'

'*I'm so sorry to disturb you, Chairman, but it's this Mr Smuttle. He insists that you do know him, that the matter is urgent, and that it concerns "The Orient Express". He said you'd know what he meant.*'

George, however, had just reached the letter's expansive heading. 'What the blazes is *this* all about?' he muttered incredulously.

'*Well, I'm sorry, Chairman, but that's what he said, "The Orient Express". He sounds very insistent.*'

'What? ... No, no, *no*! I'm talking about the *letter*. Oh, good grief! What are *you* talking about?' And then, some points in his brain were switched and a vital stock of information flowed out of its siding onto the mainline of his consciousness. He became uncharacteristically alert. 'Put him through *immediately*,' he snapped.

'*The Chairman, Lord Weetwood, will now speak with you, Mr Smuttle,*' said Miss Spigot grandly.

A silence followed: neither party appeared to know what to say to the other. The caller finally plucked up courage and spoke softly.

'*Lord Weetwood, is that you? This is Smuttle. ... Well, you know ... it's me. ... May I report on the progress of the Orient Express?*'

Conspiratorially, George scanned his palatial office and cupped his hand around the mouthpiece. 'Yes, of course it's *me* speaking. How dare you phone me here. I told you never to phone Soap House. *Never*! Really, Dumpwell, this isn't good enough. It's a serious breach of security, you know.' He picked up his pen from the silver tray strategically positioned by Miss Spigot a few inches to one side of the telephone, and scrawled 'SECURITY' on the nearest available piece of paper – the Post-It recently removed from the faxed letter.

'*I know, sir, but in view of what's happened, I firmly believed I should contact you without delay, rather than await our usual weekly call. Incidentally, shouldn't you be calling me "Smuttle"?*'

George ignored the question: he resented the implication of breaching his own Security Directive for Project Orient Express. 'What do you mean, "in view of what has happened"?' He heard Dumpwell inhale deeply.

'*Well, early this morning Section B reported that – this is just provisional, you understand, and the other sections haven't had any results like–*'

'Dumpwell – Smuttle – what did Section B report? Now careful, don't break the Security Code!'

'*In brief, they reported ... well, Section B seems to have been "derailed", sir, and it looks as though there have been ... casualties.*'

A few seconds passed before George asked: 'What do you mean? Have there or haven't there been "casualties"?'

'*It seems so. Well ... yes. There have ... to be honest.*'

'What sort? ... Fatalities?'

'*Um, there are some, I'm afraid. Yes.*'

'How many?'

'*It's quite bad.*'

'How many?'

'*A lot. In fact*' – Dumpwell lowered his voice to a whisper – '*all of them, sir.*'

With its wood panelling and double glazing, few sounds ever penetrated the Chairman's office. But now the silence was almost too much for George to bear. He felt alone and vulnerable. What was that awful American expression? ... 'The buck stops here'? It was inconceivable. It had to be an error. Orient Express couldn't go wrong – it just couldn't. Rotating his high-backed leather chair to face the window, he looked out at the mighty industrial complex which he controlled. All his working life it had functioned perfectly. WSD had just steamed on like a great ocean liner – unsinkable, unchallenged, unstoppable – day after day through the dangerous waters of the market place. And now this! If Orient Express had really malfunctioned, the outcome could be disastrous. And on this occasion, he'd no one to turn to for assistance – or to blame, for that matter: none of his colleagues at Soap House knew anything about the project.

'*Lord Weetwood, are you still there?*'

'Yes, er ... Smuttle. Look, have your chaps any idea as to the cause of the ... er ... the derailment? Are they sure it was the product? Perhaps the "passengers" could all have been struck down by a disease or something. After all, it's jolly hot out there, isn't it?'

'*Not really. It's winter – Southern Hemisphere. Today there's a forecast high of–*'

'Yes, yes – of course! What about the food or the water they were given?'

'*Um, good points, sir, but we've checked all those and they've proved negative. Anyway, these matters were not unique to Section B. All the ... passengers on the other sections have experienced the same conditions and consumed the same food – and drink. No, it looks almost certain to be the product, I'm afraid. I'll be able to give you a definite answer by this time tomorrow.*'

George pondered the issue for a few more moments and then asked plaintively: 'But damn it, er ... Smuttle, if it's the product, why haven't the other sections been, you know, derailed? It doesn't add up.'

'*Not necessarily. After all, sir, the Section B passengers had more delicate skins and were subjected to more – how can I put it? – more frequent visits to the washroom. In any event, I suppose it's always possible that the passengers of the other sections might suffer a similar fate in due course.*'

'And yet, Smuttle, when we spoke a fortnight ago, you said everything was "proceeding normally", that all the passengers were "enjoying the experience", and that you foresaw "nothing untoward".' George was momentarily emboldened by the thought that here, perhaps, was someone to blame after all.

'*Well, yes. Two weeks ago that was the position, but as you were well aware, Lord Weetwood, the project was incomplete, and I cautioned against making any irrevocable decisions.*'

'It was only "incomplete" in the sense that there were a few more weeks to run of a project that had already been operating for almost a year. And frankly, I don't recall *any* caution when we last spoke. On the contrary, Dump – *Smuttle*, you expressed – quite emphatically – complete confidence that the project would be a total success, and–'

'*Perhaps, Lord Weetwood, this isn't the time or place to engage in–*'

'Don't interrupt *me*, you–!' But George stopped just in time: arguing with this minion was demeaning. He needed to think. 'I'll contact you tomorrow using our normal channel of communication. I expect a clear and succinct final report. Goodbye.'

This time, George slammed down the receiver with such force that it cracked. He was about to remove himself to his sanctuary in the Directors' Washroom – it invariably assisted in resolving irksome issues – when there was a delicate tap on the door. Miss Spigot entered holding a piece of paper.

'Chairman, while you've been on the telephone, I've identified the optimum time for a board meeting. Dame Diana can't attend – she's got a meeting of the Trustees of the Royal Stamp Collection – but all the others could be here at two p.m. Mr Brancepeth-Tring will have to leave by half-four because he's–'

'Miss Spigot! Just a minute, *please*. What *are* you babbling about?'

'Oh ... sorry, Chairman. ... Well, in view of FoamFay's imminent launch and the contents of the American lawyers' faxed letter, I thought you would definitely want to discuss the problem with the directors – and, indeed, our solicitors. I've phoned Mr Grimshaw's secretary, incidentally, and put her on notice that you may want Mr Grimshaw–'

George raised one hand and gestured like a policeman ordering traffic to stop. Miss Spigot recognized the command and fell silent: the Chairman was obviously suffering from one of his usual Monday morning moods; she'd have to play the role of punch bag for the rest of the day. So many worries and responsibilities, she thought. How on earth did the great man cope? He was an inspiration.

In truth, however, George was a single-issue man: if required to deal with several matters simultaneously, a painful buzzing would sound in his head. Above all, he hated the unplanned, the unexpected, the surprise. Now, with his queasy secretary standing before him, awaiting instructions, he strenuously attempted to put the Orient Express crisis to one side. Finally, it dawned on him that the Dallas fax demanded his attention. He picked it up.

'I think I should read this.'

'Oh, I'm sorry, Lord Weetwood. I thought you had. I *did* mark it "urgent" – in bold – and had intended to speak to you about it immediately, but, as I said before, I was powdering my nose when you arrived. In fact, I've had to do so quite a few times this morning. I can only think it was that wretched pâté I–' But noticing the Chairman's icy stare, Miss Spigot terminated her defence.

'I'll let you read it in peace,' she continued softly. 'No calls. Give me a buzz when you're ready.' She attempted a smile, but her master – with eyes bulging and open-mouthed – was already scanning the document. Just as she reached her adjoining modest office, another surge of pain erupted in her tormented stomach, and she dashed off to run down three flights of stairs to the nearest ladies' washroom.

George's heart was pounding as he reread the heading to the letter from Swinehart, Crudge, Idol & Purkey: '**Re SI Corporation (SI), Groovy Soaps Inc. (Groovy) and Ms Vosene Pesto (Pesto)**'. Five pages of verbose American legalese followed, but, in essence, Swineharts were claiming that their client SI believed that WSD was about to launch a new product; that it had been invented by one Vosene Pesto while employed by either SI or Groovy; and that, as successors to Groovy's business, SI would, in either case, be the invention's owner. Contractual provisions, statutes and case law were quoted *ad nauseam*. Furthermore, Swineharts were alleging that at the time Pesto entered into her agreements with WSD, 'senior WSD executives' knew she'd made the invention during her employment with Groovy or SI. Thus, they knew she didn't own the invention, and, furthermore, that her disclosure of it was unlawful.

With beads of perspiration breaking out on his brow, a mouth devoid of saliva, and a churning in his stomach, George scanned the letter's final paragraphs with terror:

Pursuant to our advice, SI has filed a patent application for the invention at the UK Patent Office. SI will file further applications in the USA and other countries in due course. Accordingly, WSD is required to give SI the following undertakings:

1. Not to exploit the invention in any country of the world;
2. To provide such assistance as SI may require to vest the invention in it; and
3. To deliver up to SI all research records, test data, and manufacturing information in WSD's possession relating to the invention.

We have instructed our English correspondent lawyers, Fancourt Utley, Solicitors, of 15 Offal Lane, London EC2. They have briefed Counsel, Sir Tudor Mudwort-Welch, QC, of Gallows Court, Temple, London. If Fancourt Utley do not receive such undertakings by noon on Monday, July 21, proceedings will be commenced claiming the relief to which SI are entitled, including an account of profits and punitive damages in view of WSD's flagrant and wilful acts. SI will also seek injunctions to prevent the launch of your new product.

94

Close to hyperventilating, George glanced at the fax cover sheet. It bore the simple message: 'Confirmatory copies of this letter and the copy documents faxed herewith will follow by courier.' He began flicking through the pages of the 'copy documents', seeking in particular WSD's two agreements with Pesto of January 1992. He found them and looked quickly at the signature sections. Thank God! It was just as he'd remembered: Barmcake had signed the agreements on WSD's behalf, and Nickel had witnessed his signature.

Miss Spigot was right: a board meeting was certainly required. He was going to have some explaining to do, but at least Barmcake was conveniently out of the way, thanks to his fatal car crash last December. That was a stroke of luck! He could prove a very useful scapegoat. After all, no one else on the board knew exactly what had occurred in Texas on that fateful night five years ago. A flicker of a smile appeared on George's face. *That's right! And apart from Nickel, there isn't a living soul who could contradict my account, seeing how the Pesto woman is also dead.*

What a nasty business that had been! George shuddered as he recollected the photographs Dumpwell had shown him. Frightful! Nickel had taken it very badly, of course. It was understandable, but his subsequent actions had been quite out of order. It had cost a lot of money to shut him up. But presumably, he was the bounder who'd now gone and snitched to these blasted Start people. That must be it.

George gulped. Start! ... *Miss* Start! A coincidence? ... Impossible! She had to be some kind of spy! But what sort of father would stoop so low? ... An American tycoon, of course – not a shred of morality among the lot of them! What had she hoped to find out? ... Had she been pumping Caroline for intelligence all these years? Good Lord! It was sickening – not that Caroline knew the foggiest thing about WSD. Had she ever visited the works? ... Soap House? Not as far as he could remember. And if Start thought his snooping brat would get anything sensible out of ... er, James, well, dream on!

Slowly walking around his office, George continued to analyse the situation. As he passed his desk, he picked up the fax again and skimmed through it. Ah ha! Just as he'd thought: the cocky American lawyers merely *recited* the fact of Pesto's death. And the more he considered the matter, the more convinced he became that Nickel must have kept his side of that particular bargain. After all, it wouldn't be in his interests to contradict the official line on Pesto's demise. And if the Americans had had any suspicions about that, they would never have instructed their lawyers to write that damned letter in the first place, would they? But where did that get him? If Nickel had told the Texans everything, they would have told him to bugger off – or even taken steps to silence him! He wondered if he himself should tell the vile Mr Start the truth, but then rejected the notion almost immediately: it was impossible, completely unthinkable. Alas, the battle would have to be fought using different tactics.

George flung the fax onto the conference table and, with a heavy sigh, sat down.

'I mean,' he muttered, 'it's probably a load of poppycock. I bet our legal chaps will demolish Start's claims with no trouble. Yes, Pesto made her invention while she worked for those nutty Groovy people, but she wasn't employed to *invent* a new kind of soap, for goodness' sake. Anyway, they and Start's outfit would probably have sent her to a psychiatrist had she gone to them with her "Pestex" story. And we've spent a fortune developing the stuff. Can't imagine any judge – certainly not an *English* judge – giving these Yanks even the time of day!'

Feeling somewhat happier, George stood up with the intention of popping in to see Miss Spigot: he needed to confirm the arrangements for the board meeting. But then the spectre of Project Orient Express and the conversation with Dumpwell returned to haunt him. He groaned and walked once more around the conference table.

'Well,' he murmured, 'there's no point trying to make a decision now. The casualties in Section B could have resulted from all sorts of things. It's happened before. And these boffins take a ghoulish delight in devising experiments to test their absurdly hypothetical worst-case scenarios, and then, when the results prove the theory, they convince themselves that the gibberish they thought of in the first place is, in fact, wholly credible.'

Smiling, he contemplated these words of wisdom and concluded that a speech based on their theme could prove popular at the next SADMA conference. He should make a note of them. But, reaching for a pen, he snapped: 'For goodness' sake, old boy, concentrate on one thing at a time!'

He was walking towards the door to Miss Spigot's paragon of secretarial efficiency when the blast hit him.

# CHAPTER 9

Caroline's scheduled flights to Ibiza via Barcelona had been bad enough – what with the Spanish air traffic controllers' dispute and the disgusting brats running riot on the planes – but it was nothing to the mounting terror as she waited by the conveyor belt in the baggage hall at Ibiza airport and watched all her fellow passengers collect their luggage. Finally, she stood alone, refusing to believe the evidence before her very eyes. Later, at the Iberia counter, she had her first experiences of the Hispanic belief that it's always better to invent a succession of good-news tales than to admit disaster outright. Thus, for almost an hour there were conflicting reports from a battery of staff working on a five-minute shift system: her luggage had been found in the airport and would materialize shortly; it had got mislaid at Barcelona, but had already been put on the following flight, which should, in fact, touch down in five minutes; it was still in Manchester – but safe and secure, and would definitely arrive before 1700 hours, when Iberia would 'personally' deliver it to her on Formentera.

And so, armed with just her flight bag, Caroline finally escaped the terminal's air-conditioned bedlam and joined a queue for a taxi in the midday furnace. How the driver avoided a massacre on the white-knuckle drive to the harbour in Ibiza Town, she would never know! But to be fair, he was only trying to get her on the one o'clock ferry. As he weaved in and out on the traffic-choked highway, she glimpsed the suburban concrete jungle surrounding Ibiza's capital. It was as bad as she'd feared; Formentera, no doubt, would be equally grim – if not worse.

Although the maniac got her to the quay in only fifteen minutes, the ferry's siren was booming, and the gangway was being pulled away from its side, just as the taxi screamed to a halt. Before she knew what was happening, her voluminous flight bag was thrown through an open door in the ship's hull, with the hysterical crew yelling and gesticulating that she should follow it and jump the gap of two or three feet now separating the door from the quayside. Something, somehow, released a long-suppressed force within her, and, suddenly, she was flying through the air into the arms of two grinning sailors.

In a state of shock compounded by the exhaustion of the journey and the baking heat – her tracksuit ensemble was not helping – Caroline made her way to the top deck as the ferry passed the harbour's outer breakwaters.

She found a wooden seat near the stern, and, taking deep breaths and shading her eyes, watched Ibiza's Old Town, the Dalt Vila, slip by. Hugging its precipitous peninsula and appearing to tower above her, it all looked very picturesque with its massive fortifications, ancient churches, and narrow streets of whitewashed houses – quite unlike the miserable suburbs she'd seen from the taxi. With just a hint of a smile on her chubby face, she scolded herself for judging a book by its cover.

The ferry picked up speed and headed for the open sea, the welcome breeze cooling and refreshing her. Ibiza's coastline drifted by, and, in the gentle swell, the small vessel began to rock rhythmically. Caroline's eyes closed...

She was at Bobbins ... standing on the terrace. It was a beautiful day and she could feel the sun burning her skin. The lake was like glass, the reflected light dazzling her eyes. As she squinted, hundreds of strange men appeared from behind the elms on the lake's far side, and as they began to walk towards her across the water, she realized they were all clones of a taxi driver. But she didn't know any taxi drivers ... unless ... unless ... She could hear terrible screaming. Was it her, or–?

A raucous convoy of seagulls abruptly awoke Caroline to a world of blinding white light. Totally disorientated, she began to focus on what appeared to be an archipelago of small rocky islands surrounding the ship – all quite barren, apparently uninhabited ... and dangerously close! Could they be off course? With her heart beating faster, she looked astern. A large landmass – it could only be Ibiza, surely? – seemed surprisingly distant, and as the seconds passed, she experienced the oddest feeling that she'd never really been there at all.

The ferry blew its siren and began to overtake a large sailing yacht. Two women and a man, who were sunbathing near the stern, looked up and appeared to wave directly to her. Unhesitatingly, she started to wave back, but, with a gasp, flung her hand over her mouth. She was not merely shocked by her unprecedented spontaneity: the sunbathers were naked!

Caroline was still trying to come to grips with all these aberrations when she saw her first tower. About fifty feet high, round, and built of massive stone blocks – some kind of fortification, she guessed, of eighteenth-century origin – it stood solitarily and dramatically near the edge of a low cliff of red rock on one of the islets. It looked oddly familiar. She tried hard to concentrate. ... Goodness only knew why, but it reminded her of dear Aunt Belinda and her bungalow at Eastbourne! She giggled. It was just a tiny giggle – quite inaudible to any other passenger with all the sounds of the voyage – but, nevertheless, a giggle. Again, she put a hand over her mouth as if she'd committed some cardinal breach of etiquette, No one, however, was paying her any attention.

*Oh dear, how very confusing. ... Why on earth does that tower remind me of Auntie? And what's all this giggling nonsense? Golly! I do hope it's not sunstroke – or dehydration! ... Heavens! There's another islet and another tower, just like the first one, and–*

*Of course! Years ago, when James and I used to spend our summer hols at Eastbourne, and Auntie took us on those day trips along the coast, there were similar towers. They're ... Oh come on! It's on the tip of my tongue. ... They're–*

'They're *Martello* towers!' she blurted out aloud with a feeling of triumph, 'named – if I remember correctly – after the tower at Cape Martella on Corsica, which in 1794–'

A bronzed young man sitting next to her, clad only in knee-length shorts and a sleeveless T-shirt emblazoned with the word **ADIHASH**, turned and smiled. Embarrassed, Caroline smiled back, and then noticed his bare feet. He pointed forward: 'Formentera ... *sehr schön, nicht war?*'

This was all getting a bit too familiar. Caroline stood up and moved to the ship's rail. At first, she wasn't sure which of the islands ahead was Formentera, but by a process of elimination, concluded that it must be the largest: there was no way any of the others could be twelve miles long. From her limited research, that was one of the few facts she could remember. As the north coast became clearer, she stood spellbound, almost as if it was hypnotizing her. Formentera seemed to consist of three sections, which, although of roughly equal length, were remarkably distinct. The eastern third looked inaccessible – a tomb-like monolith with massive cliffs, hundreds of feet high, rising sheer from the water. At its western edge, a thickly-wooded escarpment dropped steeply to a low strip of land – perhaps no more than thirty feet above the shore line at its highest – which connected this 'tomb' to another elevated mass at the island's western end. The latter, however, presented a softer face – an undulating landscape with gentle slopes; a windmill seemed to crown its highest point.

A novel feeling of excitement began to build within Caroline. What lay beyond this coastline? What would she find on the plateau of the eastern monolith? And–?

But before she could ask herself whether there might be any Martello towers to explore, she spotted one ... and then another. She let out a cry of joy, gripped the ship's rail tightly, and pushed herself up onto the tips of her toes to get a better view.

'*Ja,*' said the bare-footed youth, who was now standing just behind her, 'Formentera *ist sehr schön.*'

Caroline managed to continue smiling. 'Um, yes. ... It's jolly nice.'

He surveyed her black tracksuit bottoms. 'You English?' he asked languidly.

She hesitated as if it was a trick question. 'Yes – yes, I am, actually.'

'OK. I am thinking you probably have good legs. Let the sun – the great life force – see them, *ja*?' He handed her a small grubby business card from his pocket. 'You will go here in Sant Francesc – friends of mine. They sell great shorts. *Hasta la vista*!' Then he turned and joined the rest of the passengers, who were queuing for the gangway and the lower decks, for the ferry was approaching the harbour mouth and would soon be docking at La Savina.

The calm of the voyage gave way to the chaos of disembarkation and the pandemonium of Formentera's only port. Caroline's romantic notions of the island quickly evaporated. For a start, 'Teeny' Kirk – Pangbourne's former protégée – was not at La Savina to meet her as arranged. Then, in the mad scramble for taxis, an excitable Italian tourist dropped a very heavy suitcase on Caroline's right foot. Eventually, she found herself sat in the back of a baking taxi on the quayside, engaged in impossibly difficult discussions with the driver as to the whereabouts of the *Villa Clementina*. And with no sea breeze to keep her cool, she felt close to fainting.

It transpired that there were several '*Villa Clementinas*' on the island. All she knew was that hers was big. '*La villa* is *massivo*,' she kept repeating. With growing frustration, she'd a horrible feeling that everything that had happened on the ferry had been a fraud. Finally, the penny dropped when she told the taxi driver: '*La villa* is *la villa de Señor* Kurt Schmückstück *et Señora* Ernestine Kirk.'

'Kurt *y* Teeny!' he laughed, a refrain he kept repeating as he put the taxi into gear. If his broad smile was anything to go by, they were all good friends.

Emerging from the *Estación Marítima*, Caroline wound down the back windows to get some air and studied her surroundings. Her initial reaction was not good. Awash with young tourists who choked the few streets with their bicycles – the hire shops were doing good business with those recently arrived off the ferry – La Savina looked modern and rather characterless. But where all these tourists stayed was beyond her, for there appeared to be very few hotels. In fact, as she subsequently discovered, most of the island's visitors were day trippers from Ibiza who rarely journeyed far from La Savina, their sheep-like instincts usually persuading them to head en masse for the long sandy beaches of Illetas and Llevant, a short cycle ride along the flat peninsula to the north of the port.

However, as the taxi accelerated up the long straight road out of La Savina, fields of goats and sheep, enclosed by drystone walls, quickly replaced the dull pueblo. Paradoxically, the scene reminded Caroline of the Pennines. And yet, there was nothing bleak about this sun-drenched landscape, for here the stones were of a glorious golden colour, and the hot air rushing in through the open windows was rich with the fragrances of rosemary, sage, thyme and other herbs she could not yet identify.

At the top of the hill, the taxi turned sharp right and, without any warning, plunged into the narrow, crowded streets of a small town devoid of anything remotely resembling a suburban fringe. The driver turned round. 'Sant Francesc!' he announced with a smile, while narrowly avoiding a coach of air-conditioned tourists with blank faces. As dramatically as they'd materialized, the shops and bars fizzled out, and, regaining the countryside, Caroline concluded it was the only 'capital' one could drive through in two minutes.

Maintaining his cavalier style, the driver suddenly took a left turn onto a narrow bumpy road. It wound its way through wheat fields and – to Caroline's intense surprise – vineyards. It was all very picturesque – quite Italianate even; Formentera's northern coastline had indeed been cunningly deceptive! Perhaps she'd been right after all – that this was a magical place. She breathed deeply, and finally began to relax.

Just as the road degenerated into little more than a dirt track, Caroline's reverie was terminated by frantic barking and a tremendous jolt: a diminutive farm dog was not only chasing them, but also making brave efforts to jump through the open window at her side. The car slowed down to negotiate the potholes, but despite the advantage given to him, the hound abandoned the chase when pinewoods closed in around them and he reached his territorial limits. With the intoxicating smell of resin raising her spirits even further, Caroline watched him for a few moments out of the rear window. Standing in the middle of the dusty *camino*, the canine sentry stared after the ejected trespassers, happily wagging his mongrel tail.

Although she found the scene spellbinding, Caroline abruptly faced forward and stared ahead: inexplicably, she knew that the sea was close by. With her excitement mounting, the track began to drop steeply, and the pines thinned out. The taxi turned a corner and emerged onto a treeless bluff. Caroline gasped and held her breath for just an instant. Below, lay a scorched terrain of rocks, scrub and a few isolated pines, but beyond it – and extending to the distant horizon – shimmered a sea of the most beautiful colour she'd ever seen, a vast swathe of almost unbelievable blue.

The track turned towards the south-west and followed the coast. Ahead, she could see a few villas – large single-storey structures built of the island's golden stone, and separated from each other by low drystone walls. Although clearly of recent construction, the villas were modelled on the traditional farmhouses she'd noticed on the drive from La Savina. At one corner of what appeared to be the largest, rose a round stone tower – no doubt inspired by the Martello towers she'd seen earlier. She prayed it would be the *Villa Clementina* – it just had to be.

Five minutes later, the taxi pulled off the track onto a gravel drive that meandered through a desert-like garden of cacti and palms. Finally, it came to a halt before the tower and an open door.

'*La Villa Clementina*!' yelled the driver triumphantly. '*Muy bonita, sí?*'

'*Sí!*' echoed Caroline as she heaved herself out. Readjusting the elasticated waistband of her tracksuit bottoms as she stood wilting in the early afternoon heat, she scanned the tower with a broad smile. 'Rapunzel, Rapunzel, let down your hair,' she giggled. But then – just for a second – the scowling face of an old woman appeared at a second-floor window.

*Bobbins – the man down by the lake, and–*

*No! Stop it! I've left all that behind ... a thousand miles to the north.*

Save for the buzzing of cicadas, everything was quiet. Caroline breathed deeply and, forcing herself not to look back at the window, rested her eyes on the stunning crimson blooms of the bougainvillea that smothered the villa's walls. She was shaking her head in disbelief at the colour's intensity, when a loud cough startled her. Realizing that the taxi driver still needed to be paid, she started to fumble in her flight bag, but all her best efforts to connect the foreign currency with the man's words and gestures were suspended by the sounds of rapidly approaching footsteps and a woman's voice shouting hysterically in Spanish. As she and the driver turned to face the open door, a smartly dressed Teeny Kirk shot out carrying two large suitcases in her muscular arms. She fired more Spanish at the taxi driver – Caroline gathered his name was Jaume – before turning to her.

'Christ! I thought you'd never bloody get here. How the *hell* did you miss Felipe and the Jeep? It's a brand-new Wrangler for God's sake! The idiot's still down at the port waiting for you – just when I need him. Typical!' Caroline noticed that 'Jaume' had grabbed the suitcases and was hurling them into the taxi's boot.

'Look, Caroline, I'm *terribly* sorry. There isn't time to explain. I've got to dash or I'll miss the three o'clock ferry. And if I miss *that*, I'll never catch the plane at Ibiza. I've written a note. It's on the dining room table. Be good and enjoy yourself, and' –Teeny was now getting into the car – 'don't *worry*. We trust you.' Jaume's taxi began to accelerate around the gravel forecourt to return down the drive. 'I'm really, really sorry,' she bleated,

leaning out of the front passenger window, 'but it's all in the letter. Bye-ee!'
And with that the car roared off at an alarming speed.

Caroline slumped to the ground before the open door, inhaled deeply, and burst into tears. It was the first time she'd cried since Burgers.

At some point, a short, plump middle-aged woman dressed in black silently materialized before Caroline, and, using both sign language and a few hefty tugs, persuaded her to come inside. She was soon to learn that the woman was the housekeeper, Maria, a formidable creature who spoke no English but managed to communicate quite effectively with dramatic gestures. As Maria led her to the dining room, Caroline assumed that it must have been her face which she'd seen at the tower window; no one else appeared to be around.

As instructed, Teeny's letter was on the table; Maria dutifully stood to attention while Caroline read it. Kurt's mother was seriously ill and dying in a Buenos Aires hospital. They'd been estranged for years, but now she wanted him at her bedside. The message had been received by telephone only at breakfast that morning, and Kurt had dashed off on the first available flight. At the height of the summer season, of course, it was very difficult to get on any plane out of Ibiza, and there'd only been one spare seat on Kurt's. He'd begged Teeny to accompany him, and had she not taken the last seat on Iberia's 17:05 service to Madrid – from where they would travel onward together – she'd have been stuck for another few days. It was either that or the ferry to the mainland, or a convoluted schedule via Mallorca. She hoped Caroline would understand.

The manuscripts, Teeny added, were locked in the library; she knew Caroline would handle them with care and honour the agreement Kurt had made with Pongo. She could stay as long as she liked. Maria, who lived in Sant Francesc, would come every day and prepare her meals. If there was anything she wanted in particular, she should just write it down and Maria would get her younger sister, Catalina, to translate it; she taught English at the local school. Above all, Caroline should make herself at home. Teeny would ring regularly to make sure everything was OK.

With Caroline still trying to come to grips with her abandonment, Maria took her to a ground-floor bedroom. It was large, tall and beautifully furnished with what she assumed were local antiques and restored rustic pieces. French windows gave on to a terrace that ran the full length of the villa's south side. Not more than fifty yards away, just beyond the garden wall, shimmered the hypnotic sea. Maria seemed perplexed by the absence of luggage, but thanks to some animated mime, Caroline explained that it had been lost by the airline. Within minutes, Maria returned with some T-shirts and two pairs of baggy shorts. Caroline had no choice: the prospect of retaining her tracksuit in that heat was unthinkable. And so, for the first time in many years, her legs were exposed to public gaze. She looked into the mirror and felt ... well, she had to admit it ... ashamed. Thank goodness there was no one there but the housekeeper to witness the grim spectacle.

For lunch, Maria had prepared what looked like a banquet of salads, seafood, cold meats and cheeses. It was laid out under a large canvas umbrella on the terrace. Caroline, however, had little appetite and wanted to get to work on the manuscripts as soon as possible. Anyway, it was far too hot to think of food. All she really wanted was some chocolate, but with the formidable Maria omnipresent and insistent, Caroline succumbed to a meal of gargantuan proportions.

It was mid-afternoon when Maria finally took her to the library. With a sense of great importance – and trembling hands – the budding historian unlocked the cupboard containing the manuscripts. She held the precious volumes reverently for some time before depositing them on a massive Louis XV desk in the centre of the room. Then, with the shutters drawn against the afternoon sun, and attended by several near-melted Mars bars and a can of Coca-Cola, she sat down ready to commence her mighty task.

Ten minutes later, a vacuum cleaner started up somewhere close by. Maria was also singing at the top of her voice – well, it was more like wailing – and the combination was deafening. After more than an hour of the same, Caroline abandoned the manuscripts, retreated to her room, and collapsed on the bed. She was soon snoring.

The sun was setting when she awoke, and it took some time to get her bearings in the now silent villa, but to her intense relief there were no signs of Maria, save for a stew giving off an intense aroma of garlic left on a low light in the oven. Alas, a thorough search did not reveal any 'personal delivery' by Iberia of her suitcase. Caroline's rage against the Spanish national carrier was, however, assuaged by the stew, which, despite its unappetizing appearance, proved to be extremely tasty.

Refreshed by her siesta, and reinvigorated by Maria's ethnic sustenance, Caroline felt that a second attempt to start work on the manuscripts could be an ideal way to conclude her first day on this strange island. Accordingly, following a meticulous tour of the villa to ensure that all doors were locked and windows shut – not only for her personal security but also to guarantee her defences against the canny mosquito – she retreated to the library.

It was after one in the morning when she finally turned in. Almost too tired to sleep, and with perspiration dripping off her, she lay in bed trying to detect the slightest hint of a mosquito. 'Damn that airline!' she cursed under her breath, pushing back the counterpane in a futile gesture to mitigate her roasting. 'I knew I should have packed the mosquito equipment in my flight bag – Ping Pong too.' She had a horrible vision of a sweaty Spanish baggage handler going through her suitcase and extracting her beloved stuffed panda for one of his many children. Since her eighth birthday, she and Ping Pong had never spent a night apart.

When Caroline did finally manage to calm down, she remained ill at ease – not because of her solitary isolation in a strange house, but due to the bizarre nature of what she'd read in the manuscripts.

# CHAPTER 10

Unofficially, the Greater Manchester Fire Brigade had already ruled out gas as the cause of the explosion which had destroyed Goblinville's Roberta Weetwood Memorial Playhouse and Picture Palace. So far, however, no one had claimed responsibility for what several organs of the media were wildly labelling 'a likely act of terrorism'. In view of the force of the blast, it was a miracle that there had been neither fatalities nor serious injuries. As for Lord Weetwood, he'd quickly recovered from the shock of awakening in the arms of Miss Spigot: the blast's boom had caused him to stumble, just as he reached the door to her office; falling to the floor, he'd hit his left temple on the handle. In fact, within the hour, and after the works' physician, Dr Ollerenshaw, had fussed over some minor bruises, George was inspecting the devastated Roberta Weetwood and giving interviews to the media. Using Churchillian language, he rashly guaranteed restoration, 'whatever the cost'.

Although the board meeting hastily arranged by Miss Spigot for two o'clock went ahead as planned, the explosion was substituted as the agenda's first item. The superficial wounds suffered by the Chairman and some of his fellow directors served to generate a remarkable air of informality – even gaiety. Theories flew wildly around the table; David Chopping suggested a disgruntled ex-employee, but, on reflection, neither he nor his colleagues could conceive of any being so disgruntled. Even Daventry Merryweather expressed an opinion to everyone's surprise, particularly as the Chairman – from whom Merryweather usually took his lead – had distanced himself from all speculation: he was content to await the outcome of the official investigations. In fact, Merryweather came up with the most extraordinary culprit, widowed Nora Barmcake. After all, hadn't she screamed abuse at the Chairman during Ernie's memorial service in Goblinville's parish church, accusing him of murdering Ernie through years of overwork?

But Merryweather silenced himself when he noticed Weetwood drawing the outline of yet another island map. 'Well, Chairman,' he spluttered, 'shall we move on to Item 2 and the letter from Swinehart, Crudge, Idol & Purkey?'

Without looking up from his doodle, George nodded, whereupon Charles Grimshaw, the senior partner of Manchester solicitors Grimshaw,

Sons & Botham, was summoned from reception. He was accompanied by one of his younger partners, Ben Turbot, the head of the firm's Intellectual Property Department, and introduced as a 'patent wizard'. The meeting was long; when it finally broke up a few minutes after eight o'clock, George felt as if he'd been interrogated by the Gestapo. Turbot, who plainly didn't care whether he ruffled feathers, had done the grilling, while old Grimshaw amused himself by flicking through textbooks on patents extracted at intervals from a voluminous old Gladstone bag at his side. Indeed, it was the first board meeting Brancepeth-Tring had ever enjoyed; it was so enjoyable that he even cancelled his dental appointment and stayed to the bitter end. Turbot asked all the questions that he'd longed to ask about Project Troll for the last five years. How had WSD first been introduced to Pesto? What had taken place at the meeting in Texas? Who had been present? What exactly had she revealed about the invention? When had she made it? How? Where? Why had she been 'spirited off' – as Turbot put it – to South America? What was Nickel's role? How had Pesto died? And why had WSD not taken steps to patent the invention?

By the time Turbot had drained his first cup of coffee, it was already obvious that the only director who had any detailed knowledge of the Pesto affair was Lord Weetwood himself: the others could only deal with technical aspects of the product, the R&D costs, the marketing plans and so forth. Despite Turbot's relentless probing, however, the primary cause of George's mounting irritation was not the requirement to disclose Project Troll's history as such, but rather that such disclosure was demanded by a young man who was obviously his intellectual superior – a young man, to boot, who failed to treat him with the sort of deference he'd come to expect of hired professionals after more than twenty years of chairing the board of one of Britain's largest companies. On the other hand, he needed a lawyer like Turbot. It was a painful admission, but deep down he knew it to be true. The Americans' allegations looked serious. Most of the Group's reserves had been expended on Project Troll. If FoamFay had to be withdrawn without a single sale, the humiliation would really be too much to bear. And then there was Beryl: he'd never hear the end of it. Moreover, if the Start people exploited the damned invention, how could WSD ever cope with the competition – at least, that is, until the Americans themselves discovered the problem that Dumpwell had just reported?

'Well now,' Turbot continued after completing his preliminary list of questions, 'before I deal with the merits of SI's claims–'

'They're nonsense, of course,' George interjected.

'–I should tackle some general issues of immediate concern. As you know, SI are threatening to apply for a temporary injunction against WSD in the English courts to stop FoamFay's launch. We call it an "interlocutory" injunction. Incidentally, you'll *all* appreciate that an injunction obtained here would have no extra-territorial effect. Anyway, the chances of SI obtaining one are problematic because–'

'There you are,' sneered George, waving a hand disdainfully over his copy of Swinehearts' letter, 'I knew all this was nonsense.'

'Please let me finish, Lord Weetwood, and I suggest you listen carefully to what I have to say before you come to *any* conclusions.'

Merryweather gasped; George's mouth fell open, but before he could respond, Turbot was already in full flow.

'Their chances are not good because whatever the merits of their claims – and I can't come to any final view on them at this stage – a court would only grant an injunction before trial in *exceptional* circumstances.'

Merryweather nodded sagely as if to indicate that Turbot was just reading his own thoughts. In truth, and despite being a solicitor, he was lamentably ignorant of litigation procedure.

'As you know,' Turbot added, 'it usually takes at least eighteen months – often longer – for a case to come to trial in the High Court. In the interim, a plaintiff with a valid claim might be irreparably damaged if the defendant were allowed to continue doing the acts which the plaintiff says are unlawful. So, a successful judgement might prove a Pyrrhic victory, especially if during the long interval between the issue of the writ and judgement, the defendant has gone into liquidation or disappeared with the profits of his unlawful activities.'

Merryweather was still nodding away.

'OK, let's imagine you find someone – "Mr Evil" – marketing poor quality soap under the name "Goblim". You'd want to stop him, so you'd try and get an injunction. You'd go to a judge and say, "We're WSD. We own the famous Goblin trade mark. Mr Evil is selling rubbish soap under a confusingly similar name. He's damaging our brand. We can't wait for a full-blown trial to prove he's an infringer. Please give us an injunction now to stop this rogue. If he's found to be innocent at the trial, which seems unlikely, we'll pay him compensation for the soap he would have sold but for the injunction."

'Now, if the judge concludes that WSD has a good claim but could, nonetheless, compensate Mr Evil should it lose at trial, then he'd probably grant the injunction, *provided* WSD has also demonstrated that the loss which it would suffer if Mr Evil were *not* injuncted would be greater than the loss *he* would suffer if injuncted. It's what we call "the balance of convenience." So, what case could SI put to a judge along these lines? Well, for a start, they haven't got a patent yet for ... for–'

'FoamFay,' sneered Brancepeth-Tring.

'Indeed. For that matter, WSD haven't got a patent either. I'll come back to that. Frankly, it puzzles me why you've never sought to patent the invention.'

'Well, Ben, we did consider–'

'As I said, Daventry, I'll come back to that. ... So, SI can't claim patent infringement as you can't sue on a mere patent application. Anyway, with Pesto dead – and with all the uncertainty surrounding the making of the invention – SI are going to have one hell of a job prosecuting a patent application in their own name. Well, that leaves them with claims against WSD for inducing Pesto to breach her contracts of employment with Groovy and SI, and unlawful use of proprietary information, whether Groovy's or SI's. Mind you, the letter from their lawyers seems to imply that they don't know precisely when or how the invention was made, but then if they do sue, they could force us to tell them all *we* know.'

George gripped the arms of his chair.

'Of course, they're also asserting that Pesto was obliged to communicate those details solely to her employer, and to keep them confidential. So, when she spilled the beans to WSD, she acted unlawfully – and that you knew that. After all, Lord Weetwood' – George almost jumped out of his skin – 'you and your then Technical Director, er ... Mr Barmcake? ... were doubtless familiar with standard research-staff terms of employment, and with employee obligations generally. And the fact that she was spirited off to South America – with even a change of identity, as I understand it – well, it hardly indicates that you thought you were acting in good faith, does it? To be blunt, it's our Achilles heel. SI and their lawyers will milk it for all it's worth.'

Shifting uncomfortably, George looked as though he was about to say something, but Turbot beat him to it.

'The fact is, Lord Weetwood, you can't go into a witness box and swear that you believed Pesto was free to contract with WSD and sell *any* rights in her invention, can you? With your knowledge of this industry, you must have known she was acting unlawfully.'

George desperately tried to think of a crushing reply, but he was tired. Damn it, he'd had a very long and traumatic day! And his head ached terribly – he'd almost been killed by a bloody explosion! And then there was Dumpwell and Project Orient Express. It just wasn't fair. He should have listened to Dr Ollerenshaw and taken the rest of the day off. The board meeting could have waited another twenty-four hours and–

'OK, we'll leave Lord Weetwood to mull over those points. Now, let's assume SI sue us for unlawful misuse of proprietary secrets, and for inducing Pesto to breach her employment contracts, and seek an injunction, as threatened in their lawyers' letter. What irreparable harm could they suffer pending a full trial, if we were *not* injuncted?'

Everyone wanted to say 'none', but perhaps it was a trick question. Even Charles Grimshaw remained silent.

'Well?'

'I suppose, Ben,' ventured Grimshaw, 'they could argue that if WSD were not injuncted and proceeded with FoamFay's production and sale, there'd be a much greater risk of the details of the invention entering into the public domain, thereby destroying its commercial value.'

'Good point, Charles, but then, as we've chosen *not* to patent the invention – for whatever reason – we've every incentive to keep the process secret, haven't we? SI, on the other hand, have chosen to file an application to patent the stuff. So, in due course, they'll have to accept the Patent Office's publication of the invention's details, and then rely on any patent rights they might secure to prevent exploitation.'

'Ah,' Grimshaw murmured.

'And, of course, there's no question of a mighty company like this going bust, is there – at least not in the foreseeable future?'

'Absolutely not, Mr Turbot!' retorted George indignantly.

'And it's not as if we're going to put rubbish on the market which might tarnish the invention and prejudice SI's future chances of exploiting it, are we?'

Heads were shaking. George, however, simply stared at the portrait of his late father and fretted about Project Orient Express.

'So, while I can't advise that SI would be bound to fail should they seek an injunction, I think the chances are against them. If WSD were injuncted, you'd suffer whopping losses – you've already invested massively in the product, and its launch is only weeks away. But if SI fails to injunct you, they won't lose any sales. After all, they're not even manufacturing the stuff yet – and won't be in a position to do so for some time – possibly years.'

'Mr Turbot,' George snapped, 'this is all most illuminating, but how exactly do you propose to respond to these American "attorneys"?'

'I was just getting to that, Lord Weetwood. Much depends on what you think SI really want to achieve and what's our bottom line. We also need to guess how much they already know. It's pretty unlikely they've disclosed their full hand, don't you think? However, we should be wary of devising our strategy on the basis that we suspect they don't know this or that fact. Presumably, we're all agreed that most of the information in their possession has come from this character Nickel. He's not a scientist, as I understand it, and so he could only have given SI the most basic details about the invention. ... Mind you, I suppose his wife could have made detailed notes and secreted them somewhere before her death.'

'That's possible,' George agreed, somewhat absent-mindedly.

'So, Nickel goes to SI and says, "Hi! My wife used to work for you guys. She made this fantastic invention, and we ripped you off, thanks to WSD. If you give me a huge pile of dough, I'll tell you all you need to know to screw those bastards and sue them for every last cent they've got." Is that what we think Nickel has done?'

Brancepeth-Tring, who thought Turbot's impersonation of a Chicago mobster was rather good, started to chuckle, but stopped when he realized that the Chairman was not at all amused. Grimshaw also seemed somewhat put out by Turbot's performance, and, with a clear indication of disapproval, cleared his throat.

'To be honest,' said Turbot, 'I don't understand why Nickel should have destroyed his relationship with WSD. After all, under the terms of her original deal with you, Pesto was entitled to receive a so-called royalty of one per cent on all WSD's sales of the product for ten years. And under the funny little agreement you and Nickel entered into shortly after Pesto's death – I must say, I can't understand why WSD did that – it was confirmed that those sums would be payable to him and his heirs. Now, from what we've learnt this afternoon, if the product sells as well as you chaps think, he could be entitled to *millions*. Well, he's forfeited those payments because he's' – Turbot turned to the relevant page of the copy of the agreement Merryweather had given him – 'because he's breached clause 4's secrecy provisions. Basically, they say he can't breathe a word about the invention to a living soul without WSD's consent. And why–?'

'Sorry to interrupt, Ben, but the "funny little agreement" was drafted by *me*.'

'I assumed that, Daventry.'

'And as is so often the case, Ben, it had to be drafted *very* quickly. And my instructions from the Chairman *himself* were quite explicit. I know that with the benefit of hindsight–'

'Let Mr Turbot continue, Daventry,' George ordered, glaring at his lieutenant.

Turbot managed a flicker of a smile. 'Thank you, Lord Weetwood. ... Daventry, what I was alluding to was the provision prohibiting Nickel from ... well ... frankly, from discussing the circumstances of his wife's death with anyone, except – and I quote – "to the extent required by law". I suppose that was meant to cover things like a coroner's inquest – if they have such things in Uruguay.'

'They don't – I mean they do – but there wasn't.'

111

'There wasn't what, Daventry?' asked Turbot.

'There wasn't an inquest.'

'Should there have been? I mean–'

'What the Company Secretary is trying to say,' George boomed, 'is that Miss Pesto's death – her *tragic* death at such a *young* age, I should add – was slightly ... unusual.'

'I thought she died of salmonella poisoning,' said Brancepeth-Tring, glancing at Turbot conspiratorially. 'What's so "unusual" about that?'

The Chairman smiled at his Export Director as if he was mentally handicapped. 'Miles is correct, of course, Mr Turbot. She was, however, *wrongly* diagnosed – one of the major hospitals in Montevideo treated her for appendicitis. Nickel kicked up a frightful fuss, and' – George glanced again at his father's portrait – 'and ... well, I have to confess ...'

Brancepeth-Tring's heart beat faster – a confession from the Chairman? How he'd waited for this day!

'...that we – that is to say, our people in Uruguay – pulled a few strings which, perhaps, should not have been pulled.'

'How do you mean exactly?'

'Well, Mr Turbot, Nickel was having difficulties getting a death certificate. Unsurprisingly, the authorities in Montevideo were just covering up for their own incompetence. They started playing silly buggers' – gasps from various quarters over their master's unprecedented language – 'and poor Nickel was frantic. He just wanted his wife buried.'

'Wasn't she cremated, Chairman?'

George gritted his teeth. 'Thank you, Daventry. ... Yes, of course. I meant "cremated". You see, Mr Turbot, Nickel wanted a proper funeral. He couldn't bear the thought of her being stuck inside a hospital mortuary week after week. So, he persuaded us to make some payments to the right people to get a death certificate. That's all. In all the circumstances, I think it was a jolly decent thing to do.'

'The terms of your agreement with him were quite draconian to deal with just a little spot of bribery, weren't they? And why didn't Nickel just bribe the "right people" himself if he was so fussed? Or was he broke?'

'Mr Turbot, I've explained the position to you, and, frankly, I resent your word "bribery". Miss Pesto had been our loyal employee. She was in Uruguay at *our* request. We felt we had a moral obligation to assist Mr Nickel. That, sir, is the sort of employer we are – and have been for over a century. We didn't think it seemly to make our assistance conditional on an examination of his bank accounts.'

The room fell silent.

After a few seconds, Turbot said: 'Well, whatever his motives, Nickel's ratted, jumped ship and waved goodbye to a small fortune from this company – well, not so small, perhaps. God only knows what SI have paid him.' He paused. 'But that's what really intrigues me.'

'What does?' asked George.

'The motives – SI's motives. What do they *want*?'

'Surely, Mr Turbot, *that* – at least – is obvious.'

'Oh?'

'To make a great deal of money, of course – to make a super profit – pure income without any investment. We've done all the work, taken all the risks. Now with the aid of clever lawyers' – George resisted the temptation to say 'like you' – 'they undoubtedly hope to reap a windfall profit.'

'Perhaps, Lord Weetwood. But then *you*, no doubt, took the decision to invest in Pesto's invention mindful of the risk that something like this might happen. You could never guarantee that neither Pesto nor anyone else cognisant of the facts would spill the beans one day to SI. Clearly, it was a risk you thought worth taking.'

*The cheeky young bastard! Another crack like that and I'll – How dare he stare into my eyes! No one ever does that. Has he no respect at all?*

Turbot stroked his chin. 'OK. What do we think SI *really* want? Do they desperately want to manufacture this stuff at any price? Have they got the resources to go into production? ... Keep this in mind, even if they were successful in stopping you from manufacturing, it doesn't follow that an English court would order you to hand over to them – free, gratis and for nothing – the details and ownership of all your improvements and know-how. I bet your technical guys have had to do a hell of a lot of work to get Pesto's invention into commercial production. And then there's all your safety testing. I should imagine that–'

'What do you mean, "safety testing"?' barked George. 'What are you suggesting?'

Brancepeth-Tring's heart beat even faster.

For once, Turbot was momentarily confused. 'I'm sorry, Lord Weetwood?'

'I said–'

'Sorry to interrupt, Chairman,' Merryweather said meekly, 'but I think Ben – Mr Turbot – is referring to our normal safety testing for dermatological purposes.'

'Exactly.'

'And of course, Ben, the product, like *everything* that comes out of our factories, has been *stringently* tested. In fact, we've had many months of testing on volunteer students – from Lancaster University, actually. The tests have been *very* satisfactory.'

Turbot tittered. 'You mean their skin turned bright orange, came off in great lumps, and now they're all six feet down!'

Some hearty laughter was silenced by George's fist hitting the table. 'What the *hell* do you mean by *that*?' he roared.

'Sorry?'

'What ... do ... you ... mean by that *fatuous* remark, Turbot?'

'It was just a joke – in bad taste. Sorry. You must excuse my sense of humour.'

'Come on, what did you mean by the students being "as good as animals"? We do *not* test our products on *animals* – not *this* company. We haven't done so for many, many years. No indeed, sir, we do *not*.'

'I'm sure you don't. I didn't mean to imply that you ... Forget it.'

While slowly shaking his head, George rolled a pencil backwards and forwards across his notepad. His eyes were firmly shut.

With a forced smile, Grimshaw said brightly: 'I think we've almost finished, George, you'll be pleased to hear – at least for today. ... Ben, you were about to give us your views on a possible response to the Americans.'

'Er ... yes ... of course, Charles.' Turbot was still looking quizzically at Weetwood, wondering what all the fuss was about. 'OK. ... Do SI really want to make this FoamFay stuff and hog the market all to themselves? Or, provided they get a cut of the action, would they be prepared to let *you* make and sell it?'

'How do you mean, Ben?' asked Merryweather timidly, with one eye on the Chairman.

Turbot groaned inwardly. 'Well, for all I know, Daventry, perhaps SI want to do a deal.' George stopped rolling his pencil and looked up. 'Their bottom line may be that for a small royalty, they would settle for a licence to use Pesto's invention. Their starting point might be a royalty-free licence with, say, exclusive rights for North America. Or they might demand that you admit they own everything, but in return they'd grant you a licence back – possibly for the UK and Europe – whatever. We'd want exclusivity – obviously. It's possible, don't you think? Or they might just want a lump sum – a capital payment and call it quits.'

'Mr Turbot,' George declaimed acidly, 'are you *seriously* telling me that, having invested hundreds of millions in this product, we should *share* the technology with these grotesque Americans – that we should even consider the possibility of becoming a *mere* licensee? Do you *seriously* imagine–?'

'I'm not telling you to do anything, Lord Weetwood, I'm just–'

114

'Don't interrupt me, young man!'

'I'm thirty-six–' but before Turbot could say another word, a sharp kick under the table from Grimshaw silenced him.

The meeting had reached its nadir.

Always the perfect diplomat, Grimshaw once more stepped into the breach. 'George,' he said kindly, 'I know this has been an *awful* day for you – the letter, the explosion and ... everything, but I think we're just looking at this *outrageous* claim from all angles. What Ben is saying is that things may not be as black as they appear. On balance, it seems that SI have less than a fifty per cent chance of stopping your planned launch through an injunction – is that right, Ben?' Turbot nodded. 'So now we're just contemplating whether they really want to make life difficult for you. For all we know, George, this whole thing might be a try-on – "Nothing ventured nothing gained. We've got a stick to beat these English with. If we spend a few thousand on lawyers' fees – even go as far as starting proceedings in England – WSD might be prepared to pay us something just to shut us up and make us go away. After all, if they've invested hundreds of millions, what's a few more hundred thousand to buy peace of mind? Those English probably envisaged some sort of claim from us, so they might have even budgeted for it." As Ben said, we've got some weak spots, but then the person who would have been their star witness in any proceedings is dead.'

'That's a very good summary, Charles,' Turbot said calmly.

*He's quieter,* thought George. *I've finally put the little tick in his place.*

'It goes without saying,' Turbot continued, 'that there's absolutely no question of us throwing in the towel at this stage. Possession is nine-tenths of the law, and *we* possess the technology. Even if SI have Pesto's formula, they don't yet have the facilities or know-how to utilize it commercially. And don't forget, we know from Pesto – at least I think this is what you said earlier, Lord Weetwood – that SI were secretly testing products on animals at the laboratory where she used to work. Would they really want a public trial where that would come out? Naturally, we'd let them know in advance that we'd spill the beans.'

To Turbot's surprise, however, highlighting this ammunition failed to revive Weetwood's spirits.

'All right. I suggest I send a short but firm reply to Fancourt Utley – SI's London solicitors – saying, um ... something like, "Thanks for your letter, bla, bla, bla. Our client WSD is firmly of the view that SI has no proprietary interests in ... um ... Pestex or any of its improvements thereto. Accordingly, we have advised WSD that SI is not entitled to any of the undertakings demanded, or to patent Pestex or such improvements, whether in the UK or elsewhere. The details of Ms Pesto's invention and WSD's improvements constitute confidential proprietary information of WSD, and any use or disclosure thereof by SI without WSD's consent would be unlawful. No doubt you will advise SI of the serious implications of any such unlawful use or disclosure, et cetera, et cetera. Yours, bla, bla, bla." What about that?'

'Sounds bloody good to me,' Brancepeth-Tring chirped.

'Obviously, I'd want to approve any letter before it's sent,' added Merryweather.

'Naturally. I suggest we send it shortly before the expiry of their deadline, and then sit back and see what happens. If they sue, then we'll defend vigorously.'

'I suppose it'll get into the press,' George said, the fury having gone out his voice.

'Possibly,' Turbot replied. 'So, Daventry, I'll send you a draft of my proposed reply tomorrow morning for your approval. ... Oh, sorry, there's one thing I've not covered.'

'Oh bugger!' chortled Brancepeth-Tring. 'I thought it was too good to be true.'

'There's the patent issue,' continued Turbot.

'Oh!' croaked Merryweather, glancing nervously at his boss.

'We have to remember that SI have just filed their own application. So, unless we do something ourselves, *they* could end up with a patent. After all, SI merely have to convince the Patent Office that Pestex was invented by Pesto and that either she was *their* employee at the relevant time, or that she was Groovy's employee and that they bought Groovy. And, of course, they'll need to prove that the details of the invention aren't in the public domain. Presumably, we believe that the only possible disclosure outside this company has been by what's-his-name ... Nickel – to SI.'

Nodding, Merryweather again glanced at Weetwood, but he seemed to be in a trance.

'OK,' Turbot continued, 'I think we should wham in our own patent application immediately as a sort of quasi-blocking measure. The Patent Office will then see two applications on file for the same invention and start asking questions. Incidentally, the British system is that where two applicants claim to be the owner of the same invention, the first to file wins.'

'Oh, God!' groaned Merryweather.

'Ooh-er!' croaked Brancepeth-Tring with obvious mock concern.

'But if it comes to a battle between us and SI,' Turbot added, 'there's no inventor – Pesto's dead. Who can give sworn evidence as to exactly how and when the invention was made? SI might force Nickel into the witness box, but his evidence would be just hearsay. And perhaps it would be possible for us to claim ... I don't know ... that when we first came into contact with Pesto, she just had a germ of an idea, and–'

'It was a damned sight more than that, Ben.' Grimshaw interjected.

'OK, Charles. I mean, we could *honestly* claim that she had come up with *something*, but the details – the chemistry of the process and so forth – were only identified *after* she joined WSD. In other words, neither she nor anyone else could have filed a valid patent application *before* she was spirited off to Uruguay. And perhaps we could also argue that one or more of our improvements to make the process commercially viable are patentable, and that without them the original Pesto invention is pretty valueless.'

Nodding almost out of control, Merryweather looked as though he might do himself an injury. 'I'll get the ball rolling, Ben,' he gushed.

'Well, George,' Grimshaw said, rising from his chair, 'we'll be off then. ... *George?*'

'Oh, Charles. ... Sorry... miles away. Goodbye, and thank you.'

'Don't thank me, George. I'm just one of yesterday's men – can't keep up with all this new law at my age. It's the young chaps, like Ben here, who are the experts now. Still, I suppose experience counts for something, on occasion.'

Turbot held out his hand. 'Well, goodbye, Lord Weetwood. I'm glad we've met at last. To be honest, it had surprised me that after more than ten years with the firm, nothing major had come my way from WSD.'

George finally stood up and shook both men's hands. Without looking at either of them, he said: 'Mr Turbot, my father used to say to me, "Whatever you do, lad, never wash your dirty laundry in Piccadilly, Manchester."'

# CHAPTER 11

When Ron Duffle dropped George at Bobbins' front door after a silent drive from Soap House, Vivian Duffle was waiting on the steps. She'd heard the Jaguar come up the drive and was anxious to empathise with her employer over the dreadful explosion; Radio Oldham had been keeping her up-to-date in the kitchen for much of the day.

'Oh, Lord Weetwood,' Vivian cried as he walked up the steps, 'I'm absolutely gutted about the Roberta Weetwood theatre. I mean, where will you hold the Goblinville Model Railway Society's annual exhibition? It's always been at the Roberta Weetwood.' But he didn't appear to hear. Instead, as she followed him into the house, he startled her with an exceptional request to bring him supper on a tray in the Yellow Room.

'I want to see the news,' he muttered. 'I'm on.'

'Do you know how to work the telly, m'lord?' she shouted down the corridor as he sped off, but there was no reply. 'I suppose it's postponed shock syndrome,' she mumbled, picking up the briefcase he'd flung to the floor.

*

George had rather enjoyed watching his television appearance, but with the news over, he'd got up to switch off the set. Although Mrs Duffle had left him with what she called the 'remote control unit', after several minutes of button pressing, he'd merely subjected himself to a highly irritating bout of channel hopping. Furthermore, no button or symbol on the TV's fascia gave him any indication as to how it could be silenced. He took a step back and glared at it.

'Do you know,' he hissed, 'you are a perfect example of so-called "progress"? I can remember television sets with jolly great knobs that one could grab hold of. And underneath them in plain, large lettering – in *English* mark you – were meaningful words like "ON", "OFF", "VOLUME", "HORIZONTAL HOLD", "CONTRAST" – not a lot of incomprehensible hieroglyphics like the nonsense on the front of you. Of course, that was when televisions were made by *British* companies here in *Britain*. ... So, you little monster, how *are* you switched off? Come on – tell me, or else!' He peered around the back of the set and spotted a cable. 'Ah, I've got you now.' He followed it to the wall socket and yanked out the plug; the sight and sounds on BBC 2 of a coke plant in eastern Poland – the

118

opening sequence of a film entitled *My Beautiful Blast Furnace* – were extinguished.

The Yellow Room was not a popular haunt of George's, but he slumped back into the armchair before the blank screen and yawned. Overwhelmed by an intense fatigue, he sat for a few moments neither thinking nor focusing on anything in particular. He wanted to go upstairs and take his mind off things with Crewe Junction, but he just didn't have the energy. It had truly been an awful, horrible, beastly, wretched day. Indeed, it had been one of the worst days of his life. For the first time in a very long time he felt unhappy, *very* unhappy – not that he was ever ecstatically happy about anything ... except trains, of course. He loved Crewe Junction, but as for everything else in life, well...

*Come on, be fair. What do I have to complain about? My life's all right. Satisfactory. I'm healthy – touch wood – never have to worry about money, and have the privilege – yes, it is a privilege – of running a vast industrial organisation. People treat me with respect – I don't care whether they like or dislike me – but respect ... that's important. 'Yes, Lord Weetwood. No, Lord Weetwood.' That's what people say. And why not? I've worked hard. WSD is jolly successful. Naturally, there are occasions when my duties bore me – like those ceremonies for employees with fifty years' service ... or is it thirty years? ... And as for those monthly meetings of SADMA, the governors of Manchester Grammar School, and the trustees of the Royal Exchange Theatre – sheer purgatory! But people in my position have to accept that sort of thing, don't they? It earns one respect, a lot of respect. And then I never have to cook a meal, or wash a dish, or ever go shopping – perish the thought! ... Duffle drives me everywhere. ... When did I last drive a car? ... Can I still drive?*

George was still puzzling over this conundrum when Vivian Duffle entered the room.

'Oh sorry, m'lord, I thought you'd be up in your ... study.' She spotted the tray deposited at one side of his chair. 'Lord Weetwood, *really*! You've not eaten your sweet. I made it specially – bread and butter pudding.' She bent over to pick up the tray. 'Ooh my poor back. We're not getting any younger, are we, sir?'

George managed a smile of sorts: he'd never been one for small talk.

'May I say, sir, I thought you looked smashing on telly.'

'Thank you.'

'Quite ... *heroic*. I mean, there you were saying such eloquent things to those TV people after having been blown up and–'

'Well, not exactly "blown up", Mrs Duffle.'

'Oh, don't split hairs, sir. You were nearly killed according to Radio Oldham. And you were very naughty not going to hospital and everything. You're probably concussed. You look a bit peaky. I said to Ron earlier on, "Ron," I said, "don't you think his Lordship looks a bit odd?".'

'Hmm?'

'I did, yes. ... Why don't I fix you a nice hot toddy, sir? And couldn't you manage just a bite of your pudding? Even if I say so myself, it's *very* good. Ron had two helpings. Mind you, he'd eat anything. ... Ooh, I nearly forgot what with all the excitement. Master James has gone off. Now what about *that*?'

'Sorry?'

'James has left – packed his bags and gone in chase of that American girl. 'course, it was obvious from the start he'd a soft spot for her. I said to Ron–'

'Mrs Duffle, *please*. I'm *very* tired. What *are* you talking about?'

'James' – George continued to look puzzled – 'your son, *James*. He decided to follow the American girl who stayed here over the weekend – Miss Caroline's old penfriend. You remember, don't you? ... Oh Lord, perhaps you *are* concussed. Look, let me phone Dr Ollerenshaw and–'

'No, no! I remember – of course.'

'Well, anyway, James was really in the dumps this morning, I can tell you, after she – Misty What's-her-face – left. Between you, me, and the gatepost, Lord Weetwood, I think things got quite passionate between them two. Well, I said to Ron, if she can get him out of that stupid stupor what he's been suffering these last two years, good for her. Actually' – Vivian lowered her voice to a whisper – 'I found a pair of his socks under her bed this morning. Fancy!'

'Mr Duffle's socks?'

'No! *James*'s socks!'

'Oh.'

'Anyway, she's flown off to Paris and Master James is determined to find her.' Vivian looked at the uneaten pudding and sighed. 'I think it's ever so romantic, don't you? It's like that film ... you know, what's-it with what's-his-name and thingy. I couldn't stop crying. Mind you, I had to lend him some money. Well, how could I refuse? He said you'd pay me back, but there's no hurry. ... How on earth he's going to find her in Paris with all them blocks of flats and squares, I don't know. They have lots of squares on the Continent, don't they? Funny that, because they must have knocked down a lot of houses to make them. I suppose it was the War. ... But as I said to Ron, where there's a will there's a way. He'll find her – I know he will. I just hope she appreciates it.'

Silence followed.

'Well now,' Vivian continued with contrived jollity, 'shall I fix you that hot toddy? And come on, have a piece of–'

'No thank you, Mrs Duffle. Nothing. And I'll give you a cheque tomorrow morning.'

Vivian knew what that tone meant – she knew it only too well: it was his 'go-away-and-leave-me-alone' tone. 'Very well, Lord Weetwood. I'm *so* sorry to have disturbed you. Good night. ... By the by, I'd rather have cash if you don't mind.'

George felt dizzy. 'My own son,' he muttered, 'and that female transatlantic spy – "passionate" indeed!' Desperately needing some fresh air, he pushed himself out of the armchair and made for the French windows. As he opened them, an almost overpowering scent of roses engulfed him. He breathed deeply and walked out onto the terrace.

'You're a fraud, George Weetwood.' The loudness of his voice startled him, and the feeling of intense loneliness that he'd experienced in his office before the explosion that morning returned. If only he had a friend he could turn to – get it all off his chest – ask for advice. If only. But he didn't have any friends, of course. In fact, if he was truly honest with himself, he'd never had a real friend in his whole life. ... Why not? And why hadn't it bothered him before now?

*For God's sake, George, get a grip! Have you **really** been unhappy? Well, have you? ... No! You reminded yourself of that before that babbling idiot came for the tray. You're not like other people. You should feel proud – no, not proud – I mean strong. You've been able to go through life content with simple pleasures and without the need of constant support from others – without having to cry on their shoulders ... without needing constant chatter and touching and being touched and ... and ... sex.*

*Yes, I should feel blessed that I can enjoy my own company. ... So why do I feel so wretched? Why did I call myself 'a fraud'? How ridiculous! Absurd!*

To his surprise, George discovered that he'd walked to the end of the terrace. He turned around to face the house. About thirty yards away, light flooded out of the French windows, but Bobbins was otherwise dark. 'I'm *not* a fraud,' he said softly, '– I'm *not*.' But a nasty little voice from somewhere said: 'Oh, but you *are*. Just think of all the terrible things you've done – things you're so ashamed of that you didn't even dare hint at them during Turbot's "interrogation". And when they come out – and they're almost bound to now – you'll be finished. Ruined. Destroyed.'

'I *won't*. That *can't* happen.'

'Don't fool yourself, Weetwood. You're not that stupid.'

121

'Stop it! Leave me alone! Go away! I'm not bad – I'd never hurt anyone. I couldn't.'

'Don't lie! For God's sake, man, you're prepared to kill *millions* of innocent people rather than face–'

'No! That's not true! I–'

Bells were ringing. ... *Bells?* George wiped hot tears from his eyes and tried to concentrate on the sound. ... It was a telephone. Something was telling him to run. Could he run? Yes, God damn it – of course he bloody could! *Go on – run!* **Run,** *damn you!*

Breathing heavily and with a jabbing pain in his right ankle, George rushed into the Yellow Room, spotted the phone on a Chippendale side table, and bounded towards it.

'Hello!' he blasted.

'*Oh, Lord Weetwood! Vivian Duffle here. I've been trying all over the house. I never thought you'd still be in front of the telly. Fancy! Anyway, there's a gentleman on the line what wants to speak to you. Won't give his name but says it's about "The Orient Express". Wasn't that the film with what's-her-name – that Agatha Thingy story set in Egypt? Oh,* **you** *know? Anyway, shall I–?*'

'Just put him through, woman, for God's sake!'

There was a brief silence. '*I really do think Dr Ollerenshaw should come over and–*'

'Put him through *now*!'

'*Yes, all right – if I can get the hang of these extension phones. Now, if I push this button, I think–*'

The click told George that the caller was connected. 'Hello? Dumpwell? Is that you? I thought you were phoning tomorrow?' George's heart was pounding. Not only had he run for the first time in years, but the fact that Dumpwell was calling *now* – well, it had to mean bad news. *Oh God, how much worse can it get?*

'*Smuttle here, Lord Weetwood. I hope you're all right. I heard about the explosion on the World Service news at lunchtime.*'

'Yes, yes – I'm fine, Dumpwell, thank you. Let's dispense with this "007" stuff for once. I'm very tired and really can't be bothered.'

'*Oh! ... Right!*' Dumpwell was taken aback: it was difficult to imagine Weetwood being 'very tired'.

'So, Dumpwell, are you phoning solely to enquire after my health, or do you have something to report?'

'*Ah, yes. ... Are you sure you want me to dispense with the code?*'

'Yes!'

'Well, OK. ... I thought I'd better call and let you know straight away. All the passengers – I mean **animals** – in the other sections have died.'

'*All* of them?'

'I'm afraid so. They just dropped like flies this morning – a couple of hours after I phoned, actually.'

'So suddenly?'

'Yes. It was just like Section B, one minute the animals seemed fine, and the next they were vomiting, violently twitching, and collapsing. Death comes in fifteen minutes at most, you know.'

'Just like ... Pesto in fact.'

'*Exactly.*'

'What the hell is it, Dumpwell? How can it be the soap? People have been using soap for over two thousand years without any serious adverse effects.'

'*My brightest assistant here, a chap called Badminton, believes he's identified a toxin. In brief, it looks like a by-product resulting from the complex chemical reactions between certain molecules in the tea liquor, and bromide compounds in the sea water. We've found high concentrations of the toxin in the animals' brains, with clear damage to the brain tissue. Our guess is, however, that for sufficient concentrations to build up in the **human** brain to cause death, one would have to use the product daily for about ten years.*'

'So, what about Pesto?'

'*Well, not only was she handling concentrated laboratory samples from the outset, but we understand she was also washing her hair with it every day. The toxin is absorbed through the skin, you see, so after almost four years of that sort of use, well ...*'

George lowered himself into an armchair. There were some small silver ornaments around the telephone on the side table, and he started to rearrange them. 'Why didn't you indicate any of this to me this morning, Dumpwell?'

'*Ah, well, Badminton had only analysed about half of the Section B brains when I phoned. He's worked non-stop for forty-eight hours, you know. I wanted to be absolutely sure in view of your concern – understandable, of course – about the **preliminary** findings I communicated to you a fortnight ago.*'

George snorted. 'Look, isn't there something we can do to remove this toxin? The compounds present in the tea and sea water which react to form it, well, can't we filter them out before the soap-producing process commences?'

'*We've thought of that, sir. One of our chaps has done the chemistry. Without those damned compounds, the process probably won't work. Anyway, filtering them out would be prohibitively expensive – ruinous.*'

A long silence ensued.

'Dumpwell, how many people know about these tests, apart from ourselves?'

'Well ... there's Badminton of course, my two other assistants – Frobisher and Googe – and ... well, that's it, I think.'

'You think?'

'I mean, there shouldn't be anyone else. The tests have been conducted at the small warehouse I rented out in the sticks – about ten miles from Montevideo. Only the four of us have been there. We did everything ourselves to fit it out – at weekends and nights. We acquired and delivered the animals. We've even done the cleaning! Badminton, Frobisher and Googe have lived together in an apartment down town, and as far as I'm aware, they've had no contact with any of our people in–'

'Do you trust Badminton and ... er–?'

'Frobisher and Googe? Absolutely!'

'And your wife? Have you spoken to her about any of–?'

'There is no Mrs Dumpwell, sir.'

'Ah yes. ... What about Nickel?'

'Nickel?'

'Yes, Nickel. When did you last see him?'

'Well, I ... um ... I last saw him some weeks ago. He's gone to the States. He told me he was going to spend some time with his sister – in California, I think.'

'Where did you see him?'

'Where? ... Oh ... er ... on the golf course.'

'The golf course?'

'Yes. We're both keen players. We've played quite a bit together since Orient Express started. You know, there's not a lot to do in Montevideo, Lord Weetwood, and not many Anglo-Saxons – at least not chaps one would want to play a round of golf with. I mean, Nickel's been pretty desperate since his wife's death. I've tried to get him out and about, cheer him up and–'

'Dumpwell, did he know about the tests? Did you tell him? Yes or no?'

'I ... well ... The point is, he was understandably concerned about the product. Obviously he had his suspicions that it might have caused Vosene's death, and from time to time he asked what we were doing by way of safety testing. He seemed genuinely worried. Well, he's a very genuine chap.'

'You told him.'

'I ... I didn't think it would do any harm. Yes. I mean he's got a vested interest in the product's success. From what he told me, he's in for a bloody great royalty and–'

'Dumpwell! Listen to me. Today we received a letter from lawyers acting for Pesto's former employers in Texas. They're claiming *they* own the invention. They're threatening us with everything under the sun. They're demanding we abandon the whole project. And they know a *hell* of a lot about Pesto, Uruguay, her death, et cetera. We're convinced that their primary source is your friend and golfing partner, Nickel.'

'*Oh my God!*'

'It's possible that he's also told them that we're conducting safety tests on *animals*.'

'*Oh fuck! Sorry!*'

'But the one consolation – if we can take *any* comfort from it – is that he's probably *not* indicated to them any concern about the product, or hinted at any possible connection between it and Pesto's death. Presumably, he's stuck to the salmonella story. No American manufacturer would want to have anything to do with an invention tainted with health risks.'

'*Absolutely not! ... But I just can't believe it, sir – Nickel – double-crossing us. I mean it's ... it's–*'

'It's happened, Dumpwell. Now I want a straight answer. Have you had any contact with Nickel since he left for America? You said he'd gone about three weeks ago. That would be before there was any indication that the tests were going wrong.'

'*No! I swear. I haven't heard from him at all. And when we spoke about the tests at the club – I mean, he'd been pressing me for months about what we were doing, if anything – well, he started crying ... at the ninth hole I think it was. ... Anyway, I just told him we were doing these tests on dogs somewhere – very intensive, that they'd been running for many months, and we'd not come up with anything untoward. ... Look, sir, if you want my resignation–*'

'Don't be ridiculous, Dumpwell. It's an understandable error on *your* part. Who knows, it might turn out to be a blessing in disguise.'

'*I ... I don't follow–*'

'It goes without saying that any leak – any hint *whatsoever* – of the outcome of these tests, Dumpwell ... well, I don't think I need to spell it out. Just wind up Orient Express quickly. I want you and your chaps to do a thorough job. We must know *precisely* what's wrong with the stuff and what happened to the animals.'

'*May I ask if Weetex is to be abandoned, sir?*'

'The new brand name is FoamFay.'

'*FoamFay? ... Right.*'

'We have to consider the future carefully. Your boffins may still come up with an answer. Perhaps the launch will have to be delayed.'

125

'*That's beyond doubt, isn't it?*'

'I – I ... I need to consult the board. ... Incidentally, Dumpwell, this new chap we've recruited from Unilever to replace Barmcake as Technical Director – Jarvis ... well – I really shouldn't be saying this, and I'm not promising anything – but I'm not sure he's the man we thought he was. ... It's time you came home, Dumpwell. We need you here.'

'*I ... er–*'

'But remember this. Beware Nickel!'

'*Naturally.*'

'If he attempts to contact you, just act as if nothing has happened. Don't let on we suspect him of anything. Frankly, I doubt you'll ever see his face in Montevideo again, but be friendly should he get in touch. And if he asks anything about the tests, just say they're going fine. And pay your assistants some bonuses. We'll talk again in a few days.'

'*Fine.*'

'Goodbye.'

George replaced the receiver without waiting for any reciprocity. The carriage clock on the mantelpiece said 10:35. It would be 6:35 p.m. in Montevideo, he calculated. What would Dumpwell be doing this evening? ... Probably boozing with his ex-pat chums at his ghastly golf club and dreaming of being WSD's Technical Director. Fat chance! The man was a decent biochemist but quite loopy. No, not loopy – louche. Which, on reflection, would tend to indicate that Dumpwell would probably not be spending his evening downing pure malts at the golf club. And that was odd, he thought: Dumpwell playing golf – and with Nickel of all people. It was more than odd: it was bizarre. Could Dumpwell be trusted? ... And his assistants, what about them? What if they also sold their souls to the Texan Devil? But then if SI found out that FoamFay was lethal, they'd back off, wouldn't they?

*Oh, this is pointless! I've already considered all these angles. Any discussion of animal testing – any at all – could devastate WSD's reputation. And the more people who know, the greater the chances of it becoming public knowledge. ... But hang on! What connections are there between WSD and the Uruguay operations? If anyone tries to investigate the matter, they'll just find a chain of apparently innocuous safety-trial contracts and subcontracts – all specifying clinical human testing – from one nominee company to another, starting in the Isle of Man and ending up in Uruguay via Liechtenstein, the Cayman Islands and Panama. After all, that's what most companies in the toiletries and cosmetics business have been doing since the animal-rights fanatics started spreading their dotty gospel. At least we've not been as stupid as SI!*

But George had to admit that, at the end of the day, one still had to worry about the people on the ground who did the testing, the Dumpwells, Badmintons and – whatever the other assistants were called – of this world. There'd always be the risk of their blabbing, whether for money or out of some misguided qualms of conscience. They could take photographs of the horrid animals, photocopy reports, record conversations, swear affidavits ...

George felt hot. Perhaps ...? No, it was out of the question! How could he even begin to think of such a dreadful thing? He stood up and walked very slowly towards the French windows. And yet, it was South America, wasn't it? By all accounts, a very dangerous place. Crime was rampant. Shootings were common. They'd tried to buy off Nickel, and where had it got them, damn it?

'But for God's sake, man,' he cried aloud before the open windows, 'even if I got rid of these people, that would still leave the core problem. The bloody product's lethal! Do we sell it? Do we abandon the whole project and capitulate to the Americans after spending virtually all our cash, or–?'

George stopped as the mantelpiece clock chimed 10:45. Yet, all he could hear was the irritating voice of the arrogant young lawyer from Grimshaws. What had he said about licences and deals? ... Could it just possibly work? After all, the Americans believed WSD were on to something big. If SI want FoamFay, why not give it to them – lock, stock and barrel? Well, not 'give' – sell it. ... But how? One couldn't be seen to be too willing to sell or they'd smell a rat. Play them along – put up a good fight – even go ahead with the launch, perhaps. Dumpwell had said it would take *years* of using the product to absorb enough toxin to suffer any serious injury, let alone death – and thereafter, WSD could start settlement negotiations. The old routine: there's no certainty in litigation for either side; we don't want the adverse publicity; we'll sell you the damned invention – the whole shooting match; it's a blow, but that's life; you buy it 'as is' – no warranties, no indemnities. Oh, and by the way, Mr Start, we won't say anything about your animal testing at Soda Flats – or wherever it was that Pesto worked. Perhaps there was some light at the end of the tunnel after all.

George yawned; he could barely keep his eyes open. It was definitely time for bed. Tomorrow his head should be clearer, and perhaps the world might start to make sense again.

'Why hasn't Duffle been round to lock up?' he muttered, closing the French windows. Perhaps he *had* been round, but finding the room occupied–

*My God! Could the cretin have overheard anything? Would he have understood? Would he –?* George jumped as the phone started ringing.

'Damn the blasted thing!' he bellowed. He'd let it ring. If it was important, then whoever it was would phone back tomorrow. He bolted the French windows, drew the curtains, marched to the door and, yelling 'To hell with you!' at the phone, switched off the lights. As he closed the door behind him, the phone fell silent. Within seconds, however, extensions began ringing and echoing all over the house. It was the final straw.

George threw open the door, switched all the lights back on, and stormed toward the wailing instrument.

'You deserve a bloody good thrashing!' he yelled, grabbing the receiver.

'*I beg your pardon, Lord Weetwood*?'

'Mrs Duffle, I don't care who it is! I do *not* want to speak to another living soul tonight. Do you understand? I'm going to bed. If I hear this infernal machine ringing again tonight–'

'*The caller says it's about the Roberta Weetwood explosion – says it's very important. Mentioned this "Orient Express" thing like your earlier caller. Definitely not the same person – very persistent, I must say. I was just off to bed myself. And Ron's not back from the Cob o' Coal–*'

'Look, you stupid, *stupid* woman, just put him through and get off the line!' There was silence. 'Put him through *this instant!*' A series of clicks were accompanied by what sounded like muffled sobs. 'Hello? *Hello?* Weetwood speaking.'

'*Good evening. Be silent. Listen carefully. We are the European Animal Liberation Front. We know all about your Project Orient Express and your vicious torture and foul murders of our canine comrades. Revenge and retribution are nigh. We have struck the first blow. Your monument to the degradation of animalkind, the so-called Roberta Weetwood Memorial Playhouse and Picture Palace, has been destroyed. You shall be hearing from us again soon. Remember my code name – REX.*'

George continued to hold the receiver for some minutes, wondering what it might be like to blow one's brains out.

*

Sitting on the terrace in the dark, not ten yards from the Yellow Room's French windows, Ron Duffle was also troubled by the evening's events – although he had yet to develop any suicidal tendencies. Picturing himself more and more as Michael Caine playing 'Harry Palmer' in *The Ipcress File*, he'd escaped from Bobbins immediately after dinner, and, with a sense of mounting excitement, had arrived at the Cob o' Coal with ten minutes to spare before the scheduled debriefing session with Ganoid and Rinderpest. Peggy Umpleby was polishing glasses and chatting to the landlady, when he entered whistling the *Harry Lime* theme from *The Third Man*.

'You're full of the joys of life tonight, Ron,' she chirped. 'The usual?' and without waiting for an answer she crossed to the Ramsbottom pumps to pull him a pint. 'Anyone would think you were pleased with today's goings-on in Goblinville. Did you see the reports? If you ask me–'

'Hang on a minute, Peggy, I'll just wait for me friends. Are they in the garden?'

'And which "friends" might *they* be, dear?'

'Lottie Rinderpest and Ken Ganoid, of course.'

Mrs Umpleby looked at her lover with surprise. 'I don't know what sort of "business" you've been up to with them two weirdoes, but your so-called friends checked out this morning. ... I hope you didn't lend them any money or something, did you, Ron? ... Ron? Are you listening?'

But Duffle was in shock. He anxiously awaited his colleagues until closing time – he consumed six pints of Ramsbottom's in the process – but they never appeared.


Now, in the gloom of Bobbins' terrace, as Lord Weetwood half-heartedly contemplated suicide, Duffle continued to speculate about his own situation. His employer's ravings were also food for thought.

# CHAPTER 12

Had Misty had the courage of her convictions and phoned Bobbins at any time during her miserable stay in Paris, everything could have been so different. After all, James himself was walking its streets within hours of her arrival, and a message left with Mrs Duffle could have been rapidly communicated to him. Indeed, for several days he bombarded the housekeeper with calls in the hope that Misty might have phoned, as she had promised. And how cruel it was that fate never threw the two of them together: like all other congested centres of rampant tourism, there are only half a dozen sights in Paris that most visitors feel they cannot miss. Cognisant of this axiom, James had devised a daily rotation involving an hour at each of Sacré Coeur, the Louvre, Notre-Dame, the Musée d'Orsay, the Arc de Triomphe and the Eiffel Tower.

The Musée d'Orsay had been a tough decision: it was either that or Les Invalides, but, on balance, James guessed that if Misty had to choose between fabulous works of art or some lousy tombs of military heroes whose names meant nothing even to most of the French – with the obvious exception of Napoléon – then Misty would choose the Musée d'Orsay. He was right.

In the early afternoon of his second full day in Paris, as he waited outside the museum's entrance, a well-dressed youth begging for spare change, or alternatively a cigarette, briefly interrupted his vigil. When he looked round after the beggar had moved on, he saw Misty stepping onto the escalator at the entrance to the Musée d'Orsay Métro station. He shouted, he ran, he searched. But Misty was nowhere to be seen. Perhaps she'd taken the Métro to Les Invalides or the Eiffel Tower, just a few stops further on. However, his searches there that afternoon also proved fruitless.

For her part, an ever-deepening perception of isolation and loneliness began to engulf Misty. Previously, she'd always made friends easily and attracted admirers. It was not just her beauty, charm and style: she was possessed of an indefinable aura that magically drew people to her and made them smile and forget their worries. None of this was the result of any conscious act on her part, which, perhaps, was the loveliest thing about her. And although her magic had only worked on one of the three Weetwoods she'd met so far, they were a rather peculiar family.

Something, however, had gone wrong from the minute she touched down at Charles de Gaulle, where no one was prepared to answer her queries about the railroad or subway links to the centre of Paris. The tetchy receptionist at her hotel, just off the Champs Elysées, denied that there was any reservation – even when Misty presented copies of the relevant faxes. The receptionist countered by alleging that Misty must have subsequently telephoned a cancellation.

'Are you calling me a liar?' asked Misty incredulously. The receptionist shrugged her shoulders. The manager was summoned, the computer was investigated, and Misty found she'd become a 'Mlle. S. Tart' and was in room 451. And that had been the next blow.

Thanks to *Gigi, Funny Face, An American in Paris* and other old movies, Misty had an idyllic vision of France's capital, and now she was ready to follow in the footsteps, so to speak, of Audrey Hepburn and Leslie Caron. Room 451, however, was a box, a very small hot box with paintwork and wall coverings the colour of milk chocolate. A 40-watt light bulb dangling from the centre of the room provided the only source of illumination; it was encased in a lampshade resembling a model of a 1960s Soviet satellite. For some time, she just stood shaking her head and repeating 'A hundred bucks a night for this dump!' The bathroom had shaken her faith in France's claim to be a major economic power – the absence of a shower curtain was beyond her comprehension – and she promptly discovered that sitting on the toilet necessitated an extraordinary feat of acrobatics: it was so close to the washbasin that she had to squeeze her knees underneath it.

Misty was, nonetheless, philosophical: the room was clean, the hotel could hardly be better situated, and she had no intention of doing anything in it except sleep, wash and store her belongings. She pulled back the chocolate-brown curtains emblazoned with pink and yellow flowers of almost science-fiction proportions, and held her breath. Heavy wooden shutters barred her way. How romantic! It *was* just like the movies. On the other side would be a panorama of zany tiled roofs and chimneys pots, and beyond them, the soaring towers of Notre-Dame, the gleaming domes of Sacré Coeur, the majesty of the Eiffel Tower. She grabbed the rusty handle and pulled with all her might. The shutters flew open and Misty gasped.

Room 451 certainly had a view – a view of a gloomy central courtyard of truly horrifying dinginess with a ventilation shaft of stainless-steel construction topped by an extractor fan at roof level rumbling ominously; a thick black goo was seeping from its numerous joints. Hot, humid air, stinking of fried fish, flooded the room. For the first time in many years, Misty burst into tears.

*

Across town in the unfashionable streets around the Place de la Victoire, James's hotel bedroom *did* feature a splendid view of many of the

131

city's great buildings from its attic window. Nonetheless, he, too, was subjected to the Gallic penchant for chocolate-brown décor; in his case, it appeared to have been attacked by someone who'd gone crazy with a finger-printing set. Moreover, he had no en suite facilities, save for a cracked washbasin and the occasional supply of cold water. But he was indifferent to the attributes of his accommodation: he was out for most of the day; after dark, he'd patrol the nocturnal tourist haunts – around Montmartre, the Latin Quarter and the Champs Elysées. Alas, he'd always return alone to his dingy attic room. Chain-smoking Gauloises, he'd lie naked on the bed, watching the smoke drift gently to the open window and then disappear. Misty was out there, somewhere. The heat was oppressive and the perspiration would trickle down his chest. Wiping it away, he would invariably find his penis erect. Was it really love or just lust? Was it all just a foolish infatuation? But the softness of her skin would always come back to him ... her heavenly scent ... the indescribable sensation of being inside her. Inevitably the release would come, and sobbing, he'd reach for the grubby hand towel.

*

The Parisian nights were equally unbearable for Misty. Being in no mood to frequent bars, restaurants or clubs on her own, she invariably ended up watching American films in original version at the Gaumont on the Champs Elysées. Like James, nor did sleep come easily: in addition to the heat and rumbling of the extractor fan, the plumbing gurgled, clanked and groaned continuously. It had just not meant to be like this, she kept telling herself. It certainly had not: she'd originally arranged to stay with an old Brynamman friend, Becky Spasfon-Lyoc, who worked in First Chemical Bank's Paris office and rented an apartment on chic Avenue Foch – no less. But just a week before Misty departed New York, Becky had phoned to say that the apartment was being redecorated, and she'd be spending July on the Côte d'Argent at her boyfriend's Arcachon villa. Pointedly, Misty was not invited to join them.

On Misty's fourth evening in Paris, and after yet another movie at the Gaumont, someone tried to grab her shoulder bag as she walked back to the hotel. That night, she didn't sleep at all; in the early hours, she resolved to cut her losses. By noon the next day she was on a train to Nice and writing postcards. She wrote one to James. It read:

Hi! Four days in Paris and I was suicidal!
On a train to Nice, so excuse the writing.
Hope you're OK. I'll be in touch.
Love, Misty

The card reached Bobbins a week later. Vivian Duffle felt tortured when she communicated the contents by phone to James at his Paris hotel; she'd always had a soft spot for him. Now she was in a dilemma: she worried about his diet, his state of mind – and laundry. Reason dictated he should return home and await further news, but the romantic streak in her was too strong.

'Well, what do you *really* want to do, chuck?' she asked James after a brief discussion of the pros and cons.

'*Go to Nice, of course, Mrs D.*'

'Your dad still thinks she's some kind of spy – industrial espionage he said – spying for her dad's company.'

'*Pa's soft in the head – or lying just to get me home.*'

So, Vivian told James to phone Lady Weetwood and tell her he was on his way to the *Villa Gobelin*. He protested, but Vivian talked some common sense: he was running out of money and needed clean clothes and some decent food. In truth, Vivian was also keen to get an objective report on what exactly went on at the villa during Beryl's visits; she'd had her suspicions ever since Lord Weetwood had abandoned his Riviera holidays years ago.

After frantic packing and an extravagant taxi ride to the Gare de Lyon – there was simply no time to telephone St-Jean-Cap-Ferrat – James found himself sharing a couchette compartment with three paralytic Danish students on the overnight express to Nice. It proved impossible to decline their generous offers of beer, gin, vodka, whisky and Cassis de Dijon. When he was awoken the following morning by a cleaner in some carriage sidings on the outskirts of Nice, James had barely any recollection of the journey – save for the first hour or so. As he shielded his eyes from the dazzling Mediterranean sunlight streaming through the windows and suffered the cleaner's raucous, incomprehensible interrogation, it dawned on him that, save for empty bottles and plastic cups, the compartment was empty. His belongings were nowhere to be seen – no holdall, no passport, no money. All he possessed were the jeans, T-shirt and scuffed Timberlands which clothed and shoed him. He felt in his pockets; he had a few francs.

It was late afternoon when James arrived at Cap-Ferrat, for it had taken some time to extricate himself from the railway officials and, through hitch-hiking and walking, find his way to the ultra-exclusive peninsula. Unshaven, unwashed and devoid of luggage, he looked distinctly incongruous as he trudged along its labyrinthine, winding lanes. At least ten years had passed since he'd last been subjected to the horrors of a family holiday at the *Villa Gobelin*, so his recollections of its whereabouts were hazy. Seeking directions proved problematic: there were very few people about, and those whom he did manage to address either ignored him as if in fear of being mugged, or professed ignorance. Nor was his quest assisted by the high walls, forbidding gates and dense vegetation that served to protect the residents' palatial homes from undesirables.

Finally, a diminutive plaque glinting in the late afternoon sunshine caught James's attention. Discreetly positioned in a stone wall to one side of fortress-like gates, it bore the words 'Villa Gobelin' in text worthy of an eye test. His attempts to gain access to his family's estate, however, proved hopeless. For a start, it took him ages to obtain any response to his constant buzzing on the electric intercom. And when his request for admission through a hoarse and weak voice was finally answered, the female reply comprised a torrent of obscenities in French interspersed with hysterical laughter. It made no sense.

Thus, despite his exhaustion, James scaled the gates.

At the end of a long drive, an Aston Martin, a Bentley and a Ferrari were parked in front of steps that ascended to the villa's columned portico. The grand double doors were wide open, and, without a second's hesitation, James walked in. The marble-floored entrance hall felt deliciously cool. It ran the entire width of the house and culminated in three huge French windows. They were also wide open, and through them came a gentle breeze on which were carried the sounds of laughter and the smell of cigarette smoke. James made his way along the hall, passed through one of the French windows, and emerged onto a spacious terrace. It was bordered by a balustrade surmounted at intervals by mighty stone urns from which white pelargoniums cascaded. James walked over and looked down.

What first struck him was the size of the swimming pool: it seemed positively Olympian. And with the vivid flowers, classical statues, fountains, verdant lawns and glimpses of the sea between the pines, all bathed in the golden light of early evening, it momentarily occurred to him that this, perhaps, was how Heaven might look. But then stereotypical sounds of a couple approaching orgasm caused James to focus on a poolside sun-lounger immediately beneath him. An expertly tanned and bony woman with her back to him was astride a muscular young man; they were bouncing up and down with expert co-ordination. As she started to yell 'Oh God!' louder and louder, an impeccably dressed waiter approached and, with complete indifference, cleared the empty glasses from the table at their side.

With a terrible churning in his empty stomach, James suddenly recognized the woman's voice and let out such a roar that, just for a second, everything in the garden stopped. And then the frozen, photographic scene disintegrated: the bony woman turned her head, looked up, and screamed;

the waiter, who'd been in the process of providing the intertwined couple with fresh glasses of champagne, dropped his tray; the young stud yelled and tried to jump up. As the woman fell onto the broken glasses and began screaming hysterically, the sun-lounger tipped up and the hunk was catapulted backwards into the pool. As he came up for air, James recognized him, for he'd seen most of this Hollywood star's blockbuster movies. It was, however, the last thing he would remember before slumping over the balustrade and vomiting his stomach's meagre contents over his mother.

*

While mayhem was erupting at the *Villa Gobelin*, a 2,000-ton yacht weighed anchor and headed east down the Gulf of St-Tropez. It was an elegant vessel of 1930s vintage built on the Clyde for King Zog, the first and last king of Albania, and named *Burgajet* after the castle of his birth. Its original steam turbines could still achieve a stately 15 knots, and with a gleaming white hull, twin masts, and a tall yellow funnel, the *Burgajet* epitomized the discreet elegance which had been the hallmark of British naval architects of the era. Paradoxically, it was this very quality that now set the *Burgajet* so clearly apart from the angular and top-heavy vessels which catered for the marine amusements of contemporary plutocrats. Indeed, she was the only yacht Misty had admired earlier that day as her noon ferry from Ste-Maxime approached St-Tropez's harbour entrance.

Misty had 'done' Nice and its environs; neither had impressed her. She had, of course, hit the Riviera at a bad time; it would shortly get even worse, she was told, when French industrial and commercial life ground to a halt on Bastille Day for a month. Be that as it may, she found the Riviera overdeveloped – to the point of tackiness. Mile after mile, the coast was lined by condominiums, freeways and shopping malls – and more were under construction. Nice possessed a narrow strand of pebbles and a hinterland of fast-food diners; the Old Town looked as though it had been blitzed by a convention of deranged graffitists – and, sadly, no one seemed to care. A day in Monte Carlo had only served to exacerbate her mounting depression: with its garbage-free streets, over-manicured parks, and carpeted pavements fronting exclusive boutiques, the principality's all-too-obvious smugness seemed calculated to engender nothing but greed and envy. It had been a relief to board the coach for the return to Nice.

Rose Water, a thirties-something real estate agent from Pittsburgh, befriended Misty on the ride back. Without any of the usual polite preliminaries – except 'I bet you're American!' – Rose had launched into an investigation of Misty's life story. There was just no stopping her. And she stuck like a limpet. It was Rose who persuaded Misty to quit Nice and make for St-Tropez. 'It's cool!' Rose had enthused, and, notwithstanding her monotonous voice and painfully slow speech, she made the resort sound quite attractive.

And so it was that, on a sweltering day, Misty found herself sitting on the pavement terrace of St-Tropez's harbour-side *Café de Paris*. Rose had gone in search of accommodation, rather than partake of lunch – 'I can never relax until my bags are unpacked,' she'd admonished. But Misty was thirsty and hungry, and, frankly, in view of the seething mass of holidaymakers choking the town's narrow streets, it seemed highly unlikely that there'd be a single spare bed for miles around.

In front of Misty, a dozen impressive yachts were moored at right angles to a quay choked with gawping tourists. They jostled to take photographs of themselves before the gangways as members of the respective crews – all impeccably clad in white – gazed down on them disdainfully. Once in a while, someone who might – or might not – be rich or famous would come on deck and stand at the rail, provoking a wave of audible speculation among the adulating flocks as to his or her identity. It was a spectacle that Misty found absolutely fascinating. She ordered another overpriced beer and a salad niçoise, and continued her observation.

'I don't believe it! It can't be! It *is*! My God! Misty! *Darling*! What on *earth* are *you* doing here? So much for charity work in Haarlem! I knew you'd see sense in the end.'

'Tubs! I–'

'Don't tell me! Um ... you're with that divine hunk Tom Babcock on the *Maid of Orleans*! I mean, what an *absurdly* ridiculous name for a floating bordello. No, you can't be – he's with that ghastly bitch whose father's in dog food.'

'Tubs–'

'I know! You're on the *Titanic* with the Culture-Vultures – from Arkansas – of *all* places. The number of churches those poor souls have visited already! Well, we call it the *Titanic* after they hit that pedalo in Menton last week. How a pedalo could do so much damage is beyond me.'

'Tubs–'

'No, no, *no*! They were all out last night at that wild little club beside the *Mairie* sipping gin and tonics and puffing on Sobranie cocktail cigarettes. Well, they were *asking* for trouble, weren't they?'

'Tubs–'

'Got it! Tony Schwartz-Bianco! Of course! How many times did he try to date you at Harvard? And all those love letters! So, he's finally got his wicked way at last and you're sailing on his floating palace – not like us on the goddam *Bounty* out there with "Captain Bligh". But what are you doing here sitting all *alone*? Where's Tony? Off your ass, young lady, and come and meet the crowd. We're sat over there – the Beautiful People I call them. We've got a Swiss, a German, an Austrian – oh it's all so *very* cosmopolitan on the *Bounty*. Come on! You'll *love* them.'

Stockard Avery – 'Tubs' – had barely changed since she and Misty had been roomies at Brynamman. Built like a shot-putter, she was five feet of volcanic power. In consequence, Misty barely managed to grab her holdall and backpack before finding herself dragged by a fierce grip to the table of the Beautiful People. Bronzed, blond and blue-eyed, the assortment of men and women in their twenties sipping Badoit and smoking Marlboros all seemed to have come from the same finely crafted mould. They attracted attention – and knew it.

Notwithstanding her hitch-hiker appearance, the Beautiful People immediately recognized Misty as one of themselves and welcomed her into their exclusive club. In any event, somewhere in her torrent of biographical details, Tubs said: 'Her old man's Start Industries!' Tubs, on the other hand, looked completely out of place, but was tolerated by the Beautiful People because she had the richest father. All this was crystal clear to Misty: after all, Tubs had been desperately trying to buy friendship for as long as she'd known her.

It transpired that Tubs and her friends had only stopped at the *Café de Paris* because of the former's raging thirst, and were about to return to the '*Bounty*'. Having ascertained Misty's current situation, Tubs invited her to lunch on board with 'Captain Bligh'; a refusal was out of the question. A message was written for Rose Water and left with a waiter, but he quickly threw it away. In any event, Ms Water was already far from St-Tropez: she'd made straight for the bus station after leaving Misty and had caught the first service down the coast towards Toulon. It had been easy getting Misty's credit cards on the boat over from Ste-Maxime, but then rich kids, as Rose had reminded herself, were always so careless with their valuables.

The '*Bounty*' turned out to be none other than the *Burgajet*, and 'Captain Bligh' was Tubs's fiancé, Paul Woodward III, whose father – senior partner of mighty Wall Street stockbrokers Woodward Brothers – had rented the yacht as an engagement present. Tubs and Paul were spending the summer cruising the Mediterranean, and were not due back in Marbella until the first week of September. Paul had encouraged Tubs to assemble an entourage of suitable youthful sophisticates of impressive parentage to accompany them, and she'd exceeded all his expectations. Paul, for his part, had brought a few of his old cronies from Andover and Princeton.

The lunch was outstandingly good, the scenery superb, and the wine intoxicating. Tubs gushed; it had been weeks since she'd enjoyed a real girlie conversation with a fellow American. The Beautiful People and Paul were left to themselves; they were already discussing their plans for the winter and skiing. Yet, the story from Tubs was that all was not going too smoothly on the good ship *Burgajet*. Woodward was turning out to be something of a spoilt schoolboy and martinet; she should never have bought him that peaked sailing cap at Brook Brothers! It had been meant as a joke, but he'd hardly removed it from his prematurely balding head since they'd set sail from Marbella. And he was driving the professional crew mad; the captain had virtually broken off diplomatic relations. The chef had gone on strike after just a fortnight when Woodward complained about a soufflé and had attempted to make one himself in the galley. There'd been a fire; an unscheduled call at Toulon had proved necessary for a minor refit, and the chef had scarpered. Luckily, Tubs's Austrian friend aboard, Otto von Geidel, had procured a replacement – a 'gem' who'd once worked for his family; he was at the *Negresco* in Nice but 'bored'. Then Woodward had become obsessed with the idea that someone had stolen a case of the Dom Perignon with which Tubs's father had had the yacht stocked for the voyage. He'd demanded a search of everyone's cabin!

'And if all that wasn't bad enough, Misty, honey,' moaned Tubs, 'although this boat is full of old-world charm, the lack of modern thermostatically-controlled air conditioning did come of something of a shock, I can tell you. I mean' – she sounded as if on the point of bursting into tears – 'all we have are electric fans and portholes! How did that king ever cope? Some nights, it gets so hot that Otto and his friend Franz von' – she flicked a wasp away from her wine glass – 'von, von... doo-dah, sleep on the deck.'

But despite the martinet and the lack of air conditioning, Misty stayed on the *Burgajet* when she weighed anchor that evening. For the next five weeks it became her home. She had originally planned to sail with them only as far as Sardinia, but Tubs was frantic that she should stay at least as far as Naples: 'We'll see Pompeii, and then, if you want, you can take the train to Rome and visit your friends there.' However, when they reached the Bay of Naples, disembarkation was not on Woodward's schedule: 'The city is rife with crime and violence,' he claimed. 'We're sailing straight on to Palermo.' He brooked no argument. The announcement of his decision to introduce daily boat drills – it had been over breakfast one morning between Spetses and Hydra – had been the final straw for some of the Beautiful People. Yet, both Tubs and those who remained after the desertion had no difficulty in recruiting substitutes as the *Burgajet* steamed majestically through the Greek islands.

Misty's replacement American Express card finally caught up with her at Rhodes – the long arm of the law never did catch up with Rose Water –

but by that time the *Burgajet* had firmly cast her spell over Misty. In particular, she'd been forced to admit to herself that she was strongly attracted to Otto von Geidel, and it appeared that he had every intention of continuing with the voyage until its bitter end, even though it was an open secret that he was Woodward's primary suspect in the Dom Perignon Saga.

Mid-August found the *Burgajet* off the Turkish coast. Shortly before the orders were given for her to turn about and begin her leisurely return westwards to Marbella, the 'Great Mutiny' occurred. While the yacht lay at anchor in an isolated and deserted bay, some of the Beautiful People – including Otto – finally disobeyed Woodward's interdict on nude sunbathing and swimming. Misty, who couldn't see what all the fuss was about, sided with the mutineers; Tubs joined them. There was a fracas, and Woodward somehow ended up fully clothed in the bay's crystal-clear waters. His peaked cap was lost. As far as he was concerned, von Geidel and Start became *personae non gratae*.

Woodward made the fatal mistake of presenting Tubs with an ultimatum: 'Either they go or the engagement's off.' He did not receive the answer he'd expected. Humiliated, he begged forgiveness; the *agents provocateurs* remained. After all, he was acutely aware that there was some connection between his engagement to Tubs and his father's plans for Woodward Brothers' merger with its Wall Street rival Avery, Avery & Avery. Paul, however, vowed revenge on Otto and Misty.

Save for her phone calls to American Express, Misty avoided communication with the outside world during the cruise, a policy reinforced when Woodwood showed her reports in the *Wall Street Journal* about SI's allegations of 'technology theft' against WSD concerning 'some goddam soap'. Naturally, she concluded that James and the rest of his family must be cursing her name, and would never want to hear from her again. As if to expunge the matter from her thoughts, seducing von Geidel swiftly became an obsession, albeit he manifested disinterest: scuba diving with his friend Franz and strumming a guitar dominated his waking hours. At Malta, however, Franz was taken off with suspected appendicitis. Thereafter, along the southern Sicilian coast, Otto finally began to succumb to Misty's charm offensive. Finally, in Sardinia's Golfo di Caglioni, they had passionate sex. On the very day she moved into Otto's cabin, the *Burgajet* set sail for Ibiza.

*

Dr Alphonse Audinette had an enviable list of patients – 'clients' as he preferred to call them – in and around Nice. A man of humble origins, he basked in their reflected glory, for he was not a physician of any great expertise. However, his good looks, charm and discretion – coupled with a large win on the French Lottery while still a medical student – had enabled him to buy a reputable practice in Villefranche-sur-Mer and build it up. Over the years, he had proved most useful to Lady Weetwood – both professionally and socially – and, in consequence, was not an infrequent guest at the *Villa Gobelin*. Indeed, at the very moment James was vomiting over Beryl, Audinette was entwined in the pool house with a leading French actress and her current boyfriend. Alerted by a waiter, Audinette was soon on the scene. Rapidly evaluating the situation, he administered a combination of injections and pills that rendered James comatose for almost twenty-four hours. Meanwhile, Beryl sped to England.

When James finally came round late the following day, Audinette was there to greet him. He played his part well and with a clear conscience: thanks to Beryl, he knew that since Peter's death James had indeed been suffering from a very deep depression, an illness for which he should have received treatment long ago. Furthermore, there'd been the trauma caused by the American girl, Misty; Beryl had learned all about that when she'd telephoned Bobbins to ascertain why on earth James was in France and to inform Mrs Duffle of her unscheduled return. Shocked by the news of James's 'breakdown', Vivian had told her mistress what she knew of his long, fruitless search in Paris, and his decision to follow Misty south to the Riviera. To this convenient cocktail of personal misery and angst, Audinette, judging by James's appearance, had added other presumed ingredients – the exhaustion of his trip, dehydration, heat, sun. In brief, it had all been too much for him.

As James tried to take in his unfamiliar surroundings, Audinette wanted to know what he could remember of his arrival at the villa. But so terrible were his recollections, he couldn't bring himself to speak of them. Had it all been just a hideous nightmare?

'How long have I been out?' asked James in a hoarse voice.

'About twenty-four hours. You were delirious and hysterical, James – what we doctors call "psychotic". Your poor mother was terrified. You said some dreadful things to her, you know.'

'Christ!'

'Now do not get the upset. You were being traumatized and–'

'I have these awful visions of horrible ... sexual ... *perversions*, Doctor, involving my mother and a ... well, a famous actor.'

'Yes, I know, James. I heard your ravings. But you see, none of that was real.'

'But it *seems* so real. I can see it so–'

'James, listen to me. Your actor was *not* here yesterday, I assure you. There were *no* actors here. Do you honestly believe Lady Weetwood could possibly be involved in ... in ...?'

'No – of course not. Jesus! What's wrong with me, Doctor? Am I losing my mind? ... Where's Mother now?'

Audinette got up from his chair and switched on the lights; the sun was sinking fast. He'd have to speed things up if he was going to make the dinner engagement in Monte Carlo with the couple with whom he'd had yesterday's threesome.

'No, James, you are not "losing your mind". And, on my advice, your mother returned to England this morning.'

'She must hate me.'

'No, you must not think that. She loves you very much – I almost had to order her to go. I feared that if you were to see her again before you were fully recovered, you might have another breakdown. You see, I think that deep in your subconscious you are trying to find someone to blame for the sadness that has engulfed you for so long. It is a woman, perhaps, who you blame for your friend's death. ... I think Lady Weetwood said he would not have got killed had he not gone to the ... how do you call it? – *la Poste* ...'

'The Post Office.'

'Exactly – had he not gone to the Post Office for you to post the card to your aunt, yes? And then it was this American girl who we hear about from your 'ousekeeper last night. She visits you in England and you think you fall in love. ... You sleep with her, perhaps?'

'Yes.'

'And then she leaves and you try to find her. And that is why you come to Nice.'

'Yes. ... Christ! She could still be here. I ought to be out looking for her. I've lost a whole day.' James tried to get out of bed, but he hardly had the strength to move.

'No, no, *mon ami*, you are in no state to go anywhere, and you have no passport, no money – nothing. You were robbed, yes?'

James nodded. 'On the train coming down here. Some drunk Danish bastards, I think.'

'So, you see, you must have complete rest and some good food. I think Madame Papet – the cook – will be bringing you something nice soon. ... Believe me, James, your hysteria yesterday against Lady Weetwood was just a manifestation of a temporary subconscious loathing of women projected onto the most important woman in your life ... the woman who brought you into the world, your mother.'

'You think so?'

'I *know* so.'

In his exhausted and confused state, James didn't require much persuasion to abide by the advice of this handsome and friendly physician,

141

namely, to remain at the villa under his care and enjoy its peace and charm for a week or two. If James was a prisoner, he was certainly unaware of it. Audinette's medication and daily counselling made him feel serene, safe and reassured – reassured that he was gradually recovering from a long illness. And in what better surroundings could one wish to convalesce? – an estate bathed in sunshine with breathtaking panoramas from every vantage point, not to mention the mouth-watering Provençal cooking of the formidable Madame Papet, a well-endowed lady of indeterminate age who looked as though she'd stepped straight out of a Toulouse-Lautrec poster for the *Moulin Rouge*.

The weeks drifted by, weeks of sunbathing, swimming, working out in the villa's gym and playing tennis with the young chauffeur, Jean-Luc. Whether it was his medication or the hypnotic effect of his surroundings, or a combination of the two, James gradually lost interest in leaving the estate. And as his exercise schedules became ever more demanding, so his thoughts of the outside world correspondingly receded. On one occasion, Audinette persuaded James to accompany him to Nice in order to buy him some new clothes, but the noise, traffic and crowds had not been to James's liking at all. It had been a relief to return to his haven on Cap-Ferrat.

Audinette claimed that Lady Weetwood was acutely concerned about James's progress – as indeed was his overworked father – and that she phoned every day to ascertain his progress. Audinette's firm advice was, nonetheless, that for the time being, mother and son should continue to have no direct contact. This suited James perfectly, as the only cloud on his horizon was the prospect of having to face her and apologize for all that had happened.

And so, by the end of August, a bronzed James had regained the superb muscular physique which he'd enjoyed before Peter's death. He was also at peace with both himself and the world.

# CHAPTER 13

'It's no good,' Caroline croaked, shaking her head. 'I just can't go any further – not another inch.'

She dismounted her bicycle and wiped the perspiration from her brow. Perhaps this wasn't such a good idea after all, she thought, as she wheeled the bike round to the north side of the old windmill and into the shade. She sat down on the rocky ground and, from her backpack, extracted a plastic bottle of mineral water wrapped in several carrier bags for insulation. She took a healthy swig.

'Good grief, the water's pretty warm too!'

After consuming almost half the bottle, she looked hard at a bag of crisps, but it was too hot to eat anything. Thank goodness she'd decided not to bring the Toblerone! She took another long swig of water, and then, realising she still had to cycle home, reluctantly replaced the top and put the bottle back.

Caroline began to take note of her surroundings; the view was breathtaking. From her hilltop vantage point a kilometre west of Formentera's 'capital', Sant Francesc, she could see much of the island. It lay shimmering under the scorching mid-August sun, strangely silent – save for the faint whistling of the light breeze through the windmill's sails. Looking northwards, the hillside of scorched, rough pastureland swept down to the small port of La Savina, with its little white houses and the stunning aquamarine of the Mediterranean – without doubt the most beautiful colour she'd ever seen. In truth, she'd gradually come to believe that whenever this sea lay before her, it was radiating some exotic energy force – a force which generated within her feelings of such utter contentment that she couldn't conceive of anything more pleasurable or uplifting which life might have to offer.

Leaving her bike, Caroline walked slowly round to the windmill's south side. Wincing as the full power of the sun hit her, she thought of the delicious shade of the *Villa Clementina*'s terrace. Could she see the villa from here? But, pulling down the brim of her hat in a vain attempt to reduce the glare, all she could see was the gently undulating landscape of parched fields, drystone walls and single-storey farmhouses extending several kilometres southwards to distant woods of stunted pines; beyond them, she guessed, would be the sea. She smiled: she'd be in the water like a shot on her return to *Clementina*!

Caroline retraced her steps to the shade, took out her map, and located the goal of her expedition, Punta de la Gavina on the island's rugged and near-desolate west coast. By her reckoning, it was only two kilometres distant. She looked up, and, edging around the windmill to get a better view, followed the coast south-westwards from La Savina. The scenery was bleak: exposed to the full force of the winter gales, not much grew along this part of the coast. ... But there it was – the elusive Martello tower! It stood isolated on a barren headland with waves crashing at its base. If there'd been a straight road or track, she could have cycled there in half an hour, but there was nothing marked on the map. Instead, it looked as though she'd have to cycle to La Savina, take a circuitous track along the coast, and then walk the last few hundred metres.

No, it was impossible: the heat was too fierce. And although she could probably freewheel most of the way down to La Savina, the long ride back up the hill to Sant Francesc would kill her. To reach the Torre de la Gavina, she'd have to set off at sunrise to avoid the midday heat. It was a shame, but she wasn't going to risk another attack of sunstroke!

How long ago all that misery seemed to her now. And yet it was only ... what, five weeks ago? ... six? ... What day was it anyway? ... She lay back against the old mill's stones, stretched out her legs, and patted them. They looked pretty brown, and, even though she said so herself, they were beginning to get quite firm. Good old Pierre! She turned to her beloved bike – a Peugeot Paris – and gave him a salute. She'd become very fond of him.

Back in England, she'd pictured herself closeted away in a magnificent library surrounded by priceless leather-bound volumes, mesmerised by her exciting research. Perhaps she'd be able to catch a few hours' sleep from time to time, and manage the occasional dinner with her hosts, Kurt and Teeny. She'd had expectations of unearthing some extraordinary historical data that would make her reputation and open doors, a research fellowship perhaps. Above all, her work would cement the bonds of friendship between Pongo and herself, for she'd been given a heaven-sent opportunity to repay the enormous debt she owed the great historian.

But things had not turned out at all as she'd expected. There'd been the dream-like ferry crossing on that crystal-clear July day, her first excited sightings of the Martello towers, the strange young German – she'd bumped into him a few times since, and gone to the funny little shop he'd recommended! – and then enigmatic Formentera itself appearing on the horizon. It had enchanted her from the moment she'd first set eyes on it. Yet, after that magical drive to the villa – she'd never forget her first view of the island's south coast for as long as she lived – there'd been the shock of

Teeny's dramatic departure and her abandonment in the large, lonely villa. And Kurt's mother was still hanging on by a thread!

Caroline was distracted by a lizard basking motionless only a few feet away. It appeared to be staring at her, but then it suddenly darted off and disappeared under a rock. In the past, anything like that would have terrified her, but here the lizards seemed such harmless little chaps. She chuckled, stretched again and tried to stifle a yawn. A sigh followed: despite the heat, she really ought to be getting back to *Clementina*. But then she remembered that Maria would probably still be there, performing her weekly comprehensive cleaning routine. Ah, so it must be Thursday!

Grinning broadly, Caroline shook her head from side to side. 'That was a stroke of genius – persuading Teeny to get Maria off my back!'

*

The first week at the villa had been impossible: Maria arrived around eight in the morning on a battered moped and departed at five p.m. – heretically foregoing a *siesta*. She dusted, mopped, polished, vacuumed and 'sang' continuously. Nowhere in the villa was safe. Breakfast and lunch were served according to a rigid timetable, whether or not Caroline was hungry or engaged in a complex piece of translation; for supper, a local dish – usually tasty, to be fair – was left for her to reheat. The villa's lack of air conditioning compounded the misery: on the third day the temperature reached 39 Celsius. To cap it all, her luggage had still not materialized, notwithstanding numerous phone calls to Iberia. It was, therefore, unsurprising that progress on the manuscripts was painfully slow. By Day Four of the purgatory, all she'd discovered was that the author, apparently Louis XIV, had enjoyed watching various courtiers perform acts of abnormal sexual intercourse – most were quite beyond Caroline's imagination – and had invented numerous words for parts of the body relevant thereto.

In desperation, she attempted working through the night, but the heat just put her to sleep. After five days she was at the end of her tether: she'd hardly been out of doors since her arrival and was beginning to fear Pongo's nightly phone calls for progress reports. So, on that fifth frustrating day when Teeny phoned from Buenos Aires, Caroline broke with tradition and poured out her heart. Teeny responded positively.

'Hey, Caroline, don't worry. I understand. ... Can you cook?'

'Sorry?'

'Can ... you ... *cook*?'

'Well, I've never really tried.'

'OK. So here's your chance. Look, I'll phone Maria and tell her you need absolute peace and quiet, and to come only once a week to do the

145

*cleaning and laundry. I don't suppose you'd mind a bit of dust around the place, would you?'*

'Of course not.'

*'Great. And as for food, just go into Sant Francesc and buy whatever takes your fancy – ham, fruit, eggs, fish. It's all there. OK?'*

'Super.'

*'Have you hired a car?'*

'A car? Well, no. I ... I don't drive.'

*'Oh! ... Right! ... Well, I could arrange for Felipe, our sort of handyman-cum-gardener, to take you in the Jeep.'*

'Ah, him. ... I think I've seen him loitering in the shrubbery. ... No – no thank you. I don't want to be a nuisance. I'll sort it out.'

*'OK ... if you're sure? ... Look, there's a small supermarket at Es Mal Pas. It's a fifteen-minute walk along the cliffs towards Platja de Migjorn – well, I guess you'll already have discovered it. It's near the old tower.'*

'Old tower?'

*'Come to think of it, there's a guy there, Lorenzo, who rents bikes and mopeds to tourists. Why don't you–?'*

Teeny sort of laughed. Caroline would never forget that horrid little laugh.

'Why don't I *what?*'

*'Oh nothing. It's just ...'*

'What?'

*'Well, I was going to suggest you hire a bike, but I have to confess I can't really see* you *on a bike, Caroline.'*

Something snapped inside her – it had been a tough week. 'Oh, *can't* you, Teeny?' And with those defiant words she put the phone down.

For a few minutes, Caroline paced around the 'drawing room' – as Teeny grandly called it – and then sat down heavily in an armchair. God, she felt depressed! The whole trip was turning into a nightmare. 'And why can't she see me on a bloody bicycle anyway!' The silence that followed her outburst was almost deafening; it exacerbated her negative thoughts. Here she was in an empty villa, miles from anywhere, hot, tired and devoid of all her personal belongings – she'd sue that beastly airline! – translating some seventeenth-century royal smut.

It was quite late by the time Caroline had worked the anger and bitterness out of her system. With a heavy sigh, she raised herself out of the armchair and went to shut the French windows. But just as she reached them, a most peculiar noise startled her. She stopped dead in her tracks. It was coming from outside and sounded like ... No, she had to be imagining it. ... But there it was again, and it did indeed sound like ... well, singing – a man and a woman if she wasn't mistaken – and they were singing in *English*!

Hesitantly, Caroline went out onto the terrace and descended the steps into the garden. The cicadas were chirping their chorus as usual, and waves were gently breaking beyond the garden wall, but otherwise all was quiet in the moonlight. Wondering whether she'd imagined the singing after all, Caroline decided to walk down one of the gravel paths towards the sea, but as she neared the low wall, she heard the singing again. And then, peering intently, she spotted two people walking slowly along the cliffs to her right, not more than fifty yards away. After a few seconds, they turned and passed through a gate in the garden wall of the neighbouring villa; she'd thought it was shut up, but now she noticed that lights were burning on its terrace.

To get a better view, Caroline moved closer to the wall that separated the adjoining properties. As the couple climbed some steps to the terrace, it was the man who stood out first: he was wearing a white dinner jacket and black bow tie. The woman, who appeared to be engulfed in acres of pink chiffon, held a long cigarette holder. They sat down at a table and poured themselves what looked like champagne from an ice bucket. The sound carried well on the still evening air.

'But, Tom, darling, the first line is "I'm walking backwards for *Easter* across"–'

'Don't be ridiculous, darling, it isn't. How could it be? It's "I'm walking backwards for *Christmas* across the *Irish* Sea". And it was Spike Milligan who used to sing it, not Peter Sellers. You've had too much Rioja, darling.'

Hidden behind a large cactus, Caroline really couldn't believe what she was hearing. It all seemed so surreal. And yet there was something extraordinarily familiar about the woman's voice. She'd definitely heard it many times before. But how? Where? Perhaps she could get a closer look.

A rustling noise suddenly froze Caroline to the spot. Something was moving about in the garden. A cat? ... A rabbit? ... Her imagination began to generate pictures of things far worse – snakes, for example. They had snakes on Formentera, didn't they? Hadn't she read that somewhere? And scorpions! ... *Scorpions*? ... What about rabid dogs? – almost bound to! And rapists.

'Oh cripes,' she hissed, 'there it is again! Something was definitely moving towards her. There really was no alternative.

'Hello!' she shouted, darting around the cactus. 'Yes, I'm over here – *here* by the wall. Help me! ... *Please*!'

*

147

Caroline gave Pierre another pat and straightened her back against the windmill's stones. 'You know,' she said, 'on reflection, I was really quite phlegmatic.'

Giggling, she glanced at her watch: almost a quarter to three. If she left now, by the time she got back to *Clementina*, Maria would probably have finished her chores. She could have a quick dip and then spend an hour or two working on the manuscripts before cooking supper. Oh, how happy and fit she felt – *very* fit! She stroked her calf muscles and looked at Pierre.

'We're a good team, you and me. We've travelled some miles on this island, haven't we? If it hadn't been for Teeny's sarcasm ... well, we'd never have become friends, would we?' She smiled fondly at him and then glanced back down the track towards Sant Francesc.

A man and a woman – both elderly, very tanned, and clad only in swimming costumes – were cycling up the hill towards her. She guessed they were about seventy. 'I bet you anything, Pierre, they're German.' They eventually came to a halt in front of her, dismounted and said in unison, '*Guten Tag!*'

'*Bon dia*,' Caroline replied in the local dialect. They looked confused and wheeled their cycles around to the windmill's south side.

Her solitude destroyed, Caroline reconsidered the pros and cons of setting off for *Clementina*, but decided to rest just a bit longer. In any event, the butcher in Sant Francesc wouldn't be open until four, and she wanted some chicken fillets for supper. Chicken fillets! ... Good Lord! That reminded her of the very first meal she'd cooked and the momentous day when Pierre had come into her life.

*

Caroline's unusual and unscheduled introduction to Tom and Gwen Blackberry – the champagne-drinking neighbours – gave them such a shock. However, they'd rushed over and stumbled round *Clementina*'s grounds like bulls in a china shop. Tom had returned for a torch while Gwen had smothered Caroline protectively in chiffon and Chanel N°5. But whatever had been tracking her in the garden proved elusive. They'd probably frightened 'it' away, Gwen asserted brightly.

Gwen Blackberry! – Jessica Muffin of *The Muffins*! No wonder Caroline had recognised her voice. She'd slept like a log that night, thanks to Gwen's tumbler of brandy – thus ended Caroline's abstinence – and the loan of a mosquito appliance: hers had been packed in the 'mislaid' suitcase, and she hadn't found anything remotely similar in the villa. And so, early the next morning, refreshed and revitalized, Caroline marched off down to the cliff path, turned left and headed east in search of the neighbouring *pueblo* and Teeny's bike-rental chap. It hadn't taken long, however, for the landscape to bewitch her. After reminding herself that she didn't have a train to catch, she stopped and looked around.

It was simply wonderful. Ahead stretched a gently curving bay, some five or six miles long – sandy for the most part and backed by dunes and pine woods. At the far end, she could just make out a long, low building – probably a hotel – and halfway along the crescent, about two miles distant, was a four-storey block – clearly a hotel. But otherwise, apart from some villas, there seemed to be little in the way of development; there was certainly no sign of a *pueblo*.

The cliff path, which proceeded above a narrow sandy beach – it was only half past eight and still deserted – eventually descended into dense pine woods. After a few minutes, Caroline rounded a small point and came to the mouth of a narrow valley. Her heart jumped, for on the far side, beyond a cluster of villas and *tavernas*, was a Martello tower! It seemed almost magnetic; it begged to be explored. She marched down the wooded hillside and found herself in sleepy Es Mal Pas.

Outside Lorenzo's hire shop, the white and blue Peugeot Paris gleamed in the morning sunshine; Caroline immediately knew she wanted him. Adjustments to saddle and handlebars were made, tyres pumped up, and paper work signed. Hesitantly at first and out of sight of prying eyes, she cycled for twenty minutes along the dirt tracks in the adjoining woods to reacquaint herself with the almost forgotten techniques of cycling. And then, at the little *supermercado* – the beach almost reached its front door – she stocked up with whatever took her fancy – including chicken fillets – and bought a large-scale map of the island and a commodious backpack. She re-emerged into the morning sunshine equipped and ready for adventure.

As the weeks passed, she settled into a happy routine. Her days at the villa would invariably commence at six-thirty with an hour of translating the manuscripts, followed by a swim with Gwen from the rocks just beyond their garden walls: 'It's the best way to get rid of a hangover, darling!' Caroline had tried desperately to wriggle out of it at first – she'd hated her swimming lessons at Burgers in the icy-cold college pool – but Gwen was not a woman to take no for an answer.

After a light breakfast, Caroline would set off on her bicycle, her goal being to explore every part of the island. Above all, she wanted to visit all four of its Martello towers and the two lighthouses. At first, the cycling had been agony: for a couple of days she'd hardly been able to sit down after her bumpy rides along the rocky tracks. She'd also got badly burnt – and experienced a mild dose of sunstroke. But she persisted. Slowly but surely, her unused muscles developed and the pains subsided. Gwen's extensive range of sun creams and after-sun-care products also assisted in the nurturing of a respectable golden tan – her first ever. By the end of her second week on the island, she was coping well with the heat – and had lost almost ten pounds.

The afternoons would be spent in the relative cool of *Clementina*'s library. Despite occasionally nodding off, she invariably managed to get a couple of hours' work done. Five o'clock would bring her back out into the sun and a further hour's swimming with Gwen, either from the rocks or down at the beach just five minutes' walk away along the cliffs. The nudism had at first horrified Caroline; had she read her guidebook carefully before leaving England, she might have been forewarned by the references to the ability to obtain an 'all-over-tan' when holidaying on the island. She soon discovered that nudity was the norm – whole families gambled naked together – and as the days passed, she began to tolerate – and then accept – this behaviour. Indeed, after a while the few people who did attract her attention on the beach were those who were conventionally attired; they looked strangely out of place. On the other hand, there was something quite beautiful about the innocence of the naked children running in and out the water, and playing so happily with their naked parents – without the least concern or embarrassment. And yet, she could never bring herself to discard the floral one-piece bathing costume that Gwen had loaned her. But then Gwen was no naturist herself.

'Oh, Caroline, don't be silly,' she chided one afternoon on the beach in reply to a query about her modesty. 'It's all right for you young people, but when you get to my age, darling, best to cover up. Believe me, it's *not* a pretty sight. Just look at those wrinkled old Germans over there and you'll see what I mean!'

Caroline's culinary skills also developed dramatically. From fried bacon and tomatoes, she graduated – with several disasters on the way – to tasty casseroles and composite salads. Soon, she was even cooking steaks and chops on the villa's barbecue. The frequent invitations from Gwen and Tom to dine at bizarrely-named *Honeysuckle Cottage* had proved useful, for Caroline would always be press-ganged into service. To her surprise, Gwen was a good cook – she seemed to get through a bottle of wine before anything reached the table – and, by watching her at work, she'd learned how to prepare quite a few succulent dishes. In fact, she sometimes surprised herself, and when she finally invited the Blackberrys round for her very first 'dinner party', their praise – together with unaccustomed hugs and kisses – brought tears to her eyes. If only her own parents had been like them, she'd reflect sadly.

In the evenings, Caroline would usually work for another hour or two after dinner – unless she got frogmarched round to *Honeysuckle Cottage* for a game of cards; Gwen thought she spent too much time on her own. Caroline scoffed, but, in truth, there were evenings when, sat at the huge desk in the library, trying to concentrate on the wretched manuscripts, she would sometimes wish that Tom or Gwen would pop over and ask her to join their little party of guests whose laughter would be drifting over on the balmy air. Gwen would probably be amusing them with more of her indiscreet reminiscences of BBC stars, and Caroline would picture Tom sitting with his glass of cognac laughing as happily as the others, even though he'd undoubtedly heard them all so many times before.

*

Caroline had almost dozed off when the sounds of a vehicle chugging up the hill from the direction of Sant Francesc brought her round with a sudden jerk. The wind had got up, and she could see white water out at sea. She squinted at her watch; it was almost four.

'Good grief, Pierre! It's time to go. With this wind behind us, we should make *Clementina* by five, even allowing for a stop at the butcher's. We mustn't miss our swim with Gwen, must we?'

An old VW van came into view to her right. *Probably hippies from the commune*, Caroline mused. Tongue-in-cheek, that was what Gwen would say of anyone with long hair, ripped jeans, sandals and beads who walked along the cliff-top path. She'd told Caroline about a whole crowd who'd come to the island in the Sixties. Many had never left, and most of the survivors – and their offspring – still lived around El Pilar on the desolate eastern plateau. They socialized at the Fonda Pepe in Sant Ferran, 'an institution with something of a reputation' as Gwen had described it.

The battered VW reached the top of the hill just as Caroline mounted her bike. Through the glare of the windscreen, she could just make out the driver. There was something odd about him, and as the rising wind began to rattle the windmill's sails, she experienced a strange sense of apprehension. The van pulled up in front of her, and the driver turned his head to face her. She gasped.

With a tremendous screech, the back doors burst open. A man – or was it a woman? – jumped out and ran to the driver's side. It had to be some kind of joke: they were both wearing gorilla masks. The man – it had to be a man, surely? – shouted something at Caroline and waved his hand. What was he holding? ... Without thinking, she began to smile nervously, but the man shouted again, gesticulating wildly. He seemed to be telling her to get in! Then she realized that the thing in his hand looked like a gun. Suddenly, he froze.

*Was ist los?*' yelled someone behind her.

Caroline yelped, but before she could turn round, the figure with the gun ran round to the front passenger door and jumped in as the van jerked forward violently. Gears crashed as the VW did a clumsy three-point turn, and then, with its rear doors still wide open and banging noisily, careered back down the bumpy track.

A hand gripped Caroline's shoulder. She spun round.

'*Was ist los, Fräulein*? Vot – is – zee – problem?'

The two elderly cyclists in swimming costumes were standing before her, wide-eyed and looking very concerned.

# CHAPTER 14

Just fifteen minutes before the expiry of the deadline specified in the letter from Swinehart, Crudge, Idol & Purkey, Ben Turbot of Grimshaws faxed his reply to Fancourt Utley, SI's London solicitors. A few hours later, Mr Perry Match of Fancourts was on the telephone expressing surprise that WSD were not using their London solicitors, Bragge & Crow, who were 'conveniently situated', as he put it, only a few minutes' walk away. And then he got down to business.

'Very sad your clients couldn't be reasonable about this, Mr Turbot. As we see it, they really haven't got a leg to stand on. We've an *excellent* opinion from Sir Tudor Mudwort-Welch, QC. *Outstanding* chap, don't you think? Who've you instructed?'

'We haven't felt the need to instruct Counsel yet, Mr Match.'

'Really? How *extraordinary*! Well, I'm afraid you're going to have to do so now. In anticipation of your chaps being uncooperative, we've had our writ and notice of motion issued. The hearing for our interlocutory injunction is next Thursday – before Mr Justice Bunker. We've prepared a few affidavits in support. Actually, my secretary's just gone off to fax them to you – to give you as much time as possible to prepare your case.'

'Too kind!'

For most of the following week, Turbot and his assistant spent much of their time closeted in meetings at Soap House with Lord Weetwood, Merryweather and Chopping. They read through the plaintiff's affidavits together, and sought agreement on how to respond. An affidavit should only contain information within the deponent's own knowledge: it should contain facts, not speculation and flights of fancy. Mr Match, however, had few – if any – qualms about bending rules: as far as he was concerned, everything boiled down to whether a particular course of conduct would help his client's case. And so, the affidavits which he and his large team of assistants had drafted for SI's executives were littered with innuendo, half-truths and gratuitous prejudice. Indeed, George barely recognized himself or his company from the pages of this testimony. A great British institution – a household name synonymous with quality and integrity for over a century, and suppliers of soap to the Queen of the United Kingdom – was reduced in these vitriolic pages to no more than an amoral leech. The peer of the realm who controlled this monster fared little better.

153

'This is outrageous!' exclaimed George during one stormy session in his office. 'Can't we sue for libel, Mr Turbot? I mean, how can this wretched little tick' – he turned to the affidavit's first page – 'Evanston Oakbrook – the names of these Americans! – who calls himself 'Chief Finance Officer', well, how can he say *this*?

'"*From my examination of the Defendant's accounts, I verily believe that the sums expended by the Defendant on research and development during the last five years are grossly disproportionate to the Defendant's Net Asset Value, and that such expenditure clearly indicates a reckless disregard for sound and established corporate financial practices. I also verily believe that as the Defendant has been under the control and chairmanship of Lord Weetwood at all material times, he is responsible for such recklessness, and that, therefore, his competence and abilities must be seriously doubted.*"

'I mean, what has my "competence" got to do with *any* of this?'

Merryweather, shaking his head theatrically at Mr Oakbrook's unbridled insolence, said: 'It's irrelevant, of course, Chairman, whether you're competent or incompetent.'

'Exactly,' added Chopping. 'And there's some pretty nasty stuff about me, too, in this ... this farrago of lies. Dash it all, I'm only the Finance Director!'

'I really wouldn't worry about all this guff,' Turbot said soothingly. 'Judges are used to it. The fact is that whatever you've spent on Project Troll – whether wisely or not – WSD has a very healthy balance sheet. The judge will see that from the most cursory glance at your accounts. Let's move on.'

But not all the allegations could be dismissed so lightly: at the centre of the case against WSD was Luke Nickel's key affidavit. In most respects it appeared to be an accurate – albeit sanitized – account of how he came to meet Pesto, learn of her invention, and introduce her to WSD. But as for her decision to abandon her 'well-rewarded employment' with SI, animal testing went unmentioned: she'd been lured away by Lord Weetwood's seemingly generous offer and her desire to be with her lover.

Nickel's decision to 'confess' to the Plaintiff was simply a question of guilt and remorse according to his affidavit. His wife's death – he stuck to the salmonella story – had made him realize how foolish and immoral he'd been: but for his inciting Ms Pesto to breach her contractual and fiduciary duties, she would never have gone to Uruguay and would, in all probability, still be alive. And what was in it for him? Nothing – or to be precise, nothing more than he could have expected to receive from the Defendant: he swore that SI had simply undertaken that if its claim were successful, it would pay him royalties on the same terms as those contained in his agreement with WSD.

'I don't believe a word of it,' George snapped huffily. 'I bet they've paid him a tidy sum.'

'Perhaps he really did have some kind of religious experience after Pesto's death,' Merryweather said without any hint of sarcasm, '– "seen the Light" and all that nonsense. Americans are prone to do that sort of thing, aren't they?'

'Didn't seem the type, I must say,' George muttered.

'Mad, bad or otherwise,' Turbot said, keen to make progress, 'do we object to any of his factual statements? Incidentally, you'll note he says nothing about Soda Flats.'

'I must stress again, Mr Turbot,' George responded, 'that Miss Pesto painted quite a frightening picture of her employment there, and we were left in no doubt as to the ruthlessness of her then employers. As I recollect it, she was gripped by fear and felt she was a mere chattel, so to speak – that SI would never allow her to leave their employment. I think she even said her life might be in danger. ... Yes, I'm *quite* sure that's what she said. Naturally, we concluded that the risks involved in her giving proper notice to SI were far too great. Actually, the more I think about it, the more convinced I am that we acted in Miss Pesto's very best interests when I sanctioned the plan to extricate her from the nightmare to which she was being subjected.'

'Very true,' Merryweather added with appropriate gravity.

Turbot looked dubious. 'Hmm. ... We'll concoct something along those lines for your affidavit, Lord Weetwood. Pity Barmcake isn't here to back it up.'

'What a tragedy,' George intoned. 'To be fair, I should say that most of the plan to ... er ... to help Miss Pesto and provide her with a new identity, well, it was Ernest's idea – always was an ideas man, dear old Ernest. If only he were here now, he'd have some jolly good ideas on defending these extraordinary claims.'

'Barmcake?' queried Chopping with obvious incredulity. 'One shouldn't speak ill of the dead, but that's the first–'

'I know ... er, David, what you're going to say,' George interjected, '– that we took him for granted – never gave him sufficient credit for his achievements and successes during his many years of loyal service to the company he loved. Yes, I'm as guilty as the next man.'

'That's interesting,' Turbot said, 'because Nickel clearly states that the plan to spirit Pesto away–'

*My God, why does the wretched man keep using that infuriating expression?*

155

'– was proposed by you, Lord Weetwood.'

'Of course it was *proposed* by me at the *meeting*, Mr Turbot – I was chairing it. But it was Mr Barmcake's *idea*. I thought I'd made that quite clear.'

They moved on, and as they waded through Fancourts' mountain of paper, they learned that, in addition to Nickel's non-technical description of Ms Pesto's invention, he'd also provided SI with some notebooks he'd found in their Montevideo house after her death. Copies were exhibited, but WSD's technical people doubted that, in themselves, they would greatly assist SI to manufacture 'Pestex' – as SI still insisted on calling the invention.

As for Sonny Start's affidavit, George branded it one of the greatest works of fiction he'd ever read, although, in truth, he was not a great reader of anything except corporate documentation and railway timetables. According to Start, SI was a world-class company at the forefront of technology in all its numerous product divisions. He also claimed that any properly managed undertaking which had proprietorship of an invention would, in his experience, take at least the preliminary steps to obtain patent protection. In the present case, where the Defendant had clearly invested hundreds of millions of pounds, the decision to do nothing to patent Pestex prior to notification of the Plaintiff's claim was explicable only if WSD believed it had no rights in the invention at all – in other words, that to seek a patent would expose its unlawful activities.

'So, chaps, how do we answer that one?' asked Turbot, grinning cheekily. 'Daventry, when we spoke about the patent issue at the outset, you said that it was "perfectly straightforward" – Lord Weetwood and his predecessors have always had an antipathy towards patents, and that the company doesn't own *any*, in fact. Is that right?'

Merryweather looked sheepishly at the Chairman. 'Um ... yes. Obviously, I've always been able to identify the advantages and disadvantages of patenting, and, when appropriate, I've set out the arguments – for and against – in my submissions to the board. On this occasion I–'

'Daventry,' George interrupted, 'could you pop out and ask Miss Spigot for some fresh coffee, please? Oh, and some mineral water for me? ... Thanks.'

Suitably humbled, the Company Secretary padded out of the room.

'Now, where were we?' queried George rhetorically. 'Ah, yes – the patent issue. ... Daventry is on the right track, Mr Turbot, in that both my father and grandfather regarded patents as a complete waste of time and money – at least in the soap business. And, in brief, that's my own view too. Of course, I'm no intellectual property lawyer, Mr Turbot, but I do have over thirty years' *practical* experience, and I think that counts for something.'

'Naturally.'

'And the proof of the pudding is in the eating, as they say.'

'Indeed.'

'Well, as is self-evident, my company has prospered without patents. After all, a patent is only worth anything if one's prepared to enforce it – to sue infringers. And then the other side say, "Oh but your patent is invalid. Mr So-and-So invented the same thing in Canada decades ago." Or, "This isn't an invention at all! It's just a cobbling together of bits of technology that have been lying around for ages." So, one spends a fortune battling it out and making you chaps rich, Mr Turbot. And if one doesn't win, then every Tom, Dick and Harry can just go and buy a copy of one's patent and exploit the technology described in it for nothing.'

'Well, that's one point of view, Lord Weetwood,' Turbot said drily. 'You sound as though you speak from bitter experience.'

'Indeed I do. I once made the mistake of ignoring the wisdom handed down to me and reluctantly agreed to my company filing a patent for some low-lather automatic powder. In fact, Barmcake was the inventor, if I remember correctly. We ended up in litigation with Lever Brothers. It lasted ten years. Frankly, I think each side forgot what we were really fighting about.

'Anyway, Mr Turbot, on balance in *this* business – something like pharmaceuticals may be different, I grant you – *secrecy* is the keyword. Do you know, we're still manufacturing Goblin soap with the same unique and highly distinctive fragrance which would have been familiar to Queen Victoria? Manufacturers across the globe have tried to reproduce it. As far as I'm aware, none has succeeded – not even got close to it. The formula is still *secret*.

'Mr Turbot, it doesn't cost much to spend a bit of time recruiting the right chaps – people of principle, integrity and loyalty – and get them to sign clear and simple secrecy agreements. As a matter of fact, we're still using the masterpieces of clarity drafted by Charles Grimshaw – ooh ... how many years ago, Daventry?'

Merryweather had just padded back to his seat. 'Our standard Secrecy Agreement, Chairman? ... Er ... before my time.'

'Yes, well anyway, it's certainly stood the *test* of time. You can keep your patents, Mr Turbot – devise and implement rigorous and effective security systems, operate on a 'need-to-know' basis, and, as I said a few moments ago, build a trustworthy workforce. That's the Weetwood System – and by Jove, it works.'

The days passed, and George grew more confident. He began to scent Victory. He had answers for everything, and as he read Turbot's first draft, and subsequent redrafts, of his own affidavit – George constantly thought of improvements – he came to believe everything stated in them with absolute conviction. It was as he'd always thought: he and the company had acted with complete integrity throughout.

Maintaining his invariable practice of keeping clients' evidence succinct, Turbot prepared just four brief affidavits. Lord Weetwood's highlighted Miss Pesto's dire plight, detonating the bombshell of 'the Soda Flats Secret'. There were also punchy paragraphs explaining how Miss Pesto had come to the company with 'a mere germ of an idea' – something vaguely connected with the almost-laughable teapot experiment back in New Jersey – and how WSD plc, a pillar of British Industry emblazoned by its Royal Warrants, had devoted thousands of man hours and expended hundreds of millions of pounds to improve, enhance and develop this little fragile seed into commercially exploitable technology. And anyway, Miss Pesto's American contracts of employment had been 'oppressive'; their invention and secrecy clauses were, moreover, void.

As for Nickel, what faith could one have in his evidence concerning the crucial timing of the invention and the work undertaken by Miss Pesto prior to her joining WSD? Her death was tragic, but after receiving reports from Dr Mark Dumpwell – WSD's 'senior employee in Uruguay' – Lord Weetwood had inevitably concluded that Nickel had experienced some kind of breakdown: he'd alleged that WSD was responsible for Pesto's demise and had sworn vengeance against her former employer. There was a short confirmatory affidavit to this effect from Dumpwell. Merryweather's affidavit reinforced the section in the Chairman's dealing with WSD's patenting policy. Chopping deposed to the robust financial strength of the mighty WSD Group: it was good for any damages.

Mr Match was very unhappy when he received these affidavits; he telephoned Ben Turbot to tell him so. He said they were 'a joke'. Then he got quite heated. He said that the references to his clients being involved in secret tests on animals at Soda Flats were 'scandalous' and 'probably actionable'. His voice was raised. He threatened to postpone the hearing as he needed time to deal with 'these scurrilous lies.'

'You have four full days, Mr Match,' Turbot pointed out calmly. 'By the way, I received yet another *unsworn* affidavit from you today. Do you really believe the Court will be interested in a statement from a former WSD nightwatchman who alleges that he once heard Lord Weetwood "chuffing along the corridors of Soap House pretending to be a train."?'

The hearing was not postponed, but the day beforehand, another bundle of unsworn affidavits arrived from Fancourts purporting to deal with all the contentious points in the Defendant's evidence. There was only one important rebuttal: as expected, Mr Start categorically denied that there had ever been any animal research conducted 'by the Plaintiff or by any of its associated companies, whether at Soda Flats or elsewhere.' In Mr Match's accompanying letter there were threats of proceedings if 'the Soda Flats allegations' were repeated. On the other hand, there were no counter-allegations that WSD had itself been involved in animal testing. George was cock-a-hoop: his gamble had paid off. Either Nickel had not told the Americans, or if he had, they were afraid to pour oil on an already burning fire.

Mr Justice Bunker disliked excessive affidavit evidence in interlocutory proceedings in general, and both Mr Perry Match and Tudor Mudwort-Welch, QC, in particular. He did not, however, allow these phobias to cloud his judgement. And while he certainly did not believe that the Plaintiff's case was nonsense, or that the Defendant was whiter than white, he was persuaded that the balance of convenience lay in the Defendant's favour. Consequently, he dismissed SI's application for an injunction. For the next few days, Perry Match made the lives of his assistants and secretary unbearable.

*

Before his receipt of Lord Weetwood's affidavit, Mr Match had excelled himself with numerous press releases about the litigation, which just managed to stay on the right side of the law. The *Financial Times*, therefore, decided to report the dispute in some detail, and the Defendant's Soda Flats revelations proved manna from heaven. Although SI issued press releases containing denials and blistering condemnations of animal testing, its stock fell sharply. As a result, FoamFay's launch achieved far greater notoriety than would otherwise have been the case. However, but for Beryl's last-minute intervention, it would not have been such a grand affair. Her unexpected return to Bobbins from the South of France ten days before the court hearing had stunned her husband, who'd been anticipating a deliciously solitary existence for most of the summer. And matters were exacerbated by Beryl's insistence on repeating *ad nauseam* the reasons for cutting short her stay at the *Villa Gobelin*.

Although George found it difficult to comprehend exactly what she was trying to tell him, it appeared that their son had suffered a 'right proper' nervous breakdown triggered by his infatuation with the Start girl, who he'd been chasing around Paris. Apparently, after his fruitless searches for her there, he'd somehow made his way to Cap-Ferrat. Filthy, unshaven and 'high on something', he'd materialized unannounced, screaming obscenities at Beryl and destroying whatever he could lay his hands on. When restrained, he'd struggled with such ferocity and been so foul-mouthed she would have thought him possessed by the Devil – had she believed in such things. Doctors – the very best the Côte d'Azur could muster – had been summoned. They'd diagnosed a whole host of psychiatric disorders. But perhaps the worst aspect of James's tragic illness was his vile hallucinations about Beryl herself. They were too awful for her to detail; it was sufficient to say that they were of a perverted sexual nature. As Beryl had anticipated, George had no desire to know more.

'I'm beginning to wonder whether that treacherous Miss Start wilfully endeavoured to engineer a family crisis,' George ventured to suggest during the first account of James's 'breakdown' over dinner on the day of Beryl's return. 'Frankly ... er, Beryl, I'm surprised you didn't smell a rat when she first spoke to you on the telephone to arrange her stay here. Perhaps the boy should return home. I suppose you've put him in some clinic or other in Nice?'

'Don't try and blame me for this carve up, George! Anyway, as I understand it, everything that "Misty" creature told me was true. You're the chump who entertained her here at the very moment her bloody father was writing a snotty letter to you – not that I've understood one word of your babbling about all that nonsense. As for James, the doctors said travel would be very unsettling for him. Anyway, he hasn't got a passport.'

George raised his eyebrows.

'All we could get out of him was something about a group of drug-crazed Scandinavians mugging him on a train somewhere or other. We've got the Consul in Nice running round in circles trying to procure a new one.'

'New what?'

'Passport of course!'

'Ah.'

'Anyway, *darling*, the poor boy is at the villa getting plenty of peace and quiet. I just hope he recovers and gets back to normal – *soon*.'

George looked up as he devoured the last roast potato in the tureen: he really couldn't remember Beryl calling him 'darling' before – ever. In any event, at least she hadn't countermanded his instructions to Mrs Duffle on the food front: they'd dined on roast beef with all the traditional trimmings.

'Shouldn't you have stayed with him?' he ventured.

'Good heavens, no! The doctors feared that if he saw me again in his current deranged state ... well, they wouldn't be answerable for the consequences.'

'I see.'

Vivian Duffle entered with a bread-and-butter pudding. She looked decidedly uncomfortable.

With an exaggerated smile, Beryl said: 'Ah, more good old English fare!'

'I'm sorry, your Ladyship, but it's what his Lordship asked for.'

'Of course, of course, Mrs Duffle! I must say it's a jolly nice change from the somewhat over-spiced Provençal food I've had to cope with recently. My husband must have what he wants.'

Vivian almost dropped a plate as she cleared the remnants of the main course from the table. 'So, *you'd* like a portion, ma'am? I could go and rustle up something special for you if you like.'

'Wouldn't hear of it, Mrs Duffle. No, I'd love some of your famous bread-and-butter pudding. And is that custard I spy? Splendid! Put plenty on mine, please. Now, George, I've had a very interesting chat with Mrs Duffle and she's been telling me all the news. I'd simply no idea you were having such a frightful time here. Why on earth didn't you phone and tell me? Not only those beastly Americans wanting to sue the company, but also the Roberta Weetwood destroyed by an explosion, and masses of preparation for the launch of some new product thing. But you're not to worry, *darling*, because *I'm* home and I'm going to *help*. Now, for a start let's prioritise. Numero Uno in my book is the party.'

'*Party?*'

'Yes, of course – for the launch of whatever it is!'

'Well, it's just for some journalists coming up from London and our foreign distributors ... and the representatives of some of our overseas subsidiaries ... and a few people from our professional advisers. Miss Spigot's organizing everything.'

'Oh my God! Who's she got for the food?'

And so began Beryl's takeover of the FoamFay Launch.

Miss Spigot's economical affair involved Slattocks, a firm of caterers in Oldham, whose cold buffet in the Directors' Dining Room at Soap House was to have been accompanied by cheap and cheerful Beaujolais and Muscadet. It was all cancelled. Instead, Beryl devised a banquet of regal proportions in a marquee on the lawn at Bobbins. With their meal, those privileged to be invited – particularly the self-important and pretentious London hacks – enjoyed Pétrus 87 and Montrachet 86. With pudding – a rather superb crème brûlée flavoured with lavender – nothing less than Château Yquem 86 would do. And thus, when the guests finally departed, it was in a golden glow of serene contentment, as golden as the exquisite Sauternes they'd consumed. Most of them fell asleep aboard the luxury coaches which returned them to Manchester Airport for the final legs of their respective all-expenses-paid trips. With print deadlines looming, there was, however, the problem of having to write something sensible for their papers. But what could they remember of a day that had started with Dom Perignon 85 at 10:30 a.m. as they started their tour of the Goblin works? Their scribbled notes of plankton and interlocutory injunctions were intermingled with now meaningless figures which might – or might not – relate to bars of soap produced per month or per annum ... or perhaps to tonnages of raw materials consumed per week at the Kenyan? ... Sri Lankan? ... factory. Dear, oh dear – it was all such a muddle! Thank God for the extremely lucid handouts WSD had given them.

Consequently, in the days following the launch, Britain's financial, trade and technical press hailed FoamFay as a miracle product. It was without doubt the dazzling technological achievement of a Great British Industrial Giant. SI's litigation was dismissed as 'sour grapes'. The rest of the world took up the story almost verbatim.

There was one reporter, however, who did not leave Beryl's binge in an alcoholic stupor. *The Sun*'s Diane Bradbury was an ambitious young lady, who, being both a vegetarian and a teetotaller, had escaped the marquee's heat as soon as she'd consumed a few crudités and some iced Malvern water. Having ambled down the gravel drive, a turning to the left led her to what she was seeking – the former stables, now garages for the Weetwoods' vehicles. In the courtyard, Ron Duffle was sat on a folding chair by the gleaming Jaguar he'd just finished polishing. A plate of smoked salmon – leftovers from the 'do' as he called it – was on his knees. Putting on her best antipodean accent, Diane introduced herself as 'Patsy Pinkerton' of Goblin Australia Pty.

Ron had a fascinating conversation with 'Patsy'. How the time flew! She seemed so interested in him and his work, and her charm rapidly disarmed him. She heard stories of a mad heir to the Weetwood Empire – a son who'd locked himself away in the dark, brooding house behind them for over two years, who – at this very moment – was incarcerated in some French 'lunatic asylum', having attempted to murder his own mother. There were tales of an introverted boffin of a daughter, who was such an embarrassment to the family that she'd been banished to a remote Spanish island for the summer. And sex-mad, rapacious Lady Weetwood couldn't bear to be in the same room as her frigid husband; it was anyone's guess what she got up to in the South of France. As for Lord Weetwood ... well, he was probably the nuttiest of the whole family.

'Do you know,' Ron whispered, leaning closer to Ms Bradbury to get a better view of her fine cleavage, 'he's slept alone on a camp bed for the last twenty years with just his bloody train set for company? You can hear it at night – whistles and steam engines and train announcements like' – Duffle imitated a female announcer affecting a posh voice – '"The nine-twenty express to Glasgow will be the next train to arrive at platform eight." Bloody crackers, if you ask me.'

'And this is the man in charge of our Group?' queried Ms Bradbury rhetorically, shaking her head.

Duffle gave her a comforting pat on the knee. ''fraid so, love.'

But there was more evidence of the madness which the Chairman had so cleverly concealed from the outside world. Diane was sworn to secrecy.

'I heard Weetwood out in the garden late at night a few weeks back.'

'Yes?'

'I were doing me rounds, making sure everything were locked up an' all, and ... well there he was – on the terrace – acting all peculiar like. Shouting his head off, he were.'

'Really?'

'Oh aye – absolutely barking – shouting he was a mass murderer – that he'd killed millions.'

'Millions? ... Millions of *what*?'

Duffle looked at her incredulously. 'Well, *people* of course.'

'Christ!'

'Hold yer horses, love, there's more. Now don't ask me 'ow I know, but between you, me and the gatepost, he's planning to evict everyone from Goblinville and sell both it and the whole bloody Group to the Germans – and they're going to turn it into a Kraut holiday camp!'

Sadly, Diane was succumbing to doubts about Duffle's own sanity, and, in consequence, the credibility of everything he'd told her. Perhaps he was a disgruntled employee working out his notice.

'Stone the crows!' she finally managed. 'Goblinville ... that's the cute little fantasy town we drove through on the coaches this morning – with the bombed-out theatre?'

'Ah ha! I notice you say "bombed-out".'

'Yeah, well I've read that the police are almost certain now it was a bomb of some sort.'

'And who do you think blew up the Roberta Weetwood?'

'I've no idea.'

'Guess.'

'I really haven't a clue.'

'Well, *I* know.' Ron looked at her triumphantly and tapped her knee twice.

'You do?'

He nodded and looked around conspiratorially. 'It's obvious – the Germans, of course!'

163

'The Germans? *Which* Germans?'

'The ones who want to buy Goblinville – Schnittblumen and Whatsits. You must 'ave 'eard of them, lass? They make them Troll sanitary towels – and aero engines ... and table mats, if I remember correctly. You see, Weetwood wants to buy rail franchises so he needs the cash.'

It got more bizarre by the second! And yet, could this old bugger really make up such a story. 'But why,' Diane probed, 'should the Germans want to blow up–?'

'Because old Weetwood is being difficult about the price, of course!' Duffle paused and wiped the perspiration from his brow; it was a very hot day. 'Or perhaps they're in it together and the Roberta Weetwood is where they want to build some 'orrible concrete 'otel. ... Or–'

'So, you're just guessing?'

'I've reasoned it out. There must be a lot of money at stake, and you know what Germans are like.'

'Look, Ron, you're a very nice guy. In the outback we call blokes like you' – Diane paused, desperately searching for some appropriate Australian-sounding term – 'a rare binkum.'

'Oh, thanks, lass.'

'But this German story sounds crazy to me, Ron. I'm sorry, but I don't buy it.'

'Oh, don't you? Well, I got it from the horse's mouth.'

'Weetwood himself?'

'No, of course not – some reporters from a leading German magazine.' Duffle told her a suitably sanitized version of the Rinderpest and Ganoid story. 'And if you don't believe me, you can check out the Cob o' Coal's register.'

'And that's your only evidence for the German connection – two odd bods who disappeared?'

'Well, the Roberta Weetwood did blow up, didn't it?

'Yep, you're right there.'

It was time to be getting back to the festivities. Ms Bradbury and Duffle made their farewells. After she'd gone, he wondered whether he'd said too much. After all, he'd given a solemn undertaking to Rinderpest and Ganoid. But then they'd deserted him, and it hadn't been easy bearing his secret for all these weeks, had it? And now that he'd shared it with the delightful young Australian, he felt as if a heavy burden had been lifted from his shoulders.

As for Diane Bradbury, she promptly organized a taxi and was soon on her way to the Cob o' Coal.

# CHAPTER 15

Misty was still trying to get her thoughts together. At least she'd finally stopped crying. The passing waiter gave her an anxious look and attempted a smile. He'd been very kind, she thought. And the girl behind the bar was a saint – she'd probably come out again in a few minutes to check on her. It was strange, Misty reflected: it was at a similar harbour-side bar that everything had started five weeks ago … five extraordinary weeks. At the time, it had seemed like a miracle – her luck changing so dramatically in St-Tropez, the holiday she'd dreamed of finally materializing. Some miracle! She drank the last of her *café solo* and took a sip from a tall glass of mineral water. What had happened? How could she have been so wrong about him?

'The bastard,' she muttered, 'the fucking, fucking bastard.'

She tried again to fit the pieces together.

*

The *Burgajet* was moored in Ibiza Town harbour, only a few hundred yards off shore. After dining aboard, they'd all piled into the launch. They visited some bars, the wilder ones which Otto had recommended, with their complements of weirdoes and eccentrics – Salvador Dali wannabes, transvestites aping every gay heroine from Judy Garland to Tina Turner, guys in leather proudly displaying pierced nipples and tattooed buttocks – and everywhere the unmistakable fragrance of weed. The Beautiful People recognized comrades from fellow wealthy European dynasties; to Paul Woodward III, some of them were more outrageous than anything he'd ever seen.

It had been the plan for all of them to go on to Ku-Ku, the best club in Europe claimed the Beautiful People, and as Tubs had said, 'They should know!' But by one a.m. Woodward had had more than enough. Misty could recall his judgement when they emerged from a bar where half a dozen rubber-clad girls had been ravishing each other in one corner to the sounds of ear-splitting flamenco singing: 'It's like a zoo where all the animals have been let out of their fucking cages.'

Woodward issued orders: he and Tubs would return to the *Burgajet* – she demurred – and the launch would return to the quay near the *Estación Marítima* at four for the stragglers. Otto protested vehemently: Ku-Ku didn't come alive until two at the earliest, nobody left before six in the morning, and – to boot – it was some way out of town. After a fierce

165

argument, Woodward relented: the launch would return at seven, but the *Burgajet* would sail at ten a.m. on the dot – *come what may*. He'd repeated it three times.

With its numerous dance floors separated by exotic gardens of fountains and flowers, Misty had been bowled over by Ku-Ku. The *Burgajet* party had quickly split up, attracted by different types of music and to make rendezvous arranged earlier in the town's bars. She recollected the ice-cold San Miguels – she didn't believe she'd drunk more than four – and Amalie, a girl with piercing blue eyes and a shaven head to whom Otto had introduced her at some stage. The three of them had ended up dancing together to the hypnotic rhythms of techno music – for how many hours? And then Otto said he needed to take a leak. A short while later, Amalie disappeared. Neither of them returned.

When Misty finally went in search of Otto, she came across one of the Beautiful People, Antonio di Dolmio-Ragu, sitting beside a fountain; he was fondling an attractive older man's groin.

'Otto? Yeah, Misty, I saw him leave ages ago with Amalie. Looks like the wedding's back on.'

'*Wedding?*'

'Didn't that German bitch tell you about Amalie? We all thought you knew. They got engaged about six months ago – it was in *all* the glossies, darling – don't you get those in Texas? They had a big bust up just before we set sail from Marbella. Apparently, she'd been sleeping with some French actress – that Sophie *quelque chose* – and Otto took offence. Mind you, I always thought he'd swallow his pride. I mean, the von Geidels are really hard up by all accounts, and Amalie may look an absolute fright, but her old man is Prince Friedrich von Wuppertal-Cloppenburg. He owns half of Bavaria! Old Wuppi has a villa here. ... Have you met my new friend, Sven?'

Misty didn't want to hang around until all her fellow shipmates were ready to go back to town. By five-thirty, and after a solitary taxi ride, she was sitting on a bench near the *Estación Marítima*. Ibiza Town's clubs and bars were winding down, and the quay was crowded with revellers, but their high spirits only served to exacerbate her depression.

When the Beautiful People began to turn up for the seven o'clock launch, it was clear that Antonio had spread 'the news'. There were no words of comfort; if anything, Misty had the distinct impression that no one cared. In the early morning light, just before seven, the launch hove to. Misty immediately noticed some items of luggage piled at the stern, including a guitar case. One of two crewmen began to unload them.

With her voice breaking, Misty said: 'Those are Otto's things, Miguel.' Someone giggled behind her.

'*Sí, sí*! The First Officer gets a call half an hour ago. Señor Otto is staying with a friend here. I have to wait for the chauffeur who is coming to collect the bags.'

When Misty boarded the *Burgajet*, she went straight to the cabin she'd shared with Otto and packed. The launch had to return for Miguel in any event. She didn't say goodbye to any of the passengers, not even Tubs.

*

Misty drank the last of her mineral water and stared hard at the spot in the harbour where the *Burgajet* had lain at anchor. The tears began to roll down her cheeks once more. She put her sunglasses back on, and, feeling the sun's hot rays on her arm, pushed her chair a few inches to one side and into the umbrella's shade. But she couldn't sit on the bar's terrace for ever: there had to be a sensible solution to her predicament. The events of the last twelve hours, however, were making rational thought difficult. And she was exhausted. Ideas came and faded. Maybe she should just fly straight home and start her new job immediately.

The roar of a powerful engine made her look up. A jet ferry was entering the harbour and lowering its hull back into the water as it slowed and made for the quay. Without any real interest, Misty followed the vessel's progress as it came towards her. It moored about fifty feet away, and its passengers, clad mainly in beachwear and clutching towels, began to disembark. They'd obviously been out on some trip, she surmised. And then the sign at the end of the gangplank caught her attention. One word in large red letters stood out: **FORMENTERA**.

*

The warm evening air was rich with the scent of pine resin. Cicadas were buzzing hypnotically, and beyond the garden wall came the sound of the rhythmic rising and falling of the swell in the gullies at the foot of the cliffs. Misty opened her eyes and watched a moth fluttering around one of the candles on the table. Opposite her, Caroline was busy arranging and rearranging the positions of her dessert spoon and fork.

'That was an excellent dinner, Carrie. Thank you.'

'Only rabbit stew, you know. Nothing special.'

'You're too modest. It was delicious.'

'Oh, it was just something I learned from Gwen.' Caroline pointed in the direction of *Honeysuckle Cottage*. 'I'll tell you all about the Blackberrys when' – she hesitated and started fidgeting with her cutlery again – '... when you're feeling better.'

'It's very, very kind of you to let me come and stay. I really don't know what I would have–'

'Don't be silly. It's the least I could have done.'

167

There was an awkward silence. Finally, Caroline said: 'I do hope you'll be able to meet Gwen and Tom. They're *lovely* people. They've just dashed back to London – something about Gwen's contract. She's on the BBC ... radio that is – quite a star. I think she's a bit worried about her part in *The Muffins*. ... They hope to be back by the middle of next week. Of course, on the programme Gwen's been in a coma at Worchester Royal Infirmary ever since her horrific collision with Cadogan Montpellier's combine harvester opposite the vicarage in Bumpstead Plumpstead. Montpellier is the snooty parvenu – not that *he* was driving the combine, of course. Seems that one of his farmhands, Kevin, had too much parsnip wine at the Heston Charlton Young Farmers' Summer Barbecue. Of course, I don't often listen to *The Muffins* but–'

Misty was crying again; she'd cried in the taxi most of the way to the *Villa Clementina*. Caroline, who'd met her off the ferry at La Savina, was still unclear as to what had happened, but it seemed that she'd had a traumatic experience in Ibiza. Caroline feared the worst, and the worst in her eyes was something sexual. Despite having long buried her head in the sand of historical texts, she wasn't completely ignorant of the harsh, real world which existed outside the ivory tower she'd so carefully constructed for herself. Even on the rare occasions when she watched television to view a historical documentary or drama recommended by Pongo, it was almost impossible to locate the correct channel without being assaulted by scenes of sickening gratuitous violence or sexual perversions. But there was something about Misty's predicament that had caused a door deep within her to unlock and creak open, and a little tenderness had crept out.

She left her seat, came to stand at Misty's side, and laid a trembling hand on her shoulder. In a quiet, yet emotional voice, she said: 'I know I'm not very good at this sort of thing, Misty, but I really would like to help. ... I wish there was *something* I could do. Perhaps if you were to tell me what happened – get it all off your chest, so to speak – well, that might help, don't you think?

'Look, why don't we go and sit on the comfy chairs over there, hmm? We can fill our glasses with some more of this lovely wine and have a good natter. I mean, I just couldn't really follow what you were saying in the taxi, and while you were resting this afternoon, my mind was going berserk imagining all sorts of–'

'Oh, Carrie,' Misty sobbed, 'you're precious! It's strange, but – now don't hate me for saying this – but in the last two months something – or someone – seems to have transformed you into a human being, whereas ... whereas *I've* become a defiled whore.'

'Don't *speak* like that, Misty!'

'No, it's true!'

A few minutes' silence passed, but then Misty dried her eyes and, with a smile, said: 'Come on then, I'll take you up on your kind offer. Let's see how good you are at counselling.'

It was three in the morning when the two women finally turned in. Caroline had heard the whole story, starting with Misty's arrival in Paris and concluding with her phone call from Ibiza's *Estación Marítima* to the *Villa Clementina* after getting the number from a reluctant Vivian Duffle at Bobbins. It was a story which Misty told with clarity and precision, almost as if it was about someone else. Caroline listened with a mixture of fascination and anger. She couldn't begin to understand how this Otto character could have been so disingenuous, mercenary and callous. There and then, she made a silent vow to dedicate herself to the task of restoring Misty's happiness.

Caroline hardly slept that night. She lay for hours going over and over in her mind the decadent scenes of life aboard the *Burgajet* which Misty had so clinically recounted – the self-indulgence, promiscuity and deceit. But was there any real difference between their nature and the royal perversions described in such lurid detail in the manuscripts she was still laboriously – and now reluctantly – translating? And what had Misty meant by all those odd comments – in her phone call and in the taxi – about the whole Weetwood family 'hating' her, thinking her a 'spy', and loathing her father, Mr Start, for suing Goblin? She'd have to seek clarification as soon as Misty was in a better frame of mind. Perhaps she was a bit unbalanced after the Otto business.

It was only as the cocks started to crow in the farms somewhere beyond the pine woods that Caroline finally fell asleep. With the eastern horizon beginning to fill with light and the promise of yet another hot, cloudless day, Rory Devlin crept out of his hiding place to return the way he'd come – along the cliff-top path. Though fortified by a half-empty bottle of wine gracing the uncleared dining table on *Clementina*'s terrace, he was not a happy man.

When Caroline finally awoke around ten, she was bewildered by the sound of clattering dishes and the delicious aroma of fresh coffee. Her first reaction was that the dreaded Maria had made an unscheduled visit. Then she remembered her surprise guest. Squinting at her Swatch, she gasped in disbelief. Within seconds, she was dressed in shorts and her favourite 'I ♥ FORMENTERA' T-shirt. She found Misty in the kitchen, loading the dishwasher with obvious competence. A full pot of coffee stood invitingly on the table.

Alerted by the patter of Caroline's bare feet on the tiled floor, Misty turn her head.

'Hi, Carrie! Sleep well? I didn't want to disturb you. I've just made some coffee. Help yourself. What a beautiful day and what a beautiful villa! Those guys really know how to live. And the views from my room in the tower – awesome! I didn't take any of it in yesterday when I arrived. You must love it here. What do you usually have for breakfast? Is there somewhere I can get fresh rolls or croissants – or whatever they have in Spain?'

'Um ... gosh! I ...' Caroline rubbed her sleepy eyes. 'How long have you been up? More importantly, how are you feeling?'

'I feel *so* much better, thanks. I guess that was the first night's sleep I've had on dry land since–'

'But you must have been up for yonks,' Caroline interrupted. 'I mean, you've cleared up *everything*. You really shouldn't have.'

'No sweat! It's the least I could do.'

Caroline pointed to the dishwasher. 'Do you really know how to use that thing? I haven't a clue. Gwen did try to explain, but it all sounded frightfully complicated, so I usually do my few dishes by hand.'

'It's no big deal. They're all basically the same. Let me pour you some coffee.'

'Thanks. It smells yummy. I usually have Nescafé – not because I prefer it to the *real* stuff, mind you – I just can't get the hang of that wretched Spanish coffee machine. I tried it once, and ... well, to be honest, it exploded. It took me hours to clear up the mess. In fact, you can still see some spots on the ceiling up there. See? I couldn't reach them.'

'Oh yeah.' But Misty was not really looking. Instead, she was studying her friend and shaking her head.

Caroline lost interest in the brown coffee spots. 'What's wrong? Why are you looking at me like that?'

'Nothing's *wrong*, Carrie – quite the opposite. I just can't get over how much you've changed. For a start, you're so *brown* – and you sure as hell didn't get that colour closeted in a library pouring over dusty manuscripts!'

'Well ...'

'And your *hair*? I mean, what happened to the Anglo-Saxon look? Hell, you must think I'm so rude, but honestly, Carrie, you've got a lovely face and that style just did *not* suit you, no siree. And are those new Armani specs you're wearing?'

'Oh, that's Gwen again. Actually, I'll pop my contact lenses in after breakfast.'

'Contacts! Who is this Gwen angel?'

'I think I mentioned her last night – Gwen Blackberry?' Misty did not remember, so Caroline gave her a brief résumé of her mentor.

'She sounds like the best friend you've ever had,' said Misty.

'Possibly. ... There's Pongo, of course.'

'Your old Prof?'

'Well remembered! But for her I wouldn't be here.'

'And how come you've managed to lose so much weight – and to look so fit?'

'Hmm? ... Super coffee by the way!'

'Well? I'm waiting.'

Caroline stared at her feet with a cheeky grin. 'It's all thanks to Pierre.'

'Gwen's fixed you up with a *boyfriend* as well! Does she have a fairy wand, or what?'

'No, no, no! Pierre's my Peugeot Paris.'

'Your compact?

'My bike, silly! He's got built-in locking *and* white-wall tyres. We've travelled the island together and never a problem – not even one puncture.'

Misty was laughing. 'So *that's* your secret – cycling! Well, good for you.'

'And swimming. I do a lot of that – every day. Oh damn!' Caroline stamped her foot. 'I've missed my morning swim. That's another thing Gwen got me into doing.'

'And I bet *she* got rid of the tracksuit bottoms.'

'Well, it was a bit hot for them.'

'And you live here all alone? How come? I thought this lecturer ... er–'

'Teeny Kirk – *ex*-lecturer, actually.'

'Sure. ... I thought this Teeny and her sugar daddy – Kurt? – were supposed to be entertaining you. Or did I get that wrong?'

Caroline adopted a serious expression; it reminded Misty of the weekend at Bobbins.

'Misty, I really don't know what sort of relationship Teeny and Kurt have.' After explaining her hosts' absence and the subsequent elimination of the housekeeper, she added: 'Kurt's mother finally died a few days ago, and he and Teeny are now sorting out her affairs. They hope to get back here before the end of the month.'

'And the research?' asked Misty with just a hint of cynicism. 'Do I get the feeling it's not exactly progressing as you had imagined?'

'Um ... one could say–' But the unmistakable screeching of seagulls directly overhead interrupted Caroline's reply. 'I know!' she snapped, gratefully changing the subject. 'How about a quick swim to work up an appetite?'

'Sure!'

'Super! We can stroll down to the *supermercado* at Es Mal Pas along the cliffs. It's a pretty walk and we can have a swim on the way – or on the way back. They should have some fresh bread. A chap brings it every morning from a smashing little bakery in Sant Francesc – that's the island's so-called capital. It's just a village really. ... You'll like it. Actually, we drove through there yesterday, but I suppose, um ...'

'No, I don't remember.'

'Anyway, how does that grab you? And I can show you my tower.' Misty looked at her quizzically. 'The towers are magic! Just you wait and see.'

Armed with towels and bathing costumes, Misty and Caroline were soon walking slowly along the path to Es Mal Pas. There was a gentle sea breeze, and about thirty feet below them the smallest of waves broke lazily along the narrow beach of white sand. With September almost upon them, there were now even fewer people enjoying the tranquillity of this part of the bay – Caroline counted only six – and after weeks on the island she was indifferent to their nakedness. But should she have warned Misty? Should she say something now? ... She shot her a sideways glance. Misty, however, looked radiant and wholly unphased by the sun-worshipping holidaymakers.

Caroline walked on. She pointed out the distant Club La Mola Hotel, at the far end of the Platja de Mitjorn. 'Awful place,' she said, '– full of Italians. Used to be full of Germans, apparently, but it dropped from four stars to three, or five to four – I can't remember – because the owners wouldn't spend the dosh to revamp it. That's what Gwen says, anyway. Not that I've got anything against the Italians, of course. It's just that they're so noisy. And they hate push-bikes. I mean, everyone cycles on Formentera, Misty, *except* the Italians. Instead, they zoom around in great convoys on those horrid noisy Vespa things, terrorising the locals. Mind you, that does tend to keep them on the few tarmac roads. I cycled down to the Club La Mola once. There they all were, several hundred Italians packed together on the strip of sand in front of the hotel yelling their heads off and churning up the beach in an orgy of organized games. Frightful!'

Misty said little. She was intoxicated by the beauty and peace of the scenery and the rich, fragrant mixture of pine resin and rosemary in the air she breathed. She was content to follow Caroline, who clearly knew by heart all the sandy paths that twisted this way and that through the woods of stunted pines. Eventually, they came to the clearing on the small promontory from which Caroline had first spied the tower of Es Mal Pas, the *Torre d'es Catalá*. She pointed with almost childish glee. 'There! What about that? Isn't it beautiful?'

Misty put a hand above her eyes and surveyed the scene: the wooded valley with its dried-up river bed; the few whitewashed buildings of the *pueblo*; the hillside beyond with its squat stone tower. ... She could just make out someone walking slowly towards it, up the rocky, steeply sloping terrain that separated the tower from the narrow strip of vineyards bordering the beach a few hundred yards distant.

'It's idyllic, Carrie. It certainly gives the place a romantic feel.'

'Romantic? Do you think so?'

'Sort of.'

'I've found it rather difficult to get any reliable information about it – or the other three towers on the island.' Caroline rattled off their names as they set off down the hill to Es Mal Pas. 'However, I've gleaned that there are similar structures on the other Balearic Islands and that they date mostly from the seventeenth and eighteenth centuries. I believe they were part of the Spanish coastal defences against the French and the English, who were constantly grabbing bits of the Med at the time. The English ruled Menorca for quite a while during the eighteenth century, you know.

'Just think, two hundred years ago there would have been nothing here except that tower. But at least it's in a relatively sheltered spot. The others are located in wild, barren places where the wind always seems to blow. Can you imagine being dispatched from Madrid or Seville to guard one of them? Nothing but miles of empty coastline, an island with just a few hundred inhabitants at most – although Formentera was actually abandoned for much of the eighteenth century – and winters with notorious storms.'

'And yet,' Misty replied playfully, 'on a day like today, don't you think some of the soldiers would have looked at the sea, smelled the air, and said, "OK, guys, how about a spot of fishing and then a barbecue on the beach with some of the local wine – and if we're lucky, some girls from the nearest village?"?'

'Perhaps. ... It really hadn't occurred to me.' For a moment, Caroline looked lost in thought. 'Misty, I really didn't understand all that stuff you said yesterday about spying and Goblin and your father, and me and the family hating you. I mean, it all sounded a bit batty to be honest.'

Misty groaned. 'Don't you get newspapers here? – radio? – CNN? Surely you've been in touch with your folks? ... James? I mean, the coincidence of me turning up at Bobbins and then all that FoamFay – FayFoam? – stuff blowing up. Woodward – Tubs' fiancé – showed me the *Wall Street Journal* and ... I think we were sailing around Crete at the time. ... Anyway, I thought, "Jesus! What the hell will the Weetwoods think?" And–'

'Stop! You're losing me again.'

'Sorry.'

'First, I haven't read a single newspaper since I've been here. Secondly, apart from some postcards to my Aunt Belinda – my father's sister – I haven't had any contact with any member of the family. Thirdly, I've never watched any television here. As for the radio, I've only listened to *The Muffins* on the BBC World Service. ... Oh, I *did* hear some news bulletins, but there were certainly no references to Goblin.'

As they continued through the woods, Misty told Caroline all that she could remember about *The Wall Street Journal*'s report of SI's attempt to injunct the launch of WSD's new wonder soap.

'Well,' Caroline gasped, 'now I can understand why you feared we might have thought you were a spy! Perhaps my father still does, what with your father claiming that this FoamFay soap – or whatever it's called – was developed from some technology Daddy – of all people – pinched ages ago – and that all the research was done "secretly" in Uruguay! Sounds absolute rot to me.'

'Me too, but then my father is a bit weird. To be absolutely honest with you, Carrie, that was what made me resolve to find out if you were still here – so that I could plead my innocence.'

'How silly! As if you could be a "spy"! Mind you,' Caroline added mockingly, 'you always asked loads of questions about Goblin soap in all those letters you wrote.'

'I just thought I might get you to write about what interested you!'

'*Me* – interested in *soap*? Come on! ... Actually, this is probably a good opportunity to apologise for all the calculated gibberish I wrote in reply. Sorry, Misty.'

'Apology accepted. Anyway, when I decided to put a face to those weird letters on my European tour, I had absolutely no idea about this FoamFay claim – you've got to believe me.'

'I *do* believe you – honestly.'

But as they reached Es Mal Pas, troubling images flashed through Caroline's mind: the man down by the lake at Bobbins; Misty's unexplained possession of a copy of *The Man In The Iron Mask*; the intruder in *Clementina*'s garden; the masked figures up at the Sant Francesc windmill.

As if awakening from a trance, Caroline suddenly realised they were standing in the middle of the *pueblo*. There wasn't much to see: amidst woods that reached right to the edge of the beach stood just a few two-storied whitewashed buildings erected during the last twenty years. There were no streets or car parks, only sandy tracks converging at the Supermercado Miramar, from which a dirt road led northwards uphill into dense woods. No one seemed to be about, although a few children could be heard playing on the beach some way off; at the Luna Amarilla restaurant, a waiter appeared and began laying some tables for lunch under a canopy of vines and old fishing nets.

Taking in the scene, Misty stood before the Miramar's steps as if she was an artist attempting to memorize it for a future canvas. The waiter got bored with the tables, and ambled to a blackboard propped against a rusty anchor that lay in the centre of a small patch of grass. Misty watched him write '*sardinas frescas*' and realized she was very hungry. She turned around expecting to find her companion, but there was no Carrie.

Presuming she must be in the little supermarket, Misty started up the steps. As she was about to go inside, however, a bizarre sensation caused her to stop and look back at the tower. A figure was standing on top of it. After a few moments, she realised it was the person – almost certainly a man – she'd seen earlier from the hill above Es Mal Pas: he was wearing the same distinctive yellow and red striped T-shirt. Suddenly, there was a flash, and it dawned on her that he was looking at something through binoculars.

'No, not "something",' she murmured, 'he's looking at *me*.'

'Oh, *there* you are, Misty!' cried Caroline, popping her head round the door. 'Come on, Señora Canaleta's got some fresh chicken. What about that roasted for dinner tonight? Or would you prefer vegetable pasta? There's an Aladdin's Cave of vegetables in there. ... Misty? Are you listening?'

'Sounds great. Yeah ... chicken pasta. ...You know, Carrie, there's some guy up–'

But when Misty looked again, there was no one at the *Torre d'es Català*.

# CHAPTER 16

An able-bodied person could walk around any of Formentera's three largest settlements in fifteen minutes at most, even at a leisurely pace. Two of them, Sant Francesc and Sant Ferran, are of ancient origin with narrow streets of small whitewashed buildings radiating from their fort-like churches. They lie just two kilometres apart and within sight of each other at the edge of the same north-facing escarpment. Below, and between them and the sea, lies the great lagoon of Estany Pudent, once an integral part of the island's former main industry, the extraction of sea salt. But now long defunct, the intricate network of evaporation ponds, canals and sluice gates – and even a little narrow-gauge railway – lie abandoned.

When the Formenterans decided to cash in on tourism at the end of the 1960s and create a coastal resort, they chose what appeared to be an ideal location, Es Pujols on the north coast, two kilometres from Sant Ferran and an easy drive from the island's port of entry, La Savina. They could not have selected a nicer spot: on one side, a beautiful sheltered bay with a sandy beach stretching for miles north-westwards and stunning views of Ibiza; on the other, the shimmering expanse of Estany Pudent. But this was to be no Benidorm, for the wise islanders stipulated that no building could exceed four floors. In any event, Formentera experiences severe water problems; tanker lorries bring the vast bulk of its requirements on the ferry from Ibiza. Consequently, only a few streets were laid out. By the early Seventies, these had been lined by uniformly drab concrete blocks of holiday apartments in the Lego style; a couple of small and similarly designed hotels, devoid of character and aspiration, completed the resort.

For the most part, these edifices have not weathered well, and Es Pujols has not become a destination for the famous or fabulously rich. And yet, because of its smallness and the island's generally low-key atmosphere with little nightlife, this tiny outpost of the Iberian tourist industry has a peculiarly magnetic charm. Families adore it, and even at the height of the season the traffic along its few streets consists mainly of bicycles. Out of season, however, Es Pujols resembles a ghost town, for few islanders live there. Hence it possesses no church, post office or hardware shop. By contrast, these three essentials of Formenteran communal life are all to be found in Sant Francesc and Sant Ferran, together with a healthy variety of bakers, butchers, grocers and other stores.

Such were the 'towns' which had gently worked their magic over Caroline. She'd got to know them well, and now she was happily introducing them to Misty. Her desire to join Caroline in cycling caused her first visit to Es Pujols: Lorenzo in Es Mal Pas only had the one Peugeot Paris, and as Misty was so enamoured with Pierre, nothing else would do. Thus, on her second full day on the island, and with Teeny Kirk's telephoned permission, the two women set off in their hosts' Wrangler with Misty at the wheel. They finally found what they were looking for in Es Pujols; Misty named him 'Pedro'.

During the next few days, as she recovered from her ordeal in Ibiza, Misty happily adopted Caroline's routine, with early-morning swims at the beach just below the cliff path, and outings with Pierre and Pedro along the tracks in the villa's vicinity. After lunch, while Caroline worked on her manuscripts, Misty would lie in the shade on the terrace, reading or staring out to sea, with just lizards and seagulls for company.

Late one afternoon, a week after Misty's arrival, and with the sun casting long shadows across the terrace, Caroline emerged from the villa with two tall glasses of chilled orange juice and set one on the table at Misty's side.

'Good grief, Misty, I've had enough of that Versailles tripe for one day.'

'You do look exhausted, Carrie. Thanks for the drink.'

'Fancy a swim?'

'Sure. Hey, I was thinking earlier on – why don't we take the Jeep and go out for something to eat tonight? There must be some good restaurants round here somewhere. My treat, of course.'

'Out? ... Golly! I don't know. I mean ... well, we've got plenty to eat in the fridge, and–'

'Oh, come on, Carrie, you can't cook *every* night, and *I'm* not in the mood. What d'you say?'

'Well, I suppose we could. ... I went once with Gwen and Tom to a rather odd place in Sant Ferran.'

'Odd?'

'The food was jolly good – tasty local fare. ... Actually, it's quite a famous restaurant in its way. It's called Fonda Pepe – always packed, apparently.'

'So, what's "odd" about it?'

'The people. It's favoured by eccentrics and hippies and ... well, all sorts of *weird* people.'

'Sounds perfect!'

The Fonda Pepe lies at the centre of Sant Ferran, cheek by jowl with the church. It's not a pretty building, and access to the restaurant is through

177

an austere bar, which never seems to close. In truth, it's an effective filtering system, for many tourists in search of food would never risk plunging into its maelstrom; those diners who do reach the restaurant on the far side would be justified in believing they'd finally reached the Promised Land.

As Misty followed her friend through the seething mass of drinkers and a veritable fog of cigarette smoke, she quickly realised that dinner was going to be an experience. She brushed past a bearded young man wearing a plush red velvet jacket and a top hat to which half a dozen rabbit feet had been attached; he was singing *Yellow Submarine* at the top of his voice to no one in particular. At the bar, a middle-aged lady, dressed elegantly in a grey suit, was having a hysterical argument in Spanish and hurling coins around like shrapnel; she was insisting that she'd been overcharged for something or other.

Misty would have liked to hang around for a few minutes to digest the scene, but Caroline was relentlessly pushing her way deeper into the melee, and she didn't want to lose her.

'See what I mean about the people being odd?' she shouted over the racket as a waiter led them at a trot to one of the few empty tables in the restaurant. He thrust menus into their hands and shot off.

The two friends looked around the large whitewashed room. At first sight, the diners appeared relatively normal: a young blond couple of undoubtedly Scandinavian origin with eyes only for each other, quietly tucking into lamb cutlets, French fries and salad; four elderly German ladies with vast bosoms and stomachs, and already replete – they'd made an early start to secure their usual table by the window – smoking, drinking large tumblers of brandy, and dissecting their bill as though they were auditing Deutsche Bank's accounts; and at the centre of the restaurant, seated at a long table and talking loudly in German, French and Italian, was a group that could have been cloned from Misty's former *Burgajet* shipmates.

But on closer inspection, a quite different picture emerged. At the table behind Caroline, a couple stared tenderly at each other and ignored their food. The man was young, tanned, almost too handsome, and dressed in a dazzling white Boss top. His female companion sported a scarlet T-shirt and, from where Misty was sitting, what appeared to be a black leather mini-skirt. Around her neck was a string of mussel shells. Her hair was long, fluorescent green, and surmounted by a woolly pill-box hat – possibly embroidered by the wearer.

'Carrie, just turn round slowly and guess the age of the woman behind you.'

Caroline half-turned with theatrical lethargy but spun back quickly. 'Good Lord!' she whispered, leaning across the table. 'I don't believe it. She must be seventy-five if she's a day. It's horrific.'

'That's what I thought.'

'And all that make up – just like Barbara Cartland.'

'Who?'

'Never mind. What on earth can that young chap see in her?'

'Money I should think.'

They both giggled and tried to study the menu; it proved impossible. To Misty's left, a table for three was occupied by a young woman of exceptional beauty and an extremely thin middle-aged man. A white clipped poodle, with a red ribbon on its head, sat between them, panting. The man stared continuously at the girl's breasts; the tablecloth was not long enough to conceal that his left shoeless foot had disappeared into her skirt.

'I can't eat langoustines without my bib,' he snapped petulantly in a high-pitched, grating American accent. 'Where's my bib, Amanda? I want my bib.'

'Amanda' barely glanced at him. 'It will be in your handbag, Oliver. Would you like me to look?' Her voice conveyed all the indicia of an English aristocratic background, as did her style.

'It's not a "handbag", Amanda, it's a gentleman's portmanteau – that's what they called it at Hermès in Barcelona, and it cost me 2,000 bucks.'

Amanda reached for the 'portmanteau', opened it, and pulled out a spotless linen bib. She got up and tied it around Oliver's neck.

'Happy now? I said it would be in your handbag.'

'It's *not* a handbag, it's–'

'Oh for Christ's sake, don't start *that* again.'

Oliver pouted. He looked at the poodle. 'Mommy's being horrid to Pop this evening, isn't she, Roosevelt?'

Misty and Caroline looked at each other and covered their mouths in a vain attempt to stifle the giggles. Finally, they ordered: to start, fresh sardines for Caroline and *Gambas al Pil-Pil* for Misty; they both fancied the *Riñones a la Jerezana* – kidneys in sherry – to follow. Seconds later, bottles of the house *vino blanco* and sparkling mineral water thumped onto the table.

The restaurant's 'bohemian atmosphere' – Caroline's description – encouraged the disclosure of confidences; the wine helped too.

'How's your brother?' asked Misty.

'James? Haven't a clue. Not been in touch with England – no need really.'

'Don't you like him?'

'He's all right. I mean, we don't really have much in common – if anything. He's always been sporty and clever, and ... oh I don't know – sort of an all-rounder. ... Do *you* have any brothers or sisters?'

'No. I had a fairly lonely childhood – like you, I think, judging from what James told me at Bobbins.'

Caroline smiled. 'You two got pretty chummy, didn't you?'

'Why, Carrie, you surprise me! I didn't think you noticed things like that. You certainly didn't act as though you were much interested in either of us that weekend.'

'Ah, Miss Start, but that's where you're wrong. ... Well, to be honest, I *didn't* at first, but I'm not a complete chump.'

'I didn't think you were.'

'Oh really?'

'Have you never been out with a boy?'

Caroline groaned. 'I just knew you were going to ask that.'

'Well, have you?'

'Yes, as a matter of fact – at Durham – Timothy Dingle, a spotty geology student at Hatfield College. Horrid breath and sweaty hands. He was a member of the Archaeological Society and he used to come on some of our digs. He asked me to his college ball. I was dumbfounded. Obviously, he'd no one else to take – which was hardly surprising – and, to my eternal regret, I accepted.'

'"Eternal regret"? Why?'

'He and the ball were awful. He spent the whole evening talking about his hobby – fishing. And we tried to dance to this frightful music. It was so embarrassing. *I* was bad enough, but Dingle jumped around and waved his hands in the air wildly like some kind of witch doctor. Everyone was in hysterics, but he didn't seem to notice. And he spilled a glass of cider down my dress. Finally, he offered to walk me back to my college. I said it wasn't necessary, but he insisted. When we got to the gates, we sort of stood there awkwardly saying goodnight and how much we'd enjoyed the evening and all that rot. Then he said, "Would you like me to kiss you goodnight." And I said, "No thank you, Timothy. I don't think so." I must say he looked frightfully relieved. He just said, "Oh that's all right then." I wasn't sure what he meant. Anyway, he never came to any more meetings of the Archaeological Society.'

Misty was laughing. 'Carrie, honey, you're priceless!'

'There! You see, Misty, *that* proves my point. The fact that you find the idea of me with a boy so funny–'

'Oh, come on, that's not why I'm laughing. It's the story and the way you tell it. It's so ... so *British*. There's no reason on earth why you shouldn't have a boyfriend – fall in love – get married – have kids. But I don't believe a person ever finds love – *true* love – as long as he or she doesn't like what they see in the mirror.'

'Well, using your mirror test, I'm condemned to be an old maid.'

'Why do you say that?'

'Look at me!'

'I'm looking, and what I see, Carrie, is a twenty-year-old woman with a super tan, a pretty face, sparkling blue eyes and – no, let me finish – a woman who's lost pounds and pounds in a couple of months – a woman who hasn't been so happy since ... hell, I don't know – probably in all her life. You see, Carrie, that's exactly my point. If you feel good in yourself, you're a different person and the rest of the world responds accordingly. It's like the song, "Smile and the whole world smiles with you."'

Caroline looked doubtful. 'But–'

'I don't like the "but" word, Carrie.'

'I'm sorry, but ... well, it's easy for you to talk like that. You're so pretty and gregarious – both waiters have been drooling over you since we arrived.'

'That doesn't make me want to flirt with them – or feel sexy.'

'But it makes you feel *wanted*.'

'So?'

'I've never felt ... wanted – I've never felt I wanted anyone either. I just don't believe' – Caroline mouthed 'sex' – 'and me go together.'

'Heh, don't get all serious on me! You had a miserable puberty in a snobby girls' school, you were cast in the ugly duckling role, and played it for all it was worth. It was easier to stuff yourself with candies and hide in the library than confront the problem head on and break out of the mould. It became a vicious circle. Here on Formentera, a chance set of circumstances has forced you to fend for yourself for the first time in your life. You've been befriended, and a transformation has got well and truly underway. Am I right or am I right?' Misty grabbed Caroline's hand and gave it a squeeze.

Caroline sighed. 'Thanks, but even if you *are* right, I can't stay here for ever. In a few weeks, at most, I'll be back in England.'

'Buy a bike, join a gym, start going to a hair stylist, get a new wardrobe. Jesus, Carrie, your folks have got enough money–'

'Oh, I couldn't ask them for money. Anyway, I've got money of my own. I get an annual allowance of £10,000, you know, but I don't spend much. ... Incidentally, they stopped James's allowance after Peter's death because they thought he'd do something silly with it.'

'You're kidding! Like what?'

'I don't know, really – go to Tibet, erect a monument. ... He was pretty loopy and–'

Something out of the corner of Caroline's eye caught her attention. A man and a woman had recently been placed at the table to her left. They were both thin, the woman particularly so. There was nothing exceptional about their attire, but she felt sure that the woman had just rearranged her mop of bright orange hair: it had been at a funny angle and now it was as it should be. The woman shot her a glance, and then looked back at her companion.

Caroline leaned across the table and hissed: 'The wrinkled old prune to your right ... is it a wig?'

'Where's that waiter?' barked Misty as she scanned the restaurant, pausing for just a second at the table in question. 'Definitely!' she sniggered. 'Maybe his lank hair's a wig too.'

The woman was certainly tanned to the point of absurdity. She lit a cigarette, tilted her head back, and blew a great cloud of blue smoke high up towards the ceiling.

'Jesus, what a neck,' Misty added under her breath, '– like a turkey!'

'You're wicked!'

The waiter suddenly appeared before them, asking if they wanted *postre* or coffee. They both opted for the *flaó* – cheesecake with honey and almonds – and a *café solo*.

As he sped away, Misty said: 'By the way, how do you get on with your mom? She seemed OK when I spoke with her on the phone months back.'

'Mother's frightful! Can't imagine why Daddy ever married her. I think she was only after his dosh – that's all she's interested in. Actually, I'm surprised she hasn't bankrupted us in view of all the plastic surgery she's had. Poor Daddy, he's not such a bad sort really. I mean, if you wanted something, I'm sure he'd give it to you. He's just a bit batty, that's all.' Caroline stared into her wine glass. 'You know, I think he's got the same problem as me.'

'How do you mean?'

'About feeling good inside and all that. I don't believe he likes what *he* sees when he looks in a mirror. And as far as I'm aware, he doesn't have any friends at all. I'm sure Mother doesn't love him, but then she only loves herself. Golly, what a family!'

'You're not unique.'

'No, I suppose not.'

Misty frowned. 'I wonder how James is. I feel very bad about how I treated him.'

'Oh? Why? I thought you'd got on really well.'

'Yeah, we did. That's just it ... too well, perhaps.'

Caroline looked into Misty's eyes. 'You mean–?'

'Yes, we did ... more than once.'

'Cripes!'

'And I promised to phone and write, but all I did was send one lousy postcard from Paris. You know, it's weird when I come to think of it, but when I phoned Bobbins from Ibiza to get your number here, that housekeeper, Mrs Danvers–'

'Mrs *Duffle*, you mean.'

'That's her ... well, it was like getting blood out of a stone. She was real peculiar – as cold as ice. I was too shaken up to give it any significance at the time, but it's just come back to me. She said something like, "In view of what you did to Master James, I don't think Miss Caroline would want to have anything more to do with you."'

'Mrs D said *that*? I can't believe it ... not *her*. What on earth could she have meant? Perhaps you misheard her. After all, you were in quite a state.'

'Yeah, I know, but I'm sure that's the gist of what she said. ... Maybe she was just alluding to my dad's law suit – me being a spy or something. Or maybe James thought he was really in love and–'

'– and had a relapse after you left, reverting to his "woe is me" routine.'

'Thanks, Carrie. That's just what I wanted to hear.'

'But you liked him a lot, didn't you? I mean, you and he–'

'Of course I liked him a lot.'

'So why didn't you–?'

Caroline was staring at 'the Wiggies' – as she'd nicknamed them – at the next table. 'I say, Misty,' she boomed so that the Wiggies could hear, 'I think *these* people are listening to our conversation. They certainly can't take their beady eyes off us. It's a bit of a liberty, don't you think?'

Surprised by the outburst, Misty stared wide-eyed at Caroline – the wine must have emboldened her – and then smiled at the Wiggies. 'Hey, guys, do we know each other?' she asked with disarming charm.

Mr Wiggy coughed and focused on the *gazpacho* before him.

Mrs Wiggy, who was lighting another cigarette, said: 'No *comprendo. Soy húngara.*' She sounded like Greta Garbo on fifty cigarettes a day.

Caroline turned back to face Misty. 'What did she say?'

'Some crap about being Hungarian.'

'Hah!'

Sighing, Caroline stared at a wine stain on the tablecloth.

'Come on, Carrie – out with it. What's troubling you?'

'Oh nothing. ... What shall we do tomorrow?'

'Don't change the subject. There's something on your mind.'

'You'll think I'm silly – that I probably imagined the whole thing. It's really not–'

'Imagined what?'

'Nothing – nothing at all.'

But Misty wouldn't let the matter drop; in the end, Caroline's defences collapsed.

'Well – I – the point is,' she stammered, 'I – er ...' She took a deep breath. 'At Bobbins, when you came to stay, and we had that chat in your room. ... By the way, I really am sorry you got that pokey dump on the third floor. I–'

'Carrie!'

'Sor-*ry*. ... Well, in your room – remember the dinner gong sounded and – and – and the book you were reading ... the French novel – it fell to the floor and I tried to pick it up but you grabbed it and ...' With her cheeks burning with embarrassment, she finally met Misty's perplexed stair. 'It wasn't *Eugénie Grandet* you were reading – it was something by Dumas. I mean – I could be wrong of course, but ... Oh dear, now you're cross. I'm sorry – I should never have mentioned it. I ...'

Misty's expression of bewilderment disappeared as rapidly as it had materialized. She began to laugh. 'You're not trying to tell me that ... Jesus Christ! Have you been fretting over *that* for all these weeks?'

'No – of course not! It's just that–'

'I always wondered whether you'd rumbled my little deception.'

Caroline furrowed her brows. 'Deception?'

'It's a fair cop, guv,' Misty said in a Dick van Dyke cockney accent, presenting her wrists. 'I'll come quietly, Inspector Weetwood. I was a fool to think I could ever pull the wool over *your* eyes.'

Although Caroline was endeavouring to smile, she felt uneasy and apprehensive.

'I have a terrible confession to make, Carrie,' Misty intoned solemnly. Caroline began fidgeting with the condiments. 'I'm afraid I already knew quite a bit about your "secret research" – as you called it – before our little chat at Bobbins. ... By the way, why *did* you give me that funny little room? James was shocked, you know.'

'I – I–'

'Oh, never mind.'

'So how did you know about Project MIM before I told you?'

Misty leaned back in her chair and folded her arms. 'It'll cost you,' she said coolly.

'Sorry?'

'You heard. We'll have to do a deal. I'll answer your question if you tell me why you deliberately wrote such transparently stupid letters to me for three years even though I bent over backwards and did somersaults to be nice to you.' Misty held out her hand. 'Is it a deal? Come on – shake.'

Caroline's day of reckoning had arrived. Hesitantly, she raised her head and glanced at her dining companion. Misty was smiling broadly – and still holding out her hand.

'Oh, Carrie! Don't look so serious. Now that we're buddies, surely we can be honest with each other?'

Caroline managed a hint of a smile, and the two women shook hands under the watchful gaze of their nosy neighbours at the adjoining table.

Misty's 'confession' was simple. After her arrival at Bobbins, she'd slept for a couple of hours until mid-afternoon. She'd gone in search of Caroline, had got lost in the huge house, and had ended up discovering James in the Yellow Room.

'Well, it's a long story, Carrie. I mean, he'd been crying. He thought I was Peter. ... Anyway, I finally persuaded him to give me a conducted tour of the Weetwood homestead, and at some stage we reached the library.'

'I never saw you.'

'You weren't there, honey. ... Didn't you spend the afternoon packing?'

'Oh yes.'

'Anyway, James started poking around the desk, and, I'm ashamed to say, we snooped. You'd made all these lists and things and James sort of impersonated you and read them out, and–'

Caroline groaned loudly. 'The pig! The rotten, beastly–!'

'I'm sorry, Carrie, but the point is, I thought that if I swotted up *The Man in The Iron Mask* stuff, you and me would have something interesting to talk about – well, something that would interest you anyway. And James remembered that he still had an old copy of Dumas's book – he'd had to study it for his French exams at school. He found it gathering dust on a shelf in his bedroom, and, luckily for me, it had an introduction setting out all the historical background stuff. So, when you burst into my room later on, I didn't want to give the game away, you see. ... *Eugénie Grandet* was the first thing that came into my head.'

Caroline was shaking her head in disbelief. 'And I thought–' she began, but exploded with laughter.

'You thought *what*?'

'I'd had this idea, Misty – since the beginning of the vac, actually – that someone was indeed spying on me. I even thought I spotted someone – a man – down by Goblin Water. All sorts of barmy ideas were going through my fuddled brain – even that you were part of some conspiracy to sabotage Project MIM! – or to steal the manuscripts!'

Caroline was now laughing so loudly that several diners were staring at her, including the Wiggies.

'I think we'd better leave,' Misty interjected playfully, 'and get you some fresh air before the men in white coats arrive.'

'Charming! And what about my side of the bargain and the notorious St Ethelburgers' letters? Or am I being let off?'

'Certainly not! You can confess all on the drive home. Anyway,' Misty added, turning to the Wiggies, 'I think these folks have eavesdropped enough.'

Misty caught the attention of one of the waiters and asked for the bill.

Caroline divided the remaining mineral water between them and took a sip. 'I was wondering,' she said hesitantly, 'how long you were going to stay.'

'Oh dear–!'

'No, no! Please don't think I'm trying to get rid of you. On the contrary, I'd love you stay. I just wondered what your plans were. When do you have to fly back to America?'

Misty told her about the job she was starting at the law centre in the Bronx the second week of October. 'I'm booked on a flight from London to New York at the end of September – the twenty-ninth, I think.'

'So, you could stay until then?'

'Well, I–'

'Oh *please*, but if you want to move on, don't worry. I know there's not much jet-set action on Formentera.'

'Hell, don't you think I've had my fill of the Beautiful People for one summer? ... No, Carrie, I was thinking of you and your research and–'

'Oh, *stuff* the research!'

'Carrie!'

'I mean, I'll get that tosh finished, don't you worry. You could even help if you like. I'm afraid some ... well, actually, *most* of the smutty stuff is quite beyond me.'

'Well, I'd love to stay. I couldn't think of anywhere nicer.'

'Smashing!'

'You don't think Teeny and Kurt would mind, do you?'

''course not. Anyway, Teeny said on the phone the other evening that she was glad I had some company at last. ... Talking of phones, it's occurred to me that we both might feel a bit better if we gave my brother a tinkle when we get back to *Clementina*.'

Misty pulled a face. 'I don't think he'd want to speak to *me*.'

186

'I bet he will – unless of course he's gone barking mad.'

'Jesus! – don't joke about things like that.'

'Oh, he'll be all right ... I think.'

Misty paid the bill and they started for the door and the seething body of drinkers visible in the bar beyond. Caroline, however, stopped at the Wiggies' table; they seemed to be in a panic to pay their own bill, as if they had a train to catch.

'I hope you've enjoyed your evening,' Caroline said grandly with a slight bow, 'and that you'll leave this establishment the wiser.'

Mrs Wiggy started her 'no comprendo' mantra, but Caroline stopped her. 'And you can forget all that foreign mumbo jumbo, my good woman. You understand me perfectly. A very good night to you both!'

Unscathed by the wild scenes of merrymaking in the Fonda Pepe's bar, Misty was still laughing and shaking her head as they emerged into the street. 'You're incorrigible, Miss Weetwood. I think everyone on earth suffering from depression or suicidal tendencies should be prescribed a fortnight on Formentera. ... Now where did we park the Wrangler? Was it left or –?'

Wide-eyed, Misty stopped dead in her tracks and grabbed Caroline's arm. 'Of *course*! I *knew* there was something familiar about that man. Come on! Quick!'

Misty was standing beside the Wiggies' table when Caroline caught up with her, but there was no sign of the eavesdroppers. 'You took your time!' she scolded. 'Is there another way out of this place, Carrie? I just don't understand how we could have missed them.'

"*Who?*"

'The Wiggies, of course!'

'Oh! ... Um ... yes. I think there's a back door that leads directly to the square. I saw it when I went to the loo, but–'

Misty was already heading for the *servicios*.

The adjacent back door did indeed lead into the square. Save for a few children cycling around the pseudo gas lamps, however, it was deserted; the old church, floodlit against the night sky, looked particularly fort-like and temporal.

'Shit! We've lost them.'

'Misty, *please*! What on *earth* is going on?'

'Oh, sorry, Carrie. It's just that ... Well, remember the first day we walked down to Es Mal Pas and you left me standing for a few minutes outside the *supermercado*?' Caroline nodded. 'And I thought I saw some guy on top of the tower looking at me through binoculars?'

'Not *that* again! He could have been looking at *anything*.'

'Yeah, I know. Anyway, the guy with the binoculars and our Mr Wiggy are one and the same.'

'Oh, come on! How do you work *that* out? I mean, you can't possibly have seen the chap on the tower that well.'

'Because they were *both* wearing the same T-shirt – red and yellow stripes – *thick* red and yellow stripes.'

'Misty, there must be loads of people with T-shirts like that.'

'On Formentera? I don't think so. White, blue, black, red – sure, but not like *his* T-shirt. I'm telling you, it's the same guy. And all that "no-speaka-de-English" shit! Trust me, Carrie, there's something weird about that couple.'

They drove back to *Clementina* somewhat subdued; penfriend confessions were forgotten. When they pulled off the main road just outside Sant Francesc, Caroline finally plucked up courage and told Misty about the incident in the garden which had resulted in her meeting Tom and Gwen, and the people in the gorilla masks up at the windmill.

'Didn't you go to the cops?' asked Misty incredulously as she guided the Jeep along the dark bumpy road.

'Well, if you think about it for a minute, what could I have told them? At the villa, there was simply no evidence of any intruder. Gwen and Tom found nothing. And as for the gorilla incident, what actually happened? I wasn't hurt or anything.'

'But you thought one of them had a gun!'

'It *could* have been a gun, but there again I couldn't swear to it. I'd been dozing. It was scorching.'

'There were those German cyclists.'

'Yes, but I didn't take their details.'

It was just after eleven when they reached the villa. They went into the living room and flung open the French windows to get some air. The soothing sounds of the sea engulfed and relaxed them. The Wiggies were put on the back burner.

'So, we'll phone my brother now, shall we?' asked Caroline grinning cheekily as she picked up the receiver.

For once Misty looked nervous. 'If you like,' she said quietly.

It took several attempts to get through to England, and when the call was finally answered by a breathless Vivian Duffle, she spent the first couple of minutes explaining how she'd been in the middle of serving a 'spotted dick': there was a dinner party for WSD's directors and their spouses.

'You're pulling my leg, Mrs D. Has Daddy gone bonkers? And it's a Sunday!'

'*Oh, it's nothing to do with his lordship, Miss Caroline, it's your mum. She organized it, a sort of farewell do before she beetles off back to France in the morning. I'd thought it would be cancelled, what with poor Diana being killed in that horrific car crash in Paris – I always knew she'd come a cropper – but you know what your mum's like, "The show must go on," and–*'

'Mrs Duffle! Stop! *Mother*? Is *she* there? Car crash? Diana who?'

The guests could wait for their spotted dick. Vivian launched into a colourfully embroidered and haphazardly edited account of the Master James saga; the tragic death of the Princess of Wales was forgotten. Caroline's intermittent croaks of astonishment, 'Oh gollies!' and gaping eyes only served to exacerbate Misty's nervousness.

Vivian's monologue concluded with a dire warning: '*I'm sorry, Miss Caroline, if that American spy has turned up out of the blue to pester you. I didn't want to give her your number, but she said it was "a matter of life and death" – or some such nonsense.*'

'But Mrs D–'

'*Knowing you, Miss Caroline, I'm sure you'll get rid of her quick enough. Mark my word, luvvy, she's trouble that girl. … Ooh, there's his lordship buzzing me. I must dash. They'll be wanting more custard, I bet.*'

'Hang on, Mrs D! What's the *Villa Gobelin*'s number?'

\*

James stood naked before the full-length mirror in his dressing room. He'd showered, and brushed and flossed his teeth. Now he was ready for bed. But before turning in, he couldn't resist the temptation to gaze just once more at his extraordinary physique. How beautiful was the reflection! He flicked his nipples and watched them go hard. He turned ninety degrees and stroked his buttocks. 'What a perfect bum,' he whispered, 'so firm, so exquisitely curved. … My penis and balls, too … exquisitely proportioned in every respect. … You're like a god.'

He moved from the dressing room to his bedroom and surveyed the packed suitcases. England. Bobbins. He had to be philosophical, that was what Alphonse Audinette had said. He certainly couldn't stay on at Cap-Ferrat, not with his mother returning with her entourage. On the other hand, she'd persuaded his father to give him a job in WSD's Export Department – an assistant to some guy called Brancepeth-Tring – Jesus Christ! According to Alphonse, there'd be lots of foreign travel and a seat on the board within a couple of years. Buying him a Ferrari had seemed a touch extravagant, but he supposed it was about time he got something to show for his position as the heir to one of Britain's greatest fortunes. Alphonse was right: he should buy a place of his own. He'd contact some agents as soon as he got home. He'd have to have a gym for sure. And a tennis court. And a squash court.

James had been asleep for less than thirty minutes when the phone on his bedside table began ringing. He was rudely awakened from a dream about Ancient Greece and naked bronzed athletes cavorting with each other in various sporting activities. He was disorientated and irritable.

'Yes!'

*'James?'*

'Yes!'

*'James, it's Caroline.'*

'Who?'

*'It's Caroline – your sister. ... Are you all right?'*

'What?'

*'Well, we've only just learned about your breakdown.'*

He heard a female voice in the background hiss 'Jesus, don't say that!'

*'I mean, your stay in Cap-Ferrat ... and everything. Golly I'd – we that is – had no idea. But you're OK now? Mrs Duffle says you're going home tomorrow. She couldn't tell us everything because of her spotted dick and–'*

'Caroline! Where are you? Is something the matter? What time is it anyway?'

*'Oh, were you asleep?'*

'Yes.'

*'Sorry. It's ... um – oh it's just eleven-thirty.'*

'"Just"?'

*'Well, you never used to go to bed before–'*

'Where are you?'

*'In Formentera – Spain – remember? ... And guess who's here with me.'*

'I don't know and I don't–'

*'Go on, guess.'*

'Arnold Schwarzenegger.'

*'Who?'*

'Forget it.'

*'Misty – Misty Start!'*

James did not compute: he sat motionless, propped up on one elbow, his mind frozen.

*'James, Misty's here and would like to speak with you. She's had a very rough time too, but that's a long story. ... I'm going to put her through now.'* Misty was shaking her head, mouthing 'no'. Caroline held out the phone, hissing, 'Come on, don't be silly.'

'*Here she is.*'

For a few seconds, James listened to a silent line. Then he heard, '*Hi! How yer doin', James?*' There was an instant explosion of memories and a barrage of conflicting emotions.

'Hello, Misty,' he muttered coldly.

\*

At *Clementina*, Caroline made a diplomatic exit as soon as a hesitant trans-Mediterranean conversation appeared to be getting under way. In any event, the anti-mosquito devices needed switching on in the bedrooms. Whatever transformations she may have undergone during her lengthy stay on Formentera, Caroline could still not retire without first doing everything in her power to create a hermetically sealed environment, notwithstanding the heat or the manufacturers' assertions that their products were effective even in rooms with open windows. Little did she suspect, however, that Misty, who loved fresh air and to fall asleep to the sound of the sea, undid all the precautions in her own quarters.

'Oh dear!' she cried, entering Misty's second-floor room in the tower: the three windows around its circular walls were all wide-open. Tut-tutting and slamming shut two of them, she moved swiftly on to the final danger zone. But leaning out to close the shutters, she caught sight of the moon rising on the horizon. A great carpet of silver light was streaming across the sea towards her.

'How can I ever leave this place?' she murmured, shaking her head slowly. She thought of England, of Bobbins, and the wind and rain that seemed to lash it for so many days of the year. She pictured her mother's face – that look of constant disdain whenever she was in her presence – and shivered. Frankly, she didn't care whether she ever saw Beryl again. Her father was all right though. ... All right? Wasn't that a tad unfair? ... As if mesmerized by the shimmering water, she re-evaluated her analysis but reached the same conclusion. In truth, he sometimes even had difficulty in remembering her name. Would he be in the least bothered if she were never to return home? The more she thought about it, the more convinced she became that Bobbins no longer had any relevance to her life. On the other hand, back in England there were her history studies, Durham and dear Pongo. Surely none of them had lost any of their magic?

A flash of orange light on the horizon far to the south caught Caroline's attention. She continued to stare at the spot where she'd seen it. After about a minute, there was another flash – and then another. Although there was not a breath of wind, and the water was like a mill pond, a storm was clearly brewing.

Her thoughts drifted slowly back to Pongo. But for her and Project MIM, she would never have discovered Formentera's magic. And yet, even on this front something was troubling her. Could it be that Pongo had simply wanted the manuscripts translating? – the performance of a tedious and purely mechanical task? And in one sense, wasn't that all she'd become to Pongo over the last couple of months – nothing more than a wretched machine? Pongo's phone calls had even become businesslike. Yes, that was true, now that she thought about them: no chit-chat, no enquiries as to what else she was up to, or whether she was lonely, happy, miserable, healthy. No, Pongo had never really bothered about anything other than those blasted manuscripts. And what did they reveal about old Louis XIV anyway? – that he got a big kick out of writing a sort of pornographic diary of his exploits with female favourites. Pongo might make some mileage out of that tosh on one or other of those pseudo-intellectual TV or radio chat shows on which she appeared from time to time as the eccentric professor – Margaret Rutherford couldn't have done it better – but was it really the sort of research with which she herself would be proud to be associated? ... And she had still to find any blasted references to the Man in the Iron Mask! And that was odd too: why had anyone ever thought that the diaries might contain such references? Was it Teeny's idea? ... Kurt's? ... Pongo's?

But perhaps she was being unfair. How could the Prof have known what the manuscripts were going to contain? And, what with her lectures at Harvard's Summer School, the October deadline from her publishers for the finished manuscript of her definitive biography of Colbert ... well, it was hardly surprising that poor Pongo didn't have time for a chinwag. Dash it all, the manuscripts might have turned out to be of staggering importance – they could still do so – and yet the critical and privileged task of translating them had been entrusted to *herself*.

That, however, was the kernel of the problem. Why *hadn't* Pongo personally dealt with what was potentially the most explosive source material ever to come into her possession – probably in her entire career? It was a chance in a million; access to such unpublished material was any professional historian's dream. She could have made arrangements to examine them later in the year, couldn't she? So why had Pongo delegated? Did she believe that the manuscripts were forgeries? Had she some reason to suspect that they contained nothing but regal smut? Or was it all to do with her taking another History undergraduate, the waif-like Miko Navette, as her 'secretary' to Harvard, a fact which Teeny had disclosed in her most recent phone call?

Teeny said she'd heard it from a friend of hers who lectured in Durham's Archaeology Department. The tone in Teeny's voice had sounded quite melodramatic – almost as if she was disclosing details of a husband's adultery to an innocent and naïve wife. ... Now why on earth had she used that analogy? And why should she care one jot about Navette anyway? She was just a silly first-year student, a Canadian with a brain the size of a pea, by all accounts, who never stopped talking about her father being minister of something or other in Quebec's provincial government.

Caroline sighed heavily. Perhaps she was just reading too much into everything. And she was tired. But damn it! – if Navette was so dim, why in God's name did Pongo have anything to do with her, let alone take her to Harvard as–?

'Oh, come on, you silly girl,' Caroline muttered, 'this is getting you nowhere!' She reached out for the shutters and peered down into the garden. From her position high up in the tower, she momentarily pictured herself in a castle, and couldn't resist the urge to chant 'Rapunzel, Rapunzel let down your hair' – just as she'd done on that first traumatic day at the villa. She started to chuckle, but suddenly froze. There was a figure in the garden, close to the gate down by the cliff path. And in the moonlight, she could tell that there was something strange about its head. It was too large for the body, misshapen, and–

The figure looked up at her, and then began running towards the villa. As it reached the illuminated terrace and looked up again, Caroline saw a gorilla's head.

'Misty!' she screamed, bolting for the door.

Caroline screamed even louder when she burst into the living room. The scene was startling in its clarity: Misty was sat on the sofa, blindfolded, gagged and handcuffed. At her side stood a man wearing a gorilla mask. He held a pistol to her head.

'Don't move or she's dead!' he shouted.

Then Caroline was grabbed from behind and something hard was pushed into the centre of her back.

'And you too will be dead if you struggle or make another sound,' snarled a harsher, shriller voice.

Within seconds, Caroline met the same fate as Misty. The last thing she saw before being blindfolded was the man's red and yellow striped T-shirt.

# CHAPTER 17

For years, the Duffles and Miss Spigot had devotedly served George Weetwood. Yet, whenever they misguidedly attempted to engage him in chit-chat he switched off. Even so, he could, if necessary, convey the impression that he was absorbing their every word through the judicious use of nods, raised eyebrows, hmms and ahs. He was doing so now, as Ron Duffle babbled while driving him to Soap House on this morning of Monday 1 September. Duffle had commenced his inane chatter immediately upon their departure from Bobbins.

'What a palaver over Princess Diana's death. I said to the wife at breakfast that–'

Unexpectedly, George cut him short. 'Very tragic, of course. However, she was *not* "Princess Diana" but "Diana, Princess of Wales".'

A silence followed. By the time Duffle commenced a fresh topic, George was already imagining nocturnal adventures at Crewe Junction. But then something suddenly struck him: for weeks now, Duffle hadn't babbled at all – he'd hardly said a word. Why? When had his routine changed? ... And why had he now returned to the tedious *status quo ante*? With the Jaguar approaching Muckley, he decided to make a determined effort to listen.

'... would 'ave thought that with all your interest in trains and stuff you'd be champing at the bit to get some of the action.'

The eyes of chauffeur and passenger met momentarily in the windscreen mirror. George raised his eyebrows. 'Ah, well ... possibly,' he responded, wondering what 'action' he might wish to possess.

'Right up your street, I would 'ave thought,' Duffle continued as the limousine accelerated out of the village. 'I dare say you've been mulling it over for quite a while. Mind you, buying a whole line – that would cost quite a packet, I bet.'

'Hmm.'

'Yes, a hell of a lot – if you'll pardon my French, sir.' Duffle fell silent: the conversation was not progressing as well as he'd hoped. He'd try a different tack. 'Perhaps you're dead against all this privatisation – I mean, lots of folk said the railways would fall apart – like what's happened in America.'

The penny dropped. It was time for George to indicate that he knew exactly what Duffle was talking about – and sound knowledgeable.

'Ah yes, the privatisation of the railways, er ... Duffle. What a very big issue – a very big issue indeed. I always said that these politicians didn't have a clue. The practicalities of running a vast railway system are *way* beyond their limited abilities. And why any intelligent businessman would want to take on the nightmare of running passenger services – the immense problems of timetabling, the maintenance of rolling stock, the complexities of apportioning ticket revenues between numerous operators for long-distance travel, the gargantuan–'

'I take your point, sir – oh why's that blasted truck stopped right on the bend?' Duffle slowed and carefully overtook with his usual degree of extreme caution. 'I take your point, but then you, sir, being an expert an' all, it wouldn't be a problem for *you*, would it?'

'Well, I ... The point is–'

'Oh, I know what you're going to say, sir.'

'The point *is*–'

'The point is, you're already running a vast industrial empire and you wouldn't 'ave the time to mess about running express trains as well – like Branson and Virgin.'

'Er ... no, that's not what I – that is ...'

The Jaguar rolled down the hill into Dribbledale towards the level crossing where the road traversed the Manchester-Leeds mainline. The lowered barrier, flashing lights, and klaxon heralded an approaching train. George peered through the windscreen with intense expectation.

'The point is, er ... Duffle, that the cost of acquiring one of these "franchises" – just one – would be very, very considerable. It's really not the sort of investment WSD could–'

'I wasn't thinking of WSD, sir, but *you* – personally like.'

'*Me*?' The horn of the approaching train reached George's ears, and he pressed the button to lower his window. Warm moist air filled the air-conditioned car. 'Good Lord, Duffle, I haven't got the resources to go buying railway franchises!'

Duffle's response was immediate and vehement. 'Come off it! If you sold WSD you'd 'ave enough to buy the whole damned lot! And I bet there's plenty of companies what would like to buy Goblin – and Goblinville, come to that – some *German* companies perhaps? The *Germans* have got more money than bloody sense now, 'aven't they? – buying up everything in sight – them and the Japs. Oh, you'd get billions! – bloody *billions*! You could be the "Railway King" – do what you like – even bring back steam engines an' all.'

Duffle had turned round to face his master. His eyes blazed. George felt uncomfortable; something was definitely wrong with the man. He'd no right to behave like this – none at all. ... And yet–

As the train roared past, George thrust his head out of the window to get a better view. A whirlwind of thoughts engulfed him. Sell WSD? ... Buy rail franchises? ... Abandon Goblin and his inheritance? ... The control of Crewe Junction – not a model but the *real* thing. ... The power to reintroduce the beautiful maroon livery of the old LMS – to build new lines and reopen some of his beloved branch lines. ... Lord Weetwood – the Railway King! Perhaps this was his destiny – to rescue the British railway system from the inevitable catastrophe of piecemeal, ill-conceived privatisation!

Some minutes later, George was finally roused from his reverie by the door opening. Duffle stood at attention before him, grim-faced. For just a few seconds, he'd no idea where he was, but then the incongruous plate-glass doors within Soap House's mighty Decorated Gothic porte cochère came into focus. He sighed, reached for his briefcase, and mumbled 'Goodbye' as he emerged from the car. But with a sneer, Duffle merely slammed the door and walked away.

Fifteen minutes later, Miss Spigot was hard at work trying to get the Chairman – grandly framed by the large Perpendicular Gothic widow behind him – to concentrate on his busy schedule. But George was still trying to come to grips with Duffle's gross impertinence. Perhaps the cretin was mentally ill? ... On the other hand, he – of all people – had suggested the possibility of saving the national rail system from catastrophe. A dark horse indeed!

*Oh what in God's name is Spigot droning on about?*

'... then at eleven-fifteen, Chairman, there'll be a brief presentation ceremony in the Boardroom. It's a Mrs Edna Spat. She's retiring after forty-two years' service. Worked her way up from Packaging and Dispatch to Senior Stationery Supervisor. It's all here in the little presentation speech I've prepared for you. And in this envelope is the solid brass key to her retirement house in Goblinville, 36 Palm Oil Boulevard – really quite a nice little house. ... I drove past it on my way home last night. ... The Director of Personnel will present her with the usual bouquet and ...'

*What tedium! At least there'll be no Beryl when I get home this evening – back to Cap-Ferrat at last! Well, via Paris, that is. I just hope she doesn't go mad at Cartier again. ... After supper tonight, I'll programme Crewe Junction for a summer Bank Holiday afternoon and then give some more thought to this railway franchise business – run over the figures – not that I'm seriously considering getting involved – so don't start counting your chickens, George, but–*

'Now there's an extra appointment at eleven-forty in Meeting Room 3, Chairman. Mr Brancepeth-Tring's International Committee have an emergency meeting to consider the tragic demise of the Southeast Asia Divisional Chief Executive and the appointment of his replacement. Mr Brancepeth-Tring would welcome your attendance, Lord Weetwood. He says it's a "rather sticky wicket".'

'Hmm? ... What is?' George looked up from the list he'd just scribbled on his memo pad. It read: *Buy franchises for "Flying Scotsman", "Cornish Riviera Express", "Royal Scot", "Manchester Pullman"?? Reintroduce "Thames-Clyde Express" from St Pancras to Glasgow via Leeds???*

'The selection of Mr Joop Yudohusodo's successor.'

'Sorry? *Who?*'

'The Chief Executive of the Southeast Asia Division.'

'Ah yes. Nice chap. What's *his* problem?'

*He really is like a little boy*, Miss Spigot thought maternally. She had a tremendous urge to admonish him gently, using the voice she reserved for her conversations with Augustus, the terrapin who inhabited a squeaky-clean glass tank in the living room of her otherwise lifeless abode.

'Well, he's ... er ... he's dead. Dreadful business – absolutely dreadful.'

'Dead? Can't be.'

'It was in the memo from–'

'I mustn't have received a copy.'

'I believe I left one–'

'It really isn't good enough, Miss Spigot. One can't have senior executives passing away without proper notification to me.'

'I think it's the pink sheet of paper under the list you're compiling, Chairman.'

George tore the list off the memo pad and secreted it in the inside breast pocket of his jacket. *Sometimes that woman notices too much for her own good.* He quickly skimmed the pink memorandum – an innovation calculated by Brancepeth-Tring to draw the attention of fellow directors to what he believed to be urgent matters.

'Heavens! Choked to death on a chicken bone – and at the Mandarin of all places! And now some cousin wants to be appointed his successor. And according to Mr Brancepeth-Tring, Miss Spigot, the cousin's brother-in-law is a minister in the Indonesian government, and if this bounder doesn't get the job, the planning approval for the extension to our Jakarta plant may be delayed indefinitely.' George sighed and shook his head. 'As if I didn't have *enough* problems to solve.'

'I know, Chairman, I know. I've managed to get the lunch with the auditors put back to one-thirty.'

'Lunch? Oh blast! Is that in Manchester?'

'Yes. As you know, they're awfully keen for you to meet the new Managing Partner, Giles Trimfone.'

'I don't suppose I could get out of it?'

'It's already been rescheduled *three* times ... but if you *really* want to–'

'No, no! I suppose I'd better face the music. In any event, I–' But on reflection, George thought it wiser not to indicate that he might use the opportunity to sound out Trimfone and his partners on the current thinking in the City on rail franchises – not that they'd know anything about railways, as such, or possess an ounce of imagination. Accountants!

To Miss Spigot's amazement, her mentor suddenly smiled. '"Into the Valley of Death",' he intoned melodramatically. Then he chuckled.

*

George's sister, Belinda Thornton – she never used the 'Honourable' to which she was entitled as a baron's daughter – rarely travelled any more, but things had been very different before her husband died. Whenever Len could take time off from his job at Eastbourne's Cleansing Department, he and Belinda would be off like a flash. For them, travel was a passion – the landscapes, savouring new dishes and wines, the fascinating local customs, the history and architecture discovered and rediscovered. They'd stayed in *adobe* houses in the Peruvian Highlands, camped in Botswana's Okavango Delta, and trekked across the Jebel Sahro Mountains of Morocco. Despite all its problems, planet earth was wonderful. They'd saved up for these memorable experiences – which might have come as a surprise to anyone with knowledge of Belinda's background or her annual dividend income from WSD – but then, not being much interested in things materialistic, the Thorntons had chosen to donate most of this unearned income anonymously to various charities.

Eustace Weetwood had adored Belinda. Consequently, after she'd run away from her third boarding school, he finally agreed that she could apply to enter the Royal Ballet School. She was accepted, did well, and graduated into the corps de ballet at Covent Garden. Then she met Len on the Tube and romance followed. An engineering undergraduate at Imperial College, he came for a weekend at Bobbins, and Eustace liked him. Within a month, Len and Belinda were married at Kensington Register Office.

After graduating, Len got a job with Eastbourne Council, and Belinda gave up the ballet: she believed that looking after her husband was more important than dancing. They were blissfully happy together, although there was a brief period of sadness when Belinda discovered she couldn't have children. Adoption was discussed but never pursued: Len always seemed less than enthused when the subject came up.

When Len died of cancer in 1978, George came to the funeral; Beryl did not. For a long time, Belinda felt her life had ended. She even attempted suicide by sticking her head in the gas oven, but natural gas wasn't up to the job. She never told anyone. The bungalow took up most of her time at first, particularly the garden. That had been Len's domain and she owed it to him to keep it looking nice. The neighbours had been kind – the Potters on one side and the Gortons on the other – but she could only take them in small doses: the Potters were too house-proud; the Gortons had spent most of their lives in South Africa. They were all retired and played a lot of bridge together; bridge was not Belinda's game. She contemplated travel, but without Len it all seemed pointless. After a few years, she considered selling up and taking a flat in London; there might be an office job at Covent Garden or Saddlers Wells. She'd kept in touch with some of her former colleagues and a few of them had got to the top. But she didn't like to ask, and what would Len have said about pulling strings?

It was Joyce Potter who suggested the Bench. 'We need younger people like you. There are so few these days willing to serve as magistrates – what with kiddies and trying to hold down a job. It's jolly interesting and one gets a lot of satisfaction putting criminals where they belong.' She left some pamphlets from the Lord Chancellor's Department on the hall table. Belinda never thought for one moment that she'd be selected, but when the letter arrived, she felt quite excited and thought Len would have been proud of her.

As far as Beryl was concerned, the Thorntons had always been *personae non gratae*: it was bad enough being ordinary and middle class, but to be so when one had the means to live in what she regarded as 'style' was simply beyond her comprehension. George, on the other hand, believed that what Belinda did with her income from WSD was entirely her own affair. Beryl's excommunication of the Thorntons meant that Belinda initially saw very little of her niece and nephew. But then, when the twins were five, Beryl phoned one hot July morning with a suggestion that her sister-in-law might like to look after them for a week. Belinda had come very close to losing her temper, but, as usual in these situations, she'd thought of what Len would have done. It transpired that 'Nanny' had been rushed to hospital with suspected appendicitis just as Beryl and George were about to leave for the airport en route for the *Villa Gobelin*; this was when they still took holidays together. There was some tiresome agency in Manchester which could procure a temporary replacement, but George was being difficult about entrusting the 'little ones' to a total stranger. And their new housekeeper had gone to a funeral in Scotland – Beryl couldn't remember whether it was the woman's father or mother – and was refusing to come back. She and George just had to get to Cap-Ferrat as they had 'an army of awfully important people' to entertain, including a cabinet minister. Belinda allowed Beryl to continue begging for some minutes, even after she'd decided to take the children; it was wicked but a joy to hear Beryl grovelling.

Ron Duffle drove the twins down to Eastbourne; it was not a journey he'd care to remember. Belinda sat in the bow window of her front room for hours, waiting for the car to arrive, wondering how she'd cope. But the three of them got on like a house on fire, right from the moment Belinda helped them out of the car, with Duffle moaning about the number of times he'd had to stop to take them to 'the toilet'.

'"Lavatory"!' the twins shouted in unison.

The week became a fortnight, and then a month. After six weeks, the nanny recovered and the twins' first schools loomed. Belinda sobbed for hours after Duffle drove her 'little angels' away in the old black Rover; they'd waved frantically out of the rear window until the car turned the corner and was lost to sight. Little could she have imagined then that, having made such an impression on the twins, their parents would willingly permit them to spend their summer holidays at Eastbourne for many years to come.

'What super times they were,' Belinda said quietly; she talked a lot to herself these days. And why not? She suspected most people did when they were alone. She'd finally found Formentera in her *Times Atlas of the World* and hoped that the scale would be big enough to locate the places Caroline mentioned in the postcard that had arrived that morning. She was prone to start reminiscing about her fun with the twins on those long summer holidays whenever she received a communication from one or other of them. They'd always written her letters and cards, and she'd kept them all; bundles of them were tied up with string and stored in old shoe boxes. There'd been quite a lot of cards from James once he started spending his holidays with Peter, but since his death they'd only spoken on the telephone intermittently. She'd tried so many times during the last two years to get him down to Eastbourne, but to no avail.

And Caroline hadn't been to stay since the summer before she went up to Durham. What a serious girl she'd become! The postcards and letters had continued to arrive at regular intervals, but they rarely contained anything other than factual reports of her historical studies. And that was how the postcards had started from Formentera – as dull as dishwater – excruciating! And then came the bombshell. It had just been one short sentence on the back of a postcard of an old tower: 'I've hired a bicycle.' In subsequent postcards there'd been further dramatic news, including references to swimming, cooking and socializing with Gwen Blackberry and her husband, Tom. Gwen Blackberry! – Belinda's favourite character in *The Muffins* – of all people!

Just a few days ago she'd received a card announcing that an American penfriend had arrived, called Misty – such an odd name! Whatever next! But there'd been even more excitement: out of the blue, a very unexpected postcard arrived from James! This summer was turning out to be full of pleasant surprises! It was a very colourful picture of a very pink house. The undated message read:

Dearest Aunt Belinda,
Hope you're well. This pile is (or was) Ephrussi de Rothschild's villa. It's next door to our place in Cap-Ferrat – as you'll no doubt remember. Now I know what I've been missing all these years! I'll phone when I get back.
Love, James

Belinda had sat for some time at the little breakfast table in the kitchen trying to puzzle it out; she'd even been late for court. She was still waiting for James's call.

Still peering at the tiny map of Formentera in the *Times Atlas*, Belinda murmured: 'Well, I'm sorry but I can't find anywhere called "Es Mal Pas". Never mind.' She decided to read aloud Caroline's latest postcard just in case she's missed something.

'"Dearest Auntie, Misty and I are still enjoying the super weather." Oh, I'm so glad Misty's stayed on. It would have been a bit lonely without Gwen and her husband. "We cycled to Cap Barbaria today." Now I've seen that on the map somewhere. ... Ah yes, here it is. Oh, that's what's on the postcard, of course. Heavens, it looks barren – wild, I'd say. And yet the rest of the island, judging from all her other cards' – she had half a dozen spread out on the kitchen table – 'looks quite wooded. I bet Len would have loved it. And he'd have had no hesitation getting his swimming trunks off! Remember that time on Bornholm when...

'Come on, Linda' – Len had always called her that– 'what else does Caroline have to say. "It should be Misty's turn to cook tonight, but she's reminded me there are sardinas frescas at the Sol y Luna in Es Mal Pas. It's a smashing little restaurant on the beach."'

Belinda scoured the map once more, but there was nothing with a name remotely like Es Mal Pas. Anyway, it all sounded so charming. And there had to be something very special about this place, Formentera, to have had such an effect on dear Caroline. She looked at the postmark on the card, but it was smudged. 'I wonder when she wrote this. She normally writes the date at the top.' But there was nothing. 'Well, the other cards took four or five days so I suppose ... Oh dear, I can't sit here all morning, not with' – she hesitated – 'not with George coming. I hope he doesn't mind a salad for lunch.'

*

George's telephone call the previous evening had come as a shock: Belinda very rarely heard from him personally, albeit in view of her position as an important shareholder, there were regular communications from WSD. In this connection, she'd been perfectly happy to keep things on a formal arm's length basis; so had George. She did not attend the Annual General Meetings – a pure formality held at Soap House each June. She always appointed George as her proxy and had never voted against any resolution proposed by the board. She received the audited accounts and studied them with great interest and care; if she had any queries, she directed them by mail to the Company Secretary, Merryweather, whose brief replies were rarely illuminating. George had only contacted her in recent years when she'd questioned the appointment of Dame Diana Tenby-Jones as a non-executive director, and the colossal sums expended on R&D. The latter had resulted in a dividend reduction; she was only concerned because of the sums she'd covenanted to pay to several charities.

It was funny in a way – 'spooky' was how she'd described it to herself when she came off the phone – because George had rung as the nightly fifteen-minute broadcast of *The Muffins* had concluded with a melodramatic phone call to Geoffrey Muffin from the smooth-talking Dr Mellon at Worchester Royal Infirmary. Jessica was still in her coma after the awful accident with the combine harvester at Bumpstead Plumpstead. Geoffrey had just got back from another traumatic day at Jessica's bedside in Intensive Care, even though he ought to have been at Home Farm supervising the harvest...

'*Hello! Heston Charlton 2263. Geoffrey Muffin speaking.*'

'*Ah, hello, Mr Muffin. It's Dr Mellon here.*' Gasping, Belinda had put down her spoon of butterscotch Angel Delight: it had to be bad news.

'*Yes, doctor?*' Geoffrey sounded very anxious. '*It's Jessica, isn't it?*'

'*Well, yes. Look, I'm just leaving the hospital now to go to the Young Conservatives' Harvest Festival bash at Upper Poxley Hall, and I thought that if you were going to be in, I'd come via your neck of the woods. You see, Mr Muffin, there's something rather important I need to discuss with you.*'

As the BBC Symphony Orchestra struck up the rousing signature tune – *An English Country Garden* at an extremely accelerated tempo

– Belinda's phone rang. She knew it would be lazy Joyce Potter wanting to gossip about Dr Mellon's mysterious call to poor old Geoffrey.

'Hello,' Belinda said in the voice she used for greeting Joyce.

'*Belinda? This is your brother George speaking.*'

'Oh! ... George! ... Hello! What a pleasant surprise. I thought you were my neighbour Joyce Potter. I was just listening to *The Muffins.*'

After a pregnant pause, George said: '*Ah ... right. ... There's something rather important I need to discuss with you.*'

'Goodness, George, I would never have imagined that *you* listened to *The Muffins* too.'

Another pause.

'*Belinda, it's urgent. I'm coming down tomorrow by car. I should be with you by midday. Is that convenient?*'

'Tomorrow? ... Well, I'm supposed to be sitting – it's a Tuesday – but–'

'*"Sitting"?*'

'In court. On the Bench.'

'*Oh, I see.*'

'I'll sort something out though – if it's important.'

'*It is.* **Very.**'

'Can you give me any idea what it's all about?'

'*No – not over the phone.*'

'Oh. ... All right.'

'*I'll see you tomorrow.*'

And with that he rang off.

Belinda had not slept well. Now, bathed and dressed in one of her best Marks & Spencer outfits, she was sitting on the sofa in the front room, the breakfast dishes washed and put away, the simple salad for George's lunch prepared and popped in the fridge with a covering of Clingfilm. She'd nothing to do but wait and speculate.

Half-heartedly, she flicked through that morning's *Guardian*. Having skimmed the endless columns on the tragic events in Paris and criticism of the Queen's alleged indifference about Diana's death, she started to read an article on violence in the classroom, but swiftly abandoned it: she got enough of that sort of thing at Court. Oh dear, everything seemed to be so gloomy and depressing. Sighing, she turned to the supplement on 'Personal Savings and Ecologically-sound Investments' – which was the only reason she'd ordered the paper from the newsagent instead of her usual *Times*. But what she thought was the supplement on the sofa beside her turned out to be *The Sun*.

'Oh damn! That silly man at the newsagent,' she giggled. 'We'd better not let George see this or–' She mouthed the banner headline: '**LADY GOBLIN GOBBLES MORE THAN GRIME!!!**' Beneath it was a fuzzy photograph – obviously taken with a telephoto lens – of a skinny naked woman kneeling in front of a naked man at the edge of a swimming pool. Not much imagination was required to work out what was taking place. The participants could have been almost anyone, but *The Sun* had no doubts as to their identities. A box at the side of the page, containing no less than six exclamation marks, informed readers that there were more photographs on pages four and five, and that a certain '**SOAP EMPIRE**' was '**IN A LATHER**'.

Belinda walked over to the bay window. A grey blanket of cloud hung over Eastbourne. 'The poor twins,' she mumbled. 'Poor *George*.' Tears began to trickle down her cheeks.

# CHAPTER 18

Rory stood at the cliff edge and peered over. The sight and sound of the waves and the swirling mass of white foam almost two hundred feet below made him jump back in terror. The wind was strong, and force of habit made him raise his right hand to push his hair back, but all he felt was the bewildering smoothness of his shaven head. He looked around, feeling self-conscious and horribly conspicuous. The flat arid landscape of rocks and occasional stunted bushes stretched up and down the coast and some way inland. There was no one in sight, but then it was still early. He looked at his watch: 7:36.

During the long hours of darkness, he'd had plenty of time to contemplate the events which had now finally taken place. When their enormity had sunk in, he'd wanted to run away – far away from *Casa Bayreuth* and its awful secret. But Ursula must have known that he lacked the courage to do that. How else could he explain her deep, undisturbed sleep? Nevertheless, he had resolved to try to disguise his identity. And so, at daybreak, armed with some kitchen scissors and a razor, he'd shaved off both his moustache and all his hair. Almost immediately, he'd panicked: a reasonably respectable middle-class Englishman had been transformed into a skinhead; now, he even *looked* like a criminal! Ursula would be furious. He'd had to get out into the fresh air – the dark, claustrophobic confines of the villa were suffocating him – and, as the night's storm had blown itself out, he'd resolved to walk the two miles northwards along the cliffs to the old tower at Punta Prima.

*

*Casa Bayreuth*'s isolation had rendered the property perfect for the kidnappers' purposes. Perched citadel-like at the edge of mighty cliffs on Formentera's north-west coast, the villa commanded panoramic views of both the Mediterranean and the scrubby hinterland plateau; it was nearly always windy, whatever the weather. A bumpy dirt track led from the villa's gates and connected it after a mile or so to the quiet tarmac road linking Punta Prima with Sant Ferran, a twenty-minute drive away. Using the 'sensitive author' ruse, the owners' agents were kept at bay; they drove out once a fortnight, but the cellar was not on their checklist. And although the coastline at this point was dotted with villas – most of them large – none was inconveniently close to *Bayreuth*. Their residents, moreover, kept very much to themselves.

Back in July at the height of the season, Rory and Ursula had thought themselves extremely lucky to find *Casa Bayreuth*. But now, after almost two months of occupation, it was painfully clear to Rory why it had been available. For a start, the villa resembled a wartime blockhouse: its German owners were devotees of concrete and functionalism. In consequence, there were remarkably few windows, and those which had been grudgingly permitted in the otherwise fortress-like walls of the structure, were tiny. Accentuating *Bayreuth*'s bunker-like appearance were the high concrete walls which enclosed its garden – a flowerless and waterless domain of cacti and stunted pines laid out in depressingly symmetrical arrangements. The villa's interior was also devoid of any semblance of Mediterranean charm: the dark rooms with their bare walls were clinically furnished in a minimalist style with high-tech furniture. And as Rory had quickly discovered, there was not a comfortable chair in the house.

Then there were the paintings – more than thirty and all by the same artist – depicting World War II battlefields liberally sprinkled with mangled corpses in a quasi-cubist style. These macabre works had provoked the first serious dispute between Rory and Ursula after their arrival. With his intense sensitivities, Rory had found them deeply distressing, and had wanted them taken down for the duration of their stay. Ursula had objected vehemently, expressing a near manic enthusiasm for their quality and themes. She'd ranted and raved. The grim scenes remained *in situ*, constantly feeding Rory's senses of servitude and inadequacy.

*

As he shuffled onwards to Punta Prima, gloomily reliving the events of the last twelve hours, Rory failed to notice the gulls swooping over his head, or their ever more menacing cries as he wandered closer and closer to the edge of the cliffs and the gulls' nests. Suddenly, one of the birds dive-bombed him with a blood-curdling screech. There was a rush of air as it narrowly missed him, and, awakened from his reveries and realizing his predicament, he began to run over the rocky ground as fast as he could towards the old tower just ahead of him, praying that it would offer some protection. Another gull swooped – and then another. Screaming, he threw himself to the ground and covered his hairless head with his hands.

When the gulls' cries had finally died away, he hesitantly looked up. There were still some birds flying high overhead, but now that he was some distance from the cliffs, they no longer appeared to regard him as a threat to their young. His knees were badly cut, however, and the sight of the blood shocked him. He began to cry, at first just a whimper, and then uncontrollably. He grabbed a rock, and, with a roar of anguish and self-pity, hurled it as far as he could. Wincing, he managed to get to his feet, and, still sobbing, limp the remaining thirty yards to the tower. Leaning against its rough stones, he slowly sat down, pulled his legs up towards his chest, and studied his knees with horror.

'Oh, God,' he cried, 'what a sodding, sodding mess! *Everything*'s a sodding mess.'

He faced the route he'd just travelled, and in the distance towards the south-east, he could make out *Casa Bayreuth*'s ugly, angular mass. 'Christ,' he muttered, 'she's probably awake by now, wondering where the hell I've got to. It'll be murder when I get back.'

In his tortured mind, he weighed up what was worse: incurring Ursula's limitless wrath, or opening the door to the cellar. ... He could still run away – even go to the police and give himself up. If he confessed and led them to the scene of the crime *and* gave them Ursula – it had been *her* idea – she'd planned everything – he'd done nothing more than what she'd told him to do. That's all he was – a mere puppet – all he'd ever been. But why should the police believe that? What difference would it make at his trial anyway?

The blood and dirt on his knees were congealing, and the fear of infection began to alarm him. He was also hungry and thirsty. A bank of cloud had spread over the island, and with the sun obscured, the strong wind began to feel cold. He studied his scuffed trainers and grubby shorts; it would be a very long and painful walk to the police station in Sant Francesc. Back at *Bayreuth*, on the other hand, there were warm clothes, Ursula's comprehensive first aid box, and breakfast. Yes, there was a lot of sense in returning. If, after some reflection, going to the police still seemed like a good idea, he could always pop down in the van this afternoon when Ursula had her siesta.

In any event, there were the two girls. He really ought to check out the cellar: he didn't trust Ursula; there was something mean and vicious about her – like the way she'd kicked that American girl in the van last night. And then he remembered the look of abject terror in Caroline Weetwood's eyes. With a gasp of pain, he pushed himself up and began hobbling back to the villa as fast he could go.

When Rory finally reached *Casa Bayreuth*, he hesitated for some time before he put the key in the lock and let himself in. Ursula was sat at the kitchen table, eating some form of gruel she'd prepared using yoghurt, oatmeal and prunes. A cigarette with an inch of ash lay burning in the ashtray at her side. She was reading a copy of *Bild*. He could hear banging and muffled shouts coming from the cellar.

'Where the hell have you been?' she snapped without looking up. 'Those girls need feeding – or the toilet. See to it. And then we'll put Phase 2 into operation.'

Rory was in a dilemma: he'd worked up the courage to confront Ursula with his attempts at a change of identity, but he could just postpone the misery by walking out and obeying her orders. However, his wounds needed dressing, and he couldn't remember where she'd put the first aid box. In any event, he wasn't sure how he was supposed to feed the captives.

A sudden gust of wind caused a door to slam somewhere in the draughty house. Irritated by the disturbance, Ursula picked up her cigarette and inhaled vigorously. 'Well, just don't stand there, Rory– *Mein Gott*! Your hair!'

'Now, I *can* explain. I–'

'Brilliant! *Wunderschön*! I like!'

Accustomed to her constant sarcasm, Rory remained very much on the offensive. 'I – I ... er ... I thought it would help sort of disguise me, but I never imagined it would make me *look* like a–'

'For once, Rory, you do something sensible. So much better than that horrible long hair and moustache. And so sexy! I like men who look like Yul Brynner. And now you can dispense with those awful fake spectacles.' Stubbing out the cigarette in her bowl of partially consumed food, she added: 'Take that bread down to those bitches, but make it clear it has to last them all day. And don't forget your mask!'

Rory snatched the two baguette-like sticks and limped away. Oblivious to his injuries, Ursula watched him go and resolved to have sex with him later in the day.

*

During the planning of Caroline's kidnapping, Ursula had decided that after the deed was done, contact between the captive and herself should be avoided. At the time, the various arguments put forward in support of this strategy seemed logical to her co-conspirator. For a start, she'd said that a 'one-to-one relationship' would probably help to calm the girl: if she never knew who was going to come through the door, it could prove very unsettling. Reading his mind, Ursula had gone on to say that it would be far better for Rory to be 'the sole interface' for two reasons. First, Caroline would instantly spot her German accent, and, as Ursula suspected German Intelligence already had a file on herself, she'd probably be put on the suspect list immediately following Caroline's release. Secondly – and this was an extraordinary admission for Ursula to make – Caroline was more likely to obey the orders of a man than 'a mere woman'.

And then, after all their weeks of careful planning, and just as they were about to make 'the grab', the American girl had turned up out of the blue. The two of them had become inseparable! In the end, they'd really had no option but to abduct them both.

'So much for the "sole interface"!' muttered Rory as he donned his gorilla mask and prepared to unlock the cellar door for the third time that morning. It wasn't fair: Ursula should help out. Damn it, *she* should take the girls to the toilet! He'd never known anyone pee as much as those two. Nerves or not, it was getting ridiculous. Perhaps they were doing it deliberately – trying to wear him out – up and down the stairs. Christ, they hadn't even been in the villa twelve hours and he was knackered. And his cut legs still hadn't been seen to.

'About time,' snapped Misty as Rory walked in. 'What kept you? This bread is shit. It's like concrete.'

'Misty, don't antagonize him for goodness' sake.'

Rory attempted to speak loudly – and half an octave lower than normal. 'Yeah, sister, you'd better listen to your friend, or else.'

Misty groaned. '"*Sister*"? Give me a break! Why don't you just speak normally and tell us what the fuck is going on here.'

Rory didn't like obscenities; he particularly disliked the 'f' word. What annoyed him most was their use by women; it was simply beyond the pale.

'Don't speak like that in front of a lady!' he shouted. Immediately the words were out of his mouth, he realized how ridiculous they must have sounded; he couldn't imagine what had made him say them.

'Excuse me? You and your friend abduct Carrie and I–'

'*Me.*'

Misty shot Caroline a mean look. 'What?'

'Carrie and *me* – not Carrie and *I*. ... Sorry.'

Misty shook her head and sighed. 'Where was I, King Kong? ... Incidentally, when's Mrs Kong going to make another appearance?'

'Mind your own business.'

'Anyway, you two geeks abduct Carrie and *me* at gun point last night, gag, handcuff and shackle us, throw us in a truck, kick the shit out of me, dump us in some windowless hole devoid of furniture – without even a john – and you get all prissy because I use some good old Anglo-Saxon words like–'

'Just shut up!' roared Rory, pulling out a pistol tucked into his shorts' waistband. 'I don't want to hear that word again, OK?'

Misty stared at him wide-eyed. 'OK, OK. Keep cool.'

'Look, Mr–' began Caroline. She paused. 'Actually, what *is* your name?'

'Carrie, he's not going to tell us his–'

'Just call me "Rex".'

'Good. Well ... Rex, I really think it would only be fair and reasonable if you gave us some idea of what's going on. As my friend has indicated, we do feel that your treatment of us has been positively beastly. I mean, are handcuffs *and* shackled ankles really necessary? And expecting us to sit on the floor is beyond the pale. Frankly, I can't for the life of me imagine why on earth anyone would want to abduct *me* – or Misty for that matter. I mean, it's not as though we're important or anything. ... I say, it's not got anything to do with the manuscripts by any chance, has it?'

'What?'

'Don't take any notice of her, Rex. It's the shock ... or the hunger. How about some breakfast? This bread really is like concrete, you know.' As if to prove the point, Misty hit the floor with one of the baguettes he'd left on his first visit. In the process, she turned her head towards Caroline and mouthed '*SHUT UP!*'. Caroline seemed to get the message and stared at her chained ankles.

Rory moved slowly backwards to the door. 'Caroline,' he said softly – she looked up – 'don't worry. It's WSD – your dad's company. It has to be punished.' Her brow furrowed with incomprehension. 'They've been torturing dogs,' he added.

'Dogs?'

Rory nodded, turned and went out, locking the door behind him.

Caroline finally broke the silence. 'I don't understand *any* of this, Misty. I mean, torturing *dogs*? WSD? Are these people crazy?'

'They may be fanatics, but crazy? ... I don't think so.'

Caroline pushed herself towards the two bottles of mineral water which Rory had left in the middle of the room. 'Well,' she said brightly, 'at least he was quite civil. That's a start, isn't it?

'Is it?' In the harsh light of the two bare 100-watt bulbs, Misty was carefully studying their surroundings. 'It's possible this room may be bugged,' she whispered.

'Bugged!'

'Shush!'

'Sorry!'

'So, we have to be very careful what we say, OK?'

'OK,' Caroline whispered back.

'Now let's try and evaluate our situation.'

'Excellent idea.'

'We're in a windowless basement or cellar ... about fifteen feet by fifteen' – Caroline nodded vigorously – 'of a house somewhere in Formentera. Judging by our trips to the bathroom, it's a fairly modern house – hideous and big. On the floor above when you get to the top of the stairs, the john is the first door on your left, and there are six other doors that lead off that corridor. It must be about thirty feet long and has no windows. Agreed?'

210

'Um ... well, to be honest, Misty, I've never really looked.'

'You've been to take a leak *three* times, Carrie.'

'I know. I'm sorry. I was concentrating on, well ...'

'OK, but *look* next time.'

'I will.'

'Opposite the bathroom door – the bathroom is windowless too, of course – the stairs continue upwards to another floor.'

'Oh yes. I remember now. I did notice the stairs.'

'Great. We know that there are at least two of them.'

'"*Them*"?'

'Kidnappers.'

'Oh yes. Sorry.'

'One of them is a guy, Rex – obviously a false name.'

'Why "obviously"?'

'I'm going to ignore that question, honey. Just believe me. ... And I'm pretty sure the other one – the one we saw last night – is a woman.'

'Why?'

'Because she *smelled* like a woman.' Caroline looked blank. 'Well, how many guys do you know who splash on So Pretty by Cartier before they go out for a spot of kidnapping? There was just a hint – but I couldn't mistake it. It's what Tubs used all the time on that yacht.'

'Oh. ... Jolly tall for a woman.'

'And she smokes. In fact, when I went to the bathroom I could smell cigarettes. Couldn't you?'

'Well ...'

'Forget it. Now, there could be more than two of them, but somehow – just a gut feeling – I bet there are just the two of them.'

'They're probably the same blighters who tried that funny business up at the old windmill ... in view of the masks.'

'Well done, Carrie.'

'Don't make fun of me. This has all been rather a shock.'

'Sorry. Have some more water.'

'No thanks. For all we know, it may have to last us *days*.'

'Any more cheerful thoughts?'

But before Caroline could voice her concerns about the lack of food, they heard footsteps and quickly separated. By the time the door opened, they were both sitting innocently six feet apart.

'Hello, Rex,' Caroline said politely. He walked over towards her and bent down, holding out a carrier bag.

'Here – something to eat. Sorry about the bread.' As he exited, he added: 'I'll be back in a couple of hours.'

'I hope this food is meant for the two of us,' Misty said sarcastically after his footsteps on the stairs had died away.

'Don't be silly.'

'Well, he did give it to *you*. I think our Rex has a little soft spot for you, young lady.'

Caroline flipped the contents of the bag on the floor. 'What? ... Oh, don't be ridiculous, Misty. ... Golly! Cakes, three Mars bars, an apple, two oranges and one of those sticky Spanish croissants.'

'So much for the weeks of sensible eating and exercise.'

They feasted, and with Caroline's blood sugar levels topped up, she began to think more carefully of their predicament.

'I suppose they're after money, Misty.'

'Boy, how do you do it, Miss Marple?'

Caroline chose to ignore the sarcasm. 'But what I don't understand is where the dogs come into it.'

'Do you know what I think?'

'What?'

'We're dealing with a couple of amateur animal rights guys.'

'Because of what Rex said about the dogs and torture?'

'Yeah.'

'But what's that got to do with WSD?'

Misty looked hard at her English friend: she was like a child – so naïve, so simple. 'Putting two and two together, I would suggest they think your dad's company has been testing soap on our four-legged friends.'

'But that's ridiculous! The packaging of all our products clearly states "Not tested on animals". I've seen it.'

'Well, perhaps someone's lying.'

'Not Daddy – that's for sure. Perhaps they've got the wrong company. That must be it. It's all a huge mistake.'

'I wish. They've obviously been planning your abduction for months. Christ, they even followed you to Formentera.'

'But how could they have known I was coming here?'

'Because they were watching you in England, of course. They probably planned to do the snatch at Bobbins. Perhaps they tailed you to the airport. Or they could have had inside information. Who knows?'

Despite her handcuffs, Caroline did her best to grip Misty's arm. 'You're right! I wasn't hallucinating after all!'

Misty stared at her in bewilderment. 'What are you talking–?'

'Someone *was* spying on me! I mentioned it in the restaurant last night – remember?' Caroline recounted how, before Misty's arrival at Bobbins, she'd felt that she was constantly being watched. 'And then – I think it was the day before you arrived – I saw this man. I mean, he was right over on the other side of the lake so I didn't see him very well. And *I* thought I was imagining it all, and ... well ...'

Misty smiled reassuringly. 'Maybe it was Rex – or Mrs Kong.'

Caroline gasped. 'Maybe Bobbins was ... you know ... bugged.'

'Possibly.'

'How ghastly! Anyhow, Misty, they haven't kidnapped *me*. With all due respect, they've kidnapped *us*.'

'*Us*. Yes. But then I just got in the way. After all, if they *are* the windmill people – and two lots of gorilla-masked weirdoes would seem unlikely on this island – their first attempted abduction was long before they'd ever seen or heard of me. In fact, I don't think they know who I am. So, Carrie, don't tell them. After all, if they wanted to double their chances of a big ransom, well ...'

'Cripes! I hadn't thought of that. I wonder what they'll ask from Daddy. ... I didn't like that word "punish" Rex used. ... Um, do you mind if I have the last cake?'

'You've eaten that lot already? You little piglet!'

'Sorry.'

'Oh, go on – have it. I just hope *this* stuff doesn't have to last us days.'

The two companions sat in silence for some minutes. Misty thought of Lord Weetwood and how he'd react to the news of his daughter's disappearance and kidnapping. Would he be devastated? Would he co-operate with Rex and his partner? What would they ask for? And how would her own father react in Weetwood's position? ... Jesus! ... But who knew she'd come to Formentera? ... Mrs Duffle ... James ... Who cared anyway?

Suddenly the room seemed to get hotter and smaller – a concrete box with just two bare light bulbs. Somewhere above them was a golden sun shining in a dazzling blue sky. There had to be a way of escaping from this hole. Rex was no heavyweight – clearly neurotic. And she knew she was right about there being just one other – a woman. The big question was: how would Caroline fare in any attempt to break out?

'Blimey! I've just thought of something, Misty.'

'Not so loud, Carrie.'

Caroline put a hand over her mouth and grimaced. 'Oops! ... I bet that chap who you saw on top of the Torre d'es Català–'

'At Es Mal Pas?'

'Precisely ... was none other than our Rex, which would mean–'

'– that the couple at the table next to us last night at the Fonda Pepe–'

'– were Rex–'

'– and Mrs Kong.'

'Exactly!' But Caroline's triumphant grin was brief. 'Hang on, how could they have known we were going to dine there?'

'Maybe they were tailing us.'

'Perhaps. ... I say, do you think the Kongs locked *Clementina*'s doors? There's some pretty valuable stuff in there, you know – not just the manuscripts.'

'Carrie, honey, sometimes I can't begin to conceive how your thought processes–'

'I was just mentally listing who might start wondering about us. I'm not expected back in England until ... well, I didn't actually fix a date for my return – I've got an open ticket on Iberia. The only commitment is the beginning of term. ... Then there's Maria. She's due on Thursday – only *three* days away.'

'She'll just think we've gone out for the day as usual – cycling or something. It's not as though the villa's smashed up, or we left a casserole on the stove.'

'No, I suppose not. ... Teeny and Kurt might come back.'

'Yes. Or they might not.'

'Teeny phones every few days.'

'She'll just think we're out, too, at least for a week or so.'

'She might phone Maria and ask her to investigate. Then she'd notice nothing had been touched since her last–'

'Maria! Be serious.'

'Well, there's Gwen and Tom. They're due back at any time. She phoned last week and said that there were just a few i's and t's to dot and cross on her new *Muffins* contract, and they'd be on the first plane – this week. She said they would definitely be back *this week*. Gwen's bound to be suspicious – immediately. Well, that's comforting, isn't it?'

'Sure.'

'You don't sound very convinced.'

'It's just–'

'There's good old Pongo! I have to report on the progress of the translation and everything. Now, she *will* get concerned. ... Misty, why are you looking at me like that? What have I said *now*?'

Misty sighed: she was beginning to sound rather negative, but Caroline had to be realistic. 'I'm sorry, honey, but Pongo has not exactly – correct me if I'm wrong – well, she's not exactly been champing at the bit recently to get the latest instalment of the Louis XIV saga, has she?'

Caroline pouted. 'She's been frightfully busy.'

'She's touring the States with some pea-brain student'

Caroline was back to staring at her feet.

'Carrie, unless your father goes to the cops when our friends upstairs contact him – which, of course, they'll strongly advise him not to do – there'll be no particular reason for *anyone* to suspect *anything* untoward – at least, not for some time. Even then, we might have hired a boat and got swept out to sea. Anyway, how could they search every villa, farm and shack on Formentera?'

'Someone might have seen something suspicious last night,' Caroline mumbled.

'I doubt it, and so do you.'

'Hang on! You were talking to James when Rex burst in. He must have been frightfully worried when the line went dead. At this very moment–'

'We weren't exactly getting on like a house on fire. He'll just think I've dumped him again – Jesus!' Misty briefly closed her eyes. 'Basically, Carrie, there are two routes to freedom. First, there's your pa and the negotiations with Rex and Co. On balance, I think he'll involve the police. That's what normally happens. Scotland Yard will be on to Interpol and within hours they'll have plain-clothes guys from the mainland dressed up as bird watchers and olive pickers covering this dump from every angle. And they'll get us out. Believe me.'

'How?'

'How what?'

'How will they know to come here?'

'They'll trace the phone calls, of course.'

Caroline was pensive. 'Won't they use phone boxes?'

'There aren't that many on the island. They'll watch them.'

Caroline smiled and shook her head. 'Somehow I suspect our gaolers will have thought of that. ... Thanks for trying, Misty. What's the second route?'

'We escape.'

*

The early morning bank of cloud, which had threatened to bring to an end a fortnight of searing heat, had unexpectedly broken up. With the sun burning his shaved head, Rory pushed his rented scooter off the dirt track and took shelter under a large carob tree. Cicadas were buzzing all around; there was a species of lizard unique to Formentera, he recollected, and perhaps there was some damned cicada that was only found on the island's west coast – with a distinctive mating call. He could picture a boffin dug up by Scotland Yard from the Natural History Museum listening over and over to a recording of his phone call. ... Perhaps Weetwood was like Nixon and had all his calls taped?

'Bloody hell,' he muttered, 'I'm going nuts!' He took the mobile phone out of the back pocket of his shorts and sat down. Where had he put the script? If he had to go back to *Bayreuth* for it, there'd be all hell from Ursula. After five minutes of frantic searching, he found it crumpled and barely legible in the same back pocket.

He glanced at his watch – 11:23 – which meant that, with the hour difference, Weetwood should now have been at Soap House for twenty minutes or so. Mouthing the words, he slowly read the script one more time. British pragmatism demanded action, but German strategic planning required the call to be made at 11:30 precisely. What possible difference it could make was beyond him.

He leaned forward and stared at his knees. What a mess! And damn it, sodding Ursula had decreed that there was no time to change the plasters if they were going to keep to the new schedule. There wouldn't have been a problem if she'd allowed him to phone from the villa yesterday as originally planned. But she'd spent the whole day reassessing everything, thanks to their being lumbered with the American twat. So, it was now Tuesday and he'd had to ride five or six miles down dirt tracks to this godforsaken spot near Punta de sa Gavina. ... Why? After all, who was going to try and trace their Spanish mobile – especially at this stage when there was no reason to believe anyone had the slightest suspicion that anything was amiss? And, from what he'd read, while his use of the phone could be traced to the Balearics – even Ibiza – it would take some time to narrow things down to Formentera. In any event, the chances of the authorities nabbing him while using the phone were pretty slim indeed. But there was no arguing with old Jackboots.

A goat was peering at both him and a desiccated bush between the two of them. There seemed little else in the immediate vicinity for the animal to nibble on.

'Piss off! I've got an important call to make.' He checked his watch –11:33! 'Oh Christ!' he bleated, pressing buttons rapidly.

The first number he rang turned out to be a pet shop in Oldham. On his second attempt, he was sure he had the right number, but all he heard was the engaged tone. He got the same responses on his third, fourth and fifth attempts, by which time the goat had plucked up courage and was tucking into the bush despite Rory's expletives. Soap House appeared to be permanently engaged, and by midday he was beginning to worry about the phone's battery level. More goats were beginning to arrive when he finally decided to use his initiative and phone Bobbins. It was Mrs Duffle who answered.

*'Lord Weetwood? I'm afraid he's not in. Who's speaking please?'*

'A friend.'

'*Oh?*' Vivian was right to sound dubious: to her knowledge, Lord Weetwood had no friends as such. '*You're not another reporter, are you? Because if you are–*'

'No! I'm not a reporter. I need to speak to Lord Weetwood urgently. Is he at Soap House? I've tried there but I just get the engaged tone.'

'*Oh, you won't get any joy at the works this morning, sir – or is it "madam"? It's not a very good line.*'

'Madam.'

'*Well, madam, not with all the stuff in the papers an' all. I suspect the switchboard's jammed. Shocking, isn't it? I said to Ron – that's my husband – I said–*'

'Get off out of it, you stinking animal!'

'*I beg your pardon?*'

'Sorry – not you. I'm talking to this bloody goat.'

'*Goat?*'

'It's nibbling at my sandals. Piss off!'

'*Look, who is this?*'

'Oh bugger! This isn't going at all right. Listen to me, love. This is a matter of life and death. I must speak to Lord Weetwood without delay. I assure you he'll want to speak to me.'

'*You are one of them reporters, aren't you?*'

'For Christ's sake! What are you talking about? Why should I be a bloody reporter?'

'*Well, I've been told some yarns over this phone this morning, I can tell you. The depths you people sink to – and the photographs! When I think of the children – gentle James and – and–*'

'Caroline? Yeah, well ... It's Mrs Duffle, isn't it?'

She gasped. '*How do you know my name? I'm not going to be in* The Sun *too, am I? Oh no, please–*'

'How many times do I have to tell you? I'm not a–'

Rory stopped himself: things were going horribly wrong; he needed to think fast; he had to make the first contact with Weetwood as soon as possible. He knew he should have overridden Ursula last night and got things moving, even if it had meant getting Weetwood out of bed at three in the morning. And what was this old bat droning on about? Reporters? *The Sun?* The woman really seemed afraid.

*To hell with Ursula. Be un-German, Rory – improvise! Use your bloody initiative.*

Vivian was still babbling. '*... I've told the others already. I've never even been to Cap-Ferrat – wouldn't even know how to find it. And **nothing***

*– absolutely **nothing** like that has ever happened here – not at Bobbins. Not that I accept one word of the story, mind you–'*

'Mrs Duffle! Just shut up and listen.'

'*Well really!*'

'OK. I admit it. I *am* a reporter.'

'*I knew it!*'

'Now, I have some very juicy pictures – lots of pictures in fact – of your husband with a certain barmaid, one Peggy Umpleby, at the Cob o' Coal in Muckley, and believe me, they're not playing tiddlywinks together in the back of his car.' There was a deep intake of breath on the other end of the phone. 'Now correct me if I'm wrong, but doesn't Ron have a tattoo on his left buttock of–'

There was a scream down the line. '*Not Ron and that Umpleby woman? Not **her**?*'

'Believe me, I'm not interested in your husband's pathetic affair – or you for that matter – only Weetwood, understand? So, is Weetwood at WSD? He must have a private number – or a mobile?'

Through the hysterical sobbing, Rory learned that Weetwood was not at Soap House but en route by car to his sister's in Eastbourne. There was a car phone, but Weetwood usually had that switched off. Rory, nevertheless, got the number – and Belinda's. Then he rang off. The triumphant look on his face immediately evaporated: some thirty goats had surrounded his scooter. He swore loudly, using the word he despised.

'*Bon día!*' barked a harsh voice.

'Oh Christ!'

Rory jumped up, wide-eyed and open-mouthed: a fierce-looking rustic stood near the goats, staring at him. Did he understand English? How much had he heard? Was he a copper disguised as a peasant? There was a canvas bag over the man's shoulder, and as he started to moved towards Rory, he thrust a gnarled hand into it.

# CHAPTER 19

George Weetwood and Ron Duffle had been on the road since six. As soon as it was light enough to read, George had opened his briefcase. He managed to get through a mountain of paper on the journey, including Ben Turbot's latest correspondence about the SI litigation. Although the Americans had failed to get their injunction, there were no signs of the substantive action going away. On the contrary, Perry Match was bombarding Turbot with endless demands for Witness Statements, Lists of Documents, 'Further and Better Particulars of the Defence' and countless other matters. Turbot, however, seemed fairly relaxed, although he was surprised by the difficulties Merryweather was having in locating all the documents in WSD's possession that were 'relevant' to the proceedings. More concerning was the news that SI were going to produce numerous statements from current and former employees to confirm that there never had been any kind of animal research at Soda Flats. Someone, of course, had to be lying.

George had almost exhausted the briefcase's contents by the time they reached Eastbourne. Perhaps he'd done too much; Belinda thought he looked very tired as he walked up the garden path, but otherwise she was surprised by just how little he'd aged since they'd last met at Len's funeral all those years ago. By contrast, George found his sister haggard and pale; her eyes indicated that she might even have been crying. They pecked each other's cheeks hesitantly on the doorstep as Duffle drove off: George had instructed him to 'amuse' himself in Eastbourne for a few hours; he could expect a call on the car phone when the meeting with Mrs Thornton was concluded – so he'd better switch it back on.

*Heavens, this is a difficult reunion,* George thought as he finished his cup of tea and looked around the small sitting room with its bay window. He suspected Belinda was not quite right in the head; she'd said some pretty strange things on the phone yesterday evening. Listening to muffins? What did she expect to hear? Of course, she was alone – not even any dogs or cats to keep her company as far as he could see.

Belinda started to say something.

'Yes?'

'Oh nothing.'

'It's ... it's ... um ... very *comfortable* here, Belinda, very ... light.'

'Would you like some more tea? There's plenty in the pot, George.' Belinda smiled briefly; her stomach was tied in knots. How were they going to start? Should she wait for him to break the ice? Did he suspect she might not have seen the article? Had he noticed her copy of the tabloid? She'd purposely left it half-folded on the coffee table immediately in front of him with the masthead clearly visible. Good God, he must have seen it!

Her brother did not require any more tea; the glass cabinet bursting with souvenirs from treasured holidays with Len appeared to be fascinating him. How she pitied George. He might not have been a romantic husband – he'd never exhibited much emotion about anything, except his beloved toy trains, of course – or a loving father, but for Beryl to do *this* to him! ... Doubtless, he desperately wanted to get it all off his chest – get advice on a divorce. After all, she was his only close family – apart from the twins – but then how could he talk to *them* about this *abomination*? ... The twins! Did they know already? Caroline couldn't have seen *The Sun* yet, but where was James? It was no good: she couldn't stand this evasion any longer.

'George, dear, I think we should–'

'Yes, I'm sorry, Belinda. We need to talk. It's been such a long time and ... well, to be frank, I'm not sure where to start.'

'Take your time, dear. And remember, I *am* a magistrate. After almost fifteen years on the Bench, there's not much I haven't heard when it comes to depravity. I'm not easily shocked, George.'

Her brother looked puzzled. 'A magistrate? Really?'

Belinda nodded. 'I'm sure the twins must have told you.'

'Possibly.'

'I had to find a substitute today – remember? I mentioned it on the phone last night.'

'Ah yes. So you did.' George wondered whether he should have a word with someone: a magistrate who listened to muffins didn't sound too good for the proper administration of the criminal law. Or was all this magistrate business a figment of her imagination? And what on earth did she mean by 'depravity'?

'It must have slipped your mind, George. I mean, the strain and ... everything.'

'Quite. You've really put your finger on it, Belinda. The point is, WSD has been my life. It's meant everything to me for so long. Indeed, I think it's fair to say that no one could have done more than I've done to steer our great family business through the dangerous waters of the global market place. Papa placed the mighty responsibilities on *my* shoulders, and even if I say so myself, I believe he would have been proud of me.'

'I'm sure, George – *very* proud.'

'Turnover and profits have gone from strength to strength. But I've not been a short-sighted accountant, Belinda, just thinking of today.'

'Of course not.'

'I have *not* squandered our inheritance. My policy has always been to think of the future, to guarantee jobs for the children and grandchildren – nay, *great* grandchildren – of our employees. In brief, to ensure the prosperity of Goblinville and the whole of south-east Lancashire for generations to come. Not for me the easy life – oh no. Not for me a fleet of private jet aeroplanes, a flotilla of yachts in the Caribbean, or a portfolio of ostentatious beach houses used for only a few weeks of the year. ... Ah, I see from the look on your face that you're thinking of Cap-Ferrat.'

Tears welled up in Belinda's eyes. 'No, no, George, not that den of iniquity – of the *twins*. When I think of all the fun we used to have down here on their summer holidays and ...'

*Poor, poor Belinda, stuck alone in this godforsaken, suburban ...* Words failed him. Perhaps he should have come before. Perhaps she was ill ... mentally ill ... certifiable.

'Yes, yes, of course, Belinda, the *fun*. That's what I was coming to. You had fun with the children, while *we* – Beryl and I, that is – were working. Yes, even at Cap-Ferrat. Of course, Papa bought the *Villa Gobelin* as a present for Mama ... and for us too – for our holidays – remember? But I couldn't afford holidays after I joined the company – oh no! Our guests, you know, were very carefully selected with marketing in mind – airline chiefs, chairmen of shipping lines, owners of hotel chains – anyone who could possibly open doors for major contracts for Goblin products. You know, Belinda, I can tell you that sometimes I found those rounds of dinners and cocktail parties at Cap-Ferrat harder work than sitting behind my desk all day long at Soap House. Well, I tried my best, but I have to admit I'm not a social butterfly. In the end, Beryl and I decided – and I assure you it was a *mutual* decision – that I was better off back at HQ. She was right of course.'

'How can you say that? She was just getting you out of the way. You must see that now?'

'Oh, I think that's a bit harsh.'

'You're too good for that ... that *woman*. You always were. Even now you're sticking up for her.'

'Now, now! I know you and Beryl have never exactly been ... I'm just trying to make the point, Belinda, that what might have been our one extravagance – especially during the last few years when dividends have been slightly lower than–'

'George, I don't care about the dividends!'

*That's what she says! What does she do with all that money? She certainly doesn't spend it on clothes or the damned bungalow.* 'Well, you say that, Belinda, but I do remember the correspondence you had with us over our R&D budgets. Even last year's accounts were queried. Of course, with the launch of FoamFay – did you get the information pack, by the way? ... The launch went jolly well. You should have come. I think Miss Spigot sent you an invitation, and Beryl organized a splendid reception at Bobbins – she's terribly good at that sort of thing. And before you say anything, I know it cost a lot, but the press loved it and the reports were worth their weight in gold. Which brings me back to my point – FoamFay's launch explains why all that R&D was necessary. It was all terribly hush-hush. I'm sorry I couldn't let you in on the secret earlier.'

'George ... dear, *dear* George, I can imagine how terribly painful this must be for you, but you can't keep on evading the issue that you've really come to talk about.'

'Well, no. But I just wanted to give you the background – the reasons why I've decided to ... to make a complete break – to cut all the ties and start again.'

'A divorce.'

'I suppose one could call it that.'

'Don't be afraid to say it, George.'

'I've never been very good with words, Belinda. I'm just not an emotional sort of chap.'

'You've every right to be emotional – cry if you want.'

'Well, to be honest, I'm feeling quite ... happy.'

'You mean you've had doubts for some time, and now that it's all out in the open ...?'

'I can't say "doubts" exactly. ... I must say you're awfully understanding about all this, Belinda. I was steaming along quite contentedly in my own way – like a carthorse in blinkers I suppose – if you get the analogy?'

'Oh I do.'

'And then – you'll never believe this – it was Duffle – of all people! – the *chauffeur*! – who started me thinking that–'

George broke off: Belinda was staring at him very oddly.

'Yes, I can understand your surprise, Belinda. At first, I could think of all the reasons why it would be impossible. After all those years – the family name, the tradition, loyalty ... severing all our links with the company, and–'

'Is that really necessary? People can be very understanding ... given time.'

'Of course, one could just sell *part* of one's shareholding and, perhaps, remain on the board. I could be a sort of Life President. ... But I really don't think that Unilever or Procter & Gamble would swallow that.'

'Oh, George, dear, I'm sure you could make a fresh start without having to sell *any* shares.'

'Oh no – I could never raise enough capital. And I couldn't do both jobs anyway. The railways would need all my attention.'

Belinda moved the cup and saucer off her lap and placed them slowly on the coffee table. 'Railways? What railways?'

George suddenly stood up, making Belinda start. 'The whole system is in a shambles,' he said, moving towards the window. 'It's criminal! You know how railways have been my passion ever since I was a small boy, Belinda. Well, here's my chance to protect and develop a vital national asset. I want to bid for as many "franchises" – dreadful term! – as possible – certainly the West Coast mainline. I want to bring *pride* back to the railways. I want style, *trains de luxe*, gleaming rolling stock, sparkling locomotives, staff resplendent in smart uniforms – oh there's just *so* much I want to do, so much I know I *can* do. Don't you see? I'm *enthused*. For the first time in my life, I really want to do something, Belinda. You'll help, won't you? *Please*. If I ask you to sell your shares ...?'

Belinda's brain was near meltdown. It was flashing *HE NEEDS HUMOURING!* 'Well, of course, dear, I'll do everything I can to help, but perhaps you need to think this through more carefully ... when things have settled down a bit. You may change your mind.'

'No! Never! Impossible! I have a *mission*, Belinda, a sacred duty. I *have* thought about this very carefully. I've seen the light at the end of the tunnel.'

'I see. ... Have you already spoken to ... *Beryl* about all this?'

'Not yet. I don't mind telling you that I'm a bit concerned she won't be one hundred per cent in favour, but I was thinking that with the railway business being so political and high profile at present, she might quite enjoy the publicity. I'm sure she'd have some interesting ideas about liveries. Of course, she wanted me to go for a flotation years ago to realize some of our assets, but–'

'George, my love, I know this is terribly difficult for you, but you've got to stop thinking about ... *Beryl*. This is a matter for *you* and the twins. It's got *nothing* to do with her. She won't be able to stop you now, whatever you want to do – even selling Bobbins, if it comes to that.'

'Well now, I grant you she isn't a shareholder – like yourself – but after all, I need to give *some* thought to her feelings.'

'I can't believe I'm hearing this! After what that – that – *slut* has been doing – probably for years – behind your back.'

'Now listen, Belinda, I know you've never liked Beryl, but–'

'Oh to hell with bloody Beryl! What about the twins? Have you spoken to them about all this? With both of them abroad – they *are* still abroad, aren't they? – you don't want them to discover it in the papers, or from someone else.'

'Naturally, I propose talking to them. But Caroline has no interest in the business as far as I can tell, and, er … James … well, he's been acting oddly for some years now. I really thought I should talk to you first and then go and see the Trustees.'

'The *Trustees*! What on *earth* has it got to do with them?'

'Everything! If a prospective purchaser wants to buy the whole shooting match – which is what I'd expect – they'll want the children's shareholdings as well. I don't think they'll be much of a problem.'

Deafening alarms were now ringing in Belinda's head. Her brother, who'd always been such a pillar of rationality, was clearly in no state to make any important decisions. He probably needed treatment; reality was slipping away from him.

'George, listen to me. We need to speak to Caroline and James *now*. I have her number. It was in one of her post–'

'We don't need to involve–'

'We *do*! They're very sensitive children. A shock like this … well, anything could happen. Caroline's so naïve, even though this Spanish trip seems to have brought her out of her shell, thank God, and James has … well, *you* know. … He's not still at Cap-Ferrat, is he? I got a postcard–'

'Ah, so he told you, then, about his attempt to kill Beryl – at the villa?'

Belinda gasped. '*What*?'

'Oh, he didn't? I thought … So, what are you referring to?'

'All that business over his friend's death and … He tried to *kill* Beryl?'

'Apparently. Had a breakdown and went berserk – earlier on in the summer. I forget precisely. He's all right now, I believe. Poor Beryl was–'

'What was he doing at Cap-Ferrat in the first place? Where's bloody Beryl now?'

'"Doing"? … James? I'm not sure to be honest. … I think he got emotionally entangled with a friend of Caroline's … an American – strange girl – quite violent – a spy, if you ask me.'

Belinda stood up abruptly. '"*Violent*"? – "a *spy*"?' She began pacing in front of the fireplace.

'Yes. I seem to remember her banging the table rather violently – and shouting … when she dined with us at Bobbins. Probably on drugs – being

224

American. She's the daughter of that bounder "Sonny" Start. You must have read the press reports of his company's Ltigation against WSD – to block our launch of FoamFay and –'

'Just a minute! You don't mean *Misty*, do you?'

'That's the one.'

'Good Lord! I don't understand *any* of this. Why did James think Caroline's friend would be at Cap-Ferrat? More importantly, in view of what we *now* know about ... *Beryl*, I can perfectly understand why James *would* want to kill her – especially if he witnessed one of her so-called "parties". Oh God! I'm in such a muddle. ...Where *is* James, anyway?'

George was looking at his sister with undisguised exasperation. It was a tricky situation: he needed her co-operation for his proposed sale of WSD to proceed smoothly. One false move now and she could prove rather difficult.

Very gently, he said: 'I'm not quite sure where, er ... James is at this *precise* moment. I think he may be on his way–'

'We have to find him, George.'

'Yes, yes, of course. ... Now, Belinda, you said something just then about understanding why James would want to kill Beryl – something about what we *now* know. What do you mean?'

'I don't understand.'

'Well, surely the question is clear enough?'

Belinda was shaking her head. 'George, you just can't keep pretending. I can understand why your mind wants to obliterate what's in the papers, but we're going to have to cope with the reporters. And the divorce lawyers will have to be instructed. Christ, if you ask me, she's got to be kicked out of *our* villa today – if she hasn't already slunk off in disgrace. But knowing that gold digger, she'll–'

'Papers? Which "papers" are these ... dear?'

'Oh please, George, don't – don't pretend. It frightens me.'

'Which "papers", Belinda? You can tell *me*. I'm your brother.'

It was Belinda's eyes that solved George's puzzle. He followed their gaze to the folded newspaper on the coffee table.

'Ah, *this* paper?' He leaned over and picked it up. 'I'm surprised you take *this*, Belinda – *very* surprised.'

'Don't get angry, George. And you don't need to read it–'

'Oh, but I shall.'

Belinda jumped as the phone in the hall started to ring. She wanted to stay with George, but the insistent tones were already beginning to irritate her.

'I'll just answer that, dear.'

George made no reply as he stared at the *The Sun*'s banner headline.

It was Daventry Merryweather. He'd finally tracked down his master's whereabouts through Mrs Duffle, after Miss Spigot had suffered some kind of breakdown earlier that morning. Apparently, a fellow secretary at Soap House had shown her a copy of *The Sun*'s story that the Chairman was dumping soap for railways because of a midlife crisis exacerbated by his wayward wife, an allegedly drug-crazed dropout son, and an exiled lesbian daughter.

'*May I speak with the Chairman please, Mrs Thornton?*' asked Merryweather frostily.

'My brother can't speak to you now.'

'*I really must insist. It's a matter of* **great** *importance. I should say that I'm speaking on behalf of myself and* **all** *the executive directors of WSD plc.*'

'I'll tell him you phoned. Goodbye.'

At Soap House, the directors assembled around Merryweather's desk awaited his news anxiously.

'She put the phone down!' he gasped.

'Phone back!' someone bellowed.

He redialled. 'It's engaged.'

'He's probably talking to Procter & Gamble,' snapped Chopping hysterically.

'More likely those bleeding Krauts,' moaned Brancepeth-Tring.

As soon as Belinda hung up on Merryweather, the phone rang again.

'Oh damn!' She glared at it for a few seconds. 'George,' she shouted from the hall, 'you don't want to speak to that Merryweather chap, do you?' The silence seemed interminable. Snatching the handset, she barked: 'I'm sorry, Mr Merryweather, but my brother does *not* – that is – he *cannot* speak to you at the present time. He–'

'*I vant to shpeak mit Lord Veetvood – now.*' Rory's over-the-top impression of Ursula stopped Belinda in mid flow. '*It is a matter of life und death.*'

Belinda was not impressed. 'Look here! If that's you again, Merryweather, I'll–'

Rory groaned audibly down the line. He knew who Merryweather was: the bastard had played a prominent role in his prosecution for criminal damage over the WSD laboratory incident.

'*No, it's not. Nor am I a reporter. Now get Weetwood – Veetvood – to zee phone. Tell him it's Rex – the person who knows all about Orient Express. OK?*'

In the living room, Belinda found her brother examining the glass display cabinet. 'I rather like this dagger,' he said quietly. 'Looks Turkish. Never been to Turkey.'

'George, there's somebody rather odd on the telephone babbling drivel about "the Orient Express". I said you–'

In the hall, George calmly picked up the handset and smiled at his sister. 'I say, old thing, why not go and get that salad organized. I'm feeling rather peckish. ... Now then, Rex, what can I do for you on this fine September day? Blown up any more historic monuments? Don't tell me – you've kidnapped my daughter! Better still, you've kidnapped my wife.'

Eavesdropping in the kitchen, Belinda almost dropped the salad bowl.

Secreted in the thick pinewoods above Es Mal Pas, far from goats and hospitable peasants offering him cheese and wine, Rory bit his lip.

'Well, come on, Rex – I haven't got all day. I have a railway system to save, you know.'

*'Just shut it and listen!'* snarled Rory, forgetting the German accent. *'As a matter of fact, we* **have** *kidnapped your daughter ... Caroline. She's not been harmed, and no harm will come to her provided you do* **exactly** *as I say. Do not contact the police. If you do, you'll* **never** *see Caroline alive again. She'll be released only if you do three things. First, you've got to issue a press release admitting that FoamFay has been tested on animals. Secondly, you have to resign from WSD and sell all your shares. Thirdly, you must pay us one million U.S. dollars in used one-hundred-dollar bills. You'll be contacted at nine p.m. British time tomorrow at Bobbins with full details of how the press release is to be worded and published and how the money is to be paid. You'll also talk to Caroline. I repeat – do* **not** *contact the police. We're watching you –* **all** *the time – OK?'*

Rory switched off the mobile and came around the side of the Torre d'es Catalá. Platja de Mitjorn's long arc of white sand lay before him, and the sea was like glass. He felt elated: things were finally on the move.

'You know what, Devlin, old chap? I think you could do with a swim.'

*

'George? ... George, dear? Is it bad news? Oh Lord! You look as though you've seen a ghost. Come and sit down in the kitchenette. The salad's all ready.'

'I need Duffle. We have to phone Duffle.'

'After lunch, dear. Come along. I've got some brandy somewhere.'

George did not want brandy; nor did he wish to discuss the Beryl Crisis. He just wanted the address book in his briefcase with the car phone's number. But there was no reply when he rang. The salad was forgotten.

Belinda spent the afternoon trying to contact James and Caroline at the *Villas Gobelin* and *Clementina* respectively; thoroughly traumatised, George failed to recall that his son should have flown home on Monday. When she was not using the phone, he repeated his attempts to get through to Duffle. When six o'clock came and contact had still not been made with him, Belinda tried phoning Bobbins with the intention of disclosing his disappearance to Vivian Duffle, but there was no reply there either.

In fact, Vivian never even heard the telephone – or anything else that evening: she'd consumed a variety of alcoholic beverages during the course of the afternoon, following her return from the Cob o' Coal, and had passed out. Her very public slanging match in the bar with Peggy Umpleby would remain the main item of village gossip for weeks.

Finally, Belinda rang Eastbourne's hospitals, but there'd been no admissions in the name of a Ron Duffle. It was when she determined that enough was enough and the police had to be contacted that her brother decided to reveal Rex's claim to have kidnapped Caroline. Belinda did have a brandy – several.

At nine p.m. they got into Belinda's battered Triumph Dolomite and drove around the town. They eventually found the Jaguar parked in the station forecourt; there was a copy of *The Sun* on the driver's seat. The booking office clerk recognized Belinda: he'd once been up before her on a charge of being drunk and disorderly after a colleague's stag night. Yes, he confirmed, at around six o'clock a man answering Duffle's description had bought a single ticket to London.

# CHAPTER 20

George spent the night in his sister's spare room, a night of terrible dreams during which Belinda had sat at his bedside and tried to make sense of his ravings. At regular intervals she would phone Bobbins, Formentera and Cap-Ferrat, but without success. As for the latter, she had no wish to speak to Beryl, but was determined to find James, for someone had to visit the *Villa Clementina* urgently, and she knew that her nephew would not hesitate to go. After all, if Caroline really had been kidnapped, they had to ensure that neither the villa's owners nor the Blackberrys raised the alarm: police crawling around the place could prove fatal. And what had happened to Caroline's friend, Misty Start? Had she left the island before the kidnapping?

At dawn, after more fruitless calls to all three numbers, Belinda roused George from a coma-like state and told him of her decision to take him home immediately. She made some domestic arrangements with Joyce Potter, who was only too happy to keep an eye on the bungalow. Indeed, Joyce even helped Belinda and her brother into the taxi booked to take them to Gatwick Airport. He was unshaven and resting on his sister's arm – so different to when he'd arrived in the chauffeur-driven limousine yesterday, as she later told *The Sun*'s reporter.

While awaiting their flight to Manchester in a secluded corner of Gatwick's VIP lounge, George's sang-froid began to revive, and as it did so, his exchanges with Belinda became more frequent and rational. Meeting the kidnappers' financial demands seemed to be causing him most concern. Belinda was shocked.

'But that must be chicken feed for you, George.'

'Hardly, Belinda. It's an *awful* lot of money. I dare say I could scrape such a sum together. ... Perhaps I could negotiate a lower figure.'

'George! This is Caroline's *life* we're talking about, not a raw materials supply contract.'

'Well, we shouldn't be seen to be too co-operative, or they'll "up the ante" – as I believe the expression is.'

George did not, on the other hand, express his concerns about the press releases Rex had demanded. In truth, he'd not even mentioned them – and hoped he'd never have to do so. They were something that would certainly have to be negotiated out of any deal!

\*

229

Bobbins was besieged by the media when George and Belinda arrived in a taxi from Manchester Airport. She had advised him to say nothing and to keep cool. She'd had every intention of doing so herself until someone in the crowd shouted, 'And is this bint your bit on the side, Lord Weetwood!' There was a flutter of laughter.

Even Belinda was surprised by the volume of her own voice. 'No, sir! I am a magistrate and Lord Weetwood's sister. You are all trespassers. Unless you are off this property within five minutes, you can expect the police to remove you. There'll be no statements or interviews today.'

With Bobbins' doors firmly locked behind her, Belinda set about organizing. Her first task was to sort out the elusive Duffles. In their flat, she found a dishevelled Vivian clad in a bright pink dressing gown slumped over the kitchen table sipping black coffee; thanks to her alcoholic stupor, she'd only just got up. Between sobs, Vivian proffered abject apologies for her misdemeanours, and undertook to leave his lordship's employment forthwith. Most of her babbling about adultery and tattoos made no sense to Belinda, who assumed she was referring to Beryl. Finally, after Belinda had reported Ron's disappearance in Eastbourne and declaimed that, for reasons which would become clear in due course, they needed her services more than ever, Vivian began to pull herself together.

Offering her a clean tissue, Belinda said: 'I bet you anything, Vivian, dear, that Ron's sought sanctuary with that Mrs Umpleby. What's her number?'

Vivian didn't have it, but a phone call to the Cob o'Coal proved productive, and Belinda's rapid interrogation of the *femme fatale* procured confirmation of her theory. As that seemed to clear up one mystery, Belinda handed Vivian several sheets of handwritten instructions and ordered her to work. Bobbins was going to be very busy for quite some time: beds needed to be prepared, provisions ordered, and meals cooked.

'Do you still love Ron?' asked Belinda on her way out of the kitchen.

'I worship him. Even after–'

'So let him stew for a few days, Vivian. But until further notice, don't answer the phone on *any* account. I'll handle the reporters – and anyone else who might call.'

Patricia Spigot was next on the list. Belinda finally located her at home; she sounded terminally depressed. The news, however, that Lord Weetwood desperately needed his loyal secretary at Bobbins in order to play a vital role in the transfer of his interests from soap to railways, provoked hysterical weeping down the line. But these were tears of joy, and, as requested, Patricia was soon packing a small suitcase as though her life depended on it.

At length, George was finally permitted to use his own telephone. Charles Grimshaw had been expecting the call: the firm's divorce and libel specialists had been put on standby, together with corporate lawyers to assist in WSD's sale and the acquisition of rail franchises. But the teams mobilized by Grimshaw and his partners were not what the noble client required: he wanted Turbot – just Turbot – and he wanted him in residence at Bobbins night and day for at least a week; there was already a room being prepared for him.

Charles politely protested, pointing out that Turbot was not a corporate lawyer.

'He understands simple contracts, doesn't he?'

'Of course, George, but–'

'And he knows how to negotiate a good deal, doesn't he?'

'Of course, but–'

'If Turbot's not here by tomorrow morning, Charles, I'm off to Bragge & Crow.'

'He'll do it. And the divorce?'

'That can wait.'

Turbot was flattered but horrified. 'Charles, I don't know a bloody thing about share sale agreements. And I'm right in the middle of a massive copyright case for–'

'Ben, if Weetwood goes to Bragge & Crow they'll get the railway franchise business too. Have you any idea of the sort of fees that work could bring in? If we lose him ... well, I'm sorry, Ben, but you won't have many friends left in this firm. Hell, you're just holding the man's hand! You'll have constant access to a dedicated team of corporate chaps here.'

Turbot worked all night to clear his desk.

Just after four that afternoon, Belinda finally got through to the *Villa Gobelin*'s housekeeper, Madame Papet. The paparazzi, she reported acidly in broken English, had invaded Cap-Ferrat; Lacy Weetwood had fled with Dr Audinette – by helicopter of all things! – within just half an hour of her arrival from Paris yesterday. Papet professed not to know where they'd gone. Assuming Lord Weetwood would be dismissing all the staff, her own bags were already packed. Belinda confirmed that this was indeed the case; she was in the process of instructing a security firm in Nice to remove everyone from the property, except, of course, her nephew. But when she asked to speak with James, Papet stunned her: early Monday morning, the chauffeur had driven him to Nice airport to catch a plane to England.

Belinda swiftly procured a confession from George that he'd forgotten that Beryl had arranged for James to join Brancepeth-Tring in the Export Department. Vivian Duffle confessed that he had indeed been expected back, but he'd phoned mid-morning Monday to say he'd changed his plans and would update her later in the week. With all the 'goings-on' during the last twenty-four hours, it had been the last thing on her mind. Thus, there was more panic and another session of frank exchanges between Vivian and Belinda over strong tea, during which George was despatched to attend to Miss Spigot: flush with excitement and accompanied by Augustus the terrapin, the faithful secretary had just arrived in a taxi.

During the remaining hours before dinner, Patricia organized an office for herself in the Yellow Room and one for Mr Turbot in the Library – both equipped with word processors and fax machines procured from Soap House. And while Patricia contacted Air France to ascertain whether or not James had flown to Manchester, Belinda made some progress in localizing the Blackberrys: thanks to her short-lived ballet career, she knew the head of Twentieth Century Ballet at BBC Radio 3, and he procured the name and number of Gwen's agent from Radio 4's producer of *The Muffins*.

The agent, Sam Panama, was reluctant to speak to Belinda at first, but the ice melted as soon as she declaimed, 'I'm Lord Weetwood's sister.'

'*If he's thinking of writing his memoirs, darling,*' Panama fizzed, '*I'd love to represent him. And to think Gwen and the daughter have spent so much of the summer together!*'

'Well, that's why I'm phoning, actually.'

'*Doesn't sound like the same girl to me from the descriptions in the papers.*'

'So, Mrs Blackberry spoke to you about Caroline?'

'*You kidding? Me and Gwen have been closeted for most of the last fortnight in a meeting room at the Beeb trying to renegotiate her contract. And don't ask me whether she comes out of that coma – my lips are sealed. Do you listen to* The Muffins?'

Belinda finally managed to explain that, thanks to Caroline's postcards, she knew Gwen and Tom had the neighbouring villa. So, in view of the newspaper reports, she wanted to have a word with Gwen to make sure her niece was all right – if they'd returned to Formentera, that is.

'*Oh yes, darling, they flew out today. Want their number? And remember – if Lord Weetwood wants to do the dirt on old Beryl and dozens of VIPs, I could secure some fabulous deals.*'

Belinda repeatedly phoned *Honeysuckle Cottage*, but there was no answer. Tom and Gwen were, in fact, marooned in Ibiza for the night: their plane had been delayed and they'd missed the last ferry to Formentera. From their hotel room, littered with English newspapers, they, too, had unsuccessfully endeavoured to contact Caroline. Gwen was so worried, but at least they'd be there to comfort her first thing in the morning – unless she'd already returned to England.

Supper at Bobbins that evening was exceptional: for the first time in his life, George ate in the large kitchen. It was Belinda's idea: she felt 'a team spirit' had to be engendered. Vivian had been stunned, whereas a dream of Patricia's had come true, albeit she'd always pictured the Chairman and herself dining alone in a romantic candlelit *brasserie* somewhere in the vicinity of the Sorbonne. In the event, there was little conversation: Vivian pondered her broken marriage; George and Belinda ticked off the seconds to Rex's promised call at nine o'clock; Patricia knew her place.

It was during pudding that Air France finally returned Patricia's call: James had not used his ticket to Manchester; nor had he rescheduled it. Although Belinda didn't voice her concerns, she began to wonder whether he, too, had been abducted. The news, however, did not appear to alarm her brother.

'Par for the course,' he muttered.

After a few seconds of furrowed brows, Vivian spoke up. 'I've just remembered something! Miss Caroline phoned me on Sunday night.'

Belinda gasped. 'Caroline called *you* – on *Sunday*?'

'Yes, Mrs Thornton.'

'Oh, *please, do* call me Belinda.'

The siblings were staring intently at each other: to Belinda's chagrin, George was insisting on a 'need-to-know' regime, which conflicted with her 'team spirit' policy.

Vivian proceeded to explain that the purpose of Caroline's unusual communication was to obtain the Cap-Ferrat telephone number. 'If you ask me, it was all to do with that American girl, Misty What's-her-face. I always thought she was going to be trouble ... Belinda.'

'And yet, Vivian, by all accounts she and Caroline have become great friends.'

George, who gave every impression of not knowing who 'Vivian' was, said: 'Perhaps, er ... James decided' – he looked at his sister conspiratorially – 'to go and visit this American girl.'

Vivian's eyes bulged. 'Oh, Lord Westwood, I do hope not. Any road, why don't we just pick up the blower and find out if he's in this Formentedterror place?'

Belinda abandoned her helping of apple crumble and fought back a tear. 'That's precisely what I've been trying to do all day, Vivian.'

George had little time for all this idle conjecture. He was turning over in his mind the letters from the chairmen of WSD's competitors that had been arriving by courier since mid-afternoon. Although bearing the hallmarks of fastidious vetting by pedantic lawyers, it was clear they were all desperate to buy WSD. They wanted to meet him as soon as possible – office, hotel, home – whatever suited him. He stared at the kitchen clock: *I can't put everything on the back burner because of the kidnapping. It's now or never.* Which brought him back to the idiocy of making that damned statement about animal testing. Unthinkable! At best, it would severely damage his chances of selling WSD at the sort of price he had in mind; at worst, it might scupper a sale – lock, stock and barrel. Damn that bloody Pesto woman! Damn her and her bloody invention!

Thoughts of the late Vosene Pesto reminded George that, so far, he'd not received any expression of interest to purchase WSD from SI in Fort Worth – or from those Germans mentioned in *The Sun*. Anyway, kidnapping or no kidnapping, he'd get Spigot and Turbot to set up meetings with all his counterparts. They could trek up to Bobbins – the lot of them. Any deal would be done in *his* home and at *his* convenience. He wasn't going anywhere. In fact, it might be quite amusing to get them all up together, put them in separate rooms, and then play one off against the other! As for the business of paying a ransom and taking delivery of Caroline, perhaps he could delegate that to Merryweather – better still, to Brancepeth-Tring: he was the overseas chap and spoke fluent Spanish – or so he claimed.

At the end of supper, Belinda reminded Vivian and Patricia of the phone ban: her brother was expecting 'a most important call imminently' concerning his proposed sale of WSD. By quarter to nine, George was seated by the telephone in his study. He'd advised Belinda that it would be best for him to talk to Rex privately – without her listening in on an extension: any sound from a third party – any hint of eavesdropping – and Rex might panic. Reluctantly, Belinda had concurred.

The call came just after nine. With Patricia having retired for an early night and Vivian tidying up her kitchen, Belinda had secreted herself in the Yellow Room. The siblings picked up their respective receivers simultaneously.

'*You haven't contacted the cops, have you?*' asked Rory, trying to sound like Sylvester Stallone. '*I wouldn't want to do nothing nasty to this pretty girl of yours.*'

'Why does your voice sound–? ... Sorry? ... What "pretty girl"?'

'*Don't mess with me, Weetwood! Now listen and listen good. Got pen and paper?*'

'Yes.'

'*OK. You're to bring the money to Formentera–*'

'I–'

'*Shut it! You are to arrive on the eighteen-fifteen ferry from Ibiza on Friday. The* **eighteen-fifteen** *– quarter past six. Understand?*'

'*This* Friday? – the day after tomorrow?'

'*Correct.*'

'But–'

'*You'll take a taxi to the Cala Beliran Hotel.*' Rory spelt the name. '*A reservation has been made for you. And don't worry, they've got a safe that can handle a briefcase stuffed with dough. Come alone. You must carry your mobile at all times. And keep it charged! Give me the number.*'

'Er, I don't have – that is – I don't know if it would work abroad.'

'*The number!*'

'If you could hold on a minute, um ...'

'*Weetwood!*'

He dictated the number.

'*There's a phone box at the side of the hotel. Stand in front of it at twenty-one-thirty – half past nine – on Friday evening.*'

'But–'

'*No buts!*'

'Rex, for goodness' sake – *listen*. I – I ... I don't have that sort of cash lying around in bank accounts. Heavens no! I'll have to realize investments. It takes time. I might be able to scrape ... ooh ... about 750,000 dollars by ... say this time next week? Would you take pounds, by the way?'

Belinda bit her tongue. *My own brother! How could he?*

'So much depends on current stock market valuations and – and – I can't just leave the country at the drop of a hat. And do you honestly expect me to carry that amount of cash–?'

'**Weetwood!** *I'm holding a long sharp knife. Would you like me to cut off some interesting piece of Caroline's anatomy and send it to you?*'

Oh, how Belinda wanted to shout obscenities down the phone!

'Please – don't do that.' George was thinking. With Turbot in residence aided by Spigot, negotiations on the WSD front could get underway. And with that mobile phone gadget, he could keep in constant touch with Bobbins. It would be almost as though he were there in person! In fact, the need for Turbot to keep referring things back by phone to himself could be quite a useful negotiating tactic. Indeed, his absence *abroad* could be interpreted as an attempt to negotiate a deal with a mysterious foreigner. That would frighten them! And he could take Brancepeth-Tring to do all the tedious chores – and potentially dangerous ones.

'Very well, Rex. I accept those terms.'

'*How very noble of you. Now, the press releases–*'

'In return, *you* have to forget all this nonsense about press releases.'

'*You what? I don't think you understand the score, you dick head.*'

'Please, Rex, let's be civilized about this. I am not – I repeat – I am *not* in any circumstances going to issue any press releases about animal testing.'

'*You–*'

'Listen to me, you dunce! What would such press releases be worth anyway? If, as I assume you would, you release my daughter once your demands are satisfied, what would stop me from immediately going public about the kidnapping, denying everything in the press releases – everyone would accept I'd issued them under duress – and get myself reappointed as chairman? ... Well?'

'*I've got pictures.*'

'We'd say they were fakes. What would connect such pictures to WSD anyway?'

'*Dumpwell's in them – coming out of that place in Montevideo.*'

George's hesitation was noted by both Rex and Belinda.

'I don't give a damn. There will be *no* press releases.'

'*So, you'll never see your daughter again.*'

'Rex, I suspect the million-dollar ransom is just a little bit more important than some silly press releases. You can do an awful lot with that to help your animal friends. I think you should consult your partner – part*ners*, perhaps – don't you?'

'*I can take decisions on my own.*'

'Really?' There was another silence. George thought he could hear some whispering. His bluff had paid off: he'd thought it unlikely that Rex would be acting on his own.

'*Weetwood?*'

'Yes.'

'*I ... er – I don't have a partner, OK? ... I'll drop the press release stuff.*'

'Very sensible.'

'*But it'll cost you another million.*'

There were a few more minutes of frantic argument. Belinda was seeing her brother in a new light, and it was not flattering. A compromise of an extra $100,000 was finally agreed.

'So, Rex, we'll talk again in Formentera. On Friday.'

Belinda's thoughts were in turmoil: *Christ, he hasn't asked to speak with Caroline! I can't believe he's forgotten.*

Sarcastically, Rex asked: '*Weetwood, don't you want to hear your lovely Caroline?*'

236

'Ah, yes. Of course. Put her on, please.'

A few seconds passed; Belinda held her breath.

*'Hello, Daddy. This is your daughter, Caroline, speaking.'*

'Good evening ... er, Caroline. How are–?'

*'I am in good health and being looked after well. Please do what Rex tells you. I love you and Mummy very, very much and look forward to seeing you very, very soon. Bye for now.'*

'Caroline?'

*'OK, Weetwood. We'll talk again Friday.'*

Belinda finally snapped: too many emotions had been bottled up. 'It's a bloody recording, George!' she screamed into the handset. 'We've got to talk to Caroline *herself* for God's sake!' There was a cry behind her and she shot round. Open-mouthed, Vivian stood in the doorway.

*

'I knew my father would be suspicious about all that "Mummy and Daddy" stuff.' Caroline didn't seem to be addressing anyone in particular in the cellar.

'He wasn't the one who was suspicious,' replied Rory through his mask. 'Christ, what a loving parent you've got there! No, it was your aunt.'

'Aunt Belinda? You spoke to *Aunt Belinda*? I don't understand–'

'You don't need to. You just have to say a few words on the phone. And don't try anything clever, OK? And you' – he pointed at Misty – 'keep your big mouth shut.'

'We need a shower and some clean clothes,' Misty muttered.

Rory glowered at her. 'You always want *something*, don't you?'

'Misty's right, Rex. We're beginning to ... to smell.'

'And we need some proper food, for Christ's sake – not these slops.'

'I'll see what I can do in the morning.'

Rory sat down cross-legged on the floor between his captives. He unlocked and removed Caroline's handcuffs and dialled Bobbins. Nothing. He kept trying but to no avail. The line seemed to be dead.

'I just don't understand it,' he kept mumbling.

Shaking her head, Misty said: 'You're so dumb. There's probably no signal down here in this bunker. You'll have to take us upstairs to make the call.'

'What do you mean, "us"? I only need Caroline to–'

'She won't go without me, will you, Carrie?'

'Well, I–'

'And I need to powder my nose, anyway. You can kill two birds with one stone, so to speak.'

Rory dashed upstairs to check with Ursula, but a frantic search of the house proved fruitless. She had to be in the garden, smoking her head off. To hell with her! He'd use his initiative. That vile living room would do.

*

George's intention had been to defend his conduct with an imaginative rewriting of history, taking inspiration from the affidavit drafted for him by Turbot. But when he reached the Yellow Room after a brisk trot from his study, he was shocked to find his sister putting her new friend in the picture. They were sat on the sofa comforting each other, with Mrs Duffle sniffling that although she'd always preferred James, Miss Caroline certainly didn't deserve being kidnapped. As George stared despairingly at the two sobbing females, Patricia Spigot appeared, clad in a thick woollen dressing gown: she'd returned to the Yellow Room in search of her reading glasses.

'Poor Miss Caroline's been kidnapped,' Vivian blurted out.

'Oh, God!' groaned George. 'Why don't we invite the whole of Muckley over? "Roll up! Roll up! Come and witness the great spectacle of the Weetwood family–"'

'Oh *do* shut up, George, and stop making a fool of yourself. I said at the outset that our little team here should be put in the picture.' And then without further discussion, Belinda proceeded to do exactly that.

'Rex should be phoning back any minute with Caroline,' Belinda concluded. 'I persuaded him to–'

The phone started ringing. Belinda picked up the receiver even before her brother had a chance to react. 'Rex? ... Yes, it's Mrs Thornton again. Put my niece on the line – *now*.'

In *Casa Bayreuth's* living room, Rory passed the mobile to Caroline, having put it on speaker; they were sat side-by-side on a sofa. Misty was sitting opposite them, in an armchair just a few feet away; Rory was pointing a gun at her. Unlike Caroline, she was handcuffed, but Rory had removed their ankle fetters in the cellar to save time in getting them upstairs.

'Hello, Aunt Belinda.'

'*Darling! Oh, I can't tell you how wonderful it is to hear your voice. Just reply "yes" or "no" to my questions. Have they harmed you at all?*'

'No, Auntie. I'm all right – honestly.'

'*Is Misty with you?*'

'Yes.'

'*Oh, thank God! I mean, I'm glad you're not alone. And she's all right too, darling?*'

'Yes, Auntie. I – I do love *you* very, very much.'

'*I know you do, darling. And I love you very, very much too. We'll soon have you both free, don't you–*'

Misty threw herself forward with all her might, taking aim at Rory's crotch. Her head scored a direct hit. With a roar of agony, his head snapped backward, and the gun flew out of his hand, clattering somewhere on the room's black marble floor.

Completely stunned, Caroline heard Belinda scream, '*Oh my God! He's killing her. Caroline! Caroline!*' Then she let go of the mobile. It hit the floor with a loud crack, just as Misty began beating Rory over the head with her handcuffed wrists.

'Get his gun, Carrie!' she yelled.

But, sickened by the sight and sounds of his beating, Caroline remained rigid for a few seconds. Then she sprang into action, and, despite the writhing bodies, managed to stand up. She swiftly spotted the gun near the open door – it was bathed in light from the harshly illuminated hallway – and dashed towards it.

Down the line, Belinda – her heart in her mouth – heard a terrifyingly loud bang. Then the connection was lost.

*

Waving her still-smoking gun, Ursula stood in the doorway and surveyed the disorder before her. The air was dusty from the shattered concrete in the ceiling where the bullet had embedded itself. At her feet, where she'd accidentally stood on it, lay the mobile. Alerted by the commotion, she'd dashed from the garden without donning her mask.

'If this phone is *kaput,* I'll – I'll ...' She picked it up and pressed 'redial'. She got connected – the phone rang twice at Bobbins – and rang off. 'That's lucky for you,' she barked at the two captives while kneeling to examine Rory, whose mask had fallen off during the fracas. He was groaning and in great pain. 'You pathetic English–!' She searched for a suitably nasty word as she snatched up Caroline's handcuffs off the sofa and snapped them around his wrists before he knew what was happening.

Still clutching his groin, he could barely speak. 'I ... She ... What the hell are you doing, Ursula? Please, I need help. I don't understand–'

Ursula was shaking her head. 'You just can't do anything right, can you, "Rex"? We could have taken this bitch in England if it hadn't been for you trying to eliminate every risk – watching that house night after night, involving that *Untermensch,* Duffle.' She proceeded to catalogue Rory's inadequacies; it was a long list culminating in his 'dumb' decision to bring both 'girls' up from the cellar without her approval, and his 'moronic' removal of their ankle shackles and Caroline's 'bracelets'.

'You could have just *held* the phone for her,' Ursula not unreasonably pointed out. 'Anyway, did you really believe that when this was all over, I'd want to share the rest of my life with a creature like you?'

The beating over his head had made Rory dizzy and queasy. He began to vomit. Caroline looked away.

'I hope you don't think I'm going to clear *that* up,' Ursula snarled. She walked over to Misty, put the gun to her head and glanced at Caroline. 'OK, Lady Caroline–'

'I'm not "Lady"–'

'You'll speak when you're spoken to – *ja?* – and not otherwise! You tell me now exactly who this "Misty" bitch is.'

'I've told you, I'm just an ordinary kid from the Bronx–'

Caroline screamed as Ursula gave Misty a mighty slap across the face.

'Ursula!' yelped Rory, trying unsuccessfully to get to his feet.

'Now, *Caroline*, let's try again. I want to know *everything* about this American. And if anything doesn't check out, you'll be *very* sorry – very sorry indeed. ... By the way, that idiot's gun is just a toy – unlike mine.'

*

It was just after eleven that night when Ursula's call to Bobbins was answered. 'You will listen!' she snapped, pressing the pocket tape recorder's play button.

*'This is Caroline. I confirm I am still OK. Please do what ... what they tell you. Please do* **not** *go to the police or they will ... kill us.'*

Ursula rang off. 'Now for the *coup de grâce*,' she hissed, redialling. 'What is it that the English say? ... "All clouds are having the golden padding"?'

*

The local time in Fort Worth was almost exactly four p.m. when Ursula was put through to Pimkie Bouchara, Sonny Start's secretary. In her cosy 'cattle pen', Pimkie was collating the few letters which the President would need to sign before he departed for the Charity Gala in Dallas. So, she politely told the caller that Mr Start was engaged, and offered to take a message. The response stunned her.

*'You don't understand. I'm phoning from Spain. It's about his daughter, Misty. She's had an accident. I need to speak to Mr Start urgently.'*

When Pimkie hovered and coughed at the entrance to the Conference Module, Sonny was summing up two hours' worth of advice from Swinehart, Crudge, Idol & Purkey's half dozen lawyers who were working on the WSD case. The meeting had been summoned as soon as the news had reached the Start Tower via *The Wall Street Journal* of WSD's likely sale. Sonny, following the gaze of the lawyers, interrupted himself.

'Yes, Pimkie.' He sensed something was wrong, and they moved over to the potbelly stove; it concealed a water cooler. As soon as she'd explained the problem, he took the call at his desk, listening calmly and with few interruptions. Then he went over to Pimkie and reported that it was nothing serious; she was not to worry. He returned to the Conference Module and concluded his summation, confirming that he'd no desire to purchase WSD or any part of it. He wanted either a cash payment or exclusive rights to the Pesto invention for North and Latin America. Weetwood's weakness at this time should be exploited. He gave the green light for suits to be filed in Kenya and Sri Lanka, the locations of the two FoamFay production facilities.

After signing his mail, Sonny took the elevator to the penthouse apartment, made a few calls, and then changed into his tuxedo for the Gala. Just after six, having already collected Carmen, the chauffeur, Dwayne, picked up Sonny, and the Cadillac set off for Dallas; Chuck and Bob followed right behind in their Jeep. Carmen, who looked magnificent, spent the journey reciting her comprehensive list of the 'Big Noises' who'd be at the Opera – including the Governor; it was vital that Sonny had a quick word with *all* of them.

The new production of *The Marriage of Figaro* – translated into 'American English' and transported to the Texas of the 1870s – made little impression on Sonny. Unsurprisingly, his thoughts were elsewhere during the performance; at one stage he convinced himself it was *Oklahoma*. Afterwards, during the raucous buffet, Carmen charmed the Governor while Sonny was subjected to a monologue on the ever-increasing costs of staging opera by the Board of Management's Sponsorship Vice-President.

When the ordeal concluded, Sonny stunned Carmen by returning with her to their mansion, *SonCar*: he rarely slept there during the week, of course, for it was his invariable routine to stay at the Start Tower's penthouse apartment, working late into the night and rising early. However, to minimise the gossip generated by separate accommodation, the couple did weekend together at *SonCar*; they even shared a double bed – albeit its exceptional proportions nigh eliminated the possibility of accidental physical contact.

As soon as Carmen got home, she scanned the telephone messages which her secretary, Courgette Pulp, had left on the hall table. One of them caused her to blaspheme indignantly in Spanish and then to stomp noisily into what she called 'the Long Gallery', where Sonny had already poured her the customary bourbon and prepared a Perrier with a slice of lime – never lemon – for himself.

'You won't believe this, Sonny, but Spasmine Jolly has phoned to say that Fuss – that chain of beauty salons, yeah? – have decided not to go ahead with their sponsorship of the new Bog Turtle National Breeding Centre in the zoo's herpetarium. Can they do that, Sonny? I'm sure we got a letter from some vice-president or other that ... Sonny? You listening?'

Sonny undid his bow tie and walked over to the music centre that was discreetly located within an early Colonial mahogany chest of drawers. 'Carmen, you'd better sit down. I didn't want to fluster you before the Opera, but ... You know I have all my calls recorded at the office? OK, well I want you to listen to this. It's a call I received just after four this afternoon.'

After Carmen had listened to the recording three times, she said: 'Well, I'm not sure either, Sonny. It's been such a long time since I've spoken with Misty. I mean, it *sounded* like it could be her voice ... but then, I couldn't swear to it. They *do* mean Spain, Europe?'

'Yes, some island. ... Have we got an atlas somewhere, Carmen?'

She thought there might be one in the Library; it contained hundreds of books that she'd bought by the yard some years back. It was a room she only visited when it was her turn to host some committee meeting or other of one of her causes; she thought it impressed her colleagues.

Carmen followed Sonny into the Library. It took some time to locate an atlas; it took him even longer to track down Formentera.

'But that's just a *rock*, Sonny! What the hell *is* it – some kinda Spanish Alcatraz? Look, perhaps this is one big scam.'

But Sonny thought otherwise. 'I made some calls ... to some people I know' – Carmen could imagine the sort of people – 'and they've done a bit of checking.'

'Oh?'

'Misty's not been at her apartment since at least early July.'

'Did we have her address?'

'We do now. My friends in New York ... well, they traced her. Seems she went to Europe. She flew to England first – Manchester of all places – then on to Paris. She must have lost her Amex card – or had it stolen. They sent a new one to some Greek island. For the last week, she's been using it in Spain.'

'My, my, you *have* been busy!'

'I snuck out for a while during that buffet to check on the progress–'

'You know, Sonny, I think Misty herself may be behind all this – a wind-up just to get attention. Or maybe she's got mixed up with hoodlums – like that Patty Hearst kid. Perhaps we should go to the cops. Do we have insurance for this kinda thing?'

242

'No. And I don't want to involve the FBI – not yet anyway. If Misty is fooling around, I think I can sort that out. If this is for real ... well, either way, we don't want any bad publicity.'

'Oh hell!'

'And what could the FBI do anyway? We'd have to involve the Spanish police – probably through the State Department and our embassy folks in' – Sonny searched for the name of the Spanish capital – 'in ... in Madrid.'

'Could it be the Mafia?'

'That's Italy.'

'OK, but on this map they're real close. ... Isn't there some PLO faction in that neck of the woods? ... The Bisques?' Carmen kicked off her shoes. 'Can you raise a million bucks – cash – in just a few days?'

'Sure. I'll get Chase to make arrangements through their ... their Madrid branch and pick up the dough there.'

'What about negotiating?'

'Why? There's no way I'm going to lose one cent.'

Carmen smiled broadly. 'That's my Sonny.' She finished her bourbon. 'I think it was very clever of you asking them for the name of Misty's pony as proof of the kidnapping.'

'Oh *that*. It was the only thing I could think of. I remember all the bills – the veterinaries, that guy we had to hire to look after it, and–'

'What was it called anyway?'

'No idea. Courgette will know.'

'And this person with the odd voice–'

'Regina?'

'Yep. She's phoning you tomorrow morning? I think she sounded Swedish – like that chef in *The Muppits*.' Sonny looked blank. '*Hombre*! You must be the only guy in the States who doesn't know what I'm talking about.'

'Probably. Anyway, I'd guess the accent was fake.'

'Hmm. So, you're gonna go to Europe – can one fly to this island? You don't want *me* to come, do you? I don't think I'd be much use, and with these dumb Fuss people trying to wriggle out of the Bog Turtle sponsorship, I'm gonna have to work my butt off on the Zoo Committee.'

'No – no thanks. And I've no idea how to get to Formentera, except that I have to take a darned ferry from Ibiza – there's bound to be an airport there. I'll get Pimkie on to it first thing.'

'What you gonna tell her – and the board?'

'I've been thinking about that. I could pursue the "Misty has had an accident in Europe" story and that I need to–'

Carmen pulled a face of mock incredulity. 'I like the concerned parent angle but–'

'But telling them to keep that secret—'

'Doesn't add up.'

'You're right. So, what about this? Remember that English business I mentioned to you, Goblin … WSD?'

'The soap thing?'

Sonny nodded. 'Looks as though they're up for sale. I'll tell the guys they've been in touch about a settlement of the litigation and want secret head-to-head discussions in Europe.'

'On this lousy island?'

'It's *all* Europe! They'll assume this Lord Weetwood guy has a villa, castle or yacht there.'

'Perhaps you really could arrange to see him – once this kidnapping thing is cleared up, I mean.'

'Possibly.'

'You're not going alone, are you? If Misty really has been kidnapped, these guys could be dangerous! That Regina sounded quite–'

'I'll take Chuck and Bob.'

'Ah.'

Sonny put the atlas back on the shelf where he'd found it. 'Do you think I should have insisted on talking to Misty directly?'

'What good would that have done? We'd be none the wiser – *you* know, whether we were talking to her or …'

'That's what I thought.'

'Bed?'

'Bed.'

Later, just as Sonny was about to nod off, his brain finally made some hesitant connection between Misty's odd flight to Manchester, England, and the crazy Weetwood folks.

# CHAPTER 21

British newspapers usually arrive in Formentera on the day following their publication. It's unlikely that this delay causes much inconvenience: there are few resident Britons, and the island's British holidaymakers tend to be folk seeking to escape the hurly-burly of 'civilisation'. However, early on the morning of D-Day Plus Four of the kidnapping, Ursula Klinker was anxious to learn whether Britain's media had – for whatever reason – any inkling that something untoward might have happened to Caroline Weetwood. And now, having ascertained the American's identity, she'd added the *Herald Tribune* to her shopping list.

Before setting off to the newsagent in Sant Francesc, Ursula checked on her prisoners. They were all suitably docile. Perhaps the communal bucket she'd left for them had generated feelings of overwhelming embarrassment, but she wasn't going to exacerbate the risks of another escape attempt by escorting those three pests to and from the toilet every few hours! She'd rather put up with emptying the bucket, albeit to perform their ablutions she'd had to remove Rory's handcuffs and ankle shackles; she'd even accepted the women's argument that it was also impractical for them to continue being chained together with the other handcuffs and shackles. To cap it all, she'd given them some air freshener, but then without it, getting the name of that stupid horse would have been very unpleasant, such was the stench in the cellar.

And so, suitably reassured, and 'disguised' in her orange wig and sunglasses, Ursula drove her battered VW to San Francesc and bought a copy of each British newspaper on sale; Princess Diana's death dominated their front pages; the newsagent didn't stock any American papers. Then she proceeded to Es Mal Pas and parked in front of the little *supermercado*. Keeping as close as possible to the trees and bushes, she made her way along the cliff path until she came in sight of the *Villa Clementina*. It all looked very peaceful; it was certainly not crawling with police. She was tempted to go nearer, but then thought better of it, making do with her binoculars. They revealed nothing of interest.

Below her, the narrow beach of fine white sand lay empty and inviting; perhaps the piles of seaweed at the water's edge had discouraged prospective bathers. In any event, the solitude was exactly what Ursula required. A steep track zigzagged down to the beach, and she was soon sitting comfortably in the hot sunshine, enchanted by the sound of the breeze blowing through the pines on the cliffs behind her. How she loved that eerie sound! It reminded her of *Forest Murmurs* from Wagner's *Siegfried* – one of dearest Papa's favourites. He was always playing it on the old gramophone in the cottage on the Baltic coast during her childhood summer holidays. There'd be the occasional mysterious guests – former colleagues from 'the good old days' as she'd much later discover, who, like Papa and Mama had also been able to assume new identities. The music was perfect, for the cottage stood amidst dense pinewoods. After being put to bed, she'd listen to both the wind in the trees and the music drifting up from the living room. And if she listened carefully, she'd hear the messages – messages whispering what she longed to do.

Humming *Siegfried's Death and Funeral March* from *Götterdämmerung*, Ursula pulled out the newspapers from the canvas shopping bag she'd brought with her from the van. She'd have a quick flick through them and then call Fort Worth and give Mr Start the name of his vile offspring's childhood pony – 'Elvis' indeed! It would only be around five in the morning there, but what the hell!

Flicking past the Diana features with disinterest, it took her over an hour to digest all the stories about the Weetwoods and WSD that filled the tabloids' inner pages and the broadsheets' business pages, including references to an industrial espionage suit brought against the company by Texas tycoon Sonny Start! Ursula's initial shock – shock at the discovery that a spotlight was now focused on Caroline and her family – slowly turned into a heady cocktail of sardonicism and opportunism. Indeed, she returned to unruffled Es Mal Pas by way of the water's edge whistling the triumphant chorale of the finale to Bruckner's Fifth Symphony, the gulls scattering before her.

Had she looked back towards the *Villa Clementina*, she would have seen the Blackberrys opening *Honeysuckle Cottage*'s shutters.

*

'I spy with my little eye something beginning with–' Caroline's concentration disintegrated due to the sounds of 'Rex' urinating into the bucket.

'Sorry,' he said.

'I spy with my little eye something beginning–'

'I don't want to play this anymore. I'm sick of it.'

Caroline pouted. 'Oh, Misty, don't be like that. We can't just sit here. We have to do *something* to keep our minds off–'

'Well, I don't want to do *anything*, OK? I'm hungry and dirty and this place stinks.' Misty glared at her ex-captor.

'Well, I'm sorry,' he whined, 'but I just had to have that crap earlier on. I *am* human. I'll spray some more–'

'I really think we should use the air freshener sparingly,' Caroline advised.

'It was never meant to be like this,' Rory sighed. 'For a start, *you*, Misty, weren't even in the plans. If you hadn't come to Formentera in the first place–'

'Oh stop arguing, you two. It's no good crying over spilt milk.'

'Sometimes, Carrie, your British phlegm is just unbearable.'

'Well, I don't see any point in getting hysterical.'

'I am *not* "hysterical",' Misty retorted, moving to the opposite wall. 'It's just that … well, that woman seems deranged to me. I'm not sure that …'

'Not sure what?' asked Caroline nervously.

'Oh nothing.'

'That's not fair, Misty. You can't start something and then–'

'*You* do.'

'I don't.'

Rory sat down as far from the women as possible; the distance was more symbolic than real. 'Look, I know you two must hate me, but we're all in the same boat now. And if Regina sticks to the original plan, we – that is, you two – should be released in a few days … once the ransom has been paid.'

'You mean *ransoms*, don't you?' corrected Misty, '– which I don't think were part of your "original plan" either. Nor was your being entombed with us. And who's going to pay a ransom for *your* safe release? Why should this "Regina" – sorry, *Ursula*, which you revealed last night – why should she let *you* go?'

'Misty! That's a horrid thing to say. And I don't think Rex ever meant us any harm, did you? By the way, is "Rex" your real name?'

'It's Rory, actually.'

'Oh … right.'

'Well, *Rory*,' Misty sneered, 'what are our chances of escaping, where exactly are we, what ransom is being demanded for Miss Stiff-upper-Lip here, and what arrangements were to be made for the exchange, et cetera, et cetera? If we're "all in the same boat", you won't have any problems telling us, will you? And by the way, you've missed two buttons – your dick's hanging out.'

Rory recounted everything about their abduction, at first hesitantly and then with growing confidence. The hours flew by as his audience sat mesmerized. They had many questions, and he answered as best he could.

Eventually, Caroline said: 'So what you're saying, Rory, is that all this is my father's fault.'

'I'm not sure I'm saying that exactly. Perhaps WSD's fault.'

'But Daddy's the boss. He controls it. And if your story is true, he must have authorized all those experiments in Uruguay.'

'I suppose so. ... And it *is* true.'

'In which case, he must be responsible.'

'Maybe.'

'But I still don't understand why these tests on dogs would have been thought necessary. It's just soap we're talking about. And they test the stuff on *people*. They always do. And why Uruguay? I'm sorry, Rory, it just doesn't add up. It really doesn't.'

'I can't answer those questions. You'll have to ask your dad.'

'What do you think, Misty? ... *Misty*?'

'I think she's nodded off.'

'Good. She needs the rest.'

'She's a bit neurotic, isn't she?'

'Golly! That's rich coming from *you*. What about you and your obsession with Dumpwell?'

'I suppose so.'

'She's normally rather laid back. ... I'm afraid life hasn't been easy for her. I shouldn't really tell you this, but ...'

Caroline didn't tell Rory everything – just enough about Misty's background to disprove any thoughts he might have had that she was just another spoilt little rich kid. He was reduced to silence for some time. Finally, he moved closer to Caroline: keeping his distance now seemed antisocial, unfriendly, at odds with the confessions which had passed between them.

She glanced at his knees. 'How did that happen?'

He told her of his trip to the old tower at Punta Prima and the gulls. It all seemed so long ago now.

'It's funny,' said Caroline, 'but right from the start I felt your heart wasn't really in this kidnapping stuff. It was as though I was watching a second-rate actor in a third-rate drama.'

'Charming!'

'Oh, you know what I mean.' Just for a few seconds she stared at his tanned legs, with their golden hairs glinting in the light of the bare bulbs. Something almost untraceable stirred deep within her.

'Is something wrong, Caroline?'

'Wrong? No, I was just thinking ... about Duffle.'

The treasonable chauffeur had been the last thing on her mind.

'What about him?'

'Oh, this and that ... like how he could have been so ... so gullible.'

'People often believe what they want to believe. Look at me.'

'Yes, but perhaps we can attribute your foibles to a rotten childhood.'

'It wasn't *that* bad. At least my parents loved me.'

'Ah ... well, you were certainly lucky in that respect.'

'I suppose you went to some posh boarding school.'

'St Ethelburger's, Cheltenham.'

'St *what*?'

'Ethelburger's.'

'Did you like it?'

'Vile.'

'Why?'

'Everyone hated me.'

'Oh, come on!'

'No, honest – they did – because I was fat and ugly. Children always hate fat, ugly kids.'

'They don't.'

'Yes they do. How would you know anyway?'

'Silly me! I thought they only hated skinny wimps.'

'Well, you're not a skinny wimp anymore.' She glanced at his legs again; the same strange sensation rippled through her.

'And *you're* not fat or ugly.'

'Oh–'

'You *were* – fat that is – not ugly. Sorry, that sounds rude. I mean before you came here – back in England.'

'I know. Don't worry.' Caroline struck the floor with clenched fists. 'That's what makes one really cross. Up there!' she cried, pointing to the ceiling, '– the sun – this island of scented woods and silver strands surrounded by translucent seas redolent of lapis lazuli, sapphire and emeralds.'

'Yes, well ... for *you* maybe. As far as I'm concerned, I've been baked alive for weeks lurking in insect-infested undergrowth keeping an eye on you – and then Misty too. I only had my first swim two days ago – after calling your dad.'

'So, the island has never worked any magic on you?'

'You must be kidding! I'll be glad to see the back of it.' He frowned. 'I wonder what *will* happen to me. I mean, even if things work out for you and Misty, whichever way you look at it, the police are going to be after me. I wonder what the punishment is for kidnapping in Spain – or for blowing up a theatre in England, come to think of it.'

Caroline remained deep in thought for some moments. 'Well, I'll put in a good word for you – Misty will too ... probably.'

'Why should you do that? Why should *she*?'

'Because you didn't harm us, as such, and–'

'Somehow I don't think that's going to cut much ice in court, do you? And anyway' – Rory glanced at Misty – 'I can't see *her* being quite so charitable.'

'Oh, she'll come round. She's OK – honest.' Caroline furrowed her brows. 'I suppose we could say ... um ... that Regina – Ursula – was going to torture us and you tried to stop her and–'

'Don't, Caroline. I got myself into this mess and I'll have to ... Anyway, even if you two are the best of friends, I don't believe Misty will go along with that.'

Silence followed. Eventually, Rory said: 'Tell me some more about your reasons for coming to Formentera.'

Misty continued to sleep fitfully as Caroline summarized her weeks on the island, how much she owed to Pierre the bicycle, Gwen and Tom, and latterly to Misty. She explained her fascination with the towers – Rory confessed to tracking her expeditions – and her growing disenchantment with her research. Eventually, she failed to respond to a question, and Rory realised that she'd nodded off. He stared at her until he, too, fell asleep.

*

Ursula unlocked the door and pushed it wide open, her gun at the ready. The cellar's three occupants each awoke with a start, but she'd already caught sight of Caroline's head resting pacifically on Rory's shoulder.

'My, my, my,' Ursula scoffed, 'what a pretty sight!'

Misty was too disorientated to believe her eyes.

Scattering a bundle of newspapers on the floor, Ursula barked: 'Perhaps you're all getting just a little bored down here. Well, these should provide you with some interesting topics for discussion. Such hypocrites, you English! But first, Miss Start,' she added, grinning strangely at Misty, 'we're going to phone your father and give him a little surprise – unless, that is, naughty Lord Weetwood has already told him that you're incarcerated with his precious Caroline. But somehow, I doubt it.'

*

When Belinda finally got through to *Honeysuckle Cottage* that Thursday morning, Tom Blackberry answered the phone. It was all very confusing at first because he got it into his head that Belinda's references to Sam Panama and contacts at the BBC had something to do with a possible job for Gwen.

'*I don't think you understand, Mr Blackberry. I'm–*'

'Possibly not. I blame the sun, the *cava* and the garlic. You really ought to talk to Gwen. She's–'

'*I'm Caroline's aunt.*'

'Oh! ... I say, this is an awful business about your sister-in-law. And such outrageous smears against the rest of the family – rubbish obviously. You must all be sickened – and Caroline must be devastated, poor thing. Actually, Gwen's just popped round to see her.'

'*On her own? Oh God!*' Belinda tried again to explain why she was phoning. As the emotion began to mount in her voice, a mist appeared to lift.

Suddenly, Tom dropped the telephone and ran out of the house as fast as he could, shouting 'Gwen!' repeatedly. It took him some minutes to locate her. She was upstairs in Misty's tower bedroom, standing in the doorway with her back to him.

'Oh, thank God you're all right!' wheezed Tom. 'Didn't you hear me calling, darling? I've–'

Gwen had put a finger to her lips. Moving to one side, she pointed to the bed.

A naked young man lay there on his back. He gave every impression of being unconscious; an empty whisky bottle stood on the bedside table.

Gwen looked bewilderedly at Tom. 'I can't find Caroline anywhere,' she whispered. 'Do you think *he's* anything to co with Kurt or Teeny?'

Tom drew Gwen back towards the landing. 'Go down to the kitchen, darling,' he hissed, 'and get the biggest bloody carving knife you can find. I think Sleeping Beauty here may be one of the kidnappers.'

\*

Ben Turbot's perusal of the press cuttings collated by one of his assistants had suggested to him – as they had suggested to millions of *Sun* readers – that Lord Weetwood had to be just a little ... well, kinky. After all, as Beryl had been the old boy's wife for over 25 years, how could he have been ignorant of her bizarre lifestyle? And it was hardly credible that her sexual adventures would have been confined to the French Riviera. Turbot's suspicions were confirmed upon his arrival at Bobbins: there appeared to be no less than three women cohabiting with Weetwood!

Turbot's first meeting with his client in the library got off to a business-like start. He received lucid instructions on the sort of deal Weetwood had in mind for the sale of WSD, brief synopses of the prospective purchasers, details of the target rail franchises, and advice on how the various balls should be kept in the air while Weetwood himself went on 'a short trip abroad'. The latter came as something of a surprise: maybe this dark horse was going to meet Beryl. But no explanation was forthcoming during the pregnant pause.

It was mid-morning when Belinda burst into the library and asked her brother to step out, announcing that she had some 'very important news'. In the kitchen, they joined Vivian Duffle and Patricia Spigot.

'George, dear, as Vivian and Patricia already know, I've just made contact with Tom Blackberry and put him in the picture. Unfortunately, Gwen had nipped round to the *Villa Clementina* only a few minutes before my call, so he dashed off to make sure she was all right. Now we're all waiting here with fingers crossed.'

George cringed at the thought of the increasing number of outsiders with knowledge of the kidnapping. 'I just hope that these nosy thespians don't set the cat among the pigeons.'

'For God's sake, George, poor Gwen could be in mortal danger – Tom too – and all you can think about is–!'

But the telephone saved George from further discomfiture in the presence of his two employees. The caller was a breathless Tom with the amazing news that they'd discovered a naked and comatose young man in *Clementina's* tower – he appeared to have consumed an entire bottle of whisky – and, judging by the passport Gwen had found in a holdall in the kitchen, the intruder was none other than James Weetwood!

After Belinda, Vivian and Patricia had regained some semblance of self-control, it was agreed that the Blackberrys should try and awaken James, get him sobered up, and then put him in the picture. In the event, for the next couple of hours, Gwen maintained a telephonic running commentary of James's rehabilitation over a hearty brunch at *Honeysuckle Cottage*, with Belinda reporting at regular intervals to 'the Team'. Kept in the dark, Turbot assumed she was the reluctant intermediary between Lord and Lady Weetwood, and anticipated instructions imminently for his divorce-specialist colleagues.

But as the day wore on, George began to doubt that James's discovery was truly good news. After all, his son had proved himself to be irrational, unstable and impulsive: once the Bohemian Blackberrys informed him of the kidnapping, he was capable of doing anything! And if the kidnappers were still watching the villa, how long would it be before they discovered he was there? They might already know! Why not kidnap him too? Perhaps he should order James back to Bobbins forthwith? ... On the other hand, he didn't want him messing up his business plans. And in view of the delicate imminent negotiations, the fewer members of his now-notorious family parading their idiosyncrasies around the place and providing the gutter press with further deadly ammunition, the better.

For the same reasons, he prayed Beryl would keep a low profile – a very low profile indeed. No doubt she'd be in touch once her funds dried up: having ensured there'd be no further transfers from his accounts to hers, there'd probably be not long to wait. Well, he was in no hurry on that score.

Mr Start, however, was quite a different matter.

*

Sat at his beloved antique roll-top desk in what looked more like a set for a Western than an office, Sonny was hard at work attempting to 'clear the decks' before setting off on his foreign trip. Well, that was what he'd told his secretary, Pimkie Bouchara. And although he was certainly ploughing through the WSD file, he was, in truth, endeavouring to find some clue in all those private investigators' reports which might help to explain how in God's name Misty and Weetwood's girl were imprisoned together on that pesky island! At least, that was what Misty had claimed – if it really was Misty he'd ended up speaking to when 'Regina' called him on his most private mobile number just before dawn this morning with the name of that darn horse. Frankly, he was becoming more convinced by the minute that Weetwood had to be behind the whole thing: it was just some weird attempt by that eccentric Limey scoundrel to put pressure on him to wind up the FoamFay suit. And somehow, he'd managed to recruit Misty to his cause. Carmen was probably right: the screwed-up kid was trying to punish them for not loving her enough, or sending her to that swanky school ... or something.

Sonny had told Pimkie that there were to be no calls – with two exceptions. Now, as he continued his fruitless search through the ransacked file, the phone on his desk rang.

'*It's him, Sonny!*' hissed Pimkie, overawed by the caller's title.

'Thanks. Put him through.'

'*Mr Start?*'

'Lord Weetwood! We speak at last! I was just on the point of calling *you*.' This was not strictly true: Sonny had resolved to phone only if he'd not heard from Weetwood by five p.m. local time.

The Englishman was nonplussed: Start's accent and style did not at all fit the picture he'd had in his mind. '*Indeed, Mr Start? I would have telephoned you earlier, but rather a lot has been going on here.*'

'I'm sure.'

George had hoped that Start would have said something like, 'I suppose you're phoning about the kidnapping', but he was obviously playing a waiting game. Frankly, he would have preferred to keep his own powder dry, but the incessant chivvying from Belinda had proved intolerable – especially since that odd call from 'Regina' when she'd confirmed that Start was now 'completely in the picture'. But at least Belinda was not listening in on this occasion: he was using the mobile; the ever-helpful Miss Spigot had provided him with a fifteen-minute discourse on its operation.

'*No doubt you know the reason for my call?*' declaimed George rhetorically.

'I suppose it could be one of three things.'

'*Three things, Mr Start?*'

'Of course! Which one do you want to talk about?'

'*The most pressing, naturally.*'

'And in your eyes, which one's that?'

'*Good heavens, Start! We're not playing a game here. There are lives at stake!*'

'Ah, you want to talk about *that*. Shoot – I'm listening.'

'*Well, firstly, I assume this "Rex" – or "Regina" – one or other of them anyway – has been in touch.*'

'Regina – I've never heard of "Rex". So, there are at least two of them?'

'*Yes. They've got my daughter, Caroline.*'

'I know.'

'*Ah, so they did tell you?*'

'Of course. And they've got my daughter too, Misty.'

'*Indeed. I've met her.*'

Sonny tried to conceal his shock. 'Oh? ... When?'

'*Surely she told you all about her visit here at Bobbins? She was barely out the door before your lawyers' letter arrived. What a coincidence! I say, you haven't been to the police, have you?*'

Sonny was still grappling with Misty's visit. 'Um ... no. ... Have you?'

'*No! I'm sure you'll agree that involving the Spanish could be a bit of a–*'

'I agree.'

'*Do they want you to go to Formentera, Start?*'

'Yes – I'm Sonny by the way. I'm flying out tonight. Should be there late tomorrow. And you?'

'*Yes. I should also arrive tomorrow evening. They're insisting I travel on a particular ferry, the six-fifteen.*'

'The six-fifteen?'

'*Eighteen-fifteen – quarter-past-six. ... You too?*'

'Yeah, with a copy of the London *Financial Times*.

'*We'll be like Tweedledee and Tweedledum.*'

254

'Excuse me?'

'*Never mind. ... Are you coming alone?*'

'Of course! They'll be watching us.'

'*Indeed.*'

'Where are you staying, sir?'

'*Somewhere called ... er ... the Carla Bell Tarn Hotel, I think.*'

'Cala Beltran. ...Well, that's great! So am I.'

'*Oh. ... I see. ... Do you think they'll object to us talking like this?*'

'No. Why should they? Regina hasn't forbidden it. ... Has she?'

'*No, I don't think so. Well, nor has Rex, I suppose. ... Look, Start–*'

'*Sonny*, please.'

'*– how will I recognize you?*'

'The *Financial Times* under my arm might help. But don't worry, Lord Weetwood, I'll recognize *you*. I've seen the English papers. Nasty business!'

'*Oh?*'

'I mean your wife and family – not the sale of WSD.'

'*Yes – naturally – that's what I assumed you meant. I say, I hope you don't think I'm being impertinent, but do you mind awfully if I ask how much they want for your Musty.*'

'Misty.'

'*Quite.*'

'I don't mind you asking, but I think I'd rather not say at present. I hope you don't take offence.'

'*Oh no – not at all, old boy, not at all – perfectly understandable.*'

Had Belinda been a party to this conversation, she would have asked Sonny whether he'd spoken with Misty, and, if so, what, if anything, he'd gleaned about her well-being – and Caroline's. No such questions, however, occurred to George; nor, for that matter, was anything of the kind raised by Sonny.

'So, sir, I'll see you in ... er–'

'*Formentera.*'

'Sure. ... Ever been to this little island, Lord Weetwood?'

'*No. To be frank, until all this bother blew up, I'd never even heard of it.*'

'Really? Well, if our daughters are still there, it's so small I can't imagine it would be too difficult to find them. Ciao!'

*

As George retraced his steps to the library to check on Turbot's progress, he mulled over his first conversation with the Start whiz-kid – wasn't that what the Americans called them? The chap had seemed awfully relaxed about the whole affair – *too* relaxed. .. Perhaps it was *all* an act.

255

The Yanks were frightfully concerned about projecting images, especially 'whiz-kids'. And the hint of surprise in Start's voice when he mentioned that frightful Musty's visit to Bobbins was so pathetic. The bounder was probably behind the whole 'kidnapping' malarkey. The same hotel indeed! – almost certainly just a ruse to get him to the FoamFay negotiating table. At this very moment, naïve Caroline was probably cruising the Balearics on Start's ostentatious yacht – lured aboard by the scheming Musty. And according to that 'Gwen' woman, love-struck James had only gone to Formentera after a call from Musty on the very eve of his return to England – a siren indeed! Hollywood had a lot to answer for.

*

Sonny removed a photograph of Weetwood from the WSD file and stared at it fixedly. The guy had sounded very stiff-upper-lip – very David Niven after having had his legs blown off in a Battle of Britain Spitfire. *Perhaps that's the way the British really are in a crisis.* But Misty visiting the Weetwoods' ancestral pad! Well, at least that explained her flight to Manchester back in July. What the hell had the kid been up to? And both girls ending up *together* on that goddam island? – and getting *kidnapped*? Come on!

No, Sonny Start did not believe in coincidences – no siree! He could smell one heck of a rat. After all, Weetwood had had Pesto abducted, hadn't he? – well, as good as. And look what happened to her!

*

In *Casa Bayreuth*'s cellar, there'd been an afternoon of shock, tears and sympathy. Caroline had coped well with her abduction, but the tabloids' brutal frontal assault on both her family and herself was far, far worse. The poor Princess of Wales's grim death compounded her misery. Misty and Rory provided support and counselling as best they could, but whenever they thought they'd stemmed Caroline's flow of tears, up they would well again.

Pongo might be a lesbian – even Caroline had had an inkling of this possibility thanks to some remarks she'd overheard in her college JCR – but *The Sun*'s claims that Pongo had lured her to 'an exclusive gay love nest a stone's throw from Ibiza – the Mediterranean's capital of kinkiness – for a sizzling summer of so-called research' were monstrous. Misty had urged her to sue; Rory had concurred. Apparently, Pongo was under siege at a San Francisco hotel, *The Dyke's Arms*, with Miko Navette, whose parents were contemplating proceedings of an unspecified nature against both the Professor and Durham University. *The Times* pompously reported that the University was seeking temporary injunctions against various tabloids whose employees were causing a nuisance both inside and outside the

256

Department of the Age of Enlightenment; a bust of Voltaire had been toppled in the foyer.

If anything, Misty was more vociferous than Caroline in the defence of James's character. *The Sun* had unearthed ex-schoolmates; an unnamed source 'close to the family' had spilled beans. Apparently, James was as bent as Pongo: he and his 'Siamese twin', Peter, had had more than 'tuck in the dorm' according to anonymous but 'highly respectable' former pupils at the all-boys 'Top-Toffs' school in Northern Scotland. The two friends had 'bummed' around Europe's 'raunchiest resorts', but as the relationship reached 'a climax', Peter had been 'conveniently blown away'. Drugs, a complete breakdown, and 'incarceration in a Lancashire castle' had followed. That summer, the 'mummy's boy' had escaped and followed 'Beryl The Peril' to the family's 'Palace of Vice in debauched Nice', where, following an attempt to murder her in a fit of drug-induced incest, he'd been subjected to weeks of 'brain-washing' by one 'Dr Audy Net'.

In truth, there was not a lot of dirt dug up about Lord Weetwood himself. In one sense it didn't matter: in the eyes of certain journalists, his relationship with 'Beryl The Peril' was proof positive that he had to be something of a dirty old man himself. And *The Sun* assumed that all men who had a passion for railways – in particular, those who owned a 'train set' – were, by definition, deviants with extensive wardrobes of grubby raincoats.

'I mean, *Daddy*?' wailed Caroline. 'I can't believe he's ever entertained a *mean* or – or a *dirty* thought in his life. You've met him, Misty. He's so – so ... *innocent*, isn't he?'

'Of course he is! I'm sure he is!' Misty tried her best to sound convincing, but she had to admit to herself that she had her doubts. Weetwood had struck her as an oddball. And when all was said and done, men were men.

'It's all crap, Caroline.' Rory had used this phrase repeatedly throughout the afternoon. Yet he, too, was not wholly convinced that everything in the paper was without foundation. After all, there was Project Orient Express. And then everyone knew about old blokes who went trainspotting – albeit unknown to him, George had not, in fact, indulged in that particular 'vice' since marrying Beryl.

Rory looked deep into Caroline's eyes. The sadness he saw filled him with an overwhelming desire to relieve her suffering. 'It's all crap,' he repeated. How utterly useless he felt!

For Caroline, Beryl was more of a problem. For one thing, there were photographs. And they were undoubtedly photographs of her mother. She wasn't exactly sure what it was that Beryl was alleged to be doing in them – both Rory and Misty were embarrassed about enlightening her – but even Caroline knew that whatever it was, it wasn't very nice.

'I bet these ... *pictures* are faked. They're probably super-imposed – or whatever they call it.'

'Well ... that's possible, Caroline,' Rory mumbled.

'Yeah, Carrie, they could be.'

'But you don't think they are?'

'We didn't say that. It's ...'

'Go on, Misty.'

'Nothing.'

But Caroline demanded an explanation.

'Well, they've named some fairly important people in that story. Do you think they'd risk doing that unless they were sure of their facts?'

Caroline exploded. 'I dare say they're pretty sure of their facts about James and me!' She burst into tears once more. There were two possible shoulders to cry on. She chose Rory's. Misty felt a little jealous.

*

In London that afternoon, Diane Bradbury cleared her desk: she'd been promoted and was moving to the other end of the open-plan office, where she would savour a splendid panorama of the building's atrium. *The Sun*'s editor, sensing that an earthquake was about to devastate a meaty chunk of both the Establishment and the Smart Set, assumed that Bradbury could play a leading role in the great muckraking endeavour that would hopefully be boosting circulation figures in the weeks and months ahead. After all, she had 'sources', and she wasn't about to identify them.

It was while Bradbury was lowering her rather sickly yucca into a carrier bag that Beryl Weetwood's call came through. She sounded remarkably cheerful.

'Where are you, Lady Weetwood?'

'*Wouldn't you like to know, Diane, dear? The bloodhounds are everywhere.*'

'I want to meet you.'

'*And I want to meet you, dear. But it will cost you – or rather your employer.*'

'How much?'

'*I think five million is a nice figure.*'

'Pounds?' You must be joking!'

'*It's a bargain.*'

'I can't see that your story is worth–'

'*Look, dear, it's not gossip I've got to sell – not tittle-tattle about some fag of a sitcom actor cruising Piccadilly for rent boys. I'm talking cabinet* ministers, *the biggest names in the movies, rock stars, princes and princesses of the royal families of Europe – I've had everyone who is anyone at the Villa Gobelin. And I've got photographs, videos and–'*

'Have you been to anyone else yet?'

'*No, but I'm sure if this stuff goes to auction, well ...'*

'Why come to me? I'm flattered, but–'

'*I like your cheek, dare I say ... style. And I can see a book – a truly* **extraordinary** *autobiography, can't you? I suspect you're the sort of person who could help me write it.'*

'I'd love to.'

'*I have to hang up. I can be contacted through my solicitor, Perry Match at Fancourt Utley.'*

'Start's solicitor!'

'*Perry doesn't see any conflict of interest. ... Must dash! Hope we can sort something out. Bye-ee!'*

Through her sunglasses, Beryl focused on Audinette as he lay soaking up the morning sun. He really had a very nice body – slim, but muscular. And how sweet he tasted! Of course, he was completely fatuous and disposable, but at least for the time being, he had his uses.

He smiled. '*Ça va, chérie?'*

'*Ça va!'*

Above them, St Bart's palm trees rustled soporifically in the balmy breeze. Within twenty-four hours Miss Bradbury would be there too.

# CHAPTER 22

When James spoke with Misty that Sunday night, on the eve of his planned return to England, he'd experienced very mixed emotions. He was angry, and intended to tell her about the misery he'd endured in the early summer – that she'd cruelly abandoned him after deceiving him with tenderness. But as he listened to her voice, the bitterness within him was neutralized and the anger dissipated. Then, just as she started to tell him about her travels, the line suddenly went dead. Assuming they'd simply been cut off, he waited for Misty to call back – in vain. He thought of ringing Mrs Duffle for Caroline's number, but as he weighed up the pros and cons, the doubts came flooding back. Perhaps Misty was just a two-faced bitch, after all. And then there was all that funny business Alphonse had mentioned – her turning up at Bobbins just days before her father started making extraordinary allegations of industrial espionage against WSD.

En route to Nice Airport the next morning, James mentioned the call to Jean-Luc, the young chauffeur with whom he'd played so many games of tennis during his stay at the villa. The Frenchman was oddly contemptuous, and, with Gallic emotion, confirmed James's own doubts about Misty's character; even he called her a bitch – *une salope*.

They were early at the airport, and Jean-Luc suggested keeping James company until his flight was called. James politely declined the offer, but just as he was about to get out of the car, Jean-Luc burst into uncontrollable sobbing.

'*Je t'aime!*' he wailed, '– *avec tout mon coeur!*'

The emotionally charged description of his feelings which followed was pure poetry, but whatever James had felt about Jean-Luc during his lengthy stay at the *Villa Gobelin*, it was certainly not love.

Suddenly, the car became very small and claustrophobic. James's head was swimming with embarrassment and fear – fear as to what Jean-Luc might say or do next. When he reached for a cigarette, James jumped out. By the time he'd retrieved his case from the boot, a trembling Jean-Luc was standing beside him. James offered his hand, saying: 'Well, goodbye. I'm sorry things have turned out like this, but I wish you the best of luck and hope you find what you're looking for one day.'

The hand went unshaken: Jean-Luc muttered obscenities in French, jumped back into the car and almost ran over James as he reversed out of the parking space. Then, with a squeal of tyres, he sped off in a haze of blue smoke.

James was in a daze. As he made his way into the terminal and tried to identify the correct queue for checking in, he kept reliving the incident. Perhaps he ought to have been more understanding – the poor guy was clearly very mixed up. Could he himself have been partly responsible for this awful misunderstanding? Maybe he'd given out some confusing signals. He pictured the heat and steam of the pool-house shower room, of Jean-Luc's muscles, his–

'I'm *not* gay,' he muttered to himself. And then, as if for reassurance, he added, 'I'm *not* fucking gay. I'm *not*!' A middle-aged gentleman dressed in a pin-stripe suit and standing in front of him in the queue, turned round and gave him a censorious glance.

'What's your problem, mate?' snapped James. But he didn't await an answer, moving swiftly away to a bank of seats, where he dropped his case and sat down heavily.

Perhaps he'd been utterly wrong about Misty. After all, he'd been wrong about Jean-Luc, hadn't he? And he and Misty had ... well, they'd done things which he could surely never have done if he'd ... if he'd been ... He couldn't bring himself to say it again – it was just too ridiculous. Jesus! He wanted to be with Misty so much. He wanted to lie with her once more – to touch her – be inside her – feel her tongue doing those incredible things to him.

James spent two miserable days and nights in Nice, moping alone in a grim, back-street hotel. Early Wednesday morning, he finally made a decision. After a flight via Barcelona, it was already late afternoon by the time he found his way down to the harbour in Ibiza Town to catch the Formentera ferry. And while he awaited the last service, he repeatedly phoned Bobbins to get Caroline's number, but, to his surprise, the line seemed to be permanently engaged.

The sun was setting as he disembarked at La Savina. It was a very small island, he kept telling himself, so Caroline and Misty couldn't be more than a few miles away at most – but where? How could he find them? With the passengers who'd accompanied him on the voyage drifting away in their taxis, minibuses and rented cars, he found a phone box and tried Bobbins once more. Still engaged! He simply couldn't understand it.

The owner of one of the two remaining taxis came out of the café in the *Estación Marítima* and asked if he wanted to be driven anywhere. In a mixture of English and Spanish, the two men endeavoured to establish some kind of understanding. All James could say with certainty was that the villa he sought housed two young women, whom he described as best he could. The taxi driver was very sympathetic. He could sense there was romance in the air and he rather enjoyed playing a cupid-like role. He felt sure that one or other of his colleagues would remember the two girls; after all, there weren't that many taxis on the island.

The investigation didn't take long. The owner of the other taxi parked on the quay was just finishing off a generous brandy in the *Estación*'s café. James was in luck: it was Jaume, the taxi driver who'd taken Caroline to the *Villa Clementina* all those weeks earlier. And not long ago, he'd brought her down here to pick up a friend. And what a friend!

The villa was in darkness when they arrived, and Jaume waited to ensure that someone was at home. When the doorbell remained unanswered, he and James decided to check the rear of the house, but there was no sign of life there either. Jaume tried one of the patio doors, and, to their surprise, found it open. Although they quickly established that no one was home, the girls were definitely around, judging by the clothes in a couple of the bedrooms. Presumably, they'd gone out for dinner somewhere.

And so, content that the young man had a roof over his head, Jaume departed with a generous tip, albeit he only took half of what James had proffered.

With a rumbling stomach demanding food, James looked in the fridge and fixed himself up with some cold meats, cheese and salad. Then he made a more detailed tour of *Clementina* and was suitably impressed; with such beautiful furnishings it was foolish of the girls not to have locked up when they went out. He tried the phone in the living room, found it was in order, and rang Bobbins. After his third unsuccessful attempt to get through, he slammed down the handset. 'What the hell's going on back home?' he muttered. In truth, he was getting just a little worried.

Out on the terrace, he slumped in a wicker armchair and tried to think of something sensible to say to Misty when she and Caroline returned. He was soon perspiring profusely with nerves; a whiff of body odour reminded him that he urgently needed a shower. Panicking, he dashed inside. Half an hour later, and now thoroughly scrubbed and dressed in clean shorts and a T-shirt, James decided to kill time with a glance at the English newspaper he'd picked up off a chair in Barcelona Airport. It had been folded to the sports pages and he'd only managed to read some of them before his plane to Ibiza was called. He'd neither had the opportunity nor inclination to glance at the paper since. It took him a quarter of an hour to polish off the sports section. Then he turned to the front page and saw *The Sun*'s banner headline and a fuzzy photo of his naked mother.

James would never be able to remember much about his solitary night at *Clementina* once he'd discovered the drinks cupboard. But the next day, after the Blackberrys had safely installed him at *Honeysuckle Cottage* and plied him with freshly-squeezed orange juice, coffee, and bacon and eggs, he did his best to explain the cause of his chronic hangover. And then, as if by chance, he drifted into the events of the long summer. In truth, he felt instinctively that he could talk to his kind hosts about almost anything – and without the slightest inhibitions. And how well they listened! Nothing appeared to embarrass or offend them; perhaps their life together in the world of entertainment had made them unshockable. In any event, they were certainly unlike any middle-aged couple he'd ever met before.

Finally, when James appeared to have come to grips with the events which had erupted around him during the last twenty-four hours, the Blackberrys made a confession: their story about Caroline and Misty going to Mallorca for a couple of days, was exactly that – a story. They broke the news of the kidnapping. Within minutes, James was talking to his beloved Aunt Belinda. It was a tearful conversation for them both. Then his father came on the line.

'It's jolly dangerous for you there, er ... James. We don't want *another* kidnapping. ... However, things are pretty sticky here too, what with the newspapers and ... everything. Perhaps these Blackberry people could put you up for a bit, and ... and–'

Belinda grabbed the phone and pleaded with James not to leave *Honeysuckle Cottage* until Caroline and Misty were released. He swore to be careful, to keep a low profile, and to stay with the Blackberrys at all times. He also promised not to contact his father when he arrived on the island the next day, Friday.

That evening, over a subdued and largely uneaten dinner, Gwen confided that she felt some responsibility for the kidnapping: she and Tom should have put two and two together at the outset and taken action of some kind. She told James how they'd first met Caroline, when she thought a prowler – or something – was lurking in *Clementina*'s garden. And then there'd been the strange incident up at the old mill near Sant Francesc involving the 'King Kong characters' and the van. It had just seemed like a silly prank at the time, in so far as they'd been able to make any sense of it. Intrigued, James asked for more details, but there was not much the Blackberrys could add.

Eventually, they moved on to exchanging ideas about who the kidnappers might be and where they were holed up – whether they and the girls were still on the island. When Gwen wondered if Misty had 'just got in the way', James revealed something of her background.

'So you see,' he concluded, 'she's from a very wealthy family too. They must have thought they'd struck gold when she turned up here.'

'That's if they knew who she was,' Tom queried.

James stood up. 'Do you mind if I smoke? I'll go out on the terrace if you wish.' They were eating indoors in case the house was under surveillance.

'Not at all,' Tom replied. 'I'll switch off the lights. I don't think anyone would be able to identify you in the moonlight.' Tom got a cigar and fetched Gwen's cigarette holder.

'Look, guys,' James said once they were all comfortable, 'we can't just sit here and do nothing. For all we know, Caroline and Misty could be in a villa just – I don't know – a quarter of a mile from here, guarded by some old codger with a toy pistol.'

Gwen nodded solemnly. 'Yes ... or by a few desperadoes with sawn-off shotguns.'

'True, but how will we ever know unless we go and look?'

Tom was shaking his head. 'James,' he sighed, 'where the hell would we even start looking?'

'Well, I think it's a fair assumption that these two goons you mentioned earlier, Gwen – the guys in the masks and everything – are probably the kidnappers, in which case they sound like amateurs. And all they have is some crappy old van.'

'Possibly.'

'Well, it can't be too difficult to trace something like that on this tiny–'

'Hang on, James,' Tom interrupted. 'Apart from the risks involved – putting Caroline and Misty in real danger for a start – there are *miles* and *miles* and *miles* of dirt tracks on the island.'

'But somebody must have seen the van. And these masks ... perhaps they bought them here?'

'Not very likely, James,' said Gwen.

It was no good: the Blackberrys were convinced they should do nothing. And, once again, they reminded James of his solemn assurances to Aunt Belinda.

That night, James hardly slept. When he did manage to doze off, terrifying nightmares would set him tossing and turning – visions of creatures like something out of *Planet of the Apes* subjecting Misty to unspeakable tortures – flashes of an old van in psychedelic colours driving over the edge of a mountainous cliff, with Caroline's face pressed screaming against a window – images of an orgy with Jean-Luc.

At dawn, he quickly washed and dressed. Then he wrote a note to the Blackberrys, explaining his need to tour the island in order to try and find some clues. He'd do nothing rash and would phone them every few hours.

There were no sounds from his hosts' bedroom as he passed their door and made his way silently through the villa. Having noticed two bikes at *Clementina* when he arrived, he sprinted over, selected one – Misty's in fact – and set off down the gravel drive. He'd no idea where he was going, but at least he was doing something.

*

That Friday morning, George Weetwood and Sonny Start were speeding towards the Iberian Peninsula in very different aircraft and states of comfort. In the forward cabin of his private jet, Sonny was engulfed in luxury, sipping chilled mineral water with a slice of lime. The plane was now several hundred miles out over the Atlantic; it lay some 40,000 feet below, glinting in the moonlight. Sonny was not tired: he'd managed to nap pleasantly on the Dallas-Atlanta leg of his journey. There was so much to think about, so much to plan. He opened the consultants' report and launched into the pros and cons of buying a chain of bowling alleys in Florida. In the rear cabin, Bob and Chuck were watching a movie.

Several thousand miles to the east, the sun was rising as a much-refurbished BAC 1-11 of British Mercia Airways dipped and dived through turbulence over the English Channel. British Mercia possessed two classes of comfort, 'Platinum' and 'Gold'. The former was limited to eight seats covered in a light grey leatherette substance at the front of the aeroplane. Separated from it by a flaming orange curtain, lurked the Gold passengers. As WSD didn't possess a corporate aircraft, jet propelled or otherwise, and George had stubbornly refused to countenance the extravagance of hiring a plane, Patricia Spigot had thought that she was doing the right thing by booking the Chairman on a direct flight from Manchester to Ibiza. Furthermore, Platinum Class had sounded perfectly respectable: the airline had assured her that as his was the only Platinum booking, Lord Weetwood would be in splendid isolation. Alas, an earlier British Mercia flight to Ibiza had experienced 'technical problems', so George found himself sharing 'his' front cabin with transferred and 'upgraded' Gold passengers. His protests had been in vain.

Although George disliked both aeroplanes and foreign travel, he had suffered significant doses of both. In view of his position, he'd had little option but to visit the distant outposts of the Goblin Empire from time to time – not to mention the occasional overseas meetings of SADMA's International Sub-Committee. But those excursions were planned and organized meticulously: there were limousines to and from the airports, VIP lounges, and what passed for luxury in the premier classes offered by the various airlines by which he'd permitted himself to be transported. Nothing, however, had prepared him for the experience of a British Mercia flight.

To be fair, he didn't feel any unease about being the only besuited passenger; it was not a matter which even occurred to him. Nor did he observe that he was unique in possessing and reading – or rather, attempting to read – a non-tabloid newspaper, namely, *The Financial Times*. What did concern him, however, was the little girl behind him, who couldn't stop herself from opening and closing the folding tray in the back of his seat. He'd turned round and given her a furious glance; she'd stuck her tongue out. He'd responded unwisely by querying her absence from school with what he assumed were the brat's parents.

The gentleman in front of George had decided to recline his seat, which because of the limited legroom – even in Platinum! – had rendered all further movement on his part nigh impossible. Across the aisle, lurked an elderly couple who demanded constant attention: the lady kept asking George if she could open the window; the gentleman, repeating plaintively 'They don't feed us at The Towers, you know!' wanted George's breakfast.

Two stewards, clad in orange and green uniforms, arrived with a trolley. The taller chirped: 'How about something in the fragrance line for the love of your life, chuck?' George glared. The shorter said: 'Are you sure you shouldn't be on the eight-thirty to Victoria, love?' With the glare continuing, he added loudly: 'Bet we see this one out on the town tonight in his leathers!' Coarse laughter erupted.

George buried his head in the *FT* and scolded himself for not having followed Belinda's advice and hired a private jet – and damned the expense! After all, she'd browbeaten him into travelling alone, just as the kidnappers had demanded. Actually, on reflection, having Brancepeth-Tring rabbiting on day and night would have been a nightmare: he'd have probed and probed. Impossible! And as for bringing Merryweather, well, the man was a functionary: any hint of trouble and he'd collapse like a soufflé. No, on balance, he was better off alone. In truth, apart from the abominable flight – Spigot would get a jolly good dressing down when he got back! – he was rather looking forward to his little adventure – Start's pantomime, in all probability – especially as his unscheduled absence from the UK would have everyone guessing. He could picture the panic at Soap House. ... How delicious!

*I wonder how Turbot's getting on with everything – especially the rail franchises. As soon as I get to Ibiza and escape from this hellhole, I'll give the cocky little tick a ring on that mobile gadget.*

\*

At Soap House, the Executive Directors and Company Secretary were hard at work delegating, setting up sub-committees, sending memoranda to each other and their subordinates, and generally avoiding any kind of corporate decision-making. With a merger in the offing, their jobs were on the line, and no one wanted to blot his copybook at this critical stage. But this morning's game of pass the parcel was proving especially troublesome for Daventry Merryweather: no matter how often he'd tried to rid himself of the hot potato that some idiot of a secretary had dumped on his desk, it just kept coming back like an unwelcome boomerang.

Overnight, an email had come in from Jabones y Detergentes Goblin Uruguay S.A: Dr Dumpwell had gone missing. His colleagues out there were rather worried; they'd even called in the police. Merryweather had tried to convince 'BT' that it was one for Exports, but Miles had correctly pointed out that, as an R&D boffin, Dumpwell fell under the aegis of the Technical Director, Ted Jarvis. Jarvis, however, argued that the problem was not, as such, a technical issue, but concerned the failure of an employee to turn up for work. So, they both agreed the matter should be handled by the Director of Personnel; Weetwood had repeatedly vetoed any suggestion that this title should be brought up to date by substituting 'Human Resources' for 'Personnel'. The DoP lost no time in telling Merryweather where he could go: as the police were involved, Dumpwell's disappearance was undoubtedly a legal matter, and he, Merryweather, was a lawyer – as he constantly reminded everyone.

So, Merryweather phoned Turbot at Bobbins, and Turbot said he'd inform the Chairman. In the meantime, he advised Merryweather to ask for regular updates from Montevideo, and take steps to inform the missing employee's family – and, perhaps for good measure, the British Embassy, just in case something 'unpleasant' had happened.

'Like what?' inquired Merryweather naively.

'Oh, I don't know.' *Jesus is this guy thick or is he thick?* 'Perhaps he's been kidnapped by Uruguayan bandits.' It was meant as a joke. Turbot really had no time for all this nonsense: he was grappling with share sale contracts and rail privatisation – and, to boot, a client who'd sneaked off on some secret mission.

Merryweather gravely repeated the 'joke' to BT in the Directors' Washroom. BT then informed Sue Pine in Accounts that the Company Secretary was worried that Dumpwell had been snatched by South American terrorists.

By noon, copies of the first edition of the *Manchester Evening News* were on the streets with '**JUNGLE GUERRILLAS GRAB GOBLIN BOFFIN**' as the front-page banner headline.

# CHAPTER 23

Ursula changed gear and began the two-kilometre switchback ascent of the La Mola peninsula's western escarpment. With the VW's badly-maintained engine straining noisily, she was so absorbed in her thoughts of prisoner exchanges and the *modus operandi* of her departure from the island that she didn't notice the dismounted cyclist at the side of the road opposite the El Mirador restaurant. It was James. He was taking a well-earned rest, scanning the glorious panorama of the isthmus, flanked by heavenly blue waters; on the horizon, shimmered distant Ibiza. But the tortured sound of the VW made him turn round. As it passed, he studied both it and the driver intently. Then he remounted his bicycle and set off in pursuit, putting his powerful legs to good use. But, despite the van's mechanical sicknesses, he couldn't keep up as it disappeared around yet another hairpin bend.

In the centre of La Mola lies the hamlet of El Pilar – just a few houses, a couple of shops, a bar and a tiny church. It's not a place which inspires visitors to linger; nor does the surrounding plateau with its small farms and fields enclosed by drystone walls. Often windy, it's a wild landscape, and wherever the land meets the sea, mighty cliffs plunge almost vertically three to four hundred feet to the foaming Mediterranean below.

With just the one tortuous and precipitous road connecting it to the rest of the island, La Mola had attracted the kidnappers from the outset. And now, as Ursula drove slowly from El Pilar to the Punta d'es Far – Formentera's most easterly point – she felt truly inspired by the utter bleakness. It was as near perfect as she could have ever hoped for. Critically, the road ran for two kilometres in a straight line from the village to the lighthouse on the point – the Faro de la Mola, an impressive white tower that could be seen from almost every corner of the plateau. Furthermore, the road descended at an almost constant gradient of just 1 in 66; Rory had calculated it from the large-scale maps of the Instituto Geográfico Nacional. Above all, throughout its entire length there was nothing for hundreds of metres on either side – not a house, not a tree, just stone walls.

Ursula managed a smile as she pulled up in front of the gates to the *far*, Jules Verne's 'Lighthouse at the End of the World' in his book *Hector Servadac*. How fitting it all was, she reflected: this windy spot, backed by desert-like scrub, and nothing but dark blue water stretching out before one as far as the horizon. It could indeed be imagined as the end of the world. And for her, one world *was* about to end: from this very spot she would rise up and launch herself into a new universe, so distant, so utterly dissimilar to that in which she'd existed so miserably and for so long.

She descended from the van and looked around. All was as it should be: the little café; the car park with just a few cars, bicycles and motor scooters; the small monument to Jules Verne. And after dark tonight, when the tourists had all returned to their hotels and villas on the other side of the island, the point would once more be abandoned to its lighthouse, the constant wind and the gulls.

Ursula had often wondered about the nocturnal habits of the keeper and his assistant; they lived at the foot of the lighthouse in a whitewashed single-storey building with bright green shutters and doors. Consequently, she and Rory had spent many a long night at the Punta d'es Far. Parked some way up the El Pilar road, they'd sat in the van for hours and watched as the dazzling light in the tower flashed its warning beam to those who'd need of it far out to sea. Rory had often waxed lyrical, imagining the lighthouse as a great beacon guiding spacecraft on their return to earth from galactic travels. The road did indeed resemble a runway – or was it that the whole peninsula was like a colossal aircraft carrier? In any event, during all those interminable hours at the point, there'd been no signs of life around the lighthouse.

Ursula made her way across the barren, rocky ground to the cliff edge, and looked down. The dark waters churned violently far, far below. How terrified Rory had been on their first visit when she'd tried to drag him to the edge – so pathetic – so weak – almost as if he'd truly thought she was going to push him over! He'd become hysterical. What a fool!

She shook her head: if this cliff, with its regular trickle of tourists, were situated in northern Europe, there'd be warning signs, railings – even a wall perhaps. But here, there was nothing. How typically Spanish! One just walked a few metres from the end of the road and then – a void. A strong gust of wind and one would be launched into space. It was wonderfully dangerous.

Ursula decided to have a coffee. Turning, she was about to head for the café when something made her freeze in her tracks. A young man was walking slowly around the van – taking more than a casual interest. Nonchalantly, she moved towards the Jules Verne monument, a stone monolith some two metres high bearing an inscription and an effigy of the author on a copper plaque.

James had pulled out all the stops to catch up with the VW, but when he finally reached the plateau, he'd had to admit that the van could have turned off the tarmac road onto any one of the many dirt tracks that criss-crossed it. So, the sensible option was to keep to the main road. In any event, the lighthouse ahead was strangely magnetic; when he found the van parked in front of it, excitement and trepidation shot through his body.

Although there were about half a dozen visitors dotted around the point – two were sitting at a table outside the café – the monument caught his eye. He walked towards it, keeping everyone under constant observation in a manner which suggested he was completely overwhelmed by the dramatic landscape. As he approached the monolith, a woman appeared from the other side and began to study the plaque with apparent earnestness. From his brief observations of the van as it had passed the Miramar, she had to be the driver: the bright orange hair was unforgettable.

Ursula pretended not to notice the cyclist, and moved off towards the café. She sat down at an empty table and ordered. There was no reason, of course, why she should have recognised James Weetwood. After all, she'd never seen him before, and there were no recent photographs of him in the public domain. Yet, there was something oddly familiar about the face of this young man ambling around the Punta d'es Far. Ursula watched him out of the corner of her eye – she'd donned large and very dark sunglasses – as she sipped her *café solo*. His legs were gorgeous – so strong, muscular and bronzed, their golden curly hairs glinting in the bright sunlight. And his thighs were out of this world. Had she seen him in a magazine? – on TV? – in a movie?

Despite her sunglasses, James felt sure that the woman's eyes were burning into him. She must have seen him studying the van. That was stupid! Or was he getting carried away? 'Perhaps she just fancies me,' he murmured. Without a second glance, he trotted back to his bike, remounted and slowly cycled away up the long straight road to El Pilar. A few hundred metres from the lighthouse, he piled on the speed, but after a minute's frantic peddling, he stopped and looked behind. Nothing. There was a stone wall running parallel to the road, and he picked up the bike and lowered it over. Within seconds, he, too, was on the other side. He didn't have long to wait. He saw the van pull out of the car park and make its way towards him. It was obviously being pushed to its limits. It soon screamed by, leaving a trail of choking blue smoke in its wake. The orange-haired driver was clearly in a terrible hurry. Was she trying to follow him?

When James could no longer see the VW, he cycled back to the lighthouse – there was clearly no way he could catch up with the van – and went into the café. Huge cured hams hung from the low ceiling's wooden beams; behind the bar, a tanned unshaven character sat on a stool smoking a hand-rolled cigarette. Dressed in a style that would have been cool at Woodstock, he looked about fifty. It didn't take James long to ascertain that his name was Tod, he hailed from Palo Alto, California, and had 'dropped out' in Formentera in the late Sixties. He talked about the musicians who'd also fallen in love with the place at that time – Peter Linfield, Harold McNear, David Allen, Kevin Ayers and all of Pink Floyd. And then things had begun to get civilized – reliable electricity, water supplies and proper roads. The tourists had followed, but Tod and his girlfriend had stayed. Now they were grandparents. Notwithstanding all the changes – in particular, the recent arrival of the Italians on their scooters – the island remained, for him, the closest thing to heaven on earth.

James finally asked if he knew the tall skinny middle-aged lady with the orange hair who'd had a coffee during the last half hour. She looked as if she could have arrived on the island with the hippie generation. She also looked familiar, he lied with a pang of conscience – a film star perhaps.

Tod laughed. 'Definitely not! There aren't many residents on this island I don't recognize. I guess by her accent she's German or something. She's been here quite a few times now – her and that geek she hangs around with – English, like you. They're always in that old VW. They started driving up here ... let's see ... about two months ago may be.'

'Do you know where they live?'

'No. Why do you ask?'

James thought quickly. 'Well ... it's sort of embarrassing.' He truly hated lying – was hopeless at it – and felt Tod was already seeing through him.

'It's a chick, isn't it?'

'You guessed! When I arrived on the island, I saw the lady and "the geek" with a beautiful girl down at the port. It's crazy, I know, but I fell for her instantly. I've been searching for her everywhere.'

Tod smiled. 'Sorry, James, but I can't help you. I wish I could.'

They shook hands and Tod wished the love-struck lad luck. 'Perhaps I'll see you in the Fonda Pepe some night!' he shouted from the café door as James cycled away.

'The *what*?'

'The Fonda Pepe, for Chrissake! – the bar in Sant Ferran! *Everyone* goes there.'

'Oh right! I'll check it out!'

Half an hour later, in the sleepy fishing hamlet of Es Calo at the foot of the La Mola escarpment, James phoned the Blackberrys on a payphone. It was Tom who answered.

'Where the hell are you? We've been worried sick. In fact, Gwen's gone out in the car looking for you. We have to be so careful, James. They could be watching the villa, and if they spot you–'

271

'I'm just cycling round, Tom. Don't worry.'

'But–'

'I'll phone again in about an hour. I think I may have spotted the VW van.'

'Oh my God! James–'

'Sorry. Run out of money. Bye!'

In the late afternoon, as post-*siesta* life began to stir again, Gwen found James dozing on a bench in front of Sant Francesc's fortress-like church. She pretended to be cross, but the relief on her face at having found him could not be disguised. And then she confessed to having been on the lookout for the VW herself, but had seen nothing. They'd both better admit, she argued, that their efforts were pointless: even if they discovered where Caroline and Misty were being held hostage, what could they sensibly do? As far as they were aware – and whether rightly or wrongly – the police weren't even involved. In any event, Belinda had confirmed that *both* fathers were about to arrive on the island. It was a very bitter pill to swallow, but they had to stand back and stay out of the picture.

Miserably, James cycled back to *Honeysuckle Cottage*. As he passed through the vineyards between Sant Francesc and Es Mal Pas, where heavy bunches of juicy black grapes awaited harvesting, he thought again of the strange woman with the orange hair.

*Could she really be a kidnapper? – someone so conspicuous? – someone so ... so old? And Tod said her companion was a 'geek'. Kidnappers with a twenty-year-old clapped-out van, for God's sake. It's preposterous!*

*And yet, that's the vehicle Caroline described to Gwen and Tom after her strange encounter at some old mill – it has to be. And the orange-haired woman and her pal have spent a lot of time up at El Pilar. Why? ... Why not? It's romantic in a strange kind of way. They could be lovers, couldn't they?*

*But then I seemed to fascinate that woman. ... Jesus Christ! I don't know what to think. And Dad arrives on the island in a few hours – Dad making 'the drop'! It doesn't bear thinking about.*

*

George's instructions were unambiguous: he was to catch the 18:15 vehicle ferry from Ibiza Town, and no other. So, with over six hours to kill after touching down, he'd requested Miss Spigot to book him into a hotel near the harbour, where he could wait in some comfort. The Royal Plaza, she'd proudly informed him after completing her task, was one of the island's few four-star hotels, and it was a mere ten-minute walk from the quay from which the Formentera ferries departed.

272

As George sped away from Ibiza Airport in his taxi, he breathed a huge sigh of relief: the British Mercia passengers were being shepherded into buses by uniformed tour guides; he prayed he would never meet any of them again. What he saw of Ibiza Town en route to collect the ransom monies from the local branch of Barclays Bank, did not inspire him: concrete and traffic; ugly apartment blocks; undeveloped plots of scorched earth littered with abandoned cars and unwanted mattresses. It all looked very third-world to him.

At the bank, he received red-carpet treatment from the manager, Señor Zangamanga; a director of Barclays Iberia, one Crispin Pitt-Flint, had even flown down from Madrid to hold Zangamanga's hand. George declined Pitt-Flint's offer of lunch but couldn't escape his monologue on the dangers of buying villas for cash from 'the locals': all of Spain was on the fiddle – Zangamanga scowled – and it was absolutely imperative that someone in his lordship's position should receive the very best professional advice.

'Who are you using on the legal and accountancy fronts?' asked Pitt-Flint as George declined a glass of champagne.

'Excellent people – meeting them shortly – at the hotel – already late.'

'Let me accompany you, Lord Weetwood – with one of the bank's armed guards – for the completion meeting.'

'No thank you. I … um… have a chap.'

After further earnest offers of assistance, a miffed Pitt-Flint bleated: 'Well, I'm afraid you'll have to give me full details of the property you're buying – and the name of the vendor – Bank of Spain regulations in the case of withdrawals of this magnitude – *and* in dollars, mark you. Money laundering, drug trafficking, terrorism – all that kind of rot, you know.'

George was momentarily thrown. Then he thought of all the information Belinda had obtained from the Blackberrys about the villa where Caroline had been staying and its German owner. Within seconds, he'd communicated the salient details to Pitt-Flint.

'Well, I'll be damned, Zangamanga!' snorted Pitt-Flint after George had sped away in a taxi with the bank's complimentary leather briefcase stuffed full of cash. 'I thought he'd turn out to be a queer cove after reading all that stuff in the papers. But if you ask me, something jolly fishy's afoot. A villa on Formentera! Hah! It wouldn't at all surprise me if the chap's being blackmailed.'

George's heart sank when the taxi reached its destination: the Royal Plaza was a six-storey carbuncle whose instantly forgettable facade was relieved only by a row of flagpoles flying the flags of a motley assortment of European Union nations; Britain's was upside down – an outrage he'd mention to the manager. The hotel's interior, however, came as a pleasant surprise: marble and dark polished wood abounded; the insult to the Union Jack was forgotten. George's room was elegant and comfortable, the bathroom – not that he would have much use for its facilities that afternoon – a veritable shrine to white marble and the finest sanitary porcelain. It was just a pity about the view, a depressing vista of a derelict bullring and an oil-fired power station belching out thick blue smoke. One could, nevertheless, just glimpse patches of blue water and the occasional yacht making its way in or out of the harbour. Frankly, he couldn't imagine any sane person wanting to holiday in such a place. But then he thought of his fellow British Mercia passengers.

George called Bobbins and spoke with both Miss Spigot and Turbot: meetings with prospective purchasers of his WSD shares and possible joint-venture partners on the rail front were filling up the diaries of many people.

'Oh, by the way,' said Turbot dryly, 'some chap in Uruguay called Dump-Something has disappeared and Merryweather is all in a tizzy.'

'Really?' It was the last thing George wanted to discuss with Turbot. Anyway, there was bound to be an innocent explanation.

Belinda had nothing to report on the kidnapping front; nor was there any news of Beryl. Ron Duffle, by contrast, had materialized begging forgiveness from 'Vivian'. Apparently, one 'Peggy Umpleby' couldn't 'cook to save her life.' Duffle had also confessed to talking to The Sun's reporter at the FoamFay launch. The domestic gossip did not interest George; Duffle's treason would certainly be dealt with upon his return. Talk of his housekeeper, however, did remind him that he was hungry. He bade farewell to his sister and changed, substituting a cream linen jacket and a pair of beige flannel trousers of indeterminate age for his three-piece suit.

The view from the Royal Plaza's rooftop complex of bar, swimming pool and 'bistro' was slightly more attractive. For the first time, George noticed the Dalt Vila perched on its hill above the harbour. It looked almost picturesque, he thought. Perhaps he would take a stroll that way after lunch. But what about the ransom monies? He glared at the Barclays briefcase lying menacingly beside his left foot. The hotel safe seemed the obvious answer – or perhaps there was a safe in his room. He was still glaring at the briefcase when the waiter arrived.

It would never have occurred to George to order any wine, but his steak and fries came with a complementary 25cl carafe of the colour of his choice. The waiter was insistent; George chose white. He was not expecting much from the rudimentary earthenware pot that hit his table with a thump, but the chilled fruity contents gave him a pleasant surprise. His worries about Dumpwell and ransom moneys mellowed – and then evaporated. His occasional glances at the outline of the cathedral atop the Dalt Vila grew longer. Light glinted off the swimming pool before him; there was a distant hum of traffic; the sirens of ships drifted up from the harbour. What a dreadful week he'd had! But now things seemed just a little brighter.

'*Algo más, señor?*' asked the attentive waiter. '*Café? Postre?*'

George was awoken from his daydreaming and asked for the bill. It was time to stretch his legs. Damn the ransom moneys! He'd take the briefcase with him.

He'd left the balcony doors open in his room before lunch, and hence, despite the air conditioning working overtime, it was like a furnace when he returned to freshen up before setting off for the Dalt Vila. He sat down on the bed and wiped the beads of perspiration from his brow. On the bedside table he caught sight of a pamphlet entitled *Ibiza Spotlight – The best resort guide in the Med*. Perhaps it would contain a plan of the town. He began to flick through it idly. There was a 'warm welcome' from the publisher: '*Good to see you here!*' read George. '*You're going to love this Magical Island. And because we want to be sure you have the sort of holiday you've been looking forward to, we've done all the spadework to SAVE YOU TIME, MONEY & DISAPPOINTMENT.*' He flicked forward a few pages. '*Our inspirational Anglican Chaplain, the Reverend Doctor Bill Maxwell and his wife Agnes, joined us last year after serving recently in Hackney and before that in Chile. They are available for spiritual help and...*'

George opened his eyes. He had no idea where he was. He lay on the bed for some moments trying to rationalize his surroundings. And then his awful journey to Ibiza came flooding back ... lunch ... the wine.

He was thirsty – very thirsty. Close to the foot of the bed and underneath the television, he spied the unmistakable fake wood of a mini-bar. It was while he was attempting to locate a bottle opener for his mineral water that he glanced at his watch. To his surprise, it read 5:20. It was time to make his way down to the port. But as he drained the glass, the panic struck. He'd not wound the watch forward an hour! The Formentera ferry would have sailed!

*

Sonny's private jet arrived in Ibiza just after four p.m. His transfer to the harbour in a private Mercedes taxi was as smooth and uneventful as the rest of his long journey from Texas. The smart slimline briefcase containing Misty's ransom handed to him by a representative of Chase's Madrid office – together with a copy of that day's edition of *The Financial Times* – lay at his side, filling the air-conditioned vehicle with the rich aroma of new hide.

Bob and Chuck – dressed in skimpy jogging shorts, sleeveless T-shirts, trainers and baseball caps – followed Sonny in a rented Suzuki Vitara SUV convertible; they did not acknowledge him in any way as they awaited the car ferry, sipping Coca-Cola at the Estación Marítima's café. Thanks to Sonny's movie-star attributes, the ticket office clerk refused to believe that the exquisitely clad American truly wanted to travel on the slow 18:15 car ferry – usually the preserve of truck drivers and the few tourists who took their cars over to Formentera. So, Sonny was given a ticket for the 18:00 jet ferry. But, eventually, with much rolling of eyes and shrugging of shoulders, the bewildered clerk acceded to his crazy request.

Just before six, Bob and Chuck drove the Vitara onto the ferry. Wondering where Lord Weetwood might be, Sonny boarded after finishing his mineral water; he'd been mildly irritated by the unavailability of Perrier and slices of lime. Warily, he deposited his Vuitton suitcase in the luggage area, climbed the gangway from the open vehicle deck, and, finding white plastic garden seats scattered liberally along the promenade and boat decks, placed his briefcase under one and sat down facing the sun. He shifted into a comfortable position and closed his eyes.

Sonny took no interest in the ship's departure, or the glorious panorama of the Dalt Vila, or the sweep of coastline to Punta de ses Portes – Ibiza's most southerly point – or the archipelago between it and Formentera; all went unnoticed as he soaked up the gentle rays of the early evening sun. Occasionally, he would glance around the decks in search of Weetwood, but there was no one amongst the dozen passengers who even faintly resembled him. Some distance away, Chuck and Bob remained engrossed in adult comics.

It was just after half past seven when the ferry docked at La Savina. Bob and Chuck drove off and parked in front of the Estación Marítima. While Bob pretended to seek accommodation at the Oficina de Turismo, Chuck acted miserable on a bench outside. It was a good performance: nothing escaped his attention. He watched Sonny – still clutching his pink newspaper – drive away in a taxi, but didn't detect anyone following. In fact, no one had paid his boss the slightest attention.

On the other side of the harbour, Ursula threw her binoculars onto the VW's passenger seat and cursed hysterically: plainly, Lord Weetwood had not accompanied Mr Start on the specified ferry. As for the Vitara, she never gave it a second glance.

# CHAPTER 24

Notwithstanding SI's corporate jet, Sonny Start was keen to avoid paying for unnecessary and unrequired luxuries when he travelled; it was one of the quirks of his character. Four-star hotels were more than adequate for his purposes and he always collected the complimentary toiletries, shoe shines, packs of tissues, and so forth with which his rooms were stocked.

The Cala Beltran, however, was not even a four-star hotel. That had been obvious from the moment of his arrival, when he'd had to carry his own bags – not only from the taxi to the reception, but also from there to his room. And what a room! While putting his last shirt on a wire hanger, he stood in the centre and shook his head: bare tiled floors, whitewashed walls, and rustic carved-wood light-fittings supporting what looked like goldfish bowls. Two single beds dominated the room. He hung the shirt in the small fitted wardrobe and emptied the remaining contents of his case. All he had to do now was arrange his toiletries in the bathroom – not that there was much shelf space – and his unpacking would be complete. That was always the first thing he did upon arriving at any hotel. It didn't matter how tired he was or how late his arrival, he simply couldn't relax until he was one hundred percent unpacked.

Sonny padded across the shiny floor to the bathroom and stood in the doorway, trying to figure out where he could put his bottles, tubes and pots of Clinique skincare products. He shook his head: it was ridiculous; there just wasn't enough room! He retraced his steps, picked up the phone, and dialled zero for reception.

'*Sí?*'

'Hello, ma'am, this is Sonny Start again in Room 327.'

'*Who?*'

'Sonny Start – remember? I'm the guy who deposited the briefcase.'

'*Ah sí.*'

'Are you sure you haven't got any bigger rooms? – a suite?'

'*Nothing bigger. All rooms fulled.*'

'OK. And where's the minibar?'

'*No minibar! Bar downstairs! You want food?*'

'Pardon me?'

'*Food! The restaurant closes now.*'

'Well, yes – of course! I want dinner, but I'd rather eat in my room tonight. What's the number for room service?'

'*No! You cannot take the food from the restaurant. It's not permitting! Breakfast is at eight.*'

'Forget breakfast – it's dinner I'm concerned about, ma'am. And I want it in my room.'

'*Too late! I see them lock the door now.*'

'What? So, where *can* I eat?'

'*In the restaurante through the trees. Bye!*'

'Now, hang on a minute–'

He phoned back, but the line was engaged. He'd speak to the manager in the morning and get upgraded.

Oh well, at least the air conditioning worked, and there was a TV with CNN. But he just wasn't used to hotel rooms without carpets. And the lights were so gloomy. And two *single* beds! When had he last slept in a single bed?

Sonny's stomach rumbled horribly, reminding him that he'd not eaten a proper meal on *terra firma* for a very long time. He'd find the restaurant the dumb receptionist had mentioned and then await the call from 'Regina' scheduled for ten o'clock.

Before showering, Sonny bit the bullet and carefully arranged his Clinique collection along the narrow bathroom shelf; the distance between each product was not sufficient for comfortable access, but it would have to do. Then followed ten minutes of fun and games with a Spanish shower with a mind of its own. The hot water quickly ran out.

Enveloped in the various discreet fragrances of his shower gel, hair tonic, skin lotions, deodorant and cologne, Sonny felt in a more benign mood as he slipped knickerless into his Boss jeans. He chose a characteristically colourful short-sleeve Versace shirt, pushed his feet into a pair of black Ferragamo loafers, and selected a matching black Gucci leather belt and a Cartier wristwatch. He admired himself in the mirror for a moment or two, smoothed out the bed cover where he'd sat to put on his shoes, picked up his mobile phone, which had been charging since his arrival, and went out.

The hotel's corridors, which were not air-conditioned, exuded the smell of fried food and garlic. As Sonny made his way to the stairs, he was surprised to find that every window was firmly shut. He opened them all wide. Descending the stairs, he stopped at the first landing and opened some more windows. Warm moist air drifted in, together with the sound of voices and clinking of glasses on the terrace below.

With the support of a walking stick, an elderly lady in beige slacks and a pink sleeveless T-shirt was slowly climbing the stairs.

'Good evening, ma'am!' said Sonny pleasantly.

'I wouldn't open the windows if I was you,' she warned in a sad whisper. 'They don't like it, you know.'

At the bottom of the staircase, some French windows led to a terrace, where groups of senior citizens sat at tables playing cards and reading paperbacks; a tall thin waiter with a glum face hovered menacingly. The predominant tongues of the subdued conversations suggested that British and German guests currently had control of this part of the hotel; judging by their clothes, they were either disinterested in designer labels or of limited means. Sonny plumped for the latter.

With the inmates staring at him as if they'd spotted an extraterrestrial, Sonny strolled along the terrace towards a monumental fountain illuminated by garish multicoloured floodlighting. To one side of it, more French windows led into a bar, where various groups of deeply tanned Italians in their twenties and thirties posing in avant-garde summer wear were sipping espressos and smoking Marlboros. Their conversations were animated; they were tactile and, for the most part, appeared to be enjoying themselves. A particularly elegant youth, with an air of disinterest in the chattering around him, blew cigarette smoke languidly into the air and looked in Sonny's direction. Their eyes met, and the Italian smiled with a flash of dazzling white teeth. Sonny smiled back and continued his progress to reception. As he approached the desk, he turned his head; the Italian was still smiling at him.

The pregnant receptionist who'd checked him in, and with whom he'd had the frustrating phone conversation, was still on duty. She was sitting in a chair, smoking and reading a newspaper. He greeted her as he passed, but she neither looked up nor acknowledged him. Outside, Sonny stood in the middle of a dark traffic-free road and tried to get his bearings. Although it had only been a twenty-minute drive from the port, the absence of street lamps compounded the impression that the hotel was in the middle of nowhere. Indeed, the tarmac terminated abruptly a few yards from the hotel's door, the spot being marked by a solitary call box, where, he assumed, he was to await Regina's communications. And yet, if she was going to phone his mobile, why did he have to hang around the payphone? Would she be watching? ... Perhaps she feared he might have gone to the police and that they'd be trying to trace her calls.

In the moonlight beyond the phone box, Sonny could make out a sandy path. It started where the road finished, dropped steeply, and disappeared among stunted pines. Perhaps it led to a beach: he'd noticed swimming costumes and towels hanging on various balconies, and thought he could hear waves lapping some way off. Opposite the hotel on the other side of the deserted road, some sandy ground served as a car park. Beyond the few cars, he could make out some coloured lights through the trees – and the sound of polite conversation. It had to be the restaurant the receptionist had mentioned, but the sand would mess up his shoes. And he really needed a torch and–

Another loud rumble from his protesting stomach made up his mind.

Half an hour later, Sonny was enjoying his meal in the Restaurante Chacala: his *lenguado* was excellent; he'd even allowed himself one glass of white wine – and had to admit that it complemented the sole perfectly. He was tempted to order another glass, but he really had to keep a clear head.

Just as he swallowed the last succulent piece of fish, a call came through on his mobile from Bob; back in the States, Pimkie had tried to book a room for the Boys at the Cala Beltran, but it had been full. The Internet had led her inexorably to the Hostal Pepe in Sant Ferran. Unknown to her, she could not have chosen a livelier spot.

'You guys OK?' enquired Sonny.

*'Sure. It's pretty damn basic but clean. There's some noisy bar across the street – the Fonda Pepe. Looks kinda wild.'*

'On *this* island? You must be kidding!'

*'No. Straight up.'*

'Yeah? Well I'm in the back of beyond – in a wood. I think it's where elephants come to die.'

*'Any contact yet?'*

'Nope. I'm about to go and wait for the promised call. Then I'll phone you.'

*'And the English guy?'*

'Still no sign of him. ... You eaten?'

*'Pizza round the corner. Quite a few places to eat in this pueblo.'*

'OK. Speak later. And stay out of that "wild bar"!'

Sonny looked for the waiter to ask for the bill. Over to his left at a far table, the Italian who'd smiled at him back at the hotel was sat on his own, smoking and playing with a cup of espresso. He caught Sonny's eye and again flashed his snow-white teeth. Involuntarily, Sonny acknowledged him with a cursory wave. Was this guy following him? Surely anyone linked to the kidnapping wouldn't be so obvious? Sonny looked at his watch: a quarter to ten; he should make tracks for the payphone. He got the bill, paid it in cash, and got up. He had to walk past the Italian to reach the track which led back to the hotel.

'*Ciao!*' said the Italian cheerfully.

'*Ciao!*'

Feeling a tingle of excitement, Sonny walked briskly on.

*

Had the seven o'clock jet ferry to Formentera not been cancelled due to engine trouble, George would have arrived on the island only minutes after Sonny. In the event, he found himself marooned on the quayside in Ibiza with the other disappointed passengers. So, when the last ferry of the day left at eight, it was packed to the gunwales.

George finally arrived at the Cala Beltran just as Sonny began tucking into his sole. Hot, tired and irritable, he had less than fifteen minutes to spare before his call came through from Regina at half-nine. Muttering something uncomplimentary, he pushed his way through a group of young Italians who were donning crash helmets in front of the hotel's glass doors in preparation for a trip on their scooters to Es Pujols; they naively suspected some exciting nightlife might be found there.

The pregnant receptionist was still on duty.

'Good evening, young lady! I'm' – he lowered his voice – 'Lord Weetwood. I have a reservation for three nights. I may possibly wish to stay longer, but there's also a possibility that two nights – or even one – may be sufficient for my purposes. And this briefcase,' he added in a whisper, 'is *frightfully* important. I want you to pop it in the safe and give me a receipt immediately.'

'Passport, please.'

'Sorry?'

'You give me passport. It is being returned on the morrow. You're paying with credit card?'

'What? … Yes, of course! Look, can we do all this later? The safe, if you please, and I need to know where the telephone box is located.'

The receptionist looked imbecilic. 'Telephone *box*?'

'Yes, where one makes and receives telephone calls. Do you understand?'

'There is phones in your chamber. You use it.'

'No, no, no, I–!'

*Sí, sí, sí*! There is phones.'

George sighed. 'Yes, I'm sure. But tonight I'm expecting' – he lowered his voice again – 'a call on the phone in the *phone box*. I believe there is one here, isn't there?'

The receptionist yawned. 'Ah, now I am thinking what you want.'

'Good.'

She directed him outside and to the left.

'Excellent! Now in the meantime, please have my bags taken up to my room and we'll sort out all the formalities after my call.' George looked again at his watch. 'Oh dear! I'd better take the briefcase with me. No time to sort out the safe.'

He was about to exit through the glass doors when the receptionist shouted with unexpected vigour, 'Your *amigo* is arrived!'

He spun round. '"*Amigo*"?'

'*Sí* – the American – *Señor* Start.'

George was embarrassed: he was not sure whether, in all the circumstances, he should admit to anyone that there was some form of relationship between himself and Start. Luckily, any comment proved impossible, for the final members of the Italian outing – late as usual due to their indecision over what to wear – suddenly appeared through the bar and swept him bodily outside. He spotted the telephone box and, as instructed, took up position beside it with just a few minutes to spare. At precisely half past nine, the mobile in his jacket pocket rang. Instinctively, he entered the phone box and picked up the receiver.

'Hello! Weetwood speaking. ... Hello?' The ringing continued. He realized his mistake just as it stopped. He removed the mobile and glared at it. 'You stupid–!' but the mobile's fresh eruption silenced the curse. 'Oh for Heaven's sake! Which blasted button do I press?' He guessed correctly.

'*You disobeyed orders!*' barked Ursula. '*You weren't on the right ferry!*'

'I–'

'*Don't ever disobey me again. You have the money?*'

'Yes.'

'*And you have come alone?*'

'Yes. Of course. When do we do the – the – exchange? Tonight?'

'*Don't be so impatient. All in good time. You must hire a car. There is a white Suzuki Vitara reserved in your name. You must collect it from the Avis agent in the hotel between nine and ten in the morning. Be outside this phone box in the Vitara at twenty-one hundred hours tomorrow evening with the roof down. Understand? And remember – keep your mobile with you – and charged – at all times. And wear a white shirt – no jacket!*'

'Is my daughter ... er – is she all right?'

'*Oh yes. She's–*'

A noise similar to dozens of outboard motors and lawnmowers being started en masse exploded around George: the Italian convoy was about to depart for Es Pujols.

'Hello! Hello! Regina? Are you there?' He wrenched open the call box's door. 'I say, you lot! Do you mind? I'm trying to–' But it was pointless: the drivers and their passengers couldn't hear him.

Back in the hotel, George discovered – like Sonny before him – that he'd have to carry his own bags: they lay where he'd left them. And as he completed the necessary forms for the deposit of his briefcase, the receptionist muttered incessantly. She was particularly displeased when he insisted on accompanying her to the safe.

It was almost ten o'clock when he set off in search of his room. After finally locating it, he then spent a few more minutes endeavouring to operate the electronic key. But when he did manage to open the door, he found himself unable to produce any electric light.

'Blast! Damn and blast these foreign electrics!'

Behind him, someone cleared his throat. 'Got a problem, mate?' It was a cockney voice. A gentleman in his seventies was standing in the doorway dressed in a lightweight beige suit, a cream shirt, a polyester regimental tie, and highly polished brown brogues.

'Just arrived, old cock? I'm Bert. You'll see me down on the beach every day. I help Manolo with the sun-loungers – not for money, of course – just for the fun of it. This is my twentieth year at the Cala Beltran. Wonderful, isn't it? I can remember when–'

'Do you understand how these wretched lights work?' snapped George.

'Oh yes! It's the key – well, more like a credit card, isn't it? You've got to put it in the master switch – *there* by the bathroom door. Fiendishly clever! Saves electricity. Very environmental – so you can't leave all the lights on – and the telly – and the old air conditioning when you go out.' Bert snatched the key out of the door where George had left it, and inserted it in the slot of the master switch. The room was instantly flooded with light.

George gasped.

'Oh!' said Bert with a mischievous chuckle. 'So, you're bunking up with a friend! Well, I look forward to meeting her down on the sands tomorrow – or later on in the bar. The Brits always assemble there after ten – plus Manolo and' – he lowered his voice – 'his *mistress*. She's just arrived from England – Fulham, actually. She's in her fifties, but you'd never think it. Reminds me of Lana Turner. Comes every year – like me. Super place isn't it? Been before? Do you like the accordion? I play requests, you know, and ...'

But George wasn't listening. He was at the end of his tether. It had been a foul day. And now this idiot wouldn't stop babbling.

'... Mind you, I can't eat much for breakfast, but they do a smashing spread. It's a buffet affair.'

George spotted a telephone and made a beeline for it.

'Hello! This is Lord Weetwood in Room 327.'

*'Yes, Señor Weetwood.'*

Bert, who wore a discreet hearing aid, came to stand in front of him. 'I'll see you in the bar later, Claude,' he whispered. 'OK?' He pointed down through the floor and then tiptoed away.

'There appears to be a mistake, young lady. Someone's *things* are in *my* room. I want them out, and I want them out *now*.'

*

Sonny's conversation with 'Regina' at ten o'clock was not dissimilar to George's, except that he didn't enter the call box but spoke on his mobile in the shadows where the path led down through the woods to the beach. Sonny assured her that he'd come alone, and she seemed content. Then she dealt with his car rental: he, too, was to pick up a Suzuki Vitara in the morning – in his case a yellow one – and to await her next call at nine tomorrow evening.

After she rang off, Sonny noticed some steps by the side of the call box and found that they led up to the hotel's terrace. In the warm pine-scented evening air, an elderly couple were still playing cards; beyond them, came a flash of white teeth. The Italian was sitting alone at a table by the gaudily illuminated fountain, blowing rings of cigarette smoke into the air. Sonny breathed deeply and continued walking. As he approached, he was on the point of saying goodnight, when the Italian said in a melodious voice:

'English?'

'Nope. American.'

'Ah, *American*. You have arrived today, yes?'

'Yes.'

'I think it. Your first time in Formentera?' He beckoned to the empty chair beside him. 'Sit down.'

It was not an order, but Sonny obeyed. His heart was pounding.

'Cigarette? I'm Paolo.' He held out his hand and pushed an open pack of Marlboros across the table. Sonny hadn't smoked since Texas Christian, but, without hesitation, he took one. Paolo lit it with a disposable lighter and looked at him expectantly.

Sonny was confused. What the hell was happening? Who was this guy? What did he want? 'I'm Steve,' he said. *Why 'Steve'? Why choose that name? Why?* 'Yeah, it's my first trip. I'm travelling around Europe for a few months.'

'I love your shirt. Versace, isn't it?'

'Yeah. I love Versace.'

The miserable waiter appeared and half-heartedly wiped a table behind them.

'What are you drinking, Steve?'

'Oh, nothing for me. I need an early night. ... I've been travelling all day.'

But Paolo wouldn't take no for an answer. They both settled on brandy, another thing Sonny had avoided since TCU.

The card players and paperback readers drifted away. After three more brandies each, and the emptying of Paolo's packet of Marlboros, life stories had been exchanged – except that Sonny's was a masterpiece of invention. He was a programmer working for a software house in Berkley – a bachelor with a passion for surfing. Paolo, who was also unmarried and worked in Fiat's design department in Turin, had a widowed mother to support. He had no pretences about being an intellectual; he readily confessed that his main interests in life were clothes and his own appearance. His candour was refreshing.

'It's quiet here, yes?' said Paolo softly, stroking Sonny's arm without any inhibitions as if he was stroking a pet animal.

'Very quiet.'

'I don't usually like quiet places, Steve. I'm one for the night life – bars and clubs.' Sonny nodded as if this was his way of life too. 'But I don't know, Steve, it's different here. You breathe the air' – Paolo inhaled deeply – 'and it's like a drug – ecstasy or good hash. After a few days, I can even cope with this hotel and its – how do you say? ... laws?'

'Rules?'

'Yes, rules. And the peoples! All these old and sad peoples. Why are they so sad? I don't know. It's so lovely here. So safe.'

*What does he mean, 'safe'? Safe from what? From whom?* Sonny stared into his empty brandy glass and reached for another cigarette. But the pack was empty.

'Oh, Steve! You want more cigarettes? I have more in my room.'

Sonny hesitated. He felt wonderfully relaxed. He knew it was the brandy and the cigarettes, but what the hell! And Paolo was funny; he was a born comedian. But the sound of a German female voice declaiming *'Guten Nacht'* at the far end of the terrace brought him back to reality.

'That's real kind, Paolo, but I'm bushed – tired. Time for me to hit the hay – go to bed!'

Paolo smiled hypnotically. 'No problem!'

Inside the hotel, they started to climb the stairs.

'I swim every morning at about eight,' Paolo said, putting his arm round Sonny's waist to help his somewhat inebriated friend reach the third floor. 'Bet you don't make it!'

Sonny came to a halt and stared at Paolo. 'Don't make it? I don't even know where the fucking beach is!' The sound of this particular expletive – the first he'd uttered in years – excited him. It sounded hard – manly. He laughed.

'Well, that's no problem, Steve. Just look out of your window in the morning. You can't miss it. It's big and blue and wet and warm and–'

Sonny was staring into the Italian's sparkling blue eyes. Paolo knew what that look meant. He moved closer to the American and kissed him on the lips. Sonny's tongue was quickly inside his mouth. They hugged each other tightly and felt the hardening of penises.

There were the sounds of footsteps below.

'I'm sorry, Jennifer,' boomed a shrill female voice, 'but your attitude is nothing short of snobbish. I don't see why you can't be nice to Mike. He's not *that* bad.'

'He's ignorant, boring and has no manners, Harriet.'

Giggling, Paolo and Sonny moved apart and accelerated up the stairs. When they reached the third floor and realized that the two bickering English women were no longer behind them, they kissed again.

Paolo said: 'I'd invite you to my room for that cigarette, but I'm sharing with a girl from my office – she's my fag hag.'

Sonny smiled cheerily. 'So, I suppose it had better be mine then.'

Paolo looked theatrically at the outline of an erection in Sonny's jeans. 'Can you wait, Steve?' he asked, stroking it. But Sonny pulled away.

'Not *here*! Come on.'

Reading aloud the numbers on the doors, Sonny finally stopped at the end of the corridor and repeated his own number.

'327. Now where's the key?'

Paolo put his hand into the breast pocket of Sonny's shirt and tweaked a nipple beneath the fabric. 'Here it is, Steve.'

The room was dark.

'Jesus!' hissed Sonny breathing heavily. 'Where the hell's that thing for the lights?'

Paolo took his hand. 'I think it's here, Steve.'

'That's no light switch, honey, it's ... Oh fuck!'

Sonny slid to his knees, but as he did so, a bedside lamp flashed on with dazzling brightness.

Paolo screamed.

Wearing a pair of yellow and blue striped winceyette pyjamas, George sat bolt upright in one of the single beds. His mouth fell open. 'Good Lord! What on *earth*–!'

With an expression of abject horror, Sonny froze for an instant and then scuttled into the bathroom and bolted the door.

'Well,' said Paolo good-humouredly as he tucked his exposed member back into his jeans, 'you older guys have all the luck. You must tell me your secret, *amore*. Sweet dreams!' As he passed the bathroom door, he shouted, '*Ciao*, Steve!'

# CHAPTER 25

Misty couldn't understand her attitude towards Carrie. After all, the sweet kid hadn't done anything unkind during their captivity; on the contrary, she'd done her very best to cheer her up, to make sure she ate her fair share of the dismal food, and to participate in the exercises she and Rory had devised to minimize the stiffness they were all now experiencing. She didn't even feel cross about Carrie's failure to participate effectively in the attempted breakout. How could she? She hadn't planned anything, or even been able to give her any warning; she herself had been surprised when Rory removed their ankle shackles and Carrie's handcuffs. But it was an opportunity she just couldn't allow to go unexploited. And yet, even if they had overpowered him, how far would they have got with her handcuffs and Ursula in the house?

Misty shook her head. Could it really have been her own bitchiness that had pushed Carrie into the arms of the spooky Rory? Jesus! What the hell could she see in him? She was bewitched – blinded. But then if this was the first guy to show any romantic interest in her – indeed, *any* kind of interest – then no wonder she was besotted. He had to be a psycho.

*Look at him, sitting there with his arm around her shoulders, wittering on about brass rubbing while still a teenager in Nottingham. It makes my stomach churn. ... Now she's staring radiantly into his eyes! How can she be so happy? Perhaps she is crazy – always has been – you'd have to be crazy to fall in love with a homicidal geek. And how can she empathize with all that nudist camp crap, and being emotionally and physically raped by that German bitch? Who does he think he's kidding? But then if I ever say anything to her, it always comes out wrong, as if I'm some reactionary parent or spinster school ma'am. It just pushes her closer to him – makes her keener to play the role of Counsel for the Defence.*

It was indeed a vicious circle: Misty just wanted to protect Caroline, but whenever she opened her mouth, a whine, a whinge or a criticism came out. Or so it sounded. She was alienating the poor girl, and that made her angry with herself. And the angrier she got, the bitchier she sounded; Caroline had even called her 'a Moaning Minnie'.

'What are you two whispering about now?' asked Misty, trying to sound light-hearted, '– or is it a secret?'

The fellow prisoners stared at her.

'It's not "a *secret*", Misty,' Caroline sighed. 'The last time I looked at you, your eyes were closed. We thought you were napping again.'

'What do you mean – "*again*"?'

'I don't *mean* anything, Misty. Don't get cross.'

'I'm not cross. What makes you think I'm cross?'

Caroline looked distraught. 'Please, Misty, we must keep our spirits up.'

'Don't talk to me like some nurse comforting a sick patient. And please don't mention the Blitz and plucky cockneys in Tube stations – or the Dunkirk Spirit again, or – or so help me God I'll–'

'Shut the fuck up!' yelled Rory. He even shocked himself.

Tears welled up in Caroline's eyes. Rory cradled her head and glared at Misty.

'Oh, Carrie – honey – forgive me. I'm so sorry. I–' Misty shut her eyes and tried to blot out the sound of her friend's sobbing. *Oh God! What's wrong with me? I'm suicidal because I haven't had a shower for ... how many days? – whatever – and those two act as though they were at summer camp. It must be an act – all a facade. Inside they're moaning like hell, dreaming of hot tubs, afternoon tea with English muffins and strawberry jam. They're hypocrites. Everyone knows the English are hypocrites. The worst!*

'Are you all right now, baby?' she heard Rory ask Caroline softly.

'Yes thanks, Rory'.

'Would you like to play *Twenty Questions* again? You can start.'

'No thanks – not just now.'

Misty wanted to say: 'I don't mind. It doesn't bother me. In fact, I'll play too, if that's all right.' She wanted so much to make amends. But it didn't matter what she said: it always came out wrong ... *always*.

The moment passed, and then it was too late.

*

George lay on top of the bed, twiddling the buttons of his pyjamas. Sleep was impossible. He couldn't decide what was worse: the heat, the lack of air, or the silence in the bathroom. He glanced again at the air conditioning's remote-control unit and weighed up the pros and cons of making a further attempt to procure some cold air. He should never have fiddled with it in the first place. Hours ago, when he'd finally decided to turn in after waiting up for Start, the racket from the air conditioning machine had proved unbearable. Inconveniently affixed to the wall high above his bed, it had taken him some time to realize that the contraption was not subject to direct control; he'd balanced precariously on a chair searching every square inch of its fascia for some form of knob or switch,

288

but without success. A futile examination of the walls had followed. Eventually, he came across a portable control unit flashing '25°', but his tampering only succeeded in raising the temperature to a tropical 33° – where it stuck. Further button-pressing merely served to increase the fan speed to jet propulsion levels, the air outlets oscillating with a raucous squeak. A flash, followed by a puff of acrid smoke, brought the proceedings to a close. George had his desired peace and was soon asleep.

Now, with his travel alarm clock displaying 3:37, he was wide awake and soaked in perspiration. He contemplated opening the balcony's sliding doors, but reminded himself again of mosquitoes. What was it that King George V had said? ... 'Abroad is bloody!' – or something along those lines. How right he'd been! No, he'd rather put up with the heat than be eaten alive.

Desperately thirsty, he scrutinized the room for a minibar. Perhaps there was one in the bathroom. Which reminded him: he also wanted to empty his bladder. What on earth was that perverted American doing in there? It was all very quiet – too quiet. Perhaps the chap had killed himself, or was in the process of dying with slashed wrists. There might be blood everywhere.

George pictured the scene for a moment. 'Oh, Lord!' he groaned aloud. There'd be police and inquests, coroners and reporters – lurid headlines like 'GAY U.S. BILLIONAIRE FOUND DEAD IN PEER'S HOTEL ROOM!'

He briefly buried his head in his hands, and then looked back at the bathroom door. A dead Start would be the final straw. And what about the kidnapping? How would he explain Start's death to Rex and Regina? Would the release of his daughter be delayed? Would he be stuck on this wretched island for days?

But alive, Start would be eminently open to blackmail – at least if he could get hold of that foreign chap – the Mediterranean type who'd stood exposing himself before a kneeling Start some two hours ago. Vile! Might he be a hotel guest? ... Actually, on reflection, how could he be sure that the man who'd scuttled into the bathroom was Start? He'd never even seen him before, and hadn't the other man called him 'Steve'? Perhaps the idiotic receptionist had made a mistake after all. But if so, who was the man in the bathroom? Was there, in fact, *anyone* in the bathroom? ... So many unanswered questions! It was high time he tried to get some answers.

George got out of bed, put on the slippers Mrs Duffle had packed for him, and shuffled over to the bathroom door. He cleared his throat.

'Hello? Start? Are you in there? This is Lord Weetwood speaking ... *George* Weetwood ... from WSD.'

289

There was no response.

'Start? Can you hear me? I'm coming in. Don't be alarmed.' He tried to open the door, but it was locked – which meant someone had to be in there.

'Look, Start, don't be a silly ass. You can't stay in the bathroom all night. Besides, I need to use the, er … the facilities. And I'm jolly thirsty. Nothing to drink out here. There isn't a minibar thing in there by any chance, is there? I'm not frightfully keen on drinking the local tap water – if one can, that is. Can one? … Start?' He banged on the door. 'Start! For heaven's sake, man, open this door!'

He thought he could hear some movement. 'Come on. If, as it would appear, we are required to share this room, we might as well be civilized towards each other, don't you think?' Silence. 'I say, I really do need to use the … um … the lavatory. Be a good fellow, Start, and let me in.'

On the other side of the door, Sonny was perched on the lowered toilet lid wondering what to do. Clearly, he couldn't remain in the bathroom for ever, but the ignominy of coming face to face with Lord Weetwood in the predicament in which he now found himself posed what appeared to be an insuperable problem. Matters were exacerbated by his state of inebriation. If anything, after two hours of self-imposed incarceration he felt worse than when he'd sought sanctuary: a throbbing headache had developed, and he, too, was suffering from a raging thirst. He'd even come close to drinking the tap water, but suspected that cholera could be a problem in Spain. Or was it malaria? Could you get malaria from water? Hell – he couldn't think straight!

What he *did* know for certain, however, was that Weetwood was no gentleman: he was as devious and as unprincipled as any businessman he'd ever come across. Which meant he'd try and use to his advantage any dirt he could lay his hands on. In fact, he was surprised that Weetwood hadn't already combed every corner of the hotel for Paolo – unless he'd been in Weetwood's pay all along! Jesus! Maybe he'd got witnesses, photographs, recordings! He could already hear his fruity, smug voice and picture that typically English supercilious look on his chinless face: *I won't expose you as a queer, old boy, and you'll drop all that litigation nonsense, what?*

But hold on a minute, how could that be? What could Weetwood have possibly known about his own inclinations? After all, there'd never been any gossip or rumours to his knowledge back home – he'd made very sure of that … with the aid of the Boys, of course, and people like them. And could he have been so wrong about Paolo? He seemed totally on the level, a really nice guy. He'd never been wrong before about pickups. … Well, OK, twice – but the Boys had sorted those scumbags out. They'd deserved everything they'd got. … But not Paolo, surely? He was different … wasn't he?

Sonny cracked his knuckles. If Paolo *had* set him up, then–

The door handle rattled.

'*Start*! I really must insist that you permit me to use the lavatory.'

'OK, OK! Give me a minute.' Sonny stood up and looked at himself in the mirror. What a mess! His eyes were puffed up with black shadows underneath. And at almost four in the morning, when he was about to introduce himself to this English lord, a Versace shirt looked ridiculous.

He inhaled deeply and opened the door. 'Good eve–'

'Yes, yes!' George screeched, pushing passed him. 'Formal introductions shortly, but first I need a pee.' The door slammed shut explosively.

Alone in the bedroom, Sonny considered changing his clothes, but donning something less casual at this time of the morning would no doubt strike Weetwood as eccentric. On the other hand, he had no pyjamas – he never wore them. What if Weetwood emerged while he was still undressing and commenced some kind of blackmail negotiations? Standing over him in traditional nightwear, the Englishman would have an obvious advantage! But any further analysis of the question of his attire was rendered impossible by a cacophony of clanking and rattling.

'Sorry about that racket,' George muttered, exiting the bathroom. 'Damned if I can get the lavatory to flush properly. Spanish not too hot on the plumbing front.' He held out his hand. 'We meet at last. How do you do?'

They shook hands: Sonny was surprised by Weetwood's firm grip; George noted the limpness and clamminess of Start's.

'Hi,' Sonny said meekly. Sensing the weakness of his greeting, he instantly added in a deeper, louder voice: 'What a hell of a way to meet! And what a dump!' That also sounded wrong. He wanted to kick himself.

George folded his arms. 'Oh, I don't know. It's not the Ritz, I grant you, but I've stayed in worse. When I was a teenager travelling around Europe during the hols, I often took a room in a station hotel. No doubt you did the same thing – the Wild West and all that. It's amazing what one can put up with when one's young, isn't it? And when I think of my travels when I first joined the company – in Africa, the Indian subcontinent, South America – well...

'You know, Start, my father was a great believer in economy when travelling on business, so some of the hotels I frequented in those days were pretty basic. I remember one in Dar es Salam ... Oh, I'm sorry – you're yawning. You must be jolly tired. I know I am.'

George sat down on his bed and fell silent. It was not that he was nervous or particularly embarrassed about sharing a room with the American: unlike Start, he'd spent almost ten years of his life sleeping in school dormitories devoid of privacy. What really concerned him was the prospect of Start raising the issue of the unnatural practices which his bedside lamp had so dramatically illuminated earlier on. Americans, he understood, had a habit of unburdening themselves – even with strangers – seeking cures for their personal problems, actual or perceived, through conversational 'therapy'. Such nonsense! Such presumption!

Suddenly, Sonny had a craving for a cigarette, and was reminded of Paolo. He began to frame an introductory question which might get Weetwood to reveal his hand, but the brief silence was shattered even before he could open his mouth.

'Oh, by the way, Start, I'm afraid the air conditioning doesn't seem to work.' George did not allude to his tinkering or the small explosion. 'I would have opened the windows, but the mosquitoes could be a bit of a problem. Any bright ideas?'

Sonny looked blankly at his roommate and wondered whether the question was for real. Was *anything* going on around him for real?

'And, I don't know about you, Start, but as I said before, I'm frightfully thirsty. Don't suppose you've found anything to drink, have you? I've searched for one of those minibar things without success. The tap water may be dodgy. What do you think?'

*What do I think? I want to be a million miles from here, preferably with Paolo's body entwined with mine.*

'George – it's OK to call you "George"? – and I'm Sonny. I mean, if we're sharing the same damn room ...'

'Of course,' responded George with an obvious lack of enthusiasm for the desired familiarity.

'Fine. ... Look ... er ... I–'

*Oh God, here it comes.*

'–I wouldn't worry about opening the windows. I always travel with one of these little electric gizmos that kills the varmints. I'll plug it in, if I can't get the air conditioning to work.' Sonny picked up the remote control and pressed buttons with obvious expertise. 'Nope, it's bust for sure. OK, George, you open the windows and I'll find the gizmo.'

With his task performed, George got back into bed and covered himself with a single sheet, having already pushed the coverlet and blanket to the bottom of the bed. He desperately wanted to sleep, and yet there were so many issues that might be usefully raised with Start. He was, however, uncertain whether he should raise any of them at this juncture.

Across the room, Sonny bent down with his back to George to plug in his appliance, whereupon the full exuberance of his shirt came into focus, causing him to ruminate over the type of man who would wear such a garment; it seemed particularly inappropriate for the father of a kidnapped daughter on a rescue mission. But then so did his disgusting antics with the olive-skinned character.

While furtively removing a pair of white Calvin Klein Y-fronts from a drawer in the fitted wardrobe, Sonny asked: 'So how come we're in the same room, George?' As he awaited the answer, it occurred to him that he'd filled all the storage space with his own belongings, which could explain why Weetwood's suitcase lay open on the floor; it looked as if it had been ransacked by a burglar.

'Ah, good question, Start.'

'*Sonny!*'

'"Sonny"?'

'Please call me Sonny, George.'

'Oh ... right – if you insist?'

'I do.'

George watched Sonny retreat to the bathroom.

'Go on, George, I can hear you in here.'

'Yes, well I'm surprised no one told us. From what I could gather from the somewhat less than helpful young lady in reception, when the booking was made – presumably by "Rex" or "Regina" – they only had one room available. Obviously our "hosts", so to speak, found that acceptable. And she claims there's still not a free room in the place – fully booked. Naturally, we'll speak to the manager in the morning. ... Or do you think our hosts require us to share a room?'

'How was the booking made?' asked Sonny from the bathroom, '– by phone, in person–?'

'I didn't ask. I would assume by telephone. I–' George hesitated as Start returned to the bedroom wearing only underpants; his trousers and shirt were carefully draped over one arm. He promptly averted his gaze and looked straight ahead, but even with his lack of interest in the male physique, he'd been reminded of Michelangelo's David.

Sonny removed the cover and blanket from his bed, folded them meticulously, and deposited both them and the single pillow on the armchair. George watched him out of the corner of his eye and concluded that Start was as good, if not better, than any chambermaid.

'Oh, if you don't want that pillow, er ... Sonny, I'll have it. I usually sleep with two.'

After handing him the pillow, Sonny dived into bed. He wanted to turn off his bedside lamp, but thought again of his thirst. 'It's a hell of a state of affairs when you can't get a glass of water in a hotel at four a.m. No minibar, no room service, and water from the faucet that tastes like the stuff the dentist gives you when he says, "Now rinse!". I've just tried some – you don't want to – believe me!'

George looked up at the ceiling. 'Oh well, to be fair, it *is* only a *three-star* hotel. We'll just have to grin and bear it. I suppose there are people a lot worse off than us – our daughters for example.' He thought that sounded rather noble, almost saintly.

'Sure, sure.'

Sonny had tried hard to sound concerned – troubled even – but was uncertain of the result. *Damn, damn, damn! I'm simply not in control of this situation. It has to be the alcohol. I'll never touch it again. It always caused trouble. Why did I give way so easily and so quickly – and on this night, of all nights? Why?* He put a hand into his Calvin Kleins and comforted himself. As soon as the lights were extinguished he'd remove them: he just couldn't bear wearing anything in bed.

'Spoken to Regina ... er ... Sonny?'

The two men exchanged accounts of their conversations down at the callbox.

'So, we'll both be parked out front tomorrow night, George. Sounds kinda strange, doesn't it?'

For some time, they silently ruminated on the import of this remark. Additionally, George wondered whether he could drive a jeep-like contraption. The seconds of silence turned into minutes, and each man assumed the other had fallen asleep. Finally, George leaned over to turn off his bedside lamp, but instead the switch illuminated the main ceiling light. He hurriedly tried another switch. Success! But that still left Start's lamp burning.

He glanced over to the other bed. Start was lying on his back with his eyes closed, and George was suddenly struck by the utter unreality of the situation; perhaps people cleverer than himself might call it 'surreal'. If – even a week ago – anyone had told him that he, Lord Weetwood of Dribbledale, would one day share a room with Mr Sonny Start of Texas, he would have been prepared to bet everything he had against such a prediction ever coming true. It was the most improbable thing he could have imagined.

*

Three miles to the south-east, *Honeysuckle Cottage* lay silent. In the Blackberrys' double bed, however, Gwen lay awake worrying herself sick about the kidnapping and what the new day would bring. She couldn't make up her mind whether it was a good or bad omen that the weekend would close with the death of Jessica Muffin; Sunday's omnibus edition of *The Muffins* was to be extended to cover the event. Of course, despite secrecy undertakings and dire warnings from the producer, it had already been leaked that Jessica was getting the chop: while attempting to make an emergency landing at Worchester Airport, a cargo plane loaded with live calves en route to veal production units in Belgium would crash into the Intensive Care Unit of the town's Royal Infirmary. Jessica would be one of several patients cremated in the ensuing inferno. In the weeks to come, sabotage by animal rights supporters would be revealed.

Gwen had sworn to keep the details secret until after the broadcast; naturally, she'd told Tom. They'd had a good laugh, but at four in the morning the end of Jessica Muffin didn't seem quite so funny. She'd miss Broadcasting House.

Wiping away the tears, she gave Tom's hand a squeeze. 'I love you, Tom.'

'I love you, darling,' he mumbled.

Down the hall, James had lain in bed smoking Ducados until his stock was finally exhausted. He felt utterly useless and pathetic. He was cursed, or perhaps *he* was the curse. Everyone and everything he came close to was doomed, corrupted, defiled. The devil was inside him. He was evil. It had begun with Peter. Then along came Misty, and as soon as he set eyes on her, a chain of events had been set in motion which had led inexorably to her kidnapping. He didn't want to think about Jean-Luc. As for Caroline, he should have made a real effort to befriend her years ago. And he should never have made fun of her fatness. How could he have been so cruel, so heartless? But for him, she'd never have become an introverted bookworm – a historian, for God's sake! – to be blunt, a complete turn-off to the male gender. He was so clearly responsible for it all.

And his father? That was his fault too. Had he ever shown any interest in either Goblin or Dad's hobby? No, he certainly had not! It was worse: he'd ridiculed, scorned and scoffed. He'd lived in his father's house, eaten his food, taken his money, and been educated at his not inconsiderable expense. He'd just taken it all for granted. Dad was a bloody billionaire by all accounts, but had never even talked about his wealth, or bought anything extravagant for himself – apart from his trains of course. He wasn't mean, and had never been cruel or lost his temper. He didn't drink or gamble, and had carefully piloted the family business – and protected his ungrateful son's inheritance – without the least grumble or complaint.

Now, thanks to himself and the evil Beryl, his father was being ridiculed and vilified in the world's media, and was on the point of abandoning – no doubt with overwhelming sadness and regret – the business which he'd tended with such loving care for so many years. This railway franchise stuff that Tom and Gwen had mentioned had to be a cry for help.

As his eyes grew heavy, James weighed up the pros and cons of going to see his father at the Cala Beltran, notwithstanding the express instructions not to do so. In fact, he had a very strong urge to go over there straight away – wake him up, and proclaim his love and admiration – give him a real hug – kiss him on each cheek, like the French. Then the spectre of Jean-Luc reappeared, and thoughts of the Curse returned: if he wanted a successful outcome to the kidnapping – and he was certainly prepared to do anything to achieve that – then he should avoid contact with anyone remotely involved. But after Misty's release, how would he ever be able to tell her – or Caroline, for that matter – that he'd moped around the Blackberrys' villa doing fuck all because he was 'cursed'? ... And yet, if he didn't want to destroy their lives too, maybe he should never have any contact with either of them again? Continuing this thought process to its logical conclusion, it was obvious that he should either kill himself or become a hermit, avoiding contact with humanity for the rest of his miserable existence.

James clenched his fists and beat the mattress repeatedly. 'Jesus sodding Christ!' he hissed. 'What is all this crap about *curses*?' He shut his eyes and tried to concentrate. Misty appeared before him, a vision of almost unimaginable beauty. He had to earn her respect, and he wouldn't get that sitting around on his butt. No more amateur sleuthing on a bike! Tomorrow at dawn, he'd take *Clementina*'s Jeep and scour every highway and byway, every nook and cranny, leave no stone unturned. He'd drive and drive ... and ... drive ... and ...

*

At Bobbins, aided and abetted by a second bottle of port, which stood almost empty on the kitchen table, the trio of anxious women had reached a decision.

'So, I'm going then,' Belinda said firmly. She drained her glass and stood up. Vivian and Patricia nodded in unison.

'I'll drive you to the airport,' said Patricia. 'I wish I could come too. I'm so worried about the Chairman.'

Belinda snorted. 'Yes, well I'm more worried about what he'll do – or not do.'

'Oh, Belinda, I think you're judging him unfairly. After all–'

'Look, you two,' Vivian interrupted, stubbing out a cigarette, 'you've done this topic to death. You'd better get yer skates on if you're going to have any chance of catching a plane to Ibiza this morning. It's already' – she tried to focus on the wall clock – 'er ...'

'It's twenty-five past four,' Belinda replied instantly. She made for the door. 'Come on, Pat, let's get this show on the road. Thank God I packed my passport in Eastbourne! I'll just chuck some stuff in a holdall and be back in two ticks.' She seemed supercharged; alcohol affected her that way.

'Right-o, captain!' chirped Patricia with a mock salute as she steadied herself with the back of her chair.

'Do you think she's fit to drive, Linda?' asked Vivian.

'No subordination in the ranks!' shouted Patricia in a fit of giggles.

Belinda marched over to the phone. 'What's Peggy Umpleby's number, Viv?'

Vivian pulled a face. 'You're not going–?'

'Viv! *None* of us is in a fit state to drive – and we're out in the bloody sticks. I'll never get a taxi at this time of the morning. I need Ron. Come on, dear, the number!'

Ron picked up the phone almost immediately. He'd been awake for hours, hunched up on the sofa in Peggy's over-furnished living room: her snoring and the lavender-scented sheets of her queen-size bed had proved unbearable. Belinda's request for his services reduced him to tears. She sounded like Lady Thatcher at her best. Orders at last! And from the boss's sister! It had to mean the beginning of his rehabilitation.

'Stop blubbing, man,' Belinda bellowed down the phone line, 'and get your arse into gear!'

Blimey! Orders from a real toff! Absolute heaven!

*

In Fort Worth, Carmen Start was unwinding at *SonCar* with a glass of bourbon in her 'Long Gallery'. It had been a very worrying day and she was all tuckered out. Her reputation – indeed her very credibility – had been at stake. And in view of all those meetings she'd had to attend, not to mention the brunch with the visiting troupe of Ukrainian mime artists – God, how she hated mime! – it was a wonder there'd been any time to make all those phone calls to Maui.

The President of the Fuss chain of beauty salons had not been pleased to have his vacation interrupted, especially by 'some dame' – his very words – babbling garbage about bog turtles. But his attitude changed as soon as he realized that he was talking to the unofficial First Lady of Fort Worth. He promised he would investigate the sponsorship mess immediately, swearing he knew nothing about it. When he phoned back, he blamed a vice-president who'd been on a frolic of his own. Mrs Start was not to worry: now that he was fully in the picture, Fuss would be honoured to sponsor the new Bog Turtle National Breeding Center at the Herpetarium.

So that problem was solved! Next!

'Oh shit!' grumbled Carmen: there was still the seating plan for the dinner she was giving for the Trustees of the Will Rogers Memorial Center, and their spouses – not 'partners', thank you very much. It was only six weeks away!

She decided to hunt around on her secretary's desk to see if Courgette had produced some drafts for her consideration, but after five frustrating minutes she still hadn't found any. Then she spotted a telephone message. '"Mr Start",' she read aloud irritably, '"phoned to confirm that he had arrived safely and that everything was OK."'

Carmen shook her head and frowned. It really was unacceptable: Courgette should have left the message on the hall table with the others. That was the second time in a month she'd slipped up. She'd have to have a word with her. And why hadn't she done something about the seating plan? What did she pay her for?

She sighed deeply. Enough! She'd done more than her fair share for the well-being of the citizens of Fort Worth for one day.

Carmen trudged upstairs to her bedroom. She tutted: a file lay in the centre of the vast bed; a note was attached with a red paper clip. It read:

Hi, Carmen!
Great news about the Turtles!!
Here are my first ideas for the Will Rogers seating plan. I know you like to play with them in bed!!
See you tomorrow, C.P.

*

The unmistakable smell of drains pervaded the faded hotel, but it was cheap and on the right side of Algiers for the airport. In his shabby room on the second floor, Dr Mark Dumpwell stroked the stubble on his chin and stared at the pile of photographs and maps of Formentera which littered his bed. The aerial shots of the island's coastline in the *Aeroguía del Litoral de Ibiza y Formentera* were excellent, but even with a full moon he doubted that they'd prove to be of much value. The key to everything was the lighthouse: he just had to ensure that he chose the right one! But unless he got some sleep, he'd be too tired to do anything.

He set the alarm for two p.m., which would give him almost eight hours rest – more than enough! And then he'd go and take another look at the plane: the maintenance guys had better have replaced those dodgy parts, but as almost a civil war was going on around him – just 150 miles from Cap de Formentera – it was a bloody miracle anything in the damned country functioned.

Dumpwell cleared the bed, stripped naked, and, glistening with sweat – the heat was fierce – lay down on top of the sheets. His last thoughts before drifting into unconsciousness were of Rory Devlin: what a loser!

Such was his exhaustion, he never heard the whining of the mosquitoes.

# CHAPTER 26

At six a.m. on what she intended to be her last day on Formentera, Ursula was awoken by the incessant bleating of her alarm clock. She'd slept extremely well and felt refreshed. Indeed, she felt so good that en route to the bathroom she began humming the opening bars of Beethoven's Fifth Symphony: Fate knocking at the door – how appropriate! She took a cold shower as usual, dressed, and completed her packing. She was not taking much – just a change of clothes and some items of sentimental value. Everything else – including Rory's stuff – would be burned in the garden, just in case they might provide clues of some kind to the police.

Over a breakfast of black coffee and her gruel-like concoction, Ursula discovered that she was about to run out of cigarettes. Angered by this inexplicable organisational deficiency, she stormed out to the van, promising mayhem for the lackadaisical owners of the *supermercado* at the junction with the Es Pujols road if they weren't open.

*

Gwen was sitting on *Honeysuckle Cottage*'s patio with a mug of coffee, watching the sun rising over the distant La Mola peninsula. She and Tom had travelled to many exotic locations around the world, but, as far as she was concerned, none of them could equal the heavenly vista materialising before her. But then, out of the corner of her eye, she spotted James padding softly across the tiles, and was jolted back to reality.

'Good morning, James!'

'Oh Christ! You startled me. I didn't think anyone was up.'

'Evidently.'

He came over and kissed her on both cheeks.

'Some coffee before you embark on your travels, darling?'

'Er, no thanks. I'm just going for ... a walk.'

'Oh *really*?'

'*Really* – along the cliffs – I need the exercise. I ... Gwen, this is something I've *got* to do. If you were in my position, I think you'd do the same. It's not in my nature to just sit here and do sweet-f-all. I love my sister, and I love Misty, and I don't want to lose either of them.' He turned his head and gazed out to sea. 'I couldn't live with myself if anything happened to them. I know it's risky – that I might make things worse – cock up everything – but there's also a chance I could find them. OK, it's remote, but if I *did* find them–'

'You'd try and rescue them? James, this isn't a game – it's not the movies, darling.'

He spun round. 'She – Misty, that is – could never respect me, sat on my arse–'

'We've been through all this. Listen to me. If Misty loves you, she'll understand that it required more courage and sacrifice to control your gut feelings and let the agreed arrangements run their course.'

'She *won't*! She'll think I'm a–'

'Do you want to do this for her benefit, or to prove to yourself that you're Mr Macho?'

James's face was twisted with pain. 'I'm frightened, Gwen – frightened that those creeps are going to kill them – that we'll never see Caroline or Misty again. I'm going to take Kurt and Teeny's Wrangler and–'

'James, please, I–'

The phone began ringing inside the villa, and Gwen immediately dashed through the French windows into the living room. James followed, watching anxiously as she picked up the receiver.

'*Gwen? It's Belinda.*'

'Belinda! Any news?' She turned to James. 'It's your aunt,' she whispered superfluously.

Machine-gun fashion, Belinda rattled off her dramatic announcements. '*So, I'm at Manchester Airport now. I've hired a private executive jet. Can't imagine why my fool of a brother didn't do the same. Pilot should be here in a few minutes.*'

They discussed flight times, ferries and accommodation at *Honeysuckle Cottage*.

'*Any news at your end, Gwen?*'

'No – nothing ... well, apart from that van James saw yesterday and ... I wish you'd talk to him.'

With the intention of putting him on the line, Gwen looked over to where he'd been standing. But he was already accelerating the Jeep down *Clementina*'s twisting gravel drive.

In Sant Ferran, a few shopkeepers were opening their shutters as James pulled off the main road and took the turning to Es Pujols and Punta Prima; he'd had neither the time nor the energy to explore that way yesterday. Racing down the hill towards the coast, he was so transfixed by the breathtaking views of distant Ibiza that he almost missed the sign for Punta Prima. It was opposite a small supermarket, and as he turned east into the sun and accelerated up a steep hill, he spotted an old van about a hundred metres ahead of him. He squinted in the dazzling light and his heart pounded. It was a VW – no, not 'a' VW: it was definitely the one he'd seen at the lighthouse! – the same colour! – everything!

With James hanging well back, the road soon reached a plateau of brown fields and pine copses. After a kilometre or so, the VW took a turning to the right. James followed slowly and found himself on a twisting dirt track, but the van was no longer in sight. After five tense minutes, he rounded a corner and slammed on the brakes: some thirty metres ahead, the track ended before a pair of wrought iron gates, flanked by a high wall. He switched off the engine and proceeded gingerly on foot.

The gates were padlocked. On the wall to the left, blue and white tiles read *CASA BAYREUTH*. At the end of a short curving drive, the VW stood in front of the open doors of a hideous villa's integral garage. James was over the gates in seconds, watching and listening for signs of activity, but save for some screeching gulls high overhead, and the wind whistling in the pines, all was quiet. He was about to approach the villa when a plume of thick whitish smoke began to billow from somewhere behind it. Moving swiftly up the drive, he crept along one side of the building until he reached the rear. Cautiously, he peered around the corner. A mighty bonfire piled high with clothes, books and assorted household debris, was burning in the centre of an arid garden. About ten metres from him, a tall thin woman with a shaved head was standing beside an open door. She was staring at the conflagration with an odd smile, a cigarette in one hand.

James ran so fast that Ursula only saw him out of the corner of her eye at the last moment. Screaming, she sprang backwards through the doorway into the kitchen; James sailed across the tiled patio, landing spread-eagled on a white plastic table. It crashed sideways, and his head hit the tiles with a sickening crack.

*

George opened his eyes and spent a few seconds taking in his surroundings. A shaft of light was flooding in through a gap in the curtains. He focused on his alarm clock – 8:16! He propped himself up and glanced to his left. Start's bed was empty.

'Oh hell!' he muttered. 'The bounder's probably gone to nobble that foreigner.' But as scenes from last night's bizarre performance flashed through his muddled brain, he detected the smell of fried bacon and eggs, and realized that he was famished and dreadfully thirsty.

Without bothering to wash, George swiftly donned his suit's trousers, a thick Viyella shirt hurriedly unearthed from his unpacked suitcase – he left the top button undone as a concession to the heat – and black socks and brogues. He was on the point of dashing off to unearth some breakfast when he heard what sounded like a chair scraping on the other side of the curtains. Drawing them back, he winced as dazzling sunlight hit him through sliding glass doors. They were slightly ajar and revealed a diminutive balcony barely accommodating a small white plastic table and two matching chairs. Sonny – barefooted, sporting a pair of dark blue beach shorts and a yellow polo shirt – was sitting there with his back to George. A packet of Marlboro Lights, a bottle of mineral water, and an ashtray full of cigarette ends lay on the table.

George flung the doors wide open. 'So this is where you are, Start. Good morning! Thought you were at breakfast.'

Groaning, Sonny half-turned. 'Hi,' he said softly. 'And *please*, George, it's *Sonny* – remember?'

'Oh, indeed, indeed. Sorry.' George stared at the water. 'I say, where did you get *that* from?'

'The bar ... almost two hours ago. I heard some folks moving about, so I mooched downstairs. The kitchen staff and cleaners were creeping into work. I finally managed to convince one of them to break some house rules.'

Sonny offered the bottle to George. His raging thirst got the better of him; he never even thought of getting a glass from the room. He drained the contents, and then stared guiltily at his brogues.

'Jesus! sighed Sonny, shaking his head slowly. 'How come everyone's so sour-faced in this hotel? I mean, look at *that*.' He swept an arm across his field of vision. '*Look!*'

George moved forward to the rail; one could almost reach out and touch the tops of the pines growing at the edge of the stone-flagged terrace below. Immediately beyond the trees, sand dunes tumbled down to a horseshoe-shaped bay some hundred metres wide with a beach of golden sand. Crystal-clear water, the colour of turquoise, motionless in the still morning air, gave way to the darker aquamarine of the open sea beyond two low headlands of reddish stone. Beneath the southern arc of cliffs, half a dozen small fishing boats, high and dry on wooden slipways laid into the rocky shore, were protected from the elements by crude awnings of timber and bamboo. On the other side of the bay, a tiny whitewashed house with a red tiled roof had been built into the gently sloping cliff face. It was almost engulfed by evergreens, but a covered terrace filled with tables and chairs bordered the beach. George could just make out the words 'Restaurante Sol' painted in black letters along the terrace-wall. What could be seen of the hinterland indicated that Cala Beltran was at the edge of dense pine woods.

The overall impression was one of tranquillity, for George had yet to spot a living soul. But then, as he was on the point of turning round, he noticed a man arranging sun loungers beneath red and white umbrellas close to the water's edge. A slight stoop suggested an elderly man. He blinked and looked harder. Shockwaves hit him.

*It can't be, can it? That's surely not what's-his-name, the babbling old fool that got the lights working? He can't be–?*

Sonny seemed to read his thoughts. 'Yeah, that old-timer down there is as naked as the day he was born. Unbelievable, isn't it?'

'What is?' responded George vaguely, still staring at the apparition of a nude Bert, albeit he couldn't remember his name.

'This place, of course ... unbelievable. ... I've been sat here since first light ... watching it come alive, like something out of the movies – know what I mean?'

George did not know what he meant.

'If they did this place up – splashed out an' all – it'd be a paradise – better than Jesus knows how many dumps I've been to like ... like the Caymans, Barbados ... Fiji. ... You know, George, I've been doing a spot of thinking. What do you reckon this place is worth? – five million bucks? ... six? ... more? If I could only persuade the owners to sell–'

George was not listening: he was staring at a man walking out of the sea and making for Bert; he was naked too. They greeted each other and then began chatting.

'So, George, that's the way I'm thinking at this moment in time.' Sonny exhaled and watched the cigarette smoke rise in the still air; he appeared sorry to see it go. 'It's one hell of a view, isn't it, George? – and so *peaceful*.'

'It's ... extraordinary,' George mumbled enigmatically. He moved back to the sliding doors. 'I'm off to breakfast now – and to see if I can do anything about our accommodation.'

'Yeah,' replied Sonny, still staring out to sea. The bay was hypnotic: everything about it was perfection. There was a kind of symmetry, a sublime proportionality – was that what he meant? – which made him feel real funny inside. He groped for the right words. ... It was spiritual – like he was close to God.

*Yeah, that's it ... the Garden of Eden! Adam and Eve were naked and everything, weren't they? God made them like that. And they weren't ashamed or embarrassed. It was as natural as ... as nature?*

A snake and an apple came into it somehow, but that wasn't relevant now – unless Weetwood was the snake and ... What could the apple be? ... Alcohol? ... Cigarettes? Sonny shot a fearful glance at the Marlboros. *Christ! How could something so good be so bad for you? ... That apple in the Garden of Eden was like that though, wasn't it?* He stubbed out his cigarette and pushed the pack over to the other side of the table.

The two men at the water's edge finished their conversation and Bert returned to his sun-lounger duties. The other one dried himself with a rainbow-coloured towel, slipped on a pair of shorts and a T-shirt, which he'd left on one of the loungers, and started to walk slowly up the beach towards the hotel. Locked in thought about the Garden of Eden and the possibility of getting the Cala Beltran upgraded to Leading Hotel of the World class, Sonny watched him approach. As he reached the dunes, he recognized Paolo and jumped up, slamming the back of his chair against one of the sliding doors.

'Shit! If that bastard gets to him first, I'm–!' He rushed in to shower and change: unlike Weetwood, he had standards of cleanliness which could never be compromised.

The Hotel Cala Beltran's inmates generally divide into two distinct groups: a select band of loyal aficionados who idolize both it and its owners and return unhesitatingly year after year; and the larger group comprising the bulk of the first-time-never-to-return package tourists, who feel cheated by the establishment's isolation. The former, who are almost exclusively British naturists aged over forty, despise the latter – a hotchpotch of nationalities whose chief occupation is moping. Then there is the Italian sub-group, but, being Italians, they're determined to enjoy themselves.

Perhaps to minimize feelings of undue favouritism between the hotel's polarized communities, the management operate a highly visible regime of rules and regulations. Notices are everywhere: inexplicably, the swimming pool is not to be used before eleven a.m.; no item of food or drink may be removed from the restaurant at any time; and corridor windows must never be opened – save in the event of 'an emergency', albeit what exactly might constitute an emergency is not particularized.

Mike Crabtree, a London traffic warden, had been a loyal supporter of the Cala Beltran for over twenty years. He knew *all* the rules and had never questioned any of them. Indeed, after so many seasons he'd even come to terms with the complex code which governed the dining room's efficient operation. And, being a matey sort of bloke, he now wanted to share his knowledge with the 'new boy' whom he'd just seen enter the dining room, and, to his horror, sit down at Table 15. From his clothes, Mike could tell that the 'new boy' was British and 'top drawer'. He so informed his fellow clan members, Harriet and her sister, Jennifer, who sat opposite him devouring mountainous portions of bacon and eggs as if they'd not eaten for days. The sisters, together with Mike and Bert, spent the same fortnight together at the Cala Beltran each September. Despite making significant sacrifices to afford this annual pilgrimage, they all pretended to be rather grand.

'That new boy doesn't know the ropes,' Mike said.

'What "new boy"?' asked Harriet in a voice reminiscent of the late Queen Mother.

'The one at Table 15.'

They all stared at George.

Jennifer gasped and grabbed her sister's arm.

'What on earth are you doing?' roared Harriet. 'You almost knocked over my coffee.'

'It's him! – that chap on the telly!'

Harriet looked despairingly at Mike. 'I can't imagine what she means, Mike. We so rarely have a chance to watch the television, you know. And then when we do, it's always the News or the ballet. We never miss a ballet. I met Dame Margot once at Glyndebourne,' she lied.

'Oh, Harriet,' said Jennifer, 'he plays that English chap in that American series on Sky One – you know! – What's-his-name! – Thingy!'

Harriet didn't have a clue what her sister was talking about, although the geezer at Table 15 did look familiar. And he was so eccentrically dressed he had to be really posh. She and Jennifer had better steer a wide berth: he obviously couldn't play their game.

'I'd better put him straight,' said Mike pushing his chair back noisily, but an officious and emaciated waiter beat him to it.

'Ah, at last!' declaimed George.

'You are not sitting here!' the waiter informed him.

George took no notice as he continued to search the dining room for Start's 'little foreign friend'. 'I'll have orange juice, bacon, fried eggs on white buttered toast, a few sausages, fried tomato–'

'Get over there!' the waiter ordered, pointing to the other side of the room and tugging at George's arm. 'This table is now reserved for Garibaldi peoples. You no Italian mens.'

'Now look here, my man–'

'Can't sit here, old chap,' interceded Mike, putting on his best pseudo-Oxbridge voice. The waiter flashed him a grin of recognition.

George looked Mike up and down and quickly came to the correct conclusion. 'Well, I *am* sitting here, unless I'm mistaken.'

Mike giggled girlishly. 'No, no, no! I mean it's against the rules, ol' man. I'm Mike by the way,' he added, proffering his hand. 'Unless you're with one of the tour operators, you have to sit over *there* ... with the Independents. There'd be chaos otherwise.'

Ignoring both Mike and his hand, George repeated his order to the waiter; he'd raised his voice; people were beginning to stare. Mike started an earnest monologue about 'us British' setting an example and the merits of a self-service breakfast: poor Manolo had enough to do without serving guests at their tables, of all things. George's heart began to race. It was all too much: the sight and smells of sloppily-attired holidaymakers passing his table with plates laden with fried food; the tugs of 'Manolo'; the idiotic ramblings of the Englishman; the two staring women – Harriet and Jennifer; the stifling heat – the windows of the airless room were also permanently sealed by proprietorial order.

The ticking time bomb finally exploded. Eyes blazing, George subjected 'Manolo' to a terrifying stare. 'Now listen to me, you silly little man' – his booming voice silenced the entire room – 'I am the Right Honourable, the Baron Weetwood of Dribbledale' – Jennifer gasped – 'and I am *not* moving from this table. You will serve me with such food as I may care to order, and I demand to speak with your employer – this *instant*! Do you understand? And for God's sake, man, open some bloody windows!'

Without waiting for a reply, George turned to Crabtree. 'I don't know who you are, nor do I wish to know. I simply suggest you mind your own bloody business and bugger off.'

It was at this point that a freshly-showered Paolo Amerigo strolled elegantly into the dining room amid a fragrant cloud of Armani cologne. All eyes turned towards him. It was a most dramatic entrance, and Paolo briefly savoured the moment, wishing the assembled guests a very good morning in half a dozen languages. No one, however, responded.

Smiling broadly, Paolo made straight for George. 'Well, good morning! I hope you and Steve slept well'. There was another audible gasp from Jennifer. 'I'm honoured – is that how you say it? – that you should sit at my table. Is Manolo being a little pest? You are having a problem, yes?'

George's cheeks were burning. The room was still very quiet, albeit a baby had started to cry, and some guests were already whispering stories recently gleaned from the gutter press and gossip magazines about the belligerent Briton.

'I told him,' Manolo whimpered in Spanish to Paolo, 'that this table is only for Garibaldi mens. I tried–' But Paolo stopped him and explained that it was all right: the Englishman was a friend.

'He still want boss?'

Paolo looked enquiringly at George, who slowly shook his head: he had more important things to discuss with the Italian than with the manager.

After Paolo had gleaned what his guest would like for breakfast, he said: 'I'll see what I can do,' and glided away. Within minutes, he was back with a plate of hot food in one hand and a plate of toast in the other. He set them down in front of George.

'There! A real English breakfast, I think. Tea or coffee?'

George looked contrite. 'Look, um ... I'm awfully sorry. I never expected you, er ...'

'I'm Paolo! No problem! Tea or coffee? Oh, I still don't know *your* name!'

Hesitating, George looked sheepishly from side to side. 'Um, it's ... George, actually,' he whispered.

When Paolo returned with two cups of coffee, he sat down and lit a cigarette; in all the circumstances, George felt unable to object to the latter. Between mouthfuls of food, he lost no time in explaining to Paolo that he and 'Mr "Sonny" Start' were merely 'on business' and had never even met before last night; that their hosts had booked them into the hotel, and that someone had made the most dreadful mistake of putting them in the same room. And, with the place being fully booked, nothing could be done about it.

Almost as an afterthought, he added: 'I'm a happily married man, you know – with two grown-up children.' Immediately, he realized the assertion sounded absurdly defensive.

A bemused smile had remained on Paolo's face throughout George's discourse. He was not sure whether to believe the Englishman; anyway, he'd met plenty of 'happily married' men in Turin.

Paolo drained his coffee cup and lit another cigarette. 'So, George,' he said finally, 'what you saw last night – Steve ... "Sonny"' – he shrugged his shoulders – 'and me, must have been shocking for you. I am sorry.'

George waved a hand dismissively. 'I'm a man of the world ... er ... Paolo.'

'Of course.'

'Live and let live is my philosophy.'

But George felt it his solemn duty to reveal a few facts about 'Mr Start': he was a ruthless, money-mad, heartless tycoon, a barbarian hell-bent on destroying one of Britain's finest companies – suppliers of soap to the Royal Family for several generations, no less. Indeed, he was a hypocrite of the worst kind – one who preached the virtues of family life to the American nation from the heart of Texas, but who ... well, Paolo knew only too well what Start got up to when the cat was away, so to speak.

George stopped beating about the bush: he needed Paolo's help; he outlined the sort of sworn statement he was hoping for. Paolo, still smiling, volunteered that it would surely be better if he were to give his testimony before a lawyer – and on video. And maybe they should procure statements from the waiter and some of the guests who'd seen Mr Start and himself socializing on the terrace.

George's face lit up. 'Excellent idea, er ... Paolo! Brilliant! I would never have thought of that. Not too good with this modern technology, you know.' He leaned across the table into the zone of scented air engulfing the Italian; it was a gesture carefully monitored by Jennifer, who nudged her sister and pointed. 'I wouldn't expect you to do this for nothing ... Paolo,' he whispered. 'I think ... a thousand pounds would be a fair fee for your trouble. I could get my lawyers to fax a draft statement today – this morning.'

Paolo stubbed out his cigarette. 'Lord Weetwood, do you know the Italian magazine *Oggi*?' George looked blank. 'No? Well, it's a silly thing full of gossips and pictures. My friend Nicola – I share a room with her here – has the *Oggi* of this week, yes? This morning I wake up thinking this man in Steve's room I see last night, where I see him before? And as we talk now it comes to me that I read all the news of your wife and strange things in a French villa. But, as you say before, we must live and let the others live. My Lord, I am not caring about the war between you and Steve – Mr Start as you call him. I don't know about these things. But I'm queer, as you English say, and if Mr Start is also like me, then to use this against him and make him look bad is to make me look bad too. Yes? I don't think I'm bad. And if Steve is a bad man, it's not because he's queer like me. OK? You understand? Now I go. Have a nice day!'

Paolo stood up regally, turned and began to walk serenely towards the exit.

'Ten thousand pounds!' yelled George – again the room was silenced – but the Italian just shouted 'Ciao!' without looking round, and disappeared through the doorway.

In his haste to follow, George didn't see Mike Crabtree in time. He was continuing 'to set an example' through the performance of his ritual of clearing his own dirty dishes; it was a habit ingrained in him after a lifetime of eating in self-service establishments. Frantically pushing back his chair, George knocked Mike violently sideways. Crockery and cutlery flew in all directions; Mike's vain attempt to catch some of the debris landed him in the lap of a buxom Hamburg *hausfrau*. The German's chair, already groaning under her weight, collapsed with a terrific crack.

George was barely aware of the chaos he'd caused. 'Must dash!' was all he could manage. Staring straight ahead, he strode quickly away.

'Well, what do you make of *that*?' asked Jennifer with a mixture of excitement and glee; in truth, she was rather pleased to see Mike discomforted.

Harriet stared at the spot where Mike and the German were endeavouring to disentangle themselves. 'Pathetic,' she muttered, '– utterly pathetic.' Turning to her sister, she said: 'Looks to me as though the Iti nancy boy is blackmailing that Weetwood geezer.'

Jennifer adopted a shocked expression. 'Oh, Harriet! I'm sure there's an innocent expla–'

'Oh, get real, dimwit! And from all the filth we've read about that dreadful family during the last week, I'm not in the least surprised. There's never smoke without fire, Jennifer.'

Harriet cast a glance over the faded items of holiday wear she'd squeezed into that morning; like most of her clothes, she'd had to make do with them for more years than she cared to remember. 'Come on, Jennifer, we've got work to do. No time to lose.'

'What do you mean, dear?'

'I mean here's our opportunity to make a small fortune. Come on! Get yer skates on! We need to phone *The Sun* – ***immediately***.'

Dripping in egg yolk and coffee, Mike plodded towards them with a big grin on his face. 'I always wanted to be in a Marx Brothers film,' he giggled, but even before he'd finished his little joke, Harriet had pushed him aside, dragging Jennifer with her.

His surprise only lasted a few seconds. 'See you on the beach!' he shouted at their receding backs, as it occurred to him that these women were about to switch allegiance to Lord Weetwood. 'They'll be lucky!' he growled under his breath. 'A ponce like him wouldn't give them posers the time of day.'

George met Sonny on the stairs; he was admiring the view from one of the windows he'd opened the previous evening.

'Jesus Christ, George,' Sonny said smiling, as he turned to identify the source of the chronic wheezing, 'what the hell have you been up to?' He assumed, however, that a frenetic search for Paolo was the cause.

George leaned against the wall at the side of the open window and breathed deeply; an explanation was slow in coming. 'Took a brisk walk – round the bay – after breakfast,' he lied.

'Yeah? Too much exercise after food can be dangerous, particularly for a guy like you, George – out of shape and middle-aged an' all. You should rest up a bit. See you later. I'm off for some chow myself now.'

George was on the point of warning him about the dining room's seating regulations but then changed his mind. He watched Start descend with exasperation: he'd caught the bounder *in flagranti delicto* – the most extraordinary piece of ammunition he could have hoped for, manna from Heaven. But that wretched little Italian catamite was refusing to co-operate. Honour among thieves! And after what had seemed like a complete breakdown last night, Start was now acting as if he'd found the Holy Grail. All that nonsense about buying the hotel – how absurd! – how typically American!

Back in Room 327, George decided to phone Turbot in England. The solicitor answered almost immediately: he'd been up for some time, preparing himself for a string of meetings lined up at Bobbins throughout the weekend.

'*Do you want the good news or the bad news first, Lord Weetwood?*' he asked jovially: he was beginning to enjoy both the change from Intellectual Property and the feeling of power engendered by his contacts with the megalomaniac head-honchos of 'world-class' conglomerates.

George bristled. 'I suggest you report first on the positive developments.'

Turbot got the message. The three serious contenders for WSD, he advised, were anxious to do deals. An outsider, the German group Schnittblumen & Käseglocke, had contacted him late last night, and representatives were flying over to meet him that afternoon. He'd also had lengthy off-the-record discussions with people at the Office of Passenger Rail Franchising – OPRAF.

'*To put it bluntly, Lord Weetwood, they're very keen to get your fortune invested in the railways – very keen indeed.*'

George wiped the perspiration off his forehead and undid another shirt button; he'd get the hotel people to fix the air conditioning as soon as he came off the phone. And, of course, he'd try and get Start moved to another room. It surely couldn't matter one jot to the kidnappers.

'So, Turbot, what on earth can there be by way of "bad news", as you called it?'

'*Ah, yes. Well, for a start there's competition law. In view of its size and Goblin's market share, any acquisition of WSD would be investigated by the UK competition authorities – and the chaps at the EU Commission in Brussels. Naturally, none of the prospective purchasers will complete a deal without green lights from all of the relevant bodies. That could take weeks – even months. Of course, conditional agreements are possible, but ...*'

There were a lot of 'buts'.

'*However, Lord Weetwood, that's what makes the German approach very interesting. They're hardly in the soap business, and being a one-hundred-per-cent European outfit, Brussels' knights in shining armour might be only too happy to support a merger with them.*'

310

Then there was the FoamFay litigation. Although the prospective purchasers said that SI's claims sounded crazy, and swore that the lawsuit didn't constitute an insuperable problem, their lawyers were less sanguine.

'*If you read between the lines, Lord Weetwood, these chaps at Unilever, Procter & Gamble, et cetera, want the litigation settled pronto, with WSD having the right to exploit FoamFay in its major markets. Otherwise, they'll retain a major chunk of the purchase price – unless and until they themselves sort it out after completion.*'

'Outrageous! How much are we talking about?'

'*The worst-case scenario is a total write-off of the investment.*'

'But that's hundreds of millions!'

'*I know. It's a pity we didn't approach Start about a settlement before you went public on this disposal.*'

'Look, Turbot,' George snapped coldly, 'I'm working on the Start problem ... as we speak, in fact.'

'*Ah, I suspected your trip might–*'

'I think I'm in with a good chance of getting him out of the picture. There are i's to dot et cetera, et cetera, but you can tell those bloodsuckers that you expect some good news on the FoamFay front imminently.'

'*I'll keep my fingers crossed.*'

'Is that it then, Turbot?'

'*Um ... I find this rather difficult to report, Lord Weetwood, but ... well, the franchising folk in Whitehall have indicated to me – off the record, of course – that the sensational media reports concerning Lady Weetwood are giving them some cause for concern. They say that franchisees have to be solid undertakings with proven track records in the transport sector ... not necessarily rail you understand, but–*'

George exploded. 'It's not Lady Weetwood who's bidding, Turbot!'

'*No, no – of course not. But these guys fear that the public, or at least a sizeable chunk of them, believe that you – it's nonsense and absurd, I know – but they believe that you had to have some knowledge of what she'd ... well, been up to for all these years and that–*'

'This is outrageous!'

'*Of course.*'

'Defamatory!'

'*Well–*'

'Why should anyone believe that I knew anything about Beryl's–?'

Turbot pulled the phone away from his ear while his lordship let off steam. Eventually, the line went quiet.

'*You have every right to be outraged, Lord Weetwood, but the point is that, for the moment, the public's mind has been poisoned against you.*

*And some of the Department of Transport's officials are saying that rail franchises are ... well, to quote one chap I spoke with, "an eccentric billionaire's flavour of the month".'*

Turbot paused in anticipation of another explosion, but, to his surprise, there was silence. *'In fact, until the scandal dies down, the Government will only accept you as a minority shareholder in any franchise – preferably through nominees – with no seat on the board. You see, they suspect your decision to abandon a lifetime's work in the soap business at the very moment when Lady Weetwood–'*

'So,' George barked, 'the world and his aunt believe I'm as debauched as my wife appears to be, and that I'm as mad as a March hare.'

After a pause, Turbot said: *'Oh by the way, Lord Weetwood, your sister's left us. And I suspect you'll be surprised to learn – at least from what I've overheard here – that your former chauffeur ... Mr Duffle? ... drove Mrs Thornton to the airport early this morning.'*

George was barely listening: an intense feeling of self-pity was beginning to overwhelm him. 'Oh really,' he replied disinterestedly. 'Gone back to Eastbourne, I suppose?'

*'Oh no! She's flown out to be with your daughter – in the Balearics somewhere, isn't she? And before I forget, SI have launched further proceedings against us in Kenya and Sri Lanka – presumably to try to shut down your FoamFay factories there. I'm instructing lawyers in Nairobi and Colombo to act for us and serve the necessary Defences in due course.*

*'And that boffin of yours in Argentina – sorry, Uruguay ... Dumpwell? ... well, I had Merryweather on the phone last night. Apparently, the chap's done a bunk – cleared out his flat and left the country. God knows why, but the evening papers here were full of stories about him being abducted by guerrillas! – in "the jungle"! – and–'*

The mobile fell from George's hand onto the bed. What was happening? Had the world gone mad? Bizarre disappearances, bombings, kidnappings! ... Coincidences? ... Did he truly believe that? Caroline and the Start brat – of all people! – being 'penfriends'? The brat's visit to Bobbins, then her arrival in Formentera just a week before the kidnapping? It was all too convenient, too–

Suddenly, George saw himself as a mere pawn in a vast game of chess in which Start was moving all the pieces. The man was dangerous – probably psychotic – certainly a pervert. He'd stop at nothing! The room seemed to be spinning. Start could return at any moment – with henchmen! He had to get away before–

There was a knock at the door.

312

'Oh God,' he moaned, 'too damned late!' Immobilized by terror, he watched the handle descend and the door open. A smiling uniformed lady with a trolley stood at attention. In a voice that suggested she'd just won the National Lottery, she blasted him with what was obviously a request to clean the room.

'Carry on, dear lady!' he cried, sweeping out into the corridor. 'Carry on!'

George did not slacken his pace until he reached reception. It was while he was catching his breath that he saw Paolo exiting through the lobby doors. He dashed after him.

Paolo was standing beside a motor scooter, putting on a crash helmet when George caught up with him. 'Enough of these silly games, my good fellow!' he cried, grabbing a tanned arm. 'I'll pay you *thirty ... thousand ... pounds* – probably more than you earn in a year.'

There were some Italian couples standing around their parked motor scooters, preening themselves in anticipation of another day's motorized fashion show along the island's highways. They started to laugh.

'Bloody hell, Paolo!' one man cried in Italian. 'What have you got between your legs that's worth that amount of money?' Then he explained to the others what the Englishman had said, and hysteria broke out.

Paolo grinned good-naturedly. 'He's not my type,' he shouted, and then, turning to George, said: 'I do not want your money. I tell you this in dining room. OK?'

'Stop teasing him, Paolo!' yelled another of his countrymen. 'Can't you see he's desperate!' The others joined in voluminously.

'For that amount of money, the Englishman can have my butt any time!'

'How much would he pay for a threesome?'

Paolo knew they didn't mean any harm – he'd spent most of his evenings with them and had enjoyed their company – but he was concerned that if Lord Weetwood understood Italian, he could be mortally offended; he certainly looked very peculiar.

As Paolo mounted his scooter and the engine spluttered into life, George yelled: '*Forty thousand*! – and that's my *final* offer. *Forty thousand*, for God's sake!'

'Take the money, Paolo!' the Italians roared.

More engines started up; the din was deafening. George tried to grab Paolo as he moved off, but, grasping thin air, he stumbled and fell to the ground. '*Fifty ... thousand ... pounds*!' he screamed as Paolo accelerated away.

Sonny, having abandoned the horrors of the dining room, looked on with mixed emotions from the hotel's entrance as George lay prostrate, sobbing. Harriet, squeezed inside the Cala Beltran call box with Jennifer, was describing the scene to someone at *The Sun*.

# CHAPTER 27

The three prisoners were dumbfounded when Ursula pushed James into the cellar. He finally proved very co-operative when she put a pistol to Misty's head. Ursula believed his story about coming to the island in search of the love of his life and the set of coincidences that had led him to *Casa Bayreuth*; it was like something out of a cheap novelette. However, with four prisoners, she now felt uncomfortable in such a confined space. With just two pairs of handcuffs and ankle shackles, sharing was necessary. She considered handcuffing and shackling the same sexes together, but concluded that Rory and James might prove a dangerously strong combination. Chained to their respective sweethearts, however, it was unlikely that either of them would feel particularly gung-ho. In any event, the cellar's rustic sanitary facilities were already overloaded; it would rapidly become a cess pit. Perhaps she'd exaggerated the weaknesses of the first-floor bedrooms as cells, despite their having mortise locks – like all the villa's rooms, a feature Rory had found particularly peculiar, she recalled. They had en suite bathrooms, albeit each mixed-sex couple would find relieving themselves a challenge – and embarrassing! And even if they managed to open a window, shouting for help would be pointless: no one would ever hear them.

So, after herding the chained couples upstairs – an arduous process accompanied by protests and barked orders – Ursula incarcerated Caroline and Rory in one bedroom, with Misty and James in the other. After double-checking that the doors were locked, she descended to the living room triumphantly, whistling Beethoven's Ode to Joy. Demanding a further ransom for James exercised her mind for the next few hours. Reluctantly, she decided against it: with the banks closed for the weekend across Europe, it was unlikely that Weetwood could procure significant extra funds before Monday. She needed to terminate matters rapidly.

Now, in mid-afternoon, having checked on the prisoners – they'd yet to use the 'facilities' – Ursula sat on a chair in front of the doors to the adjoining bedrooms and wondered what on earth she was going to do for something to eat and read: she'd destroyed every book, magazine and morsel of food on the bonfire. And come to think of it, was there any bottled water left? – the salty muck from the tap was only fit for cooking and washing. Perhaps she'd been too thorough in her efforts to destroy incriminating evidence. Then she remembered seeing a packet of potato chips in the VW and a bottle of water under the front passenger seat.

Caroline and Rory were sitting on the floor, with their backs resting against a bare double bed.

'That sounds like her going downstairs,' Caroline whispered. 'Perhaps she's fetching us some food.'

Rory sighed. 'I can't believe you're thinking of food at a time like this.'

'Well, I'm hungry.' Caroline shook her head. 'I still can't believe it – James! – here in Formentera! – and in search of Misty! It's very romantic, isn't it?'

'Very.'

'I do hope he's all right. From what I could see, he had some nasty bruises and cuts. And that awful bang on the head–'

'Oh, he'll be OK.'

Rory squeezed Caroline's arm with his free hand and focused on her breasts. Out of the blue, he experienced a flashback to that bizarre moment months ago at Bobbins, when, secreted in a rhododendron bush, he'd seen her topless at her bedroom window. How overweight she'd been then! 'Fat' was the only word for it. In fact, she'd borne a remarkable resemblance to Miss Piggy. Would he be feeling randy if she was still a blobby bookworm?

'Rory, what are you thinking about? You look terribly serious.'

'Oh nothing.' He shifted uncomfortably: having a wrist and ankle chained to Caroline, was proving extremely trying.

'Are you worrying again about whether she'll let us *all* go? You said the plan was to release Misty and me if–'

'Of course you'll be released. Ursula doesn't want to be at the centre of a murder investigation.'

'And if that reasoning is correct, then she wouldn't want to do ... um ... anything to you either, would she?'

Avoiding her gaze, Rory stared at his feet. 'No, I suppose not. Anyway, if she was going to get rid of me, I think she'd have done it by now.'

Caroline laid her free hand on his, saying plaintively, 'Oh, Rory, I wish you wouldn't be so morbid.'

He looked up. There were tears in his eyes. 'I love you, Caroline – I love you *very* much. You *do* love me, don't you?'

Although it wasn't the first time he'd used these words during the last few hours, the emotion in his voice took her by surprise. She hesitated. *Do I truly love him? ... Do I? ... What is 'love' anyway?*

Rory gripped Caroline's hand. 'Even if you don't feel the same way about me now, you do feel *something*, don't you? Can't you at least say there's a chance you may love me one day?'

Caroline sighed, bowed her head, and tried again to formulate an answer. Yes, there was a degree of physical attraction ... but 'love' after just a few days? She'd heard about people falling in love 'at first sight', but it had always sounded like a contradiction in terms. Surely, anyone whose emotions could be so excited by a mere glance had to be utterly superficial – or even plain stupid. One might see a painting for the first time and immediately find it beautiful. One might say that one 'loved' it. Was that the sort of 'love' Rory felt for her? Not that she could possibly conceive of herself as 'beautiful', but if this was how he felt, it couldn't amount to 'love', could it? At best, it was an infatuation with something transient – like her appearance.

No, the more she thought about it, the more convinced she became that if she were ever to love anyone, it would be an emotional state that could only blossom after a lengthy period of careful cultivation. Did this mean that all Rory's professions of 'love' were the empty words of someone who was utterly superficial? And was her family's fortune truly of no concern to him? But if she were wrong, then her own doubts about his feelings would be shameful. Indeed, the very consideration of all these possibilities made her feel cold, calculating and unworthy of any man's love. Fleetingly, she scanned Rory's tanned legs; she didn't need to rationalize her spontaneous emotions. Her gaze returned to his face: it reminded her of a golden Labrador puppy. Then to her shame she thought once more of what might be bubbling away beneath the surface.

'Your silence,' Rory murmured sadly, 'speaks volumes.'

Caroline sighed. 'Rory, you can't expect me to trust my instincts in the middle of all *this*, for goodness' sake. You *did* abduct me – and Misty – with the intention of trading us for a load of dosh.'

'You'll never be able to forgive me for that, will you? I can understand. I don't blame you. But can't you give me another chance? I swear on the lives of everyone dear to me that I've never felt this way about anyone else. I just know – don't ask me how – that you and me are destined to spend the rest of our lives together. What can I do to make you believe me? I'd swear on the Bible. I'll ... I'll *marry* you – as soon as this is all over – whatever you want.'

Caroline had been brought up in a world devoid of sentimentality. What she was now hearing conjured up images of television soap opera, albeit her knowledge of such things was minimal. In truth, Rory's protestations of love were beginning to irritate her. Nervous exhaustion, lack of food, and physical discomfort were not helping matters. She finally snapped when he began to talk of having children together.

'For God's sake, Rory, shut up and listen to me!' There was silence for a few moments as he came to grips with the anger which manifested itself both in Caroline's eyes and her voice. She, for her part, tried to make some sense of the jumble of emotions which gripped her.

'I ... I don't really know where to start, Rory, but I *do* know one thing for certain, and that is – I can't tell a lie.'

'I don't want you to–'

'*Please*. Don't interrupt. I'm not any good at this sort of thing. ... Rory, I'm not sure what "love" is, but it must be something very special, something more than just liking or being fond of someone. And obviously it's not the same thing as being attracted to someone. Now, I like you – in fact you're the first bloke I've ever got close to. I *am* prepared to forgive you for getting me into this horrid mess, and, if and when we get out of it, I hope we'll see each other and get to know each other a lot better ... in a *normal* environment. But I can't say I love you – I can't. It's possible I might *grow* to love you ... I don't know. And I ... I ... well, I do think you're quite good looking.'

'Well, I think you're beautiful, Caroline, and the kindest, sweetest–'

'Oh stop it! I'm *not* beautiful! Or kind! Or sweet! How can I believe anything you say when you use such absurd words?'

'They're not absurd!

Rory pulled Caroline towards him, buried his head between her breasts, and started to sob. Her shock and frigidity slowly gave way to tender, maternal instincts. She began to stroke his arm.

'Don't cry,' she murmured. After a few minutes, he mumbled something. 'What did you say?' she asked softly.

'I don't want to die,' he whispered.

'Nobody's going to die, Rory.'

'I wish I could stay in your arms for ever, Caroline. I feel so safe.'

She took a deep breath as he began to suck on a nipple through the cotton of her T-shirt. There were alarm bells ringing and words of protestation forming, but the novel sensation of intense pleasure flowing through every vein of her body rendered speech impossible. She made a half-hearted attempt to push his head away.

With the sucking growing stronger, Caroline thought she heard Misty's voice in the adjoining room. 'Rory, don't,' she pleaded, '– please don't.' Yet even to her own ears, her voice lacked conviction. The nibble became a bite, and as the pain began to electrify her, all resistance ceased. Her head fell back and she began to groan.

Rory felt her body relax and heard her breathing quicken. Instinctively, he attempted to get into position, but as he moved, the handcuffs and shackles went tight. 'Oh Jesus Christ!' he hissed. He couldn't stop now: Caroline had to taste the fruit that had been forbidden to her – or which she'd forbidden herself – for so long.

Managing to push up her T-shirt, he let his tongue slide down her abdomen. The sensation of his unshaven face brushing against her skin detonated an explosion of desire. Within seconds, their free hands were clumsily pulling down shorts and underwear. When he entered her, she left this world and was transported to the zenith of pleasure.

Such a momentous journey in Caroline's life, and yet it took only a few minutes.

*

Although James and Misty were similarly handcuffed and shackled together in the adjoining room, they were sat on the floor with their backs to a wall; a bare double bed stood on the other side of the room. The passionate embrace which each had longed for when they were finally alone had failed to materialize. It was Misty's observation of the briefest moment of hesitation on James's part which had triggered a chain reaction. The thought flashed in her mind that if James was truly in love with her, he would have smothered her in kisses as soon as Ursula was out the door. Yet it was James's detection of her own hesitation which instantly set alarm bells ringing inside his head. The result was a clumsy embrace and kissing of cheeks; an embarrassing silence followed. Each desperately tried to think of something witty to say in order to break the ice, but to no avail.

In truth, James's hesitation was no more than a symptom of how foolish and humiliated he'd felt from the moment Ursula had regained control of events in the garden. Finding Misty and Caroline had been the most amazing stroke of luck, and he'd been given a fantastic chance to rescue them: just one middle-aged woman to deal with! Had he used his brain, he could easily have surprised and overpowered her. His stupidity disgusted him. And he believed that Misty's aloofness towards him indicated that he disgusted her too. He also wondered whether she and Caroline had learned of the awful newspaper reports about himself and the rest of the family. Was Misty labouring under the impression that she was manacled to a mentally disturbed homosexual?

Alas, James had yet to discover that Misty had never believed for one moment what she'd read about him in *The Sun*: it had all been risible as far as she was concerned. And she'd concluded that the failure of his 'rescue' was just bad luck. After almost two hours of debriefing each other on their long, separate summers, she was actually in a deep depression. She hated herself. Why did things never work out as one had imagined them? Why had she hesitated for that briefest of moments after Ursula had finally left them alone? If *she'd* truly loved James, she'd have smothered *him* in kisses – well, at least those parts accessible in their present state of bondage.

So, the inescapable conclusion had to be that neither of them loved the other – just dreams, wishful thinking, and temporary infatuations.

Sinking ever deeper into despondency, Misty tried hard to concentrate on what James was saying.

'... and I think that Ursula bitch is still going to ask for the money to be delivered somewhere around the lighthouse up at El Pilar, or exchange you – *us*, I hope – for the money there. The guy who has the bar at the lighthouse said she and that Rory geek – Christ! I still can't believe what you said about him and Caroline. I mean, Caroline? – and a *guy*? – one of the bloody kidnappers! I know I've said it a hundred times, but she must be unbalanced.

'Anyway, the hippy who has the bar said that Ursula and this Rory spent *hours* up there – which fits in with what he told you about their plans.'

'You've got a great body,' Misty murmured. 'It's been transformed since I last saw it.'

James looked at her with sadness in his eyes. She wasn't even listening to him anymore, and the tone of her voice indicated total indifference. Perhaps she was nothing but a sex machine after all – an American bimbo in an intellectual's clothes. He couldn't avoid a sarcastic chuckle to himself.

'Care to share the joke?' she asked acidly.

'It's nothing – nothing at all.'

After an unpleasant silence, Misty finally said: 'She'll have to do something different, now that she's on her own. According to Rory, your dad was to take the money late at night up to La Mola – he'd be led there in stages via various pay phones around the island. Rory was to lie in wait for him at each one to make sure he was on his own and keep Ursula posted – she'd have the mobile. Anyway, from El Pilar down to the lighthouse it's a straight road–'

'I know.'

'– and Ursula would be able to see your dad coming from her vantage point behind some wall. Meanwhile, Rory was to keep watch down at Es Calo for any suspicious vehicles going up the hill to El Pilar, and to wait for your dad to return, once he'd made the drop. As soon as Ursula saw the coast was clear, she'd collect the money, and then, provided Rory confirmed everything was OK at the Es Calo end, drive down to meet him. A dinghy would pick them up from the beach and take them to a yacht lying offshore. Apparently, she'd hired one on a "cash-no-questions-asked" basis in Marbella. Rory said the whole Costa del Sol is just one huge money-laundering operation – mostly from narcotics coming in from North Africa.'

319

'So I've heard. And where was this yacht going to take them?'

'Across the Atlantic to the Caymans, where the money would be deposited. After that, the world was to be their oyster.'

James looked thoughtful for a few moments. 'Frankly, it all sounds a bit hare-brained to me – full of holes – amateurish.'

Misty raised her eyebrows. 'How come?'

'For a start, if Dad *had* involved the police – and they'd surely have hatched their plans with that in mind – there'd be police launches or disguised fishing boats – whatever – circling the island in anticipation of an escape by sea. They'd easily intercept any boat moving around at that time of night.'

'Yes ... perhaps, but–'

'There are no buts about it. And then, hiring a yacht capable of sailing across the Atlantic! Come on! Where would they have got the money? And all those suspicious crew members! You're not telling me they're part of some larger organisation – not those two idiots?'

'Whoa! This isn't *my* plan, you know. You asked me what Rory had told us and–'

'Why are you getting so uptight?'

'Because you're sounding pretty aggressive, and from where I'm lying shackled and manacled, it sounds as though that aggression is directed at little old Misty, OK?'

'That's ridiculous!'

Misty sighed and looked away.

James groaned. 'I'm sorry. I – I ...' For a few seconds he picked at some pieces of gravel in a cut on his knee. 'So,' he finally inquired contritely, 'when were you and Caroline to be released – and how?'

'Once they were well out to sea – a phone call to your dad.'

James shook his head. 'Do you think dimwit Rory believed all this crap?'

'Sounded to me as though he did. After all, who in their right mind would go halfway round the world to pursue a vendetta against his former boss, have the hots for a Teutonic witch who'd have made an ideal concentration camp warden, and get himself embroiled in a so-called animal liberation front kidnapping?'

'And this is the muppet my sister's fallen for!'

'Oh, he's a reformed character now.'

'No doubt! I suppose that huge fire must mean Ursula's hoping to get her money very, very soon – tonight perhaps.'

But just as Misty was about to agree, a strange groaning caused the captives to stare at each other wide-eyed.

\*

320

Ursula had become rather horny, thanks to the erotic sounds generated by Caroline and Rory, and partial sight of their gyrations through the keyhole. She would never have imagined that being fettered and handcuffed so inconveniently would have had that effect on him: bondage hadn't done so at La Jenny. Perhaps she should have persevered; perhaps she'd underestimated him after all. No, the real problem with Rory was that he was too nice: he had too many scruples; he had limits – lots of them – beyond which he would not and could not go. It didn't matter whether the issue was alcohol, sex or violence, invisible bars always imprisoned him. And the end could never justify the means – never. So British! No wonder the Weetwood girl thought he was Mr Right, the sad cow. 'Enjoy it while you can!' she hissed.

Anyway, soon she'd be off the island – rich and enjoying life – well, provided Dumpwell performed his side of the bargain, that is.

Mark! Now, there was a man she *could* respect. Yes, he was British too, but so untypical – amoral and prepared to try anything. It was such a glorious paradox: the more Rory had vented his spleen about his former superior, the more she'd liked the sound of him. And as for his involvement in nasty research on cute little dogs, she couldn't have cared less. All those suckers she'd recruited to 'the cause' over the years! What a pathetic bunch of losers! On the other hand, the life-savings and other assets which they'd naïvely handed over to her for the alleged purpose of funding her 'organization' and its activities had enabled her to live very comfortably since her retirement. They were all so trusting, so childlike.

But the people with *real* money were surrounded by lawyers and accountants who would raise questions about any significant transfer of funds. In any event, she didn't move in the sort of circles frequented by the filthy rich. It was people like Rory – misfits – for whom she'd always had to be on the lookout. La Jenny was a Mecca for them; it had been her most fertile recruiting ground.

Ursula had long been contemplating blackmail and kidnapping, but identifying a target had been problematic: every candidate she investigated proved to be too well-protected, too high-profile – in effect, they were too obvious. So, when Rory first mentioned his hatred of the Weetwoods, she felt sure that they'd turn out to be as impregnable to her schemes as all the other plutocrats she'd considered. In the event, she discovered a perfect bunch of eccentrics.

However, although Ursula had been satisfied with Rory's assistance in the planning stages of the kidnapping, she'd begun to have grave doubts about his reliability when he first voiced concerns over the manner in which Caroline was to be incarcerated. His inherent softness shone through; if and when the going got tough, she knew he'd crumble.

Substituting Mark for Rory first crossed Ursula's mind at the Cob o' Coal: she'd often looked at the candid photographs Rory had taken of him with pretty youths at secluded beaches near Montevideo. And then there was all Rory's talk about the way Mark kept dropping his pilot's licence into conversations at Soap House. 'Desperate to impress!' was how he'd put it sarcastically, diagnosing a chronic inferiority complex. That was rich!

In mid-July, Ursula reluctantly concluded that she'd grossly underestimated the problems of getting herself and a million dollars in cash safely off Formentera and out of Spain to South America – and at that time they still only anticipated one victim and one ransom. Half-witted Rory, however, was content with her bogus boat-across-the-Atlantic-to-the-Caymans plan, but then he was utterly naïve, so naïve that he couldn't even spot its idiocy.

The real problem was Formentera itself: it was so small – too small. There was no way off it other than by boat – or swimming. Naturally, she had to plan for the worst-case scenario – that Weetwood would involve the authorities, and that the ports at La Savina and Ibiza, together with the coastal waters, would be swarming with police. So, even if she could have afforded an ocean-going yacht and had known the sort of people who organised such things, an escape by sea – whether to the Caymans or anywhere else – would have been fraught with unacceptable dangers.

The miracle occurred one scorching afternoon up at La Mola as they heatedly discussed for the umpteenth time their preferred option for the ransom's delivery and collection. As usual, Rory got sidetracked. There was always something: the age of the drystone walls, the tinkling of goat bells, the smell of herbs. On this occasion it was his much-rehearsed reflections on Jules Verne and his visions of the La Mola plateau as a gigantic take-off and landing zone for spacecraft – or some such nonsense.

Ursula was on the point of telling him to belt up when the vision came to her.

It hadn't been hard to convince Rory that she needed to wind up her affairs in Germany and then return via Marbella to finalise the arrangements with the yacht people for the Caymans voyage. She'd be away just a week; he saw her off at La Savina. Twenty-four hours later, she was talking to Mark on the phone from her Montevideo hotel room and arranging a meeting with him.

Ursula liked the way Mark laughed when he flicked through some of the reports which Rory had carefully typed of his spying activities, and the genuine pleasure he manifested while studying the more compromising photographs. His choice was clear: he could join up with her and possibly become a millionaire, or be blackmailed; copies of the salacious photographs would go to WSD – and any future employers she got to know of. Additionally, some of his 'conquests' were minors; the queer-hating Montevideo police were pretty hot about that sort of misdemeanour. As for the jolly snaps of his involvement in animal 'research', they'd be sent to every tabloid newspaper and crackpot animal rights organization he could care to think of. At best, the latter would hunt him down and make his life a misery for years; at worst, they'd put him on their death lists.

Mark said he was sick of Goblin anyway – sick of his stuck-in-a-rut, middle-management life. Ursula's proposal sounded rather exciting. And a skinny woman who looked like a pensioner with a free bus pass, should be a perfect candidate for ejection from a light aircraft – provided, of course, she didn't chain the loot to her wrist.

Organizing things in North Africa was so much easier than Ursula had ever imagined. Algeria was Mark's idea: when he looked at an atlas, the proximity of Algiers to Formentera was startling. Then he remembered Omar, the Air France steward who'd regularly flown on the Paris-Manchester service for several months and who'd declared his undying love after being picked up in a Manchester club. He was of Algerian extraction and in his last flowery letter had recounted how family tragedy had forced him home and into the miserable employ of Air Algeria.

How helpful Omar had been in making all the necessary arrangements in Algiers! He'd been well rewarded with reciprocal assurances of undying love and a new wardrobe of the best that Amani, Calvin Klein, Boss and Versace could offer. Indeed, Omar was currently anticipating a long and prosperous relationship with his English friend.

# CHAPTER 28

Sonny had come across the Restaurante Juan y Andrea at Platja de Ses Illetes by accident – well, almost. He was in the neighbourhood in search of Paolo, who'd told him at some stage during last night's proceedings that he spent his days at Platja de Llevant, a gay nudist beach near a bar called the Tanga on the island's long and narrow northern peninsula. Sonny, however, had missed a turning somewhere and had ended up on the wrong side – the west coast – albeit only a few hundred yards from his goal; according to his map, Llevant lay just beyond the high dunes to the east.

It was now coming up to one o'clock, and Sonny was hot and hungry. From a sandy car park almost engulfed by dunes, the rear of Juan y Andrea looked unassuming – just another beach bar. The entrance was through a gap in a high bamboo fence, but when he reached the other side his first reaction was that he'd walked onto a movie set – *South Pacific*? – *Lawrence of Arabia*? Could this really be Formentera, with its unsophisticated hotels and simple villages?

Beneath bleached tarpaulins supported by a semicircle of date palms, highly polished wooden tables stood in coral-white sand. Just a few feet from the edge of the restaurant lay the glassy waters of the sea, where half a dozen large yachts lay at anchor between three rocky islets. On the horizon, the jagged outline of distant Ibiza constituted the vision's dramatic backdrop. Most of the tables were taken, and around them sat a cosmopolitan selection of yachting folk exuding wealth and general well-being. It was a society which Sonny instantly recognized, and they, too, instantly recognized him as one of them.

He was shown to a table by one of the barefooted waiters, all of whom were clad in spotless, dazzling white trousers and T-shirts; they looked as beautiful as their clientele. A household name, who'd been big in Hollywood in the early Eighties, was sat at one of the larger tables. His eight male guests – all considerably younger, fitter and better-looking – were dressed exotically in a colourful array of bandannas and kangas, their theatricality being enlivened by a constant supply of chilled rosé served by an over-attentive waiter. But it was the vista that made it impossible for Sonny to concentrate for more than a few seconds on the menu; three times he had to send the waiter away orderless.

It was well past two o'clock when he finally finished his excellent grilled *dorada*; he'd foregone any wine. The former Hollywood star and his

324

camp followers, having become bored with Juan y Andrea, had started to make their way down to the water's edge and the restaurant's water taxi. Savouring the delights of a Marlboro with a *café solo*, Sonny watched them go, and thought of butterflies. Had any of them a clue where they were? Where would they go next? Did they care?

Glancing wide-eyed at his watch, Sonny swiftly paid the bill, returned to the car park and scanned the massive sand dunes that rose some way off; the peninsula's eastern shore, the Platja de Llevant, had to lie just beyond them. Then he noticed three figures, fifty or sixty metres apart, walking slowly along the ridge; unless he was mistaken, they were all male ... and naked. Suddenly, one of them dropped down into a thicket of stunted pines that covered much of the dunes' western slopes, and was lost to view. Another followed, while the third remained stationary on the ridge, staring in the direction of the thicket. Sonny smiled wryly: find any shore backed by dunes and woods and there'd be guys cruising each other. He just hoped Paolo wasn't one of them.

*Jesus! I'm already thinking of him as my property!*

Grabbing a towel and a pair of swimming shorts from his rented Suzuki, Sonny set off for the ridge. After five minutes, he entered the scrubby woodland of evergreens, twisted and bent by the fierce winter gales. He was not alone: naked figures moved slowly and silently along the maze of narrow sandy paths which criss-crossed the terrain. In one small clearing, two men were having sex. He quickened his pace.

By the time he reached the ridge, at least one man was following him – mid-thirties, as white as a sheet, and a stomach that proclaimed an addiction to beer and starchy foods. While the blob hovered a few metres away touching himself, Sonny self-consciously took his bearings. To leeward, in the direction of the Juan y Andrea, the sea was waveless, a perfect mooring place for the yachts lying at anchor. But turning to face the wind, the dunes fell steeply to a wide sandy beach with waves pounding the shore. Every twenty or thirty metres lay naked sun worshippers; others were cooling off in the sea, some frolicking like dolphins amidst the breakers. And at the edge of the beach, a few hundred metres away to the south, he noticed a bar; it had to be the Tanga.

The blob had moved closer. '*Sprechen Sie Deutsch?*' he asked.

Without a word or a second glance, Sonny made a quick descent to the beach.

Like several other sunbathers, Paolo lay on his stomach with his back to the sea, raising his eyes intermittently from a paperback – an Italian translation of *Breakfast at Tiffany's* – to monitor the activities along the ridge. It amused him to guess which of the men soaking up the sun around him would succumb to its magnetic pull, and who would cruise whom. He was invariably correct. A bronzed hunk, rapidly descending the dunes, caught his attention. Within seconds, the newcomer reached the beach and, barely slackening his pace, began striding towards him, looking from left to right at the naked bodies. Paolo smiled to himself when he realised that the guy was none other than 'Steve' – Sonny Start. Yet, it didn't occur to him that he, himself, might be the American's goal.

When Sonny was about twenty metres away, Paolo half-raised himself, waved, and smiled broadly. He expected Sonny to be engulfed by embarrassment: he'd probably ignore him and walk past or turn on his heels. But, to his amazement, Sonny stopped in his tracks and waved back, his face lighting up. He trotted over, almost breaking into a run. Both men spoke simultaneously.

'Hello,' said Paolo, 'what a big surprise to be seeing *you* here!'

'Hi, Paolo. I've been looking for you *every*where.'

They laughed and stared into each other's eyes.

Paolo's first thought was: *I bet – you and that Englishman! Now you'll be offering me money too.* But what he saw in Sonny's eyes stunned him. He'd seen that look before – not often, but enough to recognize it: unless he was completely crazy, the American was hooked. It was rare for Paolo to be nonplussed by anything, but now words momentarily failed him. Something, however, was telling him to be very careful: whatever was going on back at Cala Beltran between Sonny and the English lord was very strange, very strange indeed.

Sonny's mind was reeling. It had occurred to him more than once that, in the harsh reality of daylight, sober and sensible, Paolo's magic – his extraordinary magnetism – would dissipate: he'd be revealed as just another available pickup, a silly Italian queen with skin-deep looks and a pea brain, only good for a one-night stand, if anything. But here he was, face to face with the enigma in the full glare of a dazzling sun, and Paolo's voice and eyes were already melting the icy doubts and suspicions which had haunted him.

'So, who are you today, "Steve" or "Sonny" or–?'

'Look, I'm real sorry about that. It's just that ... I'm *Sonny*, OK? Try and forget all that Steve shit, will you? I have to be careful.'

'Because you're rich and famous?'

'Not famous – rich, yes. ... How much did the Brit tell you?' There was a hint of anxiety in Sonny's voice, but before Paulo could answer, he added, looking around: 'May I sit down? The whole beach seems to be watching us.'

Paolo gestured hospitably. 'Of course!' He sat up and got into something close to a lotus position.

Sonny, despite his embarrassment, couldn't avert his eyes. He had to admit that Paolo was not the type he usually went for – guys who obviously worked out, guys one could imagine on a football field or in marine combat fatigues. Paolo was more the emaciated model-type – tall and wiry with little body hair. He suddenly felt awkward: his clothing made him stand out like a sore thumb on a nudist beach. But, despite all the unconventional things he'd done in private over the years, he'd never had the courage to go naked in public – nor, if truth be told, had he ever had any inclination to do so.

Oblivious to Sonny's issue, Paolo simply sat and watched: it really was up to Sonny to make the first move and explain why he'd been looking for him. There was, however, a conflicting emotion ... pity? The sight of a powerful businessman – if Lord Weetwood was to be believed – reduced to a fidgeting silence on a foreign shore was indeed a pitiful sight.

Paolo swiftly opened a pocket in his backpack, extracted a packet of Marlboros, removed two, and handed one to Sonny.

'Thanks,' he said with relief.

When the cigarettes were lit and Paolo had exhaled his first deep intake of smoke, he said: 'So, Sonny, you are looking for me in all places?'

Sonny nodded.

After another silence, Paolo tapped Sonny on the knee as the obese German returned from his ramblings on the ridge. 'Now is the Frankfurter's second week on the island and I am thinking he gets desperate. It's sad really.'

'He was cruising *me* when I arrived,' Sonny snorted with contempt. 'He should cut out the beer and fries.'

Some ten metres away, the Frankfurter spread himself out on a fluorescent orange towel and smiled.

'Have you never cruised someone and failed, Sonny? Do you not know the emptiness, the – how you say it in English? ... "rejection"? – the feeling of failure? We can laugh, sure, but these are lonely people, Sonny ... sad and lonely.'

After dwelling on these words for some moments, Sonny said: 'Look, Paolo, I owe you an explanation.'

'No, you don't.'

But Sonny felt differently. Above all, he wanted Paolo to be absolutely clear about his relationship with Weetwood. But the more he told Paolo, the more ridiculous it sounded, particularly when he learned that Paolo had read about Lady Weetwood's antics in the Italian gossip magazines. And it was undoubtedly absurd that two billionaires locked in commercial warfare should be booked into the same room in a three-star hotel by 'a mutual business partner', as he put it.

'I hope you don't think *I'm* here to offer you money too,' Sonny protested when Paolo finished recounting Weetwood's bizarre performance at breakfast – and subsequently outside the hotel.

'I don't know what I am thinking,' replied Paolo quietly. He looked into Sonny's eyes and sighed: the American was hypnotized; he could see kindness and sadness, warmth and suspicion.

Returning the gaze, Sonny could feel the straitjacket in which he'd felt so long imprisoned begin to unbuckle and loosen. It was both thrilling and frightening, for he knew that Paolo could completely disarm him – could make him do or say anything ... anything at all. Never had he felt so impotent. If he wanted to retain any semblance of control – perhaps even of his own destiny – he had to avert his gaze immediately. And having explained Weetwood's presence in his room – albeit without alluding to the kidnapping – and sworn that he trusted Paolo and would never insult him with offers to buy his silence, shouldn't he leave now and draw a line under the whole business? Everything he'd dreamed of since their first encounter was nothing more than a frustrated fruit's foolish infatuation in a quasi-vacation atmosphere. He had to get a grip on reality.

Paolo was smiling broadly. 'You know, Sonny, you are sitting here for over an hour in those elegant shorts and shirt, ruining my reputation in front of all these people.' The mock indignation was theatrical. 'I'm thinking you should – how do you say? ... "unclothe"? – if you are staying.'

'Un*dress*,' Sonny corrected, and then felt himself blush like a high school student. An overwhelming sense of foolishness burned within him. What was his problem? Why did nakedness seem so natural to all these Europeans – young and old alike?

Slowly, with awkward solemnity, he began to unbutton his shirt.

With a view to easing the American's embarrassment, Paolo rummaged around in his backpack for a bottle of mineral water and some apples which he'd unlawfully removed from the Cala Beltran's dining room. By the time he'd finished his pretence of searching for them, Sonny had removed his shorts and was sitting cross-legged at the edge of Paolo's large beach towel.

Paolo grinned. 'So,' he said jovially, avoiding any obvious examination of Sonny's impressive torso, 'why are you *really* on this little island?'

*

Side by side, Paolo and Sonny were lying on their stomachs, sharing the last of their joint stocks of Marlboros. The wind had dropped, but the waves breaking on the shore remained impressive. Only a handful of people were left on the beach – including the Frankfurter, who, overdosing on naïve optimism, had convinced himself that his neighbours would

328

remain until everyone else had departed and invite him to join a threesome; for over an hour now, he'd been endeavouring to maintain some semblance of an erection. Paolo and Sonny, however, were barely aware of his existence.

'I do not understand you, Sonny,' Paolo said softly, shaking his head, '– how you are so ... so *cold* about your own daughter. She is being kidnapped and you are being like you are on the holiday.'

Sonny had never intended to mention Misty, but holding back on Paolo had proved impossible: whatever Paolo asked, he felt bound to answer. Indeed, although he'd yet to fully understand what was happening to him, he *wanted* to talk, to explain *exactly* what he was doing on Formentera, to tell Paolo *everything* about his life. He'd bottled it all up for decades; now was the moment to unburden himself – to confess. Maybe he'd never be given another opportunity. And the more he talked, the easier it became. It was exhilarating. There was no pressure or probing, no interrogation: Paolo just listened and occasionally helped to clarify or crystallize his thoughts with a seemingly simple yet pertinent question.

Sonny pushed his cigarette end into the sand and tried desperately to think of a credible response that would explain his attitude towards Misty. But there was just a void. ... He had to come up with something – Paolo mustn't be alienated. ... Jesus! How could he be more concerned about someone he'd known for barely twenty-four hours than his own daughter? But with the seconds ticking away, his silence condemned him. Paolo would be disgusted.

Peering at his watch, Paolo finally said: 'It's almost fifteen minutes before the seven o'clock. We should return to the hotel, perhaps. You have an important night, and at nine–'

'I *am* doing everything I can to get her back, Paolo,' Sonny blurted, sitting up abruptly. 'I don't want her to die – if this kidnapping is for real, that is. Like I said before, I strongly suspect that Weetwood is behind the whole thing.'

Paolo raised his eyebrows. 'Yes ... maybe ... maybe not. But anyway, it is not for love that you want her back.'

'For God's sake, why should I love someone – or feel anything special about someone – just 'cause that person's the end result of me getting horny one night? I was canned! And how come you're so self-righteous, Paolo? I bet you didn't ask for your mom's blessing every time you went cruising men's washrooms.'

Paolo stood up and grabbed his shorts.

'Forgive me, Paulo! I'm sorry – *real* sorry. Don't get mad. I ... It's just–'

'I want my towel.'

Sonny raised himself and watched Paolo shake the towel and pack it with his other beach things in the backpack.

'Paolo, *please*. I want so much for us to be friends. ... This thing about my daughter – I know it pisses you off. I want to make you understand. I don't want you to hate me because I can't give you some deep fancy reason for not loving her – some Freudian shit an' all.'

Paolo stood still and stared coldly at Sonny. 'I did not ask you to tell me all your life story, but I have listened. I am not a head doctor. And I do not have a magic pill for you. I'm only a simple Italian on my holiday. When I first see you yesterday I am thinking, "Yes, Paolo, this man is attractive. He looks interesting. He may be nice for you. We could have some fun together."

'You know, Sonny, I have not been with another man for many months. I am human and I want the contact – like this poor Frankfurter.' Paolo half-turned, glanced at the German and shook his head sadly. 'But it becomes all very difficult. And why? I don't know, but I'm thinking it's because you do not like yourself, maybe. You do not like *anything* about yourself and you are empty inside. All your work, your money, your nice things – all these are only to stop you thinking about these secret thoughts. And you don't think about Misty all these years because she is reminding you of how much your life is false. Everything about you is false.

'If I am understanding, the daughter is made only because you are jealous of the woman of your lover, this Garth. You want to take her from him – I don't know – and make him jealous – make him want you. But it didn't work. So, Misty traps you in a relationship – a marriage you never wanted. And you don't want to be reminded of all this. You want her out of your life. ... You'll *never* be happy, my friend. You *walked* into the cupboard – "closet"? – and *you* locked the door. *You* have the one key. You can unlock it whenever you want, Sonny, only *you*.'

Paolo picked up the backpack and slung it over his shoulder. 'How exactly is the – the – making of Misty, I don't care. But I know she is born only because of *you*. You created her, Sonny Start. And now she is in the danger – I don't think Weetwood kidnaps her – it is just the feeling in my ... my stomach, OK? – and only you can help her. I am thinking that perhaps she might be your best friend – if you are honest with her like you do with me.'

Paolo started to walk towards the Tanga bar, where he'd left his scooter. After a few steps he looked back. 'Mr Start, when I told my mother some years past why I would not be a husband or father, do you know what she is saying?'

Sonny shook his head.

'She says, "Paolo, I am your *madre*. I know *everything*. I am *always* knowing. And the only thing that is making me the angry is that you are afraid to tell me because you think I no love you no more. How can you have so little of the faith?".' Paolo smiled. 'I wish you luck. *Ciao!*'

For a few minutes, Sonny watched Paolo make his way along the firm sand near the water's edge. Then he began to sob.

The Frankfurter quickly packed up and made a hasty retreat to the dunes.

# CHAPTER 29

Shortly after his public humiliation in front of the Hotel Cala Beltran, George had stumbled, as if drunk, down the track to the beach. Secreted in the adjacent phone booth, Jennifer and Harriet had watched him go, Harriet colourfully reporting the same to *The Sun*'s eager hack in London.

By the time George reached the rows of sun loungers near the water's edge, he was mumbling like a madman. Some mothers grabbed their children; a few sunbathers laughed; a German family watched in disbelief as he devastated the soaring towers and curtain walls of a vast sandcastle they'd laboriously constructed for their offspring over several days. The father raced after the vandal, yelling obscenities, but when he attempted to block George's path, he lashed out and knocked him to the ground. A dozen or so Britons cheered, for the castle's ever-expanding territorial ambit had ruffled feathers.

Reaching a path on the bay's south side, George climbed to the top of the low cliffs. Had he turned, he would have seen Mike Crabtree running up the beach to the hotel, intent on persuading the management to phone for the police: the dispute between the pro- and anti-sandcastle camps was becoming ugly. But wholly unaware of the chaos he'd caused, George marched on. He followed the path for a while, but then, for no particular reason, veered off and headed inland. The stunted vegetation grew progressively thicker and taller, and soon he was surrounded by dense woodland. Low branches and thorny bushes scratched his face and hands and tore into his clothes. Yet, none of the pain or damage registered, for he was wholly obsessed with what he saw as the total implosion of his universe into a terrifying black hole. What dominated his thoughts was the speed of it all – just a matter of weeks. *Weeks*! It wasn't possible, surely? And it certainly wasn't fair after decades of uneventful, blameless, decent existence. Never a cross word; never a bout of bad temper ... well, perhaps a little tetchy once in a while with Miss Spigot ... and Mrs Duffle – but nothing the Almighty could in all reason get worked up about. He'd done all that could fairly have been expected of himself, both at work and at home, hadn't he?

Was it God's punishment for the Project Orient Express debacle? But if so, God had to remember that he hadn't *wanted* to make or sell soap that was lethal. It simply wasn't his damned fault. And then by all accounts, the wretched stuff was really harmless – unless one was a cleanliness fanatic and consumed thousands of bars over a lifetime. And what about Beryl? ... and Caroline? It also wasn't his fault that one was a strumpet and the other silly enough to get herself kidnapped.

'Oh, dear God, it just isn't *fair*!' he shouted, leaning against a tree as perspiration dripped off him. He searched for a handkerchief, but all his pockets were empty. Reduced to wiping his forehead on his shirt cuffs, he then decided to roll them up to his elbows – something he'd not done in years. All of a sudden, it occurred to him that he'd no idea where he was or how long he'd been walking. He looked around. ... Trees – nothing but trees. ... And save for the buzzing of insects in the still air, there wasn't a sound. Oh, how he hated insects!

A large bumblebee circled him menacingly. 'Buzz off!' he muttered, twisting and turning. But he only succeeded in exciting it – and then attracting another. He started to run, only to trip and fall flat on his face.

'Leave me alone, won't you?' he shrieked. 'That's all I want – to be left alone!'

Having had their fun, the persecutors appeared to accede to his request, and, following voluble expressions of relief over their departure, George returned to his repetitive monologue on the unfairness of his plight. As chance would have it, however, chanting 'It's all so unfair' proved soporific. And so, screened from the full glare of the midday sun by the branches above him, the tortured industrialist lay down and fell fast asleep.

He dreamed of his beloved model railway. Something, alas, was terribly wrong: every item of rolling stock – be it a locomotive, carriage or goods van – was hurtling along the tracks at terrifying speeds. They roared through tunnels and cuttings, flew across viaducts and embankments, thundered through stations and goods yards. And there, inside a dining car – one of twelve coaches hauled by his favourite locomotive, the *Duchess of Sutherland* – were two diminutive figures locked in combat. He looked closer and entered their world...

The belligerents looked familiar, but their movements were so fast as they ducked and weaved that he couldn't get a good view of their faces. Tables and chairs were knocked over; glasses and crockery smashed. He saw blood; it wasn't a clean fight. The shorter, plump figure dressed in some kind of school uniform – he could see now it was a young girl – was doing her best to abide by the Queensberry Rules, but the older person – a nurse? – would have none of it. She hit below the belt, stamped on the girl's fingers when she was down, and threw a scalding pot of coffee in her face. God, she was wicked, and how he hated her!

'Of course!' he heard himself cry. 'She's not a nurse – it's Nanny Blotch! No wonder she's fighting dirty, the old witch – the beastly cow!' What did he used to chant when she wasn't about? ... *Nanny Blotch has a smelly crotch.* That was it – Smelly Crotch Blotch!

Now the train was accelerating across a parched Mediterranean landscape. It was an unfamiliar part of his layout, and the thought occurred to him that some mischievous intruder had taken the liberty of rebuilding his sacred private domain. He returned to the scene inside the coach, and, being convinced that he was a mere observer, felt safe enough to vent his spleen at his former tormentor.

'Go on!' he shouted to the girl – she seemed on the point of being vanquished. 'Give her one from me! Don't let her beat you! Have courage! Smash her bloody face in!'

Both combatants looked up. As George recognized his daughter and shouted her name, Nanny Blotch rushed towards him.

'You dirty, nasty little boy!' she screeched, grabbing a knife from one of the tables. 'You know what happens to dirty, nasty little boys who touch themselves *there*, don't you?'

'Ha! You can't hurt me now, Blotch – not now! I'm grown up. I'm – I'm rich and powerful. And you're dead anyway. So there!'

Blotch cackled hysterically. '*You*, Master George ... grown up? Don't make me laugh!' Waving the knife backwards and forwards, she moved closer. 'What do we do to boys who touch themselves *there*, Master George? ... We cut it *off*! We cut it *right* off! Remember?'

Then the window vanished, and George found himself inside the carriage. With his protection gone, and standing just inches from Blotch, he was seized by fear and panic. 'Caroline! Help me! Quickly! It's Daddy! Help me!'

But the schoolgirl didn't move. 'I don't know *you*!' she cried, trying to make herself heard above the roar of the train. In fact, it was now moving so fast that the world beyond the carriage windows had become just a blur. 'You're not *my* father! I don't *have* a father!'

'Oh, but you *do*, Caroline, darling,' George pleaded. 'I am he!'

'That's right, Little Miss Fatty,' snapped Nanny Blotch with obvious contempt. 'This snivelling excuse for a human being, who plays with those disgusting things that only *boys* have – foul, *horrid* things – *is* your father.'

Blotch lunged with the knife; it came within inches of George's groin. He tried desperately to move, but it was exactly as he'd remembered those same moments of abject terror in the nursery at Bobbins: he'd lost all control of his limbs.

With extraordinary dexterity for one so obviously overweight, Caroline grabbed a claret bottle as it rolled past her feet and flung herself onto Blotch's back. As the bottle came crashing down on Nanny's head, the opening bars of Vivaldi's Gloria in D burst forth over the train's PA system.

'*Gloria! Gloria!*' sang the choir of angels joyfully.

With open mouths, George and his daughter watched as Blotch fell to the carriage floor and was transmogrified into an impressive pile of Goblin soap bars.

'I say,' shouted Caroline, 'how absolutely spiffing! I wonder if Château Gloria might have the same effect on all one's enemies? Not bad for an unclassified St-Julien!'

George could feel tears in his eyes. 'Bravo, Caroline! That was terribly clever – and *so* courageous. I knew you'd turn out to be a credit to the family.'

'Sorry? Do I know you?'

'Oh, Caroline, don't start that again.'

She stamped her foot. 'Silly me! Of course – you're my father ... or so it is said. ... Prove it!'

'Don't be childish, dear.'

'Come on! Do something *fatherly*.'

George felt his mind go blank. 'I ... I'm not sure I know what you mean ... "fatherly"?'

'Yes, like ... well ... I know! Give me a big hug and a kiss!'

'Now, now, my dear – in *public*? Let's act our ages.'

'I knew it all the time – game, set and match. You're *not* my father. You're boring. You're–' Caroline's happy face disintegrated and she started to cry.

'No, no, darling! Please don't. Heroes don't blub. And you *are* a little hero. ... Come here – come to Papa.' George opened his arms wide, and smiled. Caroline hesitated, but the train jolted violently as it crossed over some points and the two of them were thrown together. He hugged her and smothered her brow in kisses.

'I love you very much, Caroline.'

'Even though I'm fat and ugly?'

'You're neither fat nor ugly, darling. You're the loveliest, sweetest–'

*'This is the conductor speaking. We interrupt this gloriously tender moment to inform passengers that our next stop will be at the dramatic cliff tops of fun-packed Formentera, where this service will terminate – that is to say, crash. I shall shortly be walking down the train handing out death certificates. Thank you!'*

George and Caroline frantically opened a window and stuck out their heads. The train was racing along a stretch of single track, and, just a quarter of a mile distant, the line ended beside a lighthouse of massive proportions. George wanted to scream, but as hard as he tried, no sound was forthcoming. He gripped Caroline's hand and looked at her face. It showed no fear at all, only love and serenity.

Everything was strangely silent. Through the window, George could see nothing but a heavenly blue sky – and then the sea rushing up to meet them.

*

'Oh, God! How horrible! ... *Horrible*!' Totally disorientated, George shielded his eyes from the light and tried to sit up. He felt sick and dizzy. 'Oh, poor, poor Caroline. She didn't die – she couldn't have.'

It took George some time to convince himself that everything in the nightmare was indeed a figment of his imagination. As he did so, his bizarre surroundings took form, and he started to remember some of the events that had brought him to wherever he was. A butterfly with wings sporting a dramatic design in orange and black caught his attention. He watched it alight some feet away on a bush covered in tiny purple flowers; rosemary was not one of the very few plants encompassed by his horticultural knowledge.

'How absolutely extraordinary!' he whispered, as if not to frighten the butterfly away. 'I've not seen a chap like you before.' As he pondered the realization that he couldn't remember when he'd last looked at *any* butterfly, he began to hum the triumphant music that had celebrated his rescue from Nanny Blotch. 'Gloria! Gloria!' he sang hesitantly in a croaky tenor voice, '... Gloria in Excelsis Deo!' He fell silent and thought hard, still watching the stationary butterfly. How on earth did he know this music – and, indeed, the words? Why had it featured in his terrible nightmare? ... Perhaps he'd heard it at one or other of those infernal sponsored concerts in Manchester to which WSD's bankers and auditors were constantly inviting him – even the damned lawyers were at it these days! Why did he go? Why did he bother? All those grotesque professionals pretending to like both him and the music, never for one second letting up on their 'marketing speak'.

'I, Lord Weetwood of Dribbledale,' he intoned solemnly, 'do hereby swear that I shall never again attend any concert, ballet, opera – *vile*! – theatrical performance, or other allegedly cultural event sponsored by any professional adviser – wherever.

'Thank you,' he said, nodding to the butterfly. 'I don't know why I'm thanking you, but–'

Just as it occurred to him that talking to a *butterfly* might suggest he'd suffered some sort of breakdown, he began squawking the Vivaldi again.

'Oh golly! What the dickens *is* that, Mr Butterfly? ... Any ideas, hmm?'

George closed his eyes. Had Blotch played it to him on her wind-up gramophone in the nursery – one of the dozen or so scratched records of what she termed 'good music'?

'Now, if I remember correctly,' he said slowly, 'there were some Strauss waltzes, various Slavonic Dances by Dvořák, and – yuck! – *Morning* from *Peer Gynt.* ... My God, how I hated that bloody tune!'

No, the evidence was pretty damned conclusive: Blotch couldn't possibly have possessed anything by Vivaldi. So, it had to be school. ... The choir? ... Of course! How could he have forgotten all that? What a chump!

'Not that I was in it for long, mind you,' George pointed out to the butterfly. 'My glittering career in that department came to a dramatic end, dear insect.' He tapped his Adam's apple. 'Voice broke, just before ... or was it just *after* my thirteenth birthday? ... In any event, thereafter I couldn't sing for toffee.'

It was all coming back to him: an end of term concert in School Hall; his parents in the audience; Vivaldi's Gloria, and – if he remembered correctly – Bach's Magnificat after the interval. Not that he got that far: his beautiful treble voice had disintegrated five minutes into the Vivaldi. He'd stood mouth sealed and glowing as red as a hot coal with embarrassment until he could make his escape at the interval.

'You won't believe this,' George said, still gazing at the butterfly as if hypnotized by its dazzling colours, 'but the wretched music master forced me to learn the violin after I came a cropper on the singing front – *me*, with about as much dexterity as a ... as a rhinoceros! Extraordinary!

'Strange places schools, you know – like labour camps – at least they were in my day. Year after year you were forced to try and learn things for which you clearly had no aptitude whatsoever. Crackers! And these teacher chaps are supposed to be the clever ones, moulding the citizens of tomorrow ... or, at the sort of school I went to, the leaders of the nation – cabinet ministers, judges, top brass of the armed forces ... ambassadors. ... Anyway, the point is, dear friend, that I ended up hating "good music", thanks to the people who were supposed to educate me.'

George pondered his conclusion for a few moments. 'That's not really true. I don't mean *hate*. I mean ... well, I suppose it brings back memories ... memories of things I'd rather forget, things like humiliation, ridicule ... bullying. Oh, I know what you're thinking – that I was too sensitive – that most schoolboys don't give these things a second thought. They don their rugby kit, go out to the playing fields, and let off steam with some rough physical contact and organized violence.'

He shook his head. 'I should imagine that's what my son James used to do. Mind you, I can't believe he had too many problems at school. I seem to remember that his reports glowed with praise – "a dazzling star", "a paragon of ...""

George's voice trailed away. A dazzling star? His son? His own flesh and blood? He furrowed his brow. Was he guilty of exaggeration? After all, he couldn't claim to have followed James's school career with any particular interest. And, of course, the last few years had seen the boy hovering on the edge of madness – or so it had appeared to him – to *everyone*. And then that extraordinary behaviour at Cap-Ferrat. ... *Cap-Ferrat?*

It was something Belinda had said at Eastbourne, but as usual he'd not really been listening. Everything had been topsy-turvy since the revelations about Beryl had exploded around him like an Exocet missile. ... Something about James and how it was no wonder he'd gone off his head. ... Well, she hadn't used those precise words, but that, no doubt, was what she'd meant. But if James had witnessed Beryl doing something along the lines of what *The Sun* had reported, then ... And what about that doctor, the one who'd been treating James? What was his name?

After a few minutes, George concluded that he hadn't the slightest idea, and that it didn't really matter. What was pertinent, however, was that he remembered some mealtime conversation at Bobbins between Belinda, Miss Spigot and Mrs Duffle to the effect that Beryl and the doctor had fled Cap-Ferrat *together*.

George gasped in horror. If James had seen Beryl doing – no, he really didn't want to imagine what the boy might have seen her doing – but, in such circumstances, of course poor James would have suffered a breakdown. And her partner in crime, the so-called doctor, would probably have prescribed all sorts of drugs to turn James into some kind of zombie. No wonder Beryl came rushing back to England and did her damnedest to convince him that his son was mad!

In truth, the last time he'd seen James – he vaguely remembered the dinner with Start's daughter ... Musty? ... Anyway, James had been ... well, cheerful, just like he used to be before the death of his school–

George thumped the ground with his fists. 'Start's daughter!' he shrieked. '*Caroline!*'

For the first time since awakening from his nightmare, he looked at his watch. His eyes widened as the lateness of the hour sunk in: it was just a few minutes before five! There were only *four* hours left before he was to receive what were likely to be the final instructions from the kidnappers. Regina had not been unequivocal, but he felt almost sure that tonight would be the night. Fear and panic began to set in. *Four* hours! He tried to stand up, but faltered: every bone in his body ached and he felt devoid of all strength.

'Oh my God! I'm ill!' He started prodding various parts of his body while conducting a rapid analysis of his predicament: he'd no idea where he was; in the last twenty-four hours he'd consumed little food and hardly any liquids to speak of; he'd tramped hatless in the blazing sun for bloody ages and had slept on the bare earth. Perhaps he'd been bitten by a snake! ... Were there snakes on Formentera? ... Anyway, he was undoubtedly suffering from chronic dehydration – and sunstroke. What use was he now? What use at all? And just at the very moment when Caroline needed him most ... if she was still alive.

'Don't ever think that!' he roared. 'Of course she's alive! She *has* to be.' The face he'd seen in the nightmare after Blotch had been destroyed came back to him – so sweet and gentle, so full of love. ... Did she really look like that – the plump, bespectacled Caroline in her dreadful tracksuits?

He stared hard at the butterfly and then closed his eyes firmly in a desperate attempt to conjure up a clear and objective image of his daughter. 'Come on, come on,' he muttered, 'you must be able to do it.' But try as he might, the only face he saw was the face in the dream as the train rushed towards its cataclysmic destruction.

Engulfed by shame and self-loathing, George slapped the top of his head. 'I brought that child into this vile world. By all accounts she's jolly bright, hard-working, respectful, law-abiding. Never asks for anything – apart from history books. Hardly touches her allowance. ... My God, all Beryl had to worry about were the girl's clothes and weight!

As the seconds ticked away, it began to dawn on him that Caroline was rather an extraordinary child – young lady really – and that he was very lucky to have such a daughter, very lucky indeed. And why should his subconscious paint a false image of her? Perhaps behind those thick spectacles there was a pretty face after all. It was simply that in his self-centred conscious world he never took any notice of her.

'You know, now that I think of it, I'm surprised' – the butterfly flapped its wings – 'all right ... I'm *ashamed* not to have thought of this before. My children *are* rather special – *both* of them.' The butterfly's wings flapped again. 'Yes, I know that sounds like a headwaiter describing the *plat du jour*. Forgive me. ... They're ... they're *precious*. They're good and decent. James did go a bit off the rails over his chum's death, but at least he didn't turn to drink or drugs – heaven forbid! – or squat in trees to stop motorways being constructed.' He grinned. 'Oh, I don't know – I might have approved of that!

'But the point is, old friend,' he said, trying again to stand up, 'I'm blessed that I'm the father of these two fine people. ... And yet, as Caroline

339

said in that nightmare, she doesn't *know* me. Nor does James. And I don't know *them*.'

George winced with pain as he willed his body – dehydrated, sunburnt and weak – to take a step forward. 'Well,' he continued through gritted teeth as waves of nausea surged through him, 'I'm going to do my very best to remedy our mutual ignorance. But first we have to liberate Caroline from the brigands – whoever they may be. And as soon as this crisis is resolved, do you know what I'm going to do?' He waited a few seconds, generously giving the butterfly an opportunity to respond. 'No? You haven't a clue, have you? Well, I'll tell you then. I'm going to withdraw that FoamFay rubbish from the market – lock, stock and barrel. There! What do you think of that, my pretty fellow? Hmmm?'

The butterfly flapped its wings and came to land on George's right arm. At any other point in his life he would have taken evasive action: without a second thought, he would have crushed the offending insect – even a harmless butterfly. But for once, he experienced no fear. On the contrary, through his veins there flowed an emotion unlike anything he'd ever experienced in his long, detached, supine life – a sense of such contentment and well-being that all sensation of his malaise dissipated.

And then the butterfly was gone, flitting this way and that, one second in shade and the next, picked out by the sunbeams filtering through the trees.

Released from his trance, the pain returned with a vengeance. 'No! Please! Don't leave me! Come back!' He tried to follow the flashes of orange, but the trunk of a fallen pine, half-consumed by voracious ants, blocked his path. The butterfly disappeared.

George made to sit down on the obstacle, spotted the ants, and thought better of it. 'Horrid insects!' he muttered close to tears, and then regretted his remark. 'I mean the ants, not you, Mr Butterfly, not you. Insects are like people, I suppose – there are nice ones and nasty ones.'

It was time to concentrate, time to get to grips. He had to get back to the hotel as soon as possible. Weaker men than he had battled their way starving, waterless and in rags across deserts. Think of Montgomery and the Eighth Army ... or was it the Ninth? ... El Alamein and Tobruk. This was a tiny Mediterranean island packed to the gunwales with tourists – in the height of the holiday season! – well, September anyway, to be precise.

'Oh, for God's sake,' he shrieked, 'stop wittering and march, you idiot! The land seems to rise over there. Perhaps there's a hill or something from which I can get my bearings. Think of Caroline. Think of the look on her face when you get her back from those fiends. Think of that smile in the dream!'

It did the trick. Within minutes, George was forcing his way up the unstable slopes of a sand dune infested with giant buzzing cicadas. Finally, after what had seemed like an eternity, he reached the baking summit. He slumped to the ground and tried to focus.

Nothing but dense woodland for miles and miles and–

*I can hear voices ... or am I hallucinating?*

In great pain, he twisted round, looked northwards, and gasped: like a lost Mayan temple secreted in the dense rain forests of Central America, not more than five hundred metres distant, peaking above the tree tops, stood the unmistakable white bulk of the Hotel Cala Beltran.

'Gloria! Gloria!' he sang – in truth, a tuneless rasp – 'Gloria in excelsis Deo!' And in his fevered mind, the cicadas' racket was transformed into the soaring notes of jubilant trumpets.

# CHAPTER 30

With Sonny still en route from Llevant, and George surveying the hotel from the summit of his sandy hillock, Gwen Blackberry brought her battered 2CV to a violent halt opposite the Cala Beltran's main entrance. Beside her – and relieved that the white-knuckle drive was over – sat a wide-eyed Belinda Thornton: having been unable to contact her brother by telephone, she was anxious to discover what the devil he was up to and to inform him of James's disappearance. Removing his helmet, Paolo Amerigo, who'd just dismounted his Vespa, turned to identify the source of the squealing tyres. With no particular interest, he watched the two women get out of the car; judging by their clothing, they had to be British.

'Oh bloody hell,' Gwen hissed, grabbing Belinda's arm and nodding towards the entrance, 'it's the sodding press!'

Loitering in the vestibule were two very white and sickly young men with beer guts, both smoking and dressed in Bermuda shorts, long-sleeved denim shirts with turned-up cuffs, trainers and brown socks. A very professional-looking camera hung from the neck of the fatter one; the other had a pen poised over a notebook. They were being lectured – or so it seemed – by two badly dressed middle-aged ladies.

Belinda and Gwen stopped dead in their tracks, just as Jennifer glanced in their direction. She'd been an avid follower of *The Muffins* for as long as she cared to remember; indeed, she proudly owned copies of every *Muffins* publication ever produced by the BBC. One of her more recent acquisitions, *The Jessica Muffin Country Cookbook*, contained over one hundred of 'Jessica's favourite recipes' – not to mention numerous photographs of Gwen dressed as 'Jessica' in tweedy clothing.

'Look!' cried Jennifer. 'I can't believe it! It's Jessica Muffin! Oh how wonderful! She must be staying here!'

While Jennifer stared rapturously at Gwen, her sister, Harriet – together with Trev the reporter and Keith the photographer – looked in bewilderment from Gwen to Belinda. Although Harriet had listened to *The Muffins* from time to time over the years, she wouldn't have been able to recognise Gwen Blackberry to save her life. As for the hacks, neither of them had a clue who or what 'Jessica Muffin' might be. Then Paolo came into view.

'That's him!' yelled Harriet. 'That's the Italian nancy boy!' As if a starter pistol had been fired, she and her three companions shot out of the vestibule.

'I think you're *wonderful*!' boomed Jennifer, galloping towards Gwen. 'It's criminal the way they've axed you.'

But no one, not even Gwen, was listening to poor Jennifer: Paolo was proving a far greater diversion. Keith was dancing around him, taking photographs from every conceivable angle, while Trev, armed with a portable tape recorder thrust almost in the Italian's mouth, was bombarding him with a barrage of intimate and aggressive questions concerning his relationship with Lord Weetwood.

'Come on, mate, everyone from the manager to the cat in this dump knows you're a fag. These two old dames' – Trev indicated Jennifer and Harriet – 'saw you an' 'im 'avin' a *very* cosy breakfast this mornin'. Then it seems you 'ad a bit of a tiff, and later the old geezer's offering you fifty thousand quid out 'ere in the street. Blackmailin' 'im, are you, mate? Got some porno pics of you an' 'im doin' it, 'ave you? 'Ow long 'ave you two been shaggin' each other then?' Trev pulled out £100 in new £20-bills from his breast pocket and waved them in front of Paolo's face. 'Yours, mate, if you give us the story, OK?'

'Scum!' snarled Harriet, wagging a finger at Paolo. 'Just what one would expect from a dirty little wop.'

'Can I have your autograph, Jessica?' pleaded Jennifer. 'I love your recipe for parsnip and nettle–'

'Look, sonny,' said Trev, 'it'd be much better for you to co-operate an' tell us your side of the story, otherwise we'll just 'ave to assume the worst.'

Paolo's confusion was turning to anger. 'Boys, you leave me alone, OK? And why you calling me "Sonny"? I am not the American. You–'

Keith had taken one too many pictures, and Paolo tried to seize the camera, but Trev was too quick for him and managed to grab his arm.

'Oh now, now! Temper, temper! So it's true that you're blackmailin' Weetwood over gay orgies at the Hotel Cala Beltran and–?'

'How *dare* you!' blasted Belinda. 'Who the *hell* do you people think you are? You've already done enough damage to my family with your lies and innuendo. My brother – with all his faults – wouldn't recognize an "orgy" – gay or otherwise – let alone participate–'

But before she could finish, Gwen had thrust a hand over Belinda's mouth in an attempt to silence her. 'For Christ's sake, darling,' she hissed, 'think of Caroline! This is turning into a circus!'

Trev's eyes flicked in bewilderment from Paolo to Belinda. 'Wait a minute! Is this fag your brother, love? Fuckin' 'ell, what's going on here?' He turned back to Paolo, who'd stopped struggling to escape and was now staring wide-eyed at Belinda.

'I – I – I ... er, I don't know this *signora*.'

Gwen started to steer Belinda back to the 2CV just as Trev finally saw the light.

'Oh, *I* get it! If this old bat isn't *your* sister, mate, then she's, she's ... Fuck me! She must be what's-her-name' – he turned to Keith for assistance – '... you know, thingy – the old geezer's sister!' As Keith swung his camera towards Belinda and started snapping, Trev pushed the £100 into Paolo's breast pocket, snarling, 'Don't move, mate, or you're dead.'

With Keith trying to position himself in front of her, Belinda panicked. It was hardly surprising that her brain was not working clearly: after all, she'd not had a decent night's sleep for days – and last night had been spent drinking port with Viv Duffle and Pat Spigot. Her punch to Keith's jaw was not particularly violent, but it was sufficient to knock him off balance, causing him to fall heavily on his left side. Crushing his arm, he emitted a blood-curdling scream and rolled onto his back. Trev rushed forward to get to his colleague, who lay groaning at Belinda's feet.

'I didn't mean to–'

'You fuckin' cow!' barked Trev, drowning out Belinda's whimper as he grabbed Keith's camera. 'You'll pay for that, bitch!'

With the intention of getting Belinda and the prostrate Keith in the viewfinder, Trev leapt back a few feet. That was when Paolo threw his crash helmet and backpack to the ground and flew onto Trev's back. The reporter collapsed onto his stomach, prompting applause from a small group of holidaymakers, together with cheers and whoops of delight from spectators on various balconies. The word that something 'exciting' – yes, *exciting*! – was happening at the hotel had spread like wildfire, and fresh onlookers were arriving in droves.

With every intention of assisting Trev, Harriet shuffled over to the wrestling men in a cheap pair of flip-flops, while Jennifer, who was visibly shocked by the turn of events – and fearful that procuring Jessica Muffin's autograph would now prove problematic – made a futile attempt to achieve a ceasefire.

'Now, now, Harriet, dear, don't do anything you might regret. This is Jessica Muffin and–'

'Oh for Christ's sake, Jennifer,' Harriet blasted as she reached Paolo and grabbed him by the neck, 'just belt up!' She began shaking his head violently from side to side, yelling, 'Leave him alone, you Iti pansy!'

'Give that wop queer one from me, love!' someone shouted from the safety of a balcony. The voice was male, coarse and cockney.

It was too much for Gwen. In a flash, she joined the melee and tried to drag Harriet off Paolo by grabbing the back of her T-shirt. 'Oh no you don't, you vulgar little woman!' she bellowed with all the volume and elocution of a well-trained trooper.

Distracted by the female fracas behind him, Paolo momentarily loosened his grip on Trev, who then rolled to one side and swiftly had the Italian pinned on his back. Trev raised one fist high in the air and was about to bring it crashing down on Paolo's face when Belinda, fired by a powerful sense of outrage, let out a war cry of such intensity that all action suddenly ceased. Even George heard the terrifying noise as he continued to extricate himself from the labyrinth of sandy paths which criss-crossed the undulating terrain between his former vantage point and the hotel. Overwhelmed by delirium, he threw himself to the ground and covered his aching head with a cry of 'Stukas!'

It was at this point that both the hotel's deputy manager and Sonny came upon the scene. The former uttered a string of Catalan expletives and rushed back to his desk to phone for the police. Sonny, who due to the blocked road had been forced to abandon his car, tapped the shoulder of none other than Mike Crabtree; with a large supercilious grin on his face, he was keeping a low profile on the crowd's periphery.

'What's going on?' asked Sonny in a voice devoid of emotion, such was his state of depression.

'Oh, one of our American cousins, I presume!' replied Crabtree flippantly. 'You ought to be used to this sort of thing,' he added, pointing towards the centre of the throng. Sonny eyed him quizzically. 'Violence, ol' man,' Crabtree explained. 'A bloody good scrap! Looks like that Italian shirtlifter is getting a damned good thrashing. I'm surprised the owners allow people like that in the hotel. He's that pervert's catamite – you know, that Lord Weetwood bastard. He's flown the nest, if you ask me, and–'

Sonny pushed Crabtree aside with a powerful shove, snarling, 'Go to hell, you heap of shit!' Gawping holidaymakers and hotel staff alike appeared to bounce off him as he raced to the centre of the spectacle. There was a cry of 'Watch out, it's Indiana Jones!' from one balcony, and 'Go and get the bloody camcorder, Mavis!' from another.

Sonny froze when he reached the battlefield. The only detail which registered was Paolo's recumbent figure seemingly crushed by the ill-clad bulk of a ginger-haired oppressor sat astride the Italian's midriff.

Broken arm or not, and notwithstanding the excruciating pain, Keith had retrieved his precious camera. Now, with a true paparazzo's intuition of history about to be made, he pointed it roughly in the right direction and pressed. He caught most of the action: Trev being lifted as if a mere child and tossed into the crowd; Sonny scooping Paolo into his powerful arms and smothering his astonished face with kisses; the shocked expressions of a few onlookers with pursed lips; and the animated faces of the majority as they cheered and applauded.

It was a blessing that when Gwen and Tom were searching for a villa on the island, they had stayed at the Cala Beltran. A fellow guest had informed the General Manager, Señor Pons, that Gwen was a star of film, stage and quiz shows. Señor Pons had thereafter bent over backwards to please the Blackberrys. And after *Honeysuckle Cottage*'s acquisition, he'd been rewarded with a couple of dinner invitations for his wife and himself. Now, roused from his office by the near hysteria of his deputy, Pons vetoed a call to the police pending his own investigation of the disturbance so incoherently described to him with colourful Hispanic exaggeration. Shooting out of the hotel, he almost collided with Gwen. Swiftly taking the initiative, she commandeered the Residents' Lounge and had all the participants in the fracas herded therein before they had time to think, let alone protest. Somehow, Crabtree ended up with them, but, being a social gastropod, he was an expert at attaching himself to people.

While Pons procured refreshments and summoned a doctor to examine Keith's arm, Gwen ascertained the strangers' identities and effected introductions. When everyone had settled down and had a glass of their preferred alcoholic refreshment, Gwen decided to explain what Belinda, Lord Weetwood and Mr Start were doing on the island; Field Marshal Montgomery would have been proud of her clarity and precision.

'Now gather round and listen very, very carefully,' she said in tones indicating that she was about to inform her audience that World War III had broken out. 'What I have to tell you is a matter of life and death. I'm sure Mr Start – may I call you "Sonny"? – will agree that matters have gone so far that we have no option but to inform those of you here who are still ignorant of the crisis just what exactly has happened on this island.' In turn, her eyes burned into those of Jennifer, Harriet, Trev, Keith and Mike. 'If any one of you should leave this room and act contrary to my pleas – I cannot *order* you to do anything – two beautiful and fine young women could be dead within hours.'

The three holidaymakers endeavoured to appear shocked, but they were all rather thrilled by this news – and their own sudden importance: Harriet was already imagining TV appearances; Jennifer could see a mass of autographs across her *Muffins* memorabilia; and Mike had a strange feeling that ... well, he couldn't quite put his finger on it, but every time he glanced at the two faggots on the sofa opposite him, his heart began to race.

Gwen succinctly recounted the events that had led up to the kidnapping and the main developments thereafter. Belinda added a few details and mentioned her nephew's presence on the island. 'I have to tell you that

James – against our advice – recommended his own search this morning and ... well, I'm afraid we've heard nothing further from him.'

Gwen looked anxiously at Belinda. 'I'll phone Tom in a minute and see if there's any news ... and bring him up to date on events here.'

'Where's that bloody doctor?' groaned Keith; everyone ignored him.

'OK, Gwen' – Trev always called people by their first names – 'it's all very tragic, I grant you, but what the 'ell's been goin' on between *this* guy' – he jabbed a figure disdainfully at Paolo – 'and Weetwood? – and Sonny here, for that matter? And can we agree now that our paper gets an exclusive on this story – these *stories*?'

'Look, guys,' Sonny said coolly, 'I can't negotiate on behalf of the Weetwood family – or Paolo, OK? But I can offer you something which I've no doubt your proprietor – I've met him many times – will jump at. I want you to call him in a minute and I'll speak to him directly.'

The deal was simple: there was to be a total news blackout on the kidnapping until it was resolved, which Sonny hoped would be in the next twelve hours, at most. Once it was over, he'd do everything in his power to let *The Sun* have the full story. But there was more: Sonny was coming out of the closet, and Trev's paper and its American associates could have an exclusive on that too – the revelations would clearly be bigger news in the U.S.

'But any reference to Paolo in your papers – one single word – without his express consent, and the whole deal's off. Get it?'

Trev couldn't believe his luck – one scoop after another! What next? Perhaps the kidnappers would do something really nasty to the two girls ... a spot of torture ... rape – even kill them. Who wanted a lousy happy ending anyway?

'Christ, I'm sorry about these kids,' said Trev; Keith nodded slowly. 'Terrible – absolutely terrible! And apologies, Paolo, for all the aggro. But you can't blame us for thinkin' that you and Weetwood ... well, you know ... in view of what we were told by old Harriet here. What a cock up!' Trev tried hard to look contrite, ashamed and shocked. He drained his gin and tonic. 'OK, let's try to get a call through to God.'

'"God"?' queried Belinda.

'Sorry, Lindy – the boss – the head honcho. ... By the way, where *is* Weetwood?'

Before anyone could answer, however, Harriet was on her feet. 'Never mind *him* – what about *us* – me and Jennifer? What do *we* get out of this palaver?' She turned to face Trev. 'This morning we were promised ten thousand quid for the dirt on Lord bleeding Weetwood. We acted in all good faith and–'

'Hypocrite!' muttered Belinda.

'Yes, in all good faith. We might have misconstrued what was going on, but when all is said and done, dear, he was hardly acting honourably – trying to buy that Italian's testimony and all.'

'There's *no* story, love,' Trev said with a smirk, '– at least not there. No story, no money.'

'Now just a bloody minute–!'

'You'll get your lousy ten thousand, lady,' Sonny cut in with obvious contempt. '*I'll* pay if *they* won't.'

Crabtree weighed up the pros and cons of asking for a payment too, but the issue of his own duplicity was troubling him. After all, everyone at the Cala Beltran believed him to be a senior police officer in the Thames Valley force. All this talk of newspapers, publicity, kidnappings, millionaires 'coming out' – where would it all end? His own exposure as a humble traffic warden? A laughing stock? Would this turn out to be the last of his annual pilgrimages to Cala Beltran?

He cleared his throat and everyone looked at him. 'It goes without saying,' he said grandly, 'that your secrets are safe with me. I require nothing. An Englishman's word is his bond and–'

'I should jolly well think so,' Jennifer interrupted. 'After all, you *are* a policeman, aren't you, Mike?'

The news caused several raised eyebrows, but before Crabtree could reply to Gwen's clipped questions concerning his rank and force, an excited Juan Pons burst into the room with a dramatic announcement: a dishevelled gentleman – seemingly drunk – had just collapsed in the reception, and, in his receptionist's opinion it was Lord Weetwood. Accordingly, all guests had been evacuated from that section of the hotel; a temporary reception had been hastily set up in the bar. Some inmates were unhappy, but free *sangría* was to be served to all and sundry for the rest of the evening.

Belinda was first out of the lounge door; the others quickly followed. The doctor summoned for Keith's arm fortuitously entered the lobby just as Belinda threw herself to the floor with a shriek of 'Georgie, darling!'

George's eyes flickered open. With a supreme effort, he tried to focus on Belinda's distraught face. His cracked lips parted. 'Gloria,' he rasped, 'Gloria ... Gloria in ...'

And then he passed out.

# CHAPTER 31

'You see, *Miss* Start,' said Ursula smirking, 'I'm not such a heartless bitch after all. I could have ignored your request to use the toilet "in private", as you put it, before I make my final departure. Rory and Caroline had no such qualms this afternoon – such intimacy together in the bathroom! – and in the bedroom! But for the remainder of your stay here, you'll just have to "hold it in" as I think the English say now that you are handcuffed to James and the other end of his ankle shackle is attached to that central heating pipe. Anyway, the 'inconvenience" should only be for a few hours – provided both your fathers behave themselves and pay the ransoms, and we get safely away.'

Despite both Misty's and James's protests as she made her dramatic exit, Ursula switched off the lights – not out of spite or for purposes of security: after a lifetime of ordered frugality, she found it impossible to leave any room wastefully illuminated. They heard her lock the door, and in the near darkness as the last hint of twilight penetrated the louvred shutters, each of them tried to think of something reassuring to say.

'It won't be long now, Misty.'

'Let's hope. I wonder when she's going to tell them – our folks – where we are.'

'Soon. I'm sure of it. She's not going to leave us here to starve to death.' Misty shot James a glance which, all too obviously, betrayed her fears that she didn't share his apparent confidence. 'And did you notice,' he continued, 'that Ursula said she hoped "*we* get safely away"? – meaning her and someone else, I assume. Obviously not Devlin. ... *Who* I wonder?'

In the adjoining room, Ursula stood a few feet from Rory and Caroline, pointing her gun directly at them. 'Don't try anything clever – either of you – or you'll both be full of holes. OK?'

Without awaiting a response, she flicked a metal keyring – just a single band one inch in diameter – bearing two small keys at Rory. They landed on his groin.

'First, remove the handcuffs, Rory.'

'Where are we going?' asked Caroline, her voice trembling with fear.

Ursula smiled wickedly. '"*We*"? ... *You're* not going anywhere. In fact, I doubt that after the number of times you've been poked this afternoon, you'd have enough strength to make it to the door. I just hope that your beloved here hasn't exhausted himself.'

There were so many things Caroline wanted to say to Ursula, so much loathing she wanted to get off her chest, but antagonizing the creature at this stage hardly seemed sensible.

Rory placed the handcuffs on the floor. 'Now what, Ursula?'

'Unlock your bit of the shackle, Rory, and fasten it to the central heating pipe beside Caroline. We don't want her doing anything heroic, do we? Hard luck if she needs the toilet again before daddy pays up tonight. Then put the handcuffs on your wrists, slide the keys back across the floor towards me, and stand up.'

Rory complied, and Ursula, without taking her eyes off the prisoners, picked up the keys with her free hand and reached round to place them in a rear pocket of her tatty jeans.

'Where are you taking him?' asked Caroline anxiously.

'Don't worry – not far. He's my security.'

'"Security"?' queried Rory.

'Well, let's just say that should anything go wrong tonight, like an escape by this creature' – she waved the gun at Caroline – 'or those couple of miseries next door, then ... Oh dear, let's not even think of it.'

Caroline gasped. 'Don't hurt him, for God's sake! *Please*. I'm ... I'm sure my father will pay you a lot of money if he's not hurt. I'll *make* him. I promise I will – cross my heart and hope–'

'Spare me this romantic nonsense! How naïve – how *stupid* do you think I am? Remember, Rory, any false move – *anything* – and I'll shoot you and come back and kill the lot of them. Understand? I've really nothing to lose. I'll get the money whether they're dead or alive.'

Caroline started to cry, softly at first, but within seconds she was wailing.

Rory made a move with a view to bending down and consoling her. 'Don't cry, baby, I'll be all–'

'Rory! Leave her and get over to the door. *Now*!' Ursula moved backwards, out into the corridor; he followed.

'I love you, Caroline! I'll *always* love you. Pray for me.'

'I love *you*, Rory! I *love* you!'

And then the lights were extinguished, the door slammed shut, and she was alone. She tried desperately to stifle her sobs: she wanted to identify any sounds which might indicate what was happening beyond her prison. 'Don't die, Rory,' she choked, '– *please* don't die.'

Having heard Ursula's barked orders, neither James nor Misty could maintain any pretence of calm.

'If that bitch has laid one finger on my sister, I'll ... I should shout through the wall and see if she's OK.'

Misty gripped his arm. 'Shush! Wait a minute. I think I heard a door bang – the van probably. They must be going. Carrie's distraught but unharmed ... I think. We'll attract her attention as soon as they drive off.'

Below in the garden, the VW now contained its cargo. At gunpoint, Ursula had ordered Rory to clamber into the back and chain himself to a reinforcing strut with one end of the handcuffs, repeating her dire warning that any attempt to attract attention would result in swift death – and the death of the other prisoners; he doubted she was bluffing. Then, with the rear doors locked, she got behind the wheel, put her small suitcase on the passenger seat, and started the engine. Within minutes she was bumping down the track, trying to remember the concluding bars of Haydn's *Farewell* Symphony.

*

It had been an enjoyable and relaxing day for Chuck and Bob. Their employer had told them to keep a low profile and await instructions: it was a tiny island, so wherever they went they'd never be more than a twenty-minute drive away at most. Hence, they'd done a spot of sightseeing, bought a few souvenirs, and then headed for Platja de Migjorn. They swam and jogged along the beach; they loved exercise and their respective muscular torsos. They left messages on Sonny's mobile, keeping him informed of their whereabouts, but, to their surprise, had received no calls from him. Bob suggested going to Sonny's hotel to make sure the boss was OK, but Chuck reminded him that they'd be contravening orders, and orders were orders. So, they stayed on at the beach and swam and jogged.

They got back to the Hostal Pepe in Sant Ferran around seven-thirty, as the sun began to set. After showering, they dressed in blue denim jeans and white T-shirts, and finally settled on a pizza at an unassuming little place across the street; the Fonda Pepe seemed a tad too exotic. As they'd still not heard from Sonny, Bob was getting worried; Chuck told him to relax. Maybe there were fresh negotiations with the kidnappers. Maybe they'd be on the island for a few more days. If so, then as far as Chuck was concerned, he'd be back to the same beach, but this time he was going naked like everyone else. Bob said Sonny wouldn't approve, but Chuck pointed out that he'd never know unless Bob snitched. Bob said he'd never snitch – never ever.

Displaying 8:43, the mobile rang. In his haste to answer it, Bob almost knocked over his glass of mineral water; he and Chuck never touched alcohol.

'Hi, boss! You OK? We were getting worried an' all.'

'*I'm fine. Look, Bob, nothing's happening tonight, OK? So, I don't think I'll be needing you. I'll let you know if there's any change of plan.*

351

*Otherwise, I'll call in the morning. Oh, by the way, you guys haven't noticed an old VW van on your travels around the island, have you?'*

Bob asked Chuck, and then confirmed that neither of them had.

*'OK. Well, let me know pronto if you do see one.'*

'You think it's ... *them*?'

*'Could be. Ciao.'*

Bob put the mobile back on the table and smiled at Chuck. 'Looks like you may get to expose yourself after all, honey.'

*

The doctor summoned to the Cala Beltran, Angel Aiguadolça, had wanted to take Lord Weetwood to the small hospital at Sant Francesc – or even have him airlifted by helicopter to a private clinic in Ibiza. He diagnosed sunstroke, dehydration and some kind of related dementia – even a nervous breakdown could not be ruled out. He was certainly not drunk, however. In the event, Belinda and Sonny persuaded Dr Aiguadolça to install a nurse and the necessary saline drips and other paraphernalia in Room 327. He initially protested, but relented once they disclosed the kidnapping crisis to him and explained the need to be able to communicate with his lordship should the kidnappers prove difficult. Moreover, the good doctor's services, they warned, might be required for the treatment of the victims of the dastardly crime. He prayed to the Blessed Virgin that this would not be the case, but, nonetheless, accepted Sonny's offer of a $500-retainer per diem until further notice.

With George clearly out of action for the duration, Sonny asked Señor Pons to bring him both Lord Weetwood's briefcase and his own from the hotel safe; Belinda agreed to accept full responsibility for her brother's.

'If the drop's happening tonight,' Sonny reasoned, 'I'll have to do *all* the running about.' He was now convinced that the kidnapping was for real: it was clear that Belinda and Gwen thought so too, and they seemed completely on the level. In fact, he'd taken a shine to them from the outset.

In the meantime, Gwen phoned Tom and learned that there was still no news from James; it was all very worrying. Perhaps there'd been an accident. Dr Aiguadolça checked at the clinic, and made some discreet enquiries through his brother-in-law in the *Guardia Civil*. Nothing. Gwen, Belinda and Sonny considered the possibility that James had indeed discovered the kidnappers' hideout. That was when Gwen mentioned the VW for the first time.

'He was obsessed about it,' she said, 'absolutely obsessed.'

Hence Sonny's reference to the vehicle when he phoned Bob and Chuck.

At quarter to nine, Sonny had to break off his discussions with 'God', who was dining with the Aga Khan in Geneva. At first, 'God' had not been too happy about the interruption; indeed, until he grasped that he was talking to *the* Sonny Start, his language had been choice. But as his anger subsided, 'God' loved what he heard down the line. Less than an hour later, a team of lawyers were working on an agreement for the 'Sonny Start Story'; 'God' had even 'suggested' a headline – '**A FRESH START**'.

Now, at five minutes to nine, a tense Sonny sat in his Suzuki and awaited Regina's call, his mind bouncing back and forth between thoughts of Paolo and Misty. Paolo was in his room packing: tomorrow afternoon, he'd be on a charter flight back to Turin, his holiday over. Sonny's intuition was that if Paolo boarded that plane, he'd never see him again. His best chance – possibly his only chance – to find happiness would disappear. The good Lord had sent Paolo, and he loved him. But how could he prove his love? – and in such a short period?

Misty, on the other hand, was the only decent thing he'd ever created in his entire miserable life: he'd learned from Gwen that James had confessed to being a suicidal, neurotic hermit before he met Misty at Bobbins; then he fell in love with her. And Belinda had said that Caroline's recent postcards from Formentera evinced Misty's assistance in transforming her niece from an unhappy introvert into a self-confident young woman who radiated joy. This was his daughter! *His*! Perhaps Misty was some kind of saint, an angel, a–

Sonny was brought back to earth by George's mobile playing *Rule Britannia*; Belinda had pointed out that he'd need it.

'Yes!'

'*Weetwood?*'

'No, Regina, it's Sonny Start.'

'*Where's Weetwood? I told Weetwood that at nine o'clock he–*'

'Now keep cool, Regina, and listen. He's sick, *real* sick. The old fool went walking in the sun all day and is delirious with sunstroke. He's in bed. He's–'

'*I don't believe you. If this is some trick–*'

'I *swear*! Please don't get mad. We're all ready to do the drop, OK? His sister's here and she's given me full authority to–'

'*His **sister**! Scheisse! Look, Start, I've got the boy–*'

'James? So–'

'*All three kids are dead if–*'

'I swear we're on the level. What the hell are we supposed to do if Weetwood gets sick? I've got the ransoms – Weetwood's and mine – right here, OK? One drop's easier than two anyway, isn't it?'

Ursula managed a brief smile: of course it was; that was exactly what she'd planned, except that she'd wanted Weetwood to make the drop and not Start. In her bones she'd felt that the older Englishman was more likely to do as he was told: Americans were devious – too clever for their own good. Be that as it may, at least she wouldn't have to persuade them to work together! She rapidly weighed up the pros and cons of going ahead but with Start substituted for Weetwood. She bit her lip: it had to work – it just had to.

'Regina? You still there? Come on, give me the goddam instructions. ... They're OK – the kids – aren't they?

'*Yes! Don't worry! Now listen! Your car is the yellow Suzuki Vitara? And the roof's down?*'

'Correct.'

'*And you're wearing a white shirt?*'

'Sure – just like you said.'

'*OK. Drive to Sant Francesc. You know where that is?*'

'The *pueblo* up the road–'

'*Go to the junction with the La Savina highway and take a right to Sant Ferran–*'

'I drove through there today.'

'*Don't interrupt! ... Keep straight on, and after a few hundred metres on the left there's a supermarket. OK? Park in front of it and wait. Bring the money and come alone. You're under constant surveillance, Start, so nobody had better be following, OK? You've got twenty minutes to get there. Now move!*'

The line went dead. Within seconds, Sonny was speeding away from the hotel, realizing as he raced through the gears that his tour of the island had been a godsend, otherwise after years of driving automatics the Suzuki's gearbox and stick shift would have been a nightmare.

Behind the net curtains of the Cala Beltran's lounge, Belinda and Gwen watched him go; each said a silent prayer. Trev, however, missed the departure: he was still on the phone to London listening to a précis of the first instalment of *Goblin in a Lather*, Beryl Weetwood's 'autobiography', which, thanks to the wonders of what her husband called 'electronic wizardry' and Diane Bradbury's creativity, would be appearing in *The News of The World* within a few hours. It was dynamite: the anticipated input from Formentera would be icing on the cake. In the background, Trev heard Crabtree suggest a game of charades 'to help pass the time'.

Sonny almost missed the supermarket: programmed by North American standards, he'd expected something with a vast parking lot out front. He squealed to a stop, invoking howls of abuse in Italian from two Vespa riders, and reversed back. Secreted behind a stone wall on rising ground a few hundred metres away, and with her VW parked well out of sight up a dirt track, Ursula watched with a sense of triumph. She had an excellent vantage point: even in the dark, she could see any approaching traffic with their headlights all the way back down the road to Sant Ferran – and almost a kilometre in the other direction.

She waited five minutes. The road was quiet: just a few cars passed in each direction; a cyclist ambled towards Es Calo; two scooters buzzed noisily into Sant Ferran. Nothing obviously suspicious.

All of a sudden, Sonny got out of the car and, leaving the door open, lit a cigarette. Furiously, she pressed 'redial'; in the still evening air, she could clearly hear the unmistakable bleating of a mobile.

'*Start!*' he snapped.

'I didn't tell you to get out of the car – or to light a cigarette.' She watched him turn and look in all directions.

'*You're here? ... We're doing it here, Regina?*'

'Shut up! We see *everything*, Start. Just remember that. And no more cigarettes, OK? And stay in the car at *all* times unless I order you otherwise.'

'*OK, OK! You didn't say that before. I'm sorry. I–*'

'Go back to San Francesc. At the junction for Cala Beltran and Cap de Barbaria, pull into the side of the road and wait. You've got five minutes.'

With a chuckle, she watched him dive into the Suzuki, reverse like a madman into the highway, and tear off back the way he'd come; she had no intention of following him. A few more cars and another scooter passed along the main road, but no one seemed to be in any kind of hurry. If Start was working with the police, there was certainly no sign of them. She pressed the redial button again. Now was the time to bluff; it would have been easier had there been two of them as originally planned, with Rory helping to keep watch.

'*I'm at the turning, Regina. Now what?*'

'Drive back to the supermarket at Sant Ferran, but go straight on and continue for six kilometres to the village of Es Calo. Turn off the road and park in front of the call boxes at the entrance to the village. There's a bar at the harbour called Can Toni. Take the money in with you. You've got fifteen minutes!' She was beginning to enjoy all this – it was like the movies, and really very easy.

After six minutes, she watched Start drive past in his Vitara; again, there was no obvious indication that anyone was following him. She trotted across the rocky ground to the VW and made a quick check on Rory; manacled and gagged, he looked truly pathetic.

'*Mein Got,*' she sniggered, remembering his sexual activities that afternoon, '*sic transit gloria.*'

355

As she drove sedately down the Es Calo road, Ursula wondered how Mark was getting on. As soon as she'd finished her first call to Start, she'd spoken to him and given the command to take to the air. Was his little plane now flying over the Mediterranean on its authorized flight to Ibiza? What if he'd changed his mind, panicked, or double-crossed her? Had she placed too much trust in him, a man she barely knew?

Shortly before Es Calo, she pulled into the side of the road, lit a much-needed cigarette, and called Start. He came on the line after thirty seconds.

'*Sorry! I've had to come outside – bad reception – and too much noise. OK, now what?*'

'Wait there until I call again.'

'*We're doing it here? ... Hello? ... Regina?*' But the line was dead.

Sonny looked around and wondered who might be watching him. The customers inside the bar had the bearing, speech and clothing of local fishermen. They were probably recounting tales of the size of their catches, or cracking jokes about the tourists seated on the terrace; avoiding the heat and choking smoke, they could savour the moonlit panorama of a few old whitewashed houses clustered around a tiny inlet hardly bigger than a good-sized pool. He spied a table of two handsome men and a beautiful girl, all laughing and playing cards. They seemed so happy, there by the water's edge on this balmy evening. If only the girl were Misty and the two men were Paolo and himself. ... But maybe *they* were watching *him*.

Out on the highway, Ursula chugged past Es Calo. Spotting the Suzuki by the call boxes, she drove on around the bend and up the hill towards El Pilar. Every few seconds she glanced in the mirror, but nothing appeared to be following her. She was now convinced that neither the local police nor any superior force could possibly be on alert: the Spanish would never be able to operate without flashing lights, wailing sirens and squealing tyres. But surely even a low-profile operation couldn't be concealed on Formentera ... could it?

To her relief, the *pueblo* of El Pilar appeared dead – neither sight nor sound of a living soul; in typical Balearic fashion, every window was concealed by closed shutters. Yet, as she rounded the corner after the tiny church of Nuestra Señora, she felt a great surge of power energizing every part of her body: there, dead ahead, two and a half kilometres distant, stood the great lighthouse, its towering bulk seemingly glowing in the moonlight. Was she imagining it, or had the van suddenly found a new lease of life? Within minutes she was parking it at the back of the dark, deserted café.

The stillness struck her as she got out and began to make her way over to the walls of the lighthouse compound: on every one of her many previous visits to Punta des Far, there'd always been at least a light breeze blowing. But tonight, there was not a breath of wind. It was odd ... disconcerting. She looked through the gates and scanned the ground between herself and the huge entrance doors to the lighthouse keepers' quarters. She knew that at least one of the employees would be in residence, but nothing visible or audible hinted at their presence. Whoever was at home was probably curled up in front of the TV.

Ursula returned swiftly to the van, unlocked the rear doors, and switched on the interior light. She'd expected Rory to be gripped by fear – even hysterical; to her surprise, he appeared remarkably self-controlled. In truth, he was terrified, but, during his enforced trip around the island, he'd resolved that if he was going to die, he'd do so with some semblance of dignity: he'd experienced enough bullies during his schooldays to know that what they loved most was the cowering, cringing victim. And in essence, that's all Ursula was – a very nasty bully. It would undoubtedly be the last thing he ever did, but he was determined to hold his head high: he wouldn't give her the satisfaction of grovelling at her feet, pleading for mercy.

Alas, when Ursula tossed a key at him and barked the order to release himself, all Rory's notions of a chivalrous and dignified departure from this earth instantly evaporated; his free hand trembled so much that he could barely pick up the key.

'*Schnell*!' she hissed.

'I can't do it,' he tried to say through his gag, but the words were unintelligible to Ursula. Desperately playing for time, he fumbled with the lock: *There's always a chance of escape – or even rescue – however remote. I–*

'Oh fuck!' he cried as the handcuffs sprang open.

'At last, you idiot! Now get out!'

With only a moment's hesitation, Rory crawled out of the van, Ursula backing slowly away as if he was a wild animal. It was just as he'd feared – Punta des Far, and she was going to shoot him and dump his body over the cliff. He wanted to weep: his life had been a succession of humiliations and disasters, and now, just when he had everything to live for – the relationship he'd established with Caroline was almost too good to be true – he was going to die and–

'*Move*!' commanded Ursula, waving her gun in the direction of the cliff edge.

As he stumbled to his place of execution, the goose pimples and shivering he'd experienced in the van gave way to intense sweating and a mouth devoid of saliva. He should make a run for it, he kept telling himself. What did he have to lose? She might even miss, firing at a moving target in the moonlight. And the shot might attract the attention of the lighthouse people. The gun might jam or–

But then there was no more ground in front of him, just a sickening blackness and, far below, the glint of moonlight on a strangely calm sea.

'Jump!' A wave of excitement shot through Ursula's body, coupled with a glorious sense of omnipotence. 'Jump!' she repeated.

Rory shook his head. 'Go to hell!' he shouted through the gag.

Guessing the muffled words, Ursula thrust the gun violently into the centre of his back, and watched him topple over the edge. She'd expected a terrible scream, trailing away to silence as the distance between them increased, but to her disappointment she heard nothing – not a sound. She peered over hesitantly.

It was as if he'd been sucked into the vacuum of outer space.

# CHAPTER 32

At Es Calo, Sonny was getting worried: more than thirty minutes had passed since Regina's last call. Something must have gone wrong. Sitting conspicuously alone with his two briefcases at a corner table on the terrace, he stubbed out a sixth cigarette in the ashtray and drained his glass of mineral water. He was taking another cigarette out of the pack when the mobile rang.

'Regina? What's happening?' He glanced at the three happy card players, but they seemed engrossed in their game.

'*Calm down, Mr Start. If you panic–*'

'I'm *not* panicking.'

'*If you panic, you might make mistakes, and that wouldn't do at all, would it? Now go to your car, flash the headlights three times, and then drive back to the main road. Turn left and follow the signs for El Pilar. When you get there, pull in to the side of the road opposite the little church and wait. You have ten minutes.*'

Parked opposite the Miramar restaurant on the escarpment high above Es Calo, Ursula had a panoramic vista of both the tiny fishing village and the main island road almost as far back as Sant Ferran, along which she could make out the headlamps and red tail lights of just half a dozen vehicles. There were three flashes from the spot where she knew Start was parked. Within seconds, he was back on the main road and lost to view; his departure didn't seem to prompt any additional or unusual activity.

With the decrepit VW's engine screaming, Ursula completed her very last ascent to El Pilar and continued down the road to Punta des Far, the accelerator pressed to the floor. Some five hundred metres from the lighthouse, she took a right onto a dirt track that led to a few remote farmsteads to the south. After a short distance, the track twisted sharply to the left, where, safely hidden from the main road, she parked. Minutes later, after crossing a field of rough pasture, she regained the lighthouse road. Gingerly, she peered over the drystone wall: save for the few lights of El Pilar away to her left, and the regular flash of the lighthouse, there was no sign of life; only the chirping of cicadas and the tinkling of goat bells some way off disturbed the silence. She pressed her mobile's redial button with a confident jab.

'You're in position opposite the church, Mr Start?'

'Yeah. Look, how much longer are we going to play this cat and mouse game? You must be convinced by now that I'm not being tailed. I'm on my own, Regina, you must believe–'

'Shut it, Start, just shut it!' Ursula sighed deeply into the phone. 'I will *not* tell you again.' She paused and looked intently up the road towards El Pilar. 'I'm going to count to three, and then I want you to flash your headlights again – twice – OK? One, two, *three*.' Her heart raced. There they were – flash, flash – exactly on cue. 'Good boy! Now I want you to continue driving down the road nice and slowly. I'll stay on the line. Now *go*!'

Sonny held the wheel with one hand, keeping the phone pressed to his right ear. His tension was mounting, and the spectre of the tall, tower-like structure looming ahead – a lighthouse? – was not helping. 'I need to know Misty's OK,' he pleaded, '– that they're *all* OK. I want to talk–'

'You're in no position to demand *any*thing!' barked Ursula, her eyes glued to the approaching headlights. 'They're not with me anyway,' she added thoughtlessly. 'I mean–'

'*What! Where are they?*'

'They're safe – OK?'

Suddenly realizing Start was only about a hundred metres away, Ursula ducked down. As the Suzuki slowly passed, she heard him ask, '*But they are on the island, aren't they?*' She ignored his question, pushed herself back up, and followed the car's rear lamps as it proceeded towards the lighthouse.

'Stop!' she screeched – louder than she'd intended.

There was a squeal of tyres as Sonny braked violently to a halt. He turned his head in all directions: plainly, Regina – or at least one of her colleagues – had to be very close. It was a desolate spot, and the lighthouse dead ahead of him compounded the eeriness and his sense of isolation. 'This must be the place,' he whispered softly; despite the heat and intense humidity, he was shivering. 'Jesus,' he hissed, 'get a grip!'

Behind her screen of stones, Ursula watched and listened: still just the incessant background noise of cicadas and goat bells. '*Sehrt gut*,' she said softly.

Sonny heard the words down the line and froze: although faint, the voice sounded cruel ... evil.

Ursula could feel herself relaxing: everything was going rather well; she even managed a smile. 'Start, there's a wooden gate in the stone wall just to your right. Get out of the car – nice and slowly please – and put the cases with the money over it and leave them on the ground on the other side. Then get back in the car and drive straight to your hotel – no stopping, no phone calls, *nada*. OK? And all the money had better be there, Start, as agreed or–'

'*It's there. Don't worry. ... And the kids? When do we get them back?*'

'Well, provided you and Weetwood have stuck to our little bargain, you can expect a call to your room at the Cala Beltran within the hour.'

'*But how can I be sure–? If you've double-crossed me, I'll track you down and–*'

'Get going, Start! If you're not back at the hotel in thirty minutes from' – Ursula hesitated, pretending to look at her watch – 'from *now*, then they're dead.' She terminated the call and grinned as she watched him dive out of the car with what looked like two large briefcases; even in the moonlight his actions indicated that they were fairly heavy. Could 2,100,000 dollars in 100-dollar bills really be such a weight? She and Rory had experimented with some scales and thousands of sheets of paper: 1,000,000 dollars should weigh about eight kilos. Had they miscalculated? Was there something else in the bags? Or was Start–?

But realizing that the drop had been completed, Ursula interrupted her train of thought. Almost before she had time to re-conceal herself, the Suzuki was shooting past her, back to El Pilar.

The engine noise died away; after a couple of minutes, the red glow of the tail lights disappeared. Ursula stood leaning against the wall, her heart thumping. If the police or any henchmen privately employed by Start – or Weetwood for that matter – were going to try and jump her, then this was the moment. The seconds ticked by. Keeping to her side of the wall, she finally made her first tentative steps towards the briefcases. She saw them from about twenty metres away – just as the sudden inky black darkness caused her to stop in her tracks and look up.

The moon had gone, obliterated by a mass of cloud. And, as Ursula stared apprehensively, the hint of a breeze rustled the leaves of some nearby bushes. Then the cicadas fell silent, as if they'd been a mere recording which someone had switched off. She felt insufferably hot, but couldn't tell whether it was simply her nerves or a genuine increase in the air temperature.

'Please, God,' she pleaded in German, 'not a storm – not now – not tonight. It wasn't forecast. You can't!'

She ran the final few metres to the cases. After another scan of the road, she switched on the small torch she'd brought with her from the van. She opened Start's impressive briefcase first. Its contents looked right: there were used dollar bills of the correct denomination – piles of them – piles and piles and piles. She fell to her knees and examined them more closely.

She pulled out a few and held them up to the torch. They had to be genuine, they just had to be. She dug down deeper and pulled out some more: they were the same. Then she opened the other briefcase. Another sigh of relief: Weetwood and Start had not tried to be clever. It would take a detailed check to be sure, of course, but her random examination ought to have revealed any duplicity.

Ursula peeked back over the wall: everything was still peaceful. If the police or any other undesirables were rushing to apprehend her, they had only one access route – the road from El Pilar, almost two kilometres distant. She'd have plenty of time to see them coming and make her escape into the pinewoods to the south. All she had to do now was to sit tight and await Mark's arrival. It was nearly eleven; he should be almost there.

She looked up again. The blanket of cloud was moving eastwards; it now filled most of the sky. But even without moonlight illuminating the island's landscape, Mark should still be able to locate his runway: all he had to do was to line up the lighthouse with El Pilar's little row of street lamps and he'd be home and dry – provided, that is, a storm didn't break in the meantime.

'*Scheisse*!' she cursed. 'Where the hell are you?'

She listened intently for any sound, be it a car, an aeroplane or – heaven forbid! – the distant rumble of thunder.

*

Relaxing on the Fonda Pepe's narrow, crowded terrace, Chuck and Bob were in agreement that a storm might be brewing: the intense humidity, the sticky heat, and the lack of wind were all telltale signs.

'This reminds me of my high school days in Galveston when a hurricane was threatening out in the Gulf,' Bob said.

Chuck groaned. 'Oh shit! What about my day on the beach tomorrow?'

'It may blow over,' Bob suggested, swirling the ice around in his glass of mineral water as he made another critical examination of the 'weirdoes' around them. 'Hey, Chuck, do you think they have Häagen-Dazs any place on this fucking island?'

Chuck looked at him disapprovingly. 'I doubt it. And Sonny wouldn't like to hear you speak like that.'

Bob pulled a face. 'Well, I'm hot. Let's go for a drive, cool off and find some *real* ice cream.'

*

Mark knew he was a good pilot, but he'd never tried anything like this before, not even in the University Air Squadron. He had to be crazy – landing on a cliff top in the middle of the night! And now it looked as if there might be a storm to contend with – so much for the Algerian Met Office! The turbulence was bad and getting worse, but at least he'd found the bloody island. He shot a glance at Ginger, the imaginary co-pilot who kept him company and helped to steady his nerves.

'I say, Ginger, old bean, that was a jolly spiffing spot of navigation. I'll mention it to the C.O. when we get back.'

'Piece of cake, ol' man – anyone could have done it. But your flying of this old kite has been positively wizard, particularly in view of your injuries.'

Mark returned to scratching his mosquito bites.

'Ginger, is that our bally lighthouse down there flashing away, or is it the chap over there at nine o'clock – or the blighter flashing away at four o'clock?'

'Pretty sure it's the first one, Captain. Count the seconds between the flashes, ol' man. One, two, three, four. Yah, that's the one, and I'll eat my hat if those twinkling lights aren't this bally El Pilar place.'

Mark had told Ursula that unless the winds were really bad, he didn't want to come in to land from the east, flying right over the lighthouse: he was concerned about the engine noise alerting the keepers, who, no doubt, were equipped with radio telephones and other hot lines to the coastguard, police, navy and God only knew who else. And in order to clear the lighthouse, his approach altitude would be such as to force him to land and come to a standstill at a point much closer to El Pilar and, therefore, much further from her preferred drop point.

And so it was that with mounting excitement and a churning in her stomach, Ursula heard the engine and watched the navigation lights of the little plane as it came in from the south-east. It circled over El Pilar, lined up the two short parallel rows of the village's only street lamps with the flashing beam of the Faro de Formentera, and, with landing lights blazing, descended to the tarmac.

It was a perfect landing, and, throttling back, Mark let out a roar of delight.

'Well done, Captain! Bloody good show!'

With surprising speed, Ursula opened the gate and dashed out into the road, waving frantically as the plane rushed towards her.

'I say, Dumpy,' said Ginger, 'there's a lady in distress in the middle of the damned fairway.'

'That's no lady, Ginger, that's my partner in crime. Hope she's got the bally dosh!'

Ursula ran forward clutching her small suitcase, and Mark slammed on the brakes, bringing the plane to a halt just few metres from her.

'Taxi, madam?' he yelled above the engine noise, sliding back his window. 'I say, old fruit, that's not much luggage! Where's the bloody loot? It's not all in there, surely?'

'Get out and help! The bags are heavy!'

Leaving the engine running, Mark dashed with her towards the gate. She waved her torch frantically at the two briefcases. 'Hurry!' she shouted. He grabbed one in each hand – he too was surprised by their weight – and sprinted back to the plane. It was while he was lifting them into the cockpit that Ursula saw the lights: a vehicle was coming towards them from El Pilar.

'*Nein, nein, **nein!*** she shrieked, pointing up the road.

Mark swiftly hoisted himself into the cockpit and grabbed his door, but Ursula already had hold of it with one hand; in the other was a pistol.

'You weren't thinking of leaving me, I hope?'

'Don't be stupid! Get in the other side! *Quick!*'

Grabbing her suitcase, Ursula took one terrified look at the roaring propeller and dashed round the rear of the plane. It was only when she reached the open passenger door that she looked back. The approaching vehicle seemed dangerously close.

'For Christ's sake – *get in, woman!*'

*

Having 'done' La Savina, Es Pujols, Sant Francesc and Sant Ferran earlier in the day, Chuck and Bob knew that the delights of Häagen-Dazs could not be procured at any of them. That was why they'd turned left towards Es Calo when their Suzuki reached the main road in Sant Ferran. In fact, they never even realized that they'd passed Es Calo until, as they unwittingly ascended towards El Pilar, they concluded that they were climbing up into some mountains.

Their request for Häagen-Dazs at the Miramar restaurant drew a blank. In the deserted one-street village of El Pilar, Chuck thought they should turn back, especially in view of the rapidly enveloping cloud cover and increasing wind.

'They got Häagen-Dazs in Ibiza,' said Bob with a hint of desperation.

'How do you know?'

'I saw an ad at the airport.'

'Oh!' Glancing suspiciously at Bob, Chuck added, 'So what?'

'Ibiza's not far.'

'Are you crazy? ... Anyway, the last ferry went hours ago.'

'Oh yeah. I forgot.'

They were debating whether to proceed down the long straight road that led towards what might be a lighthouse, when, to their surprise, an aeroplane flew right over their heads and appeared to land some way between them and the lighthouse.

A door across the street opened, and an old man looked out. Assuming they were responsible for the noise, he gave them a fierce stare and growled something unintelligible.

'I thought this island didn't have an airfield,' Chuck said.

'Me too.' Bob removed his baseball cap and scratched his head.

Chuck thumped the dashboard. 'Hey! Perhaps there's a terminal with an all-night diner – or even an air taxi service to Ibiza. Let's go see.'

*

Shortly before landing on Formentera, Mark had radioed Ibiza Tower and told air traffic control that there was a change of plan: he'd just heard from Algiers that the Algerian businessman whose yacht was to have put in at Ibiza and whom he was then to fly to Malaga, had sailed on to Mallorca. And as he had a client who needed to be flown first thing in the morning from Algiers to Oran, he was turning for home. Algiers Tower had got the same message; Omar's friends had promised to procure some supporting documentation.

All that remained to be explained were the strange movements on Ibiza Tower's radar as the plane had circled over Formentera for the purpose of returning to Algiers, and its subsequent brief disappearance. In fact, fearing a crash, Ibiza was already attempting to contact the island's emergency authorities stationed at their headquarters in Sant Francesc. But no one was answering the phone.

Now, as Mark accelerated his craft down the road to Punta des Far, he listened on his headphones to the incessant demands from Ibiza Tower for him to make contact. He'd do so as soon as the plane was in the air and tell some story about an inexplicable but temporary technical problem which had put the plane into a spin and had brought him down almost to sea level.

Ahead, the great flashing beacon loomed ever larger. Ursula gripped the little suitcase on her lap containing the remnants of her long stay on the island – indeed her long life – and experienced an intense wave of terror. '*Was ist los?*' she cried. 'Take off for God's sake! *Take off!*'

'It's this bloody tail wind!' yelled Mark. The end-of-summer storm had gathered momentum with extraordinary rapidity, albeit the torrential rain had yet to materialise. There was a sudden gust and the plane swerved to the left. A terrible grating noise filled the air as the port wing tip clipped a stone wall, but Mark swiftly got the plane back to the centre of the road.

The lighthouse now seemed frighteningly close, the vast stone edifice dominating the cockpit windscreen. Mark pulled back on the controls, and

365

as the plane rose steeply, he put it into a sharp turn to the right to avoid hitting the structure. But then, everything – land, sea and sky – was dazzlingly illuminated by an awesome bolt of lightning that scored a direct hit on the lighthouse. Ursula screamed. Simultaneously, a colossal force hit the plane – as if the outstretched hand of a giant was pushing the craft back to earth.

In German, Ursula screeched: 'We're going to die!' Staring in horror out of her side window, she saw the road rushing up towards her – with a vehicle speeding directly beneath them! And then she looked forward and saw the gates to the lighthouse – a man standing behind them frozen with fear – like a rabbit picked out by headlights at full beam.

Yet, still with all his wits about him, Mark skilfully got the plane over the south-west corner of the compound's perimeter wall. Just another few centimetres, and it would never have touched the cables that supplied the electricity to power the mighty beacon. There was a series of flashes and explosions as the cables came down and the plane flipped onto its back. It flew on over the cliff top and then dived.

Distracted by the spectacle of the plane's somersault, Bob didn't have enough road to stop the Suzuki in time. It was still doing some twenty miles per hour as it crashed through the compound's gates and came to rest in the scrubby garden before the keeper's residence. The keeper, who'd had the foresight at the last moment to dive into a yucca, fired off expletives like a machine gun as he limped back to his quarters to ensure that, with the loss of mains power, his emergency generators had started automatically. Minutes later, he was phoning everyone he could think of for assistance, both in Formentera and Ibiza.

Anxious to ascertain what had happened to the plane, and ignoring the damage to their vehicle – it was significant – Chuck and Bob jumped over the devasted gates and sprinted past the Jules Verne monument with all the athletic vigour they could muster. It was a miracle that Bob stopped himself in time and managed to grab Chuck, who was just a few paces behind him. As the storm raged around them, they stood a few metres from the cliff edge and peered into the void beyond, fearful of being blasted to the plane's watery grave.

Pulling Chuck further back, Bob yelled: 'We'd better phone the boss!'

'Thanks for saving my life!' roared Chuck. Then he gave Bob a crushing bear hug and a passionate kiss.

# CHAPTER 33

With the wind rising, and the whistling of the pines growing louder, conversation through the wall between Caroline and her fellow captives had become ever more difficult. Indeed, after several hours of mutual exchanges of somewhat hollow-sounding words of optimism, all their voices were hoarse and painful. And without electric light, the darkness in the two rooms compounded their unspoken anxieties.

Caroline was experiencing a bewildering mixture of deeply conflicting emotions, tossing her like a fallen leaf in an autumnal wind. She'd convinced herself that the best thing to hope for in life was to be spared any form of intense pleasure or happiness. Both were curses – the devil's tools – guaranteed sooner or later to generate the worst pain and suffering imaginable. Certainly, her pre-Formentera life had been dull, drab and dreary – even pathetic – yet, never having known anything better or different, she *had* been content, hadn't she? She'd certainly never suffered bouts of depression or sobbed herself to sleep. On the other hand, the Blackberrys' apparent kindness and love – not to mention Misty's and Rory's – had brought her nothing but tragedy and misery, for it was they who'd invoked her fleeting glimpses of this hitherto unknown world of excess with its intense friendships, passionate romances and sexual fulfilment.

'I wish I'd never set eyes on this horrible place,' Caroline had kept repeating. But then she would feel even more distressed: after all, even if she'd never met Gwen, Tom, Misty or Rory, she would have still come to Formentera. And so, to blame them for any of the grief which she was now experiencing must make her the most horrid, selfish person on earth.

It didn't take her long to find a new scapegoat – Pongo Pangbourne – whereupon the whole tortured process began again. The fact that Rory was a better candidate as the devil's agent, and that without his involvement with Ursula her trip to Formentera might have been less problematic, was conveniently censored by her brain, such was the power of the demon Love. The blessed Rory had simply been corrupted by the she-devil.

But shortly before the first flash of lightning filtered through the shutters' slats, even this censorship cracked under the strain. Within minutes, Caroline's undying love for Rory was converted into a loathing of at least equal, if not greater, intensity. Shocked, she began weeping.

Then she shouted insults at herself for thinking such wickedness about a man who had probably gone to his execution. ... On reflection, however, hadn't he really brought it upon himself?

Finally, she became convinced that she was having a mental breakdown. Thus, her original thesis about the evils of happiness and so forth had to be correct. ... No! Incorrect! She was unbalanced. ... No! *Correct* because – because...

Only after the fourth lightning flash did it occur to her that she might have seen something shiny on the floor. Yet such was the ferocity of her own internal storm that she didn't dwell on the matter. But after several more flashes, a hint of inexplicable curiosity registered in her tortured mind. She stared at the spot where she'd seen the reflection and waited for the next burst of light. When it came a few seconds later, she couldn't believe what she thought she'd seen in that brief instant. It was impossible – a trick of the light, perhaps even a hallucination. As deafening thunder shook the villa, a burst of lightning bolts in rapid succession confirmed that she had indeed seen two small keys on a ring – keys which had certainly not been there during daylight. Logically, they had to be the keys which Ursula had picked up off the floor just before departing with Rory. Hadn't she put them in a pocket in her jeans, though? Caroline tried to recall the scene, but she'd been focused on Rory. In her fumbling, had Ursula missed the pocket? Or was there a hole in it? If they'd dropped on the tiled floor, surely Ursula would at least have heard the clatter?

Another lightning bolt revealed that the keys lay near the furthermost edge of a small carpet masquerading as a Persian rug. Yet Caroline doubted she'd be able to reach them. If only she could somehow swing her free leg outwards and get a toe – or, even better, her heel – to reach the rug's tasselled border. She might then be able to drag it towards her. She considered shouting her plan to James and Misty above the noise of the storm, but finally concluded that there was no point in building up their hopes only to have them dashed. So, she removed the loafer from her right foot – she'd been wearing the pair since Sunday night's outing to the Fonda Pepe – stretched her leg until it ached, and pushed herself forward as best she could with her hands behind her back and her palms outstretched on the floor, each flash of lightning helping to guide her.

The closest tassel was now just millimetres away; time seemed to stand still as she began to anticipate failure. But then she felt it! The hard skin under her big toe caught some threads, and she pulled with all her might. The rug moved a fraction. She tried again, and got a better grip. After a few more attempts, it was close enough for her to grab it with one hand, and the keys came within her grasp.

'Bloody brilliant!' she shouted.

Aided by the lightning, Caroline briskly pushed one key into her ankle shackle's lock. With bated breath, she turned it, and the shackle sprang open. For a few seconds, she stared in disbelief at her liberated limb. Then she let out the loudest whoop of joy of her life, prompting cries of alarm from her neighbours. So, the other key must be for Rory's handcuffs. Did Ursula need it to unlock them? Might she return at any moment? Did she have a duplicate? Caroline tried to stand up, but so numb were her joints that she almost fell over and had to steady herself against the radiator. After a few delicious stretching exercises, she shuffled to the wall separating the two bedrooms and thumped on it fiercely, shouting, 'I'm free! I'm free!'

Startled, James and Misty gripped each other in the darkness; it was their first tactile gesture.

After locating the light switch, and with her voice straining, Caroline shouted a description of both the method of her release and her room to the fellow captives. But there was clearly no way she could batter down the door, and the windowless bathroom was a waste of time. She finally opened the bedroom window, pushed back the shutters, and contemplated the wild scene outside. To her surprise, however, there was no rain, but judging from the satanic clouds so terrifyingly illuminated by the lightning, the deluge had to be imminent.

She searched for a convenient method of descent to the garden: a drainpipe, some climbing vegetation, an adjacent tree – anything. It appeared, however, that the key was to be her only luck that night. And the room itself was almost bare; there weren't even any sheets or curtains to tie together. She contemplated shouting to attract attention, but swiftly realised that it would be pointless: Rory had graphically described the villa's isolation. Moreover, any noise she might manage to make would be drowned by the raging tempest.

'I'm going to jump!' she finally yelled through the wall.

'Don't be a fool, Caroline!' begged James.

'You'll break your goddam neck!' shrieked Misty.

Despite their increasingly frantic pleas, Caroline began to crawl cautiously out onto the window ledge. But, although she'd certainly lost much weight since her arrival on the island, the window was barely large enough for her to squeeze through. She was half way out when a fierce gust of wind blew back one of the shutters, hitting her a terrific blow to the forehead. Stunned, and with a yelp of jabbing pain, she toppled and fell.

During her earlier brief reconnaissance, and notwithstanding the lightning, Caroline had failed to identify the precise nature of the flora beneath the window; in her state of high tension, it just looked like a very large bush. The prickly pear did indeed break her fall to a degree, but she paid dearly, her flesh being pierced by hundreds of vicious needles; even James and Misty heard the screams when she impacted with the succulent.

'Maybe she's just sprained an ankle,' Misty suggested. 'Maybe she's just winded and can't shout loud enough.'

'Knowing her, she's probably broken a leg – both legs – her back. Oh God!'

'James, you have to remember she's not that tub of lard you used to know. She's lost pounds and been pretty athletic and–'

'I know, I know! I did see her earlier today – remember? ... And I don't think it's very nice to refer to my sister as "a tub of lard".'

'For Christ's sake, I was just trying to make a point!'

'Well, all right, but ... I'm sorry. I'm very worried. She could be out there badly–'

'I'm worried too. It was very brave of her to jump. ... She's a great kid, you know.'

'Yes, I know.'

'Do you? I don't think you know her at all.'

'And I suppose you do? She is *my* sister, Misty.'

'Sure. And when did you last have a conversation with her?'

'Is this a competition or something?'

'Don't be childish.'

With a view to changing the subject, James began to tug again on the chain that secured him to the central heating pipe. 'Let's try one more time. Perhaps if we both pull with every ounce of energy left in us, we might be able to rip it from the wall or snap the chain, or–'

'It's hopeless and you know it.'

James groaned. 'Why do you have to be so negative about *every*thing?'

'I'm not.'

'You *are*. Whatever happened to the Misty Start who pulled me out of my self-indulgent apathy back in England, the Misty full of optimism and–?'

'A German "aristocratic" pig crapped on her – and she got kidnapped.'

In the momentary burst of illumination as another bolt of lightning earthed itself nearby, James caught a glimpse of the sadness in Misty's eyes.

'I'm sorry, Misty. I'm so ... so insensitive. I keep forgetting that you've had a terrifying experience for days and days, and that before that ...' His voice trailed away.

'Let's just forget it, James.'

'Sure. Sorry.'

'I wish I was dead,' Misty muttered. 'I wish Ursula *had* shot me. I hope I'm never rescued from this dump. I've got nothing to live for and nobody would give a shit if I died.' She started weeping.

'Misty ... *please* – please don't cry.' With some difficulty, James stretched his free arm around her shoulders and pulled her close to him. 'And don't talk like that. It's wicked ... and untrue. I'd be devastated if anything happened to you. And Caroline obviously loves you too.' Brotherly, James kissed her on the cheek. 'Come on, everything's going to be fine. ... Caroline's probably OK. ... Hey, I bet someone will want to make a film about this mad caper. What do you think?' He kissed her again, but this time in the darkness his lips met an eye, salty with tears. He kissed the other one. 'They'd probably want you to play yourself. ... Who would you choose to play me?'

Misty tried hard to stifle a sob. 'I ... er ... I don't know.'

'Sure you do – you're crazy about films. Remember that discussion we had over dinner at Bobbins about *The Piano*? Christ, you got mad! My father virtually accused you of assault.'

Between sniffles, Misty said: 'Did he? I ... I don't remember. ... I'm sorry I messed you around.'

'What do you mean?'

'You know, seducing you when you were so vulnerable. ... Jesus! I wish I could blow my nose.'

'I think I've got a handkerchief in my pocket.' James tried the right side of his shorts, but it was empty. 'Must be the left.' A complicated manoeuvre produced results. 'Here – have a good blow.'

'Thanks. ... And then I made those promises to write and phone. Well, I did write ... eventually.'

'Yeah, I know.'

'I still don't understand why you came to Formentera – I mean after ... after Cap-Ferrat and ... and what they said in that lousy paper.'

'I only found out about all that when I got here. Didn't I say that earlier on? ... You didn't believe that crap about me, did you?'

Misty blew her nose again and dabbed at her eyes. 'Of course not!'

'Anyway, I came because of you.'

'Me?'

'Misty, weren't you listening to *anything* I said this afternoon?'

'Sure! You just said something like you wanted a break – a vacation or something ... somewhere peaceful away from the madness of Cap-Ferrat.'

'I said it was because of *your* phone call, the way *you* sounded.'

'The way *I* sounded? What do you mean?'

'Oh, come on – *you* know.'

'What?'

James paused. 'Like, well ... like you still ... you still felt something for me. Obviously, I was wrong. ... God! I hope Caroline *is* OK.'

371

They were silent for a few moments.

'James?'

'Yes.'

'Why didn't you kiss me when we were first alone today? And what did you mean when you said just a minute ago that Caroline obviously loves me "*too*"?'

'I ... Why didn't *you* kiss *me*?'

'I asked first.'

'Well ... because ... because I realized I'd made one hell of a mistake. Because it was obvious you didn't feel ... well, you didn't feel the same way I felt about you.'

'You mean you thought you were still in love with me when you–?'

'Yes. I did. I do. I worship you. ... I can't help it. ... I'm sorry.'

Misty sighed. 'Well, you've got a weird way of showing it.'

'I don't get this. You said just then – I mean ... Did you *want* me to kiss you – when we – after my balls-up of a rescue?'

'Of course I did.'

James pressed his mouth against what he hoped were Misty's lips and found her nose instead. Then he hit the mark with such a burst of passion that the back of Misty's head banged against the radiator.

'Hell! I'm sorry.'

'Shush! Don't stop.'

Just as the intense physical contact – for which they'd both so long craved – began to dissipate all the doubts and suspicions generated during the day, the door burst open. Misty, almost blinded by the light flooding in from the corridor beyond, let out a blood-curdling scream. It was immediately surpassed by the sinister figure silhouetted in the doorway.

*

Dazed, bruised and bleeding, it had taken Caroline some time to extricate herself from the horrors of the prickly pear; in the process, even more needles had penetrated her flesh. Walking as best she could on the edges of her feet, she'd painfully made her way to the kitchen door. Mercifully, it was unlocked: in a final display of Teutonic order, Ursula had left all *Casa Bayreuth*'s keys – meticulously labelled by the villa's German owners – in a neat row on the kitchen table.

'I'm sorry,' Caroline repeated, 'but I couldn't help screaming when *you* screamed, Misty. Anyway, I thought you'd have both heard me hobbling and groaning up the damned stairs – and turning the key in the lock.'

'Not with this storm!' said James, emerging from the bathroom after a heavenly emptying of his bladder. 'Thank God those two little keys you spotted next door unlocked *our* handcuffs *and* shackles. I was bursting.'

'Keep still, Carrie. I can't get these thorns out of your feet if you keep wriggling about.'

'Sorry.'

'And stop apologizing, my dear sister. I'm ... I'm bloody impressed! We felt sure you'd killed yourself, or–'

'Oh *really*? Well, it didn't look to me as though you two were overwhelmed by grief when I interrupted your romantic–'

'We were comforting each other, Carrie. And keep still, for God's sake!'

'You're bloody wonderful, Caroline. How you coped with the pain after landing in that bush is beyond me. But I'm afraid we can't stay here any longer. We've got to get away – *now*. That bitch could be back at any moment – if only for the handcuffs' key. She might not have a spare for Rory. So, we're going to have to carry you somehow. You can put your arms round our shoulders.'

'James, let's just get a few more of these thorns out.'

'We haven't got time, Misty.'

'But Carrie can't–'

'James is right, Misty. I don't give a damn about the pain. Let's move.'

The keys to *Clementina*'s Wrangler were not on the kitchen table; nor were they in the vehicle itself, which Ursula had secreted in *Bayreuth*'s integral garage.

'There's no time to search the house,' James said anxiously as he rejoined the others in the kitchen. He opened the back door and was almost knocked over by the force of the wind. 'I'm sorry, guys, but we're going to have to walk it.'

After a lively discussion, it was finally agreed that the simplest course was for James to follow the track to the Punta Prima road, and then go left and proceed to the junction with the Sant Ferran-Es Pujols highway, where he could call the police from the call box in the supermarket car park. In the meantime, Misty and Caroline would take cover a few hundred metres from the house, in the undergrowth at the side of the track, and await his return. James promised to run all the way – and was good to his word: he covered the mile to the junction in less than ten minutes. It took him another five, however, to get through to the *policía local* on the emergency 092 number. But to be fair, they were having a rather busy night.

The long-expected rain began while James was endeavouring in a cocktail of languages to convince the officer at the other end of the line that the call was not a hoax. After only a few minutes, the phone box had become a beleaguered island in a raging torrent, and he prayed for the authorities to arrive before his refuge was swept away. The prayer did not go unanswered. Within the hour, James and Misty were holding Caroline's hands as she received treatment from a paramedic in an ambulance battling its way to Sant Francesc through a deluge of Biblical magnitude. Meanwhile, in good English, a young policeman tried to ascertain what had happened to these three drenched Anglo-Saxons, and whether there was any connection between their bizarre predicament and the plane crash up at La Mola. He was unable, however, to answer any of Caroline's poignant questions about Rory's fate.

By midnight, Sant Francesc's small police station was the scene of frenetic activity – albeit none of it was particularly productive. The island's entire force had been mobilized, and several excited spouses had also been drafted in to provide all those involved in the crisis with the necessary sustenance and dry clothes. Unsurprisingly, news of the plane crash had spread like wildfire through Formentera's bush telephone. One rumour circulating among the bars of the 'capital' was that an airliner with hundreds of passengers aboard had tried to make an emergency landing in the storm. But it had ripped through El Pilar, devastating the village, and had then proceeded to roll on like a fireball all the way to the lighthouse, which it had demolished before tumbling over the cliffs. The police, however, would only confirm that a plane had crashed into the sea in the vicinity of La Mola and that two foreign men were being held for questioning.

Yet, there was definitely something fishy going on: everyone knew that 'a horribly mutilated foreigner' had been rushed to the island's tiny hospital and was now being guarded by an armed police officer. In truth, the ubiquitous Dr Aiguadolça was examining Caroline. He'd just returned from a pointless trip to La Mola, having expected to treat the anticipated air crash victims. Now, upon learning of Caroline's claimed identity, he proudly informed her that he was treating Lord Weetwood for sunstroke and related ailments up at the Hotel Cala Beltran – a disclosure which did nothing to ease her state of anxiety.

Despite the storm, a small crowd of bedraggled congenital gossipers had assembled outside the police station by the time the Cala Beltran contingent arrived in the hotel's minibus; an escorting *Guardia Civil* SUV added fuel to the onlookers' fire of speculation. Sheltering in the doorway, Tom Blackberry was already on hand to watch Trev and Keith emerge from the minibus and start organizing photographs of the dramatic gathering.

To everyone's relief, Harriet, Jennifer and Crabtree had been left behind at the hotel: thanks to the management's hospitality, they were far too intoxicated to embark upon an excursion to the police station. When Sonny's mobile had rung shortly after eleven, they were already paralytic. He'd hoped that it would be Regina with the promised news of the captives' whereabouts. Instead, he listened incredulously to Bob's account of 'the accidents'. But, as Sonny began to realize where they'd occurred, his incredulity turned to horror. He finally exploded, temporarily bringing to a halt the game of charades which the inebriates were playing with alcohol-induced over-enthusiasm. Gwen and Belinda had been too worried to participate; in any event, they – and Paolo – thought it appallingly bad taste.

Once Sonny had explained to Bob that, for reasons which would become clear in due course, he'd already handed over the ransom moneys to the kidnappers, and that the plane had crashed in the vicinity of the drop, Bob and Sonny were on the same wavelength: it was highly probable that Regina and the money had been aboard.

'Why the hell did you chase them?' Sonny roared.

'We *didn't exactly chase them, boss. We were only after some Häagen-Dazs.*'

A blast of screams from behind Sonny caused him to shoot round, only to find Gwen, Belinda and Paolo dancing together hysterically in front of the hotel manager: the police had just telephoned to say that three persons calling themselves 'Jams Weedwood', 'Carolina Beetroot' and 'Misery Cart' were in custody at Sant Francesc claiming to be the victims of a kidnap *and* related to two hotel guests; officers were already on their way over. With impressive dexterity, Keith and Trev started pouring more drinks to make 'some well-deserved toasts' before the 'pigs' arrived.

By the time Sonny, Belinda, Gwen and Paolo had finished kissing each other, Bob was no longer at the other end of the line: he and Chuck had been arrested and their phone confiscated by the police, who'd arrived at Punta des Far in the meantime. The Boys were 'under suspicion', their proud and vociferous claims to be American citizens only compounding matters; the words 'narcotics' and 'Mafia', which had been bandied about with relish by the lighthouse keeper, had not helped.

In the police station, a cacophony of sound contributed to the atmosphere of organized chaos. A group of officers were arguing about which of them should perform certain important tasks, such as contacting superiors in various parts of the Balearics and on the mainland, interviewing the foreigners, and translating the questions and answers. The identities of all those demanding to see the three self-claimed kidnapping victims also had to be verified: an ambitious junior officer had suggested that one or other of the former could be a homicidal kidnapper wishing to silence the latter. It was not very plausible, but someone's sick joke about Lee Harvey Oswald and Jack Ruby had been enough to keep the two parties well and truly apart. After all, the suspicious Americans in captivity were now claiming to be employees of the man who said he was Misery Cart's father.

And then there was the daughter of the insane English lord, who claimed that she'd jumped out of a first-floor window! What in God's name was that all about? ... Drugs, of course – it just had to be: there were Americans at every corner. Or was some cult involved? Lowering their voices, a couple of officers nearing retirement agreed that nothing like this would have happened if Franco had still been alive. In any event, the island's Director of Tourism would have a fit if any of this stuff got out and tarnished the carefully nurtured image of Formentera as a crime-free, family-holiday destination.

At length, the officer who appeared to be in charge got into a rage because the correct statement forms couldn't be found, the manual typewriter – which most of the officers could use – jammed, and the word processor – which was universally regarded with suspicion – blew a fuse as soon as it was plugged in. Matters were not helped by Trev trying to take pictures under his injured colleague's direction. Trev, however, was not very good with cameras, and resented both Keith's instructions and his increasingly acrimonious criticisms of everything he did. It all ended in an ugly stand-up row, with Trev being arrested for contravening a law proscribing photography on government property without due authorization, and Keith being evicted unceremoniously from the building into the torrential rain.

At some time between two and three in the morning, and after several power cuts and candlelit interrogations, the clouds of suspicion slowly lifted and the pieces of the jigsaw began to fit together. There were reports from officers on the spot concerning *Casa Bayreuth* and its obvious use as a hideout and prison; Ibiza Airport confirmed the movements of the missing plane; the claimed identities of Belinda, Sonny, Paolo and the Blackberrys checked out; Dr Aiguadolça – a pillar of the local community – trudged over from the clinic to examine the other two 'kidnapees', and reported he'd no doubts whatsoever that the young lady claiming to be Caroline Weetwood was indeed Lord Weetwood's daughter. And the Cala Beltran's elusive manager, Señor Pons, was finally contacted – thanks to the free *sangría*, he'd been preoccupied since midnight with drunken hostilities between the Regulars and the Rest – and added his weight to the claims of all those ensconced in the police station.

On the other hand, *Clementina*'s maid, Maria, would only provide her evidence well after sunrise – and once the storm had subsided: as the chief of police's treasured aunt, no one dared rouse her, even though she lived only a stone's throw from the station.

So, no longer under suspicion as dangerous criminals, Belinda and Gwen were finally taken to the neighbouring clinic to see Caroline. But due to her physical and mental exhaustion, together with the painkillers liberally prescribed by Dr Aiguadolça, she was already fast asleep. They were, however, allowed a peak from the doorway to her room. Much to the police guard's embarrassment, they promptly burst into tears of joy. A nurse signalled to them to be quiet and leave; they could talk to the patient in the morning.

'I'm staying here, Gwen. I don't want her to wake up in a strange hospital surrounded by soldiers and police and doctors – not after what she's been through, poor love.'

'I'm staying too, Belinda.'

'No. You've got enough on your plate. If Misty and her father *and* James – bless him! – are going to spend the night at *Honeysuckle Cottage*, you can't leave Tom to cope with everything, can you?'

It was not until the early hours, however, that the senior officer permitted James and Misty to leave the station, albeit on condition that they remained on the island pending further enquiries. They'd been well looked after, but, nevertheless, felt that for much of the time they'd been treated like criminals – not victims. There'd been strong words from both of them; their exhaustion had not helped. But, in the end, even they could see that in order to do their job, the police needed detailed statements. Sonny's interview had been particularly problematic. It had started badly due to the police rejecting his repeated demands to see Misty. But then, as they angrily reminded him, he'd failed to inform them of the kidnapping – a reckless error now compounded by his payment of the ransoms. There was, moreover, no way in which Sonny could deny that his 'minders' had accompanied him to Spain for the purpose of taking the law into their own hands. Indeed, the officers warned him that by failing to report the commission of a very grave crime, he himself had committed a serious offence; so, too, for that matter, had Lord Weetwood, the Blackberrys and Mrs Thornton – technically, even James Weetwood – and Paolo Amerigo.

Sonny was standing in a corridor, apologizing to Paolo for his own absurd detention and questioning, when a door opened a few yards away. Out walked Misty and James with two police officers. As the eyes of father and daughter met, there was a flicker of recognition. Sonny rushed forward and, with tears rolling down his cheeks, embraced her.

'Misty, honey! Thank the Good Lord you're safe!'

*He must be doing this for the cameras*, Misty thought; she even looked down the corridor, expecting to see them. Then she eyed Paolo suspiciously.

Notwithstanding the warm, friendly smile flashing at both James and herself, she concluded that he had to be one of her father's PR people.

James's first thought was: *Who is this good-looking smarmy American bastard?* He found out almost immediately.

Releasing Misty, Sonny engulfed James in a fierce bear hug. 'And you must be James Weetwood! God bless you for trying to rescue my daughter!'

James felt the man's hot tears against his own skin, and the brief tremor of jealousy subsided, only to be replaced by an aftershock of irritation. Wasn't there something pejorative about the word 'trying'?

# CHAPTER 34

Patricia Spigot stepped back and admired her handiwork: the roses she'd picked in the garden really looked glorious and their scent was heavenly. She wondered whether Lord Weetwood would notice them.

'I do hope so,' she murmured.

She began to rearrange the three separate piles of papers on the desk for the third time, but couldn't make up her mind whether the Chairman would prefer to study the documents from the local council first, or the menu and seating plan for this evening's dinner party. On the other hand, there were the faxes from Ben Turbot; they ought to be answered at some point during the day.

Searching for inspiration, she scanned the study, and noticed that one shelf of a bookcase near the French windows was in need of a good dusting.

'Dear oh dear, oh dear,' she muttered. 'That so-called housekeeper! I really ought to say something ... but then I'm not sure it's my place.' After weighing up the pros and cons of fetching a duster, she finally decided to leave things alone. She certainly didn't want to risk being caught red-handed again by that woman from the village and provoking another scene. She looked back at the desk: she'd put the papers in a single pile with Turbot's faxes at the top, otherwise there was a serious risk of the Chairman never dealing with them.

Through the open windows she heard her master's unmistakable whistling. It was the tune he invariably whistled or hummed when he was in a good mood. Sometimes he'd even sing, and if he did so, Patricia knew that there was a good chance of the Chairman remaining cheerful for the rest of the day. She poked her hair nervously and pointlessly with a pencil – it was already a paragon of the art of sensible hairdressing – and prayed for Lord Weetwood to burst into song.

Her prayer was instantly answered: the refrain 'Gloria! Gloria!' was followed by some impressive whistling as George did his best to interpret the jubilant trumpet *obligado* of Vivaldi's composition. 'In excelsis Deo!' he continued joyously on entering the study.

'Ah, good morning, Patricia, and what a *wonderful* morning! How are you today? Did you sleep well?'

Patricia moved from one foot to the other, gripped by the excitement she experienced whenever Lord Weetwood uttered the magic word

'Patricia'. 'I'm *very* well, thank you, Chair' – his eyes bulged with a highly theatrical glare – 'I mean ... *George*. Oh, *dash* it! I don't think I'll *ever* get used to calling you that – not first thing in the morning, anyway.'

'Tish and tosh! ... I say, what lovely roses! You really do spoil me, Patricia, but if you continue at this rate, the poor garden is going to be a wilderness in a fortnight.'

She managed a brief chuckle. 'Oh, I don't think so. There are so many, what with all your replanting.'

'Hmm. ... And how did you sleep?'

'Fine, thank you – absolutely super! I love that room in the tower – such a wonderful view. ... And yourself?'

'Excellent! Always sleep like a log here.' George glanced at the desk and pulled a frown. 'Ugh! What's all that you've piled up for me, Patricia? Is there no escape? And do I spy faxes? I thought Turbot would–'

'Don't worry,' Patricia interrupted, 'we can certainly get through this lot before breakfast – if we put our minds to it. Would you like a cup of coffee now? I'm sure there's some made.'

'No thank you.'

'Some orange juice?'

'No, no. I'll wait for breakfast – our very *special* breakfast.' George glanced at his watch: it was just after eight. 'Right! Let's get started.' He trotted over to the desk and sat down, while Patricia made herself comfortable in a green leather armchair on the other side, her notepad and pen ready for action. George scanned the communications from Turbot, and, without looking up said: 'That's a very pretty frock you're wearing, Patricia, very ... summery.'

She blushed. 'Thank you.'

'It's new, isn't it?'

'Yes. It's only something from Marks & Spencer. I got it in the sales.'

'Really? Just the ticket for this sort of weather. Looks like it's going to be another jolly hot day.'

'Hmm.' Patricia was delighted with the Chairman's observations, but unless she steered him back on course, he'd never achieve the nine o'clock deadline. 'As you can see, Mr Turbot is mainly reporting on the progress of the sale of the FoamFay production facilities in Kenya and Sri Lanka. You'll note the figures – quite significant write-offs, but in view of the very special processes they were built to operate, he's done well to find *any* buyers for them, if you ask me.'

'Indeed, indeed. I'm impressed. I thought at one stage they'd only be fit for scrap.' George read on. 'Good Lord! Allied Lyons are taking the Kenyan plant off our hands to manufacture iced tea! And Dupont want

Sri Lanka to expand their Far East air freshener business. How does Turbot do it, Patricia?'

She shook her head. 'It was certainly an inspired move appointing him Chief Executive, if you don't mind me saying so.'

'Thank you, Patricia. You know, I don't think I'm being immodest when I say that I've always been a jolly good judge of character. And, of course, the paramount virtue for success in senior management is the art – or should I say "science"? – of delegation.'

'Absolutely.'

'So that's it then. With these disposals, that will be the end of FoamFay – thank God!' George leaned back in his chair and placed his fingertips together. 'I know you were shocked about all that animal testing stuff in Uruguay, but you can see now, can't you, the ultimate wisdom of my having taken that decision? My God, how I agonized – the sleepless nights, the ... the–'

'The awesome responsibilities of leadership.'

'Exactly. Just think, without those frightful tests on those poor, dumb creatures, WSD might have been unwittingly responsible for the deaths of thousands – nay *hundreds* of thousands – nay *millions* – of innocent users of our product.' George shook his head and adopted an expression of utter wretchedness. 'Still,' he said brightening rapidly, 'all's well that ends well.'

'Absolutely.'

'And the remarkable thing is, that by coming clean and admitting the problem with FoamFay, we've actually boosted our sales of good old Goblin soap – bars and liquid – world-wide mark you – by ... er–'

'The figures are in Mr Turbot's second fax.' Patricia half-rose and leaned across the desk. 'Um, just here.' She turned pages until she found the unaudited management accounts for the last quarter.

'Good griffin! As much as that? ... I say, Patricia, have you seen those new television advertisements that Turbot's commissioned extolling the virtues of WSD's open, honest, caring policies – you know, the usual "marketing-speak" – and the traditional values of Goblin soap? Terrific stuff! And sheer genius to put the royal warrant in *colour* on all the packaging. It's cost a pretty packet, but it certainly is eye-catching.'

'Very posh, I think,' enthused Patricia with immense pride.

'Posh' was not a word which George cared to use, but he let it pass.

'So,' Patricia continued, 'I can reply then to Mr Turbot that you approve the FoamFay plant disposal plans?'

'Certainly!'

'Fine. Now, moving on to ... I think it's the third page of his first fax – yes, that's it – the three candidates shortlisted for the post of Company Secretary. He recommends–'

'Er ... which is the third page?' Patricia leaned across the desk again and found it for him. 'Thank you. ... That's a *very* pleasant scent you're wearing today – very pleasant indeed.'

'Why, thank you! It's ... it's the one *you* gave me for my birthday.'

'Oh? Well, Caroline chose that.'

Patricia looked slightly crestfallen. 'Did she? ... I thought *you'd* ...'

George continued reading, and then started to giggle. 'Oh, poor chap! Merryweather's found a new job at last.'

'Yes. ... Why "poor"?'

'That ghastly Tenby-Jones woman has put in a "good word" for him and got him a job as head of the Legal Department at the Root Vegetable Marketing Board.'

'I didn't think Mr Turbot would put up with him for long. He didn't really know much about the law, did he?'

George pretended not to hear. 'Well, I think we should follow Turbot's recommendation for Company Secretary – a young chap from Grimshaws who, he says, is "as keen as mustard". That's good enough for me.'

'Jolly good. I'll communicate your decision immediately after breakfast, as Mr Turbot is anxious to get the new appointee in place.'

'Excellent.'

'Now–'

'Can't see anything about James in all this stuff.'

'Yes, there is – I was coming to that. There's a brief extract from a memo to Mr Turbot from the Personnel Director commenting on his good progress in the Export Department. Actually' – Patricia lowered her voice slightly – 'I've heard from Mr Brancepeth-Tring's secretary that he's doing *very* well. And he's organizing a Goblin Soccer Tournament with teams from all Group companies – *worldwide*.'

'Is he *really*?' George visibly glowed with pride. 'He never mentioned that when he last phoned. ... By the way, when does everyone arrive? And what *are* we doing about dinner tonight?'

'That's next on the list ... George.'

He tutted. 'Please don't speak my name as though you're uttering some taboo expletive.'

'Sorry, but after all my years at Soap House ... well, you must see how difficult it is for me.'

'Stuff and nonsense!'

'Next item.'

George sniffed the air like an excited terrier. 'That really is *jolly* nice perfume. I must congratulate Caroline. Are they all travelling together? And what about Belinda, or is she coming directly from–?'

'*Next item*!' It was Patricia's turn to tut. 'You *are* still Chairman of this vast company – and its controlling shareholder. Just because it's a cloudless day outside and you're wearing a rather fashionable short-sleeved shirt–'

'Without a tie!'

'– without a tie – doesn't mean we can take our eyes off the ball, you know. Which reminds me, Mr Turbot has the agreement of the Weetwood Trust's other trustees about the Roberta Weetwood.'

George groaned. 'I *promised* – on *television* – that the Roberta Weetwood would be rebuilt.'

'Yes, but what the people want–'

'"The *people*"! Ha!'

'Yes, but they were *asked*, and they'd prefer a proper sports stadium, a swimming pool, an athletics ground – the lot. It would breathe new life into Goblinville. I think it's a smashing idea. So does James. Everyone does.'

George sighed. 'I'll think about it.'

'They need an answer! You've been putting it off for long enough. And if the Goblin World Cup is to be held in Goblinville in two years' time as James plans, they'll need to start work immediately.'

'Oh all right, Miss Bossy-Boots. I'll talk to James about it when he gets here. You have my word.'

Patricia smiled. 'Thank you.'

There really wasn't much to discuss about the dinner arrangements: Patricia had drawn up an excellent menu, the wines sounded admirable, and the table plan was unobjectionable – save for one rather important omission, which George immediately spotted.

'This won't do at all! I'm sorry, Patricia, but I'm astounded that *you*, of *all* people, should have made such a shocking blunder.'

Patricia was horrified. The warmth of the Chairman's voice had evaporated, and memories of all those frosty years at Soap House flooded over her. She was speechless.

George flung the seating plan across the table. 'Look! One of the most important guests has been omitted.' She stared in bewilderment at the document. 'Well?'

'I ... er ... Oh dear, I ...' Desperately searching for a clue, she tried to focus on the Chairman's wide-eyed face. He began to smile, and just for an instant, the grinning expression seemed so sinister that she felt genuinely afraid.

George realised he'd gone too far. 'Oh heavens! I'm *so* sorry. My odd sense of humour has misfired again. The missing name is your own, of course, you sillyosity. We couldn't have such an important celebratory dinner *sans toi*, Patricia. After all, without the loyal, honest, discreet Patricia Spigot organizing me, I would have steered WSD onto the rocks years ago.' Tears welled up in Patricia's eyes. 'Now, now – no crying today.'

'I – I ... It's just that ... Well, thank you for your kind words, but it really wouldn't be right for me to dine with you all tonight. It's ... it's ... it's a *family* occasion and–'

'That's enough! I won't hear another word on the subject. Oh, and before I forget, you're also *lunching* with me today. There's a ... a *personal* matter I would like your views on before the family arrive. I thought somewhere informal ... somewhere off the beaten track. ... Now, what remains to be covered before breakfast?'

Patricia dabbed her eyes with a small embroidered handkerchief; she was hardly listening. 'I really haven't got anything suitable to wear.'

'Rubbish! You're always *perfectly* attired for *every* occasion – always have been, my dear.'

*

In truth, prior to his return to Soap House after the convalescence necessitated by his 'breakdown' on Formentera, George didn't have the least idea how Patricia had dressed at any time during her many years of loyal secretarial service. It was not that he'd lost his memory: in the past, Patricia had simply been of little consequence. But almost three months of rest on the island under both her and Dr Aiguadolça's ministrations had proved remarkably successful in transforming George's character. The peace and quiet of those autumnal weeks, when Formentera was repossessed by its residents – both indigenous and adopted – did more for his devastated nerves and tortured mind than any of the medications prescribed by the good physician. But then, as a native of the island, Aiguadolça had known that all along.

At the outset, however, things had not augured well. For several days after the kidnapping's resolution, Belinda, Caroline and James had tried their best to communicate with him, but he gave no indication of recognizing any of them. The only thing he ever said was 'Gloria', and the family began to suspect that he had a secret mistress. Be that as it may, they listened to Dr Aiguadolça's diagnosis and prognosis, and all agreed that a Formenteran convalescence would be for the best. *Casa Maryvent*, a pleasant villa only a few hundred metres beyond *Honeysuckle Cottage* towards Cap de Barbaria, was rented for the purpose, and George and Belinda were soon in residence.

For weeks, George hardly spoke: he desired nothing but silence and solitude. In early November, however, he began to engage in rational conversation with Belinda, albeit speaking hesitantly. He made a fuss about returning to England and getting to grips with WSD, rail franchises, and divorce. But after many arguments, he reluctantly agreed to a compromise: he would remain on Formentera for the time being provided that (1) Miss Spigot was flown out to perform 'much-needed secretarial duties'; (2) Belinda returned to Bobbins to act 'in loco parentis vis-à-vis the twins', as he put it; and (3) Ben Turbot joined WSD's board as a non-executive director and acting chairman.

The conditions were promptly fulfilled.

In reality, however, George had no desire to return to England: the mere mention of it – or for that matter of Bobbins or Soap House – filled him with dread. But he kept his fears to himself; nor did he tell anyone about the terrible dreams which tormented him night after night.

*

'There's a very supportive letter from the local council,' Patricia said as she racked her brains, desperately trying to imagine herself at the dinner party in any of the outfits she'd brought with her from home.

'And about time too! They've been promising a decision on our planning application for weeks.'

'Well, to be fair, they've been waiting for the views of the lawyers of the Govern Balear in Mallorca. It now looks as though a special statute won't be necessary to reopen and extend the line to Es Pujols. I've translated the letters by the way – the translations are attached to the originals.'

'Good Lord! You must have been up half the night. I don't know how you managed to learn Catalan, Patricia. I think it's one of the most peculiar languages I've ever heard – sounds like a tortured mixture of Welsh and Swedish to me.'

Patricia laughed. 'You really ought to try and learn it yourself.'

George snorted. 'Never mind the lecture – am I going to be allowed to reopen the railway or not?'

'Well, they don't give an absolutely one hundred per cent definite answer, but it looks like it. Perhaps you should read the translations.'

*

It was Patricia who had introduced George to the small paperback book which was to have such a salutary effect on him. She'd discovered it in a small bookshop in Sant Francesc shortly after she'd first arrived on the island. As her secretarial duties had not proved onerous, she'd much free time on her hands. So, as the November weather was perfect for walking, she resolved to see as much of the island by foot as possible. But when she visited Sant Francesc in search of guidebooks and maps, she was surprised by the paucity of suitable publications. Among the few candidates in a cramped bookshop was a short history of the island, but the quality of the printing was poor; indeed, it all looked rather home-baked. Furthermore, as she rapidly flicked through the pages, she realised the text was in Catalan, a language she had yet to master. There were, however, a few old photographs of locations still unknown to her, and some of them looked worthy of a visit. She made a mental note to add them to her itinerary, coupled with a prayer that they remained undeveloped. She bought a map, identified an alternative route-march back to *Maryvent*, and, with her bobble hat unwittingly positioned at a jaunty angle, left the shop humming *The Happy Wanderer*.

She was strolling through the square when the image of a steam engine flashed in her mind. She rushed back to the bookshop, grabbed the unpretentious history booklet, and quickly found what she was looking for: a poor reproduction of a slightly out-of-focus photograph. But there was no mistaking its subject matter – a funny little train, complete with engine and trucks; it looked like something out of a cartoon to her.

The elderly gentleman behind the counter was of great assistance. There had indeed been a railway on the island – he could remember it quite clearly – but it had only been used to transport salt from the salt flats around Estany Pudent to the harbour at La Savina.

'All gone now,' he said sadly in Castilian, 'but there are still some rusty rails and trucks lying around near Sa Síquia,' and he pointed to a spot on Patricia's new map.

She thought it was worth a try: Lord Weetwood needed to get out and about, to get exercise and fresh air, to get an interest in something. She bought a copy.

When she first showed George the photograph and told him about the old mineral line, he exhibited total disinterest. But she left the publication with him anyway. Almost a week passed. Then he hesitantly suggested the possibility of Miss Spigot taking him for a drive. He said he wanted to see the spot where Sonny Start had left the ransom moneys and the house where Caroline and the others had been imprisoned. It was the first time he'd mentioned anything to do with the kidnapping in her presence. Patricia, who thought the proposed itinerary unwise, consulted Dr Aiguadolça: he felt it could prove therapeutic.

The day for their unusual excursion was cloudless and calm with a comfortable high of eighteen degrees Celsius. With Patricia at the wheel, they set off after breakfast in the Range Rover that George had had shipped over from Ibiza, and drove first to El Pilar. Although he'd not previously visited the arid La Mola plateau, nevertheless, as they drove towards the hypnotic lighthouse standing guard at Punta des Far, he experienced a strange and troubling sense of déjà vu. When they stopped briefly at the spot where the drop had taken place, Patricia sensed that Lord Weetwood was deeply disturbed, and advised against driving on to the point; he was adamant they should proceed. And then, as they approached the tall white structure, he suddenly realised that he had indeed seen it before. But how – and when?

The café was closed for the winter, and there was no sign of life as far as the eye could see. The wind had got up, and with it ruffling their hair, the two nervous visitors stood in silence beside the Jules Verne monument and stared eastwards across an agitated sea. But as George looked into the distance, the turbulent Mediterranean faded, and in its place appeared a vision of a young woman blessed with a smile that would have melted the iciest of hearts. A dam seemed to burst in his mind, and scenes from the nightmare he'd experienced in the woods around Cala Beltran at the time of the kidnapping flooded his thoughts. Gripping Patricia's arm, he began to steer her back to the car.

'We shouldn't have come,' she opined, shaking her head. 'So foolish of me. I–'

'Don't you feel the energy?' interrupted George, staring with burning eyes at the lighthouse. 'You do, don't you?'

Completely taken aback, Patricia was lost for words. 'I ... We ... We'd better go home.'

'No!' he shouted, tightening his grip on her arm. 'We *can't* go back.' His gaze remained fixed on the mighty tower. 'Not now! Never!'

It was almost noon by the time Patricia located *Casa Bayreuth*. The depressing house was all shut up; they didn't linger. Hoping to raise her employer's spirits, Patricia rapidly improvised what she termed 'a scenic route' for their return trip to *Maryvent*. Soon, they were bouncing along deserted dirt tracks that weaved this way and that across the now verdant autumnal landscape. She made repeated attempts to make conversation, but George was uncommunicative. Patricia was, therefore, startled when, approaching Sant Francesc, he suddenly asked her to motor on to La Savina.

'It might be interesting to see what's left of that old railway,' he offered by way of explanation.

Within days, George was considering plans for reopening the line for passengers and extending it all the way to Es Pujols! He was amazed that neither the local council nor the Tourist Board had thought of doing so themselves: it would not only be a major tourist attraction but also provide some much-needed and environmentally-friendly infrastructure. Traffic on the La Savina-Es Pujols road would be reduced, and, as it bordered the Estany Pudent nature reserve, the reduction in noise and pollution would be good for the wildlife.

Patricia and George were soon engrossed in a major research project to discover as much as they could about the old railway. She brushed up her Castilian and began studying Catalan, while lawyers in Madrid and Palma were instructed to assist in negotiations with the authorities. At first, the family welcomed George's apparent return to normality, but then feared that his new enthusiasm could be symptomatic of incipient insanity. After all, building a narrow-gauge railway on minuscule Formentera seemed bizarre. However, Patricia reassured them that the plan was not as daft as it sounded; that, after some initial scepticism, the Formentera Tourist Board was very supportive; and that thanks to the new project, Lord Weetwood was, in her humble opinion, growing stronger – both physically and mentally – by the day. Dr Aiguadolça concurred.

*

George looked at his watch: it was 8:58. 'Have we received those estimates yet, Patricia, from the Germans?'

'For the construction of the locomotives?'

George nodded.

'Afraid not.'

'Damn!'

'I'll phone them. They promised to fax them yesterday.'

Smiling broadly, George pushed his chair back and stood up. 'Come on! We've done enough. Breakfast!' He removed a pair of sunglasses from his shirt's breast pocket, saying: 'We're promised "Buck's Fizz" this morning, you know.'

'Really? How lovely! They spoil us.'

Side by side, the Chairman of WSD plc and his faithful secretary passed through the study's French windows and emerged onto the terrace. George donned his sunglasses and inhaled deeply. 'Smell that air, Patricia. Pure ambrosia! If anyone had told me a year ago–'

'– that you'd fall in love with Formentera and buy the *Villa Clementina*, you'd have had him or her certified. You must say that at least twice a day!'

'Excuse me for being so predictable! And don't exaggerate.'

Patricia started waving. 'Oh look! Sonny and Paolo have already arrived.'

George followed the direction of her gaze and focused on *Honeysuckle Cottage*'s terrace. He waved too, and, as he did so, Tom and Gwen Blackberry joined their guests – carrying ice buckets that glinted enticingly in the morning sunlight.

George fondly took Patricia's arm. 'Onward, my dear, and let the merrymaking commence!'

# CHAPTER 35

Paolo had returned to Turin on his charter flight some fourteen hours after he'd witnessed Sonny embrace Misty in the corridor of the Sant Francesc police station. Paradoxically, it had been Sonny himself who'd laboured to persuade the police that the Italian had absolutely no involvement in the kidnapping and should be permitted to leave the island. Paolo had agonised over his decision to fly home: although Sonny had appeared to cross a watershed in his life during that momentous weekend, Paolo had finally concluded that he wasn't in love. In truth, bearing in mind the circumstances of their meeting and the duration of their acquaintance – he couldn't really call it 'friendship' – Sonny's assertions of love had probably amounted to nothing more than an infatuation which would die as rapidly as it had blossomed.

The phone calls started within hours of Paolo's homecoming at his mother's apartment. Thereafter, Sonny called every morning and evening – and sometimes even during the day as he toiled in Fiat's design department. Sonny maintained his solemn declarations of love, and kept Paolo up to date on the many developments in his public and private life. Paolo was keeping abreast of these himself by reading *The Herald Tribune, Time, Newsweek* and various British newspapers and magazines; Signora Amerigo found it all rather exciting.

It took a fortnight before the letters began arriving. At first, Sonny's handwriting and style were hesitant – it had been decades since he'd written more than a few sentences in manuscript – but he soon became quite fluid, almost poetic in a homespun kind of way. Paolo found them charming, but remained unconvinced; he didn't put pen to paper himself.

Then, in the first week of November, representatives of the Italian media arrived at the Amerigos' apartment. Although *The Sun* had kept its part of the bargain about naming Paolo as 'the other man' in *The Fresh Start* story – and the snooping journalists had got nowhere with the good people of Formentera – a generously bribed Garibaldi Tours employee had no compunctions about handing over a computer printout of clients who had experienced the Hotel Cala Beltran's delights. The floodgates opened.

Within twenty-four hours, Sonny arrived to find Paolo's apartment building under siege; it looked as if the entire world wanted to see, interview and photograph the Italian 'hunk' who had bewitched an

American billionaire – *the* American billionaire whose daughter had been kidnapped, whose wife was suing for divorce and claiming everything he owned, and whose decision to 'come out' and liquidate all his interests in SI Corporation had sent shockwaves through Fort Worth society and Wall Street.

Signora Amerigo liked Sonny from the moment she first set eyes on him. And his suggestion that she and Paolo should proceed directly to the 'farm' – a *finca* – he'd bought on Formentera and remain there until the storm blew over, received her immediate support; Fiat thought it made sense too, for their offices were also under siege. And so, within a few hours, mother and son had packed what they thought they would need for a week's stay.

This was the period when Sonny was still involved in an exhausting three-way shuttle between Fort Worth, New York and Formentera – for which purpose he'd bought a second-hand executive jet. There were innumerable meetings with lawyers, accountants, brokers and bankers to implement his decision to sever his links with SI – not to mention effecting an amicable divorce from Carmen. Having no quarrel with her, he wanted a fair settlement that would recognize the vital contribution she'd made to his career. But the way in which her Texan friends and colleagues had snubbed her as a result of Sonny's revelations quite turned Carmen's head. Aided and abetted by a pack of aggressive lawyers, she became bitter, greedy and litigious. And the media circus expanded exponentially as Carmen became an overnight star on network chat shows with her tearful tales of living with a deceitful husband and coping with a sham marriage.

Inevitably, Misty was dragged into the miserable business. She was hounded and followed everywhere. She stopped answering the telephone – except the mobile Sonny had given her, its number remaining a secret between them. Refusing to accept her implacable position of 'no comment', there were undignified scenes as reporters and interviewers invaded both her humble New York apartment building and place of work at the neighbourhood law centre. In the end, she compromised her principles, and sought refuge in the well-protected penthouse her father had rented on Central Park West, a move which outraged Carmen, who'd been trying desperately to recruit Misty to her own camp.

The law centre was initially sympathetic. But as the cameras and lights began to drive away the very people they were trying to help, her boss finally lost patience and asked Misty to take unpaid leave of absence until the excitement died down. Sonny's advice that she should return to Formentera and stay at his 'farm' sounded to her like running away. In any event, the island held too many sad memories for her. Consequently, secure yet imprisoned in the Manhattan fortress with her 'protectors', Chuck and Bob, Sonny left Misty to reconsider his proposal while he flew off to Italy to rescue Paolo and his mother.

During dinner on the day of the Amerigos' arrival at the Formentera 'farm' – the conversion to luxury villa was already well advanced – Sonny had pleaded with Paolo to call Misty.

'Try and persuade her to fly over, Paolo. You're my best chance.'

As Sonny appeared close to tears, Signora Amerigo demanded a translation from her son. Then she promptly ordered Paolo to phone New York.

During the hours following her escape from *Casa Bayreuth*, Misty had only spent a few minutes in Paolo's presence. And yet, she felt she knew him inside out: her father seemed unable to converse with her on any subject for more than five minutes without mentioning him. In truth, she'd found the habit irritating – even pathetic – and suspected that the Italian was a gold-digger playing hard to get. Nevertheless, when Misty answered her mobile and found herself talking to Paolo, his voice and manner proved hypnotic. She kept telling herself that she was being manipulated and to resist his oily charm. But resistance proved impossible. Within minutes, she was revealing some of her most secret thoughts: she confessed that her love for James had not died – far from it – notwithstanding the angry dispute between them which had marked their separate departures from Formentera back in September.

For his part, Paolo probed diplomatically, paying careful attention to Misty's replies.

'So, Misty, what you are saying is that you want to help people the best ways you can do the helps, yes? And as you are American lawyer this is how you wanna do the helps – working with poor people in the USA who have the law problems. Now, James believes he must help his father and all the family by working in the Goblin company. And so he says he must go to England and not to America, and you must be joining him there.'

'Exactly.'

'Why you not go to England and learn English law?'

'Why the hell should I?'

'Because you love James.'

'But why should *I* make all the sacrifices? Anyway, I'm not sure he wants me in England.'

But Paolo told her that Mrs Thornton had told Mrs Blackberry, who had told Sonny that this was exactly what James wanted. Sheepishly, Misty confessed that Caroline was telling her the same story in their regular transatlantic calls.

Then she told Paolo that she was pregnant; he swore he'd not tell a soul.

The *finca* that Sonny had bought at Caló d'en Trill had at its core an old farmhouse which had been refurbished and much enlarged. It lay in splendid isolation just a kilometre along the coast to the north of the Hotel Cala Beltran. He had not, however, intended it to be a mere holiday home: within days of the kidnapping's conclusion, he'd purchased the hotel itself. It closed in mid-October and work began immediately to convert it into what the French call *un palace*. Sonny's *finca* – promptly renamed *Fresh Start* – served as a site office and hostelry for the architects, interior designers and landscape architects of international repute whom he had shipped in. Although they all had wonderful ideas – at least as far as Sonny was concerned – each of them had, with varying degrees of tact, rubbished the impressive artwork of the others. In consequence, Sonny had found himself acting as the umpire of an incomprehensible game. He'd soon begun to feel lost and out of his depth.

So, when Paolo arrived, Sonny showed him all the plans, designs and sketches littering the long table in 'the conference room' – the *finca*'s former barn. Paolo was initially hesitant in expressing an opinion, but within only a few days, and having proved himself to be both a genius at pouring oil on troubled water and a natural 'team leader', he was chairing meetings of 'the design team'. He fell in love with the project; then he fell in love with Sonny.

Paolo's resignation from Fiat quickly followed, and the contents of the Amerigos' Turin apartment were shipped to Formentera. Signora Amerigo moved into *Fresh Start*'s guest cottage on condition that she'd be allowed to do her own cooking, cleaning and laundry. She loved the island, for it reminded her of her native Sicily and the halcyon days of her childhood. Indeed, to live again by the waters of the Mediterranean filled her with a new zest for life.

Meanwhile in the main house, Paolo and Sonny began to share a bed.

The Blackberrys, who soon became close friends of the Start-Amerigos, kept them informed of developments on the Lord Weetwood front, thanks to the recent arrival of Patricia Spigot, whom they'd also befriended. It was Tom who surprised the dinner guests at *Fresh Start* one evening – Signora Amerigo had insisted on cooking her own recipe for a sausage-meat pasta – with the news that he was convinced Patricia was in love with his lordship, who, since her arrival, had begun to show signs of 'going native'. There and then, a resolution was unanimously passed to invite the putative lovers to dine at *Honeysuckle Cottage* the following week, when the

Blackberrys would reciprocate the Start-Amerigos' hospitality. Everyone was even more surprised when both Weetwood and his secretary accepted the invitation. Sonny, however, had already smoothed the way by negotiating the outlines of a deal with Ben Turbot for a mutual termination of all legal proceedings between SI and WSD over the FoamFay business.

The dinner was a very decorous occasion with all the obvious matters of commonality left undiscussed. In fact, George and Patricia monopolized most of the evening with explanations of the plan to reopen Formentera's long-lost railway. The enthusiasm with which each of them spoke on the subject fuelled their respective fires, and although the subject matter of the discourse was of little interest to their listeners, the latter all found the performances entertaining; they even sent secret signals to one another – winking, raising eyebrows, and kicking ankles under the table – to stifle giggles. But whatever its commerciality, the plan was clearly proving to be of great therapeutic value to his lordship.

Just as the party was breaking up with a final soliloquy from George on the probable need for the new steam locomotives to have oil-fired boilers rather than coal, the telephone rang and Gwen went into the hall to answer it. After a minute she returned to the dining room looking somewhat bemused.

'It's James, Lord Weetwood.' The peer had still to invite any of the fellow diners to call him 'George', albeit Sonny had done so in any event, but then they had shared a hotel room. 'He'd like to speak to you,' Gwen added. 'He tried your villa and got alarmed when there was no reply. He thought we might know where you were. Actually, he's phoning from New York.'

When George rejoined the diners a few minutes later, he looked shaken and pale. 'Your daughter ... er, Sonny ... she wants to speak with you. ... She's with my son.'

Sonny almost knocked over his chair as he rushed to the phone.

'Everything's all right, I hope, Chairman?' enquired Patricia nervously.

'Well ... yes, I suppose so. ... Sonny's daughter ... she ... she really is called "Misty", is she?' Everyone nodded. 'Oh ... right. Well, Sonny and I are going to be grandfathers.'

A week later, George and Sonny met again, this time at *Casa Maryvent* for a working lunch; there were just the two of them. It was a cold, wet and windy day, so they ate in the dining room with a roaring log fire to keep them company. Both men were still trying to come to grips with the realization that within a few months a child would be born who would inherit something – however small – from each of their respective genes. And whether their own children got married – Misty and James had yet to communicate what their intentions were on that issue – George and Sonny would, in a sense, become related. The incredulity of the situation was not lost on either prospective grandparent.

It was unsurprising, therefore, that the first hour or so of their meal should have been spent discussing what Sonny was already calling 'the family'. The frankness with which he spoke about his relationships with both Mrs Start and Misty initially embarrassed George, and then disarmed him; a few glasses of Gran Viña Sol also helped to loosen George's tongue. Indeed, as Sonny himself had first noticed over their *fino* aperitifs, George appeared less relaxed than at their last meeting; he conjectured whether the absence of Patricia from the lunch had anything to do with it. But by the time they'd consumed their first course of grilled turbot in capers – that was Patricia's little joke – both men, to a lesser or greater degree, had admitted their inadequacies as fathers.

George made the lesser confessions, for he still had a mental block when it came to talking about his family. Sonny did not press him: only the night before, Gwen had phoned to remind him to tread carefully. She and Belinda were of the same mind: George's 'nervous breakdown' – or whatever it was – had a great deal to do with his failure to play any role in Caroline's release; at the time, of course, he was unaware of James's incarceration. Hence his refusal to have any contact with her, or to permit any mention of the kidnapping in his presence. Patricia appeared to be bringing him out of his shell, but any therapy should be left to her; Sonny should steer a wide berth, Gwen warned. Above all, Caroline's 'relationship' with Rory Devlin should not in any circumstances be mentioned or alluded to.

'Well,' said George as he helped himself to some cheese and fruit, 'you and I, er ... Sonny, have a bit of business to discuss, haven't we?'

'We sure have. Thanks, but no cheese for me – got a bit of a weight problem what with all that pasta back at the ranch.'

'Ah yes, Signora Amerigo and er ...'

'Paolo.'

'Yes. Paolo. Of course.'

'They sure love the old pasta, those guys. How Paolo stays so slim, I'll never know.'

'Quite.' George poured some mineral water into Sonny's glass and then topped up his own. 'Sonny, Ben Turbot has sent me the ... er ... the draft "Heads of Agreement" – how I hate that expression.'

'I think they reflect what Ben and I talked about, George. I spoke with him directly, by the way, rather than through my Dallas lawyers. A bit unconventional, but–'

'Indeed. I understand that chap at your London solicitors, er ...'

'Perry Match? What a creep!'

'Hmm ... Match. Well, I understand that he even telephoned Turbot and complained about him talking to you, *and* insisted that all the negotiations should be done through *him*.'

'Yeah. He winged to Swinehearts too. He's been told to lay off.'

'I see. Good. Now, I want to be reasonable, er ... Sonny, but SI started this litigation and we've been put to a lot of expense defending it, and–'

'Be fair, George. It was *our* technology – legally.'

'Well–'

'But what's the point of arguing about that now? You don't want it – you've trashed FoamFay publicly – and you're withdrawing it. So, *we* don't want it either. *Nobody* wants it. We've both spent a lot of money on lawyers, OK? We should each bear our own costs.'

'You said some awful things about me and WSD in your affidavits.'

'That's lawsuits for you, George. Sorry. And you caused SI one hell of a nightmare with all that stuff about animal testing at Soda Flats. That's why we want the retraction – it's only fair.'

George shook his head. 'Oh come on! We acted in good faith. We only repeated what Pesto told us. She seemed sincere. You're not really trying to tell me that SI was *not* testing products on animals at that place, are you? Why should she have made it up?'

'I don't know, George. Perhaps she was trying to put her theft of our technology in a better light. Perhaps she was crazy.' Sonny sighed. 'Anyway, the poor kid's dead. ... Boy, that product was cursed, wasn't it? Pesto, Dumpwell–'

As soon as Sonny uttered Dumpwell's name, he knew he'd made a terrible mistake. He looked anxiously at George and bit his lip: Dumpwell; the plane crash; Ursula Klinker; the kidnapping; Caroline.

'George, you OK? ... I'm sorry. I – I...'

But it wasn't Sonny's reference to the former head of Project Orient Express which had unsettled George: being reminded of Vosene Pesto's death – something he'd not thought of for many weeks – had triggered horrible images of skin and hair coming away in handfuls, and piles of dead and disfigured dogs.

A few moments later, George was still gazing vacantly out of the dining room's rain-splattered windows. 'What a dreadful business,' he muttered, shivering. 'I'll put another log on the fire.'

'Perhaps it would be for the best if you were to forget all about it, George.'

George looked Sonny straight in the eye. 'Forget? How can I? Don't you see' – his fist hit the table – 'I'm responsible for all these deaths!'

Sonny was alarmed: he'd ignored Gwen's warning and things really had gone too far. 'I'll get Patricia,' he said darting towards the door.

'No! I don't want her to see me like this. Sit down ... *please.*'

Sonny resumed his seat. For a while, both men sat silently and watched the fire's dancing flames. Outside, the wind increased in strength, and the waves crashing beyond the garden wall threw up ever-higher jets of spray.

It was after four and getting dark when, in a state of near exhaustion and staring once more into the fire's flames, George said: 'So, Sonny, now you know it all – the whole saga of Vosene Pesto, Project Troll, *and* Project Orient Express. I've schemed, plotted, lied – I even thought of getting Dumpwell done away with *and* handing over that lethal technology to you as part of a settlement of the litigation. Good Lord, I was hoping to blackmail you through Paolo!'

'George, *don't*. Enough is enough. You'll make yourself ill again.'

Sonny rose from his seat on the other side of the fireplace and came to stand by George's side. Feeling humbled and ashamed, he placed a hand on the older man's shoulder; he felt like a priest who, having heard someone's confession, was sickened by the thought that his own sins were far, far worse. And to remain silent now – after George had bared his soul to him – would be so shamefully hypocritical: it would imply some form of moral superiority, an attribute he clearly did not possess.

'You're not an evil man, George. You didn't kill *anyone* – certainly not Pesto. It was an accident. You never wanted to harm anyone.'

'What about Dumpwell?'

'Oh, forget him. You might have *thought* about it, but you'd never have gone through with it – never in a million years. And as soon as you suspected there could be a problem with FoamFay, you checked it out. Animal testing was the only sensible route. You would have withdrawn the stuff before any harm was done – Formentera or no Formentera.'

'And sold the damned technology to *you* – or tried to.'

'For Christ's sake! Do you honestly think we wouldn't have tested the stuff on animals too?'

George stopped gazing at the flickering flames and looked up. 'You mean ...?'

'Of course! Come on, everybody in the industry does it. I bet you use a chain of innocuous-looking contracts stretching halfway across the world through nominee companies.' George nodded. 'Well, so do we ... *now.*'

'"*Now*"?'

'George, Pesto wasn't lying. ... I'm so sorry. See, even until' – Sonny glanced at his watch – 'two hours ago, I was still trying to rip you off. Sure we were doing animal tests at Soda Flats. She was on the level. We must have been crazy – thinking we could do all that stuff in-house and keep it secret. We were new boys in the cosmetics industry at that time. We didn't know the ropes. We thought we could keep it all under wraps with a few handpicked eggheads who'd keep their mouths shut with the right financial inducements. You know what I mean ... like Pesto herself.' George nodded. 'Well, it didn't work. We ... I ...' Sonny's voice drifted away. It was his turn to become mesmerised by the flickering flames.

'No, George, you didn't kill anyone,' he said as if to himself, 'but I ... I was prepared to. ... I could have done.'

George didn't become angry as he listened to Sonny's original plan for 'the Boys' to entrap the kidnappers and 'persuade' them to reveal Misty's whereabouts, thereby endangering both her life and Caroline's. On the contrary, George began to experience something akin to empathy; with a tingle of expectation, he wondered whether their mutual baring of souls that afternoon might even bond them in a unique form of friendship.

Finally, he said: 'Good Lord! We're sitting in the dark. I'll switch the lights on.' As he passed Sonny, he unhesitatingly gripped his shoulder, surprising both Sonny and himself.

'So now you know what sort of guy I am, George – a gay felon. Not exactly ideal material for a grandparent, is it?'

'Sonny, we've both done bad things,' George replied as the lights came on. 'I'm sorry. That sounds trite. Look, we have to – what do those awful accountant chaps say? – "draw a line"? Or am I thinking of something about "bottom lines".'

Sonny managed a laugh. 'You won't tell Paolo, will you?' he pleaded suddenly.

George was visibly shocked. 'What has been said this afternoon, Sonny, dear boy, will, for my part, remain within these four walls. You have my word.'

'Sorry. And you have mine.'

'I believe you.' With a sigh, George added: 'But I would suggest that one day – not now, perhaps – you should tell him. Secrets between ... between *partners*, Sonny, are not–'

'I will. Promise.'

The two men stood facing each other in front of the fire. Sonny took a step forward and gave George a mighty bear hug. His eyes welled with tears: he couldn't remember ever being hugged by anyone. He wanted to reciprocate, but something inside him was holding him back. Then the moment passed and Sonny crossed to the door.

*One day – one day soon,* George thought. *I am changing. I must change – like a chrysalis and a butterfly. ... What a silly analogy!* And then he remembered the woods near Cala Beltran, the summer heat and–

'Thanks for a great lunch, George, and ... and *everything*.' Sonny had already opened the dining room door. 'I suppose we should both contact our lawyers and get that settlement agreement finalized.'

As they reached the entrance hall, Patricia popped her head around the kitchen door – she was practising her Catalan with the housekeeper – and smiled.

'I'll be with you in a minute, Patricia,' George said returning her smile.

'See you soon, Pat!'

'Goodbye, Mr Start.'

'*Sonny!*'

'Sorry! Goodbye, Sonny.'

Patricia returned to her language lesson, and George opened the front door. They looked at the rain and shivered.

Sonny shook his head. 'The glorious Mediterranean!'

'It's good for the garden.'

'You sound like Paolo!'

They both laughed.

'By the way, Sonny, I think I have you to thank for the troubles my witch of a spouse is experiencing with her vile so-called autobiography.'

'Oh *that*. Well, only in the sense that I lent my weight to get *The Sun* to dump it. They've even sacked that Bradbury dame.'

'So I believe! I only heard all this recently – thanks to Miss Spigot – Patricia.'

'I think Beryl's problem, George, is that she's trying to destroy too many powerful people. She should have limited herself to a few big names in show business, or one or two royal hot shots. But half the western world's Great and Good was bound to lead to an almighty conspiracy to destroy her. The lawsuits have showered down like confetti on both her and Bradbury. Apparently, they've gone into hiding – understandable with the death threats.'

'*Death* threats? Really? I almost feel sorry for them.'

'Don't. Anyway, when I get back from the States, you and Pat must come over to *Fresh Start*. I'll call you from New York. Take care!'

'Bon voyage! And please give my love to James and Misty!'

George watched Sonny sprint to his car through the torrential rain, and then waved as he drove off. Momentarily, he considered a *siesta* before dinner, but then the warmth of the house enveloped him and he thought of Patricia. 'I think a nice cup of tea is in order,' he murmured, smiling, '– in the kitchen.'

# CHAPTER 36

Ever since her father had suggested 'a grand reunion and first anniversary dinner' to celebrate what he called 'the positive by-products of the kidnapping', Caroline had had grave doubts about the whole venture. He'd first broached his scheme at Bobbins where he'd spent July and August in order to avoid the worst of the Mediterranean summer heat and the peak of Formentera's tourist season. In any event, with most Spaniards on holiday, there was no hope of material progress on the railway front.

Now, as Sonny's yacht, *Fresh Start II*, made its way out of Ibiza harbour on a cloudless September afternoon and set course for Formentera, Caroline began to feel nauseous as a sense of mounting panic gripped her. She wondered how she could have been so stupid to allow things to get this far. It might not have been so bad, had her father not bought the *Villa Clementina* a few months back when Kurt Schmückstück decided that Formentera was 'out' and Mallorca was 'in': he wanted a house at Port d'Andratx near Claudia Schiffer and Michael Schumacher.

*Clementina*! – where the whole nightmare had started! Why did he have to go and buy *that* – of all places? It was the question Caroline had repeatedly asked herself. And yet, while the rest of the family had expressed some sympathy for her point of view, they didn't share her concerns. Surprisingly, Misty proved the most phlegmatic: Caroline had to come to grips with the past and accept that, for everyone else, Formentera and the kidnapping had been the catalysts for the most wonderful transformations of their lives. And Caroline – if she thought about it objectively – would see that, on the whole, it had been a good thing for her too.

Caroline looked aft and watched Misty and James cooing over their three-month-old baby boy, Sonny George Weetwood. He was protected from the afternoon sun by a pretty white cotton hat – a present from Aunt Belinda, who stood beside him pulling comic faces; Sonny Junior gurgled appreciatively. They'd all been so festive on Sonny Senior's jet flying down from Manchester – the adults sipping champagne and tucking into platefuls of smoked salmon, the baby enjoying the constant attention. But Caroline, who'd not indulged, had begun to resent their fun and the way they made her feel like a party pooper.

Paolo, who'd met them at Ibiza Airport, turned from the party of baby admirers, noticed the pain on Caroline's face, and came to join her at the rail. She groaned inwardly: the last thing she wanted was more 'agony aunt' therapy from the soft-spoken Italian. She made a move towards the saloon's open door, but Paolo intercepted her.

'It's such a beautiful harbour, isn't it?' he said smiling warmly, '– especially on a day like this. I remember the first time I came to Ibiza and sailed out on the Formentera ferry–'

'I was just going to see Rory,' Caroline interrupted with a hint of irritation. 'I need to make sure he's all right. He might ... recognize something.'

Paolo stood his ground in front of the door. 'I'm sure he'll be OK for a couple of minutes. Chuck and Bob are keeping the eye on him.'

'But ...' It was impossible to argue with Paolo: the voice, the smile, the amazing blue eyes; he was hypnotic. Perhaps, she wondered – and not for the first time – this was how he'd conquered Misty's father – hypnotism. She tried to break the spell: looking through one of the saloon's large windows, she focused on Rory. He was sitting motionless on a long sofa between the two American 'minders', Bob and Chuck, who were reading bodybuilding magazines and sipping glasses of fruit juice. A tumbler of ice-cold mineral water remained untouched on the coffee table in front of Rory; his wheelchair stood empty to one side of it.

'He still does not speak or walk?' asked Paolo as Caroline suddenly found herself being led by the arm back to the rail.

She wanted to protest at the Italian's audacity, but felt powerless to resist. Angrily, she shook her head and watched the harbour breakwater slip past. As the yacht began to roll slightly in a gentle swell, she turned and looked anxiously towards the saloon.

'Don't worry, Caroline. He's in good hands with Chuck and Bob.' Paolo stroked his chin for a few moments. 'Do you think he has any idea where he is?'

Caroline shrugged. 'I don't know. I never know. He hasn't shown any signs of recognition ... yet, but then ... well, he rarely shows emotion – sometimes just the tiniest smile if I've been away from him for a while. When I come back, his face looks ... I can tell the difference. Or if he hurts himself, there's a tightening of the muscles in his cheeks.' She tried to illustrate. 'Otherwise ... nothing.'

'And the doctors remain convinced it's just shock?'

Caroline looked sharply at Paolo. '"*Just* shock"?'

'I'm sorry. I didn't mean to – I'd never realized people could be paralysed and made dumb – is that the word? – by shock – and for so long. Sonny and Misty have told me, of course, what the doctors have diag ... diag–'

'Diag*nosed*.'

'*Si*, diagnosed ... and I'm praying that he is recovering. But now I am thinking you worry because in Formentera Rory could recognize something, perhaps, and have another shock, yes?'

Caroline nodded and steadied herself on the rail: the yacht's rolling was becoming more noticeable as they headed for the open channel. 'It's possible. But then the opposite could happen – or so the consultants have advised. In fact, Paolo, that's the only reason I agreed to come. Everything else has been tried over the last year. And God only knows how many damned doctors – good ones and bad – have examined him.'

Suddenly, she turned towards the bows and scanned the horizon, but the heat haze still concealed their destination.

*

At Punta des Far, the emergency services had been unable to do much until daybreak on that Sunday morning, when the storm abated as suddenly as it had blown up. Apart from oil slicks and a few pieces of debris that had been washed by the currents northwards around the peninsula, there were no visible indications of a plane crash below the mighty cliffs. However, the crew of a Spanish Navy helicopter despatched from Pollença on Mallorca eventually spotted a body lying precariously on a narrow ledge about ten metres below the cliff top to the north of the lighthouse. Everyone assumed it was a victim of the accident, although its position in relation to the aircraft's reported trajectory was puzzling: the corpse was on the wrong side of the lighthouse – unless blown there by a tremendous gust of wind.

It took much dangerous manoeuvring in the updrafts around the Punta before the body could be lifted. And then the mystery deepened: the victim – a young man lacking any identification – was still alive, and his injuries, though severe, seemed inconsistent with a fall from an aircraft. The helicopter flew him directly to Ibiza's principal hospital, where X-rays revealed a broken leg, fractures to both arms, and several cracked ribs. It was a miracle, the doctors said, that every bone in his body wasn't broken – that he was alive at all.

Meanwhile that Sunday morning at Sant Francesc police station, James and Misty's questioning recommenced. Learning of the apparent crash survivor, they concluded that he had to be Rory Devlin. During the afternoon, photographs of him arrived from Ibiza on a coastguard cutter: despite the severe facial injuries, James, Misty and an ecstatic Caroline identified him. Two days later, Caroline was at his bedside.

It took a further week to locate and raise the aeroplane, its proximity to the cliffs making access dangerous for the salvage ships. It lay almost intact on the seabed in thirty metres of water. Ursula and Dumpwell were still strapped in their seats; both had sustained horrific injuries. The briefcases containing the $2,100,000 were also in the cockpit.

Although Rory made a good recovery from his physical injuries, he remained in a coma for weeks: Caroline stayed with him in one of the hospital's private double rooms, maintaining an exhausting vigil at his bedside; Aunt Belinda paid. In the interim, both the Spanish and British police tried to decide what should be done about prosecuting Devlin if and when he recovered sufficiently to be charged. He was clearly guilty of numerous crimes under Spanish law. Greater Manchester Police thought they, too, might have a few charges to throw at him, including conspiring to abduct the Honourable Caroline Weetwood on their patch, and blowing up the Roberta Weetwood theatre. However, the chances of a successful prosecution for any crime in either country seemed poor, thanks to Devlin's own incarceration by Klinker and her attempt to murder him – not to mention the likelihood that Caroline would be a hostile witness due to her apparent infatuation.

Finally, in the second week of November, Rory emerged from his coma. But Caroline's joy soon turned to grief when it became clear that he couldn't speak, and was paralysed in both legs. All his symptoms accorded with a diagnosis of catastrophic shock: he was emotionless and recognized no one. Shortly afterwards, the Spanish and British authorities confirmed that no charges would be brought against him, whereupon Caroline had him flown home to England; James raised no objection to him being installed at Bobbins.

Having by now missed the Michaelmas Term of her final undergraduate year at Durham, Caroline resolved to postpone her studies: she couldn't put her mind to anything, save ministering to Rory – day and night; she slept at his side. In any event, Pongo Pangbourne had been persuaded that her own talents could be put to better use elsewhere: a 'visiting professorship' at Berkeley was in the offing; Project MIM was defunct.

None of this was reported to her father; even after he'd recovered from his own mental illness and finally learned of Devlin's existence when the Formentera police interviewed him about the kidnapping, Dr Aiguadolça ensured that nothing was said about Caroline's passionate entanglement. But when George announced his intention to celebrate Christmas at Bobbins with both his own family and Misty – she'd accompanied James on his return from New York – Caroline telephoned Formentera and told her father everything. She feared the worst. To her surprise and relief, however, he appeared remarkably unconcerned about the prospect of coming face to face with one of the kidnappers – and in his own home. But then, after so many weeks on Formentera alone with his thoughts, his mission in life was now crystal clear: to forge a united, loving and happy family.

On an emotionally charged Christmas Eve, George confirmed to Caroline that he would fund whatever medical treatment she believed might help Rory. Caroline hugged and kissed him – for the first time as far as either of them could remember. He'd had to wipe the tears from his eyes; he said it was the best Christmas present she could have given him. She said it was just as well: there was no present for him under the tree; she'd not been away from Bobbins since returning from Ibiza. Nonetheless, there was a wonderful surprise on Christmas Day: James and Misty announced their plans for a late-January marriage in Muckley parish church. Within hours, the Start-Amerigos – including Paolo's mother – were en route from Formentera. They stayed until New Year, which proved to be the most memorable that Bobbins had witnessed for decades. And although Vivian Duffle and her rehabilitated husband were rushed off their feet, they loved it too.

But as the months passed, none of the many eminent physicians who deliberated over Rory's zombie-like trance and paralysis managed to prescribe any effective treatment. They were, however, all of the view that isolation at Bobbins was unlikely to be conducive to a recovery. So, with the assistance of agencies specializing in holidays for the disabled, Caroline and Rory began travelling. George even chartered yachts and private aircraft to take them to exotic destinations, accompanied by trained staff – albeit Caroline invariably pushed Rory's wheelchair and always washed and dressed him.

Vivian thought Caroline and Rory were like something out of a film she'd once seen, but couldn't remember what it was called or who was in it – possibly Grace Kelly and James Stewart, or maybe Ali MacGraw and Ryan O'Neal. In any event, it had been terribly romantic. Ron was more sanguine: he generally referred to Miss Caroline as 'Florence Nightingale' and Devlin as 'The Invalid'; he thought the former a fool and the latter a fake.

*

From *Fresh Start II*'s rail, Caroline studied the Martello tower on the southern tip of Ibiza and shook her head as if to awaken herself from a bad dream. 'I never did get there,' she murmured.

Paolo looked at her quizzically. 'Where?'

'Oh nowhere.' She sighed sadly. 'Well, you'd think I was silly.'

'Try me.' He pointed to the tower. 'There?'

'No, another tower – not far from your place, actually.'

'The one at Punta de la Gavina or down at Cap de Barbaria?'

403

'The Torre de la Gavina. I fell in love with Formentera's towers – don't ask me why. I tried to visit all of them, but I could never find the way to Gavina. Strange really. ... I met Rory the first time I tried.' Paolo looked surprised. 'Well, I didn't know it was him *then*. It was when he and ... that woman made their first attempt to kidnap me. It's a long story.'

'I remember. Misty told me.'

'Really?' Caroline looked back at the tower receding in the distance astern.

'You can walk to the Torre de la Gavina along the coast from *Fresh Start*. Sonny and me have walked there many times. It's very romantic.'

'Oh?'

Through the heat haze, Formentera's outline finally appeared on the horizon. Paolo saw it first and Caroline followed his gaze. She shivered. It was exactly how she remembered it – inviting yet mysterious. Just for a moment, she thought of asking Paolo to get the yacht turned back, but behind her she could hear James, Misty and Aunt Belinda shouting and cheering 'Hurrah! Formentera! It's great to be back!'

What short memories they had, Caroline reflected. She watched as the island took form, almost hypnotized by the familiar landmarks: the towers, the old windmill up at Sant Francesc ... the great tombstone mass of La Mola.

Paolo gripped her hand. 'Welcome back, Caroline. Don't be frightened. This is a *good* place. The island will bring you luck. I know. Trust me.'

The yacht didn't put into La Savina but steered to starboard and followed the low cliffs of Formentera's west coast. And although it passed the Torre de la Gavina, Caroline didn't see it: she'd replaced Chuck and Bob in the saloon and was reading to Rory as the old tower slipped by. There were various stories on the International News pages of *The Times* which she thought might interest him: despite his blank expression, Caroline had long ago convinced herself that Rory heard and understood everything around him. There was simply a switch in his brain which was temporarily malfunctioning, and which prevented him from responding in any way to the stimuli to his senses. Constantly, she imagined the complete frustration and helplessness that he had to bear.

At the entrance to the bay of Cala Beltran, the yacht dropped anchor and a large rubber dinghy with an outboard motor sped away from the shore, piloted by Sonny himself; George remained on the beach, waving with untypical enthusiasm.

James seized Misty's arm and pointed. 'Bloody hell! That can't be Dad, can it? ... It is! He's wearing *shorts*! They look like something from the

Thirties. Where the hell did he get them? I'm surprised he's not wearing a pith helmet as well.'

Over the laughter, Belinda said: 'Now, now, you two, don't make fun of him when you disembark. I understand it's been a major effort on the part of Pat to get him out of trousers.'

James and Misty exploded.

'I think,' Misty spluttered, '– you'd – better – rephrase that, Belinda!' And then Belinda saw the joke and creased with laughter too.

Anxious and unsmiling, Caroline stood a few feet from them. 'Paolo, I do hope we can get Rory into that ... that *thing* without any mishaps. If he falls into the water–'

'Nobody's going to fall into any water. Don't worry.'

With Sonny whooping with delight, the dinghy circled the yacht twice at speed. 'Look at the hotel!' he roared. 'Isn't it great?'

The work remained unfinished, and a tall crane was still in position, but the drab functionalism of the old hotel had been swept away. The local council had vetoed a complete rebuilding or any extension in the total floor area, but the hotel was now entirely clad in stone, the flat roofs had been replaced by pitched ones covered in local tiles, and at each end of the facade soared a tower resembling the island's Martello towers.

'Fantastic!' cooed Belinda.

'Bloody brilliant!' added James.

'You're a genius!' purred Misty, hugging Paolo.

'Me? I didn't do nothing – *anything*, I mean.'

They all groaned and tut-tutted.

Sonny manoeuvred the dinghy to the yacht's rear landing stage and jumped aboard. 'Sorry I couldn't meet you folks at the airport – a last-minute crisis with the guys doing the sanitation.' There were hugs and kisses all round. Caroline, however, did not emulate the others' enthusiasm. Sonny sensed it, looked meaningfully at Paolo, and then turned his attention to Rory, who sat bolt upright and expressionless in his wheelchair. Sonny ruffled the invalid's hair and kneeled before him. 'How yer doin', partner? You look great. I'm glad you've come. You're going to have a ball, OK?'

Everyone saw Caroline wince – and pretended they hadn't.

Sonny turned to Chuck and Bob. 'Right, guys! Let's get Rory onto dry land first and then the others. The luggage can follow. And one drop of water on our star, and you two are on the first plane back to Fort Worth.'

'No sweat!' said Chuck and Bob in unison.

'And, everyone, listen real good. George is wearing his *best* shorts. So, say they're great! OK?'

There'd been a lengthy debate between George, the Start-Amerigos and the Blackberrys as to where everyone should stay and the venue for the anniversary dinner. Their primary concern had been to cause the minimum distress to Caroline, whose coolness about the event was common knowledge. Sonny had offered the services of his hotel's top chef, who'd already been recruited and was on the island organizing the fitting out of the new kitchen. And, subject to some minor finishing touches, a private dining room was also available. But George was adamant that he wanted the evening to be 'a homely affair', and argued that the deserted, unopened hotel would appear less than welcoming. He'd set his heart on the *Villa Clementina*, and that was that.

James and his family, together with Aunt Belinda, were more than happy to be accommodated in *Clementina*'s spacious quarters. Caroline, however, wished to limit both her own and Rory's exposure to the scene of the abduction – at least until she'd ascertained what effect, if any, it might have on him. Hence her acceptance of the Start-Amerigos' invitation to stay at *Fresh Start*.

Consequently, the decline of her father's hospitality was weighing heavily on Caroline's mind when he greeted her and the rest of the party on the beach. And her wretchedness was compounded by the extraordinary warmth of his welcome and the joy he obviously felt at having his family around him; more than ever, she saw herself as an outsider. And so, she trotted disconsolately behind Bob as he carried Rory up the beach to the awaiting cars.

Patricia was standing beside the Range Rover, ready to drive the *Clementina* party home; to George's annoyance, she'd returned to the vehicle when *Fresh Start II* had dropped anchor.

'They're *your* family, for goodness' sake!' she protested. 'You don't want a glorified secretary hanging about when you greet them. It will look too official, too formal.'

'You *are* part of the family,' George retorted angrily, '– since *lunch!*'

But for once she defied him, even though the words had enraptured her.

Now, with Patricia still flushed after having had her cheeks kissed by all the new arrivals – bar Rory – George was about to join her in the Range Rover's front passenger seat when he paused and looked back at the Start-Amerigos' Jeep. 'Come over to *Clementina* as soon as you like, Caroline,' he shouted, '– later this afternoon, I hope. You don't have to wait until dinner.'

'Possibly,' she replied with a forced smile.

*

It was late afternoon and Rory was still fast asleep. But then, as Caroline had remarked to Bob after he'd gently lowered him onto the double bed in one of *Fresh Start*'s guestrooms, both the long journey and the heat had exhausted him. Almost immediately, Rory's eyes had closed; within minutes he was snoring. Caroline also wanted to rest, but being too stressed she slumped into an armchair beside the open window and gazed at the view. Beyond the garden, which Paolo had transformed into an oasis of colour and chiaroscuro, lay the sea with its heavenly shades of intense blue. Looking northwards, she could make out the Torre de la Gavina. Intoxicated by the scent of countless roses, Paolo's words of comfort came back to her: she wanted to believe him. She closed her eyes and prayed. Some two hours later, after reliving her weeks on the island, she finally nodded off.

Rory was dreaming. It was the dream he invariably had – of his passionate lovemaking with Caroline in their final prison at *Casa Bayreuth*, the two of them bound together by chains and manacles. As his moaning grew louder, Caroline awoke with a start. She knew what to expect. And when the spasm awoke him, she said what she always said while stroking his damp brow:

'Don't worry, darling. You're all right. You're safe now.' And then she went to the bathroom for a towel.

Rory smiled as soon as she'd left the room. *It's almost over*, he thought comfortingly. Soon he would savour again the real thing with dearest Caroline. And roll on dinner! He could eat a horse!

*

Sonny had rarely felt so happy or relaxed. It was an evening of perfection: food, wine, company and conversation. Yet again, he admired the magic of *Clementina*'s terrace, illuminated by scores of flickering candles and graced by displays of hundreds of flowers from *Fresh Start*. Beloved Paolo! A genius. So creative and so kind. ... And so, so loving.

Lighting a cigarette, Sonny said: 'That was a superb meal, George. Perhaps I could have saved a fortune and hired your Maria for the hotel.'

'Don't even think about it, my dear chap,' George replied, smiling broadly.

'OK, but at least François could have a word with Maria about some of her recipes. We want some good local dishes on the menu, don't we, Paolo?' Sonny smiled at his lover sitting opposite him.

'Sure – and lots of Italian ones!'

When the laughter subsided, George turned to Misty. 'How are the law studies going?'

'Great! I'm on an Open University course, so it's all correspondence and videos. And then sometimes I go into Manchester for seminars organized by the various universities and the local law society. Belinda looks after Sonny Junior, of course, now that she's sold the Eastbourne house. She's wonderful with him.'

'Excellent! And your aim is still to qualify as a solicitor?'

'Sure. But I wouldn't take a full-time job – or even part-time – until Sonny starts school.'

'I'm glad to hear it. A mother's place is with her child. Don't you agree, Caroline?'

Gwen, who was conscious that George had constantly endeavoured to bring his daughter into the conversation all evening – albeit with little success – looked anxiously at Caroline. In Gwen's view, his latest attempt was tactless: it was obvious that Caroline would do anything to have Rory's child and was deeply envious of her brother's good fortune.

'*Really*, George,' Gwen retorted before Caroline could think of an answer, 'you're so old-fashioned! There *are* women, you know, who have to go out to work in order to support their children. Then there are those who'd go mad and be rotten mothers if they had to stay at home all day changing nappies and–'

'Whatever happened to the good old-fashioned principles of Jessica Muffin, my love?' interrupted Tom.

'She got incinerated, darling. Remember?'

'Oh, Gwen,' said James, 'tell us about the time – years ago when the broadcasts were live – when you were supposed to be shopping in some department store in Worchester. You wanted a present for–'

'My husband, Geoffrey.'

'– but instead of the noise of shoppers and ringing tills, the sound effects man pressed the wrong button or something, and all these cows started mooing and sheep baaing.'

Gwen was about to get underway when George began striking one of his wine glasses with the edge of a knife. 'Sorry to interrupt, everyone, but before we all descend into howls of uncontrollable laughter with Gwen's story, which I'm sure – and hope – will lead as usual to many, many more–'

'Hear! Hear!' seconded James.

'– there are just a few things I'd like to say.'

There were several groans and shouts of 'No speeches!'

'No, I'm *not* going to make a speech, so don't worry. I just want to say how happy I am to see all of you here. Now, I know that this island has brought each one of us his or her share of happiness ... and grief. But when we look back objectively, I feel that those dark moments were ... well, I'm not a religious man – never have been. ... Anyway, I feel that those dark moments were a supreme test of our wills. If there is a God – and please,

Paolo and Signora Amerigo, I know you're both devout Catholics – and you too, Sonny, are a bit of a bible basher – well, if there *is* a God, I think he must have a very special interest in *this* place.

'After all, everyone must admit that the circumstances which brought us together here were ... well, to be frank, so bizarre as to make one doubt that coincidence had anything to do with them. Our wretched lives – yes, they *were* all wretched – excluding dear Gwen and Tom, of course – were plainly exposed to us in the dazzling clarity of Formentera's magical light. And we changed – all of us – for the better. And to crown it all, we've united together in bonds of friendship – and, indeed, love – which, I think it's fair to say, none of us would ever have thought possible.

'Caroline, my darling, everyone around this table loves, respects and admires you. And your love for Rory is an inspiration to us all. And don't think me foolish, but I do not doubt that in his way he loves and worships you too.'

'Please, Father, don't–'

'No, Caroline, hear me out. You should thank God that the prayer you undoubtedly made a year ago tonight was answered – that this man, who'd been instrumental in your awful incarceration – and Misty's – would be saved from death in circumstances where survival seemed impossible. He *was* saved, he *is* alive, and one day he *will* – believe me – have all his faculties restored to him. We will not rest until that is achieved.'

There was silence, save for the nocturnal sounds of cicadas and the gentle churning of the warm waters of the Mediterranean around the rocks and through the gullies at the foot of the cliffs beyond the garden wall.

George cleared his throat. 'Well, that's quite enough of that! And now I have a very special announcement to make.'

'The eleven-fifteen to Es Pujols,' boomed Belinda in an attempt to revive the festive atmosphere, 'will be departing from platform seven!'

'Oh, you can laugh, my friends,' George responded good-humouredly, 'but when my new line opens down at La Savina, you'll be laughing out of the other sides of your faces. ... Come on! A bit of hush, *please*. ... That's more like it. Well now, I believe this is a most propitious moment to tell you that ...'

George hesitated and glanced at the other end of the table, where Patricia sat nervously. She'd been in good form all evening, albeit he'd detected signs of tension: several times she'd excused herself to 'powder her nose'.

He took a deep breath. 'Dear family and friends, this afternoon I asked Patricia to marry me – once, that is, the juggernaut of the law has ground a certain existing relationship into dust – and the sensible lass has graciously accepted.'

A second's silence was followed by acclamation – and then pandemonium as bodies flew around the table, with the prospective spouses being subjected to a barrage of hugs and kisses. Only Caroline and Rory remained seated.

Belinda came over and placed both hands on Caroline's shoulders. 'Please be happy for him,' she whispered into her ear, '– for *both* of them, dear. *Please.*'

With a supreme effort, Caroline rose and made her way to her father, who still appeared stunned by the impact of his own words. 'It's wonderful news, Daddy. I'm so happy for you.' She kissed him and then turned to Patricia, who'd finally managed to join her betrothed. Embracing her, Caroline said: 'And I hope you'll be very happy too, Patricia.'

George and the future Lady Weetwood gazed at one another, both glowing with platonic love. It had taken him more than twenty years to realize that Patricia's devotion went far beyond what could reasonably be expected of a loyal employee. And when his eyes had finally been opened and he'd realized that her enthusiasm for the Formentera railway project was not only genuine but also a manifestation of her deep affection for himself, he'd felt blessed – and then frightened at the thought of losing her.

Caroline turned away and looked sadly at Rory. He sat expressionless, immobile. But then his hands began to move the plate in front of him. With its remains of cheeses and bread, he pushed it slowly, this way and that. Only Caroline noticed. She recognized the sign: he needed to relieve himself. She moved swiftly and disengaged the break on his wheelchair. As she began to push him towards the French windows, Paolo came over.

'Anything wrong? Can I help?'

'No! ... No thank you, Paolo. I just have to take Rory to the lavatory.'

'Oh, I see. I can do that for you.'

'No. It's all right.'

Caroline emerged into the spacious living room and snorted as she suddenly remembered that the former owners had grandly called it 'the drawing room'.

'This is where the kidnapping started, isn't it?' a man said quietly.

Caroline spun round. 'Oh God! You startled me! I–'

But no one was behind her.

Rory turned his head and looked up. 'Yes, it was definitely *this* room. I remember quite clearly.' And then, as if frightened by his own voice, his mouth fell open and he began to breath rapidly. 'Jesus Christ! I can talk! I can *talk*, Caroline! Oh, Caroline, darling, I *love* you!'

Caroline felt the room begin to swirl round and round. 'Rory? ... Oh, *Rory*! Darling! I love *you*!' And then she slumped to the floor.

Posing for photographs and standing with his back to the French windows, George heard Caroline's strangely raised voice and turned round just as a camera flashed. 'Oh my God!' he cried rushing forward. 'Caroline! What's happened?'

Rory smiled oddly. 'Hello, Lord Weetwood. I think Caroline's fainted.'

In bewilderment, George's eyes darted repeatedly between Rory and his daughter as he groped for words to express his conflicting emotions of fear and joy.

In the adjoining study, James had just loaded one of his CDs into George's brand-new Technics music centre. He'd turned the volume to maximum, his intention being to liven up the celebrations with some party music he'd had the foresight to bring from England. But now, momentarily distracted by the sight and sounds through the open French windows of guests scattering from the terrace, and anxious to join what he assumed to be spontaneous fun and games, he jabbed erroneously – but perhaps providentially – the tape deck's start button. And thus, instead of the expected raucous explosion of *Sizzling Ibiza Hits*, James blasted the villa with the jubilant first bars of Vivaldi's choral masterpiece.

'*GLORIA! GLORIA!*' sang the exuberant choir, '*GLORIA IN EXCELSIS DEO!*'

In front of the open-mouthed congregation which had stampeded into the sitting room, George dropped to his knees beside his recumbent daughter. And then, with a saintly expression on his boyish face, Rory rose from the wheelchair and placed his hands papally on the peer's head of fine golden hair.

'God bless you, Father,' he intoned, '– for *every*thing.'

## THE END